SONGS FOR THE COLD OF HEART

Eric Dupont

SONGS FOR THE COLD OF HEART

Translated from the French by
Peter McCambridge

QC FICTION

Revision: Katherine Hastings
Proofreading: Elizabeth West, Riteba McCallum, David Warriner, Arielle Aaronson
Book design: Folio infographie
Cover & logo: Maison 1608 by Solisco
Fiction editor: Peter McCambridge

ISBN 978-1-77186-147-2

Legal Deposit, 3rd quarter 2018
Bibliothèque et Archives nationales du Québec
Library and Archives Canada

Published by QC Fiction
6977, rue Lacroix
Montréal, Québec H4E 2V4
Telephone: 514 808-8504
QC@QCfiction.com
www.QCfiction.com

QC Fiction is an imprint of Baraka Books.

Printed and bound in Québec

Trade Distribution & Returns
Canada and the United States
Independent Publishers Group
1-800-888-4741
orders@ipgbook.com

We acknowledge the support from the Société de développement des entreprises culturelles (SODEC) and the Government of Québec tax credit for book publishing administered by SODEC.

To my big sister, for her winter travels.

Teal

Years before her mother bundled her onto a coach bound for New York City in a December blizzard, Madeleine Lamontagne had been a little girl who loved Easter bunnies, Christmas trees, and the stories told by her dad, Louis Lamontagne. Nothing out of the ordinary there. After all, everyone loved to hear Louis "The Horse" Lamontagne's tall tales. Before television, his stories were the best way to pass the time in Rivière-du-Loup.

As any drinking man in Rivière-du-Loup will tell you, it was TV that killed the Horse, not the combustion engine. They'll also tell you—and there's no reason to doubt them—that any man's story, wherever he may be, never finds a more attentive ear than his daughter's, especially if she is the oldest and as such occupies a special place of her own in her father's heart. All of which is to say that Louis "The Horse" Lamontagne, or Papa Louis as the children of Rivière-du-Loup liked to call him, never had a more attentive audience than his little Madeleine, sitting right there on the sofa in her father's funeral home on Rue Saint-François-Xavier, in the parish of the same name, in the town of Rivière-du-Loup in the province of Quebec.

Amid the 1950s furniture stood a ghastly ashtray mounted on an honest-to-goodness moose leg. A cousin had made it after carving up the carcass of the animal that Papa Louis had killed in the fall of 1953, when Madeleine was just three years old. She was now eight. Papa Louis was sitting in his armchair, and her two brothers on the bottle-green sofa. In her left hand, she held a full glass of gin that Papa Louis was eyeing thirstily.

"Get a move on, Mado! We wanna hear the story!"

It was Madeleine Lamontagne's oldest brother Marc, age seven, who had just told his sister to hurry up and get Papa Louis a drink so the story could at last begin. The other brother, Luc, watched a dust mote drift through the air.

"Cut it out!" Madeleine retorted before sitting down to his right.

Marc slid his hand in under her thigh. She twisted his finger back, just enough to get her point across, not quite enough to dislocate it. Madeleine grinned. The gin was having its effect. There would be a story. To her left, Marc slipped his hand back under her thigh, and this time she let him. "His fingers must be cold," Madeleine reasoned, thinking that if she picked a fight with her brother, Papa Louis might suddenly decide to send them all off to bed. Fortunately, Marc turned his attentions away from her and watched Papa Louis knock back his gin. To Marc's left, little Luc, his dark-haired head leaning against his big brother's frail shoulder. He was going to fall asleep from one moment to the next. Luc, age five, had come into the world the day of the Coronation of Queen Elizabeth II: June 2, 1953. The sofa was almost full, but there would have been room for the cat if their mother Irene had allowed it.

"No cat on the sofa. It's not hygienic," she had decreed one day.

There had been cake for supper. Luc had eaten too much of it—he had eaten Madeleine's share as well as his own—only to vomit it back up all over his brother Marc. So Luc was already in his PJs. Madeleine had changed him out of his dirty clothes; their older brother had had to get cleaned up. Little Luc was nodding off. It was looking like he would miss the end of the story, but that was perhaps for the best, considering how sad it was. Maybe the dead man in the adjoining parlour would find the story entertaining.

"Tell the one about the dune!" whined Marc.

"I told you that one last month," said Papa Louis as he emptied a spoonful of sugar into his warm gin.

"Tell it again then!"

"Don't you want to hear a Christmas story instead? Hang on! We'll ask the dead guy what he wants to hear! Hey, Sirois! Wanna hear a Christmas story?"

The children fought back giggles. Papa Louis only fooled around with his customers whenever his wife Irene wasn't around; she found his jokes to be in terribly poor taste. Papa Louis took Sirois' silence as a formal request for a Christmas story, appropriately enough in a room still decked out for the nativity. A scrawny Christmas tree was still standing, its lower branches providing shelter to a porcelain crèche whose figurine of Saint Joseph had a chip missing from its face. A lamb had been toppled. On the radio playing softly in the background, the family rosary ticked by with the regularity of a Swiss timepiece... *full of grace. The Lord is with thee. Blessed art thou amongst women, and blessed is the fruit of thy womb, Jesus...* Once a month, when the time for the family rosary came around, Papa Louis would find himself alone with his three children while his wife Irene went off to visit an aunt who was a nun at the Sisters of the Child Jesus convent. Since he was supposed to be reciting the interminable rosary with them, he preferred to keep the wireless on. It was a cunning plan since the valves took at least five minutes to warm up. By leaving the radio playing softly on the walnut dresser right beside him, Papa Louis would always have enough time to throw himself to his knees if, by some misfortune or other, his wife were to come home early from the convent. Papa Louis had given the kids strict instructions: at the first sound of footsteps on the wooden staircase, everyone was to throw themselves to their knees in front of the radio, rosary beads in hand, and pretend to swoon with emotion. Or else that would be the end of his stories. And so it was with the rosary playing in the background that Papa Louis would always start telling his children stories. One time it had happened. Irene Lamontagne had come home early to collect a coat she wanted to donate to the nuns. Papa Louis' plan had gone like clock-work. At the first thud on the steps, Papa Louis had cranked up the radio, the cardinal's voice reverberating so hard off the living-room walls it could probably be heard outside on the street. The father and children fell to their knees before the radio, rosary beads in hand, already intoning a Hail Mary, eyes half closed as though in a spiritual trance. Madeleine prayed especially fervently, stressing each syllable: "... born of the Virgin Mary. He suffered under Pontius Pilate, was crucified, died, and was buried..." adopting the nasal tone she had learned at the convent. She might have laid it on a little thick, but the ploy worked like a charm. Irene opened the door without a sound, not wanting to disturb the touching scene of family devotion. She crept upstairs to collect the forgotten garment and, index finger pressed against her lips, crossed herself as she left in silence. When he realized he was out of harm's way, Papa Louis turned down the radio, sat back up on the armchair, picked up the glass of gin he had hidden behind the dresser, and sighed.

"Keep going! What happened to the Lady with the Big Melons?" Madeleine and Marc had chorused.

But tonight Irene would not surprise them by coming home early. There would be a Christmas story. Once a month, the children got to hear a fan-tastically fabulous story from Papa Louis, like the time he had narrowly beaten Manitoba Bill—the Blackfoot with the blue eyes—at arm-wrestling, or the tall tale about the Saint-Jean-Baptiste night when he had danced with the Lady with the Big Melons on the Trans-Canada Highway on the far side of Saint-Antonin. Madeleine was expecting to hear for a second time how one evening he had ended up by mistake at the Malecite reserve and how the Indians, stunned at the sight of the remarkable Louis, had grown angry, because you can't just pop up on people's doorsteps unannounced. There would be a price to pay, and that price would be to dance with the Lady with the Big Melons. If he hadn't, Papa Louis would never have made it back from his trip to New Brunswick alive! Not a chance! But he wasn't going to tell them the one about the Lady with the Big Melons, because the last time he'd done that, little Luc had delivered a flawless summary to their mother; not with all the juicy details admittedly, like the actual size of her melons, which the child had felt compelled, following the example of his father, to mime with his hands, but at the very least the circumstances leading to the events of that evening (and the accompanying hand gestures). Irene Lamontagne had been forced to go to confession, and to appeal to what remained of Papa Louis' common sense so that in future he might leave the juiciest details out of his stories.

"Do you want them to go around telling that story at school, Louis Lamontagne?"

Irene had gotten her husband to agree that he would tell other stories, even though, all things considered, the damage had been done. Luc would remain a rather vulgar child until the end of his short existence. But that evening, Papa Louis wanted to tell a Christmas story. The children were surprised because Papa Louis' stories usually didn't touch on religion. Those kinds were the exclusive preserve of Irene Lamontagne and Sister Mary of the Eucharist—better known as Sister Scary—a figure cloaked in black and white who, two or three times a year on a Sunday afternoon, would glide silently into their home on Rue Saint-François-Xavier.

It was probably Marc who—like father, like son—was the first to call her Sister Scary, because she always appeared when least expected and without making the slightest sound. You turned around and *bam*! There she was! Sister Mary of the Eucharist would suddenly rise up in front of you, an unnerving shadow in the doorway, beneath the clock, sitting outside on the wooden porch, or on the stairs leading up to the bedrooms. The ghostly Sister Mary of the Eucharist also seemed to have a gift for being everywhere at once. Regulars at the Ophir bar on Rue Lafontaine would say they had seen her stepping onto a train at such and such a time, while others would swear she had been standing outside the church of Saint-François-Xavier at the very same moment. The Lamontagne children were about to learn, on that December evening in 1958, why exactly Sister Scary would come to pay homage to Louis "The Horse" Lamontagne three or four times a year, most often shortly before Corpus Christi, a day or two after All Saints' Day, and on or around the feast of Saint Blaise, the patron saint of throat ailments.

In the living room on Rue Saint-François-Xavier, Madeleine, too, demanded to hear the story of the Lady with the Big Melons. Papa Louis straightened himself to his full height and raised an index finger to quell the protests. There would be a Christmas story that evening.

"So I can tell you, at last, how your father came into this world. Because we've had it up to here with all those nun stories."

Papa Louis glanced back at the door, to be sure his wife hadn't slipped in silently just in time to receive the full brunt of the blasphemy. The silence lasted for two seconds while Papa Louis hoped an angel would come down and erase from his children's memories his jab at the Sisters of the Child Jesus, whom in reality he considered almost real sisters. He waved his empty gin glass under Madeleine's nose so she could run to fill it, adding just the right amount of warm water. "I'll speak up so you can hear me from the kitchen," he promised, giving her a peck on the cheek. Madeleine poured the gin and warm water into the glass, devoting her full attention to the story so as not to miss a single word.

"I'm going to tell you the story of my birth!" began Papa Louis, slapping his knee.

"You weren't born in Rivière-du-Loup?" inquired Marc, who thought there was nothing left to be said once a person's place of birth had been revealed.

"I was, but back then it was called Fraserville."

Papa Louis was a little Baby Jesus. It was a well-known fact. But his mother—known as Madeleine the American, not to be confused with Old Ma Madeleine and all the other Madeleines that came after the arrival of this particular ancestor on Canadian soil—and his father, Louis-Benjamin Lamontagne, well, they had no advance warning. Everyone thought Papa Louis would be born long after the three kings had come and gone, so they weren't paying too much attention.

The story was going to be a good one, there was no doubt about it, what with their mother out, a second warm gin on its way, and that holiday feeling in the air. The signs were all there. It was going to be quite the story all right. It's not that the story was completely devoid of interest, but others would have dismissed it out of hand as a legend, an awkward tall tale thrown together by an attention-seeking forty-year-old who'd had a little too much to drink. "Twas Decemburr 1918 an erryone was dyin ah Spanish flu. Fullin like flies, they was," he went on in the language that people of Madeleine's generation were the last to understand perfectly and that there would be no point reproducing here in its exactitude, since so many turns of phrase would only bewilder minds used to the standardized tongue we speak as an official language in this land.

It was December 1918 in Rivière-du-Loup, then known as Fraserville. Louis-Benjamin Lamontagne and his wife Madeleine the American were expecting their first child during that glacial, silent Lower St. Lawrence winter.

"Why was Grandma Madeleine called 'the American'? And why are the ladies in your stories always called Madeleine?"

The question came from the kitchen. And a good one it was, too. Why was Madeleine Lamontagne—mother to Papa Louis and grandmother to Madeleine Lamontagne—known colloquially as "the American"? Quite simply because she came from the United States. That was reason enough. But beneath the innocent tone of this perfectly reasonable question, Papa Louis sensed that his children could no longer distinguish between members of their lineage—the result of a Lamontagne family obsession with always having at least one living Madeleine in their ranks. And kids are like that: they want to understand everything and are forever forcing storytellers to go back further in their stories and justify what just happened. Or was it nothing more than a clever ploy to push bedtime back further?

"My father, *my* dad, was Louis-Benjamin Lamontagne. My mother was Madeleine the American. It's not hard to wrap yer head around!"

"But the other Madeleine?" groaned Marc, perplexed.

"Well, there's Madeleine your big sister!" Papa Louis shot back.

"No, no, there was another one," the boy insisted.

"Ah! Old Ma Madeleine, my grandmother. Louis-Benjamin's mom. The one who, quite by accident, brought the American to Canada!"

"What was that Madeleine called?"

"Well, just like your sister! 'Madeleine' is what we called her!" he said with a loud guffaw that warmed the ears of his daughter, who had just set his third hot gin down on the arm of his chair. She rolled her eyes. Papa Louis softened.

"We'll call her Old Ma Madeleine so as not to make a mystery out of nothing. Don't worry, you'll be able to follow it all. I'll draw you a picture if I have to."

Madeleine Lamontagne—a.k.a. Old Ma Madeleine, mother to Louis-Benjamin Lamontagne, grandmother to Louis Lamontagne and great-grandmother to Madeleine Lamontagne—wanted her son Louis-Benjamin, born January 14, 1900, to marry a Madeleine, like his father before him.

"The Lamontagnes need one Madeleine every generation," she had proclaimed.

The story was repeated several times throughout the childhood of Louis-Benjamin, the first baby to be baptized in the twentieth century in the church of Saint-Patrice following a shorter-than-usual mass. The boy came to understand relatively early in life that he would be better marrying a Madeleine than a Josephine, and so, in the springtime of his life, when he became, like other boys his age, more acutely aware of the song of the black-capped chickadees, he felt the urge to marry a Madeleine. It wasn't that this particular spring arrived any more or less quickly than the others, but it was—let's put it this way, because Luc is not quite asleep yet—the spring when every boy comprehends the precise nature of his aspirations and when the words to the hit songs of the day begin to take on a whole new meaning.

The day Old Ma Madeleine surprised her oldest, ahem, swashbuckling behind a stack of firewood, his black tuft of hair rocking left and right like a woodpecker's head, she realized the time had come to find him a Madeleine of his own.

Old Ma Madeleine's choice fell upon a sickly, weak-lunged young thing by the name of Madeleine Lévesque, who had the distinct advantage of being her niece. The young lady from Kamouraska had no sooner given her consent than the parish priest gave his own. He signed in December 1917, and the records of the parish of Saint-François-Xavier leave no doubt: it was the third time that month special permission was given for first cousins to marry. The engagement party was held on January 1, 1918; Madeleine Lévesque's funeral, in Latin, on the fifteenth of that same month. The Spanish flu had taken the girl in less than a week as it decimated the villages along the coast. But Louis-Benjamin would have his Madeleine. Old Ma Madeleine took this fateful blow as a challenge thrown down to her by God himself.

"Son, your mother won't let you down. I'll find your Madeleine. Even if it means rowing across to the lands your German forefathers left behind."

Old Ma Madeleine recalled that a younger brother had left Canada for New Hampshire in 1909 and had once mentioned in a letter the existence of a little Madeleine he had adopted in the town of Nashua, the orphan of a French Canadian couple. Might the little girl already be of child-bearing age? She must be at least sixteen by now... Old Ma Madeleine had the priest write her a letter in which she asked for news of her younger brother, wondering, at the very end, if young Madeleine might not be, by any chance, ready to start a family. She enclosed a recent photograph of Louis-Benjamin, his cowlick standing straight up across his forehead, his ears sticking out a little, his fleshy lips pressed into a little wave. Looking positively thirsting for affection. The letter was mailed on January 17, 1918. The answer was not long coming. On March 1, Father Cousineau of the parish of Saint-François-Xavier knocked on Old Ma Madeleine's wooden door. He held in his hand a distressing telegram sent from New Hampshire the previous day and announcing the arrival of a certain Madeleine from the United States. She was to be picked up at Fraserville station *tomorrow*.

"Tomorrow, that's today?" Old Ma Madeleine asked shyly.

"Yes, tomorrow means today," squawked the priest.

Marc loved it when his father quoted the characters in his stories verbatim, wondering all the while how he could be sure of the words since he hadn't even been born that freezing morning of March 1, 1918, when the parish priest announced, throwing up his arms at the imminent arrival of a bride sent by railroad. He figured Papa Louis probably made up the odd bit to keep things interesting. Old Ma Madeleine and the priest stood staring at each other for a minute on the wooden steps outside the Lamontagne home, she thinking this was more than she had bargained for, he wondering how it was all going to end. Time did not afford them the luxury of putting together a little scheme to delay the bride's arrival. The train would arrive that same evening. Upon hearing the news, Louis-Benjamin, terrified yet delighted, felt an electric current surge through him. By this time, his belle must already be on Canadian soil. With a little luck, they would be gazing upon the same star barely minutes before meeting.

Old Ma Madeleine, her oldest son Louis-Benjamin, her other son, Napoleon, his four sisters, so small that the youngest could barely stand, and Father Cousineau stood shivering at Fraserville station. The father of the Lamontagne household hadn't been able to make it back from the logging camp where he was working all winter. Every screech of the locomotive sent shivers through Louis-Benjamin's body, in parts that until then had not been overly insistent, that is, no more so than he had become accustomed to, but he was in no position to judge objectively, having no one with whom to strike up a frank and open discussion on the matter. He was poised to discover the extent of this inclination just as soon as the train from Quebec City pulled into the station. He felt the ground begin to shudder underfoot as the locomotive ground to a halt, a glistening beast in the dark night. A century passed before the car doors opened, spilling out sombrely dressed passengers, a handful of Sisters of the Child Jesus holding each other by the arm so as not to slip on the damp ice, men returning home from their work in the capital, shivering shadows half asleep.

The American girl kept them waiting. Outside the station, flanked by her horde of kids, clutching her youngest children tightly underneath her coat to shelter them from the cold, like a penguin on an ice floe, Old Ma Madeleine was ready and waiting for the devil himself to step off the train. All the expressions a person's face can bear when they know they are about to meet their destiny were on display from left to right. Once they concluded there had been a mistake, that the priest had misread the telegram or else the American girl had missed her train, talk turned to which road they should take back home.

She stepped out of the third car, carrying a single leather suitcase in her right hand and a box in her left. She wore a beaver fur hat and a long fur coat, the fur ripped from an animal that Old Ma Madeleine could not identify at first glance, but that later turned out to be a marten. The young woman looked right then left, the cloud of steam produced by her mouth following her head's movements in the pale light of an uncertain moon and the locomotive's headlamp. The priest took the initiative of casting out into the night air the traveller's first name, a cue to which she promptly responded. The creature then approached the welcoming committee, which could now make out her features. Madeleine the American had pale skin that was covered in freckles, even in the middle of winter. She removed her gloves to extend her hand like a lady. Louis-Benjamin, who must have been a good two heads taller than her, had never seen a hand so white nor eyes more teal. In fact, he had never really seen teal-coloured eyes before. The American girl smiled at him, deducing this must be the boy promised her at the end of the long journey. Judging by her smile, everyone understood it to be a done deal. Louis-Benjamin, a big strapping lad of six foot six, looked the little lady from the south up and down; his mother had parted his hair to the left, as she did for high masses, and ironed him a clean shirt made from warm fabric already soaking wet beneath his long beaver coat.

With a wave in his hair that, on particularly windy days, transformed into a small tuft, with the long eyelashes inherited from his mother, with shoulders as broad as an ox, with his pale complexion and cheeks turned rosy by the cold, the young man, had he not already been promised to the American lass, would have had no trouble at all finding a wife for himself from among Fraserville's six thousand souls. The catch was that she had to be called Madeleine, a condition that disqualified the vast majority of admirers at a time when, as Papa Louis put it, "No one ever dreamed of changing their name."

"You were born Louis, you died Louis. Not like young what's-her-name. That Norma one who calls herself Marilyn for the movies. Anyhow, if the girls of Fraserville had known that just by changing their name the way Fraserville changed its name to Rivière-du-Loup in 1920 they would have stood a chance of catching young Louis-Benjamin's eye, well they'd all have changed their names to Madeleine overnight. He was a good-looking young lad was your grandpa!"

And yet Papa Louis had been through his fair share of name changes himself. Papa Louis might have been born Louis Lamontagne, but then he became Louis "The Horse" Lamontagne—the name everyone throughout the region respectfully called him as soon as he started performing public feats of strength—then, once tamed by Irene Caron, Papa Louis it was until the day he died. Between "The Horse" and Papa Louis, there had been, depending on where he found himself, other nicknames: The Incredible Lamontagne, *Cheval Lamontagne*, The Great Canadian, and others that had never reached his ears. But he was still yet to be born in his own story.

"Papa, it's complicated enough as it is…"

And so it was a bolt out of the blue, or its Nordic equivalent, a Northern light, that marked the first encounter between the sturdy Lamontagne boy and Madeleine the American as she took from her purse the photograph of Louis-Benjamin sent by Old Ma Madeleine. The American looked down at the photo then up at her model, then back down from the model to her photo. Her face lit up as though she had just seen an apparition. With not a thought to good manners or the rules of etiquette, Louis-Benjamin scooped up the traveller as if to see how much she weighed, like he did with his cousins and sisters several times a day to build his strength, the little girls having become something akin to living dumbbells that had only to be caught as they ran by. Louis-Benjamin held his new bride tight against him, because this was the girl he would marry, the doubt in his mind having several minutes ago given way to a certainty as implacable as winter, as strong as the squall from the east that had just picked up in the starry night. The bride's feet floated a foot off the ground, like those of an angel in flight. During the warm but brief embrace, Madeleine felt through her marten fur coat precisely why she had been summoned from so far away. When he set her back down onto the ice, a giggle could be heard, then Madeleine said in the prettiest New England accent:

"I see you're happy to meet me."

She spoke English. Old Ma Madeleine coughed, cleared her throat, and inquired:

"*Vous parlez français, Mademoiselle?*"

By way of response, the young lady twirled around three times, gazed up into the starry sky, and sang in a thick American accent: "*À la claire fontaine, m'en allant promener...*" Jaws dropped to the floor. Father Cousineau piped up in English. He explained to the girl that she must be on the wrong car: they were waiting for "a French girl" promised to "this young Catholic man." The young Catholic man felt as though his heart was about to burst through his ribcage and explode into the March night. Madeleine was still laughing. She produced a letter from her purse and handed it to the priest.

My dear sister,

We were glad to hear from you. Your letter arrived yesterday. We were sad to learn that Louis-Benjamin lost his bride. We understand his grief and sorrow. The flu is also killing many here in New Hampshire. Thank you for your good intentions for our little Madeleine. You are right. We adopted her in 1909 after the death of her parents, who were from the Beauce region in Canada. She will make a perfect little wife for your Louis-Benjamin. She is very happy to go live in the land of her natural and adoptive parents. She was baptized in the one true Church and still understands the French from back home. She will turn seventeen this spring, and I told her all the men in the family make good husbands. I entrust her into your care and into the care of your son, whom I imagine to be as fine a person as you are, my dear sister. May they be very happy together in our beautiful Canada!

Your brother,

Alphonse

Illiterate though she might have been, Old Ma Madeleine demanded to see the piece of paper as if able to detect some detail the priest had missed.

"It's not exactly what I was expecting!"

Louis-Benjamin paid no heed to the details. He was already tossing the American girl's bags up into the priest's sled, followed by his sisters, one by one, like bales of hay. He plunked the American lass down between two of the girls to keep her warm. The journey to the lower end of town went by in a silence that held a different meaning for each of the sled's occupants.

Back at the Lamontagne home, Old Ma Madeleine required all her maternal authority to separate Louis-Benjamin from his bride—as he now considered her—come bedtime. They realized, after dropping the priest off at the presbytery, that the young woman did indeed understand French, but there was absolutely no way she had been born into a French Canadian family that had recently immigrated to the United States. Where did her red hair come from? And the freckles and teal eyes?

"She looks more like a Scotch!" Old Ma Madeleine had remarked in a fit of pique.

Scotch, English, or Irish, the newcomer was clearly of Nordic descent. All she would ever say on the matter was that she had been born in New Hampshire in 1900, she was as old as the century, and she had been adopted by a French Canadian family at the age of nine, which led people to believe she was probably Irish Catholic because the Americans would never have put a little Protestant girl in the hands of a hopelessly papist French Canadian family.

In Fraserville, soon-to-be Rivière-du-Loup, news of the American girl's arrival spread like syphilis through a Berlin whorehouse. Fraserville was never one to pass up on a bit of gossip. The finest idle tongues from up and down the town relayed the tale like an Olympic torch. After the inevitable laughter sparked by the story of the young girl's arrival in response to a simple letter from Old Ma Madeleine inquiring if a daughter-in-law might possibly be available, each had his or her own interpretation of events. And so it was that a great many extravagant rumours did the rounds about Madeleine the American, only three of which survived until that night of December 28, 1958, in Papa Louis' living room.

According to the first version of the story peddled in the parish of Saint-François-Xavier, authorship of which was attributed to a gossip answering to the name of Dumont, the Lamontagnes had fallen victim to a dastardly plot hatched by Old Ma Madeleine's brother. There must have been vengeful thoughts behind it, because who sends his own daughter, adopted or not, hundreds of miles away into the arms of a stranger? The young woman must have been insufferable, her adoptive parents had jumped at the first chance they got to be rid of her once and for all. Now who knew what might happen? And Louis-Benjamin would be left to pick up the tab.

The second version of the story, perhaps a little more refined and more shrouded in mystery, cast Madeleine the American in the role of the woman of passion, flitting from one widower to the next unsuspecting bachelor, amassing inheritances and leaving funeral processions and grieving families in her wake. She had, of course, stolen Old Ma Madeleine's letter at the post office, before having someone pen a reply to take in the Lamontagnes. Old Ma Madeleine would have only to perform the usual checks by telegraph in order to be clear in her own mind and be rid of the parasite. In its darkest versions, this story prophesied an accidental death for Louis-Benjamin in the near future. All bets were off.

And finally, more twisted minds ascribed darker intentions to the little schemer. Probably a lady of the night, she had, they said, met Madeleine the American on the train, made sure she was well and truly *out of the picture* (there's just no stopping those kinds of vermin), and taken her belongings to organize the whole sorry sham. The rest was nothing but theatre and strength of conviction. No matter, uniformed men would soon be arriving to write an epilogue to the improbable tale.

"No one ever got to the bottom of it," sighed Papa Louis, staring at his glass of gin.

The following day, March 2, Old Ma Madeleine wrote to her brother Alphonse, demanding an explanation for the previous evening's events. Who was this girl? Had he really sent her packing to a foreign land without even inquiring as to the worth of young Louis-Benjamin? Was the young lady really that docile? Was he absolutely certain he had made the right decision? In the meantime, the American girl would have to be housed somewhere. Neither the Sisters of the Good Shepherd nor the Sisters of the Child Jesus had room for the poor thing. As for the priest, it was out of the question that he put up such a strange creature about whom virtually nothing was known and from whom the most surprising revelations might well be expected. And so the Lamontagnes resolved to let her stay with them. From the day after she arrived, the girl began to behave in a most unusual manner. First of all, she confirmed by way of a particularly nasal early morning rosary that she was indeed of the true faith. Then, every morning at the crack of dawn, she would cook dishes the Lamontagnes were not in the least used to. On the first day, she went to the general store for provisions since it appeared she had brought a modest dowry with her from the United States. On the second morning, she set to work in the kitchen, humming all the while a heartwarming song for the cold of heart:

Will you love me all the time?
Summer time, winter time.
Will you love me rain or shine?
As I love you?
Will you kiss me every day?
Will you miss me when away?
Will you stay at home and play?
When I marry you?

The little waltz in three-quarter time was so catchy that it stayed in your head for hours after hearing it. Papa Louis sang it for his audience, which was beginning to shrink as time ticked on. Luc was now asleep, collapsed on top of his brother Marc, who was himself fighting a battle of epic proportions against Morpheus. Madeleine, eyes wide as saucers, was gripped by the tale of horses and deadly epidemics and entirely under the storyteller's spell. She hummed along to the American girl's song, which their father sang to them in their little beds at night. The whole of America, a whole century, used to fall asleep to this lullaby that sang of worry, doubt, promises, and love.

Marc watched his sister Madeleine's head nod gently as she began to drift off. He was suddenly gripped by a terrible fear: Papa Louis, realizing his audience was asleep, would bring his story to an end so that he wouldn't have to pick it up again the following week. The boy was dying to hear what happened to his grandparents next.

"Madeleine, go make Papa Louis a gin!" he cried, shaking his sister like a plum tree.

Madeleine went off to mix the toddy.

"But what did the American girl cook?"

The question came, once again, from the kitchen.

"Breakfast. Pancakes, beans, fried eggs, you name it! And the people of Fraserville had never known the like of it," Papa Louis replied, gazing off into the distance.

The American had gotten it into her head that the way to Canadians' hearts was through their stomachs. But she would have her work cut out for her. Without ever having read it, she knew full well the contents of the letter Old Ma Madeleine had dictated to the parish priest the day after she had arrived. They would have to be won over one by one, calorie by calorie, carb by carb... On the third day, the American girl baked a sandwich loaf that relegated Old Ma Madeleine's bread to the rank of mere ship's biscuit. That American bread was white and fluffy as a cloud. It caressed Louis-Benjamin's lips like the wings of a dove. On the fourth day, the girl baked hot cross buns topped with caramelized sugar. Their aroma alone had the young man foaming at the mouth from the wood shop where, as Old Michaud's apprentice, he crafted small, simple pieces of furniture to order for the people of Fraserville. Cribs more than anything else. And always to the melody of *Will you love me all the time?*, which the parish priest had agreed, after much beseeching and imploring, to translate, whispering into his ear so that people would not think he had succumbed to an unspeakable, unnatural vice before the handsome Louis-Benjamin. The aroma of the hot cross buns, the American girl's red hair, the baby cribs, *Will you love me all the time?* ... It was all enough to make his head spin. The poor boy, who had never known the torments of love, was so distracted he flattened his thumb with a hammer. The cry of a wounded animal reverberated from one side of the St. Lawrence to the other. On the north shore, people thought it was the cry of a drowning man, and a search was launched on the snow-covered ice of the enormous river for the poor devil who had fallen into the water.

But the drowning man was Louis-Benjamin...

"Drowning in an ocean of love!" exclaimed Papa Louis, beating out each syllable with his left hand on the arm of his chair.

On the sofa, the peals of laughter from Madeleine and Marc were almost enough to stir Sirois from the dead. Luc remained buried in his impenetrable sleep, his body occasionally convulsed by a passing bad dream.

Old Michaud was saddened to see the young man so devoured by desire. How many times had he tried to reason with the lad? He even went as far as to explain that sometimes burning blazes could be snuffed out, temporarily at least, and that it sufficed to find some place or other where you could be certain of being alone to "plane the big beam" until your ears buzzed. Louis-Benjamin listened politely to the fellow's advice, not daring to admit that, in this particular case, a mere plane would be but a droplet of water on a burning stone. He confessed to his master that he was considering eloping with the American girl to marry her in another parish, before a priest who did not know them. Old Michaud explained to him that the plan was destined to fail, that he would only bring disgrace upon himself, and that, in any case, no priest in the province of Quebec would agree to marry a young tenderfoot to a mere slip of a girl without their parents' consent. When he saw the young boy's eyes fill with water, Michaud promised to put in a word for him with the priest. He himself had no idea what this initiative might bring, but speaking to the priest never did any harm.

Father Cousineau received Old Michaud just before mass. Michaud tried to find the words to make the man of the cloth understand that young Louis-Benjamin was languishing with love for the young American girl and that the nuptials between the two lovebirds should be celebrated without delay. He himself had taken a wife at nineteen; it wasn't at all out of the ordinary. He also tried to get the priest to understand that some trees grow more quickly than others, an allusion that was somewhat lost on him. Nevertheless, Michaud added that his main concern was getting the boy back to working at the same pace he had been at before the American girl arrived. Nothing less than a marriage before God—and before Pentecost—would settle the matter. The priest waited patiently for Old Michaud to finish. At the end of the discussion, he invited the cabinetmaker to pray with him for the intervention of the Blessed Virgin. Before leaving, Michaud made an offering to the parish, which, that day, took the form of a sugar pie his wife had baked that very morning, knowing that her husband was off to the presbytery with a request. It was only fifteen minutes until the start of mass. Taking one look at the pie, the priest calculated that by sending Michaud on his way and hurrying just a little, he might have time to eat just the tiniest slice, Lent or no Lent. Old Michaud walked into the church, and when the priest appeared in the sacristy five minutes later, he still had crumbs on his belly.

The sermon was sweeter than usual.

Meanwhile, Old Ma Madeleine was at her wit's end. On the one hand, the young American was as nice as could be, showed an uncommonly healthy appetite for work, and had won the approval of Louis-Benjamin's young sisters, with whom she shared a room. She helped the girls get dressed in

26

the morning, braided their hair, kept them clean, and taught them good manners. To say thank you. To clear the table. To smile. On the other hand, no one knew the first thing about the woman. Where had she come from? Why hadn't she learned French like everyone else? Had Alphonse's family taken to English to fit in better in the United States? And what about the girl's past? Was she going to transmit some terrible disease to her Louis-Benjamin? And in the improbable event she agreed to hand over her oldest son to this mysterious American, would their children grow up to look down on their Canadian father?

One month passed. Then, on the morning of April 2, Easter Tuesday, Father Cousineau knocked on the Lamontagnes' door, holding a letter mailed in New Hampshire. The torn envelope was proof that the priest had already read and translated its contents. Delicious aromas wafted in from the kitchen. Eggs, Father Cousineau was quite certain, and unless he was mistaken, fresh bread, baked beans, cretons, some kind of pork glistening with fat, and a full and generous teapot were standing by. The American girl was at work. He noted happily that everyone in the Lamontagne family appeared to have gained weight, even though Lent had just ended. Well-rounded cheeks, tight clothes, generous bosoms… Old Ma Madeleine's sons and daughters had spent an anti-Lent to which the American cook's arrival was surely no stranger. The breakfast table had not yet been cleared when Madeleine the American asked the priest to take a seat. "Please, Father…" She disappeared into the kitchen, returning with a plate piled high with pancakes, eggs, and slices of ham. All swimming in a half-inch of maple syrup. The priest, a man used to a leaner diet, dug courageously into the mountain of treats that towered before him. The rich food gave him the courage to announce the news he had come to tell the Lamontagne family. While continuing to eat—because, truth be told, he had never tasted pancakes so fluffy, so light, nor ham so tender—he first asked to speak to the American girl alone. The rest of the family piled into the kitchen. Three of the children spilled out onto the lawn to play in the early rays of the April sun.

From the kitchen, the priest's low voice could be heard as he spoke hesitantly in the English he had learned at the seminary. It went on for some minutes. Then a prayer went up. Next, after a short silence, three sighs from a woman were heard, followed by a sob. Upon hearing the sobs of the woman he so desired, Louis-Benjamin wanted to burst into the dining room and take her in his arms. Old Ma Madeleine looked daggers at him. "You, you stay put!" she hissed at her excitable son. After a moment's silence, the girl swept into the kitchen, her face streaming with tears, sobbing uncontrollably. Intrigued, Old Ma Madeleine and her son went over to the priest, who was busily mopping up his yolk with a slice of toast. He wiped his mouth before he spoke.

He had received a letter from the United States, penned in English by the priest in the girl's parish of Nashua. Shortly after their adoptive daughter's departure, Alphonse's family had suffered much misfortune. First, their youngest son had been struck by a terrible fever that no remedy had managed to cool. They realized too late that the boy had, like so many others, contracted the Spanish flu. The boy of twelve was dead within a week. But the Grim Reaper did not stop there. Two days before the boy breathed his last, his mother felt the beginning of the end stir in her throat. Then it was the father's turn, and he lasted no more than four days. In all, the flu had plundered four members from a family of only seven, including Madeleine. The Spanish flu had left her an orphan again, depriving her of a father and mother for a second time. Of the three children death had spared, two had already left the family home to get married. The remaining daughter had watched death take the home's occupants one by one, only to find herself alone. The priest was careful to note in his letter that Clarisse, the unfortunate survivor, was now in the care of the nuns of the state of New Hampshire.

"Are there any of those divine pancakes left?" Father Cousineau inquired.

"I think there are indeed!" said Old Ma Madeleine, getting up.

Father Cousineau waited until she was in the kitchen before giving Louis-Benjamin a wink. Between two Americans sobs, the sound of utensils in the kitchen reached them. The priest ruffled the young man's hair.

"So, my boy. If someone asked you to choose between a trip to France and the American girl, what would you do?"

The boy reddened. He looked down at the wooden table, trying to hold back tears with a weak laugh.

"France is real far!" he said.

"Yes, my boy. Much too far," the priest replied, taking a sip of tea. "And it's infested with Germans," he spat.

"We're Germans too, Father."

"I know, but that was before the war, long before. Do you remember Germany?"

"No."

"Your father neither, nor his father before him. It goes all the way back to the eighteenth century. I don't think there can be much German left in you."

"Is the eighteenth century far back?"

"As far away as Germany. And if I were you, I'd keep quiet about it," he concluded.

Old Ma Madeleine set down a second plate in front of the priest, who didn't even wait for her to take her hand away before he swiped a piece of pancake, voraciously eyeing a slice of ham glistening in the springtime sun. Outside, the gulls' cries became more piercing, a few chickadees announced better days, and melted snow ran down the streets, comforting those in mourning. The priest chewed noisily enough for Old Ma Madeleine to consider putting a word in the bishop's ear the next time he visited. Wasn't the seminary there to teach good manners? With a nod, the priest signalled for Louis-Benjamin to leave the room so that he could speak in private with Old Ma Madeleine. The youngster leaped up to join Madeleine the American in the kitchen while the priest seized the opportunity to swallow an enormous mouthful of ham.

"There was trouble in Quebec City yesterday," he announced gravely.

"What sort of trouble?"

"The army is looking for young men to conscript, Mrs. Lamontagne. They sent soldiers from Toronto, English-speaking men who opened fire on an unarmed crowd. Five innocents are dead. It won't be long until they cross the river and come looking up here. They'll be after Louis-Benjamin. That good-looking son of yours is eighteen years old."

Old Ma Madeleine sighed. What could any of this have to do with the drama that had been playing since the priest had arrived?

"The girl no longer has a home to go back to," the priest said.

"Are you asking me to keep her, Father? She doesn't understand half of what we tell her."

"The army doesn't go around taking fathers from their families, Mrs. Lamontagne."

There was a silence. Old Ma Madeleine looked outside, where two of her daughters were throwing snowballs at Louis-Benjamin's brother. It seemed to her that only yesterday her oldest boy had been doing exactly the same thing. She smiled.

"Would you like another cup of tea, Father?"

"I wouldn't be so impolite as to refuse," he replied.

Truth be told, the priest would have happily taken some more ham, and perhaps a pancake, but he kept quiet, lest the woman take him for a glutton. Old Ma Madeleine stood up to refill the teapot in the kitchen. Walking through the door, she let out a cry.

"Louis-Benjamin Lamontagne!" she exclaimed.

The priest hoisted his two hundred and twenty pounds up off the chair to see what was going on in the next room with his own eyes. There was Louis-Benjamin on a kitchen stool, holding the American girl by the waist as she sat straddled in his lap. The latter, as brazen as you please, had undone the second button of her suitor's shirt, and was removing her hand from the boy's clothing just as the priest's head appeared in the doorway. Blushing with shame, the two children didn't know where to look. The girl tried to free herself from the embrace of her fiancé who, for reasons only young men understand, reasons directly related to the spring breeze blowing through Fraserville that day, desperately wanted her to screen him for just another minute. He clung to her like a lifebuoy. Then suddenly he was infuriated. He grabbed hold of the girl with the firmness of a cowboy wrangling a heifer.

"I don't wanna go to France, Ma!" he yelled in a tone Old Ma Madeleine had never heard before.

His mother stood there looking helpless, between the two entwined lovebirds and the priest, whose belly could now be heard rumbling. The priest had looked away from the young couple. He was now eyeing up the breakfast leftovers. He noted with no small amount of interest that there was a pancake on the griddle, untouched and still warm.

"You're not going to throw that pancake out, are you?" he inquired innocently, pointing a finger at the object of his desire.

It was no time until the two youngsters, who had been only one word short of bliss, were united before God. For the fourth time that year, Father Cousineau sped things up a little, putting an earlier date on the banns, smoothing out the rough edges the hands of the authorities wouldn't help but feel when they came across a young man still practically beardless but in possession of a marriage certificate. On April 3, 1918, before a sparse audience, Louis-Benjamin and Madeleine the American were pronounced man and wife before Father Cousineau, who was as proud as a peacock.

"That's another one they won't get."

In the whole parish, he knew none finer, none sweeter, than the young Lamontagne boys. The very idea that such a handsome young man would have a bomb dropped on him or, worse still, be sent home an invalid or gassed simply because the king didn't know how to wage a war, was abhorrent to him. Old Ma Madeleine thought it best to wait until her husband had returned home from the logging camp before doing something so momentous for all concerned, to which the priest retorted that the army spotters could step out of the train at any minute or spring up like jack-in-the-boxes on the road. And once they were in Fraserville, there would be nothing for it but to hide her boys like hens hide their chicks. The priest was thinking that, judging by what he had heard from Louis-Benjamin at confession, the young American girl was about to feel a spring wind blow, the likes of which she had never felt, or at least find reward for all her attentions in the kitchen. With the resignation of the birds, Old Ma Madeleine, sitting stiffly in a pew, shed not a tear, tears not being her forte, and wondered instead how she was going to explain everything to her husband when he came back from the logging camp at winter's end. Piled in beside her in the freezing-cold church, Louis-Benjamin's little sisters dozed, stared at the Madonna out of the corner of their eyes, or counted the cotton flowers stitched onto Madeleine the American's white dress, which had been hastily rented the day before from the Thivierges' general store, meaning that Old Ma Madeleine had been up part of the night adjusting the waist (much too ample for such a tiny slip of a thing) and ironing her girls' calico dresses. Her face wan and her head filled with sleep, Old Ma Madeleine entrusted the fate of her oldest son to the hands of God and the wedding photos to Lavoie the photographer.

Their wedding photo—the one that Papa Louis is pointing to with an insistent index finger at this very moment, right beside the photo of Sister Mary of the Eucharist's twin sister who died in Nagasaki—shows the newlyweds in profile, still almost children, Louis-Benjamin with his cowlick standing straight up in the air and smiling blissfully, perhaps because he was wearing a bow tie for the very first time, perhaps because his dearest wish was going to be realized when he walked out of the photographer's studio on Rue Lafontaine, which the bridal procession had entered headed up by Old Ma Madeleine, followed by her girls, each in their Sunday best, then the main attraction, the undisputed superstars of this strange Easter carnival.

The photographer had them sit very close to each other, close enough for the girl to feel on her neck the breath of the strapping Louis-Benjamin doing his level best not to go mad with happiness. They were like two children dressed up as adults to get a laugh out of their parents. The collar on Louis-Benjamin's shirt was slightly too big for him, his bow tie almost as broad as his smile. As for the girl, she looked like she'd just been told a risqué joke. The blissfully happy expression that was to mark that day still shone clearly in December 1958 in Papa Louis' living room, in the soft light of the fringed floor lamp that enveloped with its yellow glow the storyteller, his children, a still-decorated Christmas tree, and, at the back of the adjoining parlour, Sirois in his casket. Little Madeleine felt her brother Marc's hand under her thigh, a restless, mischievous, reassuring presence.

Her mind swimming back and forth between two distinct worlds, Madeleine took her brother Marc's hand so as not to lose him, so as not to be ejected from this downy nest confected from Christmas trees, gin, little brothers, and stories of brides arriving by train on a winter evening. She wanted to know how Papa Louis had come into the world, because that's what he'd promised to tell them: how he had come into the world against all odds that Christmas of 1918. She wanted to hear the story just once, then grow up.

"Hold my hand. I don't want to fall asleep," she whispered into Marc's ear.

As if to celebrate the impromptu wedding of Louis-Benjamin and Madeleine the American, Papa Louis lit a cigarette, twirling it several times before going on with the story. The air in the living room filled with an acrid, carcinogenic smell, lending the room a solemn feel, as though Papa Louis had wanted to show they had moved into the adult world and the story was about to get darker. He closed the door to the parlour where Sirois was resting.

"Cigarettes are bad for the dead—and for the living!"

He slapped his broad thighs. Old Ma Madeleine had set up a bedroom for the newlyweds in her home on Rue Fraserville. What is there to say about Louis-Benjamin other than that his boss, Old Michaud, saw all his wishes come true in the first week after the wedding ceremony. The boy had rediscovered his composure and constantly wore a little smile, the one he was known for before the American arrived. In Old Michaud's workshop, he carved and sanded down one little cradle after the other. His young wife had been caught throwing up into a wooden pail one morning, looking gloomy and preoccupied.

In the meantime, Vilmaire Lamontagne, Louis-Benjamin's father, had returned home from logging over the winter to find his son married to an American. He had arrived back one rainy afternoon to a deserted house.

Alone in the kitchen, a young lady was busy preparing rabbits. Vilmaire asked what she was doing in his kitchen. The stranger put down the carcass, rinsed her hands, and tried to sum up in her stilted French the events of the previous weeks. He looked at his daughter-in-law, perplexed and a little worried. The newcomer served him a bowl of hearty stew and a mug of tea. Tired after his long journey, he chewed on his meal as he looked the young woman over. Little Louis-Benjamin married? Where had his wife gotten to? And the girls? All these questions were answered after a long nap when the rest of the family came back from yard work at a cousin's house. When it was confirmed to him that his son was indeed married, Vilmaire Lamontagne smiled, looked the American up and down, and lifted her up off the ground as though checking her worth in weight.

"You're my daughter now."

The summer went by in a state of bliss that was barely interrupted by the pregnancy troubles of the young wife, who substantially increased in volume. On the days her husband received his pay, she would be seen wearily dragging herself back up Rue Lafontaine from the stores. Louis, for his part, had been thrust by his father into the world of woodwork. A similar-looking home was built beside his father's because they were starting to get under each other's feet. That September, Father Cousineau started putting in appearances again with the family. They had long since understood that the man had to be fed regularly, if only to express their gratitude to him for having spared Louis-Benjamin a senseless death at Verdun or Vimy. Nothing reprehensible or out of place for a parish priest in 1918, though, because sometimes they grew bored, these good men in their big, ghost-ridden presbyteries, where the clocks sounded for vespers, confessions, communions, funerals, and blessings. While not hopelessly nostalgic, Father Cousineau rather enjoyed being in a dining room teeming with snot-nosed children. The Lamontagne home was a place of comfort, a refuge that allowed him to escape, if only briefly, the cold, impersonal surroundings of the presbytery. On such evenings, he was especially fond of recalling his days at the Rimouski seminary for the Lamontagnes. He had been ordained there, hailing from the nearby Matapédia Valley as he did. He spoke of the camaraderie among the seminarists, without of course going into all the details of the special friendships that tended to flourish.

Ten years before being sent to the parish of Saint-François-Xavier in Fraserville, Father Cousineau had belonged to the seminary's theatre troupe, where he had spent his happiest hours. Aside from the pleasure he felt performing scenes from *Lives of the Saints* or the New Testament, Cousineau really came into his own making sets and costumes. People in Rimouski still remembered the grandiose outfit he had made himself to play King Charles VII in *The Maid of Orleans*, a pious drama penned by two Brothers of the Holy Cross in 1882 that paid tribute to the victorious king who had managed to rid France of the English plague. For his court costume, young Cousineau had made himself a magnificent doublet from maroon felt, trimmed around the collar and sleeves with fox fur he had begged one of his aunts for. A talented couturier and designer with a keen fashion sense, he hadn't stopped there: he had also made himself a large black hat with a broad brim upon which he had painstakingly embroidered the white lines that make up the starred pattern of that particular historical headpiece. He drew much of his inspiration from a portrait of the French sovereign that appeared in *Lives of the Saints* and even went so far as to wear old-fashioned stockings—borrowed from the same aunt who had loaned him the fox fur—under the salmon-pink petticoat breeches that made him vaguely resemble a peony and, the one and only anachronism in his otherwise wholly convincing attire, Charles IX shoes that had also served the year before when the senior students had put on *Le Malade imaginaire*.

The seminarist who played Joan of Arc, a fellow by the name of Levasseur whom his peers cowardly referred to on occasion as Father Ganymede, had advised Cousineau to wear a pair of plain leather or white canvas bearpaw shoes, but Cousineau thought the Charles IX shoes gave him a regal stride that the king who had liberated France from the English was surely deserving of, even if that meant flouting the fashion rules of the fifteenth century.

"Those shoes weren't in fashion at the time of Joan of Arc," Levasseur had grumbled.

"Yes, but they're more comfortable. Besides, they put a little spring in my step," Cousineau had retorted, clicking the little black heels of his Charles IX's together.

"We are portraying the life of a saint. We must remain faithful to the spirit of the time," Levasseur had insisted. Cousineau pursed his lips and glared disapprovingly at his colleague.

"Father Levasseur, if we are to follow the spirit of the fifteenth century to the letter, then we shall have to stop washing for two weeks and burn you alive for what everyone saw you doing with Brother McNeill in the sacristy the day before yesterday. A fat lot of good that would do us!"

Levasseur had let the matter drop. Cousineau would wear his Charles IX's.

And so the troupe of seminarists gave the actor who had triumphed as Toinette in *Le Malade imaginaire* the role of Joan of Arc in *The Maid of Orleans*. The irony being, Father Cousineau remarked, that the Brothers of the Holy Cross, who had written the play, had included one rather lengthy scene depicting the trial of Joan of Arc, particularly her indictment, in which she was reproached, among many other offences, for wearing men's clothing. So it was that when the young seminarist played this role dressed up as a woman, a sigh or gasp always went up from the audience, as a train of thought arrived in the station. But in *The Maid of Orleans*, Father Cousineau had stolen the show from the cross-dressing seminarist thanks to his magnificent costume and the deep voice he had used to reply to Joan of Arc when she was crowned.

"Your Majesty, we absolutely must take Paris. Our victory is unimaginable without Paris."

"Joan, above all else we must be careful," Charles VII had replied, under the approving gaze of the audience, Cousineau's presence so eclipsing poor Levasseur that people almost began to hope he would be burned as quickly as possible.

And so Father Cousineau belonged to those who you could say had missed their vocation in life, even though his Sunday mass attracted four to five hundred souls, rain or shine. To a liturgy as regular as clockwork and in which there was on the face of it no place for creativity or improvisation, the ingenious Father Cousineau always found a way to introduce a dash of theatricality to the proceedings, as though the popes had not already personally seen to it that Catholic mass remained the best show in town. On the feast day of St. John the Baptist, for instance, Father Cousineau made sure that the altar boys were all very young, with curly blond hair. He had arranged it so that the Sisters of the Child Jesus, newly arrived in Fraserville, joined a very active choir that parishioners would turn out to hear at the drop of a hat.

And so it was that on Sunday, November 17, 1918, a very special mass came to be sung at the church of Saint-François-Xavier. Father Cousineau, always with a keen eye for staging and an ear for music, had demanded that each parishioner be at the mass, adding that absentees had better be on their deathbeds. They were going to give glory to God, ask forgiveness for their sins, and praise the Virgin Mary for having brought an end to an interminable war, a senseless, horrifying war, and no grounds would be deemed acceptable for failing to attend the ceremony. Without a word of explanation to the parishioners, Father Cousineau asked the couples he had personally married during the war to fill the first pews, thereby upsetting an established order determined by how much the faithful had contributed to the parish finances. He had also tasked the choirmaster with having the choir sing a *Te Deum*, a hymn sung on various occasions, notably at the end of a smallpox epidemic or whenever a siege of a city had been lifted, an heir to the throne had been born, spring had arrived after a particularly deadly winter, a shipwrecked crew had been saved, a harvest of oats had been especially bountiful, or an end had come to a war that no one had wanted and that had brought nothing but death, sadness, and pestilence down upon humanity. Father Cousineau's sermon was clear: "My fellow *Canadiens*! Go forth and have children to replace those the war has taken from us!"

And he addressed his message to the first rows of the congregation in particular, for the most part sprightly and willing young men married to very young women deprived of all means of contraception.

The *Te Deum* was magnificent. Papa Louis chanted in Latin to impress his children:

"*Te æternum Patrem omnis terra veneratur!*" he sang in a tuneful tenor.

"What does it mean?" chorused the children, who belonged to a time where people still wanted these mysterious phrases translated.

It means, "All the earth doth worship thee, the father everlasting!" Papa Louis replied, proud to prove that not only was he able to lift a horse clean off the ground but he could translate from the Latin, too.

In a way, the parishioners, and especially those whom Father Cousineau addressed on that first Sunday following the armistice, were singing for their priest a silent hymn full of thanks to a man who, through some sleight of hand, falsification, and manipulation had managed to unite before God and man an unrivalled number of couples, a good many of whom had not yet reached adulthood. With their chubby, smiling faces, not the slightest grey hair among them, their hands still plump, sometimes already expecting, unsuspecting though they were, they wanted nothing more than for the interminable mass to end so they could get on with the task Father Cousineau had set them in the intimacy of their wooden homes. Everyone would remember the impeccable organization behind that armistice mass, the emotion that had washed over the congregation, and Father Cousineau's touching affection for young people, family, and music. Could there possibly be, east of Quebec City, a parish priest more pleasant, more determined, more kindly? They had their doubts. At any rate, in the hearts of Louis-Benjamin and the American, Father Cousineau was truly a saviour, a guardian, an indispensable guide.

The last few leaves still clinging to the maple trees were now carried off by the breeze. On their way out of the church, Madeleine the American, her sense of smell made keener by her pregnant state, said to her husband:

"Louis-Benjamin, I smell snow!"

The residents of Fraserville peered up at the grey sky and smiled blissfully.

But Cousineau still had an idea or two to ensure his masses would live long in the memory of his congregation, masses as unforgettable as opening night at the theatre. It goes without saying that he considered Louis-Benjamin and the American something of a creation of his own making, that is to say that he proudly attributed to himself—and not unjustly—the happy ending of a story that could easily have turned out differently, ending in the worst-case scenario with a terse, sorry telegram from the Canadian Army. From one Sunday to the next, he could see how the pretty American was thriving, developing more curves, and illuminating with her hopeful face the gazes of the other parishioners. With her bulging belly, rosy cheeks, and glowing complexion, the American exuded maternity and joy. According to the priest's calculations, she would bring her child into the world after New Year's Day, which gave him cause to consider realizing a dream he had cherished for years: a live nativity scene at midnight mass. Never had he dared bring up this desire with any of Fraserville's young couples, fearing they would refuse outright or misinterpret his intentions. But he was so close to the American, and young Louis-Benjamin was, out of all his flock, the closest thing to the son he would never have. And so in September he revealed his plans to them. It wouldn't be a big deal for Louis-Benjamin and his young wife: between the ox and the little donkey they would come in from the sacristy and walk calmly toward the altar. They would, of course, be appropriately attired, faithfully harkening back to the days of the nativity.

"With real lambs, I promise!" Cousineau had assured them.

He had already spoken to a farmer on Chemin Témiscouata, who had agreed to supply two of them. They would be led by young shepherds, the same who had played the role of Saint John the Baptist.

"There will be singing, and music, Bach, Balbastre... Fraserville will still be talking about this mass in one hundred years' time!"

37

In the Lamontagne household, the thought had brought a smile to the little girls' faces, already imagining their big brother as Joseph and his wife as the Virgin Mary. Old Ma Madeleine immediately expressed her clear disapproval: the young woman would likely not be able to live up to the priest's ambitions. And it would cause the whole parish to turn its attentions to the pair when all eyes had already been on them for months. At any rate, if the project was to go ahead, it would do so without her consent.

"People are talking. Saying the girl was put in the family way by my Louis-Benjamin before the wedding."

What Old Ma Madeleine did not know, but what anyone in the parish could have told her, was that that was the most harmless rumour doing the rounds about Madeleine the American. The town gossips had come up with whole new chapters for the tall tales surrounding her origins and the real reasons why she had turned up in Fraserville.

Nobody had officially bought the story of the family decimated by Spanish flu. For scandalmongers, the idea that Madeleine the American had been a victim of circumstance was much too bland. It didn't fit with the story they had already scripted for her and so they came up with two explanations for her pregnancy. The first had it that the child had been conceived out of wedlock, the very night the American first set foot in the Lamontagne home. The sorry reputation the women of America held in Canadian eyes only added fuel to the fire. An American! Just imagine! The young lad had surely been seduced from the first minute by the red-haired devil. Two reliable witnesses had even seen them kissing on the lips, right under the noses of Old Ma Madeleine, Father Cousineau, and Louis-Benjamin's little sisters, whose salvation had surely now been compromised by such debauchery. They would have to be watched carefully. But that was far and away the least hurtful of the tall tales circulating along Rue Lafontaine.

There was much worse.

Among the many stories Old Ma Madeleine had never heard about her daughter-in-law was the vile rumour that she had come to Fraserville already carrying the child whose paternity was now being ascribed to Louis-Benjamin. It goes without saying that this version nicely complemented rumours that the American had led a loose life before repenting and winding up in Fraserville. The rest was said to have been a ruse on her part: she seduced Louis-Benjamin, they said, so that he would raise the child whose real father would never be known. At any rate, Old Ma Madeleine was against the idea of a living nativity and did not mince her words. Louis-Benjamin's father, for his part, was completely indifferent to the whole affair. Only the little Lamontagne girls seemed keen on Father Cousineau's project. Perhaps they would be allowed to take part themselves?

"The angels are boys," Old Ma Madeleine snapped, nipping in the bud her daughters' dreams of the theatre.

Louis-Benjamin's young brother Napoleon wanted to know if they needed a shepherd, making it clear to the priest that any support for his project would come from the youngsters. Louis-Benjamin and the American had laughed long and hard at the priest's plan and were largely in agreement, provided they had very few lines to deliver. The priest had reassured them immediately: they would have very little to say, the whole thing would be narrated by a nun from the Sisters of the Child Jesus, who would read the story of the nativity from the gospels. This eased the American's mind in particular. Her hesitant French caused her to blush every time she had to speak in public.

The priest remarked that the young woman was wearing a very simple gold cross on her ample bosom. He had not noticed it when she arrived in the spring. Perhaps it had been hidden by layer upon layer of clothing. But now he could see it shining in the light. The cross was about an inch long and made from real gold. Seeing the priest staring at the piece of jewellery, the girl tried to explain its provenance in French peppered with English. Louis-Benjamin had given it to her for her birthday, on June 24, the feast of St. John the Baptist. She unfastened the gold chain and handed it to the priest, saying, "Could you please bless my cross, Father Cousineau?" The priest fingered the pendant. There was an inscription on the back, its owner's initials in cursive script: M.L. The priest, well used to being asked to bless entire farms, new homes, telephones, and even locomotives, didn't think twice about blessing the piece of jewellery, especially since he felt that by performing this simple task for the naive little soul, he would surely improve the odds of her taking part in his living nativity. He blessed the small cross and returned it to its owner, pink with gratitude. How much must it have cost? Much more than Louis-Benjamin was earning at Old Michaud's, that was for sure. But Louis-Benjamin had not let material considerations dampen his ardour for his Madeleine. The cross was brilliant, scintillating proof of it. The priest told the American to be very careful, to never go out in the evening wearing her cross too ostentatiously, and to take good care of it.

"I will, Father Cousineau."

Much to Old Ma Madeleine's chagrin, the deal was sealed quickly. They agreed on a dress rehearsal in December and then the meal was served, to Father Cousineau's great delight. At last he would have the midnight mass he had always dreamed of.

And so autumn passed, the first snowfall came, then a second, then another. Little by little, soldiers and officers came back from Europe; some had seen Paris with their own eyes. Despite the cold of winter, a wind of hope blew in over the St. Lawrence Valley. Father Cousineau thought about his living nativity every day, had costumes made, sat down with the nun to decide on which text to read, did everything in the church to make sure the scene would have every bit the impact he hoped for, even for those who would be sitting at the back or standing. The American was now enormous. She dragged herself with more and more difficulty from one chore to the next. Sometimes she would be caught sleeping on a stool, her head leaning against the kitchen wall, as the soup she had begun to heat up boiled over. On days like those, Old Ma Madeleine would excuse her from all strenuous tasks and order her to remain seated or lying down, to keep away from the stove at any rate, a miserable sentence for a woman used to cooking morning, noon, and night.

With December came Advent, celestial organs, and red cheeks. The Lamontagne family put the building of Louis-Benjamin's new home on hold. The shell and structure were ready, and the final touches would come in the spring. Even the mountains of Charlevoix, which could be seen gathering snow on the other side of the St. Lawrence, seemed to agree with how things were in Fraserville. In the afternoon, the setting sun gave a rosy hue to the snow and the locals before disappearing. No country was more beautiful.

Then came Christmas.

On December 22, the fourth Sunday of Advent, Father Cousineau again stood up the Sisters of the Child Jesus—the nuns having set up home in the church of Saint-François-Xavier's sacristy while waiting for their first convent in Fraserville to be built—to dine with the Lamontagne family. The Lamontagnes now considered the man of the cloth one of their own. By this stage of her pregnancy, the American was praying every day to be delivered from the burden she carried, a burden that kicked and wriggled around inside her. She sometimes wondered if the child, so often did it keep her awake at night, was not trying to warn her of some imminent danger.

She could feel some sort of battle being waged inside her, she was sure of it. Forced to rest, she was served food by Old Ma Madeleine. It was much less tasty than her own, but had the advantage of being prepared for her. As the priest chewed away on a slice of pork, he politely reminded the married couple he was expecting them on the afternoon of the twenty-fourth for the nativity scene dress rehearsal.

On the morning of December 24, the American was rudely awakened by her child, who was kicking with such frenzy that Louis-Benjamin could see the baby's foot bulging through his wife's skin with his own eyes; he could even count five tiny toes. The couple laughed off the incident, Old Ma Madeleine having explained that all her children, particularly the boys, had elbowed and kicked with varying degrees of violence. Painful though it might have been, it was nothing to get worked up over. Around two in the afternoon, as the sun's angled rays were already starting to turn the snow-covered shores of the St. Lawrence pink, a telegram arrived from Quebec City, warning of most inclement weather for the following day. But the telegraph operator on duty that December 24 had fallen ill and was unable to record the message that might have helped avoid the worst.

The dice had been cast by a much higher authority.

In the church, the couple found the parish priest in hysterics, raising his voice *in front of the Madonna* to berate a visibly dismayed workman. The priest had had a beautiful wooden set made for the nativity scene. Just to the right of the altar stood a miniature stable, complete with a little roof of coarsely planed boards—a nod to the cold, destitution, and poverty the Saviour had been born into. A tiny cradle made of branches and filled with straw had been placed beneath this approximately six-foot-high structure. And above the stable there shone a huge star, its wooden frame some five feet across covered by a white sheet. The object fascinated the American for an instant, as she watched the custodian open one of the sides fastened by two tiny metal hinges to hang an oil lamp inside. Perched on a wooden stepladder, the man struck a match and drew it closer to the wick. Once the lamp had been lit, he closed the side of the star, now shining brightly and casting out its yellow light. Madeleine the American had never seen the like of it.

"Beautiful!" she exclaimed, as the priest puffed up with pride.

To read the text of the nativity according to Saint Luke, the priest had chosen a nun whose sweet and gentle voice was sure to charm the faithful, but she had been confined to her bed by an unexplained illness. During the previous night, she had suffered from frightful dreams, at the end of which she had awoken as white as a sheet, her face haggard, in a sweat, and without even taking a bite to eat she had begged her Mother Superior to intercede with the priest on her behalf to relieve her of performing the reading for the nativity scene. She had described her nightmare: a terrifying scene where, standing on the terrace of a stone fortress on the shores of the Tiber River in Rome, she watched, powerless, as a man was executed, his hands bound behind him. In the background stood St. Peter's Basilica, which she recognized from pictures she had seen. A drum rolled; soldiers took aim with their rifles. Scarlet blood against a white shirt. A body collapsing. Cries ringing out in the sacristy. A fall from a great height.

"The rifles fired real bullets," sobbed the nun, head in hands.

In a trembling voice, she had explained her helplessness and confusion to her Mother Superior, who found it impossible to reason with her. A little alarmed herself by the shouts and cries of the young nun, and fearing for her protégée, the Mother Superior had advised the priest to call on the services of another reader for his nativity scene, even recommending another nun by the name of Sister Mary of the Eucharist, who had volunteered to do the reading, but of whom nothing was known other than a boundless love and respect for the Holy Scriptures. Nobody in Fraserville in that December of 1918 managed to come up with a satisfactory interpretation of the nun's nightmare.

The organist was at the dress rehearsal. He held in his hands a few loose sheets of paper, some scores, and the list setting out the order in which the pieces chosen by Father Cousineau were to be played. Louis-Benjamin and Madeleine the American felt as though they had been admitted to an inner circle of actors, and followed the priest's orders with the diligence of dilettantes. After two hours of practice, false starts, and retakes, they agreed to meet in the sacristy at nine o'clock that evening for the final preparations. The priest was still nervous. Sister Mary of the Eucharist had not been able to attend the rehearsal. A birth had held her back in Cacouna (she was also a midwife). She had, however, promised Father Cousineau she would be at the ceremony and would take her time reading whatever section of the gospel she was asked to. That evening, Old Ma Madeleine went outside and contemplated the overcast sky.

"Looks like snow," she said in her husband's direction.

"That's nice, snow at Christmas."

Then they decorated the tree, the little girls were dressed in their Sunday best, big Napoleon in a suit, and they waited for the birth of Christ. Louis-Benjamin and Madeleine the American were already in the sacristy. Sister Mary of the Eucharist still had not arrived. The priest was pacing around in circles, praying that a mishap hadn't befallen her on the way to Fraserville. The actors got into their costumes. For Joseph they had chosen a loose-fitting beige shirt and moleskin pants. By way of props, a set square and a small saw hung from a braided cord at his waist to remind everyone he was a carpenter. Louis-Benjamin felt very much in character. Sitting in a corner, two blond angels, brothers from the same family, helped each other adjust their great white wings as they hung from a harness. Both were to play the Archangel Gabriel. The priest had at first wondered whether the audience would be confused if he had the same character played by two different actors, but neither of the two was prepared to give up a speaking part to his brother. The role was therefore divided into two equal parts. To avoid the whole thing dragging on for hours, the performance would follow the regular midnight mass his parishioners had grown used to.

Sister Mary of the Eucharist arrived just as mass was about to begin, which meant that the priest didn't have a chance to introduce her to the other actors. Madeleine the American spent the whole mass wondering why Father Cousineau, a man who placed such stock on appearances, had asked such a frightening-looking woman to take part in a nativity scene. From the front, the sight of Sister Mary of the Eucharist could elicit the odd snigger. But from the side her silhouette recalled that of a crow or some other large-beaked bird. Her nose, upon which sat a small pair of round glasses, seemed to go on forever. And it would have been impossible, even if one were to mime, to describe her face without first mentioning that nose, just like it would be impossible to speak of Paris without mentioning the Eiffel Tower. Young or old? It was impossible in the penumbra of midnight mass to put an age on the bleak, tortured, and downright alarming face. In contrast to her black and white Sister of the Child Jesus habit, the pale skin of her face shone in the church like a moon in June; the image would have been reassuring, and calming, in this particular context, had the nun been careful not to smile: instead, the determined contraction of her facial muscles made her look as though she had swallowed a boomerang in full flight. The American recalled the legends of New England, terrible tales of pregnant women who, startled by some hideous monster or other who had appeared out of nowhere, had given birth to appalling, deformed creatures. While Sister Mary of the Eucharist sang about shepherds watching their flocks by night, the American felt a stirring in her breast, a dull, deep trembling that in other circumstances would have scared the wits out of her. Sister Mary of the Eucharist's voice, nasal and sharp as a bayonet, broke away from the rest of the choir.

But the young woman had no more time to continue with her questions. Her belly filled with pain, she stood with the others to hear *O Holy Night* being bellowed by a townsman whom a fellow parishioner, seeking to flatter, had foolishly complimented one day on his voice. At "Fall on your knees! O hear the angel voices!" the American felt another stirring inside her, as though the words had been addressed to her personally. While the church was only three-quarters full, it was not for a lack of devotion from the parishioners, nor because Father Cousineau had failed to promote his show. Rather, around ten o'clock that evening, heavy snow had begun to fall on Fraserville. After a quarter of an hour it lay already an inch or two deep in front of the church and showed no signs of letting up.

For fear of seeing the first gust of wind transform this touching scene into a hellish storm, many parishioners had not made the trip to midnight mass, even if that meant being refused communion for a week or having to go to confession. When the mass ended, the wind picked up in Fraserville and if those in attendance had taken the trouble to open the doors to the church of Saint-François-Xavier, they would have realized the visibility outside was so poor that they were trapped in their place of worship. The snow was now falling in dense flurries. And yet it was only when the wind began to whistle over the church roof that the parishioners really began to worry. No doubt about it: Father Cousineau would have excommunicated on the spot the first person to dare suggest they leave the church earlier than planned. The nativity would go on!

As the Latin mass ended quietly with Christmas wishes and hopes for greater fraternity that bore more than a passing resemblance to those of the previous year, the actors gathered in the sacristy to make their entrance. The American felt a little light-headed. Only Sister Mary of the Eucharist had stayed with the choir, looking over the pages of the New Testament she was preparing to read. But fear was beginning to get the better of the faithful. As the wind whistled more and more insistently, they feared they would no longer be able to make it home. A handful of families excused themselves politely and exited via the main aisle under the wrathful stare of Sister Mary of the Eucharist, her pale, haunting ugliness glinting in the low light.

The runaways had waited for Father Cousineau to disappear into the sacristy, but were forced to turn back once they realized, upon opening the church doors, that a terrible blizzard was beating down on Fraserville. You couldn't see more than ten feet ahead, the wind flinging to the ground any brave souls who might have preferred the prospect of a nice warm meal in their cozy homes to a nativity scene in a poorly heated church while the wind howled ominously outside. A few families who lived in neighbouring homes took their chances with the snowstorm. The rest returned to their seats, informing those who had stayed behind of what they had seen. The congregation was seized by panic. Were they all going to have to spend the night in the church? A worried murmur went up from the two hundred or so people who had resisted the temptation to slip out.

Sister Mary of the Eucharist cleared her throat to attract everyone's attention. She had just heard Father Cousineau signal that they were ready to begin. Someone turned down the lights. Between two gusts of wind, the nun's nasal voice rang out in the church.

"There was in the days of Herod, the King of Judaea, a certain priest named Zacharias, of the course of Abia: and his wife was of the daughters of Aaron, and her name was Elizabeth.

"And they were both righteous before God, walking in all the command-ments and ordinances of the Lord blameless.

"And they had no child..."

No one in Fraserville could claim they had ever heard Sister Mary of the Eucharist read out loud. People vaguely knew the nun, a ghostly, furtive figure sometimes glimpsed striding down Rue Lafontaine. Behind closed doors, Sister Mary of the Eucharist was referred to, depending on people's imaginations, as The Crow, The Raven, The Wicked Fairy, or, quite simply, Sister Scary. It would never have crossed anyone's mind to cast her in a living nativity. Far from evoking the grace of an angel in flight, her face recalled more the fall of the walls of Jericho than it did the Annunciation. As for her voice—a husky growl escaping from an ashen, wrinkled throat—it seemed to come straight from the deep, smoking crater of a devastated land. A shiver ran down the spines of the faithful.

The characters appeared stage left as their names were called. Father Cousineau had given himself the role of Zacharias, while Elizabeth was played by a young woman by the name of Marie Plourde, the notary's daughter. The nun rolled her r's terribly, stressing the final syllable of each phrase as though it were a judgment of apocalyptic proportions. Worst of all, she was afflicted by a tragic lisp. It was, as someone was to say forty years later when describing her sepulchral voice, "as though a Brussels sprout had started to talk." In the darkness, the two little blond boys had silently ascended the pulpit, the tiny balcony attached to a large column in line with the first pews, its staircase wound around the column on the left. The thought of leaving the church in the terrible storm was momentarily pushed to the back of the congregation's mind. The nun droned on:

"And there appeared unto him an angel of the Lord standing on the right side of the altar of incense.

"And when Zacharias saw him, he was troubled, and fear fell upon him."

The nun delivered the last sentence in the same tone storytellers adopt to say, "and the wolf gobbled her up!" A murmur ran through the congregation while the organist, high up in his jube, attacked the opening notes of the accompanying music whose chords, far from reassuring or calming them, only made everyone more nervous. In the pulpit, the two angels began to speak at the same time, not giving a thought to the priest's instructions.

"Fear not, Zacharias: for thy prayer is heard; and thy wife Elizabeth shall bear thee a son, and thou shalt call his name John."

Father Cousineau, playing Zacharias, responded to the Archangel Gabriel's long tirade in his deep voice: "Whereby shall I know this? For I am an old man, and my wife well stricken in years."

The congregation pondered, and for good reason, a certain number of questions, namely: Why does the Archangel Gabriel have two heads? And why four wings? Why is *one* angel being played by *two* boys?

The priest, when he heard the boys parroting the gospel as one, looked up and could not prevent an expression of surprise from spreading across his face, an expression so in tune with the scene that someone was heard to mutter, "You can tell he's no stranger to acting, eh?" But the poor director's troubles had not ended there. Aside from the fact they were both speaking at the same time, the little archangel boys did not have the clearest diction, so that "thy prayer is heard" came out as "thy bear is bared" and instead of "thou shalt be dumb" the congregation heard, "thou shalt be a bum," but these mispronunciations were quickly forgiven. The Elizabeth-Zacharias procession fell silent, giving way to the Annunciation. In the half-light, stage right, Father Cousineau prayed to all the saints that the boys would begin taking turns. But his prayer was not heard over the howling wind. When Louis-Benjamin's brother Napoleon made his entrance, leading two lambs on a leash, cries of delight rang out. The young man smiled beatifically, conscious of the effect the charming animals were having on a Catholic audience whose imaginations were largely composed of bucolic scenes and who, more than anyone, were inclined to accept the animals as a happy omen. To general hilarity, the lambs bleated as if to announce their entrance. People turned to look at each other:

"Ah! Dear old Father Cousineau! Is there anything he wouldn't do?"

"Are those the Lévesque lambs there?"

"All that's missing is an ox and a donkey!"

The latter did put in an appearance, but only in song. The choir of nuns struck up a crystal-clear rendition of *Silent Night*. The spectacle was a feast for every sense. Somewhere myrrh was burning. Thick, perfumed smoke rose slowly in the air, wafting through the church.

Just as she was about to make her entrance on stage, the American was struck by such a violent cramp in the lower abdomen that she fell to her knees before the Archangel Gabriel, stretching out a trembling arm toward him. "My word, the girl's got talent!" Father Cousineau thought to himself. He hadn't seen such a powerful performance since his own Charles VII in *The Maid of Orleans*. Then the two-headed archangel cried:

"Hail, thou that art highly favoured, the Lord is with thee."

The howl of pain that went up from the American was drowned out by the organ as it launched into Balbastre's *Joseph est bien marié*, the music temporarily calming the electric atmosphere in the church. The archangel went on, "Thou shalt conceive in thy womb, and bring forth a son, and shalt call his name Jesus. He shall be great, and…" The nun continued to rhyme off the gospel like a bailiff delivering a death sentence. The pain had left the American groggy and stunned. Louis-Benjamin helped her to her feet. Among the congregation, people said she was a born actress for being able to swoon so convincingly before an angel that wasn't even real. After a fashion, they finally got to the birth of Jesus.

"And it came to pass in those days, that there went out a decree from Caesar Augustus, that all the world should be taxed."

At these words, the American girl let out a scream that is still echoing around the church of Saint-François-Xavier to this very day. Standing in front of the make-believe stable, she gripped Louis-Benjamin's shoulders with both hands, pulling his fake beard off in the process.

"My God! Oh my Gooooood!" the pretend Virgin Mary roared, as though pierced by spears.

Before the horrified gaze of the congregation, the poor woman fell onto the straw, rolled herself up into a ball and continued to scream.

"Her water's broken!" shouted Elizabeth, who had edged closer, now certain that the cries were not part of the production.

A frightened snort made its way around the church. Her water? Already? A particularly nasty gossip seized the moment to whisper to her sister-in-law in a slanderous tone, "I thought she was supposed to have it *after* New Year's Day." On the altar, the nun had stopped reading and made her way over to the American. Louis-Benjamin, down on his knees beside his wife, was imploring her to calm down. Father Cousineau's heart had skipped a beat when he heard the frightful cry.

"Somebody fetch a doctor!" a voice rang out.

Two strapping lads opened the main doors, engulfing the inside of the church in an ice-cold blizzard. From outside could be heard the sound of part of a building being torn off by the storm and now making a terrible din as it clattered against the stone. A maple bough as big as a man, only just ripped from its trunk, flew into the church to the shouts of women who huddled together, prepared to face the apocalypse. On her bed of straw, Madeleine was now howling desperately, her body shuddering from the powerful contractions. Sister Mary of the Eucharist had placed her head in her lap and whispered a hoarse prayer "…blessed art thou amongst women, and blessed is the fruit of thy womb…" to the irritation of Father Cousineau, who could see his nativity was going to end in drama. The bulk of the congregation had gathered at the door to throw the maple bough back outside. Others strained to close the doors that the wind had slammed against the outside wall; it took no fewer than four men to a door. By the time the doors had been shut, the two hundred or so who had stayed behind for the nativity scene were bitterly regretting their decision. Fetching Doctor Lepage, who lived at the lower end of town, was out of the question. Neither man nor beast would be able to convince him to make his way up the hill to the church. Rather than feeling sorry for the American, the congregation was busy planning its escape from this house of pain. Whether prudish, irritated, or disgusted, they'd had enough drama for one night. Some one hundred people, most of them bright young things with no fear of God or high winds, faced with the choice of watching the American bring a child into the world or freezing to death in a blizzard, had chosen to brave the elements without a second's hesitation. The church doors were opened one last time to let the runaways escape. Most of them lived nearby and would probably manage to make it home. For the others, those who lived more than five hundred yards away, escape was unthinkable.

"We must pray!" proclaimed Old Ma Madeleine, drawing a set of white rosary beads from her pocket.

"Yes! A rosary! A rosary for the American!" another woman chimed in.

Those who had left their pews sat back down, casting a discreet eye over the terrible scene unfolding before the altar. Now writhing in pain on the straw, Louis-Benjamin's young wife was panting like a thirsty dog, giving out the occasional shriek in between the odd heartrending "Nooo!" and "Help me!" Her husband was sobbing in the arms of the priest, who was trying to console him. The two little angels, still high up on the pulpit, were crouched beneath the balustrade so as not to have to witness the scene. Only the tips of their wings could be seen trembling in the half-light. Two nuns came running from the sacristy with towels and assorted metal instruments. The American had to be brought to the sacristy right away, they gasped. But the American was not for moving.

"I can't move! Help me! Oh Lord, help me!" she shrieked. Her cries echoed three or four times around the almost-empty church.

Sister Mary of the Eucharist took the situation in hand.

"We must save the child!" she said in a voice that instantly made everyone fear the worst.

She knelt before the American, and with the dumbfounded congregation, the priest, and Louis-Benjamin looking on, lowered the American's stockings and underwear to spread her legs.

"Don't be afraid, Madeleine. This child is going to be born. I know a thing or two about bringing children into this world. Pray to the Lord and breathe as I tell you. And when I tell you to push—push!" she told her in her back-from-the-grave voice.

"You have to push, Madeleine!" someone shouted from the third row, even though the American had understood well enough that the nun was also a midwife and that she was going to give birth on this pile of straw. Powerful contractions rocked her body. Joseph had regained his courage and rested his wife's head on his broad chest. On a nun's orders, the congregation broke into a rosary.

"The rosary!" she cried, brandishing her beads.

And the prayers went up, forming a musical backdrop that was occasionally interrupted by a shriek from the woman in labour. Sister Mary of the Eucharist felt the mother's belly, as though searching for something. She looked contrite and disapproving. A full hour of intense labour went by, while the prayers continued in the pews. The American appeared exhausted. Half opening a frightened eye, she flattened her hands in the straw and moaned miserably.

"The baby's facing the wrong way. When was the last time he moved?" she asked the American, who was suffering too much to reply. "This child should have been turned three days ago!" the nun shouted, lubricating her hand with a greasy substance a fellow nun held out to her. "Madeleine, I'm going to have to put my hand inside you to turn the child. It's not facing the right way at all."

Sister Mary of the Eucharist slowly put her hand up into the American's dilated vagina. A flood of amniotic fluid cascaded out onto the straw. A man sitting in the third row fainted. Madeleine screamed blue murder. "Push," the nun shouted. She removed her hand from deep inside Madeleine, who, her mouth wide open, was now begging to be put out of her misery. From time to time, she would crane her neck to glance down at the nun who was helping her bring her child into the world, only to let out a cry of terror at the sight of her hideous face.

"Try to calm her down!" the nun hissed at the father.

Louis-Benjamin sang into his wife's ear the only English song he knew: *Will you love me all the time?* The song did seem to soothe her a little, and there was almost the hint of a smile on her lips. Sister Mary of the Eucharist seemed quite irritated.

"Madeleine, you have to push. Push as hard as you can!"

The congregation held its breath; the little angels sobbed in the pulpit; the women who had given birth themselves felt Madeleine the American's pain as their own. The men did their best not to rest their eyes on the terrible scene. Madeleine wasn't making it easy for them: she wouldn't stop screaming. Suddenly a terrible spasm went through her body and her piercing yell gave way to a thin, reedy sound, a *pianissimo con forza* howl that shattered Louis-Benjamin's eardrums. Sister Mary of the Eucharist shook her head. A small, grey arm could now be seen between the American's legs. The child had chosen this position to be born into the world, but that seemed the least of Sister Mary of the Eucharist's worries.

"The child has been dead for a while. Now we must try to save the mother."

Sister Mary of the Eucharist leaped up and ran to the sacristy, where she lived with the other nuns. She re-emerged after a minute armed with a peculiar instrument. It looked like a pair of metal pliers, glistening like a jewel in the half-light. The nun ran a determined hand along the little dead arm and pushed her own arm in until she could feel the whole child in its mother's womb. The manoeuvre caused a terrible ripping and tearing, and the girl began to bleed profusely. The smell of excrement mixed with the scent of the Christmas candles. The nun's bony fingers found the child's neck and gripped it firmly. Then, very carefully, with her right hand she picked up the instrument she had brought from the sacristy.

"What is *that*?" Louis-Benjamin gasped.

"Forceps. We use them to turn and extract babies when they are being born. Madeleine, I'm going to use this instrument to get your baby out. Don't be afraid. I use them all the time. It's absolutely normal. Even kings and princesses are delivered using forceps."

The nun inserted the forceps into Madeleine's body, found the dead child's head, and caught hold of it. Then she waited for the next contraction to pull the baby from its mother's belly.

"Push, Madeleine! Push!"

Resistance was spongy and strong. The baby's head, spattered with mucus and blood, appeared, lodged between the forceps' metallic arms. In front of the traumatized onlookers, the nun managed, with a painful grunt, to extract the dead child from the body of its mother who, after arching violently, had fallen onto her back, exhausted from the pain. Madeleine's wounds continued to bleed horribly, despite the nun's efforts to contain the hemorrhage. Someone in the congregation began to vomit noisily. The nun looked up at the ceiling, wondering which saint to turn to next. She motioned for Father Cousineau to come forward. She spoke softly into his ear. The priest nodded twice, then knelt down beside the American to give her the last rites. Every gaze followed the same trajectory, tracing a triangle from the dead child, then to Madeleine, before falling inevitably back to Sister Mary of the Eucharist's sad, frightful face. As soon as it was extracted from its mother's body, the child was laid on the straw. All eyes were now on the tiny, stiff, greyish white form, its eyes closed.

"It was a girl," someone said.

Hands covered in mucus and blood, the nun had her eyes locked on the mother's open belly, still shaken by contractions. The audience was stunned. Moments before the birth, some had made a break for the jube, clambering up the stairs four at a time to find refuge and escape the gaze of the American and the priest, trying to forget they had ever been witness to the scene. Up above, Louis-Benjamin's little sisters sobbed in each other's arms. Two women tried to console them.

"Your brother will have other children. Hush now. Let us pray to the Lord."

A man stood with his hands over his ears, trying to block out the prayers and the shouting. Of all those the storm had trapped inside the church of Saint-François-Xavier that Christmas night, very few escaped without lasting psychological damage. The parishioners huddled together in the jube tried to strike up a conversation that would have distanced them, in mind if not in body, from this cursed place. But even from up there, any escape from the terrible racket that followed was impossible. After five minutes when nothing but crying, sobbing, and the voices of the obstinate few who persisted with the rosary could be heard, a cry of unprecedented force rang out in the church. The American's body had started to convulse once again, as the nun held her legs apart. The nun appeared to be no longer aware of anything else around her.

"Jesusmaryandjoseph!" she gasped.

A tiny foot could be seen kicking the American's still-enormous belly. This one was very much alive, and apparently demanding their attention.

"Madeleine! Madeleine! You need to push! Push harder!"

The American had no strength left. She tried to contract her muscles one last time. The nun plunged her arm back inside her to grab hold of the living child and waited again, patiently, for the last contraction to come. By this point, all life seemed to have abandoned the mother's body. She was now breathing only feebly to the sound of the prayers mumbled by Father Cousineau. And yet, something in her was still alive: the second child whose existence she had only just learned of.

"Madeleine, push..." murmured Louis-Benjamin.

Then Madeleine pushed, slowly and painfully, helped by Sister Mary of the Eucharist, who had a firm grip on the second child's head. A cry tore through the church. "She's having another! And this one's alive!" Every head, which out of respect for the stillborn child had been bowed, suddenly rose again. A drumming of feet could be heard from those who had sought refuge from the horror in the jube and were now racing back down the stairs to see the miracle for themselves. Kneeling on the blood-soaked straw, Sister Mary of the Eucharist, herself dumbfounded at the turn of events, struggled to pull the second child out of the American. From the front rows, people had already seen the child's huge head emerge, then its shoulders and pelvis, and last of all its tiny feet. Pale pink in colour, the baby was already moving its arms, as though to reassure everyone of its health. Sister Mary of the Eucharist patted it on the back a few times, holding it by the feet. A subdued, sombre, sinister silence fell over the congregation. The little one's birth had been a total surprise, but there were already very precise though modest hopes for him: that he let out a cry. They waited another five seconds, then Papa Louis' voice was heard for the first time, strong, clear, and resonant, immediately followed by one "Thanks be to God" after another, ending the very short period of mourning in memory of his twin sister.

In Louis-Benjamin's lap, the American showed no signs of life. Her face, glistening in pallor, was even whiter than the statue of the Madonna. An inversed *Pietà*, the couple was no longer of interest to anyone. Madeleine had passed away in the arms of Louis-Benjamin, who had tenderly closed her eyes. Attention now turned to the child, to the huge baby wailing at the top of its lungs, turning its head right and left like an old man in the throes of a nightmare. "It's a boy!" Old Ma Madeleine cried from the pew where she was sitting, rosary beads still in hand. Beneath the wooden shelter, Sister Mary of the Eucharist passed the child to his father, whose arms trembled as he reached out. The American's head fell back against the floor with a dull thud. The nun leaned over and kissed her on the forehead. Before moving away, discreetly, quickly, furtively, she removed the gold chain and little cross that Louis-Benjamin had given her for her birthday on the feast of St. John the Baptist. The piece of jewellery disappeared into the folds of her voluminous habit.

Two or three hours after the child was born, the wind ceased battering Fraserville. Everyone took the opportunity to go home. Madeleine the American and her stillborn child could not be buried right away, so their caskets were stored for the winter at the charnel house. It was only in spring, once the ground had thawed, that mother and baby were buried. Old Ma Madeleine searched high and low for the little cross the deceased had been given as a gift by her husband. But she could not find it anywhere. She asked all those present at the scene, even Sister Mary of the Eucharist, who claimed never to have set eyes on it.

"She should be buried with her little cross," Old Ma Madeleine sighed in vain.

The Fraserville undertaker engraved *Madeleine Lamontagne (The American)* on her tombstone, which was solidly planted in the ground that spring at a funeral ceremony Louis-Benjamin did not attend, since on March 1, 1919, one year to the day after Madeleine the American first arrived in Fraserville, his body was found in the *rivière du Loup*, at the foot of the waterfall where he had thrown himself to his death, inconsolable, desperate, resigned to his fate. He was given the burial reserved for those who chose death over life, interred in a small, separate cemetery, far from the mortal remains of Madeleine the American, who, having died of natural causes, had been given a Christian burial. The child was baptized Joseph-Louis-Benjamin Lamontagne on the very day of his birth, but his grandmother, Old Ma Madeleine, always called him Louis, and raised him alongside her remaining five children.

Of the American there remained only a handful of objects, items of clothing, a prayer book, wedding photos, and *The New England Cookbook*, which the young woman had had in her bags the day she arrived in Fraserville and which Old Ma Madeleine did not have the heart to throw out, and which she could not make out a word of in any case. She packed all the items away in boxes and had her son Napoleon drop them off at the Sisters of the Child Jesus to be given to those in need.

Louis was an unusually robust boy. At birth, he already weighed twelve pounds, a very respectable weight for a boy born in 1918, and a twin, to boot. By the time Fraserville had calmed down, by the time Old Ma Madeleine had mourned her daughter-in-law, and then her son, it was spring of 1919, the first year of peacetime after a long war. Father Cousineau had lost the pounds he had put on during the American's brief stay in Fraserville. Old Ma Madeleine did not really know what she should tell the child. The people of Fraserville would no doubt take care of that for her soon enough. She took care of him, but there was always a doubt at the back of her mind; she was suspicious of a boy who was too big and would eat enough for two, already managing to sit up by himself barely a few weeks after he was born. Nonetheless, Old Ma Madeleine had other things to be worried about. One day in June, after the American's funeral, she insisted on meeting Father Cousineau alone at the presbytery with the child. She wanted, she said, to ask his opinion on a matter concerning the baby. Nothing serious, just a nagging doubt, a question sparked by that sixth sense somewhere between the heart and the mind that serves neither to think nor to love, but that allows a woman to feel rightfully worried.

The priest was only too happy to meet her.

And so Old Ma Madeleine arrived at the presbytery the following day with the child she had difficulty carrying and who was already demanding to be fed even though he had eaten barely twenty minutes earlier. Strangely, the baby stopped bawling as soon as the priest took him in his arms.

"How may I be of assistance, Madeleine?"

By way of reply, Old Ma Madeleine took the child, set him down on the table, and began undressing him. Once he was wearing nothing more than a cotton diaper and babbling *ga-ga-gaa*, the priest repeated his question.

"The child seems perfectly normal to me," he added. "A little hefty for such a young thing, but when you think of so many other children being born all sickly and skinny, it's nice to see one so robust! He'll be a strongman, your Louis!"

The priest gently pinched the child's plump thighs between his thumb and index finger as Louis smiled, revealing what looked like a tooth on its way. Old Ma Madeleine sighed and undressed the child completely to show him to Father Cousineau as God intended. She pointed between little Louis' legs. Father Cousineau squinted, then put on his spectacles because he was rather far-sighted. His jaw dropped. There was a moment of silence, then he looked Old Ma Madeleine in the eye and muttered: "May God preserve it for him!"

In the living room on Rue Saint-François-Xavier, Papa Louis' impression of Father Cousineau had the children rolling about laughing.

"And then in 1919, Fraserville became Rivière-du-Loup," he went on. "Officially, I'm as old as our town! You children should know that!" he said, finishing his fourth gin of the evening and already a little tipsy.

In the meantime, Madeleine and Marc had undressed their brother Luc. He was already sound asleep. He barely made a sound when his sister Madeleine slipped his undershirt off. Then they pulled their pants down and inspected each other. Madeleine buried her face in her hands in shame.

"Papa Louis! I don't have one!" Marc lamented.

"Not all three of you have one," Papa Louis responded. "Only your sister and your little brother."

They all gathered around Luc first, still asleep on the sofa. An inch above his ankle, he had a small birthmark about the size of a dime and shaped somewhat like a bass clef.

"What is it?" he asked, waking at last.

"A bass clef," replied Papa Louis. "It's for writing music on staves."

The children looked at it, wide eyed. In their excitement they hadn't heard their mother Irene return home from the convent. This was how she found them, bedtime long since passed, Papa Louis tipsy, Luc stark naked, Madeleine and Marc with their pants down. Too late, they turned to see her, standing fuming at the living-room door. If it is possible to describe such an expression in words, it could be said Irene had the end of the world written all over her face. In a flash, she grabbed her pantless son by the scruff of the neck and marched him upstairs to his bedroom. Without a word—just a look—she picked up Luc and ordered Madeleine up the stairs, where she closed the door to her daughter's bedroom and told her in no uncertain terms to go to sleep.

"We'll talk about all this tomorrow."

In a dream, half awake, little Madeleine could hear her mother's shouts rising from the living room. The glass thrown against the wall shattering into pieces. A "Christ Almighty!" from Papa Louis. The dull thud of a woman's body flung against a wooden floor. Once. Twice. Then silence. The sound of water running. In the parlour, Sirois' body went on decaying to general indifference.

The dead mind their own business.

A Black Eye Is Watching You

Years before a journalist dubbed her the "Queen of Breakfast" at the opening of one of her restaurants in a Toronto suburb, Madeleine had been a little girl almost like any other. Lots of people could have told you that, people like Siegfried Zucker, a kind of door-to-door salesman who once a month travelled the length and breadth of the Lower St. Lawrence in a truck chock full of foodstuffs that he hawked at knock-down prices that could be knocked down even further if you were ready to bargain. Zucker, an Austrian who came to Canada after the war, had decided to make the Lamontagne home the last stop of the day. He was always welcomed by Irene Caron, a hardened negotiator, and her little girl, Madeleine. It was probably the Austrian who first picked up on Madeleine's nose for business. When she was eight, Zucker once offered Madeleine a barley sugar lollipop in the shape of a maple leaf. They were standing outside on the steps while her mother carried what she'd bought into the kitchen.

"Can I have one for my brother Marc?"

"Why of course!" Zucker replied, handing over a second candy.

When Zucker came to deliver Irene Caron's order the following month, there was no sign of little Madeleine. Instead, he found her brother Marc playing on the porch with a cat. The boy thanked him for the previous month's lollipop.

"At that price, you're practically giving them away!" he laughed to Zucker, who realized that Madeleine had sold the candy to her brother.

Far from being shocked, Zucker developed an instant fondness for Madeleine. In some ways, she became his favourite customer. He would often haggle with her over imaginary wares, testing the child's perspicacity, and she never let him down. Madeleine in turn grew fond of the man she came to associate with abundance, profit, and barley sugar.

Aside from Zucker, no one in the parish of Saint-François-Xavier could ever have imagined that the undertaker's daughter would one day turn the restaurant world on its head, revolutionizing how North Americans defined breakfast. Madeleine seemed predisposed to nothing but the ordinary, tedious, and laborious life of any French Canadian woman. But from the moment she entered the convent school, the nuns discovered she had a gift for mental arithmetic. It was astounding. As it happened, her brothers had been the first to realize her talent the day all three of them had been watching The Horse do a bench press and Marc had wondered out loud how much the barbell weighed.

"How much do you think, Madeleine?"

In a split second, Madeleine had, to her brother's astonishment, added and multiplied the round weights plus the bar.

"Two hundred and thirty-five pounds."

Then, at the age of eight, she had, without really meaning to and in the offhand way that only little girls can manage, surprised an entire grieving family with her math skills. It was at the wake of the widow April. Madeleine, holding a tray of cookies, was following her mother about while she poured coffee into the cups of the family come to keep vigil over the wrinkled corpse of the old woman whose niece had found her sitting dead in her rocking chair, still holding the little blue mitten she had been knitting. The niece, a woman in her thirties whom grief had made voluble to a fault, chattered incessantly while the other relatives, absorbed by their rosary, seemed oblivious to her.

"It's strange just to go like that. She wasn't even ill. Of course, considering her age… Good Lord. I'd asked her if she'd like me to do a little weeding around the garden to help her out. At her age, you know, bending down like that… She might have ended up stuck between two rows of onions. How old was Aunt Jeanne anyway? Let's see, she was three years younger than her husband and he was born in 1891, so that would make her, uh…"

"Sixty-four," Madeleine piped up, as she proffered the tray of cookies, instantly reducing the woman to silence, much to the relief of the rest of the family.

Besides this gift for numbers and the effect the stories of Louis "The Horse" Lamontagne—a man she considered a demigod—had on her, Madeleine had only one other exceptional character trait: she had a jealous streak, a poison she had begun imbibing without reserve the day the letter from Potsdam, New York, arrived. In theory, the letter from Potsdam should never have fallen into Madeleine's hands, but fate had decided otherwise. On that particular day in September 1958, Irene had kept her daughter home so that she could catch chickenpox from her little brother Marc, who had caught it at the boys' school.

"Better to have it at her age than once she's an adult. It'll be over and done with."

Irene tucked the still-sleeping Madeleine into the bed of her crying brother, whose hands Papa Louis had tied behind his back to keep him from scratching himself raw. There he was, trussed up like a turkey and itching all over, when his sister arrived in his bed. Irene had to go out for a few minutes and Louis had left to pick up a corpse from a house on Rue Saint-Pierre. Which meant that the children were all by themselves when the letter dropped into the letterbox on Rue Saint-François-Xavier. Madeleine heard the metal click and the postman's footsteps on the wooden porch. Curious, she went downstairs, ignoring Marc's pleas.

"Scratch me or untie me, will you!"

The envelope with the red and blue border caught her attention. It bore an American stamp with an old man on it. And the address, which wasn't easy to read for a youngster of eight:

Louis "The Horse" Lamontagne
Rivière-du-Loup
Province of Quebec, Canada

The sender, a lady by the name of Floria Ironstone, had written the return address on the back of the envelope. Potsdam, New York. Madeleine read the name one syllable at a time, stumbling when she got to the impossible-to-pronounce Ironstone. She took an instant dislike to the name Floria. This person—she could feel it—wanted to steal her Horse away from her. She immediately sensed the letter was a threat to her happiness and decided then and there that it would never reach its intended recipient. Seeing her mother at the end of the road, she scampered up the stairs, holding her booty at arm's length. She barely had time to hide the letter behind a baseboard and race back to her brother's room (where poor Marc was being driven mad by the itching) before Irene opened the door downstairs. Apart from this letter from America that she had intercepted in the nick of time, Madeleine used to hide all kinds of valued finds behind that board, little treasures she had "discovered" here and there, and that glinted and gleamed. Sometimes at night she would pry back the board, the door to her secret safe, to admire her fortune by the light of a polished-glass lamp. And this is what she would see there, shining in the magpie's dusty nest:

—a wedding band stripped from a dead man's hand at a boisterous wake where the grieving relatives had decided, just before closing the casket for the last time, to settle a few old scores over fisticuffs on Louis Lamontagne's lawn. While Papa Louis separated the men, Madeleine had snuck up to the casket and pocketed the shiny ring that had been calling out to her with every ray it had for the past two days;

—a silver spoon given to her brother Luc and every other child in the Commonwealth who had been born on June 2, 1953, to commemorate the coronation of Her Majesty Queen Elizabeth II;

—and a cheap flower-shaped earring her brother Marc had found in the mud in spring 1957.

Irene was upstairs now. Madeleine pushed the board back in place.
"Put that on your brother's spots, Madeleine. It's calamine lotion, it'll help."
Madeleine made a face. Marc begged his mother to untie him.
"It itches so bad!"
"It's perfectly normal. It'll pass."
Ten days later, it was Madeleine's turn to be smeared in pink calamine lotion, her wrists tied tight behind her back.
"It's for your own good."
Now, you may well wonder why Madeleine refused to open Floria Ironstone's letter. The explanation is quite simple. She was convinced that its contents, for as long as they remained imprisoned inside the envelope, wouldn't be able to disrupt things. To the little girl's mind, a letter is only a letter once it has been opened. By opening the envelope, she risked setting free a virus that she knew would prove fatal to The Horse.
Far from Rivière-du-Loup, in St. Lawrence County, New York, Floria Ironstone waited and waited to hear back from The Horse, until she finally came to the realization that he would not be writing. The letter had been delivered to the wrong stallion. At least she'd tried.
"He was French Canadian, your daddy," she would later tell her daughter.
She'd christened her Penelope, the perfect name for a little girl who would wait her whole life to hear from her father. Floria had been a singer before becoming an acrobat, but it hadn't taken long for her to realize that her future was on the trapeze. Penelope must have heard the story a dozen

times, "He was French Canadian, your daddy..." and so would begin the story of the time her mom met her dad in 1939, a frightfully odd-numbered year. What makes the story so tragic is that Madeleine would never get to hear it, Madeleine who so loved Louis "The Horse" Lamontagne's stories. She had, of course, heard snatches of it from the Horse's mouth before, but not all the details, not those that Floria Ironstone would share with her teal-eyed daughter, Penelope Ironstone. It happened at the county fair.

The St. Lawrence County Fair was, until the invention of the television, both the most predictable and the most surprising fair in all of New York State. The 1939 edition was no exception, so much so that for a long time afterward many believed that the devil himself had marked the date on his calendar. Floria Ironstone wouldn't have missed the St. Lawrence County Fair for the world. She had checked with Old Whitman no fewer than eight times: he had promised to come by to pick up her and her sister Beth in his truck on the first Saturday in August at 7 a.m. sharp. When there was no sign of the truck at the time they had agreed on, Beth sighed.

"We'll go next year. There'll still be music next year, Floria."

Floria was in tears on the porch. She hadn't missed a single St. Lawrence County Fair since she'd turned eighteen. She'd always found a way to get there, in Old Whitman's truck or by bus, and writing it off altogether was out of the question. Now where had Old Whitman gotten to?

Just as all seemed lost, the Ironstone sisters heard the truck's engine rev and splutter.

"Sorry I'm late, ladies. Little Adolf here wasn't too keen. He's a bit of a nervous nelly, but if you ask me that's a sign of character."

"Why, Mr. Whitman! He's absolutely enormous! You won't be coming home empty-handed this year, I'm sure of it! Now what do you think of my skirt? Mamma made it."

"Not bad at all. But why so red? You'll be seen for miles around!"

"Let's just say I don't plan to go unnoticed."

The truck had pulled up in front of the two young women, both dressed in their Sunday best, now radiant in the morning sun. Behind the slats a curious black eye looked out at them. It belonged to Adolf, an oversized calf that had been lovingly fattened on a steady diet of grain. Whitman's every hope rested on the calf that Saturday in August 1939. An ardent admirer of Nazi Germany from the very beginning, Old Whitman had named his calf after the Führer, the same Führer whose photograph he had pinned above the calf's paddock and stall in the hopes that the dictator's unwavering stare would work the same magic on the animal that had saved Germany from destitution and famine. His hopes were realized beyond even his wildest dreams. The animal thrived and grew, valiantly turning into muscle all the grain and hay that could be found for him. Its coat took on the sheen of a ribbon-winner and the animal, through some inexplicable phenomenon of transubstantiation, developed the same gaze as the man whose first name it bore: it was as though the calf could peer right into the depths of your soul, a certain jaded affection in its eyes, with a *je ne sais quoi* of Alpine ingenuousness that had convinced Whitman that glory was lying in wait, that he would be returning home that very evening brandishing the three-coloured ribbon of the St. Lawrence County Fair. Where there is discipline and self-sacrifice there is hope, as would soon be proven to the state of New York.

"He's as clear-sighted as the Führer!" Whitman thundered as he slammed the door of his Ford.

No, Whitman would not be returning home empty-handed. He looked the two sisters up and down. It all depends how you look at it, he thought to himself: in the eyes of the young men of St. Lawrence County, the girls, so eager to whirl their skirts at the county fair, could pass for two fine ladies; but to the ladies of the Temperance League, they'd be denounced as a couple of shameless hussies.

"Dressed like that, you might not be coming home at all!"

Old Whitman was fond of the girls, even if they were a bit odd. They had been raised by a crotchety Hungarian widow who'd lived in an old wooden home on the outskirts of Potsdam since 1933. Born a Nowak in Vienna and later married to an Eisenstein from Budapest, the Hungarian lady had become an Ironstone in America. The name, it seemed to him, brought to mind her strong character and robust constitution. The two girls, born in Budapest to different fathers who happened to be sworn enemies, had come to America before they had time to form a single memory of the Old World. First came Floria, the eldest, named after the heroine of *Tosca*, an opera that Mrs. Eisenstein—now Ironstone—had seen several times in Vienna and that had shaken her to the core, particularly the scene in Act II in which the heroine, Floria Tosca, stabs to death the frightful Scarpia, head of the police in Rome, before removing from his still-warm clutches the safe conduct that will allow her to flee the city with her lover. Floria Ironstone's sister Beth, born two months before the family left for America, was named after Elizabeth of Bavaria, Empress of Austria and Queen of Hungary. Every summer, Whitman would take the Ironstone sisters to the St. Lawrence County Fair out of Christian charity. "If I don't, who will?" would say the old cattle breeder who, in 1939, after a series of lean years brought about by lean cattle, was about to present handsome Adolf, the biggest, the fattest, the strongest, and the most mouth-watering calf ever seen south of the St. Lawrence and east of the Mississippi.

At the behest of Old Whitman, who wanted to get his calf in the right frame of mind for the fair, the Ironstone sisters sang as they made their way along the road to Gouverneur, then the old cattle man gave them a lesson on hard-working Germany and its great Führer, explaining among other things that the German chancellor had managed to accomplish in four years what no American president would ever achieve in a lifetime: give every citizen a motor car.

"They all have Volkswagens. The people's car! And just look at our jalopies, still dragged along by horses. America the beautiful indeed!"

Flooring his poor old Ford pickup, Whitman overtook a buggy drawn by an emaciated grey mare, and as he passed it he bellowed out a "Heil Hitler!" loud enough to be heard the other side of the Adirondacks. The poor countryfolk, who could see nothing but the head of the hulking brown calf staring out at them from the back of the truck, thought for a moment they were under attack as the driver struggled to prevent the startled horse dragging the carriage and its occupants into the ditch.

Whitman and the girls arrived at the fairground around eight o'clock, agreed to meet that afternoon at the paddock where the ribbons and awards were to be handed out, then joined the crowds of fairgoers. Floria and Beth spent the first hour walking arm in arm between the shooting galleries, canvas tents, and enclosures where terrifically fat peony-pink piglets sniffed and snorted. Beyond the stands that had been erected for the occasion and beneath a sky alive with swooping swallows, there stood columns of cages filled with farm-yard birds and their comical-looking feathers: spherical guinea-fowl speckled with white, immaculate Cochin China chickens, Rhode Island Reds with their scarlet combs, geese that stuck out their necks to nip at Floria and Beth's stockinged legs, quails that clucked tenderly, a handful of domesticated par-tridges, and ruling proudly over the rest of the farmyard, having left its cage to parade before the people of New York State, a large, magnificent peacock whose beauty instantly turned the Ironstone sisters into pillars of salt.

"Look, Floria! A peacock!"

"How handsome he is. He's the handsomest of all the birds."

"Do you think he'll fan his tail?"

"We'll have to find him a peahen."

"No peahen… Poor little peacock."

"Don't you worry about him, Beth. When you're that handsome, being unhappy isn't even an option."

As though to show the Ironstone sisters he could read their minds, and for their own pure wonderment, the peacock half displayed its feathers, without completely straightening its large, multicoloured tail. Fairgoers bunched around the crates to admire the huge, vain bird that was visibly aware of the commotion it was causing. Then, around ten o'clock, the miracle happened: the peacock fanned its tail wide, to the applause of the crowd. The bird seemed more surprised than anyone at how big its body had become, as though this morning pavane was the very first time it had ever unfurled its feathers. The bird swayed, twirled around, and haughtily studied the people who were so fascinated by its colours. One idiot, no doubt jealous of the attention, thought it a good idea to throw the bird a piece of bread as a reward. The peacock took it as a provocation, stood stock still, looked out at the crowd, and drawled: Leooon-a! Leooon-a! Floria and Beth Ironstone clapped in delight. The audience, charmed by the display, looked on at the young girl in the red skirt who was filled with wonder at such a simple spectacle.

"His bride-to-be is called Leona! Ha! Ha!"

Soon they grew tired of admiring the peacock. After showing off its plumage and crying "Leoon-a!" a few more times, it had nothing more to offer an audience hungry for excitement.

At noon, after the first horse and buggy races were over, the Ironstone sisters ate the hunk of dark bread and the apples they had brought with them from Potsdam, and bought lemonade. Sitting on the grass beneath a maple tree, they discussed handsome Adolf's chances of winning the three-coloured ribbon. What they had seen in the enclosures had worried them. Other animals from Utica, Watertown, Canton, and even Canada might just as easily take home the honours. Beth was pensive.

"Do you think Adolf realizes he's being watched and judged? He's only a calf, after all!"

"Of course he does. The peacock knew we were watching, didn't it? Why wouldn't the calf?"

"You're right. Handsome Adolf is probably polishing his hoofs as we speak."

On the main stage, the Ogdensburg brass band had just given way to a square-dancing performance that was boring Floria and Beth silly. They redid their hair, shook off the dust and straw that clung to their skirts, and decided to explore the parts of the exhibition they had never visited before, on the other side of the horse-racing track.

A large tent of coarse canvas loomed before them, identical to those serving as concert and dining halls. This tent was set a little back from the fairground and from it emanated occasional deep manly cheers, rounds of applause, dull thuds, and, now and then, for no more than a second or two at a time, absolute silence. Whatever was happening there appeared to be taking the audience's breath away. Each silence was followed by a spontaneous explosion of shouting, whistling, and exclamations of astonishment and amazement. Floria and Beth approached the entrance to the tent, which had been tied closed with rope. Consumed by curiosity, they called out four or five times before a portly gentleman with a moustache came to untie with his cylindrical fingers one of the cords that was keeping the mysterious performance hidden away from curious eyes.

"And what can I do for you ladies?"

"We want to see what's in here," replied Floria.

"It's a show for gentlemen."

"What do you mean, *gentlemen*?" asked Floria, more curious than ever.

"Strongmen. It's no show for ladies."

"Well then, today we're no ladies," Floria retorted, shoving the huge man aside.

The man watched the sisters walk inside, his gaze lingering on Floria's red skirt, and thought to himself: "Not today, and not tomorrow either."

The older sister took the younger by the hand and now they were pushing their way through a crowd of men, all of whom were taller, bigger, and sturdier than they were. An indefinable perfume of leather, sweat, and testosterone hung in the air. Floria noticed right away that the doorman had lied: they weren't the only women in the crowd. A few old biddies were sitting in the lowest tiers, one of them shaking her fist and shouting something in a Slavic language. As her eyes took in the stage, Floria realized that they had stumbled upon a strongman contest and they were nearing the end of the first event, which involved lifting off the dirt floor a black weight on which "300 lb." had been painted in white. A tall blond man with blue eyes stood to let the newcomers take his place in the stands. "Please, ladies…" How many people were looking on from the V-shaped stands? Three hundred? Four hundred? One thousand, by the sounds of it. A master of ceremonies—black suit, bow tie, slicked-back hair, shiny shoes, gold watch, eyes puffy from the heat in the tent—announced the upcoming contest.

"And now, ladies, *girls*—he peered over at the two young sisters, their white stockings sticking out like a sore thumb in the sea of men—and gentlemen, now that our contenders have warmed up, we can get down to business. Bring in the heavy loads for the real men!"

The tall blond man who had given up his seat explained to the newcomers that they had missed the first event, a jaw-dropping bent press that a Canadian had won handily. A man known to all as The Warsaw Giant and a certain Idaho Bill had finished second and third.

A pair of scrawny men set up two wooden sawhorses three yards apart and lay a thick oak door on top. It left just enough room for a man to squat down between the door and the ground. The master of ceremonies called down from the stands the stoutest men he could find. Soon, seven strapping men were sitting on the wooden door, which didn't budge. A murmur rippled through the audience. There was no doubt: they were in for a squat lift. Beth's neighbour guessed out loud that the seven giants must weigh at least fourteen hundred pounds, all told. But the man sitting behind him disagreed: the big guy sitting on the left end of the door, Lipincott was his name, must surely weigh three hundred pounds all by himself. No, if you asked him, there was two tons of flesh, bone, and muscle sitting on top of that door. In the voice of a tormented tenor, the master of ceremonies tried to calm the din rising from the stands.

"The next event consists of squat-lifting the wooden door, including passengers, for ten seconds. They shall be allowed to touch the door with their hands and rest it against their upper back. We ask our distinguished volunteers to please hold still and show nothing but the utmost calm throughout this extremely dangerous manoeuvre. We do not wish to see a repeat here in Gouverneur of the unfortunate incident that left one poor fellow in Buffalo with a broken tooth! And I am counting on my distinguished audience to help me with the countdown! Now, without further ado, please welcome Michigan's very own Samson: The Great Brouyette!"

A short, stocky man strode into the tent through an opening in the side. The striped costume that left his shoulders bare threatened to come apart at the seams. Floria and Beth burst out laughing at the sight of the little moustachioed man intent on lifting over a ton. Brouyette crouched beneath the door and the tent fell silent. Then, after a few deep breaths, the unthinkable happened: the door and its seven passengers were lifted a few inches up into the air. Floria let out an admiring whistle.

"My word. Did you see that, Beth?"

Beth had indeed seen it, too, and there was more to come. Three strong-men followed, one after the other. Each managed to lift the seven men, their faces lighting up with incredulity every time they felt the wood they were sitting on shift beneath them. After The Great Brouyette came Idaho Bill, The Warsaw Giant, and Alexander Podgórski, a Pole whose name meant "of the mountain." Podgórski, a strapping curly-haired fellow who wore a black costume and must have been six foot four, was cross-eyed, which brought a smile to the faces of the Ironstone sisters. Remarkably, his squint disappeared the very moment he lifted the door, as though the effort had realigned his eyes.

"Look, Beth. He looks a little like Adolf, Old Whitman's calf!"

Beth pinched herself so hard she drew blood as she tried to stifle a laugh.

A triumphant Podgórski thanked the cheering crowd. After The Warsaw Giant, it was he who had lifted the weight the longest and the fastest, so easily in fact that he had not even been heard to moan or groan like the men before him, especially Idaho Bill, who had let out a pained whinny as he struggled to hoist the load. The crowd had counted down—"ten, nine, eight, seven, six..."—while Idaho Bill collapsed under the weight of the men. A stricter master of ceremonies would have disqualified him for giving way too quickly.

To announce the fifth and final contender, the emcee took on a deeper tone.

"And finally, ladies and gentlemen, please welcome for the first time in the state of New York, the iron man of Canada, Louis 'The Horse' Lamontagne!"

As he said the word "ladies," the master of ceremonies had again looked straight at Floria, as though to stress that the man he had just announced was a sight for sore female eyes. Floria felt the crowd turn to look at her as one. To keep her composure, she adjusted the little cloth flower above her right ear while she pursed her lips and did her best to look dignified.

And so appeared Louis Lamontagne. For the crowd at the St. Lawrence County Fair, Louis would go down in history as "The Horse." That's how the master of ceremonies had introduced him and that's how he would remain in the minds of the Americans. The applause lasted longer than for the other contestants who, behind the canvas, must have been wondering what the audience saw in the Canadian, a greenhorn not yet turned twenty-one who it was virtually impossible to hold a conversation with because, as his name suggested, he was French Canadian. While Louis Lamontagne's rivals refused to ponder aloud what made the Canadian so special in the crowd's eyes, it was certainly no mystery to the Ironstone sisters. Least of all to Floria who, until the day of her sudden death while watching the NBC newsreader announcing John F. Kennedy's election on November 9, 1960, used to describe Louis Lamontagne as the handsomest man in America. It was that simple. Between that Saturday in August of 1939 and John F. Kennedy's election as U.S. President, Floria Ironstone must have proclaimed at least thirty times to a great many people, including her own daughter, Penelope Ironstone, that Louis Lamontagne had swept her off her feet. If she happened to be there, too, her sister Beth would nod as if to confirm what her sister said was true, and that she had seen it with her own eyes.

The emcee stepped back to reveal the beast. Louis Lamontagne must have been over six foot six. His hair dark and wavy, the hair of the Roman emperors in American black and white movies. Unlike his rivals, all of whom seemed to have been moulded from a barrel, Louis Lamontagne was nothing but muscle and bone. But what bone! When he flexed his right arm, a bicep as big as a cantaloupe sprung up, and an appreciative murmur rippled through the tent. Clad in a skin-tight navy blue leotard, Louis Lamontagne did not appear to believe in the virtues of humility and prudishness cherished by a certain segment of society. But no one in the audience seemed the least concerned about that. His body was offered up for their admiration just like that of Adolf the calf, who was at that very same moment, only a few hundred yards away, being observed, assessed, judged, and graded in every respect. Acutely aware of the effect he was having on his audience, Louis Lamontagne advanced, feet slightly apart to display his shapely thighs and improbably round calf muscles. "Legs like a horse," muttered the old men in the third row. And what can be said of the hands of this colossus, other than that they would have surely made him, in another time, in another place, an Olympic swimming champion? Chiselled from marble, the body of Louis Lamontagne was almost entirely hairless, with the exception of one or two little tufts on his broad chest. The boy grinned the grin of one too good-looking to hold a grudge. And like the peacock that had strutted for the Ironstone sisters that morning, Louis Lamontagne spread his arms wide before the hypnotized audience. Their admiration for this body was stealing the show, and the poor devils sitting on the wooden door were quickly forgotten as they waited patiently to be hoisted by the Canadian. Louis Lamontagne appeared more concerned with the admiring looks taking in his body from head to toe than by the feat of strength he would have to win if he wished to remain in the competition.

It would be unfair to the memory of the Ironstone sisters not to mention Louis Lamontagne's face. Because while it might have been his perfectly defined muscles that won over the men at the fair, it was his grin that forever transformed him into an object of desire in the minds of the few ladies present. Like a child. To picture him in your own mind's eye, it sufficed to imagine a slightly gentler side to Clark Gable, whose fine and elegant whiskers Louis Lamontagne also shared. And the eyes. Teal. Achingly beautiful. Eyes of a colour so rare that one day a woman would cry, "If you walk out that door, don't bother coming back!" and another, "I exist only for you…" and another still, just before she took her own life, would write as her last words, "I loved you, Louis. With all my heart."

Floria ovulated.

Not knowing the term, she could never have put it quite like that, but that's what happened. She felt it down below, a sensation that brought a smile to her lips, perhaps at the precise moment when Louis Lamontagne's gaze met hers. Fate's fatal error. It was the beginning of the end for Floria Ironstone, as a wink smacked her full in the face. To an audience well used to seeing strongmen from all over the world on parade, Louis' appearance was as pleasing as it was astonishing: as handsome as Charles Atlas—from whom the French Canadian must have, there was no denying it, learned the basics of Dynamic Tension by mail order—and built like Eugen Sandow, the Königsberg-born father of body building, Louis had a face with all the innocence of the angels who escorted the Virgin Mary. Without the slightest hesitation, anyone would have confided their wildest dreams in Louis in the hopes that he might find a way to make them come true, because to have developed a body such as his in the 1930s was really something. Who but a countryman's son would ever have gotten his hands on enough animal protein to go about putting so much meat on his bones?

"He's the new Louis Cyr!"

Hogwash. Louis Cyr might have been the world's strongest man, but never its most handsome. Louis Cyr had never caused the young ladies of the state of New York to spontaneously ovulate. Louis Cyr did not have Louis Lamontagne's angelic smile. Cyr had been a brute force straight out of the Old Testament; the Canadian colossus now crouching down under the wooden door looked more like an attempt by God to seek forgiveness for the flood and the regrettable excesses of Deuteronomy.

"But he's too tall to be Louis Cyr's boy!"

Indeed he was. Unless, of course, Cyr had married a giant, which hadn't been the case at all. Louis Cyr's wife was tiny; as anyone who followed strongmen knew. "So where did he come from?" the regulars wondered. The need to find an answer to the question lost all significance as soon as Louis shouldered the door and its seven passengers into the air. He looked up mischievously, smiled at Floria Ironstone, gave her another wink, then gently set down the load after more than twenty seconds had elapsed, without any of the passengers so much as feeling the door settle back down on the sawhorses. The audience went wild, jumping to their feet as they shouted and applauded, boisterously signalling that the rarest of events had just taken place. The Ironstone sisters rose along with the crowd and found themselves clapping until their wrists threatened to give way, shouting loud enough to be heard all the way to Buffalo: "Bravo! Bravo! Bravo!"

The remaining feats of strength were to be held outside that very same afternoon. The Ironstone sisters' hearts were well and truly aflutter. They had followed the enthusiastic crowd outside, behind the squadron of strongmen and the master of ceremonies. Come! Come, one and all! Who will be the quickest to pull a car one hundred yards? Which of these five giants will manage to hoist a horse to the top of a telephone pole? There were four events in all: the bent press, the squat lift—both of which had just been won by Louis Lamontagne inside the tent—then the car pull and the horse hoist. First place would earn the winner three points; second place, two points; and third place, one point. The man who completed all four events with the most points would be taking home two hundred American dollars. After the first two events, Louis was top of the leaderboard. The Warsaw Giant, who had twice finished second, was hot on his heels, with Idaho Bill and cross-eyed Alexander Podgórski sharing third place.

The crowd leaving the tent did not go unnoticed by the fairgoers, some of whom, men for the most part, peered over at the curious procession led by the master of ceremonies, closely followed by a bunch of strongmen in leotards, some of whom bore more than a passing resemblance to the cattle vying for the winner's ribbons at the county fair. Just behind the mega-phone-wielding master of ceremonies was handsome Louis, as happy as could be, bearing Idaho Bill's right buttock on his left shoulder, the left buttock resting on the right shoulder of Alexander Podgórski, who was squinting for all he was worth. Bringing up the rear were The Great Brouyette—the Samson of Michigan—and The Warsaw Giant, who flexed their biceps to the amused looks of the fairgoers. A stream of tinny words spewed forth from the master of ceremony's megaphone.

"Ladies and gentlemen, people of the state of New York! After stupefying Iowa and Ohio, these strongmen are now going to dumbfound this great state of yours! Who among them will prove the strongest? Who among them will be crowned New York's strongest man? Come watch the last two events at the county fair's annual strongman contest and see who will be crowned champion. Will Idaho Bill manage to defend the title he fought so hard for last year? Will he be dethroned by his long-standing rival, The Great Brouyette? Or perhaps by the dashing young French Canadian, Louis 'The Horse' Lamontagne? With the first two events completed under the Big Top—the bent press and the squat lift—'The Horse' is leading the way! Will he manage to keep such an impressive gathering of rivals at bay? We'll all know in just under two hours' time! And now, ladies and gentlemen, let's head out to the field for the car-pulling event! Come one and all. Come admire these forces of nature at work!"

Every last spectator that had witnessed the first two events followed behind, which is to say two or three hundred people who were still picking their jaws up off the floor. Their eyes still round with admiration and won-der, they aroused the interest of other fairgoers. They too began to follow the procession, first the young men, then their fathers, and then, finally, the women that Idaho Bill and Louis Lamontagne had been winking madly away at. Soon, there were at least two thousand people standing under the August sun around the perimeter of the field, which had been set up for the car pull. On the freshly mowed grass stood five brightly shining cars, loaned out for the duration of the fair by a handful of local bigwigs. The contenders' task was quite simple: each man would be hooked up to a cable and harness, which were attached to a bumper. Upon the signal, the men would have to run the hundred yards like a devil knee-deep in molasses, dragging the car along behind them through pure brute force. The event was usually against the clock, but to the crowd's great delight, for the St. Lawrence County Fair a car had been found for each of the contestants: five black 1938 Oldsmobile Coupés, borrowed from Buffalo, Gouverneur, and Potsdam. Bringing the spectacle outside, where the strongmen could be seen by everyone, had been a masterstroke. Nobody could possibly have missed the strange and noisy procession, led by a man in tails hollering into a megaphone, followed by creatures who were half-man half-beast and by a crowd that was visibly in their thrall. There was but one thing to do when confronted by this carnival-esque scene: join the glorious parade. The irresistible spectacle drained the crowd away from the other attractions, notably the giant pumpkin contest and the brass band. The band was performing a military march and its conductor—a man with a moustache and an impeccable uniform—motioned to his musicians to fall in line behind the procession of strongmen. In no time at all, the shooting galleries, games of skill, and picnic tables were all deserted. Every visitor at the St. Lawrence County Fair, with the exception of those attending the ribbon ceremony by the horse and cattle enclosures, was now standing around the five black Oldsmobiles, each of the cars hooked up to a strongman. In each car sat five men, each man having weighed in at one hundred and eighty pounds right before the public's eyes, just to ramp up the suspense while the contenders were hooked up to their vehicles and harnesses. The Ironstone sisters, who had ringside seats to this extraordinary race across the field, held up their hands to shield their faces from the sun's unrelenting rays. Their hearts were no longer their own, not since the Canadian had sent a wink in their direction during the squat lift. It was hard to say which of the sisters, Floria or Beth, had the highest hopes for this beast of the north. Silence fell. The cars' passengers put on a show of their own: "Come on! Pull, Horse! Show us what you're made of!" The master of ceremonies drew a pistol from his belt, which calmed the crowd. "On the count of three!" And the shot rang out in the scorching-hot sky above Gouverneur. The five contenders took off like rockets. At the end of his rope, whose length he had clearly overestimated, The Great Brouyette lurched backward, felled by the weight of his load. The crowd roared. He picked himself back up, but it was too late: Alexander Podgórski already enjoyed a comfortable lead ahead of him in fourth place… and he was no longer squinting, a miracle that came about every time he had to give his all. Unfortunately for him, his squint returned with a vengeance as soon as he relaxed his muscles.

Louis Lamontagne also got off to a difficult start, but for reasons unrelated to the weight of his load or the length of the cable that bound him to it. He had been distracted by the high-pitched shouts of Floria and Beth Ironstone as they chanted his name in an American accent that was not without its charms. The two sisters' voices rang out in harmony, reminding Louis of a liturgical chant from his childhood, angelic tones that brought him back to the church of Saint-François-Xavier in Rivière-du-Loup. An elusive image of a communion procession flashed before his eyes like a movie, and for a second too long he lost contact with reality and slipped into third place behind The Warsaw Giant and Idaho Bill.

Wheezing like a galloping horse, almost sucking in his leotard in the process, handsome Louis Lamontagne advanced, his determination kindled by shouts of encouragement from the passengers in the Oldsmobile he was pulling. Part of the crowd had noticed the flirting between Louis and the Ironstone sisters, who were by now making no effort to conceal their love for the handsome Canadian.

Swept along by the innocent charm of the two young women—now in raptures over the colossus—in a voice at first muffled and hesitant, coming from the area where the sisters stood breathlessly, then spreading like a rumour that was soon on everyone's lips until it reached the shores of the human sea surrounding the field in ever more powerful waves, the crowd chanted the winsome young man's name along with the two sisters. Halfway through the race, the rest of the crowd began to chant "La-mon-tagne" as one, as though calling for a sacrifice.

Puffing and blowing like a steam engine, Idaho Bill was radish-red and making headway in second place. Of this interesting character, it should be said that he did not in fact hail from Idaho, but rather from California, where he had been baptized Everett Sterling in Sacramento in 1918. How had he wound up competing as a strongman in the Midwest and Northeastern United States? The answer depends a lot on who you ask. What we do know is that Idaho Bill did live at one time in Idaho, where he had been a cowboy or a lumberjack—accounts differ—and that he had decided to call himself Bill after a price was put on the head of a certain Everett Berling (in the wake of a sordid sex scandal that also involved the governor of Oregon's brother) in four states right at the start of the Roosevelt administration, an event that dealt a severe blow to his career as a strongman. It is this version of the story that was told most often; when Bill was around at least. And just in front of him was The Warsaw Giant, advancing with no apparent effort, a man whose nickname required no explanation: standing more than six foot six inches tall, he towered over most of his fellow contenders by at least a head, sometimes two, meaning that his regular walking pace was enough to win him the car-pulling event, a feat he accomplished to the sounds of a crestfallen crowd that was rooting for the Canadian out of sympathy for Floria and Beth. Aware that his victory had disappointed the crowd while putting a little spice back into the contest, The Warsaw Giant looked around sadly. In his native Poland, his victory would have been met with adulation, but here it seemed only to stoke the fairgoers' desire to see the Canadian win the day, an outcome that was looking increasingly uncertain. With a ballerina-like flourish, The Warsaw Giant crossed the finish line that had been whitewashed onto the warm green grass, as Floria and Beth Ironstone looked on in dismay. Not wanting to break the titan's heart, the crowd applauded all the same. Idaho Bill finished far behind, cursing the heavens for not being taller. Then came Louis Lamontagne, Alexander Podgórski—whose squint returned as soon as he was freed from his harness—and finally the now Not So Great Brouyette, who never did manage to make up the ground he lost by falling on his ass two seconds after the race started, caught up in his own harness. The passengers who had been used as ballast stepped out of the Oldsmobile one by one, swapping notes on the incredible race, laughing at the master of ceremonies' quips, and waving to the crowd, feeling a few crumbs of the Polish champion's glory fall on their own shoulders. The passengers from the winning car scoffed at the losers, taking credit, however undeserved, for their beast of burden's win.

But outright victory still wasn't completely in The Warsaw Giant's hands, far from it. His long legs might have won him the third event, but this easy win wasn't enough to surpass Lamontagne's triumphs in the first two events, the bent press and the squat lift. Which meant that Lamontagne had come out of the first two events with six points, comfortably ahead of The Warsaw Giant, who had only four points to show for having twice finished second. After his victory in the car pull, The Warsaw Giant now had seven points, tied with Louis Lamontagne, who had had to make do with a solitary point for his third-place finish. Disappointed but not disheartened, Lamontagne vowed he would do better in the final event.

Among the crowd of visitors to the St. Lawrence County Fair, the Ironstone sisters weren't the only ones praying with all their might that the Canadian might take a shine to them. Louis' guilelessness, youth, vigour, and simplicity had conquered the hearts of every last fairgoer. They loved him for all kinds of reasons: languidness, admiration, a fascination for his extra-ordinary physique. And while it is undeniable that certain young ladies would have immediately taken the handsome devil up on an offer to dance, parental consent be damned, it would not be true to say that all of St. Lawrence County was drawn to him for reasons of the heart. Louis Lamontagne's presence was a source of fascination, inexplicably soothing and exciting at once. A mere glance from Louis was enough to awaken the best and the worst of the man—or especially the woman—his eyes happened to fall on. Louis was to the St. Lawrence County Fair what Marlene Dietrich was to the American troops: the charms, at once sophisticated and unrefined, of a vague elsewhere, a promise of something new. At a time when Uncle Sam was recruiting men the length and breadth of the United States, a handful of his agents were naturally at the county fair and, scattered throughout the crowd, had immediately remarked the five rivals in the strongman competition and were now waiting for events to follow their course.

The master of ceremonies decreed a two-hour break to let the strongmen recover and allow the crowd to refresh itself, what with the heavy air that foretold a late-afternoon storm. No doubt to maintain the air of mystery that surrounded him and seemed to have worked to his advantage so far, Louis Lamontagne took care to keep a safe distance from the crowd that had gathered around the competitors as soon as they were out of their harnesses. People scrambled to see him up close, to touch him with their own hands, to see him with their own eyes, but the Canadian preferred to play hard to get, heading off to the privacy of a trailer a little to the side of the field, flanked by his cross-eyed colleague. The Ironstone sisters sighed.

"Come on, Floria. Let's go talk to them! I'm sure they have whisky in that trailer!"

"Mmm. A little shot of Canadian whisky. They're bound to have some."

Beth was taken aback at her own daring. Her sister followed behind, trying to hide her jitters. Both men disappeared into the trailer. Two scrawny horses grazed a few yards away. How many times did Floria rearrange her hair as she approached Louis Lamontagne's trailer? Which of the two was more nervous at the prospect of speaking to the young man? Who among the rest of the crowd had failed to notice that these brash young things had plucked up enough courage to do what they all dreamed of doing? So many unanswered questions. A door on the side of the trailer opened with a loud crack, revealing Louis Lamontagne and Alexander Podgórski sitting on wooden stools in surroundings that were far too small for two men of their size. Before them on the table was what looked like an enormous turkey, which Podgórski had brought back with him from Buffalo. Strangled and roasted the day before by a helpful woman from Gouverneur (the strongmen were welcomed like kings wherever they went), the bird was equal to the two huge appetites. For the Ironstone sisters, it made for a moving scene: two strapping young men who had given their all and were now sharing a gargantuan meal in a trailer where trapeze artists, lion tamers, bearded ladies, and dwarfs would not have been out of place. Louis was busy tearing one of the thighs off the huge bird. Floria, her hopefulness winning out over bashfulness, as was her way, got straight to it:

"I so wanted you to win, Horse!"

"So did I," her sister Beth chimed in. "But I'm certain you'll win the horse event! We saw you in the tent. You're so strong! I'm Beth, and this is my sister, Floria. We're from Potsdam."

Beth pointed east. Both men, who were busily wolfing down their meal, glanced up at the two women, chewed some more, then swallowed. They wiped their lips and smiled. Lamontagne's English was fairly basic. He would intersperse his speech with snatches of French—which Podgórski would translate, sometimes hesitantly due to the often mystifying Canadian accent—then go on, giving the impression the sisters were speaking to a two-headed man, one speaking something akin to English in a thick Slavic accent, the other impeccable Frenglish, embellished with sweeping hand gestures, facial expressions, and mannerisms that formed the grammar of his language every bit as much as his vocabulary. Floria and Beth wanted to know everything: Where from? How? When?

Podgórski told them he had been born in Warsaw in 1918 to an unknown father and an uncertain mother. He had been raised by anyone and everyone, fed more often than not by the nuns in the Praga neighbourhood, the first to become aware of young Alexander's uncommon strength. At the age of twelve, he was hired by the convent and received full board in exchange for his brute force. When he became too old for the nuns to keep him in their service, he was given the chance to join a religious order in Warsaw. But young Alexander had already begun to display his might in the main squares of Praga, in nearby neighbourhoods, and even beyond the Vistula in the more stylish parts of the city. It was at a feat of strength that involved hoisting a barrel of sauerkraut that young Podgórski caught the eye of The

Warsaw Giant who, back then, was still known as Wlad. Impressed by the performance of young Podgórski who, without batting an eye or losing his footing, had, before a crowd of four thousand, managed to heft the barrel brimming with sauerkraut off the ground, the Giant had always remembered him and, once established in America, realized the country was big enough for more than one Polish strongman and wrote to the young man back in Warsaw, inviting him to cross the ocean and join him in Baltimore. A whole continent awaited him, a continent partial to shows of strength and muscle, a continent where a Slavic accent was enough to get you hired as a fairground entertainer. The Giant liked to recall the delightful scene in Warsaw: up on the platform, Podgórski's pronounced squint had left the crowd come to admire the strongmen's feats in stitches. But their boorish, hurtful laughter gave way to stunned silence once the young man took hold of the barrel, knees bent. At that very moment, his eyes returned to their normal axis, his gaze straight and steady for as long as his muscles were contracted.

"Look! He's not cross-eyed anymore!" they cried, pointing up at him.

And as the people of Warsaw looked on dumbfounded, Podgórski had not only lifted the barrel of sauerkraut, he'd stopped squinting too. The potential was not lost on The Warsaw Giant.

Alexander had been kind enough to share the barrel of sauerkraut—it was the winner's to take home—with the sisters of Praga, who received his mail and read his letters to him since the boy, unlike The Warsaw Giant, was completely illiterate. The nuns had been sad to see their protégé and supplier of foodstuffs leave them (the barrel of sauerkraut was not the only bounty that Alexander had brought back to the convent over the course of his last few months in Warsaw). Beer, sausage, unripened cheese, milk, eggs: the youngster's exploits tended to be rewarded in kind. The nuns of Praga would never again eat so well, and their sadness was great—as was their hunger—when they gathered on the platform at Warsaw station to bid their final farewells to the young man who looked out at them in cross-eyed fondness from the seat paid for by a generous archbishop.

"I'll come back, sisters! I'll come back a very rich man indeed!" the boy cried from the window of the train as it pulled slowly out of the station of the hometown he would never see again.

The call of America had long been ringing in Podgórski's ears, but he decided to give one last chance to Old Europe before crossing the ocean. And so Alexander left for Krakow to join a travelling circus.

It was the Great Krysinski, tamer of big cats and business associate to the owner of a famous German circus, who snatched him away from Poland and had him hit the roads of Germany. Podgórski was a hit wherever he went. "The Cross-Eyed Pole! Come see him cured through hard work!" In Berlin in 1936, Podgórski was the hottest ticket in town, the platform close enough to the crowd that each and every one of them could see the miracle for themselves as he lifted eight *Fräulein* sitting on a door.

To the delight of the Berlin audience, Podgórski's cross-eyed squint disappeared the very instant he lifted his head. The usual stunned silence was followed by a burst of laughter and applause. The circus continued on its way through Germany to Strasbourg, where Podgórski decided—following an argument with the manager, a jealous sort who suspected Podgórski of having one eye on his wife, a Ukrainian trapeze artist—to leave the troupe, as the atmosphere had become stifling. After two weeks of aimless wandering, Alexander was picked up by a French circus, which was delighted with his number that aroused at once admiration, astonishment, and general hilarity, an exploit in itself for a fairground entertainer. And Podgórski thus roamed from town to town in the Third Republic. From Troyes to Sète, from Orange to Angers, and from Cannes to Vannes, he discovered the beautiful country that was France and learned the language of the people—or more specifically, the women—who lived there. The German circus manager had been right about his Polish performer: Podgórski was a randy young fellow, a fact that went completely unnoticed in 1930s France. And if amused reports from any number of his French lovers were to be believed, the Pole also lost his squint at the very height of passion. But Podgórski skipped over this particular detail as he recounted his origins to the Ironstone sisters in the field in Gouverneur. Something told him that, with a little luck and a helping hand from his Canadian colleague, Beth might very well have an opportunity to witness this rare, inexplicable phenomenon for herself by sunrise.

As he explained how fate had brought him to this New York field to drag a black Oldsmobile one hundred yards, a crowd had begun to gather. The onlookers had followed the Ironstone sisters, curious to see just how far the unseemly young ladies would go to win the handsome Canadian's heart. While their behaviour may have been unbecoming, in America's outlying counties where there was nothing but Deathly Boredom to be had, agricultural fairs had become carnival-like events where propriety and decorum tended to be set aside. After all, weren't fairs a place to celebrate nature's bounty and generosity?

Standing outside the open trailer, twenty-odd people were now hanging on Podgórski's every word. Lamontagne used the distraction to gobble up the rest of the roast turkey, tearing it apart, bit by bit. Podgórski ended his story by recounting how in Calais, at the end of a tour that had threatened to take a dramatic turn—another case of ending up in the wrong bed—he had gone to England in the hopes of finding a ship to take him to America. And that's how he set sail for New York in May 1937, unable to sit still at the thought of discovering a whole new continent of women. In the United States, the Pole discovered a drab, boring country, its cities rough and filthy, its people of no interest to him. The Americans, on the other hand, were fascinated by him. Despite being illiterate, he managed to track down The Warsaw Giant, whose nickname amused him no end. The two men were delighted to meet, happy to find a compatriot on American soil, but the Giant was of no great use to Podgórski. The troupe he had been travelling with had gone bankrupt in the wake of the Great Depression and all the two men could do was travel across America from town to town, from Sioux to Cheyenne, from Miami to Toledo, from Bismarck to Lafayette, entering strongman contests and renting out their brute strength to industry, agriculture, and the occasional mine. Their trajectories separated, but sometimes they met up again, as in August 1939 in Gouverneur, New York.

Podgórski and Lamontagne had first met at the Montcalm Hall in Montreal, on the corner of Saint-Zotique and De Lorimier. Both were entered in a bent press event that Lamontagne, newly arrived from the depths of the countryside, won hands down. Podgórski, dumbfounded by the young man's might, wanted to get to know him better in order to uncover the secrets of his strength, and so an admirable symbiotic relationship developed between the two. Young Lamontagne, absurdly handsome and well built, attracted the young women of Montreal to him like a magnet. He would keep his favourite—who, strictly speaking, wasn't *always* the prettiest since he was especially partial to big brown eyes, curly hair, and slender hands—and toss his second choice into the waiting arms of Podgórski, who became Lamontagne's commensal: one who lives and eats at the same table with another, content with leftovers and causing no harm. In return, Podgórski would interpret into English for Lamontagne. Louis seemed to be on the lookout for what others might have termed "imperfections" among these one-night stands. A gap between two teeth, a few merry pounds too many, a surfeit of freckles… every conquest had a particular trait that lingered in his memory. Because, for Louis, that's what grace was all about. Like braille to the blind man, all that mattered were the little rough spots on the smooth surface of a beautiful woman. He wanted to feel them all. Together Podgórski and Lamontagne had bought the blue wooden trailer from a family of New England dwarfs that had opted for the comforts of sedentary life and now ran a home near Albany where, in return for fifty cents, it was possible to observe them at leisure through a one-way mirror. Tired of staying in seedy hotels, Podgórski and Lamontagne had bought the vehicle—complete with a couple of old nags—for next to nothing and now moved at a snail's pace along America's roads.

"And what about *you*, Mr. Lamontagne. Have you always been so strong?" Beth Ironstone was desperate for the Canadian to speak.

Louis set down the turkey leg he had been picking clean to explain that he couldn't recall ever being weak. He stood up and, in front of a crowd of onlookers that was growing by the minute, began to explain how he had become known as Louis "The Horse" Lamontagne back in Rivière-du-Loup. Louis flung an apple at a little boy who had been hungrily eyeing the half-eaten turkey. Now, whenever Podgórski interpreted one of Louis Lamontagne's stories, he would put all his cognitive faculties into the tale, making every effort to come up with just the right word, the best possible expression. His Slavic accent imbued Louis Lamontagne's stories with an exotic perfume that the American public couldn't get enough of, fascinated as they were to hear what went on in a land so close recounted with such a distant accent. No matter the hall or field where Lamontagne performed, he always seemed to attract two or three brazen young ladies, and sometimes even a few boys eager to develop a similar build. Saving a young lady for his travelling companion was no hardship. And he couldn't have dreamed of a more dedicated interpreter to bring the stories from his land of snow to life.

"Do you have a wife, Horse?"

The fateful question slipped out of Floria like a belch and amused the crowd no end. Bracing themselves for disappointment, they expectedthe Canadian to reply that he was married and to pull a miniature tutu-wearing French Canadian out of a hat for them. They laughed nervously. What could Louis Lamontagne's wife possibly look like? What Delilah of the North had managed to tame this Samson? Without letting the crowd stew too long, Podgórski delivered the sweetest word in the world to the ears of Floria and Beth: unmarried. The word brought with it hope and promises of better tomorrows. He was young, of course, but didn't they say that Catholics went about nature's duties with the utmost diligence? It was conceivable that, despite being only twenty years old, Lamontagne had already sired lots of children. The truth was not far off, but Podgórski knew only the truth that Lamontagne had chosen to reveal. He strongly suspected that his Canadian pal had, just like him, left more than one kid behind along the way, and twice already, in the space of eighteen months spent wandering America, he had witnessed the same scene: a tearful woman would find Louis after two or three months of desperate searching. Show up at an event with the longest of Lent faces. Wait patiently until the very end of the contest, then ask to speak to Louis in private. Would sob. And would leave, defeated. Teal-coloured eyes in Ohio, Iowa, Michigan... And soon in New York, too. Podgórski, born in similar circumstances and himself father to a multitude of little American bastards, found nothing reprehensible about the matter. The sisters of Warsaw had always told him he was a child of God, and for this simple reason he had nothing to fear from men or their judgment.

"But Louis, wherever did you get those teal-coloured eyes?"

"My mother was an American, from New England. She had teal eyes."

The three hundred or so people now assembled outside the trailer turned to look at each other. An American? So this marvel actually had red, white, and blue roots? With his mysterious past and the innocence associated with every recollection of him, Louis had found a place in the hearts of the visitors to the St. Lawrence County Fair. To the young ladies listening attentively to the two strongmen recount their adventures, Louis was practically an American. A sheep strayed north of the border. And to the two U.S. Army recruiters, who hadn't missed a word of the story from the back row, Louis was more of a lamb ready to be brought into the fold.

In his thick Polish accent, Podgórski interpreted the story of the birth of Louis Lamontagne on December 25, 1918, in the church of Saint-François-Xavier in Rivière-du-Loup. Louis didn't skimp on the details. He described how his mother, the enigmatic American, had wound up in Canada in the spring of 1918. How she had managed to put Old Ma Madeleine in her back pocket, no matter how wary the matriarch had been, no matter how many times she'd been around the block. How she'd charmed the gluttonous priest, and how, with the horrified parishioners looking on, she'd given birth to Louis Lamontagne at a live nativity scene with the help of Sister Mary of the Eucharist, a midwife whose countenance was enough to stop a haemorrhage in its tracks. Louis pointed to the faint traces the forceps had left on his cheeks: two minuscule furrows across his pink skin, just an inch below his teal-coloured eyes, Madeleine the American's eyes. By the time his story was over, tears were streaming down the women's cheeks. If Louis had managed to win over the crowd by dint of his handsome features and generous physique, the story of how he came into the world at the tragic midnight mass of 1918 transformed him into a mythical hero who would be spoken of for years to come the length and breadth of St. Lawrence County.

"But if your momma died giving birth to you and your daddy died not long after, who raised you, Horse?"

They were lapping it up. After the tragic demise of Louis-Benjamin Lamontagne—father to Louis Lamontagne and widower to Madeleine the American—the question of who would raise the orphaned boy was in need of a quick answer.

"Sure I'll keep him. I won't have lost a son for nothin'. And at least he didn't die over in the old countries!"

And so Old Ma Madeleine raised him as her own. She even waited until he turned ten before telling him the story of his birth, a tale he already knew every word of, having picked it up from the local gossips. But it wouldn't be entirely true to say that Old Ma Madeleine raised the boy alone; after all, it takes a village to raise a colossus his size. Louis Lamontagne was raised as much by his uncle Napoleon Lamontagne, his aunts, his grandparents, the Sisters of the Child Jesus in Rivière-du-Loup, and Father Cousineau, who was particularly fond of the boy. The priest had actually been the first to detect the boy's natural stage presence, not to mention his incredible strength. And Podgórski told how, in August 1932, at the age of thirteen, Louis, already over six foot tall, had begun to go by the name Louis "The Horse" Lamontagne.

It was on the wedding day of Alphonsine, one of the late Louis-Benjamin's sisters who had been handed over to a merchant from the lower part of town with a house on one of the streets alongside the bay, a man from Saint-Patrice looking for a devout and industrious housewife. Father Cousineau, saddened to see young Alphonsine leave his parish, offered to take the Lamontagne family in his buggy, a cart owned by the priest but drawn by a mare who belonged to the Sisters of the Child Jesus, a weary, unpredictable old beast who was older than even the nuns could remember. And so they all went, Old Ma Madeleine and her husband, Old Man Lamontagne; their son Napoleon; the three daughters yet to be married off; and, of course, young Louis, who walked beside the buggy. At the end of the ceremony, as the party was preparing to head back to the upper town, the old mare decided to breathe its last. Just like that. Dead as a doornail.

It must have happened at the very moment young Alphonsine agreed to the yoke of marriage. At any rate, all they could do, when they emerged from the church, was note the poor animal's passing. Malicious tongues immediately pointed the finger at Father Cousineau, who was fatter than ever and never thought twice about taking a cart ride all the way out to Cacouna. But the truth was much more mundane: the mare's time was up, plain and simple. It was sheer chance that it had happened to drop dead during Alphonsine's wedding. But then again, luck is often no stranger when men are made into heroes.

"Why, our handsome young Louis can pull us up into town!" Father Cousineau had joked, but the young man took him at his word.

Old Ma Madeleine protested loudly and scolded her grandson while his grandfather egged him on, perhaps eager to dish out a lesson in humility to his little Louis, who was a strapping young man indeed, but who was certainly incapable of dragging a whole family back up into town in a cart, with a spherical parish priest on board to boot. The old man laughed up his sleeve. Louis was champing at the bit. Outside the church, the guests looked on in amusement at the antics of the Lamontagne family. In her white dress, young Alphonsine tried to talk Louis out of it.

"You'll make a mess of your nice clothes!"

The argument didn't carry much weight. Not as much as Father Cousineau was carrying anyway. He was already in the cart, on the orders of Old Man Lamontagne, squeezed in beside Old Ma Madeleine and her four daughters who were preparing to be humiliated in front of the whole wedding party. To lighten the mood, Father Cousineau gave out a loud "Giddy-up!" and young Louis reacted instantly, thrusting his massive frame forward. And the miracle happened. As smooth as you like, to the gentle creak of axles in need of a good greasing, the cart moved forward, as much to the astonishment of its occupants as to those looking on. Without batting an eyelid, Louis Lamontagne climbed the long slope up Rue Lafontaine, between two rows of spectators decked out in their Sunday best, then onto Rue Saint-Elzéar, finally bringing the cart to a standstill outside the family house on Rue Fraserville, to frenzied applause from a jubilant crowd. Breathless but bursting with pride, Louis Lamontagne was known from that day on as Louis "The Horse" Lamontagne. Podgórski didn't mention the fact that there was another version circulating in Rivière-du-Loup about the origin of the nickname. Louis, some said, had acquired the name for an entirely different reason. But it was the first version of the story Louis preferred to tell at the strongman competition. The wedding went on for another two days, during which time half an ox, twenty-two chickens, just as many quail, and two hundred ears of freshly picked corn were eaten, with Louis wolfing down twenty by himself.

But it was at the funeral of his grandmother, Old Ma Madeleine, that young Louis Lamontagne provided the most irrefutable demonstration yet of his Herculean strength. On the morning of January 30, 1933, Podgórski explained to the crowd at the St. Lawrence County Fair, death struck Old Ma Madeleine down in her prime.

"The day Adolf Hitler came to power!" a particularly well-informed onlooker felt compelled to share with the others.

On that same day, no one in Rivière-du-Loup had an inkling of what was brewing in Berlin, but news of Old Ma Madeleine's demise struck everyone like a blow to the heart. No one, not even her husband, was saddened more than Father Cousineau, the first to be called to chant funeral orations over the deceased's body. It was not yet midday. Old Ma Madeleine had yawned, announced that she had not had enough sleep, that she felt a little worse for wear, that a morning nap would have her feeling right as rain in no time at all.

"And my arm hurts too! It hurts like the dickens."

At noon, the whole family—Napoleon, Louis, the three girls, and Old Man Lamontagne—sat down, absolutely famished, to an empty table. The table hadn't been set, there wasn't a plate in sight. They looked at the clock. Were they mistaken? They found her in bed, smiling, feet and hands crossed, head wrapped in the mauve kerchief she always wore when taking a nap. They took off the scarf. Her eyes were staring out at the bare branch of a maple tree swaying in the winter breeze. A bright light, bleak and cold, flooded the room. It was Old Man Lamontagne who closed her eyes. Father Cousineau arrived soon after.

"Her heart?"

"Or her soul?"

"And how old was Old Ma Madeleine anyway?"

Podgórski translated as best he could the fact that no one in Rivière-du-Loup was altogether sure of Old Ma Madeleine's age. Born in Kamouraska to a family that had long since passed on, she had lived her life without a birth certificate. On the day of her wedding, she had made up a birth date to keep the priest happy and never spoken of her roots again. Her husband was puzzled. Her heart? Yes, no doubt her heart had suddenly stopped beating.

The wake was held in the Lamontagne home. There filed past Old Ma Madeleine's open casket, in order, three of her cousins who were still alive and had made the trip over from Kamouraska, all the Sisters of the Child Jesus, Father Cousineau, the worthies of Rivière-du-Loup, her children, her son-in-law, and, finally, young Louis Lamontagne, the last to kneel before his grandmother's casket and mumble his way through a prayer amid the crying and the wailing. Since the cousins from Kamouraska were there, the others took the opportunity to ask them a few questions of a practical nature.

"What should we put for the year of birth on the gravestone?"

"We don't know. Madeleine was our older sister. She was already married by the time we were women."

"Did she leave behind a birth certificate? A certificate of baptism?"

"Nothing. All we have left of her is a pair of socks she knit for her father in 1898 or 1899, we're not exactly sure."

"But she must have a date of birth."

"She never spoke of it. She never talked about herself. She was a humble, simple woman."

Meanwhile, Louis stumbled his way through the Our Father, skipping a syllable or two. "Give us this day our bread and forgive us our trespasses..."

"Our *daily* bread!" Old Ma Madeleine cut in, lying there in her casket and causing everyone at the wake to fall silent.

"She's right, Louis. You missed a word. It's 'our *daily* bread.'"

Shamefacedly, Louis corrected himself and closed his eyes. Father Cousineau gave him a clip around the back of the head.

"...our daily bread and forgive us our trespasses as we forgive those who trespass against us and deliver us from evil. Amen."

"Amen," chorused the twenty or so people gathered in the Lamontagne's parlour.

A little white cloud escaped from every mouth because, at Old Man Lamontagne's request, the windows had all been opened wide so that Old Ma Madeleine's remains would not decompose before her far-flung relations could make it to the wake. It was just as well she'd died in January: those who die in July are buried before there's time for their grandchildren's prayers to be heard. The deceased's daughters served hot tea while Father Cousineau continued the orations alone, this time in Latin, a language in which he was unlikely to be contradicted by a dead, illiterate old woman. A handful of contemplative nuns from the Order of Saint Clare, who had just settled in Rivière-du-Loup, were next to visit the dead woman in the cold house, notably Sister Mary of the Five Wounds, Sister Mary Saint Paul of Jesus, and Sister Jesus Mary Joseph, formidable prayers every one of them, come to relieve the mourners of their duties toward the departed. Not that the Sisters of the Child Jesus were lacking in piety, far from it. Their orations were every bit the equal of the Order of Saint Clare's, but let's just say that when a Poor Clare begins to pray anyone else is destined to finish a poor second. If it had been a matter of teaching someone to read or bringing a child into the world, they would have been spared the visit from the contemplative nuns, but instead there they were, brought up from the lower town by sled along icy, dangerous roads. They arrived just as Father Cousineau's stomach was beginning to rumble.

"I have some roast and potatoes left over in a pot," Old Ma Madeleine muttered to the parish priest, no stranger to his insatiable appetite.

The old woman sighed. Now they wanted to know—since she seemed clear-headed enough—what she had done with the sugar. Instead of wearing herself out giving instructions she'd only have to repeat the following day, Old Ma Madeleine got up to fetch the sugar bowl herself before returning to her casket.

Cousineau and Louis took refuge in the kitchen—the only warm room in the house—to vie for the leftover roast, while the Poor Clares, indistinguishable in identical habits that revealed only the middle of their bloodless, angular faces, took turns reciting a series of rosaries that went on for three days and four nights, until they were absolutely certain that Old Ma Madeleine's soul was resting in peace. Old Ma Madeleine, meanwhile, joined in fervently with the Hail Marys and the Creeds, delighted to see such a fuss being made about her. The Poor Clares eventually returned to their monastery, leaving behind a house in mourning and a perplexed Old Ma Madeleine. Sister Mary of the Five Wounds whispered some words of reassurance in the dead woman's ear on her way out.

"Real rest is still to come. This first death has freed you of your earthly obligations. You can stay on for a long time yet, until your real rest begins. But rest assured: we only die twice."

What she meant by that, while not in so many words, was that Old Ma Madeleine would never again have to sweep a floor, knead dough, nail down a shingle, shovel snow, bring children into the world by the dozen, knit their clothes, chop wood, haul rocks, take care of the poor and the innocent, train animals, drag home huge slabs of meat to satisfy Louis' appetite, watch over the sick, console the unfortunate, suffer through the itchy dry skin of winter and the insect bites of summer, crush beneath her heel the mice that nibbled away at her flour reserves, beware her neighbours, pray on her knees, pray lying down, or pray standing up. In short, she had been freed from her life as a French Canadian woman.

There was not a hint of the fragrance of flowers in the air of the Lamontagne parlour: it was January. Only a handful of funeral wreaths of willow, fir, and cedar released a resinous perfume into the frigid air. And so died Old Ma Madeleine, on the very same day that Adolf Hitler was named chancellor in Berlin. The good woman wasn't one to make a fuss, and so she answered the nun with no more than a weak "That's what I was wondering, too." By this, she meant that she had understood. She would take it easy until she died a second time. She would be allowed to do some light housework: hulling strawberries, shelling peas, coring apples, that kind of thing, to relieve the boredom at harvest time. They asked Old Ma Madeleine what she thought of it all, if she was glad to be dead or if she would have liked to have lived a while longer.

"I have to say, I'm mighty relieved," came the reply.

In Gouverneur, the temperature was reaching a record high, but nothing in this world could have persuaded the crowd to move from the trailer where Podgórski regaled them with stories of an ice-filled world, a cooling breath on foreheads that glistened with sweat. They imagined the soothing caress of snow on damp skin, they began to dream of frost-covered windows, of the echo that can only be heard in wintry lands: the crisp clarity of a shouted voice across a snowy field, the sound of the cold. Better than a rain shower in May, the story of Old Ma Madeleine's funeral had brought relief from the oppressive heat to the people of Gouverneur and beyond. Louis was doing them good and Floria was more than willing to pay him back in his own coin on New York's behalf. A photographer's flash went off: two strongmen immortalized in their trailer, sitting around a half-eaten turkey and grinning. The contest would be starting up again. The crowd left the men to their stretching.

Excited to the roots of their hair, Beth and Floria Ironstone were the first to reach the venue for the final event: the horse lift. The animal in question was already standing beside a pole similar in size to a telephone pole, in which iron rods had been inserted about a foot apart. Each competitor had to mount the horse—the most docile animal in the county—then, secured to the saddle with a harness whose broad straps covered his shoulders, hoist himself thirty feet up off the ground—with the terrified animal strapped on to his rear end—while clinging on to the post's iron rods, the post itself securely anchored in the ground. It was known in the industry as a "summer event," quite simply because it was difficult to organize in the theatre halls that hosted the shows once the cold weather set in. Another challenge was to find a sufficiently obedient animal that would put up with a slow skyward ascent five times in a row; plus, needless to say, an owner with nerves of steel who would allow their animal to take part in the dangerous game. As luck would have it, all these conditions came together in Gouverneur, and the master of ceremonies beckoned the crowd to come gather around the strange-looking pole. The Warsaw Giant, Idaho Bill, The Great Brouyette, then Podgórski and Lamontagne formed a ring around the master of ceremonies and drew straws to determine who would hoist the horse first. The Giant got the nod, followed by Podgórski, Idaho Bill, Brouyette, and, lastly, handsome young Louis.

The horse bore The Warsaw Giant's two hundred twenty pounds without complaint. The contender was strapped to the saddle with the harness and the horse's saddle straps checked one last time. Then everyone held their breath. This was an especially dangerous event: once the strongman reached the top of the pole, he could lose his grip at any moment and come crashing down to the ground with his mount. It was up to the Giant and the others to use their heads and be a good judge of just how strong they were. The Giant got halfway up the pole, but was forced to turn back before reaching the top. His forearms had begun to shake, a clear sign that he was close to letting go. A nervous murmur rippled through the crowd. With a tear in his eye, the Giant waited until he was released from his harness before uttering what must have been a Polish profanity. Podgórski crossed himself and looked offended. The Giant spat angrily before striding off. He was known to be a proud man; it was better not to stand in his way whenever the red mist descended.

Podgórski looked Beth in the eye as he was hooked up to the horse. He had secretly decided she was prettier than her sister. But Beth had no idea the Pole was eyeing her so greedily. The sad fate of the Warsaw orphan meant that, due to his squint, girls could never tell when he was looking at them. Determined to engrave himself in Beth's memory forever, Podgórski grasped the first iron rod with a firm right hand. His muscles went hard and his eyes immediately returned to their normal axis. The crowd aahed in admiration. A few laughs rang out. As he climbed the rungs, Beth couldn't help but admit he was actually quite a dashing young man. Podgórski couldn't believe it himself.

"Such a shame that he's cross-eyed the rest of the time," she whispered to her sister, who had also fallen under the spell of Podgórski's unwavering gaze as he strained to lift the calm and sleepy horse off the ground.

Invigorated by the thought of Beth Ironstone, Podgórski reached the top of the pole without even realizing it. He climbed back down slowly and the crowd sighed in admiration once the horse's hoofs touched the ground. Beth quivered with joy.

Next, Idaho Bill took his turn. He huffed and he puffed, and managed to haul his load almost to the top of the pole, higher than The Warsaw Giant at any rate, but not right to the top like Alexander Podgórski. He had to turn back four rungs from the top. The Great Brouyette, meanwhile, went into the horse lift with nothing to lose. He had barely gotten over his shameful fall at the start of the car pull, and this time only a win would allow him to save face. The good man also managed to lift the horse higher than The Warsaw Giant, but not quite to the top of the pole. He still had three markers left to climb when he made the decision to come back down, to the crowd's applause.

And so Louis Lamontagne was firmly attached to a horse that would now be subjected to its fifth ascent in a half hour. But an animal has only so much patience. When the mare felt the Canadian's weight on her backbone, she felt what one, without exaggeration, could only call exasperation. Louis, trailing in the standings, had to win the event if he was to beat The Warsaw Giant. Perhaps he paid too much heed to the distance between the rungs on the pole and not enough to the starts of the animal that was growing restless between his thighs. In any event, he was barely halfway up the pole when the horse awoke from its torpor, whinnied, arched its back, thrashed its legs, thrust its head around, and kicked out, exerting, in short, a tension that was simply too much to bear on Louis' aching arms. The distraught animal forced him back down the pole. The crowd groaned with disappointment: the favourite had just lost a make-or-break event. Some tried to convince the master of ceremonies to give Louis Lamontagne a second chance, but all of his rivals were up in arms at the idea, apart from Podgórski that is, who had no hope of winning the contest anyway. The crowd's pleas failed to move the master of ceremonies. The contest rules were clear. To win the horse lift, a strongman needed to rely not only on his muscles, but on his ability to calm his mount, which Lamontagne had manifestly failed to do. Three points went to Alexander Podgórski, two to The Great Brouyette, and one to Idaho Bill. The two great rivals, Louis Lamontagne and The Warsaw Giant, were tied. But there's nothing more disappointing than an even number at the top of the standings. There can only be one winner. The master of ceremonies was ready for this eventuality and announced that, per official contest rules, the men would arm-wrestle for the title. The match would take place immediately, on the outdoor stage where a brass band had just massacred a Viennese waltz or two.

One wooden table. Two chairs. Two arms. One referee.

The only people who remained in the wooden stands had no choice but to be there. The rest of the crowd stood before a stage draped in red, white, and blue and waited to see how the arm-wrestling match would unfold. At the other end of the fairground were stalls and paddocks, where prizes had just been handed out to the cattle and poultry. A turkey answering to the name of Jeanette and an ox called Moby Dick had taken home top honours. A special mention was awarded to the owner of the proud peacock. And to Old Man Whitman's great distress, poor Adolf had come third in his category.

"He's a fine-looking animal is your Adolf, but he's no match for the competition."

The judges had shown no mercy to Whitman when he burst into tears. No match, his Adolf? Adolf, whom Whitman had bottle-fed since birth, cuddled, pampered, and loved? They needed their eyes tested. There was just no way! Are you sure? I don't think he's any smaller than the others, far from it. And what about his colour? Did you see his rich, deep brown? And those big eyes of his? The intelligence behind those eyes. You could almost call it determination. Yessiree! Determination in spades! I demand to see the fair president! What do you mean it's too late? You haven't heard the last of me! I'm not going to take this lying down! You have my word! I wasn't born yesterday, you know. Look me in the eye and tell me, if your balls are big enough, that my Adolf isn't the finest-looking bull calf in this here county! What am I saying? In all of New York! Come on, who are you trying to kid? I demand to speak to the president! Open this door!

Old Man Whitman had lost it. He was fuming with rage, panting for breath, clutching his left arm, desperately looking around the paddock—anywhere—for someone to stand up for him, lend him moral support, tell him it was all a dream, nothing but a bad joke. Alone in the paddock, waiting for his owner to come get him, Adolf brooded. He was a sensitive soul, feeling Whitman's every emotion as his own, as though the two were one on a metaphysical level. Whitman wrapped his arms around Adolf's neck, whispering words of consolation into his ear between heartrending sobs. Embarrassed onlookers began to drift away. And the animal, just like Whitman, began to feel that the dice were loaded, that he was part of a sorry production whose sole aim was to hold him up to ridicule, to humiliate and insult him. And to what end? Why such injustice? Adolf began to stamp his feet. He could no longer bear to see Whitman sobbing. He grew restless, and instead of returning quietly to his bullpen, he broke into a run, all forelegs, letting out a bellow, a D-sharp announcing the end of the world.

Up on stage at the other end of the fairgrounds, Louis Lamontagne, sitting across from The Warsaw Giant, was thanking the heavens that he wouldn't have to face his trusty companion Podgórski. His squint would no doubt have put him off, perhaps even have left him rolling around with laughter. Of all the feats of strength he had accomplished, this arm-wrestle would live longest in his memory. Getting the better of The Warsaw Giant would be no mean task, but he was counting on the energy the crowd was sending him to unsettle his rival and give him the upper hand. He would stare at him with his teal-coloured eyes, show him pupils like those of the stained-glass Madonnas and martyrs the sun shone through in Catholic churches. Would he fall under his spell? The Giant awaited the signal from the master of ceremonies, eager to be done with this trifling Canadian who, not content with stealing his fellow countryman away from him, was now resorting to cockamamie stories to get the crowd behind him. Who said this greenhorn was handsome? And what of the moustache that made him look like he was trying too hard to be Clark Gable? Wasn't that enough to give everyone a good laugh? And what gave this young upstart the right to be winking at the ladies in the crowd? Ladies? I'll give you ladies. When I've smashed your wrist against this table, when the boards have shattered under the phalanges of your fingers, when I've ground your metacarpus to a pulp, you'll see why they call me The Warsaw Giant. If the crowd had been able to read the two men's thoughts, it would likely have booed the Giant for all it was worth.

"I love you, Horse!"

It was a woman's voice. Beth stared hard at the grass, ashamed to death of her sister. The Giant frowned while the emcee's frail little hand clutched the men's wrists.

"Ready and go!"

The first few seconds were unbearable for the Ironstone sisters, the Giant almost managing to pin Louis' hand to the table. But Louis, having lost his composure for an instant, recovered himself at the last moment to pull his wrist up and away from the table. The Giant's strength was colossal. Straining for all he was worth, Louis felt his toes spreading apart like the five arms of a starfish. Red in the face, muscles bursting at the seams, the two strongmen put on a spectacular show for Gouverneur, one that would surely last no more than a few seconds. Prayers went up. People shouted the Canadian's name. The Giant foamed at the mouth. Some onlookers began to take bets, while others quite simply lost their heads in the suffocating heat. They wanted one thing and one thing only: for a winner to be declared so that they could go jump into the water to cool off. They shouted, they yelled, they kicked up such a racket that both men struggled to keep their concentration. The Warsaw Giant rolled a rather worrying black eye. An eye that had never been so big, so black. It was the eye of an animal. Just as Louis thought he had mustered enough strength to overpower his opponent, a frightful howl came up from the public enclosure.

"Adoooooolf!"

The cry was repeated, swelling until it became a clamour through which appeals to God himself could clearly be heard. Alarmed at a din that no longer bore any resemblance to shouts of encouragement, Louis and The Warsaw Giant stole a glance at the crowd. And what a sight they saw: Old Man Whitman running along behind his bull calf as it galloped full tilt toward the terrified spectators.

There was no doubt about it: the animal was charging straight toward the stage, apparently excited by the red, white, and blue banners adorning it. The crowd split in two like the Red Sea before Moses's staff, leaving the Ironstone sisters alone at the foot of the stage, petrified, staring at the furious bull as it charged at them, head down. The calf stopped twenty yards from Floria—now reduced to no more than a squeal—hypnotized by her red skirt. The shouting and screaming stopped suddenly. The crowd could actually be heard breathing in time with the calf. Then, without warning, it rushed forward! Alexander Podgórski, courage his only guide, dashed out from backstage where he had been watching the arm-wrestling contest and swept in like an acrobat before Floria and Beth. His years with the circus had not been in vain. Squinting like crazy, he stood there, his huge arms wide, waiting for the bull to advance. He didn't have to wait long. It charged! It struck! Its little horns gored the Pole! The animal was furious! The crowd ran for its life, leaping over fences, escaping the frightful carnage as best it could. Podgórski was unsteady on his feet, but still standing. He didn't see the second charge coming. And now Adolf's violent blow knocked the poor boy to the ground. It was the painful snapping sound of Podgórski's bones being trampled by Adolf that brought Louis Lamontagne out of his torpor. The despairing shouts were growing louder.

"Help him! *Do* something!"

Lamontagne was only too happy to oblige. He planted himself directly in the path of the animal, which looked up at him. God was again called upon, more insistently than ever. And perhaps the devil, too, because the bull had less luck with the Canadian. Wild with rage, Adolf ran full tilt at Louis. The strongman stepped aside at the last second, and the calf went crashing into the oak planks. The animal disappeared beneath the stage, seemed to whirl around once or twice, and let out a bellow that was amplified by the wooden structure that held it prisoner. Then Louis quickly made up his mind and slipped beneath the stage himself.

"Don't go, Horse! It's still alive!" Floria cried.

And that's exactly what Louis was hoping for. He stuck his head out and shouted something at the master of ceremonies, who had hidden underneath a tarpaulin at the first glimpse of the animal steaming toward them. He handed Louis a thick cable that had been used to attach one of the strongmen to an Oldsmobile. The Canadian dived back in under the stage. A thunderous but short-lived battle ensued, of which nothing at all could be seen. The calf bellowed, stamped its feet, struck out. Louis could be heard swearing in French. Then nothing. After what seemed an eternity to Floria and Beth, Louis slowly emerged into the daylight, dragging the bull behind him, its feet bound tightly and its eyes round with surprise. In no time at all, twenty armed men surrounded the animal, each vying to be the first to plant a bullet between its eyes. Age won out.

"But that's my Adolf. You can't just—"

Nobody listened to another word from Old Man Whitman. Four shots rang out. Adolf was no more. The words "filthy beast," "good riddance," and "may the devil take him" travelled from mouth to mouth. A silent crowd formed a circle around Podgórski's body. Someone went to look for a priest. Dismayed murmuring. It was a sad spectacle. Podgórski was rid of his squint once and for all, his belly torn open, his ribs broken. Beth, tears in her eyes, held his hand, and, kneeling down just in time to bless his soul, a Catholic priest mumbled a few words in Latin over the orphan so far, so very far from Warsaw. The body was still twitching. A death rattle rose high into the American sky. Louis approached, repeating in French the prayers the priest had reeled off in English as though to be sure they were understood by God, because French Canadians are the only people in the world who believe that God is a French speaker. And Podgórski went on dying, determined to leave the world behind him.

"We only die twice, Podgórski," Louis muttered pointlessly, forgetting in his grief that a miracle is no longer considered a miracle if it happens too often.

And in vain he intoned "our daily bread, our daily bread, our daily bread, our daily bread" until he was led gently away.

Louis was declared the winner and pocketed the tidy sum of two hundred dollars. Given the circumstances, there were no celebrations. Louis returned alone to his trailer, at once victorious and defeated. The Pole would be buried in the nearby cemetery the following day; the priest who had performed the last rites had agreed to officiate the funeral. The Giant promised to write to the nuns of Warsaw, who would long lament the fate reserved for their beloved strongman. But they wouldn't receive the letter until months later, after the capitulation of Warsaw, in the midst of the martyrdom of Poland. Perhaps God had wanted to spare Alexander from having to watch his people die, they told themselves. The Giant didn't go into detail about his compatriot's death, referring only to an unfortunate farm accident. The recruiters from the U.S. Army, astonished by Louis' exploits, kept a close eye on him as he organized his friend's funeral. They waited, patient as Sioux, for the young man to go back to his trailer. They even hung back and let Floria knock on the door and spend the night with the Canadian before introducing themselves.

Louis was lying in his trailer, alone in prayer. There was a knock at the door. He was going to have to speak. He really didn't want to. Don't answer.

Say nothing. Keep your arms crossed. Doesn't matter who's standing on the other side of that door. He could hear a woman's voice. A pretty woman's voice.

"Horse! Open up! It's me, Floria."

"I'm praying."

"Let me pray with you then. I'm so upset. Such a narrow door for a man with such broad shoulders."

"But we can't stay here alone. Who saw you come in?"

"No one. Beth is with the priest. She wants to help with the funeral. She was very fond of him. No more than a wink from him and her heart would've been his. I would never have thought my sister capable of such a thing."

"Floria's your name, right?"

"Yes, as in Floria Tosca. It's an opera. Do you like opera?"

"Never heard one. Can you stay with me a while?"

"Of course. That's why I came. To keep you company. It's really awful what happened to that poor boy... Why, you're crying, Horse!"

"Who's going to translate my stories? Just listen to me! My English is terrible. Who's going to pull the trailer while I sleep? Who's going to keep me company?"

"But your English is not so bad. Give it time. Let time take its course. Here, take my hankie."

"Thank you. You're very kind. Podgórski was a poor sleeper. Whenever he couldn't sleep, he'd say, 'Hey, Lamontagne, tell me one of your cock-and-bull stories from Canada.' And I'd tell him a story, any story."

"And he'd fall asleep?"

"No! He'd want to hear the end. Then he'd fall asleep. That's how it was. He knew lots of my stories by heart. What a tiny nose you have, Floria..."

"Why the cheek of you, Louis Lamontagne!"

"I'm serious! I love your nose! It's such a cute little nose."

"And my legs are too thin. That's what Momma always says."

"Your legs are magnificent. And now you're crying too."

"Do you know what would do us good?"

"No, what?"

"A little whisky! If only we had some..."

"Well, actually I do. Right over there. The good stuff, from Canada."

"Why, what a stroke of luck! I was just thinking that a Canadian must never travel without his whisky."

"Would you like some?"

"Sure, why not? Twist my arm!"

"Here you go."

Glug, glug, glug.

"Hey! Easy does it. Not so fast!"

"Oh! This whole business has me so upset. Thank you, Horse. Not only are you the handsomest man I've ever laid eyes on, you're a gentleman too. Oh your hand is so big and strong."

"A woman in Michigan once told me that."

"Kiss me, Louis."

The night Podgórski died, it rained in Gouverneur. Torrential storms straight out of a Wagner opera. Thick clouds sent to cleanse the earth of the stains of humanity. Once Floria left to spend the night in Gouverneur ahead of Podgórski's funeral, Louis slept like a baby amid the thunder and lightning. The U.S. Army recruiters were waiting for him the next morning.

"Your mother was an American, we hear…"

Two years later, wearing an infantry uniform and having piled on a few extra pounds at Uncle Sam's mess, handsome Louis set sail for England aboard a ship accompanied by a minesweeper, *Will you love me all the time?* playing in his mind, his knowledge of Europe amounting to no more than a blurry, quaint image of a small country densely populated with nothing but Polish nuns, strongmen, and mad dictators. Of all the members of his division, Louis Lamontagne was probably the only man there out of love for Poland. He was also the most attractive man aboard. That was beyond a shadow of a doubt.

It wasn't until December 31, 1999, at the age of forty-nine, that Madeleine decided it was safe to open the letter from Floria Ironstone she had intercepted in 1958. She found two plea-filled pages covered with kisses. The word *please* appeared six times. Attached to the letter was a photograph of a little girl who had been conceived at the St. Lawrence County Fair in August 1939—Penelope Ironstone, who would wait for her father's reply for the rest of her life. Madeleine never did try to contact her half-sister, thereby missing out on one of Louis Lamontagne's most colourful stories.

Like Puccini's heroine Floria Tosca, Madeleine Lamontagne wasn't fond of competition. Although it must be said in her defence that most of the women who fell head over heels in love with Louis "The Horse" Lamontagne never did manage to completely recover. His daughter was no exception to the rule.

The Neighbour

She saw her for the very first time over the willow hedge. She was five. They hadn't started school yet. On Sundays, the Lamontagnes would drive out to the Point in Papa Louis' Oldsmobile to eat ice cream. Irene Caron, their mother, would invariably slam the car door on her way back into the house. Hiding behind the willows, just a few feet away, Solange Bérubé first set eyes on Madeleine Lamontagne's face. Madeleine was clinging to her dad's grey pants. Her dad was a kind of fine-whiskered giant, a legendary beast of burden, an undertaker by trade.

"Solange, you're not to go over to the Lamontagnes'. Do I make myself clear? You're not to go to the undertaker's. Tell Mommy you won't go over to the Lamontagnes'. Tell me right this minute. Or you won't be having anything to eat."

Solange didn't eat.

Since it was June and the willow leaves had come out a little earlier than usual that year, nobody spotted Solange Bérubé, which already gave her a certain advantage. She and her brother Marcel were used to spying on Louis Lamontagne from the willow hedge, watching him bring the caskets down from his porch and slide them into the hearse, usually unassisted. She also loved, safely hidden behind a lilac bush, watching mourners file into the Lamontagnes' for a wake. From her hiding place, Solange could hear Old Ma Madeleine greeting the relatives with a few words of comfort.

A dead woman acting as a welcoming committee for a funeral home only stood to reason. Who better to reassure a grieving family than someone who had passed to the other side herself? But on that particular Sunday, the Sunday of first contact, the funeral parlour was empty. Not a soul. Alone in the yard, Madeleine Lamontagne seemed to be looking for something.

She turned around. From the corner of the big house, a little cat had begun to walk toward the willows, threatening to reveal the spy. Luc had stayed behind in the car and now his mother came to fetch him. And the little cat continued on its uncertain path toward Solange.

"If I don't move, it'll never see me."

But curiosity killed the cat. The animal approached the hedge and sensed the presence of a child. Madeleine ran over to stop the cat going next door, bent down to scoop him up, and, as she stood, set her teal eyes on Solange Bérubé for the very first time. Pretending not to have seen a thing, she left with the little grey and white cat, which was still staring at Solange. At the door to the house, just before going back inside, Madeleine Lamontagne, all of five years old, turned around one last time and looked Solange straight in the eye. One second later, the little Bérubé girl collapsed in silence among the tender green willow foliage in Rivière-du-Loup.

Old Ma Madeleine, as old as time itself and stooped over like a venerable oak tree, was struggling to push a rocking chair across the Lamontagnes' porch to sit down on. It was she who first noticed Solange's body lying in the grass on the other side of the willows. She knocked on the Bérubés' door, scaring everyone half to death, as she was inclined to do.

"Your little girl isn't well!" she informed the Bérubé family through the screen door. They didn't hear her at first because since her sudden death in 1933, Old Ma Madeleine spoke only when absolutely necessary and her voice came out as little more than a croak. Mind you, anyone would have had a hard time making themselves heard over at the Bérubés', even someone equipped with an entirely normal vocal apparatus.

Were there ten or twelve of them crammed into the smoke-filled kitchen waiting for a ham to arrive? Solange, the youngest, wasn't always able to squeeze a word in. Old Ma Madeleine, as she watched everyone bustle about, gesticulate, cough, talk, explain, laugh, and belch, was losing patience. She banged three times on the doorframe.

"You'd best go get your daughter before the ants do!"

They fell silent at last. A woman armed with a broom came out onto the porch to chase the old Lamontagne woman away. They'd been clear enough with Papa Louis: he was to keep his grandmother to himself. Yes, people were grateful to him for working as the parish's undertaker, but still, he shouldn't get carried away, and he really shouldn't go around thinking that people were overjoyed to be living beside a funeral parlour, not when a dead woman might come knocking on your door at any moment to bother you at suppertime. But the old woman didn't move. She just pointed to the garden, whistled, dodged Mrs. Bérubé's broom, grabbed hold of her sleeve—causing her to shriek like a distraught virgin—and demanded to be heard.

It was the Bérubés' simple-minded fourth son who found Solange passed out beside the willows. Madeleine Lamontagne watched the scene unfold from her bedroom window. So many people gathered around the young neighbour she had just smiled at. Had she suddenly fallen ill? Solange, who was laid out on the living-room sofa, gradually came around. Ice-cold water. Face-slapping. Prayers. Old Ma Madeleine had gone back home, much to everyone's relief. Mr. Bérubé had thanked her all the same. Solange felt as though she had a pumpkin for a heart, a whale in her head. Mrs. Bérubé shook her. "Well, speak then, would you? What's the matter? Will you live?" Solange had two choices: the first was to diligently describe the harm she had just suffered, the second was to lie. Telling the truth would have meant explaining to the twelve heads leaning in over her that she had just seen the rest of her life flash before her eyes, that it had happened in the instant Madeleine-Lamontagne-Holding-Kitten-Standing-In-Front-Of-Door had looked her up and down with her teal-coloured eyes. Solange lied. She didn't say the words that would come to her only years later—when so many witnesses had disappeared—which just goes to show that our best thoughts always come too late. She wouldn't have been able to adequately describe the experience anyway. She hadn't started school yet and still didn't have the words to say: "I've just seen a quite incredible person, who looked at me like no one has ever looked at me before. I saw, in the depths of her teal-coloured eyes, the answers to my fraught existence. Never again will I be able to begin another day without first dedicating it to this being of light who lives in the house beside mine. In her absence, I will be no more than a lost, hopeless animal. I understood as I fell to the lush green grass that never again would I be the same, that life without this being would be nothing more than a dreadful, tiresome sham. Needless to say, I will spend the rest of my existence praying to God for this being to set eyes on me a second time. Until then, every move I make, every word I speak, every person who passes through my life, everything I eat, the stars in the sky, the animals of Creation—all will be relegated to the realm of nonsense and foolishness. My name is Solange Bérubé and I exist only for the eyes of Madeleine Lamontagne."

Mrs. Bérubé scolded her daughter anew. "You're not to go over there. I forbid it. You are not to go to the Lamontagnes' house. Do I make myself clear? Now eat your potatoes and don't even think about going near those willows." Every mother in Rivière-du-Loup used to repeat the very same words to their children. Ask anyone who can remember and they'll tell you.

"He was an undertaker, you see… and the bodies were right there in his parlour…"

"And that's not all. He liked to have a drink or two, did old Louis Lamontagne. And he had a real temper on him!"

"Especially after he came back from the war. Never spoke a word about it. But he wasn't the same man. Did you know he liberated Dachau?"

"And you're forgetting the wife! Irene Caron! Pure poison…"

"And Madeleine's brothers, Marc and Luc. They weren't all there either. Strange, the pair of them… Not quite right in the head. Unhinged."

"But as strong as oxen!"

"Not crazy enough to set the place on fire, but in no rush to put it out either!"

"I wouldn't want them for neighbours, I'm telling you!"

"And the grandmother who just won't die! Hanging on to them like a ball and chain!"

And yet the Lamontagnes were rather quiet folks. Apart from Old Ma Madeleine who would sometimes knock on the neighbours' door to tell them to keep an eye on their kids, the Lamontagnes kept themselves to themselves. On Sunday mornings, they occupied pew number four in the church of Saint-François-Xavier, just yards away from where Madeleine the American had died giving birth to Louis. On Sunday afternoons, Papa Louis would take the family out to the Point for an ice cream. Despite his past as a strongman and his work as an undertaker, Louis Lamontagne made a point of behaving in a way that was never anything but normal, that nothing he did might be interpreted as an extravagance. With a grandmother who belonged to the ranks of the living dead, there was enough to set tongues wagging already, without him adding to it. Old Ma Madeleine didn't much like ice cream and preferred to stay home and rock herself on the veranda and wave at passersby. To put on a bit of a show, she would sometimes pretend to puff on a snuffed-out pipe. Solange barely knew Old Ma Madeleine. Her only memory of her was of the old woman who had died in 1933 and was still there, rocking away on the Lamontagnes' veranda in 1955.

The first time Madeleine Lamontagne had spoken to Solange Bérubé was at the convent. Grade One Class A. In September 1957. Mrs. Bérubé had been very clear:

"Just you be careful, Solange Bérubé. If that little Lamontagne girl speaks to you, you don't answer. Do you hear me? Don't go near her, don't sit beside her, and don't go talking to her on the way home either. Not to her and not to her brother Marc. I know we're neighbours, but that doesn't mean we have to be friends. You take the other sidewalk on the way home. If Mommy catches you talking to Madeleine, you'll be in trouble, understand? Just as much trouble as last Saturday, remember?"

The child didn't reply.

"Solange Bérubé, I'm talking to you! Do you understand?" she shouted, twisting the little girl's arm.

"Yes, Mother."

Mrs. Bérubé was referring to the punishment to end all punishments she'd handed out to her youngest daughter two days before. A regrettable situation that could have been avoided if attention had been paid to detail. But Mrs. Bérubé, in baptizing her ninth child Solange—because it rhymed with *ange*—had sworn deep down it would be her last. Saint Solange, the virgin martyr, was decapitated for rejecting the advances of the Count of Poitiers' son, who carried her off while she tended to her sheep. A proud and fierce girl, she had struggled until her kidnapper decapitated her with his sword. Mrs. Bérubé would never have suspected that her little girl would become, in her own way, a reincarnation of the saint. By 1950, she had brought nine children into the world. Two girls and seven boys. Knock-kneed and tubercular, the Bérubé kids tended to live for ten or twelve years before coming down with some incurable, albeit not deadly, disease or other: diabetes, emaciation, polio, bronchitis, various and varied degrees of ataxia. Only Solange was an exception to the rule.

"Always something wrong with those Bérubés!" the gossips of Rue Lafontaine would say as they watched one of the sickly boys shuffle past.

The family's eldest daughter, the picture of ill health, was a tall, wan girl by the name of Antonine. She cried with joy when her little sister Solange was born. At last someone to fuss over, someone whose diapers she could change, someone to shape in her image. She was delighted to take over from her mother, exhausted after nine pregnancies in twelve years, and proclaimed herself little Solange's nanny, throwing herself into the role of big sister. The doctor having declared a general boycott on cesareans, Mrs. Bérubé had taken four months to get back on her feet again after the birth.

"She's had eight already. I don't see why the ninth wouldn't make it through just fine!" he'd said, in between Mrs. Bérubé's howls.

Solange had been heftier than the rest, and a repeat of the Christmas drama of 1918 was only narrowly avoided in Rivière-du-Loup. But her mother survived. Antonine took charge of the little girl immediately, unaware that disappointment was just around the corner. It wouldn't be fair to Solange to say that she had been bad-tempered from birth: after all, it takes a few good years of fight on this earth to form character. They say that for infants, we should refer instead to their *nature* and, in the case of Solange, her nature was, to put it mildly, untameable. The kind of nature that's bound to get a freethinker into trouble.

For instance, when Mrs. Bérubé warned Solange off the Lamontagne family on the first day of school and brought up the incident of the previous Saturday, she had been referring to the unfortunate tutu episode.

Antonine might have been twenty years old and still living with her parents, though she was engaged to be married, but she had not given up on the idea that Solange was a doll that the Lord himself had given her in the springtime of 1950 after a few timely novenas. Antonine had prayed with a martyr's fervour to the Almighty that He might send her a little sister. She'd had enough of sickly little boys that had to be dragged from the sanatorium to the hospital to the next pilgrimage (and back again), boys who would grow up only to have sons with hacking coughs of their own. And now she saw little Solange as an outlet for her own artistic inclinations. No surprise then that on the Saturday before Solange's first day of school, Antonine decided to give her the most girlish of surprises. She led her into her room, dressed her in a ballerina costume complete with a tutu she'd found at the haberdasher's, made her up like Shirley Temple, and adorned her with broaches, barrettes, and other assorted sparkly accessories.

More than a little proud of her handiwork, she then had the little girl get up on a chair to gaze at her reflection in her dressing-table mirror. The scene that ensued passed into the annals of Bérubé family lore. Antonine had forgotten that two weeks previously the whole family had been at a wake for a cousin, Annette Rossignol, who had died at the age of twelve from fever and a stomach ache. The image of the dead girl, lying in her casket in a white dress, had remained fixed in Solange's memory. When she saw herself in the mirror, all made-up and adorned in chiffon, she thought she must be dead, too, and that her big sister was getting her ready for her funeral. She began to shout and scream, turned Antonine's bedroom upside down and tried to wipe off her makeup with a corner of the bedspread, biting and hitting her sister all the while. Finally she whacked Antonine over the head with a drawer from the dresser. Alarmed by the racket, the entire Bérubé family came limping and hobbling into the room. Three of the brothers held the furious child while Mrs. Bérubé administered twenty lashes of the cane, the usual sentence for such misbehaviour. It wasn't until much later, only once she had moved to Montreal, that Solange dared apply makeup to her face, on the advice of an image consultant.

"Otherwise you'll look like a corpse!" the well-coiffed young man had told her, utterly oblivious to the irony of his remark.

The first time she'd worn makeup, Solange had thought she was dead. The second was so as not to look like a cadaver. She clearly had a troubled relationship with makeup and all traditional signs of femininity.

Solange had agreed to the convent braids and the dresses, too, provided they were just one colour—no motifs, no flowers, no tiny giraffes. Age eight, she had been given twenty-five lashes for trying to start her father Armand's car while he napped one winter's afternoon. The little girl had slipped up beside him, moving closer each time he snored, and stolen his keys with a single catlike movement. Sitting behind the wheel of the 1952 Dodge, she had managed to start the engine and was getting ready to put the car into reverse when Irene Lamontagne spotted her from the kitchen window and alerted Mrs. Bérubé. But the little girl was not about to concede defeat, and swore, between her father's fifteenth and sixteenth stroke of the cane, that she'd try again soon enough. Her father, an otherwise mild-mannered man, beat her not with any conviction, but rather because his wife's screams had roused him from a deep sleep from which he had emerged grouchy, impatient, and irritated. Solange's long-standing fascination for motor cars had always amused him, truth be told, but a man's sleep is a sacred thing.

When Mrs. Bérubé had forbidden her daughter from hanging around the Lamontagne home, when she slapped her and forbade her from speaking to Madeleine, when she closed the drapes so that her daughter would not even see her house from their living room, it was not so much because of Luc Lamontagne (a loud, obnoxious, vulgar, and violent child), nor because Louis Lamontagne ran a funeral parlour out of his home on Rue Saint-François-Xavier (a funeral parlour that, if you asked her, was all too popular), nor because of Old Ma Madeleine (who first died in 1933 and was still waiting with her grandson to be free at last of her earthly sorrows), nor because of little Madeleine (a quiet little girl who spent the better part of her time in a shed behind her house); no, none of these things, as strange and unusual as they might appear, bothered Mrs. Bérubé in the slightest. What she was so keen to protect her daughter and her long-suffering sons against was Irene Lamontagne, née Caron.

"If that Caron woman so much as looks at you, you come straight home. You don't say a word to her. Do you hear?"

Mrs. Bérubé twisted her daughter's arm. They passed in front of the boys' school, turned left, and walked toward the convent. In the courtyard, the nuns were rushing around, trying to round up the girls, excited to be back at school, into neat lines. The bigger girls were either helping or terrorizing the little ones, depending on their *nature*.

The convent. A brick cube that was home to the Sisters of the Child Jesus, complete with kitchen, parlour, refectory, and laundry room, as well as a school for girls. You went in through a side door, the front entrance being reserved for visitors to the parlour. At the sight of the sea of women and girls, little Solange panicked, dug her heels into the gravel, and refused to take another step. She wouldn't go. Why hadn't she been enrolled at the Christian Brothers School with her brothers? To be taught by men so clean and handsome that everyone wanted to be like them? Why this? And those awful cashmere tights! The sea of girls was already drawing closer in threatening little waves; a nun welcomed Mrs. Bérubé, who was only too pleased to be relieved of her burden. Solange didn't cry. On principle. She recalled, not without a twinge of regret, the Saturday afternoon outside in the yard when her brother Marcel had explained to her, proof in hand, why she was off to the convent and he to the Christian Brothers School. While he did up his fly, Solange had wondered when that thing had grown between his legs and, especially, how it had grown so fast? What prayer had been answered in return for it? What good deed had it rewarded? The thing—it looked so small, topped with a sort of bishop's hat—seemed to endow its owner with such incredible powers and privileges: he could drive a car, wear a cowboy hat, snore on the living-room sofa, speak at the table, exist.

"If the Lamontagne girl speaks to you," her mother was saying again, "tell the nun. We'll take care of it!"

As though the trauma of having been abandoned in a place peopled exclusively with women was not discouraging enough, fate would have it that Madeleine and Solange would sit beside each other in Grade 1A, right in front of their teacher, Sister Saint Arsenius, who was now barking out the pupils' names.

"When you hear your name, say 'Yes, Sister,' and come take your books. Don't drop them. Don't damage the corners. Take good care of them or you will be punished! Silence! Raymonde April!"

"Yes, Sister!"

Solange glanced around the room, trying not to look in Madeleine Lamontagne's direction. Little footsteps could be heard. Raymonde April was shaking as she was handed her first textbooks. Posters covered in letters lined the walls. A map of the world. A crucifix. The nun had explained that these were photos of holy people: our Holy Father Pope Pius XII in his mitre. His hat looked like her brother Marcel's penis, Solange thought to herself, except Pius XII was a penis that wore little round glasses. Yes, they were definitely the same shape. The masculine presence reassured her a little.

"Solange Bérubé!"

"Yes, Sister."

Solange stepped forward and saw the image of Sister Saint Arsenius grow as she handed her a catechism and a reading book with a smile. A few of the girls giggled at Solange's lumberjack-like stride. Solange looked daggers at a little blonde girl and went back to her seat.

"Marie Castonguay!"

"Yes, Sister!"

Madeleine Lamontagne smiled. Solange couldn't see her, but she could hear her smile. Just like she could hear her breathe and perspire. Her gaze fell on her neighbour to the left. The girl was still whimpering at being separated from her family.

"Simone Dumont!"

"Yes, Sister."

The cry baby's name was Simone. The show of tears exasperated Solange. But where else could she settle her gaze without risk of being dazzled by the light emanating from Madeleine Lamontagne? She stared hard at the photograph of the archbishop of Sainte-Anne-de-la-Pocatière for a moment, a man with a reassuring face.

"Madeleine Lamontagne!"

Absolute silence. Madeleine got up from her chair and walked toward the nun. The nun seemed to know her already and smiled at her perhaps a little more sincerely than she had the others. Madeleine sat back down. Thirty girls each paraded by Solange in this way. Then it was time for the skirt test.

In alphabetical order, the girls were told to come kneel one by one before the rest of the class. Once they were on their knees, the skirt of their sober uniforms was to fall in line with the floor, without touching it, and without creasing. Madeleine and Solange, both daughters of scrupulous mothers, passed the test hands down. Others were less fortunate and met with their first threats. "Rectify the situation, Miss, or there will be problems."

Sister Saint Arsenius began the first reading lesson. It wasn't until the afternoon that things took a turn for the worse for Solange. Until then, she had managed to completely ignore Madeleine Lamontagne. She hadn't so much as looked at her. Not even when Sister Saint Arsenius had had her recite a prayer to the Virgin Mary. But then disaster struck poor Solange. While the nun barked out the first letters of the alphabet, banging a wooden ruler against the blackboard, Madeleine started to take an interest in Solange. She was discreet at first, then she said her name. Once in a whisper, once out loud.

"Solange!"

Solange ignored her neighbour at first. She must have recognized her from Rue Saint-François-Xavier. Perhaps she had just learned her name and wanted to try it out. Sister Saint Arsenius shot the two girls a fearsome look. But Madeleine wouldn't let it go.

"Solange! Solange Bérubé!"

Why must she suffer so? Why, Lord, why? Solange looked up. Sister Saint Arsenius was now standing between her and Madeleine's desks. It was then that Solange made her mistake: she looked Madeleine in the eyes. Into the depths of her teal-coloured eyes. And in them she could clearly make out a promise.

Madeleine smiled. Two seconds later, the contents of the Bérubé girl's stomach spewed out of her mouth in a powerful yellowish stream and splashed against Sister Saint Arsenius's immaculate wimple.

"Oh dear! No prizes for guessing which disease-ridden family you come from, Solange Bérubé!"

And so, groggy from having thrown up and feeling more than a little unsteady on her feet, Solange was dragged by the arm to the infirmary and the nurse, Sister Mary of the Eucharist. While the first hours at the convent had terrorized her, and hearing her name come out of Madeleine Lamontagne's mouth had caused her to projectile vomit, the sight of Sister Mary of the Eucharist overcame what remained of her composure and courage. A nose. A huge nose. A sort of hook of flesh and bone. That's all she saw leaning over her before she lost consciousness.

"We'll have to keep an eye on her. Your daughter is a fragile one," Sister Mary of the Eucharist told Mrs. Bérubé when she came to pick up her daughter, who'd fainted on the first day of school.

Mind you there was nothing unusual about the little girls of Rivière-du-Loup fainting or vomiting at the sight of Sister Mary of the Eucharist. In fact, the nun in question was surprised to be brought a little girl who had already vomited. Barely a few hours after throwing up her breakfast over Sister Saint Arsenius's wimple, Solange threw herself wholeheartedly into a novena to Our Lady, asking for a favour almost too shameful to mention, not at any rate to her mother or her brothers, let alone the nuns at the convent, who would probably be the last to understand Solange's childish desire for God to give her a penis. If she had a penis, Solange would be sent straight to the Christian Brothers School with her brothers like a normal person. And she would no longer have to sit beside Madeleine, who unsettled her so. The following morning, Mrs. Bérubé decided to keep Solange home. The child wasn't sent back to the convent for another two days, her heart heavy. Upon her return to Grade 1A, the photograph of Pius XII was waiting for her, thumbing his nose at her with his big, firm papal mitre that was probably soft, warm, and spongy on the inside.

Solange's lack of enthusiasm for the convent hadn't escaped Mrs. Bérubé's notice; she was growing worried at seeing her youngest daughter more demoralized by the day. It wouldn't be long before the little girl outright hated the convent and everything it stood for. But shortly after joining Sister Saint Arsenius's class, Solange made a fabulous discovery: schoolyard gossip, disparaged by some, enjoyed by others, practiced by all. And so, one October morning, never suspecting the exquisite pleasure awaiting her, Solange intercepted the muttered conversation of two up-and-coming Grade 6 gossip artists in the covered part of the playground.

"The undertaker's been playing around. My sister told me."

"And how would your sister know?"

"She didn't say. But what I do know is that Mrs. Lagacé's youngest son… You know, Mrs. Lagacé, the fat cow who lives over on Saint-André? Well, he has teal-coloured eyes, just like Madeleine Lamontagne's. Take a good look the next time you're talking to him."

"You're kidding!"

"Word has it they met when The Horse went to pick up Grandpa Lagacé's body. It was Mrs. Lagacé who called him and she was home alone. The neighbours heard it all! The body wasn't even cold!"

"As long as he doesn't do it with dead women."

"Yuck! You're disgusting."

Pricking up her ears at the sound of gossip from every corner of the convent schoolyard, from every alcove, from beside every statue of every beatific saint—Saint Blandina and Saint Lawrence being her favourites—Solange learned more about the Lamontagne family than any other subject, on or off the curriculum. Whenever she noticed that one girl seemed to know a little more than another about Louis Lamontagne, she would arrange to bump into her as often as she could and try to win her trust. How many friendships did she force between grades 1 and 6 just to hear snatches from Louis Lamontagne and Irene Caron's past and present? Had it not been for this playground gossip and the whisperings in the refectory, Solange Bérubé would probably have died of sadness and terror at the Sisters of the Child Jesus convent. But every recess, every trip down the building's hallways, every moment spent standing in line in the schoolyard brought with it the possibility that she might learn a little more about the Lamontagnes. The child lived only for these snatches of conversation; they were the sole reason she paid the slightest bit of attention at school, all the way up to Grade 6. From one such conversation she learned how Louis Lamontagne met Irene Caron; from another, all there was to be known about the strained relations between Old Ma Madeleine and her daughter-in-law. As reliable as any intelligence service, the convent girls probably knew more about the Lamontagne family than Madeleine did herself. And tongues wagged and wagged... Sometimes indulgent, sometimes vicious, always informative, the gossip piled up over the years until it constituted—without Solange ever having to ask a single indiscreet question—the sum of all she knew about her neighbours, which is to say the story of Louis Lamontagne since his triumphant return to Rivière-du-Loup on Saint-Jean-Baptiste Day in June 1948. Scraps of gossip and intercepted love letters nevertheless have the peculiar drawback of not recounting stories in chronological order.

When Louis Lamontagne returned to the country in 1948, three years after war's end, he found the family home almost deserted. His uncle Napoleon had married and gone off to live in a remote village by a lake; a lake where, legend had it, there lived a monster. His aunts, all younger than him, had married farmers and men who worked for the railway. Old Man Lamontagne had died in 1946 while Louis was still waiting to be repatriated. All alone in the vast wooden house on Rue Fraserville, Old Ma Madeleine was busy hulling strawberries when her grandson Louis Lamontagne reappeared. She hadn't felt so relieved since the time they told her she had died, thirteen years earlier. He had just come from Rivière-du-Loup's Saint-Jean-Baptiste Day parade, he told her.

The first thing she asked him was: "Are you hungry, Louis?"

One chicken, eight potatoes, and four glasses of cider later, she began asking about the old country she would never see. The dead don't travel, you see. Louis had little to say. Madeleine told him about her husband's funeral, Napoleon's wedding, and a few recent baptisms. Louis had brought a gift back from Europe, a strange little painting. Sitting at the wooden table where they had changed his diapers when he was a baby, he gave it to Old Ma Madeleine, who looked at it curiously. It was a religious scene the old woman had never seen before. Someone—a woman—was lying on a slab of granite. It was Mary. Yes, of course it was. Covered in a loose-fitting garment, some sort of blue sheet. Her eyes were closed, probably once and for all. The apostles were gathered around her. Old Ma Madeleine recognized Andrew, tall and strong, Peter, and the others. Bending down over his mother's body, Jesus was holding a baby in swaddling clothes. A few seraphims were flying in the upper left-hand corner.

"Did you draw it? Is that your mother?"

Louis laughed for the first time since the liberation of Dachau. He hadn't the faintest idea what the scene might mean. He had been given the picture over in Europe. All those men standing over a dead woman's body had reminded him of Old Ma Madeleine's wake; the bright halo around Christ's head, of the statues in the church where he was born. Everything about the painting brought him back to Rivière-du-Loup and, without knowing exactly why, the scene of the Virgin's entombment had inspired him, after five years of service in the U.S. Army, to return to the calm of his northern shores.

"If you're not the one who painted it, then who did?"

Old Ma Madeleine held the painting in her bony hands. Louis hadn't a clue. The picture was all he had brought back with him from Europe. And in the stories he continued to tell, he often spoke of the old countries, of the Germans and French. Only once did he speak of the liberation of Dachau, years later, sitting at the Ophir bar. Some idiot had shouted something at him, made some stupid remark or other about concentration camps. The idiot became a projectile, and then he shut up. For a very long time. When he came around, weeks later, he found himself another bar.

Old Ma Madeleine had followed her grandson, the only living human being who remained with her in this world, to the house on Rue Saint-

François-Xavier, a bigger and more modern home than the one on Fraserville. Louis had bought it with all his earnings from the United States, all the prizes brought home from county fairs, his pay from the U.S. Army, and the money he made from selling the house on Fraserville, bought by a perfectly uninteresting family. It was shortly after he came back from Germany that he opened his funeral home. From Dachau, he had brought back the fragrance of death. The smell stuck to his skin until he become one with it.

His interest in the dead had come about, by his own admission, on a particularly grey day in Bavaria. It had been snowing and he was advancing across a field with the other foot soldiers when he stumbled on a rock that let out a moan. The rock was surrounded by other rocks, though those ones were dead. The rock said its name was David Rosen. He had marched with other prisoners from Dachau for six days, escorted by the SS. The German guards eventually realized they would never reach Tyrol: the Americans had them surrounded. All around him, prisoners were dying of exhaustion. Those who tried to escape were shot dead. The following morning, the Germans ordered them all to lie down in a clearing, and then the miracle happened. Big, fat, Alpine snowflakes began to fall, lazy and dense. Rolled up in his blanket, Rosen had fallen asleep on the ground, hoping to die at last. Realizing the Americans were no more than a few hundred yards away, the Germans fled, though not before firing a few rounds into the bodies lying in the clearing. But so much snow had fallen that they hadn't seen Rosen's body buried beneath it. When he awoke, he pulled back the blanket and saw only a huge white mass that he took to be death, and was happy to find himself there. But the white mass gave way beneath his fingers. Before him stood a giant of a man with teal-coloured eyes. His teeth were the same colour as the snow that had saved him from the German bullets. Louis was tasked with piling the frozen bodies into a truck. They all wore striped pyjamas, all had their eyes open, their hands sometimes frozen mid-movement. Some had died on their bellies, with one hand raised as though to bid a final frozen farewell to the world. The bodies were hard to stack in the cold, like trying to pack tiny lead soldiers into a cigar box. Then the truck left, leaving behind the American soldiers and David Rosen, the only survivor of that death march.

"If it hadn't snowed that morning, the Germans would have seen me and shot me. The snow saved me," David told Louis.

That was all he said, over and over.

There were shortages of just about everything in Germany in 1945, but not of bodies. There were mountains of them. Some young, some old, some nice, some halfwit, some nasty, some stupid, some shrewd, some slow, some keen, all of them disappeared without burial into the depths of the German soil.

It was this injustice that Louis was determined to right upon his return to Canada. "We should never be ashamed of our dead" had been his first slogan. And that's why Louis had made a long stopover in Quebec City before coming home. It took him six months to learn—at the hands of Henri Bellerose, an experienced undertaker if ever there was one—how to minister to mortal remains and run a funeral home. It really wasn't so different from a strongman contest: make everything appear entirely natural in spite of the circumstances, never pass up on an opportunity to introduce an element of theatre, and speak parsimoniously. At the master undertaker's in Quebec City, Louis learned that a single misplaced word can spread like a disease through a family and end up depriving you of customers. You even have to be careful how you look at them, Bellerose had often told him: even the most stoical can become highly emotional at a time of mourning. Before letting his apprentice go, Bellerose had one last piece of advice for him:

"You're a fine-looking man, Louis. That's important for an undertaker. Stay elegant. The dead will thank you for it. Don't just count on your natural good looks. And remember: you can't go wrong with black."

The Bérubés, neighbours to the Lamontagne funeral home, were not in the least enthused by the new business on Rue Saint-François-Xavier. Dead people? How ghastly! They shook their heads every time they saw a casket in the street or Papa Louis smiling at the disgusted family from behind the wheel of the hearse. And that Irene…

To fully comprehend the visceral hatred that Mrs. Bérubé—and many other women in Rivière-du-Loup—harboured for Irene Caron, we need to go back to that very same Saint-Jean-Baptiste Day in 1948 when Louis Lamontagne made his triumphant return home.

He arrived via Route 2, down below by the river, without letting anyone know in advance. News of his arrival began to wind its way up through the streets of the town. It started at the corner of the church of Saint-Patrice, then spread from store to garage, from gossipmonger to fishmonger, from fishmonger to fishwife, all the way up to the top of the town, climbing Rue Lafontaine like a salmon leaping its way through the rapids of the river where it was born to spawn and die.

"The Horse is back in town!"

"That can't be! Handsome young Louis, the American's son?"

The whole town was already in the mood for a party, as it geared up to watch the Saint-Jean-Baptiste parade on Rue Lafontaine, but all talk turned to Louis. The crowd was divided into clearly defined groups. First, those who knew Louis and had even been there for his birth on December 25, 1918, in the church of Saint-François-Xavier: his immediate family, people who went to school with him, the Sisters of the Child Jesus (including Sister Mary of the Eucharist, positively squirming with happiness at the wonderful news); then those who had rubbed shoulders with him without really ever getting to know him: neighbours, a great many distant relatives, the town's businessfolk, his very first adversaries at the county strongman contests, a handful of priests who knew of him through legend, and countless perpetual gossips, ever hungry for more. Lastly, the biggest group of all was made up of families who had made Rivière-du-Loup their home after the Great Depression, a majority who knew of Louis Lamontagne only through the fantastic tales they had heard. Strangely enough, it was this group that was most overjoyed by his return. Those who knew him were of course proud to welcome home a son they had no reason to be ashamed of, but they were apprehensive nevertheless. Had Louis changed? They would find out soon enough.

But anyone who imagined Louis Lamontagne just happened to turn up in Rivière-du-Loup right in the middle of the Saint-Jean-Baptiste Day parade was naive indeed. They were obviously unaware of the man's theatrical flair. Even more naive were those who thought it was modesty that had compelled him to parade *on foot*, wearing his U.S. Army uniform for the very last time. The floats, the Lacordaire procession, the luxury motor cars, even poor little St. John the Baptist (an altogether adorable child), all had their thunder stolen by the prodigal son's return. The American Army had robbed him of a little of his naivety, that's the first thing the Sisters of the Child Jesus noticed. When Sister Mary of the Eucharist saw Louis walk past Moisan's florist shop, she ran toward him, unable to hold back any longer. He was surprised to see the woman who had brought him into the world. She was as ugly as ever. With a smile that was enough to frighten anyone, Sister Mary of the Eucharist shouted to the crowd, imploring them to applaud the lost son. And the clamour grew. Perhaps louder still than at the victory parade when Canada's soldiers returned from Europe. Louis had been fighting for the real winner. Make no mistake about it! Maybe Hollywood had been too kind to the U.S. Army, but in the eyes of the locals it was Louis Lamontagne who had strangled the fascist snake with his bare hands. Move over, Stalin! Unlike his fellow citizens, Louis had served in a real army, an army that anyone could see for themselves on the big screen! A beaming Louis paraded before the eyes of the whole town, an ecstatic nun hanging from one arm. Because the poor woman had worked herself up into quite a tizzy. She thought of the boy as almost her own. For the first and last time in her life, Sister Mary of the Eucharist shed a tear. A single tear, furtive and happy, that evaporated before it hit the ground. Louis was moved, too, and broke away from the jubilant crowd to join Old Ma Madeleine, who never missed a parade.

"It tires me out and it's so noisy, but I enjoy it."

She wasn't wrong. Irene Caron also came out to every parade.

"It's fun and it doesn't cost a cent!"

Irene Caron. She hailed from the parish of Saint-Ludger, already cause for suspicion in the eyes of honest folk. The Carons had never been the type to lose count of anything. They were people who could always be asked flat out how much they had in their bank account. Because they knew. Just like they knew with terrifying precision how much was in the savings accounts of a fair number of people living in Rivière-du-Loup. The Carons knew how many houses there were in town, how many plots of land, how many addresses. They knew where every car was parked, they knew how much it had cost, and they could put a price on every piece of farm machinery cur-rently being paraded down Rue Lafontaine on Saint-Jean-Baptiste Day. The Carons were in the know. All in all, they had seventeen children. Thirteen girls and four boys. Their piety was beyond reproach, and their stinginess virtually unimaginable. It was not uncommon to see a Caron wearing clothes stripped off some housewife's scarecrow. Nothing all that unusual when times were hard, but enough to set tongues wagging in 1948.

Another story about the Carons bears telling, not just because it speaks volumes about the family, but because it is backed up by documents that Solange was able to read for herself. Irene Caron, the youngest child in a family that went on and on, had a brother who was one year older. He was a nice boy, sound in mind and body, whose humble origins destined him for the clergy, military service, or hard labour. The boy had taken a while to babble his first words, much longer than the others. Whenever you spoke to him, he would look up at you with those big brown eyes of his, smile, then his attention would fall on a bird or butterfly and he would laugh. Sitting at the frosted windows of the boys' bedroom on winter mornings, Armand would trace the snowflakes' winding trajectory with his finger and smile blissfully. At school, he learned to read in no time at all, but, alas, showed no interest in numbers. His father, an old man who had already turned bald and lost his teeth and hearing, was in no condition to step in. His sisters Irene and Martha tried to get him caught up in math, but it was no use. Soon arithmetic had the boy tormented. But his mother was not for turning. "Knowing how to count is all that counts." He was no idiot. He mastered the basics, even a multiplication table or two, but couldn't manage to apply what he'd learned to everyday life. One day, sitting at the table, Mrs. Caron lost patience. She nodded at the plate of roast rabbit she had just set down on the table and put young Armand to the test.

"Armand, how many feet are on the plate?"

"I don't know."

"Try."

The boy counted slowly.

"Seven!"

"What do you mean, seven?"

"There are seven feet."

"What do you mean there are seven feet when I can count four heads. If there are four heads, then there must be…"

Silence.

"Well? Go on!"

"I… uh… six feet?"

Somewhere other than at the Carons', in a loving, indulgent family, the answer would have been met with a gentle cascade of laughter, perhaps a comforting pat on the dunce's head or a kiss on the forehead. Not at the Carons'. Mrs. Caron stood up, grabbed Armand by the ear, and sent him to stand in the corner for two hours without supper. And that wasn't the end of it. As the boy grew, it became clear that he would never master the subtleties of arithmetic. And so he was thrashed by his brothers, and by his sisters, too. He became a punching bag to the family of math whizzes. In addition to his lack of aptitude for numbers he had scant regard for frugality. One day, his sister Irene caught him throwing away the peel of a large onion that their mother had just finished dicing. The little girl told on him right away and he was severely punished. Nothing too alarming: just a few strokes of the wooden spoon and two heartfelt smacks.

"Onion peel is for blowing your nose with! What a waste, throwing it away like that!"

He wasn't allowed any of that night's stew either. And since he was crying, Mrs. Caron let him wipe his nose on the onion peel he'd been silly enough to throw away.

Realizing his abnormality and limited intellectual capacity, poor Armand began looking for ways to get on his family's good side. He discovered a knack for telling funny stories, cracking jokes, and coming up with skits that featured all the Rivière-du-Loup bigwigs. One night when he was sixteen and Irene was fifteen, he decided to tell a story at the dinner table, a neatly turned anecdote that was sure to draw a laugh, inspired by an incident he had witnessed in the parish of Saint-Patrice. He told his family what he had heard Old Ma Madeleine, still as illiterate as ever, dictating to the postmaster to put in a short letter to her grandson Louis Lamontagne, now in the U.S. Army and stationed somewhere in the old country. He repeated every word the old woman had said, mimicked her old-fashioned way of talking, and even managed to pull off a passable impression of the postmaster's mannerisms. When he finished, he realized his family had barely been paying attention.

Irene looked up from her plate of stew.

"How much did the stamp cost her?"

"Um…"

He didn't know. He couldn't remember because this particular piece of information had seemed insignificant, of little interest to him at the time. His intention had been to re-enact a scene that he alone had witnessed because his father had sent him off to mail a letter. He had thought he might amuse them, transport them beyond the walls of their living room via the magic of storytelling. Nothing had escaped his attention: the worry on the old woman's face, her imploring tone ("tell him his grandmother's waiting for him and looking for a good little wife for him"), the postmaster's vain attempts to hide the beginnings of a smile. But nothing had stirred his brothers and sisters from their torpor, or for that matter, their mother, who hadn't even been listening. Irene brought an end to the ordeal.

"Anyhow, those Lamontagnes have time to waste and money to spend, that's for sure!"

At the age of seventeen, since he'd been born much too late to sign up for the Papal Zouaves and much too soon to go off to hide at a city college, Armand was only too eager, willing, and overjoyed to join the Canadian Army, which promised a chance to get away from the whole lot, two months before Mackenzie King's government introduced conscription. He wrote a series of short letters from Holland, in which he sought to put his mother's mind to rest about his health and the advance of the Canadian troops.

After the war, instead of returning home, and without anyone knowing exactly why, Armand boarded a merchant ship at Halifax, destination unknown, and wasn't heard from again until a letter reached Irene Caron in 1950. Armand went far. He explained in his letter that he had worked out Rivière-du-Loup's "antipode," a calculation that had brought him to southwestern Australia where, he said, he had married and started a family. He was never seen again. He gave no address. Irene read the letter several times over without understanding a word. She was already pregnant with Madeleine at the time, and asked Louis to explain it to her.

"What's an *antipode*? I just don't get it."

"Well, it's like he said. It's as far as you can get away from here."

"Right, but why did he go so far instead of coming back here?"

"Because he wanted to travel!"

"And how do you even get there?"

"If you take him at his word, all you need to do is start digging a tunnel and after a while you'll end up at your brother Armand's."

"At his house? I thought if you did that, you ended up in China."

"That's not what he says."

"Who's going to go to the trouble of all that digging for nothing? What good does travelling do you anyway?"

Armand's letter survived long enough for Madeleine to inherit it once Irene died. She too read the letter from her enigmatic uncle several times over without being able to grasp its meaning. Armand became a captain on a whaling boat and, in 1976, unbeknownst to his family in Canada, died at sea not far from Rivière-du-Loup's antipode. He was survived by his wife, an Australian of legendary loveliness, and four children, none of whom, Solange was quite sure, had become accountants or bankers.

It was true, however, that Old Ma Madeleine was on the lookout for a nice little wife for her grandson Louis Lamontagne during his long absence. Because, in her mind, it was obvious that the reason Louis had left Rivière-du-Loup in 1936, after winning every strongman contest in the region, was to find a Madeleine of his own. And so she'd started to keep an eye out, in case he came home empty-handed. She'd inspected every nubile Madeleine in the county, she'd even extended her reconnaissance missions to the backcountry, where winding lanes were dotted with homes that heaved with kids. None was suitable. Too thin, too bony, too much of a dreamer, too devout, every last one of the weddable Madeleines of 1948 fell short in at least one regard, in the old woman's eyes. But she didn't despair. Proof that the double coincidence of wants really does exist, Irene Caron, who had turned twenty in 1948, was actively looking for a husband after her mother served her an ultimatum:

"Marry this fall or it's off to the convent with you."

Louis' arrival in the middle of the Saint-Jean-Baptiste parade had not been lost on Irene. When someone mentioned to her that the woman who had brought him into the world was none other than her own aunt, Sister Mary of the Eucharist, Irene turned an interested eye to Louis—and to the nun. Needless to say, she first approached Old Ma Madeleine to get the lay of the land. Having limited dealings with the dead and no inkling of what might irritate or antagonize them, Irene went with Sister Mary of the Eucharist to officially submit her candidacy to Old Ma Madeleine. Louis was already someplace else, off with schoolfriends.

Old Ma Madeleine received Sister Mary of the Eucharist politely, while making it clear that her Louis was spoiled for choice. But the old woman was rather fond of the hideous nun and felt something of a communion of the soul with her.

"But your Irene, she's… well, she's not called Madeleine, is she?"

"No, but she could bring a Madeleine into this world."

Old Ma Madeleine pulled a face. Bring a child into this world? Now that was putting the cart before the Horse. And that's exactly what happened at that particular Saint-Jean-Baptiste parade in Rivière-du-Loup in 1948. Handsome Louis was marching up Rue Lafontaine to applause from the crowd when the cart carrying little St. John the Baptist, sitting on a bale of hay, came to a standstill. The two horses yoked to the cart, usually staid and dependable, were suddenly spooked, as though they had just seen the devil in person. The halter, buckled by a man in too much of a rush, came undone and the cart and its holy occupant began rolling back down the hill and picking up speed. Louis let go of Sister Mary of the Eucharist's arm for a second to grab the back of the runaway cart with both hands. He leaned forward and, acting as a counterbalance and smiling all the while, pushed the load up to the top of Rue Lafontaine. A photograph of the exploit still exists to this very day in the archives of the Rivière-du-Loup Historical Society. It shows little St. John the Baptist clinging to his lamb, the hulking figure of a uniformed Louis Lamontagne grinning as he pushes the cart, and dozens of people, laughing, pointing, and generally having a grand old time. In the upper left-hand corner of the photo, Sister Mary of the Eucharist is holding a hand to her mouth in astonishment, clutching her wooden cross in her right hand, no doubt imploring divine intervention at such a difficult time. You don't see photos like that anymore.

It was all in a day's work for Louis Lamontagne. The feat of strength reminded anyone who might not have recognized him, perhaps thrown off by the Clark Gable moustache, exactly who he was and why others hadn't forgotten him. So that now those in the know could explain to those who weren't, and to those who knew only the legend, that Louis Lamontagne, son of the late Madeleine the American and the late Louis-Benjamin Lamontagne, was back in the country, showered in military glory and ready to settle down with the right woman; at least, that's what they thought or hoped. Irene Caron had seen the whole thing. The chatter around her was music to her ears: the handsome young fellow has come home a rich man, they say he plans to buy a house in the parish of Saint-François-Xavier. Apparently he made his money at county fairs in the United States, lifting barrels full of water and pulling Oldsmobiles across fields.

Irene waited for the parade to end before she introduced herself to Louis, and it was outside the church of Saint-François that Irene Caron first looked her future husband in the eye. He sized her up, seeking the flaw that would make her desirable. It was hard going: needless to say—and difficult to say, though it is—Irene Caron was a very attractive young woman. Years of deprivation and an education built on frugality had made her an unusually svelte woman in this land of plenty. Thrifty to be sure, but not to the point of leaving the house dressed in any old thing, on this particular Saint-Jean-Baptiste Day Irene was wearing a pretty floral dress her mother had made for her out of a length of fabric exchanged for a crate of radishes. Blonde, her teeth straight and numerous, she could have posed for a catalogue or stood in for a mannequin in one of the stores on Rue Lafontaine. Louis kept looking for any charming imperfection, a stutter that would make him desire her, a squint that would win him over. Nothing. Irene behaved like a well-mannered young lady and spoke of the number of people she estimated had watched the parade, and of the money it would have cost to replace the cart if Louis hadn't been there. No woman is perfect, the handsome young man said to himself. Her imperfection was surely her ability to hide her imperfections, there you had it. Irene asked how much an American soldier earned. "Enough to want to do something else with his life," Louis said with a smile. Then he thought to himself that he wasn't going to treat this lovely girl differently to all the rest, all the same, and before going back to find Old Ma Madeleine on Rue Fraserville, he arranged to see Irene again at Sunday mass.

"There's nothing I like more than the sight of a woman wearing a hat," he was careful to explain, by way of an invitation.

The following Sunday, Irene ignored her suitor's wishes and showed up at church in a blue silk headscarf. Sitting beside Old Ma Madeleine, Louis chuckled at poor Irene's attempts to resist him. Outside the church, Irene went out of her way to ignore Louis, going so far as to turn her back on him as she pretended to wave to someone in the distance. Louis and Old Ma Madeleine approached the young lady, who turned to them with a harried look. Louis smiled; Old Ma Madeleine pursed her lips.

"You know my grandson, Louis..."

"Yes, I saw him at the parade. Did you know he pushed little St. John the Baptist's cart all the way up Rue Lafontaine? He's such a strong man!"

"I know all that. My Louis would like to invite you round for supper with us tomorrow night. Will you accept, Miss Caron?"

"Tomorrow night? No thank you. I'm afraid that's impossible."

"The supper won't cost you a cent," the old woman insisted, well aware of the Carons' legendary penny-pinching.

Irene hesitated. Louis stared at the ground, embarrassed. He wasn't a shy man, but he didn't want to give the impression that, no sooner back in the country, he was already laying claim to all the best-looking girls, playing the role of conquering hero. That's why he had asked his grandmother to invite Irene over.

"No, thank you. I can't."

Louis went back home a little irritated. Old Ma Madeleine was gloating silently as old women know how. Not only had heaven above removed the spectre of her finding herself with the Caron girl underfoot, now no one could ever accuse her of sabotaging the marriage. Madeleine couldn't have cared less about the reasons that had led the hateful, insidious child to turn down an invitation to have supper with the most eligible bachelor in the entire history of Rivière-du-Loup and probably the whole Lower St. Lawrence region too. Louis was wondering where he had gone wrong, whether he smelled bad or whether Irene had been put off by his moustache. More aggrieved than saddened, it was his pride that had been wounded more than his heart.

The following Sunday brought Louis a fresh helping of humiliation, giving Old Ma Madeleine new reasons to sing the Lord's praises. Irene came to mass with her entire family in tow (minus Armand), accompanied by a stranger from the parish of Saint-Ludger, a scabby, scrawny, foul-mouthed little man who, to the parishioners of Saint-François-Xavier, was nothing more than a walking eyesore. A handful of gossips saw right through the Caron woman's game. Because that's what she was called and what she's still called to this day in the parish of Saint-François-Xavier: the Caron woman. The poor fellow was nothing more than a flimsy alibi, a puppet who was only there to up the ante. As for the Caron woman, the men and women of Saint-François-Xavier parish shot her the same distrustful, frightened look a philanderer reserves for a venereal sore.

To give young Louis pause for thought, that Sunday Irene wore a magnificent hat. It had been loaned to her by a neighbour in an effort to seal her lips about an embarrassing affair. She was even vulgar enough to introduce her companion to Louis and Old Ma Madeleine, as calm as a picture of Good Saint Anne.

"They're a perfect match," Madeleine hissed scornfully as soon as Irene had turned on her heels. "They can go back to their own parish and live happily ever after!"

It had indeed been strange to see Irene, a child of Saint-Ludger, at mass in Saint-François. And if the church steps could repeat what they'd heard in that summer of 1948...

"If she's only out to thumb her nose at our handsome Louis, why doesn't she just stay home?"

"Yeah. Why else would he come back if not to marry a girl from the parish? Come on! And who could possibly imagine a Lamontagne-Caron union?"

No, no, no, and no. They shook their heads. They laughed. A Lamontagne marrying a Caron seemed as improbable in the eyes of the gossips of Rivière-du-Loup as the King of England wedding a bullfrog, the bullfrog being, due to its aggressive, territorial nature, naturally associated with Irene.

Others scarcely bothered to conceal their spite as they pointed out Irene's little game. Others still remarked that there's no mixing maple syrup and vinegar, leaving it up to whoever they were talking to to decide which of the two was the maple syrup.

And what about Louis? Did he lose any of his panache? Did he keep his own counsel? That summer, at a corn roast which virtually the entire parish of Saint-François had been invited to, Louis began, to everyone's great delight, telling stories again. And he had plenty to tell! His tales of Idaho Bill and The Warsaw Giant alone lasted an hour. And he longer needed an interpreter: his audience understood his every word! Poor old Podgórski had his hour of glory as the sun set over Rivière-du-Loup, the moment Louis chose to describe how the cross-eyed Pole had met his tragic end.

Solange's parents and older sister happened to be at the party as Louis, perched on a wooden crate, explained and mimed exactly how he had gotten the better of Adolf the bull calf and saved two poor American girls from a terrible end. His stories were picked up, transformed, and performed again, just like any other story in Rivière-du-Loup. It was Solange's mother who told her the story from the corn roast over at Louis Lamontagne's place in 1948, out the back of Old Ma Madeleine's house. According to Mrs. Bérubé, Irene wasn't even invited. She'd just shown up, as innocent as could be. Also according to Mrs. Bérubé's version of the facts, Irene arrived just as Louis was wrapping up the story of poor Podgórski's (she'd called him Podborovich) tragic demise. The sadness that washed over the party gave way to the natural disdain inspired by Irene Caron. Cool and supreme, Irene apparently went over to sit on a bale of hay that was part of the decorations. Upon spotting the uninvited guest, a mightily piqued Old Ma Madeleine went straight back into the house. The gossip later told her daughter how Louis had saved the day by rousing the musicians he had hired for the occasion. He had danced the night away with every woman there, apart from Irene that is, who didn't budge from the bale of hay, nibbling away on her corn.

"The Caron woman's so miserly, we were surprised she didn't eat the whole thing, cob and all."

On the stroke of midnight, when the party-goers had forgotten her, Irene Caron disappeared, like a devil of legend.

Solange's mother had, of course, added a detail or two of her own to the corn roast story. Fact: Irene turned up uninvited. Proven fact: Louis looked sad when he saw her arrive. Reality: When she saw the uninvited guest, Old Ma Madeleine stormed back into the house, slamming the door behind her. Rectification: Irene actually ate *two* cobs of corn and slipped a third into her purse. Correction: Handsome young Louis only danced with nine of the twelve women present. Detail: The Caron woman left the roast well before midnight to make it home in time for curfew. What is no lie, though, is that the next morning Louis was dreadfully hungover and Irene Caron had become his one and only obsession, his woe, his personal disaster zone. Never before had Louis' charms encountered any resistance. Even the women of conquered lands where he had been to war had welcomed him like a prince. Hadn't he just been sent a passionate letter from a splendid, voluptuous *Fräulein* he'd encountered in Bavaria? *Wann kommen Sie wieder, Louis?* When will you return, Louis? The last time he had met with such stubborn resistance had been in Gouverneur, New York, and it had come from a beast with four legs and a tail.

In August 1948, Louis, determined to stay in shape, had a set of dumbbells and weights delivered, the like of which his neighbours had never seen. To show that Caron woman what he was made of, he bought a forest-green Chrysler Windsor, which he liked to drive up and down Rue Lafontaine, even all the way to the parish of Saint-Ludger. He quickly became the unofficial driver for the Sisters of the Child Jesus, who had always considered him to be their own darling. Truth be told, Louis felt that having the nuns on his side would help him win over the recalcitrant Irene's heart more easily. And so he drove the nuns everywhere. To Cacouna so they could wade in the river, out to the peat bogs to pick blueberries, and even to Sainte-Anne-de-la-Pocatière to visit His Grace.

Solange never found out exactly, at least not from her mother, when and how Louis and Irene started going steady. Rumour had it the two had been spotted out walking at the Point and then by the lake in the first week of September 1948. Then came the morning in November 1948 that Old Ma Madeleine had dreaded—the dead can feel that kind of thing coming—the morning when Irene Caron showed up at the Lamontagnes' house, flanked by her mother.

It was not a good sign.

"Louis, my poor Louis, now you're in a fix!"

Old Ma Madeleine would happily have strangled the two women. They sat in glum silence in the living room. Mrs. Caron, still straight enough for her age, held her cup of tea with a perhaps too-confident hand. Louis stared at the floor. Barely a word was exchanged. They would have to be quick about it.

"Yes, before the snow," snapped Mrs. Caron.

And the clock went tick-tock. It chimed ten. Irene held Old Ma Madeleine's gaze, but the old woman wasn't about to back down. She would have rather died a second time than go through this. The Caron woman and her mother talked numbers for ten or fifteen minutes. What this and that were going to cost. Who should be invited. Where. What to wear. Old Ma Madeleine decided there and then she would be wearing dark grey and looking as dead as could be. And so it happened, in the church of Saint-François. Irene was Louis Lamontagne's first and last conquest, in the strictest sense of the word. Which just goes to show it can sometimes be less dangerous being the hunted than the hunter. You never know what you might catch.

"Try to make sure your children don't turn out like her."

That was how Old Ma Madeleine blessed Louis Lamontagne's marriage to Irene Caron, the undesirable young woman of easy virtue from the parish of Saint-Ludger.

"And if you think that Caron woman didn't know what she was up to, Solange, then you're just as naive as that poor father of yours!"

In Rivière-du-Loup, Louis and Irène's wedding might as well have been a funeral. And so died hope in the heart of every woman. And so was born everlasting resentment toward that Caron woman from Saint-Ludger. Even Louis' rivals, the men who envied everything he had—his strength, his good looks, his bravery, his moustache, his Chrysler Windsor, his house, his money, his stories, and his songs—even they pitied him. And it was with not a hint of irony that they sent him, anonymously of course, gallons upon gallons of gin in which to drown his sorrows and ready himself for the days ahead.

"I'm telling you, Solange, she wasn't from this parish. You need to get that into your head! From Saint-Ludger, she was. We'd never have believed it. Poor, poor Louis!"

Mrs. Bérubé pointed over to the Lamontagne house. Things had moved along very quickly. It was agreed that Old Ma Madeleine would move in with the newlyweds and, despite its vocation as a funeral parlour, all of Louis Lamontagne's children were born in that home. Madeleine was born on June 6, 1950, three months after Solange Bérubé. But the Caron woman wasn't done yet. Marc followed in 1951. Then, in 1953, Irene gave birth to Luc, a frail, sickly child whose first five years of existence were a litany of fevers, coughing fits, diarrhea, and ear infections.

She named the boys after the Evangelists to please Father Rossignol, the poor things...

Now let it be said and understood that Mrs. Bérubé in no way felt she was gossiping, merely doing her daughter a good turn with a series of warnings that would in any case soon be part of the education of every little girl in the parish of Saint-François-Xavier. Louis' story served as a cautionary tale to the young folk of Rivière-du-Loup, right up there with Maliseet legends and priests cautioning against listening to music on the radio.

"You're putting your souls in peril!"

But none of these stories prevented Louis Lamontagne from making a living with the dead. The parish gossips can say what they like, but never was a business in Rivière-du-Loup better managed than the undertaker's. Irene Caron might not have been the life and soul of the party, but she turned out to be a hard worker. She had a face like a wet weekend, which served her well at the wakes that were held almost every evening in one of the house's three large parlours. Two vehicles were permanently parked in the driveway: a hearse and a Chrysler Windsor. In what was Solange's earliest memory, a convertible was soon added to the collection. By the age of four she was already in the habit of spying on the Lamontagne household, their comings and goings, the countless bereaved traipsing up and down their front steps, shouts from the Caron woman, always scandalized by the price of something or other, Old Ma Madeleine walking back and forth across the veranda, the perfect welcoming committee for the families of the deceased.

Louis and Irene had set up a parlour where friends and family could sit waiting for the prayers to begin or chat over coffee that Irene served them with cookies. Old Ma Madeleine never missed a funeral and became the key to Louis' success. She had endless reserves of patience when questioned by grief-stricken relatives about crossing the great divide. Is it painful? No more than giving birth. Do you really see a light at the end of the tunnel? No, not a thing, especially not at night. Is it true you hear a choir of angels? Unless you die in the middle of mass like my first daughter-in-law, no. Would you be prepared to die a second time? Naturally. Go ahead and die in peace! I loved it. I'd recommend it to anyone, but everything in its time. What advice would she give those who had just lost a loved one? Pray. Pray for the salvation of their soul, give thanks to the Blessed Virgin, and take communion regularly.

The competing undertaker on Rue Lafontaine was none too keen on the strongman's arrival on the funeral parlour scene, accusing Louis of exploiting a dead grandmother, an unfair advantage if ever there was one. But the customers came. To lie in repose at Louis Lamontagne's became a not-to-be-missed rite of passage for the deceased in the know. Louis' affordable prices helped many a Rivière-du-Loup family hold a wake outside the home for the first time, an unattainable indulgence for most before 1945, and proof that the war had well and truly changed people's approach to death. A significant chunk of the population, made up of skilled workers, salaried employees, and storekeepers, suddenly realized that the treatment once reserved for the better off was now within their reach too.

But who exactly was Louis burying? Who was he laying his powerful hands on? Those whose bodies ended up at Louis' tended to be followers of fashion. They often owned a radio and record player and were fond of American music. Louis' corpses went to the movies, rarely went to confession, and had—for the most part—experienced heartbreak at some point. In wealthy families, many a slap was handed out by mothers to sons who, looking to provoke their parents, declared over supper that they wanted to lie in repose at Louis Lamontagne's once they died.

"Over my dead body! Do you hear me? Never!"

Notaries, doctors, priests, and other worthies never ended up at Louis', because this well-heeled clientele went to the competition instead, a gentleman by the name of Quévillon whose legendary inflexibility over payment and generally sullen mood discouraged more humble folk from visiting his establishment. As for the nuns, well they buried themselves when the time came, without bothering a soul. Young widows could also be seen making funeral arrangements with Louis. One day they'd end up in Louis' arms one way or another, they told their closest confidants. Perhaps not in this world, no, but who on earth gets everything they desire? Louis' clients also included men with a thirst for adventure, meaning that his parlour was the scene on more than one occasion of embarrassing revelations, a place where wives would come face to face with improbable lovers who insisted on being allowed to pay their last respects to their beloved. How many scenes of rage and anger had he had to defuse whenever there arrived, behind a black veil, a woman whose existence had long been suspected but whose boldness had been underestimated? Louis would beg them to show respect for the dead, calming the hotter heads, and often—once a strongman, always a strongman—throwing out a young cock of the walk whom death had left cuckold. It's also said—and no one, neither Louis, nor his wife, would have denied it—that men who were fond of a drink preferred to go out on one last bier over at Louis'. This was another not inconsiderable clientele he had made his own.

Much to his wife's dismay, Louis' prices were slightly cheaper than his competitors' and he would offer to pick up bodies free of charge, no matter the hour, day or night. You only had to call or knock on his door. Louis was flexible as far as money was concerned too, and would certainly have gone bankrupt in his first year had it not been for Irene Caron's gift for arithmetic and her tendency to suggest oak over pine, silk instead of wool, and insist on the need to give distant relatives time to come pay their respects to the dead. The longer the body lay in the parlour, the higher the fees. What did it matter if Irene had to put up with a few irksome odours around the house for a while! When you make a living off death, some things don't affect you quite the same way.

Old Ma Madeleine almost always sat with visitors at the second parlour for the wake, the body dressed and coiffed according to the family's means and the talents of Irene Caron, her daughter-in-law. She liked to leave a white carnation in men's buttonholes. For the children called back by God, Irene always managed to get her hands on a few white flowers, whatever the season. It was Old Madeleine who would lead off the rounds of prayers and novenas. Sometimes, if you rubbed her the right way, she might even chant a few forgotten prayers for the dead herself and even, on days when she was feeling in particularly fine fettle, openly weep for people she knew only by name. To be sure, Louis and Irene were terribly indebted to Old Ma Madeleine. Which meant that Louis didn't have to badger his wife for very long to ensure his only daughter would be christened Madeleine.

And so Solange found herself sitting next to Madeleine in Grade 1A, right in front of Sister Saint Arsenius, who had been keeping her distance since the incident at the start of term. Other little girls made up the rest of the class in their immaculate blouses, sixty braids hanging either side of thirty heads that were filled with prayers, hymns, and questions to which there were no answers. Sister Saint Arsenius regularly lost control of the class and it was for this very reason that she had been put in charge of the youngest girls, who were presumed easier to manage. If Mother Mary of the Great Power, Mother Superior and principal of Saint-François-Xavier School, was to be believed, the older girls would have eaten Sister Saint Arsenius alive.

"We could give her Grade 3 if push really came to shove," she would sigh in irritation.

Despite everything, Sister Saint Arsenius never quite managed to impose the reign of calm the principal dreamed of for her class. Mother Mary of the Great Power would often burst in unannounced, more often than not coming across an ill-disciplined rabble, little girls chatting away and sometimes even wandering around the room. She ordered Sister Saint Arsenius to use more effective methods. By way of reinforcement, the Mother Superior would ask Sister Mary of the Eucharist to patrol the convent's hallways, listening out for uproar and intervening as necessary. The nun took to her task diligently. She would slip in when least expected like a cornet-wearing ghost and mastered the art of appearing from nowhere as if by magic. She owed her authority to her sinister face, with eyes that, once directed at an unruly girl, had the power to scar her for life.

When Solange and Madeleine reached Grade 4, they were delivered into the hands of Sister Saint Alphonse. Of a more robust psychological disposition than Sister Saint Arsenius, Sister Saint Alphonse ruled with an iron fist. No more whispering between the rows, no more slips of paper passed along on the sly, no more heads propped up nonchalantly on hands.

"You are not made of rags, young ladies! And you, Madeleine Lamontagne, are you in need of one of your father's caskets? Sit up straight, for Heaven's sake! Lift up your head and think of the secrets of Fatima!"

Sister Saint Alphonse always went for the jugular. When a girl did something she didn't approve of, she didn't think twice about shooting a poisoned arrow in her direction. How many times, listening to Solange cough her way through the first colds of the season, had she passed a snide remark about the Bérubé family's poor health?

It was in that Grade 4 class, specifically during the memorable events of fall 1960, that Solange Bérubé and Madeleine Lamontagne became firm friends. The bond between the two girls might have frittered away like almost every friendship, sworn for eternity, that develops in a convent class, but fate would ensure otherwise. Truth be told, if ever an explanation were required to describe the ties that bound the girls since November 1960, it could be summed up in two parts: the end of the world and the Chinese. Two things that made Solange and Madeleine friends for life, inseparable atoms, a binary number that nothing would ever split.

Despite Sister Saint Alphonse's withering nastiness, the class began to stir between Thanksgiving and the All Saints' Day holiday. The nun's classroom was slowly transformed into something more approaching a clandestine tea house. The girls' attention began to flag after afternoon recess, and she even found—horrors!—a picture of His Holiness Pope Pius XII lying on the floor, a Hitler mustache drawn on by one of the shameless little girls. There had been no witnesses to the strange moment when Madeleine Lamontagne, the picture's owner, drew a short black line under the pontiff's nose, then smiled. Without knowing why. She had had the impression at that very instant that her hand had been guided by an angel, an outside force telling her, "Give the old guy a mustache!" Then, as though frightened by what she had done, she had flung the picture under a shelf in a corner of the classroom to make it disappear. Holding it up in her right hand for everyone to see, Sister Saint Alphonse was spitting more than speaking.

"And to think that we have only just bidden farewell to our Holy Father the Pope and someone has been bold enough to besmirch his memory in this way! Who was it? I demand that the guilty party reveal herself immediately!"

Silence reigned in the classroom. The nun walked up and down the rows of desks, thrusting the picture of the mustachioed pope under each girl's nose. They could feel her ready to explode into a thousand black and white pieces. Impassive, she opened her desk drawer and pulled out her cane. Solange swallowed. Simone Dumont, a girl who had learned too late to keep her mouth shut, got it into her head that it would be a good idea to reason with the nun. As her classmates looked on aghast, she raised her hand. The nun took a deep breath.

"Yes, Miss Dumont!"

"Sister, maybe no one touched the picture. Perhaps you're getting all worked up over nothing!"

"Whatever do you mean, you little dolt?"

"Perhaps the pope already had a mustache like that. I…"

"You mean *Our Ho-ly Fa-ther the Pope!*" the nun thundered, hammering home each syllable with a whack of her cane on the desk.

"I'm sorry, Sister. I mean perhaps Our Holy Father Pope Pius XII used to have a mustache like that and the picture dates from back then? Maybe that's why…"

Throughout the class, the nun could be heard sweating with rage. Had it not been for Simone Dumont's naivety and the clergy's thin skin concerning Pope Pius XII and his facial hair, Solange and Madeleine would probably never have known the apocalypse, or the Chinese, and might never have become the best friends in the world. The nun ordered Simone Dumont to her feet, to stand in front of the class, hold out her hand, and take twenty well-administered lashes of the cane.

"Stop snivelling! This is what happens when you spout such nonsense, Simone Dumont! Did Our Lord cry on the cross? No! You'll just have to put up with the pain, you little tramp!"

The little girl couldn't contain her sobbing, which earned her a slap. That didn't help. She went on crying. Tired of the spectacle, Sister Saint Alphonse seized the garbage can, emptied its contents over the bawling girl, and pulled it over her head. The only sound in the room was a distant, hollow sobbing, its lower notes slightly amplified by the wooden garbage can.

"That will teach you to think before you speak."

Simone remained like that for a half hour before being sent back to her desk. But Sister Saint Alphonse wasn't done yet. She was determined to get her hands on the culprit. Overweight, blind as a bat, and unflatteringly nicknamed Sister Fatty, the nun was not one for backing down. She was seen that very afternoon in the infirmary, having a few strong words with Sister Mary of the Eucharist, who had dared to smirk at the defiled picture of Pius XII. The Hitler mustache, she had said, perhaps without thinking, suited him rather well. Sister Saint Alphonse bridled.

"So you think it's funny, do you, what's going on in my class?"

"No, no, of course not. And you can count on me to help. I'll be there at eight thirty tomorrow morning. Stay calm: we'll soon catch your budding artist!"

"I wouldn't expect anything less from you, Sister Mary of the Eucharist!"

The next morning, Sister Fatty, wearing an especially severe face, gave her students a dictation exercise entitled "The Ascension of the Virgin Mary." There was nothing like a little dictation to get everyone in the mood for what was to follow.

Solange was looking over her copy when suddenly Sister Mary of the Eucharist appeared out of thin air. A chill ran through the panicked girls. One of them cried out. Simone Dumont soiled her uniform.

"Girls, we've just been told that our Holy Father Pope John XXIII will be addressing the world's faithful. Let us pray for good news. I will be here to keep you informed."

Sister Mary of the Eucharist let her news sink in and came back at the end of the afternoon. Once again, no one knew where she had appeared from. On that afternoon in October 1960, she wore a gloomy expression, gave a little cough or two to clear her throat, then delivered the following news in a weak, flat voice:

"Girls. I have dreadful news for you. The Holy See informs us that the end of the world is nigh! We already know the date: the morning of Thursday, November 10. Flaming blocks of ice will rain down to punish humanity. Only the pure of heart and the God-fearing will be saved. Our Holy Father the Pope has asked us to pray continuously so that as many souls as possible might be spared. It is time, girls, to see that all is in order in your hearts! Get out your rosary beads! Open your missals! Repent!"

She went through the same spiel in the other convent classrooms, so that by three o'clock that afternoon, every last schoolgirl was gripped in the clutches of terror and fear of the Last Judgment. For the younger ones, the weeks leading up to the fateful day were marked by feverish prayer, novenas in rapid succession, and trembling confessions. Solange and Madeleine were swept up in the panic along with the others. Strangely enough, Solange was reassured by the thought that the end of the world was near. Until then, she'd always had difficulty distinguishing between God and the Lamontagne family. But now there was a more powerful being than even the undertaker who lived next door. And she realized that Madeleine was mortal like all the rest of the girls, kneeling beside her desk and begging for clemency from the Lord, just like her. So it was in part thanks to this whole morbid production that Solange plucked up the courage to approach Madeleine Lamontagne, after four years of holding back, managing not to faint, pee her pants, or vomit over a nun's wimple in the process. Defying every single ban imposed by her mother, Solange ran to catch up with Madeleine Lamontagne on the way home. Madeleine didn't say much. She was terrorized by the thought of the end of the world, she confided in Solange, and devoting all her free time to prayer and acts of contrition.

"I put a picture of Good Saint Anne in the shed. I'll go hide there when the end of the world comes. Surely God will make sure nothing happens to Good Saint Anne!"

Solange was beaten that night on her mother's orders. Someone had ratted on her. Probably her brother, who'd been walking behind her.

"Who did you walk home from school with today, Solange?"

"No one."

"Look me in the eyes, you little..."

"I was by myself!"

Solange must have had LIAR tattooed across her forehead. Twenty lashes of the belt, which seemed like a bargain if you asked her. The next day, it was Madeleine who caught up with Solange.

"You're not allowed to talk to me. My dad beat me because I spoke to you yesterday."

"Come meet me in the shed behind our place. Knock five times."

Solange went home, wrestled with her conscience for all of twelve seconds, then as though propelled by an outside force, opened the window of the bedroom she shared with one of her sisters, caught hold of the drainpipe with her left hand, and slid down to the lawn. As nimble as a cat, she slipped through the willow hedge that separated the Bérubé property from the Lamontagnes'. Instantly, she felt as though she'd crossed a border with no possibility of return. A breathless Solange gently knocked five times on Madeleine's shed door. Three centuries went by, then the door opened a crack.

"That was quick!"

"I came down the drainpipe. I could have killed myself."

"We're all gonna die anyway. Come on in."

The door closed behind Solange, who found herself in the darkness of a little shed Louis Lamontagne had first built to house his tools and lawn-mower, but that was now Madeleine's hideaway. As her eyes grew used to the half-light, Solange sniffed the air. There was definitely a cat and another animal, probably a rabbit, in the shed. Her suspicions were confirmed soon enough. Madeleine lit a candle, its light illuminating a wooden hutch where an enormous rabbit was nibbling at some freshly picked clover. In her lap, the little grey cat was all grown up; it was the same cat Madeleine had been holding on the balcony the day when one look from her teal-coloured eyes had been enough to floor poor Solange. Holy pictures were pinned over the hutch: Saint Anne, the Miraculous Virgin of the Smile (who cured little ten-year-old Thérèse), Saint Veronica holding her veil, and Saint Joan of Arc had all been carefully pinned in a row, looking down tenderly over the big orange rabbit who went on munching his clover. Pinned to the frame of the hutch was a piece of wax paper with the animal's name—Lazarus— written on it.

"His name's Lazarus," Madeleine whispered as she grabbed him by the ears.

Solange winced in pain.

"You have to pick them up by the ears or else you hurt them. I'll set him down on your lap."

Solange had never touched a living rabbit before. She stroked Lazarus, who right then seemed to her to be the gentlest, most charming thing to ever have walked this earth.

"We'll pray that when the end of the world comes the blocks of ice won't fall on Lazarus or the convent," Madeleine declared.

"Yeah. Well, all the girls will ask God to spare the convent, the nuns too. It should work. But what about Lazarus?"

"That's why I put the pictures above his hutch: so that God doesn't destroy the shed."

"What about your house?"

"Well, my great-grandma is dead already, and I told the others to pray."

"So did I."

Out of Madeleine's pockets slipped two sets of cheap pink rosary beads, the kind you get for your first communion.

"My brother Marc took them from the little girl who was laid out for viewing at our place last summer. He nabbed them when Dad asked him to close the casket. Mom said the little girl was a saint. Her rosary beads are bound to work better than mine. Here, you can have them."

Horrified yet intrigued, Solange gently picked up the rosary beads that had been stolen from the dead girl. She lifted them up to eye height. The first drops of a chilly late-afternoon shower were beginning to strike the shed's sheet-metal roof. The small, pink rosary beads glistened in the half-light. Solange stroked Lazarus the way you would finger the petals of the first spring lily, the first peony. The orange rabbit slowly closed and opened its eyes contentedly. Like Clare sisters, Solange and Madeleine chanted their incantations, one answering the other, a heavenly duo beneath an autumn shower. Lazarus fell asleep on Solange's lap.

"Do you want to be my friend?" Solange murmured after an Our Father.

"Yes, but I'll be your one and only friend," Madeleine replied after a Hail Mary.

For Solange, that went without saying.

They had made a few rounds of the rosary beads when they heard a shout outside in the yard.

"Madeleine!"

It was the Caron woman calling for her daughter. Lazarus woke up, wriggled, bounded down off Solange's lap, and started running every which way. Madeleine barely had time to warn her new friend.

"You have to go, Solange! Come back tomorrow. But don't mention Lazarus to anyone. Dad gave him to me. Mom doesn't even know I keep him in the shed!"

Solange waited until the Caron woman was looking for her daughter in front of the house to slip out of the shed and make her way back to the other side of the willow border. She ran through the rain, snuck into the house through the cellar door, and walked up into the kitchen with an armful of potatoes that she began to peel in front of her mother.

"Decided to make yourself useful, Solange?"

Mrs. Bérubé didn't know if she should be surprised or pleased to see her tomboy of a girl doing housework for a change.

"The end of the world has finally knocked some sense into them," she thought with a smile, silently thanking the Sisters of the Child Jesus.

Outside, the Caron woman kept on hollering after her daughter. Still bathing in the afterglow of the time she'd spent with Madeleine and Lazarus, Solange thought that the Lord could happily send all the ice in Greenland crashing down onto her head. Now she had truly lived.

From that day forward, the heavy, tiresome days at the convent went by like beads on a rosary. Every morning, Sister Mary of the Eucharist would spring up from nowhere to remind a class of terrorized girls, her index finger in the air, that the end was near, before disappearing again just as quickly as she had appeared. As a direct consequence of these terrifying apparitions, the atmosphere was now appreciably calmer in the convent's classrooms and hallways. Skeptics, for fear of being punished, dared not contradict the nuns' promises of apocalypse, which meant that the week leading up to Thursday, November 10, 1960, was as long as the road to Calvary for all involved. Almost every evening, Solange managed to escape her mother's watchful eye to meet up with Madeleine and Lazarus in the shed, where they continued to pray to Good Saint Anne. At the Bérubés' and the Lamontagnes', the girls were noticeably better behaved, displaying newfound attention to propriety and decorum. Solange was surprised to find herself enjoying humanity's last days because they had brought her closer to this being of light that Madeleine Lamontagne represented in her eyes.

On Thursday, November 10, Solange and Madeleine went separately to the convent. One by one, the Grade 4 girls arrived in the schoolyard, looking crestfallen. They stood and said their morning prayers, which echoed through the whole school louder than usual on that particular day.

"Sit down, girls."

And the morning went by. A sky that had been bothered by a smattering of white clouds at nine o'clock gradually clouded over, inevitably so in the girls' eyes, as the morning advanced. At 10:40, a mass of dark grey clouds covered the sky of the Lower St. Lawrence, daubing everyone and everything with a pale, whitish hue, the light of November in northern climes. Above the huge river, the mountains of Charlevoix disappeared behind a thick apocalyptic fog. In the classroom, its windows overlooking the schoolyard, there reigned a greasy, silent sadness that no one wanted to interrupt, not with a word, not with a movement, not with a single noise. They waited for eleven o'clock to strike like Zacchaeus waited for Jesus: shaking in their boots.

Twelve minutes before the appointed hour, Solange begged the Lord to spare her a stinky end to the world by ensuring that Simone Dumont did not soil herself again. It was only natural to fear the worst from poor Simone: she hadn't said a word for two days, nothing but endless prayers driven by fear of the Last Judgment, and had begged her mother in vain to keep her home that morning so that she might live out humanity's final moments by her side.

The nun, who had a knack for stagecraft, had prepared for the occasion by giving her students, fifteen minutes ahead of time, a task to complete in silence. They were to copy the following passage into their notebooks as often as time permitted:

"Lord, I am but ashes and dust. Suppress the stirrings of pride that rise in my soul and teach me to be scornful of myself, you who heed not the arrogant and give grace to the humble."

A nervous giggle arose from the third row. Solange had torn off the corner of her notebook and decided, before being sent to hell, to pass it on to Madeleine Lamontagne, who was copying into her own notebook the act of humility that Sister Fatty had written on the blackboard. The nun, her face set in a particularly ghastly expression for the occasion, caught sight of the tiny white butterfly flitting from hand to hand, making its way up and down from Solange's desk over to Madeleine's.

"Madeleine Lamontagne!"

"Yes?"

Madeleine looked up, her concentration interrupted.

"Yes what?"

"Yes, Sister."

"You Lamontagnes are well used to death. The end of the world can't have you too worried!"

Madeleine didn't understand what the nun meant. Was she talking about her great-grandmother, her dad's customers, or both? A ruler appeared in the nun's hand.

"Are you going to answer me? You don't have much time left... I can see right through you. You think you can do whatever you please because your father served in the U.S. Army, isn't that right?"

"No, Sister. Not at all, Sister."

Madeleine's insides were starting to cramp.

"You think that looking after the dead gives you the right to defile pictures of the saints!" the nun roared, brandishing the Hitlerized photo of Pius XII.

"I... it wasn't me, Sister," Madeleine sobbed.

"You think you're stronger than everyone else because your father can pull the Saint-Jean-Baptiste cart along behind him? Is that it? Well, I've got news for you, you nitwit. The only thing that young beefcake of a father of yours is lifting nowadays is his glass of gin! Right up to Heaven! And his sins are clear for all to see in the way you behave, you little demon!"

Sister Saint Alphonse held up the holy picture of the pope, staring down at Madeleine like a chickadee considering the worm it's about to swallow.

"Bring me that piece of paper!" she bellowed.

Madeleine walked forward while her classmates looked on in concern. Simone Dumont was biting her lip, clutching her stomach with both hands. Madeleine held out the scrap of paper and the nun snatched it with her chubby fingers. No one was laughing now. Beads of sweat were gathering on Simone Dumont's forehead. The paper was unfolded, slowly, and read out loud.

"For always. You, me, and Lazarus. S."

A veil of incomprehension slipped over the nun's face. Solange's heart was pounding.

"What's that supposed to mean? And who is S?" the nun hissed.

A Sylvie and a Suzanne immediately proclaimed their innocence as one. Simone Dumont held her head with one hand, her stomach with the other, whimpering like a Queen of England with her head on the block. Solange couldn't breathe.

"Sister... I..."

"Be quiet, Solange Bérubé. I'm waiting for the guilty party to step forward. For Louis Lamontagne's daughter to own up!"

Sister Saint Alphonse shook Madeleine like a plum tree. At that very moment, soft, lazy snowflakes, the first of the season, began to fall outside. A raucous cry rose up from the schoolyard, electrifying an already charged atmosphere.

"It's the end of the world! Repent!"

Without a thought to their teachers' authority, the girls in every classroom overlooking the schoolyard raced to the windows. Down below, her arms stretched out in the form of a cross, Sister Mary of the Eucharist was welcoming the first snow with gales of laughter.

"Repent and say your prayers! Welcome the snowflakes that announce the end! Minutes from now, they'll grow bigger, as big as houses, ready to punish all of humanity!"

In the upper grades, where the girls had seen through the nuns' little charade a few days previously, laughter rang out and made its way down to the lower classes. The Grade 4 girls pressed their noses against the glass, like goldfish against the side of an aquarium. Sister Mary of the Eucharist laughed one last time.

"Don't move! I'm coming up!" she cried.

She made her way to the covered part of the playground, leaving a trail of footprints in the snow behind her.

The girls' faces turned as one to the front of the class, a horrible scene unfolding before them: Sister Saint Alphonse was beating Madeleine's hands with the ruler, frantically, forcefully, feverishly. The little girl was in a trancelike state and didn't feel a thing, taking the blows like Saint Blandina, the blows from the Roman legionaries' swords.

"That'll teach you!"

And on the count of twenty-five, Sister Mary of the Eucharist appeared, shaking snowflakes from her shoulders. The torturer stopped in her tracks, ruler in mid-air, hypnotized by the look on her colleague's face. Sister Mary of the Eucharist nodded for Madeleine to go back to her seat. The little girl hadn't shed a single tear the whole time, her mind focused on the image of Saint Blandina in the arenas of Lyon. The two nuns eyed each other. Sister Saint Alphonse lowered her gaze, then her forehead, then her chin.

"As you can see," Sister Mary of the Eucharist told the girls, "the Good Lord has once again spared humanity. It is a quarter past eleven and the world is still standing!"

A girl raised her hand at the back of the class.

"Sister, why isn't it the end of the world?"

Sister Mary of the Eucharist smiled.

"Thanks to your prayers, girls. You saved yourselves. Now everyone follow me! Let's go outside and play in the snow! I'll see you in the schoolyard!"

The girls went outside, shrieking with joy. Sister Mary of the Eucharist had rules she lived by and understood as well as any French Canadian nun the mechanics of punishment and humiliation. She also knew that it was Madeleine who had drawn on the mustache. She herself had given the girl the picture of the Holy Father to add to her collection. She had recognized the picture's slightly dog-eared edge. As to what might have driven or inspired Madeleine to give the pope a Hitler mustache, she hadn't the faintest idea. What she did know was that Madeleine wouldn't do it again. Once all the girls were outside, she found herself alone with Sister Fatty, who was still sweating from her efforts. She walked up to her slowly, wiped the smile off her face and pursed her lips, looking uglier than ever. Sister Saint Alphonse was trembling, stammering something inaudible. Sister Mary of the Eucharist got close enough to blow her cold, fetid breath into the other nun's nostrils.

"If you ever lift a hand to that child again, you'll be the one praying for the end of the world, Sister Saint Alphonse."

Sporting her apocalyptic smile once again, she went back out to the girls frolicking in the snow. In the classroom, a fruity, fecal aroma wafted up, whirled around, and hung in the air, without Simone being in any way to blame. Having lost the battle if not the war, Sister Fatty went back to her room to change.

The snow continued to fall outside, now whipped up by a westerly wind. Sister Mary of the Eucharist walked to the church, where she met Old Ma Madeleine, come to pray for the souls in purgatory.

"Come outside with me," she said to the old woman. "Come see this land of ours all in white!"

And both women stood outside the church of Saint-François-Xavier, straight and black in the storm, their hands in muffs, looking north in silence.

The snowflakes gathered on their veils and shoulders, inexplicable smiles spread across their faces. Old Ma Madeleine spoke of snowfalls of years past.

For a long time, Sister Mary of the Eucharist had always watched the first snowfall alongside her heterozygous twin, Sister Saint Joan of Arc who, shortly after taking her vows, had volunteered as a missionary abroad.

"They were already sisters before they became sisters," Papa Louis liked to joke, a quip that only the under tens were able to fully appreciate.

A photo of Sister Saint Joan of Arc before she left for Japan in 1934, off to live in the Nagasaki provincial house founded by the Sisters of the Child Jesus. Right beside the armchair where Papa Louis would mix sugar into his gin as he told his stories, an art deco walnut dresser covered in framed photographs. A gloomy-looking nun in front of a Japanese home, a peach tree in bloom; the last picture of Sister Mary of the Eucharist's twin sister, taken June 16, 1945, by a nun who was about to return to Canada. Then came the terrible pain for Sister Mary of the Eucharist, the pain that washed over her on the night of August 10, 1945, in the provincial house of Rivière-du-Loup, the night of that atomic day. A sudden weakness come from the west, she must have thought, heartfelt sadness in her rosary. There had been no need to tell her. The lines of communication between saintly sisters have never had need for telegraphs or humanity's other crutches. Of the pain felt by Sister Mary of the Eucharist, no portraits were painted, no pictures taken. But Irene, her niece, remembered, and every August 9 until the day she died, instead of saying grace she would tell those gathered around the table:

"She was standing there, just in front of the convent, leaning against a tree. Under the beginnings of a moon, her face was radiant, shining like a thousand suns. She didn't cry, she didn't laugh. She just said: 'My little sister in Japan.'"

No one had even told her yet. And there was no way of knowing; they didn't find out right away. It wasn't until weeks after the atomic bomb went off that Sister Saint Joan of Arc's death was confirmed. But Sister Mary of the Eucharist already knew. She didn't feel it; she *knew* it.

And Papa Louis had confirmed it more than once himself: Sister Mary of the Eucharist shed no tears when they told her that her twin sister had died in Nagasaki.

"Sure she knew already! Why would she suddenly have burst into tears? Just for show?" he would ask, raising his finger to shoulder height and pointing it heavenward, as though to indicate an unfathomable mystery.

After that, there had been no news of Nagasaki for a long time, not until a young priest returned one day from a Canadian Christian mission in Japan with news for Sister Mary of the Eucharist. He had been to Nagasaki and spoken to people who knew the late nun, children she had helped in the Japanese countryside just before taking refuge in Nagasaki, which people were certain would never be bombed. In fact, all the local Christians had been foolish enough to flock to the city, where misfortune awaited them.

"The Americans could very well pay dearly for this affront to the Lord," the young priest had reasoned, staring at the floor.

Strangely enough, Sister Mary of the Eucharist's bitterness wasn't directed at the Americans, if the severe disapproval that only nuns are capable of can even be called bitterness. No, it was the whole of Japan that she resented. In her mind, there was no denying that those godless people were guilty of a terrible crime that the Americans—Christian neighbours of impeccable hygiene, their fairness widely reputed—had been well within their rights to punish with the fires of divine wrath. Sister Mary of the Eucharist secretly cultivated a contempt for all matters relating to Japan, the Japanese, and any words or objects that might serve as a reminder of the Land of the Rising Sun, a feeling that was at odds with her commitment to the Lord, but that she nurtured with the patience and diligence with which some people will torture a bonsai. And so, when the Sisters of the Child Jesus convent decided to buy a television in 1966 to listen to and watch—yes, watch!—John XXIII's papal address to Canada's missionaries (the squeals that could be heard at the convent that night!), the convent's treasurer chose an RCA model made in the United States. Sister Mary of the Eucharist was one of the convent's first nuns to become addicted to the small screen. She would sometimes be spotted alone, kneeling before the screen, stroking its convex glass with her white hand to feel the magnetic field, a blissful smile on her face. When in 1975 the television was replaced by a Japanese model, the nun abruptly lost all interest in television programs and even begged off watching Paul VI's funeral. She was unwell, she said. Needless to say, she would rather have traipsed four miles through the March snow than taken a ride in a Toyota, would rather have been eaten alive by a pack of sharp-toothed wolves on a winter's night in Canada than spoken to one of the nuns who regularly came over from Japan to pay their Canadian colleagues a visit. On those days Sister Mary of the Eucharist would confine herself to the laundry room; her hatred of Japan and every sign of it had become for her an act of mortification that she knew would leave her cleansed. She never mentioned it to anyone, not even to Father Lecavalier during her confession in July 1968.

Every nun carries a little atomic crater around inside. Her own private disaster area.

And on that October day when the young missionary had come to talk about her twin sister's final hours of suffering in Nagasaki, the sister in mourning had already taken on the waxy complexion of the irradiated, already distilled all the grief the death had caused her. Her face was green as grass; her eyes were ringed with lilac, as if they too had perished in the American attacks on Hiroshima and Nagasaki. Sister Mary of the Eucharist had smiled at the missionary as though urging him to go on, to tell her what he knew of the people who had known her twin sister. How had she spent her final moments? Had she suffered? So many questions in just one smile! And how a priest's words, so lovely, so poetic, so tender and soothing, can sometimes fall like drops of water on a burning stone! The young priest was sorry to have made such a long trip to deliver such a gloomy gospel. By way of reply, he gave her the photo that could now be found on Papa Louis' art deco dresser, a copy that Irene Lamontagne (née Caron) had had printed for her eight brothers, now scattered throughout the county of Rivière-du-Loup. For all eternity, Madeleine and her brothers would remember the woman as "our aunt Sister Mary of the Eucharist's twin sister... what was her name again? Marc, do you remember her first name? Yeah, I mean Sister Mary of the Eucharist's name. No? And her twin sister? You know, the one who died in Hiroshi— no, no, Nagasaki, that's the one. Her, the one in the photo? Caron? Yes, I know she was a Caron, but what about her first name? You don't remember? Marie? Who kept the original photo anyway? You don't remember either. Ah." Sister Saint Joan of Arc's name was quickly replaced in the family's memory, and in the memory of all those who lived in Rivière-du-Loup, by Saint Mary of Nagasaki, a much more evocative name for the poor woman from Quebec who died in hostile territory serving her faith.

But the fact remains that the young priest, so proud to have returned from Japan to describe exactly how the nine Sisters of the Child Jesus met their deaths—not there and then, but later of radiation poisoning—once he was standing before Sister Mary of the Eucharist, who smiled at him the way the saints smile in holy pictures, kept this detail to himself. She knew. Few answers are as evocative as the one she gave the young priest on that fall morning:

"And there appeared a great wonder in Heaven; a woman clothed with the sun."

That's how Sister Mary of the Eucharist had imagined her twin sister's ordeal: like the image from Revelations. The young priest wasn't brave enough to ask what she meant.

Sister Mary of the Eucharist did not cry, but she did lose all her hair. By Christmas 1945, her head was entirely bald and the rest of her body was completely bare, a fact that naturally no one could confirm. It meant that, even once the order of the Sisters of the Child Jesus allowed its members to wear lay clothing, the nun clung to her habit. Lacking eyebrows and eyelashes, with no down to protect her from the cold, she had a face like a moonscape, a face that many former students at the Saint-François-Xavier School in Rivière-du-Loup still see on nights when they awake with a start from disturbing dreams.

It was perhaps out of pity that Old Ma Madeleine enjoyed keeping her company as they watched the first autumn snow settle on the church grounds.

"Do you think we'll be freed this winter?"

"I don't think so, Madeleine. I think it'll come with the cold. Perhaps not this year."

"How long have we been wandering this land, Sister?"

"I stopped counting a long time ago."

"This snow is so soft, this glacial wind such a comfort. When will we be free at last? Tell me! When will we join that sister of yours who died in Nagasaki?"

"First young Madeleine will have to leave, then come back, then leave for good. We have another few years left after that. We'll know when the archangel visits."

"When who visits?"

"The good-looking young man. The archangel. Everything in its time. It will be a cold night. I promise you one last winter journey, Madeleine."

The afternoon felt like no other in Solange and Madeleine's class. Now wearing a clean habit, Sister Saint Alphonse had used cunning and psychology to make the most of the hullabaloo created by the aborted threat to end the world and the first snowfall to proceed with the weekly sale of Chinese babies. She had pinned a huge poster on the wall. It was covered in shadowy grey outlines: faces to be coloured in. Chinese babies sold by the Association of the Holy Childhood for missions abroad.

"Girls, as you know, the Association of the Holy Childhood lets you save, through your generosity, the soul of a Chinese baby that would otherwise go straight to Hell. By buying a Chinese baby, you are allowing the foreign missions to baptize it and give it a soul. It will, unfortunately, remain of the Chinese race, but at least it will have a Christian soul and a Christian name, which will mean it no longer has to burn in the fires of Hell like *certain other people.*"

An accusing glance at Solange, then Madeleine.

"When you buy a Chinese baby," she went on, "you will get a blue booklet if it's a boy and a pink booklet if it's a girl. You'll also be given permission to colour in one of the little faces on the poster. Remember that Good Saint Anne has just spared us the end of the world. Do not let her down! Last year at the end of Grade 4, it was Lucie Cotnam who bought the most. Two hundred and fifty of them! Just imagine! You'll have your work cut out to beat her record: this year the price has gone up. Now we are to sell them at twenty-five cents, up from ten. So, girls, I'm waiting. Anyone who wants to buy a Chinese baby should raise her hand immediately!"

Buying Chinese babies was, everyone knew, a simple but expensive way of earning the nuns' esteem, the number of smacks of the ruler being inversely proportional to the number of Chinese babies acquired over the school year. This easing-off of corporal punishment was accompanied by increased goodwill and special favours like religious books and an avalanche of holy pictures of the Virgin Mary and Saint Francis Xavier, the patron saint of foreign missions. What's more, such transactions often guaranteed special privileges, like joining the nuns in their own private dining room. A sprinkling of hands went up, one or two girls from better-off families who happened to be carrying loose change. Perhaps to put the morning's events behind her, Madeleine bought herself a little Chinese girl and bought a little Chinese boy as a present for Solange, who turned red with delight. They didn't say a word to each other as they stood in front of the poster, colouring in their new acquisitions.

The rest of the afternoon was devoted to what Sister Saint Alphonse called "the battle," a duel between two girls standing face to face. Their subject? The times tables. The stakes? A Chinese baby boy. The nun got them started.

"Six times eight!"

The fastest answer earned a point. The girls had to win three of five to advance to the next round. Madeleine had invariably come out on top since

September. Woe betide any girl whom fate put before her. In French, geography, and catechism, she barely managed to keep her head above water, and was even considered something of a dunce, in spelling especially, but she always emerged victorious from these mathematical jousts. With first place out of reach, the rest of the girls would aim for a place in the final alongside Madeleine Lamontagne, the perpetual champion of these predictable contests that the pupils, surprisingly, never tired of: the girl's neurons were as much a source of fascination as her father's muscles. That day when the world had been supposed to end proved no exception: Madeleine crushed all before her. But for the first time—and much to Sister Saint Alphonse's dismay—Solange Bérubé managed to take second place, finding herself up against Madeleine in the final. Madeleine was tempted for a moment to let her friend and neighbour win, until she remembered her father's words:

"Pity is for the weak."

Solange and Madeleine walked home together, not caring what admonitions it might earn them from Mrs. Bérubé. Solange's heart was a carnival of contradictory emotions: happiness at seeing the end of the world averted, the thought of spending the rest of the school year in a classroom with a raving lunatic of a nun, and then this closeness with Madeleine, a girl who, with all their shared prayers in the shed, had become so friendly, so approachable, that Solange had, albeit somewhat reluctantly, been forced to set aside her inertia and shyness. Nothing is so foreign to the heart of the tormented lover than seeing the pain of absence disappear, as though her heart had been fuelled by this angst ever since she first laid eyes on Madeleine from behind the willow hedge. Now she would have to work on getting the ban lifted on visiting the Lamontagne house. The two girls threw snowballs at each other and slid along Rue Fraserville's steep sidewalks, breaking into a song for the cold of heart as they revelled in winter's arrival right down to the very last snowflake:

"It's not the end of the world

Oh no, no, no, no!

The nuns' heads are full of lice

Na, na, na, na, na!"

Madeleine grabbed Solange by the shoulders.

"I'll tell my dad to invite you over for supper on Saturday."

"My parents will kill me."

"No, it's my mom they hate, not my dad. Everyone loves Dad. Everyone loves Louis 'The Horse' Lamontagne!"

"I know, but if you invite me for supper, my dad will beat me again!"

"I'll take care of it!"

And their happiness lasted all the way to Rue Saint-François-Xavier where, worried by the November storm, Mrs. Bérubé was waiting in her glassed-in veranda for her daughter to come home from school. Her heart skipped a beat at the sight of her daughter frolicking with the Lamontagne girl. Would she really have to beat the stubborn little girl again? She'd almost put her shoulder out the last time. If she loved the Lamontagnes so much, why didn't she just go live with them! She could go let Irene Caron's crazy old woman lock her up in a casket!

"Solange Bérubé, come inside this instant. You're soaking wet. What on earth were you doing throwing snow at each other? You'll get sick! What were you thinking? Do you want to end up in a box at the Lamontagnes'? Madeleine, you get on home, you'll catch your death!"

She was hopping mad was Mrs. Bérubé.

"Catch my death? I'll be sure to tell Grandma Madeleine. That's a good one!"

"Just you do that, you insolent child. And leave my Solange alone."

Solange ran to her mother, clutching the holy picture that second place in the math contest had earned her, hoping the reward might spare her a lash or two of the belt. Her mother was unimpressed.

"Multiplications? Go multiply me some peeled potatoes, you little devil! And stop walking like your brothers! You're a girl, Solange!"

That night, the Bérubés were treated to a side of Solange they'd never seen before. Her words came out with newfound aplomb, she sounded like her dad when he was twenty. The defiance of youth. She followed the rules and didn't speak at the table, but she made up for it as she did the dishes. She recounted her day in the tone a witness to an air disaster might use to describe what they saw; Solange even broke a glass as she attempted to mimic Sister Mary of the Eucharist gulping down the first snowflakes of winter.

"And word has it Sister Fatty shit her pants!"

"Solange Bérubé, you watch your mouth," Mrs. Bérubé roared, brandishing a wooden spoon covered in soap suds.

Just steps away, the atmosphere was very different in the Lamontagne household. Madeleine had told her family before supper how her prayers had saved the world. She also told them about the first snow, the math battle she'd won again, and how the price of Chinese babies was up fifteen cents.

"To twenty-five cents?" Irene Caron gasped.

"Well, Sister Saint Alphonse says the price went up because christenings are becoming more expensive."

"Is that so?"

Irene was working herself into a tizzy. Madeleine could feel her chances of inviting Solange over for supper on Saturday night slipping away. She would have to find a way to make herself seem adorable, pitiful even. She nonchalantly revealed her hands, still red from the caning that morning. Irene's eyes grew wide.

"My God, Madeleine! What's wrong with your hands?"

"It was Sister Saint Alphonse. She caned me."

Madeleine held up both hands while offering a passable imitation of Saint Blandina's face as the lions surrounded her. Irene didn't seem much moved, but Madeleine was used to that.

"Are you trying to make me feel sorry for you?"

"No, no, I…"

"Why did she hit you?"

Madeleine froze. Now she'd have to own up to what she'd done, admit how her hands, driven by an outside force, had grabbed the felt-tip pen and drawn a little mustache on Pope Pius XII, and she'd have to describe how the tiny black line had infuriated the nuns.

"It's all because of Pius XII."

"What do you mean, Pius XII? Pius XII is dead!"

Madeleine decided that sobbing was the best course of action. She had come to the realization that sobs expressed the emotion that generated the greatest respect from others. In her mathematically inclined mind, Madeleine had categorized possible behaviours according to the feelings and emotions they were likely to arouse. "Looking like Saint Blandina" was at the very top of the list, almost as effective as kneeling by the radio during the family rosary, although needless to say the latter tactic worked much more effectively on Irene Caron than on Papa Louis. But generosity, thought Madeleine, a condition essential to her undertaking's success, was a quality more readily associated with Louis Lamontagne.

"Where's Dad?"

"Your father has gone down to pick up a body in town. The old Lévesque woman died this morning. Your father's happy. He was practically praying for someone to be killed on the roads."

So the old Lévesque woman, found as stiff as a poker on the morning of November 10, 1960, had been the end of the world's only victim. Madeleine decided to wait for Louis to come back in his hearse. He wasn't long coming. From the kitchen window, she saw her dad and brother Marc carrying the old woman into the basement, a place no one was allowed to go while Louis got the mortal remains ready before laying them out in his funeral parlour. Madeleine thought to herself that a new corpse arriving in their home couldn't hurt her plan to invite Solange over for supper that Saturday. She bided her time. Louis would be back up soon enough. Irene, meanwhile, had gone out, explaining to her daughter that she had an errand to run before supper.

"Peel a dozen potatoes and set the table, Madeleine. Keep an eye on the soup, while you're at it."

Irene had gone out without even buttoning up her coat. Whatever it was couldn't wait, by the looks of things. Louis found his daughter spreading a tablecloth. Madeleine ran the numbers, looked for Louis' Achilles heel, how best to get what she wanted out of him. Asking straight out "Can Solange Bérubé come over for supper this Saturday?" would never work. "How come? Don't the Bérubés' have anything to eat?" That's what he'd say. No, she'd have to do better than that. Louis washed his hands.

"Where's your mom?"

"At the store."

"So... how was the end of the world?" Louis grinned.

"It was just some snow. The nuns said it was down to our prayers."

"That's probably it."

Louis was still grinning. Things were looking good.

"I made a new friend."

"Oh yeah? Anyone we know?"

"Solange Bérubé."

Louis suppressed a laugh. Back when he was a child, he had known Mrs. Bérubé, though she was a Cormier back then. He'd flirted with her when she was twelve, back in 1930. Too shy. Too tough. He'd turned his attentions elsewhere.

"Oh, you mean our neighbour!"

"Uh-huh. She's always talking about you," Madeleine lied.

"What do you mean, she's always talking about me?"

"Her mom told her you're always telling stories, and she loves a good story."

"Well, you'll have to invite her over sometime, if she likes stories."

Madeleine flicked the black eye out of a potato, unsettled by her own power. "Be quiet now," she said to herself. "Let things take their course."

Louis wiped his hands and bent down to his daughter's height. His teal-coloured eyes looked into hers.

"Look here, Madeleine. Don't tell a soul. This Saturday I'm working on a big surprise for the whole family. If you want, I'll talk to Mrs. Bérubé and have Solange over too. What do you think?"

Madeleine was stunned: she'd played him like a fiddle. She gave her father an astonished look, which he took to be barely contained joy. Ten minutes later, Louis rang the Bérubés' doorbell. Well aware of Mrs. Bérubé's feelings for his wife, he insisted on speaking privately to Mr. Bérubé in the living room. In the kitchen, where the family was eating, Solange held her breath. She could hear both men laughing. She heard the words "Saturday" then "Whatever makes you happy, my dear Louis." Her heart was pounding. After five minutes, The Horse left again. Mr. Bérubé sat back down at the table.

"Solange is having supper at the Lamontagnes' Saturday," he announced.

Mrs. Bérubé twisted her apron nervously.

"Oh no, I don't think so! I don't think so!"

"Annette, Solange is eating at Louis Lamontagne's on Saturday and that's that. Do I make myself clear?"

A heavy silence fell over the Bérubé kitchen. Solange wondered if the world actually had ended without them noticing. She thought that the Lord, in all his goodness, might have reserved a death so quick for his creation that no one had noticed. "We're all up in heaven and I'm off to Madeleine's for supper on Saturday," she thought as she peeled a turnip. Her mind was a Chagall painting, her times tables spinning by with orange rabbits and flying nuns above Madeleine Lamontagne's sweet face.

Just as these intense negotiations were taking place on Rue Saint-François-Xavier, Irene Caron was braving the elements to settle a matter that couldn't wait. She crossed Rue Fraserville without looking right or left. Continued on to the convent and went up the steps to the parlour. After wiping her boots and shaking her coat, she waited for someone to come out to meet her. It was her lucky day: her aunt, Sister Mary of the Eucharist, came to greet her. Irene pulled every string she could to get what she wanted, which was for the Mother Superior, Mother Mary of the Great Power, to see her right there and then.

"Really, Irene! You need to make an appointment to speak with the Mother Superior!"

"Tell her Louis sent me," Irene replied.

With only her husband's name to guarantee her safe passage, Irene Caron was admitted to Mother Mary of the Great Power's antechamber at four thirty in the afternoon. A teenage girl sat on a chair. Her eyes were red and she was biting her nails. With her free hand, she kept putting on and taking off a shoe that was too big for her. Indistinct words could be heard from the Mother Superior's office. "I expect you to change..." then, nothing. The door opened and out came a woman in her fifties, visibly the nail-biting student's mother. Mother and daughter left the antechamber without a word, disappearing down the hallway, from where there came the sound of a slap followed by a yelp.

"Hello, Mrs. Lamontagne."

Irene stood. While she had been waiting in the antechamber, the snow that had clung to her boots had melted and formed a puddle of water just in front of the chair she'd been sitting on. Mother Mary of the Great Power eyed the mess and pursed her lips. Irene stepped into the principal's office.

The door was closed by an invisible hand. The nun with the bellicose chin smiled from behind a large desk. What to say of this upstanding woman other than that she couldn't abide laziness, that she had been to a papal mass in Rome in 1953 (a story she wheeled out every chance she got), and that she never ate in the presence of her colleagues? Instead, she would have her lunch brought into her office on the stroke of noon and chew each mouthful in the strictest privacy. The eucharist was the only food she would take into her mouth with people looking on. And even that couldn't be considered "eating" in the strictest sense. The Mother Superior would no doubt have preferred the term "nourishment." Not a soul had ever seen her nibble on a fillet of sole or sip a tomato juice.

If she was smiling, it certainly wasn't with delight. She was showing her teeth for an altogether different reason. Irene had been well used to the convent since childhood. She would go there with her father two or three times a year to visit with his half-sisters in the parlour. Mother Mary of the Great Power was often on the receiving end of Louis Lamontagne's generosity as he provided the convent with donations, transportation, and other sundry services. In theory, Irene and the Mother Superior should have gotten along just fine, but there was something about the waif from the parish of

Saint-Ludger that profoundly irritated Mother Mary of the Great Power. Was it the feverish fervour with which Irene had thrown herself at Louis upon his release from the army? In the nun's eyes, social mobility was no sin, provided you went about it the right way, a basic rule that seemed to have escaped Irene Caron. And it wasn't the first time today that she had been reminded of the Lamontagnes.

Shortly after lunch, Sister Saint Alphonse—yes, now she was quite sure, she'd put on weight again—had come to confess having committed a "regrettable" act against little Madeleine, without, of course, the Mother Superior inquiring as to the precise nature of the act. A few too many strokes of the cane, Mother Mary of the Great Power assumed. But the portly nun had insisted on the details, even shedding a few tears in the process. Now that the cat was out of the bag, it was holding a defiled picture of Pope Pius XII in its mouth. There it was on Mother Mary of the Great Power's desk, stirring in her an outrage that defied description. She'd found the whole story so far-fetched that she'd been about to send for Louis Lamontagne when she'd been told that Irene had just arrived. So she was here to discuss the Hitler mustache. Imagine her surprise when she realized the real motive for her visit.

"What can I do for you, my dear Irene? And how is our Louis?"

"Very well, Mother. I…"

"You realize that the Sisters of the Child Jesus consider him to be something of the son we never had. I hope you're taking good care of him. Hasn't he put on a little weight?"

The implication behind this last remark raised Irene's hackles. She struggled to hide her irritation. Take good care of him? What did she mean by that? What was the meddling old crow sticking her beak into? Throughout their short meeting, Irene thrice declined Mother Mary of the Great Power's invitation to sit. She stood there, straight as Lady Justice herself come down off her pedestal.

"He's doing very well, Mother. I don't want to bother you for too long. I came to talk to you about quite a delicate matter."

"I know, I know. I've been informed of what went on today in the classroom. I find the whole affair most regrettable, but there are two sides to every story. Madeleine has probably given you her version of the facts. Perhaps you'd like to hear ours?"

"You mean that Madeleine would have lied to me?"

"Not at all. But children, you know, often feel they are punished unfairly. They tend to recount events to their advantage."

"I suspect that's what's going on here. I don't think that Madeleine, or her family, deserve what happened at school today."

"I couldn't agree more. I spoke with Sister Saint Alphonse. She told me about the whole thing, in tears… Just imagine! Breaking down in front of me like that! But please sit down, Irene…"

"I'll stand. So it moved her to tears, did it?"

Irene quivered. A few drops of water tumbled from her coat.

"But it's not worth getting all worked up about, Mrs. Lamontagne. I'm sure that Sister Saint Alphonse had her reasons. This isn't her first year teaching! Please, sit down."

"No, I won't stay long. I find it hard to take at any rate."

The Mother Superior raised her eyes heavenward, not out of exasperation, but to indicate the source of all earthly authority.

"So do I, Mrs. Lamontagne, so do I. Sister Saint Alphonse assures me it won't happen again."

"I should hope not! Just imagine! Making money off people's backs like that! We're talking fifteen cents, all the same," replied Irene, testily.

The Mother Superior's face froze in a perplexed expression.

"Fifteen cents? What exactly are you talking about?"

"Well you're the school principal, are you not? The Chinese babies have always cost ten cents. And now, all of a sudden, they're up to twenty-five cents a head! What on earth has happened in China to warrant such a price hike? It's too expensive, if you ask me, Mother. I know you all think that Louis is made of money, but he has overheads too. If his three children have to start buying Chinese babies at twenty-five cents instead of ten cents each, he's going to have to raise his prices or find more dead people to bury! The poor man is having a hard enough time of things as it is! We're barely managing to make ends meet."

Over the course of two seconds, Mother Mary of the Great Power's face went from perplexed to astonished to flabbergasted, without even landing on amazed. So that was it: the price of Chinese babies had gone up.

"Keep a hold of yourself," she thought.

"But Irene, *we* don't set the price of Chinese babies. It's out of our hands…"

Irene wouldn't let it go, though, as insistent as a fly in October.

"You don't understand," she interrupted. "If you want to sell Chinese babies, you're going about it the wrong way, if you ask me. Unless you intend to start selling products that no one can do without, like milk or butter, you really need to keep your prices under control. 'Cause no one is in desperate need of a Chinese baby! We don't buy them because we're hungry. They're the ones that are hungry! If they want to sell them, it needs to be at the right price! Now, take—" (Irene stared at the ceiling, as though performing a difficult feat of mental arithmetic.) "Yes, that's it. Let's say I give you seventeen cents per head. Do we have a deal?"

At that very moment, haggling over the price of Chinese babies for the Holy Childhood seemed to make about as much sense to Mother Mary of the Great Power as the question of whether marsupials were fond of Ravel. She looked around for a means of attracting someone's attention, wondered for a moment if she shouldn't simply cry for help. What a day! What could she say to the poor lunatic in front of her as she continued to go on and on?

"No? What if we bought five for the price of four? Still no deal?"

The nun's jaw fell down onto the floor. Irene picked it up and give it back to her.

"You drive a hard bargain, Mother," she went on. "That's a lot of money for us ordinary folk. But I'm sure we can reach an agreement. Hah! I've got it! What if the girls were to team up to buy the Chinese babies..."

"Team up?" the nun asked, curious to see where this woman's warped mind would lead them.

"Yes! In teams! If my Madeleine teamed up with the Bérubé girl, for instance. Just the other day I saw them hiding in the shed to say their prayers. By the way, what a great idea that was, the end of the world! It sure calmed them all down! But don't play that card too often or they'll stop believing you. Anyway, let's just say that my Madeleine buys a little Chinese boy, or girl—they cost the same, don't they?—at ten cents, like before, and sells it to Solange for fifteen. Madeleine then gives you the fifteen cents that Solange gives her and you have your twenty-five cents! Not only will you meet your price, but Solange and Madeleine will pay less than the others! Although that would remain between the two of us... If they're the only two to do it, your sales won't dip too much."

Mother Mary of the Great Power found herself listening to Irene's sales patter the way some might catch themselves listening to the dialogue in a porn movie: with much shame and no small amount of interest. She mused

155

to herself. Barely ten minutes ago, when Irene's untimely arrival had been announced, she had thanked the heavens for not sending her The Horse. Truth be told, she'd been expecting to have to explain away Sister Saint Alphonse's overzealousness with the cane, having already reprimanded the nun in no uncertain terms. "Hit someone else if you have to! Not our Louis' little girl!" she'd shouted at Sister Fatty. She could already picture Louis tearing the convent to shreds with his bare hands.

She'd also expected Irene to go on and on about the story the nuns had come up with about the end of the world, a story they had trotted out at least two or three times in ten years. Nothing calms the nerves of a class of schoolgirls better than bringing the world to an abrupt end, as every nun knows.

In short, she had no use for the arguments she'd prepared since Irene's mind was entirely taken up with the price of Chinese babies. "I'm getting off cheaply," Mother Mary of the Great Power thought to herself, smiling at her play on words. After all, poor Irene was deserving of her pity; hadn't God sent her a simpleton of a child, little Luc, to test her, a child who would never learn a thing?

"I accept, Irene. Your last offer seems reasonable. It is not entirely to our advantage, as we will sell slightly fewer Chinese babies. But Madeleine and Solange will learn the virtues of saving and the nobleness of working together, like all of us here in the convent!" she smiled, pinching one of her ample buttocks hard to stop herself laughing.

Irene beamed with pleasure. Mother Mary of the Great Power had accepted her deal! What joy! The two women shook hands and the Mother Superior blessed Irene before she left her office. As she closed the door, the Caron woman, determined to have the last word, delivered this heartfelt message to the nun:

"Oh, Mother, do you think you could you ask Sister Saint Alphonse to beat Madeleine over the *back* of the hand? Otherwise she can't peel the potatoes and mop the floor properly. She says it stings too much. I'd be eternally grateful, Mother."

The door closed. The Mother Superior didn't move for a full three minutes. She watched the snow come down, imagining Louis Lamontagne driving into Heaven behind the wheel of an American convertible. Alone. Completely and utterly alone.

"Not every Hell is deserved," she said to herself, before yawning profusely.

Irene, meanwhile, went home with a spring and no little pride in her step, her head held high. On Mother Mary of the Great Power's desk, the mustachioed picture of Pope Pius XII no longer seemed so pressing. No one cared about it anymore.

When they heard that their sister had been invited to the Lamontagnes' for supper, the Bérubé boys observed a minute of silence. It was as though they had just learned she was going to die, which wasn't far from the truth, if death can be considered a new departure. The incredulity that followed Mr. Bérubé's announcement gave way to a joke or two about what she should wear for the occasion. Black, what else?

The jokes washed off Solange like water off a duck's back. They were jealous, that's all. And it was admiration mixed with envy she saw in their faces as they watched Papa Louis lift his weights on summer days out in the yard. Not one of those braggarts could claim that the hearse and convertible parked outside the Lamontagne house left him indifferent. On Friday night, Solange bellowed her catechism from her bedroom to be sure she would be heard all over the house.

"Envy is the sadness at the sight of another's goods, and the immoderate desire to have them for oneself."

To which one of her brothers, between coughing fits, shouted out in reply:

"Pride is too high an opinion of one's self, attended with an inordinate desire of being above others!"

Still annoyed with her husband for having overruled her, Mrs. Bérubé listened in silence to the children bombard each other with descriptions of the capital sins. She had managed to convince her daughter to wear a brown skirt with a white blouse to supper at the neighbours', then explained that certain topics were off limits at the table: her brothers' illnesses, the man her big sister Antonine was engaged to (who now spent all his time at the neighbourhood bar), and not a word either about how many days her father worked a week. That was nobody's business.

"I'd also tell you not to discuss money at the table either. It's not polite. But since you're going for supper at that Caron woman's…"

And around six o'clock on Saturday, November 12, Solange walked across the snow and through the willow hedge, armed with a bouquet of white carnations as an offering. Louis had pulled out all the stops to make the neighbours' girl feel welcome. Irene, surprised not to have been consulted, unenthusiastically accepted the presence of this intruder in her daily routine.

She had begun by protesting that they were in no position to feed the whole street (which wasn't true: back then, Louis could still have had the whole parish round for supper without dipping into his savings), that the Bérubés hadn't said a word to them in ten years (another lie: Mr. Bérubé often had a beer with Louis in the bars along Rue Lafontaine, as Irene well knew), and that the boys had nothing to wear (also not true: Louis had just had them dressed entirely respectably at the local tailor at an unbeatable price). Finally, Irene pointed out that Old Mrs. Lévesque was to lie in repose Saturday in the living room, that a guest at the Lamontagnes' might upset the family in mourning, and that—fiddlesticks!—the Bérubé girl, unaccustomed as she was to funeral vigils, might be traumatized by the gloomy atmosphere.

"Gloomy? What's so gloomy about wanting to bury the dead? Anyway, Old Mrs. Lévesque will be in the parlour, far from the dining room. No one will be bothering anyone."

Louis won the day. Solange was welcomed like a queen. Music played in the living room beside the funeral parlour. It was Louis' favourite: Bach's *Jesu, Joy of Man's Desiring*. A musical choice that might lead one to believe that Papa Louis was a keen follower of baroque music. Not a bit of it. It was in fact the one and only baroque record he owned. And how did *Jesu, Joy of Man's Desiring* become Louis' favourite piece of music? Germany, *natürlich*. The country from where you could bring back the very best, providing you survived.

While Solange sat on the green sofa in the living room, Louis "The Horse" Lamontagne told her how he'd come across the little painting he'd given Old Ma Madeleine when he came back from the war. When she moved into Louis' house, the old woman had naturally hung the painting in the room where the bodies were laid out. There was something about the picture of a dead Virgin Mary, lying on her tomb with Jesus and the apostles looking on, that brought comfort to families in mourning. "In death, no one is alone," the painting seemed to say. It was a way of underscoring the importance Louis Lamontagne gave to burials and funeral rites. Solange, overcome with happiness, listened to The Horse tell his story, her eyes as wide as saucers.

It was the day after they'd found David Rosen, the death march survivor who'd been saved by the morning snow in the mountains. Papa Louis had wanted to leave him at a hastily constructed Allied Forces camp by Lake Starnberg. The camp had been built to welcome deportees from Eastern Europe awaiting emigration to more hospitable lands. It was built on the site of what had once been an elite school for the Hitler Youth and left a real impression on Louis: thousands of haggard faces, stunned at the fact they were alive. Skeletal hands reaching out to him, brushing against his G.I. uniform, the women who had narrowly escaped the flames of Auschwitz speaking incomprehensible languages and throwing him warm-hearted looks.

"And the dead. Everywhere. They were everywhere, Madeleine..." he told his daughter years later, after a night's heavy drinking, just before collapsing into sleep.

At the Feldafing refugee camp—Feldafing was the name of the Bavarian village—he was told there was no room for his David Rosen. He would have to bring him to a grand Bavarian villa built on top of a hill closer to the village. Louis left Rosen up there, in a villa that looked like a cuckoo clock from a distance: wooden balconies, an onion dome, frescoes on its whitewashed walls. A postcard for a dying man.

Louis drove the military vehicle right up to the door of the villa set in a magnificent garden overlooking the lake. The wind whistled in the branches of majestic hemlock trees. Rosen, who had just been given a cup of clear broth, was clutching his stomach, his intestines unused to digesting the slightest morsel.

"I feel heavy," he said.

Louis hoisted him over his right shoulder, as you might carry a drunken companion on New Year's Eve. In the villa, he was told there was no room for Rosen: the house was already full of sick people, other deportees from camps to the east. He would have to try elsewhere. That was when Louis lost patience. On top of what he considered to be lies was the trouble he was having making himself understood by the locals. While his English had improved since the St. Lawrence County Fair, he still had to articulate every single word to get the people at the villa to understand him. They weren't German; they were there to manage these warehouses for the living dead, and that was, in fact, the first thing they said to Louis:

"Calm down. We're not German."

Louis finally got permission to set Rosen down on the floor, in a huge bourgeois dining room that had been emptied of all its furniture. He took the time to make him up a makeshift bed of hemlock branches and blankets, then hid some chocolate rations, sugar, American chewing gum, and a handful of cigarettes in Rosen's clothing, and whispered into his ear that he wasn't to eat too fast, that it might kill him if he gobbled everything up at once, because his stomach had shrunk at Dachau.

"Just a little in the morning. To see you through the day, David."

Rosen, half conscious, smiled up at the giant who had saved his life.

"Are you French?" he asked.

"Canadian."

"You sound like you're French."

Louis briefly explained where he came from, leaving out any mention of his German roots. He stayed with David Rosen for a little while, to make sure that the people in this house full of refugees understood the man he'd taken under his wing was important. Rosen's breathing slowed. He knew he could trust Louis and he fell asleep.

On the villa's ground floor, in a dark, windowless room, a portly woman was crouching down to light a fire in a huge earthenware stove, the likes of which Louis had never seen. The woman stood up and looked the soldier in the eye without saying a word. She was blonde, maybe twenty-five. But the war had left her looking forty. Her build was at odds with the emaciated bodies lying all over the villa. She seemed to be the only German there. Louis realized she must be the housekeeper or perhaps the caretaker. Life in these hilly parts had given her a shapely pair of legs, which The Horse had been quick to notice. Charmed by the sight of him, she introduced herself. Maria. She led him down to the cellar, where she lived in a tiny, dank room. It was in that dingy room reeking of mould that they got to know each other better. Needless to say, Louis skipped over this part of the story in front of Solange and Madeleine. The villa's huge basement had been used to store away the paintings and furniture that had once adorned the upper floors. Louis inspected the pictures leaning against the wall. Almost all of them were wrapped in brown timeworn canvas. The only one actually visible was the small 15" × 8" painting. Maria noticed Louis' interest in the picture. As she bundled her heavy bosom back into her blouse, she pointed at the picture and said, "*Die Grablegung der Maria,*" the name by which the piece was known in German, which is to say *The Entombment of Mary*. Louis thought that Maria meant the picture belonged to her. He couldn't take his eyes off the painting of Mary, an image that brought him back to his native land. Around the body, Christ and his apostles. For the first time in his life, he felt the urge to be nearer to them. He grabbed the painting with his huge hands and asked if he could buy it.

"Me buy the Maria?"

Which Maria took to mean: "Goodbye, Maria." She was well used to American soldiers leaving as soon as their business was done. But she found this one so handsome she wanted to give him a parting gift. She produced some canvas, wrapped up the painting, and handed it to Louis, who thought, perfectly reasonably, that the picture must belong to her. It took him a week to realize the misunderstanding, but he was far away by then and the painting was en route to America. To Solange, he explained that he'd exchanged the painting for a pack of cigarettes. Which wasn't entirely untrue since he'd given Maria a Marlboro when they went back up into the kitchen. The painting under his arm, he left the villa without incident. The U.S. Army then had it shipped to New York City, where he picked it up on his return. It never occurred to him that he might have stolen something, any more than Maria realized she'd embezzled part of her masters' fortune. She asked Louis to write down his name on a scrap of paper, along with his address in *Kanada*.

On that freezing-cold morning, Louis told his fellow infantrymen that he wanted to walk, to get his head straight. He walked along the road to Feldafing until he reached an old church. He stepped inside just as the organist was attacking the first notes of *Jesu, Joy of Man's Desiring*. And he stayed, with the rest of the faithful, to listen to that music from Bach that seemed to make up for all the aberrations he'd seen since Dachau. When mass was over, the people stared at him, contemplating him in all his Americanness. He went up to the organist, a young woman paralyzed by this strapping man with teal-coloured eyes who spoke pidgin English. Who wrote the music? Did I? Is that why this brute is pointing at me? Are you poking fun? But what can I tell the poor man other than one word:

"Bach!"

Out of fear that he might fly into a rage, they'd given him the sheet music. He'd mailed it along with the painting the very next morning, once again at the U.S. Army's expense. It was Mother Mary of the Great Power who played it for him on the organ in the church of Saint-François-Xavier, two weeks after his return to the land of his desiring.

"Why, don't cry, Louis. It's such joyous music!"

Louis didn't say a word to the Mother Superior about David Rosen, the church in Feldafing, or the big house with the wooden balconies filled to bursting with concentration camp survivors. Moved by how the music seemed to swell her Big Louis' heart, Mother Mary of the Great Power instructed the church organist to play the piece regularly. And so from that day on, it could be heard during Advent, on Louis' birthday on December 25, at the end of Lent (the priest had refused it be played on days of abstinence), and, of course, at Easter.

"But isn't that music by and for those cold-hearted Protestants?" a particularly annoying parishioner could be heard complaining one Sunday in December.

"Perhaps, but there's enough joy to go around for everyone," came the reply from an irritated Mother Mary of the Great Power.

For Christmas 1950, as a thank-you for all the errands he ran for them, the nuns gave Louis a recording of the *Herz und Mund und Tat und Leben* cantata, of which *Jesu, Joy of Man's Desiring* is the final movement, that they had secretly ordered from Quebec City. Ten years later, hoping that the music might have a calming effect on Solange, Papa Louis played the cantata's final movement for the thousandth time. The whole family knew it by heart. The record crackled and even skipped a little. Luc's head nodded in time to the music while Marc and Madeleine pretended they were holy statues to draw a laugh from their father. Madeleine excitedly showed Solange around the house, even the parlour where Old Mrs. Lévesque's body was lying, Irene having done her hair that very morning. No one had turned up for the wake yet. The old woman was laid out like an Egyptian queen, features deformed by her passing, surrounded by chrysanthemums and carnations. The two girls paid their respects in front of the old woman for an instant and mumbled a quick prayer before going back to join the rest of the family in the living room.

Old Ma Madeleine, whom Solange touched for the very first time, smiled as she stood beside the dead woman, waiting for friends and relatives to arrive, as was her wont. Solange had enjoyed the feeling of the dead woman's cold skin on hers when she had shaken her tiny hand.

"Her hand's cold. Just like Sister Mary of the Eucharist's!" she whispered into Madeleine's ear.

With Irene busy cooking, Louis was free to do as he pleased.

"Do you like a good story, Solange?"

There was a twinkle in Papa Louis' eye; his sons began to fidget...

"Tell the one about the tornado in Kansas," Madeleine begged.

"No, I wanna hear the one about the calf named Adolf!" Marc grumbled.

Solange sat, tiny and immobile on the bottle-green sofa as she listened to an hour's worth of stories that took her to places with unpronounceable names: Wyoming, Ohio, Iowa. Names that bore all the poetry in the world: Idaho Bill, The Warsaw Giant... and the incredible tale of Podgórski, or the time when Papa Louis was chased by a furious Cheyenne man up and down the roads of Nebraska. The storyteller was inspired by the little girl from next door and took her visit as an excellent excuse to share a new story with his children, an older one this time… but then he heard Old Mrs. Lévesque's friends and relatives moving around in the parlour beside them. There was a heavy silence, and words that drifted over to them… Solange listened closely to Old Ma Madeleine's voice as she tried to console what sounded like two or three people on the other side of the wall.

"She's better off now, you know that, don't you?" Old Ma Madeleine began.

"Yes! And so are we!" a woman's voice cut in.

In the living room where Louis was sitting with Solange and his children, they tried not to laugh.

"The Lord calls his favourite children back," Old Ma Madeleine went on.

"He took his time about it! Eight years we were looking after that old dame!" the same woman countered. "Now we'll finally be able to put the television in her bedroom."

"If you would like to join me in prayer… Oh merciful God who watches over us…" Old Ma Madeleine went on, without skipping a beat.

Irene brought the invisible theatre to an end, ordering them all to sit at the dining-room table. Solange was seated between Madeleine and Papa Louis, who she couldn't take her eyes off. Irene wanted to know if Solange liked pea soup. More used to meals where no one was allowed to speak a word, Solange took a while to adapt to the jovial mood at the Lamontagnes' table. Everyone talked over each other, a ladle held by a steady hand piled the plates high, and hunks of bread travelled north and south along the boisterous table where no one seemed to listen to anyone. Between the soup and the main course—chicken, Solange was delighted to see—Louis got up to put in an appearance with the Lévesque family. He came back from the parlour smiling. The family had already gone, leaving Old Madeleine to watch over the body by herself. She could be heard demanding a bowl of soup.

"Why don't you eat with us?" Louis asked, looking pointedly at the place reserved for the old woman beside Irene.

"The dead are best left with the dead," was her only reply.

Louis looked at his wife.

"You could make a bit of an effort, Irene."

Irene sighed, stood up slowly, and with the fervour and enthusiasm of a woman on Death Row, went off to find Old Madeleine, who refused to budge. She could be heard speaking softly to her and a few words made their way to Solange's ears:

"I'm sorry I spoke to you in that tone... disrespect... with us."

Then the footsteps of the two women coming back toward the dining room. Old Ma Madeleine, lips pursed. Sitting right across from Solange, she stretched out her chin to tighten the wattle hanging down off her throat, smiled at the guest, and even asked how she was getting on at school.

"Your little friend is a math whiz. Her mother trains her. Nothing gets by her..."

Irene took a deep breath. The two women were barely on speaking terms, Madeleine explained later to Solange. Not a day went by without Old Madeleine threatening to move into the old folks' home or the convent. Louis was constantly having to step in between his wife and grandmother.

"The soup's a bit thin," Old Madeleine went on.

Irene didn't turn a hair. Solange almost found her courageous. Louis, visibly keen to entertain his new audience for the evening, insisted on recounting, to his wife's despair, how, when Madeline was nothing but a slip of a girl, the archbishop of Rimouski had sent him a letter.

"The archbishop!" Solange repeated in amazement.

The Lamontagne children and their mother ate their chicken in silence. They already knew the story by heart. One day, in 1954, Louis was working up a sweat with two pals in a garage on Rue Fraserville. The garage was chilly, but they had set up a bench and a few weights there. Louis had always refused to let himself go, believing paternity was no excuse for piling on the pounds. So he'd stayed in great shape. Passersby with nothing better to do would sometimes gather and watch the three men work out. It had become a free show that anyone could take in. Scantily clad in the summer months, the three hulking men would put on, in addition to a show of strength, an anatomy lesson to anyone who showed up in front of the garage on a given Saturday morning. The lesson was revealing enough for the priest in the parish of Saint-François to have gotten wind of it in a confession from a man who had felt "degraded" after watching Louis lift his weights.

"But Louis is a strongman. It's a matter of constitution. My predecessor, Father Cousineau, told me he came into this world that way. He was so big his mother didn't survive the birth," the priest had murmured through the grill in an attempt to console the poor man.

"I don't mean that! We all know he's well built! We all know about his broad shoulders! My own mother was sitting in the church of Saint-François the night he was born in 1918!"

Father Rossignol, a puny runt of a man produced by the seminary in Sainte-Anne-de-la-Pocatière, wanted to be clear in his own mind. A few minutes were enough for him to understand what his parishioner had meant by "degraded." Then again, it's all about proportion, he thought to himself, but it was a matter best discussed with someone you could trust. And so what any woman could have told you in a heartbeat travelled from confessional to sacristy to convent to parlour to refectory. News spread through every echelon of the Lower St. Lawrence clergy, the result being that the archbishop of Rimouski got wind of the matter from a young seminarian who had heard it from Father Rossignol himself.

One day, Louis received a handwritten letter from the archbishop in the mail. To support his claim, Louis rummaged around in a dining-room dresser drawer for a moment before producing the document. His Grace, who had heard tales of Louis' exploits "both beyond these shores and within Canada" was intrigued and honoured to learn that there lived such a force of nature so close to Rimouski, only a few hours away by car. "I would like to invite you, Louis Lamontagne, to come train before me at your convenience at the archbishop's residence in Rimouski, so that we might all witness your God-given talent."

As proud as a peacock, Louis had gone down to Rimouski, bringing weights and a small cast of extras with him along the bumpy road that wasn't even paved in places to put on a most convincing display of force for His Grace and a handful of other priests: a couple of bench presses, a snatch, and two or three bent presses. From this athletic excursion, Louis returned with a photograph of himself standing beside the archbishop, an amiable man wearing a black cassock. Louis looked magnificent in his leotard and tight-fitting shorts, grinning from ear to ear. In the background were a few young priests Louis had nicknamed the "Vobiscums" and brothers he called the "Orapronobisses." There were also other, smaller, photos of Louis. One of them showed him at the peak of his powers in 1955, age thirty-seven. A wave running through his hair. Muscles bulging.

"I was bigger than Eugen Sandow in that one! You know who I mean? The father of modern bodybuilding."

Solange shook her head. And without knowing where her question—or daring—came from, Solange asked Papa Louis if she could keep one of the photos. Sitting around the table, Madeleine's brothers grinned. Such a handsome man, well used to dealing with women, could not very well refuse.

"Whichever one you like, Solange."

She killed two birds with one stone: Papa Louis flanked by the archbishop of Rimouski. The photo slid into her pocket. Solange looked at the strange family around her, so different from any to be found in her manual of civility.

Not that the Lamontagnes were ill-mannered louts, far from it! Irene saw to it that each of her children was courteous and polite. At the far end of the table, sitting ramrod straight, was Marc, a tall, quiet boy with an aura of mystery about him. It was already clear that he'd be as handsome as his father, only with brown eyes. Luc, age seven, seemed to live in a world all his own. Marc was cutting up his chicken for him. In fact, Luc seemed to be more absent than usual, as though in another orbit. Sometimes the little boy would drum his knife against the table (which his mother quickly put an end to) or seek attention by making noises with his mouth, bursting into spontaneous laughter, or making other sounds with different parts of his body. Peace would be restored after a swift slap and a growl from Papa Louis. Luc barely spoke, at least not in complete sentences that made any sense. He was content to listen, laugh, and interject with little "hah!" sounds to express astonishment or disappointment, for instance, when he realized there were no peas left. Solange was overcome with emotion at the sight of this family portrait. She would have to compliment Mrs. Lamontagne once the last bite was swallowed, just like her mom had told her, then leave no more than ten minutes after dessert. It was basic etiquette. Old Ma Madeleine, who had just begun picking at her plate, suddenly changed gear.

"At any rate, Irene, you have no idea how to make pea soup. And you can take that how you will. But your rabbit! I don't know what you did to it, but I've never eaten a tastier one, not even my own mother's. Was it the big fat orange one you roasted? Isn't it simply delicious, little Solange?"

Solange had just swallowed her last mouthful. For an instant, she felt all the air had been sucked out of the room. She couldn't feel her legs. Lazarus. She'd just eaten poor Lazarus. Papa Louis bounded up out of his chair.

"You cooked Lazarus? What's gotten into you!"

He was roaring now. Madeleine, used to these outbursts, interrupted.

"I asked her to, Dad. For Solange."

"What do you mean 'for Solange'?"

"Solange wrote me a note in Sister Saint Alphonse's class. Hang on a second. Here it is."

And Madeleine produced from her pocket the little scrap of paper that had caused such an uproar at the convent. *For always. You, me, and Lazarus. S.*

Louis peered at it. His breathing slowed, the story seemed to charm him. He lifted his glass of cider.

"Well, dear Solange, it looks like you got your wish! You'll always be together, you and Lazarus."

"Not just Lazarus. The two small ones and another that my Jew from Montreal sold me are in there too," Irene said, her mouth still full. "He was big, but not big enough to feed all of us. And he sold me potatoes at half the price you'd pay at Damours, and just wait till you see the veal in the fridge. Want to know how much I paid? Guess. Go on… give me a number."

Siegfried Zucker. The Jew from Montreal was neither a Jew, nor from Montreal. He was a Catholic from Linz, a young travelling salesman who had given Madeleine her very first business opportunity that day he gave her a piece of barley sugar. Since his prices were unbeatable and he was open to negotiation (unlike Canadian grocers who tended to be dogmatic when it came to price) and he spoke with a thick Austrian accent, Irene called him the Jew from Montreal. If you asked her, all Jews were from Montreal and spoke like he did. The name had stuck. Irene called him "Mr. *Zouquère*" when talking to him, but otherwise he was known as the Jew from Montreal. Irene harboured feelings for the salesman that were too shameful to mention. And word had it that Zucker was not altogether indifferent to Irene's charms.

"Don't vomit, don't vomit," Solange was repeating to herself.

"And it wasn't as if we were going to keep them all winter!" Irene went on. "Do you know how much they cost to feed? No, I thought to myself, the Good Lord made smaller animals for the bigger ones to eat. Isn't that right, Mother? It's just a rabbit, Louis. You can find her another one in the spring once the snow's gone."

As though caught up in her mother's momentum, Madeleine chimed in.

"Last year, we ate Thomas the rabbit with some chicken, Solange. I really wanted you to be there for Lazarus, since you knew him and all."

"The Lamontagnes love rabbit," Marc added.

"And it was me who named him Lazarus, my favourite character from the New Testament!" Old Ma Madeleine concluded.

Solange's world was spinning. Did Madeleine really have to take her message literally? Were they all mad? Dangerous? She was no stranger to the notion of eating an animal you'd raised in your own backyard; people in the country did it all the time. But did they really have to go and give it a name? One thing was for sure: she was just as determined to become a Lamontagne as she'd been the day before. Lazarus or not. As much to disguise her faltering composure as to show the Lamontagnes what she was made of, Solange sat up straight in her chair, set down her fork, and asked in a crystal-clear voice:

"Is there any rabbit left?"

Her words were met with a round of applause. Knives tinged against glasses as bravos and laughter rang out. The Lamontagnes were simple folk at heart. Fortunately for Solange, all that was left, at the bottom of the dish, were a few bits of overcooked carrot. That night, she was welcomed into the Lamontagne fold like a lost sheep. The note that she had slipped Madeleine took on its full meaning: *For always. You, me, and Lazarus. S.*

Over dinner, Solange also learned that Madeleine's first word had been a number. Before saying "Mama" or "Papa" she had said "twelve."

Then out came the coffee cake and the kind of entertainment that only Louis Lamontagne could provide. Once the tablecloth had been folded away, Papa Louis took Luc upstairs to bed. He returned looking solemn, and announced to the rest of the family that he felt sorry for Old Mrs. Lévesque. She had lived for so long and brought nine children into the world only to find herself alone in an unfamiliar parlour in the middle of November. That's not how death should be. He suggested they hold a wake for the old woman, that they treat her as a member of their own family, that they give her a proper send-off. Irene raised her eyes to heaven, but did not protest.

"Well, I suppose it doesn't cost anything!"

They stood around Old Mrs. Lévesque's casket, praying in the half-darkness. The clock struck nine. Louis thanked everyone. Solange assumed that the evening was about to end there, that it was time to put on her boots and coat and run along home like a good girl. But that just showed how little she knew Louis. Never had Solange been so glad to be in the company of the dead. Louis slipped out of the parlour without saying a word. Off to the bathroom, Solange thought to herself, as she intoned her prayers for the dead. Louis was taking forever. Old Ma Madeleine led the rosary...

"Hail Mary, full of grace..."

Irene had lit a few candles around the casket, and the children's voices rang out in unison, ending each prayer started by Old Madeleine. For a moment, Solange thought she saw a smile cross Old Mrs. Lévesque's lips. Might she be another Lazarus? And where were the poor woman's children? Wouldn't it be better to pass on at the end of one's life, swept away by the currents of the St. Lawrence and out toward the magnificent, ice-filled ocean, than end up alone, surrounded by strangers, even ones as kindly as the Lamontagnes? Between a Hail Mary and an Our Father, a soft clicking sound could be heard. It came from the living room and was followed by a loud snap, as intense as it was brief. After a return to silence, a background noise could be heard, softer and more fluid this time. And then as crisp and clear as the March snow:

"The cardinal of Montreal is delighted to see a Catholic elected to the White House and invites the faithful to include America, henceforth and more than ever, in their prayers."

The rosary stopped dead.

Irene and the children ventured into the living room one by one. Louis was standing in front of a wooden dresser with a screen in the middle of it. A man was reading a news bulletin. In the blue light, the Lamontagne family and Solange Bérubé watched the first pictures of the victorious presidential couple. The crowd was ecstatic, people were shouting in English. A cold wind blew through the house.

"Television!"

Marc and Madeleine had fallen into their father's arms. He had just been promoted from Papa Louis to the Emperor of All Galaxies and Creator of All Happiness. Irene ran a finger across the wooden box.

"So we can afford this now?"

"Come on, Irene. Almost everyone in the parish has one… Everyone except the nuns!"

"How much did you pay for it?"

"It's my surprise, Irene. For the children."

"Could you please explain to me how we can't go about our lives without one of these things, Louis Lamontagne!"

He nodded toward the dead body in the parlour, as if to tell his wife that the old Lévesque woman's funeral had paid for it.

"Do you think the store will take it back?" asked Irene, to the children's despair.

"Come on, Irene!"

"You figure it out however you please, Louis, but it's madness. Now I've told you. I don't want it in the house."

From the funeral parlour, there came a noise, a wheezing sound. Someone was having trouble breathing!

"Grandma isn't well!"

Madeleine had run in to see what was happening. She found Old Ma Madeleine sitting down, trying to catch her breath, finger pointed at the television, her eyes rolled back in her head. Guttural sounds... spittle... more wheezing... the old woman passed out.

"Turn off the television, Papa," Madeleine begged.

Old Ma Madeleine came round as soon as Louis did so.

"What *is* that thing?" she moaned.

Never, not since she died for the first time in 1933, had Old Madeleine fallen ill or complained of a single ailment. But as soon as Louis had switched on the infernal machine, the old woman had felt an unbearable pressure pushing down on her skull, she'd heard screaming voices, found herself short of breath, begun to tremble.

"It's the television, Grandma."

Old Ma Madeleine walked into the dark living room. Stopped in front of the television, now turned off, peered at the faces of her grandson and his children, where she saw nothing but joy and contentment. For the first time in her life, Old Ma Madeleine felt overtaken by events, in orbit, far from her world. At the very idea of having to endure this contraption straight from the bowels of hell, Old Madeleine grasped her head in her hands.

"You said the nuns don't have one?" she asked her grandson.

"No. They don't want one."

Old Ma Madeleine slowly walked upstairs. The thing was there to stay, that much she could tell from the look in her grandson's eyes. She would be the one to go. The dead have need of few things in this life, but peace and quiet is one of them. The tinny voices, the flickering blue and grey images of other worlds foretold the worst. Old Ma Madeleine packed a small case and took the painting, *The Entombment of Mary*, that Louis had brought her back from Europe. They thought she'd gone upstairs to bed, but she took the kitchen stairs out, noiselessly, like a ghost in the night.

As she made her way to the convent—for that was where she was off to—she stopped from time to time in front of homes bathed in the same blue-tinged light. It gave everyone the blueish complexion her son Louis-Benjamin had had when they fished him out of the river he'd thrown himself into after Madeleine the American had died. While it never crossed her mind to follow his lead, she felt a pang of sadness for all the people sitting in front of the same pictures, each in their own home. And she could hear the death of endless stories, chatter, and questions. "Nothing of interest left to be said now," she thought.

The dead are so quiet that her footsteps didn't even squeak, instead elegantly sliding above and below the snow that God sends down on the northernmost countries. In the distance, the moon shone on the St. Lawrence the same way it shines over Lake Starnberg: with extreme violence.

At the convent, the nuns were getting ready for bed when Old Ma Madeleine rang the bell. It was Sister Mary of the Eucharist who would take her into her room until she died a second time, years later. Mother Mary of the Great Power had no objections to accommodating Louis' grandmother. After all, she thought, that Irene—peculiar and money-grabbing though she might have been—was well within her rights to rule over her household like any other mother. Why should she have to endure a mother-in-law whose definitive departure date remained unknown? Old Ma Madeleine had no vows to take: death would be her safe conduct. Henceforth, the nuns shared their porridge and raisins in the morning, their ground meat in the afternoon. In return—and much to the delight of all the nuns—Old Ma Madeleine hung *The Entombment of Mary* on the refectory wall, where it would be admired by all for years to come. The painting intrigued them. In the beginning, each and every one of them would stand in front of it, as though to unearth a detail that had eluded the others. Some counted the apostles, tried to identify them by their first names. No one could agree on which one St. Andrew was supposed to be. No one was indelicate enough to admit to Old Ma Madeleine how uneasy the painting made them feel. Hadn't the Blessed Virgin ascended into Heaven? Why linger on the decomposition of the flesh? What would His Grace make of it? The painting served as a daily reminder that every living thing must rot away, a thought to which they reacted by praying even more fervently than before.

At Louis' house, Old Ma Madeleine's disappearance went unnoticed until the following morning. Louis searched everywhere for his grandmother, panic-stricken, calling out left and right until Sister Mary of the Eucharist appeared in person to explain the situation. Papa Louis protested. After all, he was perfectly capable of looking after his own grandmother! And Sister Mary of the Eucharist looked over at the television as if to say, "Even enough to get rid of *that*?" The point wasn't lost on Irene, ever present and alert. Without giving her husband time to compromise this happy ending, she hammered the final nail into the casket:

"The television has become absolutely indispensable. Now is the time to look forward. Besides, Mother will be fine at the convent. As for the funeral parlour, we'll manage. The whole business was beginning to wear her out, I think."

And that was how Madeleine saw her great-grandmother leave for the convent. The dead woman's wrists were still sturdy enough and she was put to work in the laundry since she felt neither hot nor cold. From then on, she appeared only very rarely before Madeleine, who almost forgot she existed.

Sister Mary of the Eucharist and Old Ma Madeleine formed a touching duo who stayed well clear of televisions; the first because she considered them Japanese devilry, the second because the shrill static noise drove her mad. Prayer was all the entertainment they needed.

And God only knew that Madeleine and Solange would soon be in great need of someone, somewhere, praying for them.

And Solange? After watching the news for the first time on television, Solange went home smelling of formaldehyde, convinced the world had no sweeter perfume. Her parents were waiting up for their daughter, worried stiff. It was another girl who came home to them, a different one. Clutching the photograph Papa Louis had given her—the one of him posing in a tight-fitting leotard alongside the archbishop of Rimouski—she looked at her still-awake brother, the same one who had shown her his willy in the garden. She burst out laughing and went up to her room to hide the photo away in a safe place. Her cry woke the whole house.

"My name is Solange Lamontagne! I love rabbits! I love dead people! I love John F. Kennedy!"

The following day, the extent of her impudence was made abundantly clear. She was ignored for almost the entire day, then, at around four o'clock, her father came looking for her.

"Your mother wants to see you in the kitchen."

The potatoes were waiting for her. And not just one batch of potatoes. On November 13, 1960, Solange Bérubé was shown to a wooden stool that was surrounded by every variety of potato available in Rivière-du-Loup.

She was given a very sharp paring knife and ordered to peel every tuber and remove every last eye.

"Every single one, Solange."

And so Solange began peeling. Days, weeks, months, years passed. Tons of potatoes, probably enough to feed all of Rivière-du-Loup for a century. As the greyish peels fell down into the tin bucket, Solange got older. Her feet eventually touched the floor, her fingers grew longer, and she became defter with the knife. Years went by without it feeling like she'd ever left her potato-peeling stool. She was given new clothes to wear, horrible skirts, even though she'd been praying to Good Saint Anne for pants. Round-neck blouses when she'd rather have worn one of her older brothers' checked shirts. And the white potatoes, eyes now removed, tumbled one by one into the huge earthenware bowl. The Corpus Christi procession passed by Solange Peeler of Potatoes. Sister Mary of the Eucharist laid a hand on her shoulder in solidarity. We all have a cross to bear, dear. Solange's hair grew longer, fell down over her eyes. Her mom cut it while she peeled and rinsed the potatoes. There were all kinds: white, yellow, red, blue, Kennebec, baby potatoes. While Louis Lamontagne drove his hearse the length and breadth of Rivière-du-Loup, while Irene Lamontagne née Caron applied makeup to the dead and styled their hair, while Old Ma Madeleine prayed at the convent, Solange peeled potatoes. Her aunts from New Brunswick came to visit, whispering words of encouragement. "Do you like the Beatles? We got you a record in Moncton!" Sacks of spuds fell beside her with a dull thud, keeping time to "I wanna hold your hand, I wanna hold your hand, I wanna hold your ha-a-a-a-a-nd!" Poking out the eyes, peeling the skins, picking up the pace. Every potato was a bead on a never-ending rosary offered up for the teal-coloured eyes of Madeleine Lamontagne. "All my loving," Madeleine. There was the occasional break: Solange went to school, Solange walked along beside Madeleine, Solange was confirmed. The kitchen radio played: "I give her all my love. That's all I do. And if you saw my love, you'd love her too. And I love her. And I love her. And I love her." Ghastly breasts grew on her, looking every bit like the potatoes she was peeling. On Madeleine too. Solange became a woman while she peeled potatoes. Sometimes aunts would come to keep her company in her gulag. They urged her on. The more sensitive ones even helped her. What she had done was no laughing matter. She'd preferred another family to her own, but a little elbow grease will atone for anything in French Canada! Peel, wretched child! The occasional

173

drive in the car with Papa Louis and Madeleine. Eating an ice cream with one hand while the other peeled. Mr. Bérubé died. They ate potatoes at the funeral. One nun replaced another at the convent, each stricter than the last, each strangely, improbably, more enamoured with God. How many winters? Five? Six? Eight? She couldn't say. And the church that began emptying slowly, then suddenly, maybe two years before the yellow submarine passed by the shores of Rivière-du-Loup.

One night while her mother was braiding her hair, just as she was nearing the bottom of a bag of Kennebecs, her aunt Louisa set down a cake on the kitchen table. There were seventeen candles on it. Solange looked up from her chore. The whole family stared at her, wide eyed, all wearing their Sunday best. Mrs. Bérubé looked her straight in the eye.

"You can stop peeling, Solange. It's your birthday. You've served your sentence. What's your name again? Can you remind us?"

"Solange Bérubé. My name is Solange Bérubé," she replied, spitting on the floor.

It was the most ladylike thing she did that day.

A New Confessor

In the family portrait taken by Marmen the photographer in June 1968, Louis Lamontagne and his wife are sitting on a love seat upholstered in a magenta floral print on a chestnut background. Irene is dressed in black, and is wearing the look of someone who has lost something important and is wondering wherever it might have gone. Between husband and wife, an empty space, large enough for a child to sit in. Standing behind them, their two oldest children. First Marc, an attractive, austere young man, looking every bit like he'd just stepped out of a Botticelli self-portrait: the same fleshy lips, the same hungry and languorous eyes, his hand on the frail shoulder of his big sister Madeleine, who's standing tall and proud as befits a Lamontagne, although everyone knows, without being able to explain exactly how or why, that her mind is occupied with some complex mental arithmetic, as is a Caron's wont. She's wearing a pale-coloured dress. A necklace. Her hair nicely done. Of course she's pretty! Doesn't she look like Mireille Mathieu with her hair cut in a bob like that? The Lamontagne parents, sitting on their love seat, are looking their age. Irene especially. Dark rings, crow's feet, practically ostrich feet. Papa Louis now has a round belly, greying temples, weary eyes. But he's still the best looking of the bunch, closely followed by his son Marc, a dangerous rival.

But where has little Luc gone? The dreamy child who needed his meat chopped up for him?

It must have happened shortly after John F. Kennedy's assassination. Luc, then nine, was playing with a Caron cousin, a boy a little younger than himself. Still in the imaginative world they had created for themselves, no one else was allowed into their childish games. Papa Louis had strictly forbidden them from running around the caskets in the basement and from getting too close to the room where he embalmed the bodies. Fear of Luc's father had kept them away, but curiosity had drawn them back. And that's how, during a game of hide-and-seek, Luc had slipped inside a huge oak casket. He'd had a hard time opening it, but it had closed over him in no time at all. The cousin counted to one hundred upstairs. Marc was looking on, having been vaguely told to keep an eye on the boys that afternoon. Papa Louis had business in town; Irene was out running errands. The cousin began to look for Luc in the upstairs bedrooms, a decision that, many would later say, played a part in the tragedy. Not finding him upstairs, he made his way down to the basement. Nothing. Alarmed, the cousin reported Luc's disappearance to Marc, who helped him look everywhere a second time. It was only when Madeleine came back from Solange's house that light was shed—literally—on the mystery. Generally more observant than her brothers, Madeleine had long since noticed the youngest child's interest in what went on in the basement and, paying no heed to Papa Louis' warning, Madeleine, with Marc's help, opened the lids of the four caskets that took up half the basement. She found young Luc suffocated in the smallest casket of all, his skin blue, his face scratched. He had ripped his hair out. It was this detail that would haunt Madeleine in her dreams. In the room beside them, a dead body was waiting for Papa Louis to return so that his wake could begin. Madeleine's first reflex was to go get Solange, who could do nothing more than call for help. Soon the shouts of the cousin, traumatized for life, began to alert the neighbours on Rue Saint-François-Xavier, then the rest of the parish. News of Luc's accidental death flowed across Rivière-du-Loup like lava spreading from above the church of Saint-François-Xavier, running down Côte Saint-Pierre and Rue Lafontaine and passing by the convent, emptying it of its nuns within seconds. The news spread from house to house, making its way in through upstairs windows and out through basement window wells. No one was spared, not even Louis as he sipped his gin at the Château Grandville, not even Irene as she tried to decide between two ties at Ernest & Paul. The further the news made its way down the hill, the more it got distorted. Still in its purest form when it reached the convent ("Little Luc Lamontagne has been found suffocated to death inside a casket"), by the time it was halfway down the hill it had become "Marc Lamontagne shut his little brother Luc inside a casket and he died, suffocated to death." And when it reached the bottom, the news had been completely distorted. Now barely recognizable, it travelled all the more quickly. Now it was "Marc Lamontagne strangled his little brother Luc with his bare hands and tried to hide the body in a casket" and "Marc Lamontagne is coming down Rue Lafontaine armed with an axe—hide your children!" The news finally spilled into the waters of the St. Lawrence, a stretch of the river that forever after would retain a greenish hue, the colour of slander.

Irene arrived on the scene a little before Louis. People still maintain to this day that she raced into the house with a full head of red hair and came back out completely white, like Marie Antoinette on the scaffold. Papa Louis had to push his way through the crowd that had gathered outside his house. A handful of the Sisters of the Child Jesus were praying out loud, hands in the air, as though warding off ill fortune. Outside on her porch, Mrs. Bérubé was staring at the ground.

"A defenceless child," she sighed.

Little Luc was buried in the casket that killed him. His wake lasted only a few hours, the time it took for half the town to file through Papa Louis' parlour. The religious service, sung by Father Rossignol, who sobbed and spluttered his way through it, stayed with those fortunate enough to attend, not only due to the horror and gravity of the event, but also because they were witnessing on that cursed Sunday the beginning of Louis "The Horse" Lamontagne's decline. The organist, thinking he was doing the right thing, decided to play a solemn, serious piece at the beginning of the funeral service. The Lamontagnes, sitting in the front row and looking the worse for wear, didn't pay the music the slightest bit of attention, except when Papa Louis stood up, strode from one end of the church to the other, walked up to the jube, and interrupted the musician.

"I want you to play *Jesu, Joy of Man's Desiring*."

The organist, a small, spindly man, as dogmatic as he was effeminate, sat dumbfounded for an instant.

"I... no. It's not appropriate. It's not for funerals, Mr. Lamontagne."

The congregation craned their necks toward the jube. Louis' voice rang out, sounding unmistakably like he had more than a few drinks in him.

"Play Bach, I'm tellin' ya!"

The organist stood, and in a scholarly, didactic tone committed the worst mistake of his existence.

"I know you're upset, Mr. Lamontagne, but that piece you're so fond of is simply not played at funerals. It's for Christmas or Easter, not for funerals."

Everyone held their breath. Was Louis on the verge of taking a man's life at the very place where his own had begun? His huge frame swayed back and forth, his arm slowly took the impertinent fellow by the throat, and the shouts—

"You little bespectacled apostle. You're gonna play what I want or God help me..."

Mother Mary of the Great Power, who had immediately foreseen Louis' intentions, raced up to the organist to prevent the worst. By the time her hand came down on Louis' arm, the poor man's feet had already been thrashing in the air for interminable seconds.

"Louis, for the love of God," she murmured.

The giant's hand opened and the organist fell to the ground like a sack of corn. Down below, people sighed with relief. Louis went back to his seat only when he realized that Mother Mary of the Great Power was going to play *Jesu, Joy of Man's Desiring* herself. He sat back down beside Irene, who was paralyzed by grief and hadn't even noticed the commotion. Madeleine was sobbing noisily, accompanied by Marc. The cousin just sat there, stunned. His eyes never left the casket. Truth be told, he was desperately hoping this game of hide-and-seek would be over very soon. It had gone on long enough. As the congregation looked on in horror, he stood up, walked over to the casket that was much too big for a child, and knocked on it three times. There's no way of knowing just how many people in the church hoped or thought they might see a repeat of Old Ma Madeleine's miraculous resurrection in 1933. But this particular casket remained unmoved. It was Marc who got up to lead his cousin back by the hand, his eyes lost in a far-off world. The music of Bach cast the scene in an unreal light that was both unlikely and magnificent.

Little Luc's death was treated as a tragedy that had befallen the entire community. For the longest time, the Lamontagnes had been the butt of gossip and idle speculation, although they were also admired by their peers. Now they were martyrs, bejewelled with the permanence of tragedy. When mass ended, the casket was carried out by the drama's survivors: Louis, Marc, and Madeleine on one side; Irene, Solange, and Siegfried Zucker on the other (Zucker had happened to be in Rivière-du-Loup on the day Luc died.). Their gaze was steady and proud, bordering on presumptuousness, betraying no sign of any effort whatsoever, as they carried the casket out of the church, slow and steady, just like Papa Louis had showed them, like American G.I.s. We are devastated, but we are strong. That was the message the funeral march conveyed to the music of Bach. "Joy of man's desiring." That's what the Sisters of the Child Jesus muttered to themselves under their breath. All had insisted on attending Luc's funeral, even Sister Saint Alphonse, who was spotted shedding a tear or two as the casket passed by. Outside, fine early-winter snow twirled its way through the air, as though to cover the ground in a white blanket evoking the purity of the soul God had called back. That, at least, is what Father Rossignol maintained once the family had gathered around the grave. One week after the funeral, when the poor boy's body had scarcely begun to decay in the casket that was too big for it, the very same Father Rossignol paid the Lamontagne family a visit. He insisted on speaking alone with Papa Louis and Irene, then alone with Irene. His intentions were clear, and he didn't back down at Irene's incredulous expression. She would have to have another child.

"But, Father. I've just buried one. I mean, how can I put this…?"

"All the more reason to proceed as quickly as possible. Your family is on the decline. Time to restock!"

"I'm thirty-five, Father."

"All the more reason to be quick about it, Irene. Plenty of women give birth at your age. Only yesterday we baptized Louisa Desjardins' eighth child. And she's the same age as you."

"Yes, but I have two already and—"

"Mrs. Lamontagne," the parish priest interrupted curtly. "You aren't standing in the way of the family, are you? Has the television filled your head with such notions? All I can do is express my joy at the prospect of baptizing another Lamontagne next summer, or perhaps he's already on his way? Little Luc was nine years old, after all… I do wonder what you're waiting for. Think of the consequences."

Irene fell silent. The priest left the living room and bade goodbye to Louis one last time, who was busy nursing a gin toddy in the kitchen. Irene no more felt like bringing another child into the world than she did drinking a bottle of bleach. Without a word to her husband, she helped him finish off what remained of the gin. That's what they'd done best together for the past few months: hit the gin. Papa Louis lit a cigarette and smoked in silence.

Three months later, when Irene's belly remained obstinately flat, Father Rossignol made good with his threats. In front of a packed church, he refused Irene communion. She didn't understand and tried to take the host, thinking it must be some kind of joke as the priest pushed her back. Irene returned to her seat, overcome with shame. A murmur ran up from the nave to the jube and back. The Sunday sermon dwelt on the dangers that new media posed to right-thinking French Canadian families. Irene was dumfounded. Humiliation slowly worked its way through the rock of her piety like a powerful solvent, leaving behind scars, opening cracks in places once presumed impenetrable. The silence was the final touch to the destruction started by Father Rossignol: Irene could now imagine Sundays without communion. Would she die of hunger? Would she perish, struck by lightning or crushed by a falling block of ice? For the first time, she was tempted to find the answer to such questions. What would be would be. Shame dogged her; people turned their backs on her for months. At last they knew: *she* was the end of the world. Priests have a knack for making things clear.

And so there was no little Luc in the photograph of June 1968. Five years after he left this world, he still seemed to be everywhere: in the wrinkles that lined Irene's face, in Papa Louis' white whiskers, in his brother Marc's stunned gaze, and on his sister Madeleine's tormented forehead.

Madeleine had just turned eighteen. She and Solange had left the convent two years earlier and were now learning to cook at the local trade school. They dreamed of opening a restaurant together. All of Solange's brothers and her sister had left home. She lived alone with her mother and could indulge in extravagances like the motorcycle she liked to rev through the streets of Rivière-du-Loup, around the Point, and along the country roads of the Lower St. Lawrence. When she wore her helmet, they called her Atom Ant, a nickname that filled her with pride. Her mother managed to get her to agree not to cut her long black hair. But apart from that, Solange walked like Louis Lamontagne, talked like Louis Lamontagne, and sped like a V2 rocket through peaceful villages where her diabolical vehicle—a canary-yellow Triumph Bonneville T120R—spread terror. All that was missing was an eagle on her back. A sometime passenger on those crazy bike rides, Madeleine Lamontagne was especially fond of driving along the river to Kamouraska.

There was practically no telling what Solange and Madeleine made of life or the feelings that bound them. In Rivière-du-Loup, Solange and Madeleine were both considered to be nuns in the making. The former had the awkward gait, while the latter had the devotion, or so the gossips said. And so they were expected to be walking through the convent's doors from one moment to the next. Their barely concealed fascination for Sister Smiley was, rumour had it, irrefutable proof of this, even after the nun in question left the Dominican Order and gave herself over to unnatural passions.

As far as people knew, there were no suitors or admirers after Madeleine, who would still do her hair in braids from time to time.

"It makes things easier when I'm cooking," she'd explain with a smile.

Irene tried in vain to introduce Madeleine to handsome young men. But the few candidates who managed to overcome their fear of The Horse then came up against Solange, a daunting obstacle standing between them and Madeleine who, for the time being, seemed to have no interest in matters of the heart anyway.

The biological clocks were about to be reset in June 1968.

"She's got plenty of time ahead of her," said Louis, who'd developed a philosophical bent after the death of little Luc. So much so that he hadn't lifted a hand to a soul since the incident with the organist. Louis was going soft. Nobody was going to complain, least of all Irene, and it turned out to be in the interests of the taverns along Rue Lafontaine. The old man would buy a drink for whoever would listen. To drink on the cheap, all you had to do was turn up at the Ophir in the afternoon, once The Horse was a little the worse for wear, say hello, exchange a few words with him and make like you were interested in listening to him. He would pay for the round in exchange for a pair of ears. Sometimes, after his gin, The Horse would fall asleep, often halfway through a story, snoring away in the middle of the tavern while the other drinkers looked on in amusement and understanding.

With Papa Louis no longer around, Solange had charged herself with keeping an eye on Madeleine. As it happens, she was waiting for the Lamontagnes when they emerged from the photographer's. It is also hard to tell what the Lamontagne family really thought of Solange. Marc found her horribly masculine and wasn't afraid to say so in that slight lisp of his. He feared, envied, and hated the virago, in equal measures. He was frightened of her the way people are frightened of rivals they know to be stronger than they are, he envied her motorbike, and he hated the hold she had over his sister Madeleine. Irene considered Solange to be a very nice tomboy who was careful with her money. Solange's ability to combine motorcycling with that pious lifestyle of hers amused her no end.

"A nun on a motorbike! We've seen it all now!"

As for Madeleine's feelings for Solange back then, no one will ever know. But what everyone did know—she made no secret of it—was how upset she was to see Louis' decline.

The Lamontagnes walked home from the photographer's, escorted by Solange. When they reached the church of Saint-François-Xavier, they were pleased to see the first lilacs in bloom. Their delicate scent wafted across the parish. They stopped for a moment to gaze at the river, its almost unreal shade of green. To their left stood the former Sisters of the Child Jesus convent; the nuns now lived in the huge provincial house that had been consecrated in 1961, a building enormous enough to get lost in. Atop the natural headland, on that balmy spring day in 1968, Solange and the Lamontagnes were about to become front-row witnesses to the event that would remain forever etched in the entire town's memory, the event that would seal their fate.

It started with an imperceptible stirring beneath a few tiny waves that washed up against the Point. On its way across the bay, the quiver barely wrinkled the water. Now it had become audible from the shore, a word, then two, then at last a few sentences. "He took the road up from Quebec City, he's here for the way of the cross." The sentence, now a rumour, had gone the wrong way along the route usually taken by gossip in Rivière-du-Loup: it had gone up the hill rather than down it. Soon it was hammering away at the doors and windows of the sad little shanties along Rue Saint-Marc, waking the idle from their naps.

"He's a painter *and* a priest, can you believe it?"

But the poor had no use for the news, which would gain more traction in the well-to-do neighbourhoods of the upper town; they didn't know how to keep hold of it and, like money, it slipped through their bony fingers. And now it was on its way up Rue Lafontaine. It was too late, a thousand times too late. The news was now audible, almost noisy, around the twenty-decibel mark. The priest walked past Moisan the florist's without stopping, and he didn't stop when he got to the church of Saint-Patrice either. It was clear he was on his way up in the world. He had ambition: the country parishes were of no interest to him. And so he climbed, slowly, pulling a suitcase full of paintbrushes along behind him, a small gold cross on his tweed lapel. He was impeccably dressed—that's the first thing Papa Louis noticed about him. Even his dog collar looked more fashionable than the ones worn by the colleagues who had funded his stay in Rivière-du-Loup. A burning question: how much would the priest-cum-painter be costing the people of the parish of Saint-François-Xavier? In dollars, the amount was barely enough to raise an eyebrow, nothing to get worked up about, but enough to appeal to the generosity of the town's businessfolk. Papa Louis was one of the contributors to the new stations of the cross. An extravagance shouted from every shingled rooftop in town that would bring him, or so he hoped, a few more bodies to help get him back on his feet again. Competition was fierce by 1968, and the people of Rivière-du-Loup were increasingly putting off crossing the great divide, starving the Lamontagnes of customers in the process. Business was tough, but by helping to fund the new stations of the cross Louis hoped to kill two birds with one stone. He made sure his name stayed in the hearts of Father Rossignol's flock, all while teaching his daughter Madeleine a lesson that would serve her well for the rest of her days, and that would become, in a way, her motto: ambition always goes further when disguised as virtue. One day, Papa Louis had, without her knowing why, spoken to his daughter about money.

"Money's no good to you in the bank, in a safe, or under a mattress. Money needs to be in circulation, needs to help people do things. You can't just stand by if your brother's thirsty. Your glass is full? You give him half. You have a slice of pie left? You cut it in two. Do you see, Madeleine? Mom doesn't think like that because they were poor when she was growing up. But poverty begins in the mind. You're not poor."

Madeleine hadn't understood much of his sales patter, only that her father had funded part of the parish's stations of the cross and that that was a good thing. Misfortune had fallen upon Papa Louis' business slowly, like cancer eating away at the elderly. Louis' funeral parlour might still have been one of the most popular places in town at the end of the 1950s, but by 1968 it was frequented only by the odd drunk who'd drowned in his gin. Only Madeleine had made the connection between the drop in her father's clientele and a few key events.

No one had ever asked her, but at age eighteen Madeleine would have been perfectly able to explain the decline of her father's business. The way she told it, Old Ma Madeleine's departure in 1960 had marked the beginning of the end. Indeed the number of customers had declined shortly thereafter, despite a significant overhaul of the pricing structure. The reassuring presence of a dead woman in Louis' parlour had appealed to a clientele that was frightened by what lay beyond the grave. A certain change in Papa Louis' behaviour added to this loss. The Horse wasn't what he had once been. There was no doubt that had the archbishop seen him in 1965, greying and potbellied, he wouldn't have bothered having his photograph taken with him and would have turned elsewhere for masturbatory inspiration. His fading physique was not without consequence for customers of the female persuasion either, who began to look elsewhere for the hands that would touch them once they were dead. Little Luc's accidental death didn't help matters. No one wanted to wind up, even dead, in a room where such a terrible drama had unfolded. "Negligence" was a word that was still on too many lips.

All of which meant that in 1968 Papa Louis was lucky if he buried one body a month. The family's savings dwindled. Irene had to go back to cleaning at the Saint-Louis Hotel, and the aura of success and glory that had always clung to The Horse gave way to the slightly nauseating smell of alcohol. Madeleine had learned an important lesson from the family's fall, however: customers need to be well looked after, alive or dead.

It is of absolutely no interest to speculate how much that damned stations of the cross cost in Canadian dollars or francs or sesterces, for that matter. After leaving Rivière-du-Loup, the priest-cum-painter left behind a liability for which Madeleine Lamontagne, in spite of all she would eventually amass through sheer grit and determination, would never manage to pay back more than one-hundredth of the principal.

And there's little point dwelling on the actual cost of his visit on Madeleine's parents, brothers, and, consequently, on all those whose world revolved around Louis Lamontagne, which is to say the Sisters of the Child Jesus, Old Ma Madeleine, Solange Bérubé, and all the other women—and men, it must be said—who had one day found themselves pining for handsome Louis' teal-coloured eyes. Women would stop in their tracks when he walked past. No, not Louis: the priest-cum-painter. They would stop the way Saint Bernadette Soubirous stopped before the Virgin. The rumour continued to gush from both sides of Rue Lafontaine, leaping up the falls like a salmon, oozing across smoke-filled kitchen walls, weaving its way around restaurants, businesses, and kitchens until it reached Saint-Ludger. News of his arrival swept across town like smallpox through the New World in the sixteenth century. No man and—especially—no woman was immune.

There was no hiding from it, no means of protecting oneself. He turned right onto Saint-Elzéar. He could now be seen making his way up to the church of Saint-François-Xavier. Someone should have taken a photograph of the Lamontagnes at that very moment. It could have been filed away between the photo of Hiroshima in late July 1945 and Christmas 1944 in Dresden—or of any other place whose destruction is imminent.

"He's not all that handsome."

That's the first thing Louis thought to himself when he got close enough to have a good look.

The stranger approached. Within four seconds it would be too late. His gaze would meet Marc's brown eyes, fall on Madeleine's teal-coloured ones, and stare right into Louis'.

"Hello. I'm Father Lecavalier. I've just arrived from Quebec City."

It was now too late.

He offered his hand to Marc first, then, after a lingering look into the teenager's eyes, to his father Louis and to the rest of the family. Solange shook his hand. She recoiled at the touch of his damp skin. He had broken into a sweat climbing the hill. She pursed her lips as though she'd just bitten into a lemon.

"Are you the painter?" Madeleine inquired, her voice trembling slightly.

"Yes, I'm the painting priest! Brother Marie-Victorin was a botanist; I'm a painter."

"And I'm an undertaker," Louis boomed, to lighten the mood, pretending to measure the handsome priest's arm. Father Lecavalier lost his regal bearing for a moment.

They spoke for two or three minutes before Lecavalier disappeared into the church, where Father Rossignol, the parish priest, was waiting for him. Father Lecavalier's arrival had interrupted a discussion, but no one seemed to remember what they'd been talking about.

The news had not spared the provincial house of the Sisters of the Child Jesus.

"He's here! It's him!"

Sister Mary of the Eucharist hammered on Old Ma Madeleine's door with her bony little fists.

"Did you see him?"

"No, but everyone's talking about him. We have to go!"

"I'm coming."

Sister Mary of the Eucharist silently cursed the day the order had moved into the provincial house. The huge building had its charms, and the view of the river from the garden and the upper floors was enough to bring tears to the eyes, but now the church was, from her point of view, an unreasonably long walk away. They reached the church at the same time as Madeleine, Louis, and Solange, all intrigued by the priest who had appeared unannounced. They weren't the only ones. A few women—a young widow among them—were wandering around outside the church as though they'd lost something. The Lamontagnes, at the sight of Old Ma Madeleine and Sister Mary of the Eucharist arriving with such a spring in their step, wondered what they'd eaten that morning to have so much energy.

"Where is he?" Old Madeleine asked, panting for air.

Marc pointed to the church. Caught up in the old ladies' excitement, they all went inside. In the church, Father Rossignol could no longer contain his joy. On a huge easel, a vast blank canvas awaited the painter alongside a statue of the Blessed Mary.

The parish priest explained, in an eager, trembling voice, that Father Lecavalier was just back from France, where he'd been studying art. Since his return, he'd been painting frescoes, portraits of clergymen, and in particular the stations of the cross all over Canada. While the priest spoke, Father Lecavalier had lost interest in every one of them and was now staring at his canvas, awaiting divine inspiration.

He would occasionally interrupt the priest to correct some detail about his travels, or to sing the praises of France and all that was to be found there.

"You should see everything the Germans stole, those animals!" he said.

"The Germans paid for all that there," Papa Louis tried to reassure him.

"Paid for it? And what might you know about it? They'll never repay their debts, never! Might I remind you it's our motherland they attacked. And don't say 'that there,' it's bad grammar," the priest retorted. "In France, people still have respect for grammar, even if they've lost some of their respect for the Church!"

"Are you French, Father?" asked Solange.

"No, why do you ask, miss?" the priest answered, gruffly.

"I don't know. You speak like a Frenchman."

"It is my way of paying tribute to our beautiful, proud language!" came Lecavalier's reply.

He went back to his blank canvas.

A somewhat embarrassed Father Rossignol explained that Father Lecavalier would probably be needing a few volunteers to sit as models for his stations of the cross.

"Perhaps your children would like to help, Louis."

Louis swallowed. Why his children? Why not ask him? Father Lecavalier took advantage of the silence to rejoin the conversation.

"I think your son Marc would make a perfect Simon of Cyrene. Show me your arm, young man."

The priest squeezed Marc's arm like you'd squeeze a pineapple to test how ripe it is.

"Yes, I think I could very well be in need of you, Marc... And you, miss. It's Madeleine, isn't it?"

"Errr… yes. I…"

Solange exhaled noisily. The priest went on.

"Would you be prepared to pose as Mary Magdalene for me? I love your eyes. What colour is that… turquoise?"

"Teal," Louis corrected him. "Your vocabulary appears to be lacking, Father."

Papa Louis' quip was met with an uncomfortable silence, except of course from Solange, who broke into virile, hearty laughter.

It was agreed that Marc and Madeleine would drop by the church over the coming days. On the way home, the Lamontagnes and Solange remained pensive, each for reasons of their own. Father Lecavalier had stirred entirely different feelings in each of them, ranging from utter contempt to romantic curiosity. No prizes for guessing which end of the spectrum Solange belonged to. She took her leave of the Lamontagne family without a word and returned home. She slammed the door on her way out, livid and brandishing the key to her Triumph, which she revved loudly all the way to Cacouna.

"I don't like it when she goes out without a helmet," Madeleine sighed.

The nuns, meanwhile, had lingered behind at the church, not to serve as models for the women of Jerusalem, but because the arrival of the new priest, a painter into the bargain, had left them intrigued. Sure, they'd been told that the fundraising campaign would result in a new way of the cross, but they'd paid little attention to what they considered to be nothing but a waste of money. Father Rossignol, though, hoped that by giving the church an original way of the cross—something as yet unseen in the diocese—he might stem the flood of departing parishioners. (Nothing alarming, mind you, but some were in need of a little persuasion.)

Then Sister Mary of the Eucharist did something that surprised Old Ma Madeleine.

"Have you had a chance to visit our provincial house, Father?" she asked.

"No, I arrived from Quebec City this very afternoon. I have seen nothing of the town as yet. Looking at it from below, I figured it wouldn't take long to see everything there is to see. This provincial house, it's the long yellow-bricked building not too far from here?"

"I think it's actually more cream in colour, but yes, that's the one. Listen, Father. The nuns would be delighted to have you over for supper tomorrow night, provided our dear parish priest doesn't mind us stealing you away for the evening, of course. Will you take us up on our invitation?"

Old Ma Madeleine found the nun more than a little bold. Lecavalier smiled. What did this frightful nun want from him? Supper with the nuns when he had so much work to do? The very idea of sitting down for supper surrounded by dozens of silent nuns ogling him out of the corner of their eye was about as appealing to him as the prospect of jumping on a hornets' nest, but curiosity got the better of him. He wondered how a nun ugly enough to turn cow's milk had ever plucked up the courage to invite him over. Not wanting to upset the locals, Lecavalier agreed. The two old women walked back alone to the provincial house.

"He really is handsome, Sister Mary of the Eucharist. Do you think it's him?"

"I'm really not sure, Madeleine. I still need a closer look at him. I couldn't make out a thing in that half-light. My eyesight isn't what it used to be, you know."

"Mother Superior will be furious when she finds out you invited him without speaking to her first! How are you planning to get around her?"

"Mother Superior will be delighted. Take my word for it."

"Give her some warning, at least! And how about a cake for our handsome young man?"

"Yes! With pineapple slices and maraschino cherries."

"You do realize that's a capital sin…"

The nun's laughter turned a peony red.

Over at the Lamontagne household, it was gin that was the order of the day, not tropical fruit. Each on their own, this time around. Papa Louis had changed out of his Sunday best and strolled down to his favourite bar, the Ophir. Irene was lying low in her kitchen, sipping on a sad tonic. And even Marc drank on his own, knocking back glass after glass of water. This was something that had escaped the attention of his mother and father, who only years earlier had been perfectly normal parents. As normal as a couple of undertakers could be. But Marc had grown up in their blind spot, preoccupied as they were by little Luc, who had needed so much care, only to be snatched away in such an unfortunate mishap, and by Madeleine, who carried on with her confessions and novenas as though the end of the world was always nigh. Handsome young Marc had grown up discreetly, his path as twisted as a larch. He preferred silence to his dad's patter, and in fact all he took after his father was a passion for bodybuilding: he envisaged a future for himself as a strongman travelling across America, even though he was well aware that strongmen had fallen out of fashion. A wrestler, perhaps. Or a hero of one of those sports that involved flattening someone on their back. In the meantime, he practiced on his sister.

He would wait until the house was empty, then slip like a cat into Madeleine's room, where Madeleine would often be sitting at her desk, busily reading a cookbook or combing her hair in front of the mirror. She always sensed him coming and would fend off the attacks as Solange had shown her how. But Marc was stronger. However much she might threaten to tell Solange—who terrified him—or, worse, tell fat Lise Thibodeau that he was head over heels in love with her, there was nothing doing.

It was round about that time that Marc's strange symptoms first appeared. Although in fine fettle, for weeks he'd been exhausted in the evenings. His father put it down to a growth spurt and the revelation of an entirely new set of sensations. The bouts of fatigue were always accompanied by a great thirst, which he'd try to quench by knocking back pint after pint of water. Polydipsia? No. Instead, Irene blamed the salty snacks the children so enjoyed.

"Sleep if you're tired."

And so Marc slept, to the great delight of his sister, who would then be left alone for a while. She'd never breathed a word to anyone about Marc's visits to her bedroom, perhaps because at first she'd confused them with their childhood games. Madeleine and Marc had grown up without ever being aware of their differences in age and sex. They were also somewhat cut off from the other children in the parish, due to both the fear and the admiration people had for the strongman. In short, few children, as Solange could tell you, were allowed or inclined to get close to the Lamontagne clan, which meant that Madeleine and Marc, as they napped together when they were eleven and twelve, felt not as though they were upsetting the divine order of things but rather that they were simply satisfying their need for sleep. Madeleine and Marc were close, to the great displeasure of Solange Bérubé, who saw nothing but a pale imitation of his father in the boy. He didn't even have his teal-coloured eyes; Marc had inherited Irene's big brown eyes, deep as shadows. Madeleine was the only one to feel something approaching empathy for the boy when he was overcome by bouts of fatigue and unquenchable thirst. She would carry up pitchers of water to his bedroom, keep watch over him while he dozed, and read while waiting for him to wake up. Marc would take advantage of those drowsy moments to let his hands wander.

"Stop it!"

"Why?"

"We're not married!"

"Do you want to get married?"

"Idiot!"

And so, Madeleine looked after her little brother, put his strange behaviour down to his unknown illness, and continued to pray for him. It was sometime in September or October that Irene began to take an interest in the classified ads in the newspaper, this one in particular:

FAMILY TROUBLES

LADIES, want to improve your family's lot? Consult a family therapist. Write with details of your family problems or worries. Please provide age, no. of children, if you work outside the home, years married, husband's age. CONFIDENTIAL advice. Whatever your worries

Consult us in complete confidence
P.O. Box 400 – Delorimier Mtl 34 Quebec

NAME_____

ADDRESS _____

TEL _____

The day after Father Lecavalier came to Rivière-du-Loup, the Sisters of the Child Jesus made an upside-down pineapple cake as per Old Ma Madeleine's wishes. Mother Superior, who had always harboured dreams of being immortalized in paint, congratulated Sister Mary of the Eucharist for taking the initiative and inviting the priest-cum-painter to the school. Now she prayed to God that the man would be inspired by her wise features. She had even put on a little powder. The guest arrived with Germanic punctuality at six o'clock on the dot. The only man amid dozens of nuns in the provincial house's huge dining room, he was for two hours the subject of thousands of unspeakable thoughts. Barely audible murmurs were exchanged between the nuns.

"His neck is a little long..."

"... but what beautiful big brown eyes he has."

"He still has his puppy fat..."

"... and the lips of a cherub."

"But our vows are everlasting…"

"Pfff, pass the salt, would you?"

And so Father Lecavalier's supper with the nuns unfolded in an altogether Edenic atmosphere. Ensconced between Mother Mary of the Great Power and Sister Mary of the Eucharist, just across from Sister Saint Alphonse and Old Ma Madeleine, the priest's gaze swung back and forth between *The Entombment of Mary* on the wall and Old Ma Madeleine's silent face. The old woman, he had noticed, was not dressed as a nun, not like the others.

"May I ask why you are dressed like that, Sister?" he inquired, his voice laden with respect.

A few giggles broke out.

"So as not to be buck naked!" Sister Saint Alphonse quipped, mischievous as ever, from her seat not far from the group. The entire convent was swept up in divine laughter, virgin and crystal clear. Father Lecavalier smiled inanely.

"Old Ma Madeleine is Louis Lamontagne's grandmother. You met him yesterday. She came here to get away from the television. In return, she helps with the laundry," Mother Superior explained to the young priest, visibly amused by his question.

"From the television?"

"Yes. She can't bear the hiss it makes."

Old Ma Madeleine clapped her hands over her ears and pulled a face by way of illustration for Lecavalier.

"Why, you have tinnitus, that's all."

The nuns smiled tenderly. The priest went on.

"So you're Mr. Lamontagne's grandmother?" he asked incredulously.

"Yes. I already died once. Now I'm waiting for the Good Lord to finish the job," Old Ma Madeleine replied as serious as could be, just as soon as she'd finished gnawing on a piece of chicken.

The priest, visibly embarrassed, tried to change the subject.

"Wherever did you get that painting on the wall?" he asked Mother Mary of the Great Power.

"*The Entombment of Mary*? It's a little souvenir our Louis brought his grandmother back from Germany, I believe. He never did tell us where he got it. We decided to hang it in the dining room. It's amusing, isn't it? The painter must have been a real beginner. No sense of perspective and just look at those frightful washed-out colours! And the drawing! A ten-year-old could do better!"

While the Mother Superior spoke, the priest, no doubt short-sighted, stood up, without asking to leave the table and without finishing his peas, to take a closer look at the painting. His hands behind his back, his neck craned, he peered as though studying a train timetable.

"From Germany, you say, Mother?"

"Yes, Germany. Although we really don't know. Louis says so little about the war. He used to say more. He gets so sad every time we mention it."

The rest of the meal was more relaxed, now that the nuns had had their laugh. Lecavalier was questioned about his plans for the stations of the cross. He twice helped himself to seconds of the upside-down pineapple cake, making sure he got a maraschino cherry each time, an act of gluttony that was not lost on the nuns, who, during the three months the priest stayed at the presbytery, sent him two loaves of raisin bread, three pounds of sugar fudge, two pies made from freshly picked blueberries, four jars of wild raspberry jam, and a lemon tart. Siegfried Zucker, their faithful supplier, had managed to get his hands on lemons even though they weren't in season, and all at an unbeatable price. It was their way of titillating the little cherub's senses without comprising their commitment to the Almighty.

Talk then turned to Paris, the fine arts, and—inevitably—the Eiffel Tower. It was to Rome that he most hoped to go one day, Father Lecavalier confided in the nuns. As a painter or a priest, he didn't care, but the Eternal City beckoned, a logical end to his existence.

"I know the Lord has bigger plans for me than these villages hiding away at the end of the world," he concluded.

Once he had gone, Old Ma Madeleine anxiously rushed over to Sister Mary of the Eucharist, who was making her way to her room in slow, resigned fashion.

"So is he our handsome young man?"

"No, Sister. You can sleep easy."

"But how can you tell?"

"He's as blind as a bat, just like me. He won't do. We need someone stronger, more... how shall I put it? At any rate, I bid thee good night, Madeleine. I'm tired. Time to rest. Pray to the Blessed Virgin. Keep praying to the Blessed Virgin."

The doors to the nuns' cells clanged shut one by one with the dismal metallic sound made by the bars of Alcatraz imprisoning their captives.

When Father Rossignol got wind of Father Lecavalier's thoughts of Rome, he offloaded a stream of dreary apostolic work on his guest, notably Wednesday confessions. To his great surprise, Lecavalier was only too pleased to take him up on his offer and, one Wednesday in late June, he sat down in an empty confessional and waited for the sinners of summer. They weren't long in coming: Father Rossignol had been kind enough to let his parishioners know about the change in personnel. The new confessor got his money's worth. Before he'd come to the parish, only a dozen old women with nothing better to do found the time to warm the seats of the church's confessionals, but when people found out that Lecavalier was taking over from old Father Rossignol, the sacrament of pardon quickly fell back in favour. There were new sinners among the men it is true, but most of all there were women, old and young, who had sinned and began making a beeline for the church of Saint-François-Xavier on Wednesday afternoons. Lecavalier quickly came to regret accepting the invitation. But Rossignol had assured him that no archbishop would ever consider recommending a priest to Rome unless he had experience. If the road to Hell was paved with good intentions, Lecavalier thought to himself, the road to Rome was clearly strewn with depravity and loose morals. The anonymous voices of middle-aged women whispered their failings to him: lies, ill will, slander, jealousy of every shape and size.

"Lord, I confess to raising a hand to my daughter."

The admissions of the younger folk ventured onto the tumultuous seas of sins of the flesh: impure thoughts, unwanted advances, adultery, orgasms of all kinds.

"My God, her breasts hung like over-ripe fruit."

Halfhearted acts of contrition that seemed to Lecavalier to come more from the lips than the heart. Which is how in two weeks he learned more about the women of Rivière-du-Loup (and women in general) than decency would have allowed him to hope, since Catholic confessions only count when the precise part of the body that sinned is specified. How exactly did the voluptuous pleasure arise? A priest who gave up the cloth would know more than enough to get by with a woman.

"He took me, Father, while I was cleaning the oven."

They cheated on their husbands. And two words were on everyone's lips: The Horse. Teal-coloured eyes multiplied across the parish. They could only mean one thing: that drunkard of a muscleman Lecavalier had met when he arrived, the father of that wonderful young man and that strange girl, Madeleine. (The girl had in fact been first in line on the first Wednesday Father Lecavalier took confession.) But what could these poor women possibly see in the brute? That's the question the young priest asked himself as he listened to the sometimes embarrassing descriptions of the risqué dreams in which Louis Lamontagne featured so often. In the darkness of the confessional, Lecavalier pinched his nose and prayed that the Lord would send him to Rome as soon as possible. And he complained to Father Rossignol that there were ten women for every man who came to confession.

"Are your men all saints?"

Rossignol had smiled.

"No, but the women take you to be an angel, my poor Lecavalier."

The stations of the cross began to take shape. With his "Jesus falls for the first time," he had completed his third painting by July 10. Lecavalier worked from dawn till dusk and insisted on painting inside the church, where the light was best, he said. It was best, he maintained, to create the work where it would be displayed, to avoid any surprises caused by a change in light. And so at every mass there stood an easel covered by a dirty sheet. As soon as they'd finished celebrating the eucharist, Father Lecavalier would pick up where he had left off, stopping only to eat, sleep, and hear confession.

In mid-July he began painting the station depicting Simon of Cyrene helping Jesus carry the cross.

"Did you know, Marc, that the real Simon of Cyrene was black? He came from Libya."

"I didn't, Father. Should I take off my pants too?"

"Yes, and cover yourself up with this sheet the nuns gave me. Wait a moment: I'll make a tunic out of it, don't move."

"Just as well it's summer! I'd be cold in winter."

"Here you are. Now hold the beam like this, in your left hand. Act as though you're walking behind Jesus… Exactly. It's not too heavy? You seem strong enough."

"I used to lift weights with Papa Louis sometimes, but not anymore."

"What? Louis Lamontagne has abandoned his weights?"

"More or less. He spends more time at the Ophir."

"The Ophir?"

"It's a bar on Rue Lafontaine. His friends go there."

"And how come you've given up bodybuilding?"

"I'm usually too tired to work out. Sometimes the neighbour's girl comes over to lift weights."

"The one with the motorbike?"

"Yes. She often comes round."

"She's a little like a sister to you, the Solange girl."

"To Madeleine, yes. But to me, she's just our neighbour."

"Turn your head a little to the side… There we go. Can you hold that for at least ten minutes? Time enough for me to make a sketch of the scene."

"No problem, Father."

"So you're not crazy about Solange."

"No, I'm not crazy about Solange."

"It's true she's a bit of a tomboy."

"What do you mean a tomboy, Father?"

"Well, like a boy. Like you."

"And like you?"

"Well, yes. But you're not too hard on her?"

"She's the one who's hard on me. She won't stop poking her nose into my business."

"What business would that be?"

"She never leaves me alone with Madeleine. Or hardly ever. The only chance I get to see my sister alone is at supper or in the mornings."

"But why do you need to see your sister alone? Are you to Madeleine what Hamlet was to Ophelia?"

"Who's Ophelia?"

"Never mind. Why are you so keen to spend time with your sister?"

"To play, of course!"

"To play?"

"To play at laughing!"

"What do you mean, play at laughing?"

"Like before, like when we were with Luc."

"Can you keep your head straight, Marc? Yes, like that. With Luc, you were saying?"

"With Luc gone, Madeleine doesn't want us to play like we used to."

"Once we've finished this pose, can you show me the game?"

"Uhhh. No."

"What do you mean no? I like to laugh too."

"But it won't be the same with you."

"You don't find me funny?"

"I... I don't know."

"And if I do this to you, doesn't that make you want to laugh?"

"Maybe a little."

"And here?"

"Haha!"

Marc's laughter was interrupted by a noisy, virile sneeze from the sacristy. Father Lecavalier rushed back behind his canvas and the church was silent again. Only the scratching of his pencil and the rumbling of Marc's stomach disturbed the peace and quiet. Soon, footsteps echoed in the church and Father Rossignol emerged. Lecavalier hated being interrupted by the priest while he was working, but it was something he'd learned to tolerate. Did he have any choice? The priest appeared surprised to find Marc Lamontagne wearing nothing more than his underpants and some sort of sheet in the middle of the church. Then again, had the Lord been given his pick of clothing for the Passion? He thought to himself that Lecavalier was indeed a very talented man and went back to the sacristy, going out of his way to thank Marc for the favour for the thousandth time.

"So long as you don't catch cold, poor Marc. Are you still tired?"

"Not today, but I slept the whole day long the day before yesterday."

"I'll have to speak to your father."

Summer 1968 went by like an Apollo rocket. Fall advanced along with Solange's despair. Madeleine appeared to change before her very eyes, sometimes even to the point of being curt with her. She evaded her questions and spent her time, a lot of time, watching Father Lecavalier paint. The priest-cum-painter had allowed the whole Lamontagne family, in return for services rendered by Marc and Madeleine, to watch him paint. Only Madeleine had taken him up on his offer, the others having better things to do. And so it was in mid-August that Madeleine lied to her friend Solange for the first time. She didn't even know why. It had just come to her, and her heart told her it was the right thing to do.

"Do you want to go out on the bike after school? We'll go up by the lake."

"Uh... I can't this afternoon. Mom wants me to help her with supper."

Solange pursed her lips and wreaked vengeance on the world, revving her Triumph up and down the length of the lake. It was also about that time that Madeleine undid her braids, cut her hair shoulder length, and gave in to the gentle delights of hair spray.

"What's that in your hair for the love of God?" Solange snorted. And the Triumph terrorized another village. A floral dress also put in an appearance, something that didn't go unnoticed by Lecavalier, who, ever the sycophant, complimented Madeleine on her purchase.

"I'm working as a cleaner at the Saint-Louis Hotel," she said, as if to justify such extravagance.

Most of the time, Madeleine hovered silently behind Father Lecavalier and watched him paint. She congratulated him on his Simon of Cyrene, the spitting image of her younger brother Marc.

"He even has his eyes, Father Lecavalier. He has Mom's brown eyes."

"But you have your father's teal-coloured eyes, Madeleine," he replied, passing his hand through her fine blonde hair.

"I have Dad's eyes and Luc had Mom's eyes, just like Marc."

"He has lovely eyes, your brother Marc. They're so dark. Look how they stand out in the painting. You could stare at them all day."

"You don't prefer teal-coloured eyes?"

"They're nice too. But Marc's have such depth. They're so—what would you call it?—so... playful. Isn't that right, Madeleine? Your brother's a playful boy, isn't he?"

"No more than Luc used to be, Father. He used to laugh most in the family, after Papa Louis. Marc doesn't laugh all that much."

"But he told me he loved to laugh... That you love to laugh together."

Madeleine was taken aback. She stared at the church floor.

"I don't know what you're talking about."

"Perhaps you should have a word with your father, Madeleine. Can you come by tomorrow? I'd like to start the station with Mary Magdalene."

By way of reply, Madeleine wiped away a furtive tear, got up from the pew she'd been sitting on, and left the priest to his work. She found her brother that same evening in something of a trance. She walked up to him. There were shouts, shouts that Papa Louis did not hear from the Ophir. The thud of a body falling to the ground, a sound that had not been heard in the house since Papa Louis had, to save the soul of his son Luc, stopped lifting his hand to Irene. "You're hurting me. You're killing me." Moans that did not wake Irene from her drunken stupor in front of the television, that never passed through the walls of the Lamontagne home, but that, strangely, the whole town managed to hear. The people of Rivière-du-Loup have a keen ear. The following morning, Madeleine refused to speak to Solange.

"I have to pose for Father Lecavalier. He's drawing Mary Magdalene today."

"Madeleine…"

"Yes, Solange?"

"Madeleine, you have to do something."

"What are you talking about? What's it to you, Solange Bérubé? You're just our neighbour. Since when has it been any of your business?"

"Madeleine, listen to me…"

"Nobody other than the nuns has ever wanted to take care of the Lamontagne children, and now you want to go around acting all holier-than-thou, is that it? You think you're better than us? When your dad was beating you with a stick and we could hear your screams all the way over here, did we get involved? No, we didn't! So don't act all smart, OK? Get on your bike and go wake the dead in Saint-Arsène!"

Solange gave Madeleine a slap of Wagnerian proportions. It was a sleepless night for both the living and the dead in Saint-Arsène. When she arrived at the church the following morning, Madeleine looked like a woman who had just attended her own crucifixion.

"You're perfect, Madeleine!" Father Lecavalier exclaimed.

Dead tired and prostrate on her knees before Christ on the cross, no more than six yards from where her father had been born, Madeleine prayed while the priest drew her.

"Tears aren't necessary, Madeleine."

"I know. I can't help it."

"Why are you crying?"

"The suffering of Our Lord, Father."

"You can speak frankly to me, Madeleine."

"I'm crying because you'll be leaving soon," Madeleine answered, without abandoning her pose. "The station with Mary Magdalene is the twelfth of fourteen. You'll be finished soon. You'll go back to Quebec City and then on to Rome."

"Oh… Rome. I can only hope. It will all depend on the kindness of our archbishop."

"You're going to leave and I'll be stuck here alone."

"Did you speak to your father?"

"My father drinks. He doesn't hear anymore."

"And your mother?"

Madeleine ignored the priest's questions. She seemed to be lost in a sort of trance, her eyes fixed on the crucifix, mumbling some prayer or other. Lecavalier would later swear he heard her say something in German: "*Zucker, ja Zucker.*" He couldn't be sure, however, because he didn't speak a word of German. He put it down to exhaustion and thanked Madeleine once he'd finished his sketch.

"When will you be finished, Father?"

"I'll have added the colour in three days. You can come back and see it then."

Madeleine left the church without saying a word, stopped by the Damours grocery store on her way home, and slipped a can of maple syrup into her bag while the clerk was busy giving a woman her change. She left after buying a bunch of turnips, two onions, and three radishes.

"Will that be all, Miss Lamontagne?" the cashier asked her.

"Yes, thank you," she replied, looking him square in the eye.

She hid her spoils in a drawer, under a pile of bras, and locked herself away for two days. She heard her brother get up to pee ten times that night.

The day circumstances compelled Madeleine to take Tosca's fate in her own hands coincided with Lecavalier's birthday. Madeleine went to the church. Solange saw her leaving home in the early afternoon and followed her. She waited for Madeleine to go into the church. Without making a sound, she slipped in through a side door and hid behind a confessional. Father Rossignol and Father Lecavalier were deep in discussion and didn't notice her come in. Madeleine watched them from the vestibule. Their voices carried over to her. From what she gathered, the men were discussing the stations of the cross. From behind a half-open door, Madeleine watched the scene unfold, the importance of which she wouldn't realize until later. Lecavalier had set up stations V and XII side by side, "Simon of Cyrene helps Jesus to carry his cross" and "Jesus dies on the cross" respectively. Even from a distance, Madeleine was struck by the resemblance between Simon and Marc. It was so remarkable that, for years afterward, the parishioners would look up and say, "That's Louis 'The Horse' Lamontagne's boy. Just look how alike they are. He has the same dark eyes." The three-quarter-view portrait of Marc even had the same look of solicitude that believers like to ascribe to Simon. On another easel to the right, the painting representing Christ's death was even more captivating. Lecavalier had opted for bold, almost brash, colours. In the background, the familiar sunset over the Charlevoix mountains. The same orange-tinted pink light that enveloped the people and properties of Rivière-du-Loup when evening fell. This poetry hadn't escaped the painter, who had even gone so far as to include typically Canadian trees such as balsam fir and a white spruce. In the centre, Christ, his face forlorn, had just expired. Below him, two women: the Virgin Mary, whose face could barely be seen, and Mary Magdalene, as faithful as a photograph of her model. Madeleine was taken aback for a second or two at the sight of her own face. She had never before seen herself in a painting or anywhere else other than in Mr. Marmen's photographs. The image before her eyes transfigured and transfixed her. No one would doubt for a second it was anyone but her, and the thought filled her with a feeling that was impossible to describe. Inner peace? Happiness? Bliss? Something rare, that was for sure. She heard the two men talking. Father Rossignol seemed delighted.

"I couldn't tell you, Father Lecavalier, which I like more. The portrait of Marc is so true to life. And the same goes for little Madeleine. As for the fir tree, I'm not so sure… Folks here tend to be quite conservative."

"Don't you think they'll be pleased to see the St. Lawrence?"

"Not in a crucifixion scene. We're not used to awful things happening here, you see. Canada is a blessed land. Misfortune is for Germany, Poland, the Middle East, sandy places… The people of Rivière-du-Loup really feel as though they are living in the land God chose for his children."

"Well, if that's how they see it. I, on the other hand, am more than pleased to have finished my work."

"You didn't enjoy your time here, Father Lecavalier?"

"Don't take this the wrong way, Father, but I find the atmosphere in the town a trifle stifling. People can't simply get on with their lives without constantly being watched and judged by those around them. And some of your parishioners are… how can I put this? I don't want to hurt anyone's feelings… Let's just say that some of them need to step outside themselves. Take the Lamontagnes. They need to get out of their funeral parlour now and again. Those children are much too close."

"But there's no harm in a brother and sister getting along, Father Lecavalier."

"You're not following me. And it's none of my business in any case. It's a shame for the boy. Lord knows what might become of him in the city."

"Marc speaks highly of you. You've made quite an impression on him. He's spoken of nothing but painting since you arrived."

"I think he's the best-looking of the Lamontagne children, Father Rossignol. Truth be told, both are beautiful. In such different ways, but they manage to complement one other. Marc is well built like his father. Madeleine has her mother's dreamy beauty. When I look at Marc, I immediately think of Bernini's sculptures and I curse the heavens that I lack his talent. And the mere sight of Madeleine is enough to make me question my vows."

Father Rossignol had lost the thread of the conversation. His eyes seemed to be drifting elsewhere. He looked at his watch.

"That's all very well, but I have work to be getting on with at the presbytery. Will you be much longer?"

"Another two days to finish 'Jesus is laid in the tomb' and we'll be able to announce the unveiling."

The parish priest left through one of the side doors. Madeleine slowly made her way between the pews and up to the nave where Lecavalier continued to paint. Thinking himself alone, he was humming a song that Madeleine had never heard, something in another language. Gaining confidence, the priest took a deep breath and bellowed:

"*Reccondita armonia*
Di bellezze diverse!
E bruna Floria,
L'ardente amante mia…"

"Father Lecavalier?"

The priest, who had had no idea he was being watched, nearly leaped out of his shoes and gave out a high-pitched girlish shriek, probably a G sharp.

"Madeleine! How long have you been there?"

"I just came in."

"Did… did you see your portrait?"

"Yes."

"And what do you think?"

"You made my eyes dark," Madeleine replied quietly.

"Yes, I gave you dark eyes. Dark brown, to be precise. Every character has them. Let me explain…"

"You're going to give me teal-coloured eyes."

"As I was saying…"

"I have teal-coloured eyes."

Madeleine's tone was glacial.

"Yes, but it's not you in the picture, it's Mary Magdalene, and Mary Magdalene had dark brown eyes," the priest explained.

"How do you know?"

"How *don't* you know? The people in the Holy Land didn't have teal-coloured eyes, my dear Madeleine!"

"People in the Holy Land didn't have fir or spruce trees either. And they didn't watch the sun set over the Charlevoix mountains!" Madeleine shouted, before catching her breath. "I've had it, Father Lecavalier! You're going to give me teal-coloured eyes right this minute or I'll tell my father! Marc got the right colour for his eyes, now I want mine!"

"Calm down, Madeleine. I'm sure this is something we can discuss. You have to understand that you're not Mary Magdalene. She's a figure from the Bible. I based my painting on you because..."

While the priest spoke, Madeleine sat down on the steps, on the very spot where her father was born, and began to sob. Lecavalier came over and took her in his arms to console her, an improbable Cavaradossi clasping an uncertain Tosca. Around them, a whiff of jealousy that percolated from Solange's skin as she hid behind the confessional, tormented by the desire to give the scene a Shakespearian ending. They remained like that until Madeleine calmed down. Crouched behind her confessional, Solange made the most of the fact that the side door was no longer in the priest's field of vision to slip outside as silently as a cat. She'd heard enough, she thought, to throw up for weeks. Twenty minutes later, she broke a new noise and speed record as she zipped down Saint-Antonin's main street. A complaint was filed with the police.

Despite his intentions of returning to the city as quickly as possible, Father Lecavalier remained in Rivière-du-Loup until November, a decision that the nuns ascribed to their culinary talents. They continued to concoct all kinds of desserts for him. The reception celebrating the new stations of the cross was held at the provincial house at the nuns' request. The last few nights of normality for all those folks, before the glacial wind swept in to upturn all that had once held any significance in Rivière-du-Loup. People fluttered around the convent's entrance hall, stopping now and then in front of a painting. Nothing so beautiful had ever been seen in the parish. Gleaned here and there were expressions of amazement and surprise, from "My God, isn't he the spitting image of Louis' son!" and "Look! The women of Jerusalem look just like the Lévesque sisters on Rue Saint-Grégoire!" to

"He even gave her the teal-coloured eyes she got from her father!" and "How sad she looks, our little Madeleine." Off in a corner, Irene was on her fourth glass of white wine, while Louis—dragged by his wife from his barstool at the Ophir—was unsteadily admiring the paintings he had helped pay for. The most notable absentee that evening was Solange Bérubé, who claimed to be suffering from a migraine. The parishioners were delighted by Father Lecavalier's efforts. Unfortunately, every single station of the cross in the church of Saint-François-Xavier was swiped by a thief in early June 1975, leaving Father Rossignol in a state of utter distress. The circumstances surrounding the theft never came to light. Sadness gave way to consternation when, three days later, a man out walking found the charred remains of the frames on the beach at Notre-Dame-du-Portage. Clearly, the heist had not been motivated by the prospect of financial gain.

Father Lecavalier's talented voice had not gone unremarked during his time in the parish, and he was asked to sing at the unveiling. Paris had not only made a painter of him, but a singer too. The church organist, the same man Louis had almost finished off at Luc's funeral, had insisted that Lecavalier sing at least once for the people of Rivière-du-Loup before leaving the town.

"I'll accompany you. You have such a fine voice."

"What shall I sing?"

"What you were heard singing in the church in Italian this summer!"

He must have sung at least a dozen Italian arias that summer, whenever he thought he was alone in the church. Believing he'd already done enough for the people of Rivière-du-Loup, he turned down the organist's invitation.

A week went by. The day before All Saints', Marc had fallen asleep on his bed after another day of exhaustion. This time, Irene had managed to get Louis to bring their son to see Dr. Panneton.

"It's not normal for him to sleep all the time," she'd protested.

The nuns were not the only ones to take an interest in French Canadian cooking that fall. It was a November evening, a little before the first snow. With both her parents out, Madeleine opened the can of maple syrup she had stolen from the Damours grocery store. The maple syrup pie recipe was quite straightforward. Just five ingredients. But Madeleine prepared it with all the care and attention to detail that the Japanese take in making sushi. She worked in religious silence, without making a mess, without spilling the flour. The sweet aroma of maple syrup soon floated over the kitchen, then the living room, as the syrup boiled with the heavy cream. A smell delectable enough to wake the dead, to make them wish they were still alive. Madeleine washed the utensils as she went, leaving no trace behind. Once the pie was in the oven, its aroma gained in strength and substance. It was at that moment that Solange rang the doorbell. Three times. Madeleine pretended not to have heard, but the neighbour was not to be dissuaded and let herself in. She made Madeleine, occupied as she was in the kitchen, cry out in fear.

"What are you doing here?"

"I came to say hello. Are you by yourself?"

"No, Marc's sleeping. What do you want?"

"Madeleine, we need to talk. Are you still mad?"

"I'm busy more than anything else. You'll have to come back later. Come back tomorrow, Solange."

Not wanting to annoy Madeleine, the young Bérubé girl left and went back home to wait. Alone again, Madeleine took the pie out of the oven and set it in the middle of the table, where it couldn't be missed. Then she walked downstairs to the basement, armed with her rosary beads, and prayed. It took no more than a few minutes for the beast to be roused from its sleep by the sweet fragrance. Footsteps could be heard all the way to the kitchen. Madeleine kept praying... *forgive us our trespasses...* She heard cutlery being taken out of the drawer, a plate, a pie server. The fridge door opening. A glass of milk. Noisy gobbling sounds. Then back upstairs to bed. Madeleine had time enough to go back up to the kitchen, where she found the pie plate empty. Nothing but a few crumbs. Quickly washed it all. Aired out the whole house so that it wouldn't smell of sugar. A suspicious stain at the back of the oven; she scraped it off with a knife. Caramelized sugar. Once everything was spotless, she went upstairs. Moans could be heard coming from Marc's room. He was calling for his sister. Madeleine went to bed. Before falling asleep, she heard her mother and father come in. And the night was long. Sleepless. Dawn arrived with a gaunt stare. When morning came, Madeleine got up before everyone to throw up, as she had every morning for the past four weeks.

They found Marc unconscious in his bed. It was Irene's cries that alerted Papa Louis and Madeleine. The boy was taken to hospital, where the doctor on duty, as soon as he caught a whiff of acetone on Marc's breath, diagnosed a diabetic coma brought on by a sugar overdose.

Three days later, Marc died of kidney failure before the heartbroken gaze of his parents. The day he died, Father Lecavalier left Rivière-du-Loup with the firm intention of never again setting foot there, thereby missing the lovely funeral organized by Papa Louis. It was also the last funeral organized by Papa Louis. "Death By Maple Syrup" might have been a suitable epitaph. Although no one ever found out that, the night before All Saints', Madeleine Lamontagne had baked a maple syrup pie that killed her brother, and nor did anyone ever know how the young woman had realized Marc was diabetic and that the dessert would prove fatal to him. There may be many things that we know, and that we don't know, but that doesn't prevent us from getting on with life.

This time, the organist spontaneously burst into *Jesu, Joy of Man's Desiring*. Marc was laid to rest beside his younger brother. Unlike with Luc's death, Marc's passing seemed to drive Irene and Louis further apart and bring Solange and Madeleine closer together. The maple syrup pie was never mentioned. At the end of November, some two feet of snow fell on the region, then again on December 1. The winter was going to be long and snow-filled. On December 3, a dangerously sober Irene waited for her daughter to come back from supper at the Bérubés'. On the table before her was an advertisement cut out of the newspaper, alongside an opened envelope, stamped in Montreal a few days earlier. On the letter accompanying the coupon Irene had filled out and sent off, a New York address was listed beside a paragraph of text.

"It's the answer to your problem, Madeleine," Irene said, in the voice of a bogeyman.

"I don't have a problem, Mom."

"Your brother Marc is dead and maybe that's a blessing. What he did to you is a terrible sin, Madeleine. What he left you, you cannot keep. Mommy's not going to let you down. I've put together the money, but you will have far to go. You'll have to be discreet."

"I don't know what you're taking about, Mom."

"You'll know in five minutes. Now go get your friend Solange. Tell her I want to talk to her. These are desperate times, Madeleine. Hurry before your father gets back."

Panic-stricken, breathless, and shaken, Madeleine reappeared two minutes later with a worried-looking Solange.

"Solange," Irene began. "You leave for New York City with Madeleine tomorrow morning to solve the problem Marc left her with before he died. I've bought bus tickets for the pair of you. You'll take the coach to Montreal. When you get there, you'll take the overnight coach to New York. You'll go to this address with the money I'll give you. It's a doctor, he's Jewish.

Solange, it's up to you to find the address. Madeline won't be able to find her way about the city. That night, you'll take the coach back to Montreal and, the next morning, another one to Rivière-du-Loup. Tomorrow morning is Wednesday. You'll be back Friday night. I'll tell your father, Madeleine, that you're off looking for kitchen work in Quebec City. Do you understand?"

Stunned, the two young women exchanged worried glances.

"I don't want to go, Mom."

Irene got up out of her seat, slowly walked over to her daughter, slapped her as hard as she could, and flung her to the floor with such violence that even Solange, no stranger to being knocked about herself, took fright.

"I don't think you understand, Madeleine Lamontagne. You can't bring that child into this world. You're carrying a monster!"

Madeleine lay there, prostrate on the linoleum, while Solange trembled.

"And one more thing," Irene added. "You will never ever breathe a word of this to anyone. Otherwise I swear I'll slit both your throats."

Irene disappeared upstairs. A door slammed. Silence fell over the house.

On the morning of December 4, Madeleine took a path well travelled by many other Quebec girls in the 1960s. Thousands? Hundreds of them? No one will ever know. Those girls never breathed a word, except perhaps after therapy, a night's heavy drinking, or as a deathbed confession. They set out alone on the roads of North America as though they'd fallen victim to the plague, and they came back changed by a journey that, for some, had taken over thirty hours. They didn't talk about it.

A light snow fell on the town. Sitting in the front row of a packed coach heading to Montreal, Solange held Madeleine's hand. The palm of her mother's hand was still stamped on Madeleine's left cheek as she stared at the asphalt, all covered in white. The driver had announced the trip was cancelled no fewer than three times before reluctantly venturing out onto the icy roads. Someone lit a cigarette behind the two girls. Madeleine threw up into a brown paper bag. Solange rubbed her back. The driver lit himself a cigarette too. Madeleine threw up again.

"Didn't ya have breakfast?" the driver inquired. He was a man who seemed to be all bones and not much else.

"It's your cigarette," Solange protested, incensed.

"I won't smoke too many then. The girl'll have to toughen up."

None of the passengers on that coach making its way to Quebec City had the faintest idea of the drama unfolding in the front row, nor would they have known what to make of it, because on that December morning nothing was more hopeless—or more delightful—than the image of those two snow geese being catapulted across the snow-covered roads of the New World. Hopelessness in the face of the poor girl being sent by force to a mysterious, unknown city to undergo the unmentionable; delight in the face of her companion, who had for so long harboured dreams of exploring the vastness of the continent, but who would never have suspected that her desire to see more of North America would be made possible by the miserly Irene. Three hundred dollars in an envelope, in American notes. A few sandwiches, a few apples. That's what they carried in their purses. Solange remembered the rare satisfaction she felt, for once feeling in control of things, for here she was, alone with Madeleine at last. After ninety minutes of snowy roads, they were already further from Rivière-du-Loup than they'd ever been: aside from the odd ride in a convertible or on a motorcycle to Cacouna, Pohénégamook, or Trois-Pistoles, Solange and Madeleine had never left the town. The few road signs they could make out in the blizzard conditions revealed destinations unknown: Saint-Roch-des-Aulnaies, Sainte-Anne-de-la-Pocatière, Montmagny. It was in that precise spot that Madeleine burst into sobs for the eighth time. The other passengers, a few gossips from Rivière-du-Loup among them, had already put up their receiving antennas. They weren't going to miss a second of the show. What on earth was Louis Lamontagne's daughter doing on a bus to Quebec City in such a snowstorm? All alone with Solange Bérubé? And ill, into the bargain! The cold air that made its way in through the drafty windows lashed their senses. Solange was wise enough to wait until they got to Quebec City before mentioning her brief visit to the convent the previous night. Once Madeleine had been safely shut away in her bedroom and the Lamontagne family home had been locked down by an unhinged Irene, Solange, who had kept her composure in the face of the madwoman, had run to the only place that still inspired confidence in those crazy times: the provincial house belonging to the Sisters of the Child Jesus, where, in spite of the late hour, she asked to speak with Sister Mary of the Eucharist.

Visibly distressed by Solange's story, the nun seemed to look to Heaven for inspiration. She left Solange to cry by herself in the parlour and came back clutching two items in her bony hands.

"Look, Solange. Seeing as this is how things are going to go..."

"What's that?"

"It's an old book that Madeleine's grandmother brought with her from New England. It was her recipe book. Leave it at your house here in Rivière-du-Loup and give it to Madeleine when you come back."

"*The New England Cookbook*?"

"Yes. She had it with her when she got off the train in 1918. It never left her side. And you'll give this little gold cross to Madeleine while you're at it. It was also her grandmother's: Louis-Benjamin gave it to her when they got engaged. Madeleine the American was wearing it when she died giving birth to Louis. I kept it all this time to protect it from covetous looks. I want you to explain to Madeleine what it is and where it comes from. Can you do that, Solange?"

"Yes, I think so."

"You have to tell her she must never take it off. Even to wash, you understand?"

The nun grabbed Solange by the wrist.

"I understand, Sister."

"Look me in the eye when you're talking to me, Solange Bérubé."

It was at the bus station in Quebec City that Solange decided to give Madeleine the cross, in the relative privacy of a waiting-room bench. A strange offering on that cursed day. Madeleine looked incredulously at the piece of jewellery, wondering how much it would go for, and tried to imagine the American girl's face, which had survived only in wedding photos, while she clutched the cross in her fist. They would never stop to wonder why Sister Mary of the Eucharist had waited until then to give the cross to the American's heiress. She must have had her reasons.

"The initials are the same. It was destined to be yours," Solange said, trying to lift her friend's spirits.

Between Quebec City and Montreal, Madeleine stopped her vomiting and crying. And the sky stopped snowing. Evening came early. Her head leaning against the window, she contemplated the world she had never seen before while Solange, her guardian angel, slept. Under a sky turned blue by the December light, it seemed to her that they had been thrust unjustly into a hell whose rings bore the names Victoriaville, Drummondville, and Saint-Hyacinthe, a cold, flat world that seemed without end, a series of concentric circles whose centre would inevitably be New York. They would know they'd arrived when the devil's forked tail, long and red, made its way up into the coach. After that, Madeleine would just have to keep a tight hold on her cross. Crossing the Jacques Cartier Bridge into Montreal gave her the fleeting impression of flying through the sky. To her left, the remains of Expo '67 that Papa Louis had watched on television and that his cousins had sent a postcard from. The bus station in Montreal shook her from her thoughts. That was where Madeleine understood why her mother had put her in Solange's care. All alone at night, she wouldn't have lasted fifteen minutes in that gloomy building that reeked of tobacco.

Solange went off to buy tickets to the United States. Alone on her bench, Madeleine attracted the attention of a man who'd had a few drinks too many, charmed by her youth and her crimson wool coat. He spoke to her in English and she didn't understand a word. His mouth was hidden behind an enormous moustache that made him look like the picture of Stalin she'd seen in history books. But Stalin proved no match for an impatient Solange and went off to join the other drunks in a dark corner of the terminal.

"We have to wait four hours for the Greyhound. We'll be in New York tomorrow morning. Are you tired?"

"No, just sad. It's not the same thing. And I'm scared, too."

"What are you frightened of, Mado?"

"Of finding myself all alone without you."

Upon hearing those words, Solange felt the bones in her ribcage open and a vibration that first stirred in her perineum ran up right through her, rocking her very foundations and rising up heavenward and through her lungs, pharynx, vocal cords, and nasal cavities to leave the back of her head trembling. The sound she produced was pure and clear, carried forth by the words "I will never leave you," which resounded through the bus station the way the song of an angel will one day burst forth into the world God promised to his followers. It could well have been the moment, in all her life, that Solange was at her most lucid, her most beautiful too.

They made the trip along Route 87 to New York in complete darkness. Plattsburgh, Albany. The customs officers wanted to know what the two young women were intending to do in New York. Do you have family there? Yes, lied Solange, who had been told that the word "family" was the "Open, Sesame" for the United States.

Twenty or so black men and women had got on and sat at the back of the coach in Montreal. Madeleine had watched them file in without wondering if her staring might offend them. Their amused smiles suggested they knew she had simply never seen anyone their colour before. She spent the first two hours of the journey looking over her shoulder at them, trying to catch what they were saying. She had never seen people more fascinating, as much for their colourful, loose-fitting clothes as their satin-smooth skin. Those travellers seldom spoke and would occasionally flash her a smile as if to say, "Are you crazy? What forest have you just wandered out of, you poor fool?", and that she took to be invitations to happiness. At the stopover in Albany, two white women who had found themselves sandwiched between the group of black people asked Solange and Madeleine to swap seats with them and let them sit in the front row.

"We're just too old for this!" the more fearful of the two whimpered.

"Too old for what?" Solange wondered. Once Madeleine understood what the two Americans wanted, she begged Solange to agree. It was all the same to Solange; all she wanted was to sleep a little longer. In the darkness of the coach, Madeleine continued to observe her neighbours, stealthily at first, then as they fell asleep, gazing at them as others might admire the paintings of Degas. One of the black women who was still awake found it all highly amusing and, guessing right away that the young girl had only ever seen people who looked like her, struck up a conversation that Solange had to interpret for both of them. They were musicians. They sang in a choir, to be exact. Were on their way back from a church in Montreal. Little Burgundy? You know it? The woman's name was Deborah. Flashed two rows of white teeth when she talked. Didn't move her hands until the very end of each sentence. Wore a white scarf around her neck. Was that wool? No, finer than wool. Quick to reply. All we know is the convent and the parish that protected us from the world until last night. Why New York? To see the Statue of Liberty. Don't forget it's just a statue. (Big laughs.) Can you sing? Hymns, prayers, but badly. Really? You've never seen people of colour? No. Not ever. Mind if we sing? No. No, please sing! For the love of God, please sing and give this trip to hell what it's lacking in solemnity and solace! Sing before I start throwing up again! Sing for my brother Luc, for my brother Marc, and for all the souls in purgatory! Sing for the repose of the soul of my American grandmother whose cross I was just given. Please, black lady, sing!

The Harlem Eternity Gospel Choir didn't wait to be asked twice to provide the musical accompaniment to the tardy migration of the two snow geese. Transformed into a Baptist Church on wheels, the coach ate up the miles in the dark of night. The snowstorm seemed to want to come south with Madeleine. Snowflakes fell with each passing stop, a sign that it was time to leave before they got caught in the worst of it. The driver sped up to put some distance between them and the area of low pressure pushing down from the north. The storm was heralded by ice-cold winds. The heat was turned up as far as it could go, but the passengers were shivering, especially the three baritones at the back. In the morning, Solange and Madeleine were treated to—what else?—*My Lord, What A Morning*, which lasted at least twelve minutes. On both sides of the vehicle, the city was beginning to take shape, to grow. The traffic was getting heavier. They felt that they were on the verge of something huge and noisy, powerful enough to quieten the singers, by now caught up in the excitement that comes with returning from a long trip. They crossed a bridge, then an expressway or two. At last, they arrived at the Port Authority Bus Terminal, officially declared the world's ugliest place on that day, December 5, 1968. By that point, neither Madeleine nor Solange had slept since the night of December 3. They could feel their powers of reasoning gradually abandoning them. Finding herself on the sidewalk at the corner of 8th Avenue and 42nd Street, Madeleine almost forgot what she was doing in New York. Her gaze searched for answers in the pallid morning sky beyond the enormous skyscrapers. Solange's hand took hers and they walked, closely followed by the singers from the Harlem Eternity Gospel Choir, who had insisted on seeing the scrap of paper that bore the address where Madeleine was expected. It was decided they would go with them. They'd get lost otherwise. Embarrassed by such concern for their welfare, the girls protested, no you're too kind, that's too nice of you. Your music has already helped us forget our suffering. A gift? Deborah couldn't help remark Madeleine's covetous glances. She took off her lovely white scarf.

"New York is a very windy city. This will protect you."

Her first gift from America: a white silk scarf.

Madeleine wondered what had compelled Deborah to give her a gift like that and felt indebted to her forever after. Deborah was now pointing out the north of the city, where she lived. Solange and Madeleine stared at the white palm of her hand in the grey New York sky.

"You know where you're goin'?"

No, no more than they knew exactly where they were. Far from home, that was for sure. And yet the sun stubbornly persisted in flinging down a smattering of sad rays across the city, through the rare openings in the clouds. The choir disappeared into a hole with a stairwell, out of which came the howl of a wounded animal. Or was it the sound of a train braking?

Alone in New York. It was their stomachs that reminded them of their humanity. They had to eat. It didn't matter what, but they had to eat. The girls set off toward the tallest towers, sure they'd find something to eat there. The search took a while. Every place they found along 42nd Street was either closed or too seedy for them to risk it. Thinking they might have more luck on another street, they walked for a good half hour before coming out onto what Solange said must be 55th or 56th Street. Madeleine was starting to show signs of impatience that could be put down to both her hunger and the fact that she hadn't slept in over thirty-six hours. So it was something of a miracle when Tosca's Diner appeared before them. They went in. Or, rather, they were sucked inside.

Tosca's Diner was opened by a family of Italian immigrants by the name of Donatello in 1927. Built in the Roaring Twenties, it originally catered to business people, then later to certain shady business people, who were often one and the same. For many a year, the fine white stripes of Italian-cut suits were a staple in the establishment. The couple bequeathed the restaurant to their only daughter, Donatella. Over time, as tastes and times changed, the restaurant became a favourite for American breakfasts and quick lunches. It looked like a brightly lit Irish pub minus the taps and kegs of beer. It was full to bursting at nine o'clock on that December 5 morning, buzzing with the sounds of hundreds of customers who were visibly happy to be there. Donatella Donatello, a woman well into her fifties whose Louis XIV hairstyle and Mae West makeup glued Solange to the spot (for a second or two she thought she'd landed in the middle of some sort of New York Mardi Gras), didn't give the girls a chance to wonder if they shouldn't find someplace else instead. Donatella Donatello had a gift of being able to tell, with extraordinary precision, two things about people, namely whether they were hungry and whether they were lying. This double gift had made her both a wealthy woman and a longtime spinster. A generous patron of the Metropolitan Opera, Donatella spent every Saturday night there, provided there was a performance. The family had nurtured a passion for opera for centuries, which is why the walls were covered with opera posters from the Met, signed photos of Elizabeth Schwarzkopf, and even, standing tall in the middle of the dining room, a mannequin wearing a reproduction of the dress worn by Dorothy Kirsten for the five hundredth showing of *Tosca*, which had just finished its November 1968 run at the Met. She clutched a wooden dagger in her hand, which never failed to draw a smile from the regulars and gave pause to any customers thinking about leaving without paying their bill.

"I know you're hungry, girls! Please! Be my guest!"

Donatella swooped down on Solange and Madeleine like an eagle catching its prey.

In no time at all, they were sitting at a table that had just been wiped clean by a young black boy. Madeleine was tempted to ask him if he knew the Harlem Eternity Gospel Choir. Donatella was a real chatterbox and detected a foreign accent in Solange's thank you that caught her ear. She clucked with satisfaction when she caught sight of Deborah's white scarf. Is that wool? We don't know. It's real pretty. A gift from a singer...

She decided to take the hungry young things under her wing. Her sixth sense wasn't deceiving her: the pair of them were starving. Donatella handed them menus and disappeared for a moment. They pointed to the Manhattan Breakfast Special for the smiling waitress and, as if by magic, steaming hot cups of coffee, silverware, napkins, and *you're welcome dears* appeared in rapid succession. Sugar for the coffee, milk or cream? Are you French? Madeleine was as excited as a chihuahua. Her brain took in everything she saw, the choreography of the waitresses, the way they took the orders. They multiplied, subtracted, and divided at speeds she hadn't known were possible. She saw at least twenty-four plates on the tables, which she multiplied by the price on the menu, subtracted what she reckoned to be the servers' and busboys' salaries, and indexed the overheads. In other words, the seeds of her dreams of a food empire were sown that day in an empty stomach.

"Solange, look around you!"

"What?"

"The place is full! And look outside: people are lining up to get in!"

"So?"

"Listen, if we had a restaurant like this, we'd be rich in no time!"

"Before we start selling eggs, we'd have to buy some first!"

"We'll ask Mr. Zucker to give us a good price!"

"Zucker?"

"Yes, Zucker. It's right there on the side of his van: 'Unbeatable Prices.'"

"Vans aren't always right, Madeleine."

Solange couldn't believe her ears, but put it down to her friend's fatigue. How could Madeleine get caught up in such mundane thoughts in such dark times? And so far from home too.

Donatella came over. She told them, as though they were bound to be interested, how the restaurant had gotten its name after her parents, still feeling the effects of the journey from Naples to New York, met while lining up for tickets at the Metropolitan Opera. The only tickets they could afford were for *Tosca*, which they subsequently declared their favourite opera for ever and ever and the rest of eternity. Donatella wiped away a tear from her fat cheek. Madeleine and Solange felt as though the rest of the room was watching some kind of show that they were part of. Plates appeared from nowhere. Two eggs, pancakes, bacon, fried potatoes, all swimming in grease.

"Would you like some ketchup, darlings?"

As they gobbled up what they would later maintain was the best meal of their lives—better even than the tender flesh of poor Lazarus—Donatella Donatello, only too aware that she had a captive and silent audience, asked if they knew the story of *Tosca*, then went on to describe how Cavaradossi and Tosca first met and fell in love, and about Tosca's deadly jealousy, vile Scarpia, and his loathsome trap.

The girls were only half listening. Madeleine didn't understand a word and Solange was too busy devouring her breakfast to devote any of her attention to the flamboyant woman. Donatella didn't stop there. To demonstrate her favourite moment in the opera, which is to say the murder of Baron Scarpia, she seized the wooden dagger from the mannequin's hand and, after exchanging a knowing glance with a waiter who was clearly used to playing the scene, mimed the murder, to the amusement of Solange and Madeleine. The scene lasted a few moments. Even the cook chimed in, shouting out like Cavaradossi from the kitchen, tortured by Scarpia's henchmen offstage. Tosca's kiss. A man collapses. Hope renewed. But for how long? Thunderous applause throughout Donatella Donatello's diner. Even the autographed photo of Maria Callas seemed to enjoy it.

Donatella, decidedly fascinated by the two French girls, sat down at their table and recounted the legendary tales of the various productions. How, for instance, the great Régine Crespin, during *Tosca*'s second run at the Met in 1965, had fallen victim to the curse that has always hung over the opera. While trying to grab a knife with which to kill the frenzied, deceitful Scarpia, Crespin ran into trouble: the props had been nailed to the table so they wouldn't shift during the performance. The props team had forgotten that Floria Tosca was supposed to stab Baron Scarpia dead. With the audience looking on in amusement, the diva tried in vain to pick up the knife, which remained obstinately nailed to the table. And so Scarpia was stabbed to death with a fork, proving it's the intention that counts, not the tool in hand.

Poor Maria Callas was less fortunate. During a rehearsal of the same scene in London, a candle set her wig on fire. Callas, whose concentration was legendary and who never went out of character, wondered, so the story goes, why the baritone Tito Gobbi was looking at her with such a panicked expression. Gobbi managed to put out the fire and the rehearsal went on.

The stories kept coming from Donatella, but Madeleine couldn't make out a word. Solange understood, but since she didn't know the first thing about opera, she contented herself with smiling at the parts she decided must be funny.

Donatella amused her. She asked them what they were doing in New York City. They glanced at each other. They couldn't remember! Tosca's Diner had made them forget for a moment why they'd travelled close to fifteen hours on a coach! They laughed. Solange took out the name and address of the doctor Madeleine was to meet at eleven o'clock, so that Donatella might show them the way. When she saw the doctor's name and address, Donatella froze, albeit imperceptibly; she knew how to control herself, after all.

"You don't have far to walk," she told them and kindly drew a map on the back of a piece of paper. "Maybe twenty minutes, twenty-five tops."

Suddenly deflated, Donatella Donatello excused herself and disappeared into the kitchen.

As they left the restaurant, bellies full and a spring in their step, Solange and Madeleine asked to say goodbye to Donatella. She was called back from her dressing room. Her eyes were red. She held Solange in her arms, then Madeleine, longer this time, intently, like an aunt. Long and hard enough to leave her feeling a little uncomfortable. She had a gift for Madeleine, a reminder of her visit to Tosca's Diner. A dried flower, a rose from Tosca's bouquet. She put it in her hair. A rose to watch over you, my little French girl. The flower came from a bouquet an admirer had tossed to Maria Callas in March 1965, Donatella explained, the night she sang *Tosca* at the Metropolitan Opera for the last time.

"People lined up for three days and three nights for standing-room tickets! Can you imagine? I was in the orchestra seats."

The diva, showered with flowers and applause, had thrown the rose to the audience. Donatella had dried it to preserve a little of its colour. The girls insisted on paying the bill. Donatella waved them away. Out of the question. Her treat.

"She's a sensitive soul," Madeleine concluded outside on the sidewalk. Six times she turned to go back to Tosca's Diner. Solange dragged her forward.

While Solange and Madeleine walked the streets of Manhattan, Papa Louis was cursing the woman who had kept Madeleine's trip to Quebec City a secret from him. He didn't approve. What had she gone off to work in the capital's hotels for? What was she going to do there? What was the point of it all?

"Her place is here with us! Why didn't you talk it over with me first?"

"I don't tell you everything."

Louis wouldn't calm down. There was no way he was going to let his daughter peel vegetables in some cheap restaurant in the city's lower town. Why doesn't she open a restaurant here? She could start by working at the Saint-Louis or the Granville if she was so determined to wait hand and foot on every Tom, Dick, and Harry!

"Two young girls from the Lower St. Lawrence all alone in town? They've a good chance of coming back pregnant!"

Irene sighed. Bit her bottom lip as she spread a lump of margarine on a slice of toast.

"Solange Bérubé? Pregnant?" she asked doubtfully.

"Why not? She's a good-looking girl! The boys'll be around her like flies."

"You think she's attractive, do you?"

"Of course, she is. In her own way. A strong girl. With Solange, you always know where you stand! She's solid. I like a girl like that!"

"That's the thing, Louis. Solange will keep an eye on Madeleine. Like you say, you always know where you stand with her."

Exasperated by such womanly secrets, Louis cursed and got up from the table. Irene raised her eyes to heaven, muttering something about the unfathomable depths of male stupidity. Had handsome Louis lived in New York, he'd doubtless have gone to Tosca's Diner every morning for breakfast. But since he couldn't afford such a treat, he went instead down to the Ophir, as he did almost every morning, and pulled up a seat. The cold weather embittered him. All that snow reminded him of Germany and the poor guy he'd found buried in it. What was his name again? Rose? No, Rosen. Yeah, that was it. Rosen was his name. The beer cloaked all his memories of Bavaria with a sepia veil. The Ophir regulars, all men, arrived one by one, and greeted Louis, a slap on the shoulder and a grunt by way of hello. Already drunk by two o'clock, Louis went from one table to the next, singing his daughter's praises, crying over his dead sons. He'd become a kind of talking ruin, a piece of shared history the place just wouldn't be the same without, tolerated like a senile professor on the cusp of retirement.

"My... my daughter's gonna be a cook at the Château Frontenac!" he stammered, drawing looks of pity from those around him.

A voice from the bar cried out:

"Is that a fact? I wouldn't be so sure!"

The drinkers fell silent. Who had dared? No one spoke to Louis Lamontagne like that, no more than you'd think of slapping an orangutan. The ignoramus was a man they barely knew. Marcoux was his name. Sure, there'd been that thing between Louis and his wife, an affair that left the poor cuckold wearing the horns, a common-enough look in the town, mind you. Louis smiled at the thought of the pair of horns on the calf that day in Gouverneur. Drunkenness beat at his temples like the axles on a German locomotive. What a day! Apart from the gin he could still indulge in, no one, not a thing, seemed to be on his side.

And the three hundred American dollars that were missing from the money he had set aside? It couldn't have been Madeleine who'd found his stash! She was a hard worker, his little girl. Just like her mother. He turned his attention to Marcoux.

"Somethin' you wanna say, Marcoux?"

Marcoux went quiet. To lighten the mood, the bartender turned on the television that normally only showed hockey games. A variety show. A lanky French singer was swinging his hips, gyrating in a manner that propriety forbade in the New World.

"Remind you of your son, Louis? What was his name? Marc, wasn't it?"

The room held its breath. For naught. It would take more than that to get a strongman to rise to the bait. The bartender turned off the television. The witnesses who were interrogated the following day had a hard time saying whether Louis Lamontagne had fully grasped what Marcoux was getting at. Louis was, they all agreed, drunker than usual that evening. Marcoux, on the other hand, had stuck to ginger ale and couldn't use drunkenness as an excuse. His words had whipped up the Ophir's smoke-filled air, chafing at eardrums, tormenting the men's consciences. Did he really have to go around shouting every bit of gossip that the rumour mill had washed up on his filthy doorstep?

"No, he looks more like the other one, the painting priest. They were together so often, you ended up confusing them, I suppose. That type of thing's legal now, or so they say."

His forehead resting on his hand, Louis gazed into space, oblivious to Marcoux's barbs. He was off somewhere else, a place alcohol sometimes brought him: the shores of Lake Starnberg. A German moon lit up the Alpine landscape.

Marcoux left the bar somewhat defeated, leaving a putrid stench in his wake. No one was vulgar enough to mention the incident or uncaring enough to try to offer Louis any idiotic words of comfort.

But Marcoux's vomit had spattered Louis' face all the same. It felt like a slap, and he soon left for home himself. He thought of Podgórski, of the blue trailer. His inebriated state took him back to the voluptuous memories of a Bavarian *Fräulein*, a sturdy blonde with an easy laugh. Maria. Pretty she was, too. Humungous breasts… She'd given herself to him and he'd given her his chocolate ration in return. It was Saint-Pierre who helped Louis into his jacket. Before he left the Ophir, he'd grinned over at the bartender again.

"You're not going after him, are you, Louis? He's an asshole." The bartender almost begged him.

"After who? I'm away home to eat, dammit!" Louis reassured the bartender. Perhaps that explains why later no one understood why Louis, instead of heading back up home, had crossed Rue Lafontaine and headed toward the train station. The snow swirled as it fell thick and fast, reminding Louis of the Jewish man he had found covered in the stuff. The men at the bar lost sight of him after a few seconds. Louis stopped to let out a sigh, humming the opening notes of *Jesu, Joy of Man's Desiring* before continuing on his way.

"By train, they took 'em by train," he muttered to himself. My God, the shriek of tortured metal must have been unbearable, he thought. When you think where the trains were headed. A haunting image lodged in his mind: frozen bodies piled one atop the other in car after car. But with the help of Bach, he managed to chase it away. He thought he could hear the wheels of German trains screeching along the track. A sound you don't forget. A sound that could be heard throughout Germany. "*Bahnhof*, that's what they called it. *Zug!*" Yeah, that was it. Trains! Don't get on the train! Whatever the destination! Don't ever take another train again! Stay home. Don't move. Don't budge from our beautiful land of snow, in the orange-rose light of the setting sun. Louis was slowly sobering up. He looked around. He wasn't on Saint-François-Xavier, or anywhere even close to home. He had drifted someplace else. Always the wanderer, he thought. Why were there rails on either side of his feet? And that white light he could just about make out through the snow? Why so much light? What was that in aid of?

Donatella Donatello had been telling the truth: Dr. David Beck's office was in the same neighbourhood as Tosca's Diner. Solange was doubly proud of herself: first for asking the choir the way, then for following their directions. Dr. Beck, she thought to herself, might even go to Tosca's Diner for breakfast. How long did it take them walking along 10th Avenue, to get to the doctor's? Twenty-three minutes precisely. Just like Donatella had said.

Solange had pictured a clinic that looked either like the hospital in Rivière-du-Loup or Dr. Panneton's office on Rue Lafontaine. Imagine her surprise when she realized Dr. Beck worked above a laundry. His name was engraved on a barely visible gold plate: Doctor David Beck. Physician. They walked up a long wooden staircase and out into a dimly lit hallway. There was an open door at the end. Not much in the way of furnishings. A few armchairs, and a counter behind which a young woman was working. She smiled and greeted Solange and Madeleine in French. Her name was Rachel Beck, she said; she was the doctor's daughter and assistant. She wanted to know if Solange and Madeleine had had a good trip. They didn't reply. Where had this girl—she was around their age—learned French? Rachel had long curly hair, tied back with a green elastic band. The rest of her exuded calm and sobriety. A child no one had ever raised a hand to, thought Solange. She explained that her father, a European, had insisted she learn French, and that she was getting ready to enroll at Columbia University, though in what exactly she wasn't sure yet. Rachel showed great concern for them. Her every gesture was a soothing contrast to Donatella Donatello; probably without realizing it, the Italian woman had made the girls feel quite frantic. No one ever walked out of Tosca's Diner feeling calm and at peace with themselves.

Rachel disappeared for a moment down a hallway they couldn't see from the waiting room. She came back with her father, David Beck. A thin man, his face hidden behind a carefully trimmed beard, Beck plucked a pair of glasses from his doctor's coat. He, too, spoke some French.

His appearance was a brutal reminder of the reason the two girls had just travelled over a thousand miles by coach. Solange clasped Madeleine's hand.

"Is she your sister?" Beck inquired.

"No, my neighbour."

Beck smiled. He motioned for Madeleine to follow him. The two girls glanced at each other. Madeleine followed the doctor to the end of the hallway. A white door closed behind them. Solange stayed behind with Rachel in the waiting room and immediately went about decimating her fingernails with her incisors. A telephone rang. Rachel excused herself. Solange decided to pray. What else was to be done? Once the call was over, Rachel was back to her friendly self. She was visibly delighted to be able to practice her French with a girl her age.

"My teachers are all so old!"

"Are they French?" Solange asked.

"Yes. Why do you ask?"

"Because you talk like you're from France."

"That's because my teachers are from France. They came here to the United States after the war."

The compliment—at least that's what she took it to be—had left Rachel blushing and given her some encouragement.

"Do you like jokes?" she asked, a sudden glint in her eye.

"I suppose so, yes. Like everyone," Solange replied, finding her remark to be out of place. A joke? Was this really the time?

"Papa always tells me a joke to get me to laugh. Would you like to hear it?"

"Why not?"

"So it's the story of an old lady who used to go to the park every day to read. One day, she sits down on her favourite bench in Central Park to read the newspaper. A pigeon arrives and begins to talk to her. The two quickly become friends, and the old lady invites the pigeon over for coffee the following day at four o'clock in the afternoon. The pigeon is pleased and says yes."

"That's funny," Solange lied.

"It gets better! At four o'clock the following day, the lady waits for the pigeon to arrive. But it doesn't come. At half past four, it still hasn't showed up. The old lady is very sad. The pigeon rings the bell at a quarter to five. The lady rushes to open the door.

'You're late! I've been waiting for you. Where were you?' she asks.

And the pigeon replies, 'I'm very sorry, ma'am, it was such a nice day I decided to walk.' Hahaha! Isn't that funny?"

Solange smiled. No. She didn't find it at all funny. She didn't understand why the crazy old woman would waste her time reading in the park. People in Rivière-du-Loup had better things to do than go around reading on park benches and talking to birds. Besides, aside from July and August, it was too cold to do that. But she wanted to be polite.

"Your French is really good."

And she was being honest. Sure, Rachel had an American accent you could cut with a knife, but she spoke excellent French for a New York City girl.

Beyond Dr. Beck's office was an examining room. Madeleine, from the other side of the half-open door, could make out oxygen bottles, a stretcher, and a tray covered in surgical instruments: specula, forceps. A pair of latex gloves lay slumped on a second stainless-steel tray. That was all Madeleine could see. Beck asked her to take off her winter coat, hat, and white scarf. Later she told Solange that he'd been very kind. His accent, difficult to understand at first, reminded her of Mr. Zucker's, Irene's travelling salesman. He asked Madeleine to sit on a little sofa.

A simple floor lamp lit the windowless room. It must have been eighteen degrees at most. Madeleine shivered. Beck chatted to her.

"You're a very young lady. You have plenty of time ahead of you, no?"

Madeleine nodded, embarrassed.

"You should see a doctor in two months, just to make sure everything is OK."

Madeleine didn't speak.

"Did you bring the payment?"

Madeleine took the envelope out of her bag. The doctor opened it in front of her. He counted the bills, looked approvingly at Madeleine, and put the envelope in the drawer of his big wooden desk. As he did so, he switched on the table light, which illuminated the items on the desk. Papers, pens, a photo of Rachel when she was small. No photos of Mrs. Beck. A smattering of books in the upper right-hand corner. A calendar. A china saucer in which something golden shone intensely. Beck disappeared off into the examining room and came back with a hospital smock.

"Time to get undressed. I'll be back in five minutes. Please take everything off."

"Everything?"

"Yes, everything. When you're done, lie down on the table over there."

Beck left the office. Madeleine slowly took off all her clothes and put on the smock. It seemed freezing cold to her touch. As she walked past the doctor's desk, she was struck by the golden light shining up at her from the china saucer. A dozen tiny gold crosses glinted beneath the table lamp's sixty watts. Some of them were initialled, like Madeleine's. Others were anonymous. The rays they projected seemed to illuminate the whole room and bathe everything in their golden light. Madeleine remembered that Dr. Beck had insisted she take off everything and so she removed her little cross. Frightened she might lose it, she set it down beside the china saucer, beneath the green table lamp, and walked slowly into the examining room, like the Greeks approaching Mount Olympus.

Beck was true to his word and came back after a few minutes, this time with his stethoscope. He stopped by the desk for a moment. Madeleine heard a metallic clink. Then he was in the examining room. A few tears fell onto the table as Beck's cold stethoscope moved across her belly. Madeleine's gaze stopped on a row of three little brown vials. Fine writing on them, indecipherable to her eyes.

"What is that?" she asked.

"*Morphium.*"

"What for?"

The doctor fumbled for the words.

"It's for... uh. When one has... *Schmerzen?* Pain?"

"I see."

La peine, that's what she'd understood. *Avoir de la peine.* To be sad. The vials were for when people were sad. The doctor asked her a few more questions then asked her to raise her knees. Madeleine felt his cold fingers on her kneecaps, then inside her thighs. That's where he was looking now. He stopped suddenly and took a step back, as though Madeleine had whispered the third secret of Fatima to him from between her legs.

"What is this?" he exclaimed.

"A birthmark. I got it from my father."

"It's a bass clef?"

"Yes. My little brother Luc had the same thing, but he's dead now."

"They say it looks like some sort of clef. I don't know. I'm not musical."

The doctor was looking at his patient differently now, a mixture of amazement and incredulity. Suddenly there came a terrified hammering on the door. Then came Rachel's voice, nervous and shrill. "Papa, Papa, come!" Steps in the hallway. Voices could be heard through the half-open door. Someone was crying, saying "No!" At least, that's what it seemed like to Madeleine. Then, as Madeleine was to tell Solange later, a long shiver ran through her, air rushed into the examining room. The wind had picked up outside.

It was impossible, she'd later say, to explain the sequence of events. Everything was hazy. Pneumonia, that's what she'd catch, lying on the table in the cold like that, practically naked. She could only think of one thing: the warmth of her clothes. She got dressed as fast as she could, like she did on the mornings Irene forgot to wake her for school. But she took the time all the same, watching herself in the mirror on the wall, to adjust the dried rose from Maria Callas, which she had taken out. She liked how she looked with a red rose in her hair. The cross was no longer where Madeleine had left it. Beck must have thought it was one of his and put it in the saucer where all the others glistened. The golden light, almost palpable in the dark room, seemed to radiate heat. It was impossible to look away; Madeleine was completely enraptured by the gold.

"Take me," the little gold crosses seemed to whisper to her. Madeleine thought back to her hoard of treasures squirrelled away behind the baseboard in her room in Rivière-du-Loup. That's where the crosses were asking to be taken, northward. Should she take them all? They jingled as they tumbled into her pocket. And now the envelope! Madeleine wasn't going to leave the doctor three hundred dollars for something he hadn't done! The drawer wasn't even locked. Now get out of here! That's what the little voice inside her had been screaming ever since they'd arrived in the city. Scram. Run like a thief and take Solange with her.

Madeleine laced her ankle boots in a rush, grabbed her bag and coat, and sprinted to the waiting room, without dwelling on the strange opera that was unfolding there. Rachel was sitting behind the counter, arguing with a man in a grey suit, a heavy-set man with a moustache who was clearly unhappy about something. He was brandishing a notebook, stabbing at it with his fingers as he shouted a flurry of words ending in -ing. Dr. Beck was trying to mollify him. Everybody had lost their temper and Madeleine knew enough about human nature to know that they would soon come to blows.

She tugged on her friend's hand.

"We're leaving. Let's go, Solange!"

They raced down the stairs five at a time, spilling out onto 10th Avenue. A mad dash forward, through shouts and blaring car horns, to the other side of the street. Dr. Beck emerged soon afterward and looked around for his patient, closely followed by Rachel, hugging herself against the cold.

"What's going on, Madeleine? Have you lost your mind?"

"We have to get out of here before they see us. Come on! Run!"

And run they did. Very awkwardly, too. If they'd simply dashed into the first store, Beck would never have found them. But how could you miss two girls running and shouting down the icy 10th Avenue sidewalk, one of them wearing a red rose in her hair and the other an orange coat? They fled with all the subtlety of a Soviet tank. Youth, yes, youth, the curse that until that day had been Madeleine's greatest handicap, would this time save her.

"They're right behind us!"

The girls zigzagged between pedestrians, bumped into grandmothers.

"Sorry, ma'am."

Beck was shouting now. His voice seemed to be gaining on them, Rachel's too.

"Come back!"

Right? Left? It was up to chance.

"Don't look back!" Solange gasped.

The wind suddenly picked up. Beck was no more than twenty yards behind them. Madeleine looked around for a way out, felt her legs go weak. Huge snowflakes then began to fall all around, as though an angel had shattered into a billion tiny frozen tears. No strangers to snowstorms, the Canadian girls kept on running, while Beck and his daughter slowed, swearing and shielding their eyes from the sudden, ill-timed blizzard.

The tops of the skyscrapers could no longer be seen, so thick was the snow. Madeleine, still holding Solange's hand, felt like they were moving through a cloud. They turned left again and went off in an unfamiliar direction. They were young all right, but sooner or later the heart can't keep up. They didn't speak. Just trudged through the snow. They'd lost them. West Side passersby, surprised by the storm—despite the forecast—could have described the two crazy young girls who, helpless with laughter, began throwing snowballs at each other. French girls. Very annoying, very loud French girls. They walked through the snow, got a little lost, as much as you can get lost in Manhattan.

"We need to go back to the station, Madeleine. If you've made up your mind you're leaving. I'll follow you."

"Ma will kill me."

"You can come live with us."

"And what about *your* mom?"

"Mom? She had nine! One more's not going to make any difference. You did the right thing, Madeleine. We'll just have to deal with the rest."

It only took Solange a few moments to work out where they were. The walk back to the Port Authority Bus Terminal seemed to take forever. They were cold now. They fell quiet, trying to save their energy. A thin layer of snow had formed on Tosca's dried rose.

Madeleine got a bad feeling the minute they arrived at the terminal. Sure enough, as soon as they set foot inside, they spotted Dr. Beck and his daughter Rachel waiting for them. How could they have been so stupid? Everyone knew that the French girls who came down to Manhattan to take care of a certain something left from the same hole they'd emerged out of: the Port Authority. For them, there was only one way into New York City. And now Beck was scanning the hall, like a cat outside a mousehole, on the lookout for an orange coat.

Solange and Madeleine hid behind a pillar. There was no way they could board without being seen. Beck knew what he was doing.

"They're here! Dammit, Madeleine, what are we going to do now? And what's their problem anyway?"

"I don't know, Solange. I took back the envelope he'd put in the drawer. Maybe that's what he's after."

"Still, they have a nerve coming here to get their money back."

There are times in life when you have to decide if you're Louis "The Horse" Lamontagne's daughter or not. The plan was simple: walk in like nothing was the matter and make a beeline for the escalators that led to the boarding gates. Success would depend on them being able to make their way unnoticed through the stream of passengers—and on the coach driver being on time. After the escalator, one last sprint to the boarding gate where, if God really did exist, they would be the last to get on the bus. Solange still wasn't keen on setting foot inside the building, convinced they'd be flushed out within seconds.

"We're taking a big risk, Madeleine."

"I know, but we can't spend the night just wandering the streets. We need to go home."

"Well, we could walk around for a while and take the coach home tonight at eleven. He and his daughter aren't going to stick around for another eleven hours!"

"Have you seen the snow? Where are we going to walk to? The bus leaves in five minutes. Come on!"

They slipped in with a group of students their age. You're never more invisible than when you look like those around you, a basic rule of camouflage that the Sisters of the Child Jesus had understood years before. The tactic paid off: Beck and his daughter didn't look in their direction, clearly on the lookout for two girls travelling alone.

Around Madeleine, the nasal voices of the New York students, words they didn't understand, "Really, I think a woman should be able to decide." She made a show of looking at them to make it look as though they were part of the group, "I agree with you. It's really up to a woman and her doctor." The hallway just wouldn't end. "This isn't Texas, after all." And then, there it was: the escalator was in sight!

They were through the danger zone, but strangers as they were to the city and to how crowds moved in general, they hadn't expected the group of girls covering them to move off so suddenly. With fifty yards to go to the escalators, Madeleine and Solange suddenly found themselves exposed. It didn't take more than three seconds for Rachel's voice to ring out: "Dad! Look! Quick!"

They were running again, across a floor now damp from the snow coming down off the passengers' clothing in little clumps. The same snow had moistened Tosca's dried rose, and it was now almost back to looking its best. Swollen and made heavy by the wet snow, Callas's flower was hanging onto Madeleine's hair by no more than the grace of God, who had grown weary of bearing the extra weight. Just as Beck was about to put his hand on Solange's shoulder—with the intrigued passengers looking on—the flower fell limply beneath the doctor's left shoe—a rubber-soled derby made from the finest quality leather, complete with cushioned insole—which skidded clumsily, sending its owner sprawling to the floor. A sprained ankle, a broken kneecap. Beck also hurt his wrist as he tried not to hit the floor with his chin. The Port Authority Bus Terminal erupted into a howl of pain that the girls didn't even hear as they raced away. Three ladies riding the escalator were shoved out of the way. At Gate 32, Archibald Jackson, a man as black as the night, glanced at his watch one final time before closing the departure gate. He didn't see Solange and Madeleine bearing down on him until the last second, breathless, their shoulders still covered in snow, their faces panicked, their hands brandishing return tickets.

The Greyhound left the parking lot at noon on the dot. Solange looked back at the city one more time, or at least at what the storm allowed her to see of it, and told herself she'd be back one day. Maybe with the child Madeleine would be bringing into the world, the child she'd tell: "This is where you were born. You're a child of New York City, a New York City boy." Because it was a boy, she just knew. Before she fell asleep with exhaustion, she imagined the teal-coloured eyes he would have.

Madeleine fell asleep too, fingering through the leather of her bag the three vials of morphine she'd stolen from Dr. Beck. She felt across her chest for her little golden cross, but couldn't find it.

When she woke up, she had to wait for Solange to fall back to sleep again before she could look for her cross among the ones she'd taken. It wasn't there. A lump formed in her throat. The cross had her grandmother's initials on it, which is to say her own initials: M.L. She could remember leaving it *beside* the saucer while she got undressed. Could she have left it behind on Dr. Beck's desk? Madeleine couldn't believe how stupid she'd been. Too late to go back now. So she'd left her cross there. Losing that cross would haunt her bouts of insomnia for years to come, until the day she stopped thinking about it.

She picked through the little crosses she'd stolen until she found the one that looked most like the one she'd lost. It was initialled L.B. Who might that be? Lisette Bernier? Louise Breault? Who was that woman? But, most important of all, how would she ever get her own cross back? The one her grandfather had given Madeleine the American in 1918? As she fastened the chain behind her neck, Madeleine was wracked by sobs that roused Solange from her sleep.

"Why are you crying?"

"I left something behind in New York," Madeleine sobbed.

"Not your cross! Sister Mary of the Eucharist made me promise you'd never be parted from it!"

Madeleine didn't know what to say. Losing the cross was unspeakable. She thought for a moment, looked around in vain for a hankie to dry her tears, then brought a hand up to her neck to where the white scarf should have been. Her face lit up.

"The white scarf Deborah gave me! That's what I lost!"

"I think you're tired, Madeleine. It's just a silk scarf. We'll get you another one. Now sleep. We've a long way to go."

The trip went on and on, punctuated by Madeleine's bouts of nausea, scheduled stops, unplanned stops forced on them by the terrible weather, the long wait in Montreal, the string of little towns and villages, Rivière-Ouelle, Saint-Pascal, Notre-Dame-du-Portage, and at the end of the white hell, the coach dropped the two girls off in Rivière-du-Loup, where they'd boarded the bus two days earlier but twenty years younger.

They found their town buried in snow, as restless as they'd ever seen it. Since they weren't expected before nightfall, there was no one waiting to pick them up. Half crazy with exhaustion, nauseous, and furious at having gone through what they would henceforth call their trip to hell and back, Solange and Madeleine walked up Rue Lafontaine, heads held high, ready to confront Irene, to spit in her face if need be.

Solange had already pictured a particularly violent scene in which she would make her pay for the humiliation she'd been subjected to two days before. People stared at them in the street. Folks who knew them didn't say hello, not even the ones they'd been to school with.

"Can you please tell me why everyone's looking at us like we're aliens from another planet?"

"Probably because I'm so green. Oh no. Hang on a minute. I think I'm gonna be… Oh sweet Jesus…"

Madeleine could no longer control her nausea and had been throwing up every hour since early morning. As they neared the parish of Saint-François-Xavier, the looks became more insistent. Women came out onto their balconies, shawls thrown hastily around their shoulders. "Go home, Madeleine. Your mother's waiting." Apocalyptic faces. Two police cars were parked outside the Lamontagne home. As the girls walked into the living room, a dozen red-rimmed eyes turned to look at them. After enduring Marcoux's pointless sarcasm, Louis Lamontagne had left the Ophir just as winter was about to set in. "Slightly more worse for wear than usual," the bartender admitted. Then Louis, without anyone knowing why, had crossed Rue Lafontaine instead of heading home and found himself on the railway tracks. There it was presumed he walked on for a while longer before being struck head-on by a Canadian National locomotive.

"He must have died on the spot."

The words brought little comfort to Madeleine, who was in shock. Louis had been missing for several hours. They had presumed he was in some mistress's bed until the railroad workers found him that morning, a bump in the snow a few yards away from the tracks. There he was, under close to a foot of snow that had fallen during the night. The gossips, magnificent in their role as professional mourners, came up with no end of imbecilic reasons to explain how he'd met his end: driven to suicide by slander.

They couldn't find a casket big enough to hold him. The one ordered specially from Quebec City didn't arrive until an hour after Solange and Madeleine came back, which meant that when they walked in Louis' body was still lying on a door supported by two sawhorses. Irene had switched the heating off so the body wouldn't putrefy too quickly. Louis' face was blue from the snow. He looked at peace, his arms folded across his chest.

"Like a king," a trembling Solange would tell her mother a few hours later.

It was feared the news might prove too much for Sister Mary of the Eucharist, so an able emissary was sent to inform the nuns. Father Rossignol flitted from branch to telegraph wire all the way to Rue Saint-Henri, wondering what to say to Mother Mary of the Great Power since she'd have to be told first.

She was superb and steady, her reaction worthy of the man who had been her protégé.

"You can tell Irene the nuns will take care of the funeral. She can rest and pray for Louis' soul."

In the convent's great hall, reduced to a palace of tears, all the nuns gathered; all that is, except Sister Mary of the Eucharist, who couldn't be found. She arrived at last, her boots covered in snow after a stroll through the fir trees that surrounded the provincial house. She wiped her feet conscientiously, took off her coat, and turned to face, without a modicum of surprise, the sixty or so nuns, Mother Superior, and Father Rossignol, who were all staring at her. Sister Saint Alphonse's double chin was still trembling, two enormous tears running down her cheeks like polar pearls. Outside in the forest, the black-capped chickadees had gone quiet. Sister Mary of the Eucharist knew already, just as she had known for her twin sister in Nagasaki. She looked at them, full of pride, almost haughtily, and proclaimed, loud and clear, so that all would remember:

"Louis, joy of man's desiring!"

The question on every tongue was as follows: who among them would have the courage to throw the first clod of earth down onto Louis Lamontagne's casket?

"Have the courage? What do you mean *courage*? Surely you mean, 'Who would have the honour of throwing the first clod of earth onto Louis Lamontagne's casket?' Well let me tell you something, sisters! I want it to be me! Because it was I who brought him into the world, who pulled him back from the clutches of death, who presented him like an offering to his speechless grandmother on Christmas night, God's way of making up for taking his mother, a poor, adorable woman come to die in a foreign land!"

Sister Mary of the Eucharist delivered her speech in theatrical tones that in other circumstances would have earned her some sort of award, trophy, or scholarship. None of the parishioners in the packed church opposed her wish, nor did any of the latecomers who had to stand through the funeral outside the church, its door left open despite it being the middle of December. Six or seven heads deep, the human tide that accompanied Louis Lamontagne to his final resting place must have been a quarter of a mile long. It took an excavator, borrowed from a building site in Témiscouata, to dig down through the dirt that was already frozen almost two feet deep.

"There's no way we're leaving him to freeze over at the charnel house. We'll bury him now."

The nun was categorical. Louis wouldn't be freezing among the living until spring put in an appearance. In the church where the Bach melody so dear to the dearly departed rang out, the remaining members of the Lamontagne family themselves looked as though they'd just been dug up that morning. Overcome with sorrow, the Lamontagnes, those Atridae of the New World, didn't say a word for days, no longer certain they spoke a tongue that God understood. Old Ma Madeleine fought back tears at the end of the family pew. Irene sat between her and Napoleon, demolished. Off to the side, because it was now out of the question that they sit next to Irene, Madeleine and Solange. The former struggling her way through a bout of nausea, the latter engulfed by unfathomable despair. Madeleine had been staying at the Bérubés' since they came back from the States. Next to them Siegfried Zucker, the travelling salesman who had everything you could possibly need at an unbeatable price. Before Louis was even in the ground Zucker had already organized Madeleine's escape. As they made their way to the cemetery, his voice covered by the sobbing of the women of Rivière-du-Loup, he reached out to the young Lamontagne girl, offering a chance to avoid the dark, deep disgrace the town's gossips intended to cast her into, bound hand and foot. Holding the two friends by the elbow, Zucker spoke in a whisper, making his Germanic accent even more of a hiss, even more mysterious. Only Solange could summon the strength to reply. That morning, Madeleine had opened the first vial of morphine she'd stolen from Dr. Beck and put a little drop beneath her tongue. He'd been right: it did make her less sad. A wave of nausea had washed over her; the colours around her had changed. Another drop before the funeral. She'd floated above the altar, heard Louis Lamontagne's laugh, watched the teal-coloured December sky. She developed a taste for morphine like others develop a taste for power and absinthe.

"Here you cannot stay."

"Here is our home, Mr. Zucker."

"The city. The city is what you need."

"We're just back from the city. We'd rather stay here."

Zucker became serious.

"You do not understand. Mrs. Irene told me… about… I mean… About your brother Marc…"

"Marc's dead."

"Exactly. Madeleine, do you want someone to throw that death in your child's face one day?"

"Mr. Zucker. Your business on one side, ours on the other. It's better that way. OK?"

"*Na!* Listen to me! You can't put your child through that! *Du hast keine Ahnung, wie dies ist, Solange.* I know. My mother, too… I… She… As well, I mean… Her brother…"

"Mr. Zucker, you're speaking out of turn. (Solange's tone was beginning to darken.) And Madeleine isn't going to keep it. She's going to give it up. The child will never know his father or mother."

"As you wish. I leave for Quebec City tomorrow, and for Montreal in a week. I've bought a building there, on Rue Saint-Hubert. There's a kitchen. You're both hard workers, no? There's an apartment upstairs. You can stay there a while. Think about it. Nobody knows anyone in the city. I don't mind if people think I'm the father."

"We're going to open our restaurant *here*."

"Ah yes? And you think they'll be lining up to eat at the undertaker's daughter's? What are you planning on serving? Cold meat?"

Zucker was possessed by the demon of sarcasm, an evil that could not be exorcised.

There's nothing like the terrifying *thunk* of earth hitting an oak casket to bring man's insignificance into focus. Louis was buried the day after the feast of the Immaculate Conception. Irene shut herself away in the Lamontagne family home, never going out more than once a week and getting by on the widow's pension the U.S. Army sent her until she fell into an alcohol-induced coma and died in March 1985. She would never speak to her daughter, or to Solange, again.

Hypnotized by the Bérubés' shiny Christmas tree baubles, Madeleine was beginning to emerge from her torpor. Zucker's words came back to her like warnings issued from a high Manhattan window. She tried to work out the mathematics behind the rumour, tried to come up with an equation. The problem was as follows: in a town there is always X number of people who know and Y number of people who don't. By virtue of the Law of Forgetting, the latter always end up outnumbering the former. The opposite is never true. In June 1919, for instance, every man and his dog knew the precise circumstances surrounding Louis Lamontagne's birth; witnesses to the event carried the story around inside them. But, as the years went by, the number of people who didn't know exactly how Louis had come into the world began to grow. An influx of newcomers, a jump in the birth rate… In short, those who didn't know were eventually in the majority—around April 1964, by Madeleine's calculations. The matter at hand was now the speed with which the population of Rivière-du-Loup would forget the origins of the child Madeleine would be bringing into the world a few months from then. The most conservative estimate she came up with was June 1990. Twenty-one years for the rumour to fade by half. The calculations were complex. Many factors had to be taken into consideration, namely the fact that she was a Lamontagne, which in itself lowered the forgetfulness coefficient by a few points. Also to be factored into the mix was the drivel people were spouting about her brother Marc, the frightening number of women Louis had loved in his lifetime, and the alarming rate at which news travelled up and down the town. Plus, the way storekeepers were already staring at her belly with eyes like sharp bayonets didn't leave much hope for a miracle. People knew, and they would know for a long time to come. "O land of fragile light, how poorly dost thou love thy children," Madeleine thought to herself. Another calculation, this time of a more practical nature, brought her back to Tosca's Diner. How many breakfasts would make her rich? That was much easier to work out.

"What does rich even mean?" Solange asked, trying to bring an end to her calculations.

"Rich enough to say we have money."

"You're going around in circles, Madeleine."

"We could do what Donatella Donatello did."

"You won't be able to all by yourself, Madeleine."

"I know. Come with me."

They left that January, not long after Solange managed to sell her Triumph. Sister Mary of the Eucharist was the only one to see them off at the coach station.

"Old Ma Madeleine made you raisin cookies," she sobbed.

They didn't look back. Madeleine would never set foot in her hometown again. Solange would go back fifteen years later to open a restaurant, then five years after that to bury her mother. By the time they turned up at Zucker's on Rue Saint-Hubert, Madeleine's belly was already beginning to show.

"I knew you'd come. I'll show you the kitchen."

The place at the corner of Saint-Hubert and Beaubien wasn't much to look at. It had belonged to a Polish family who'd left to make their fortune in Toronto. They'd run a lunch joint, which went by the uninspired name of Polska Deli Counter, that they'd been trying to get rid of for five years. Any would-be buyers who hadn't been overcome by the stench of grease continued their visit only to discover the place was coming down with mice. The rusty, faded sign creaking in the wind was the last straw for even the keenest prospects. Zucker had bought the place for a song, complete with an apartment above that cried "Paint me!" and a parking space behind, where rats and bums could be found sleeping helter-skelter in the morning. Despite Solange's skepticism, Madeleine was determined to make her restaurant a miniature version of Tosca's Diner. They spent that first winter in the apartment upstairs, heads buried in *The New England Cookbook* inherited from Madeleine the American. Among other things, they found the recipe for the pancakes—light and fluffy as clouds—that the other Madeleine had been renowned for in 1918. Though the pages on seafood were of no use to them, the sections that dealt with breakfasts were an invaluable source of inspiration.

"Look at those huge windows! Have you seen how many people walk by this place? Imagine each of them paying two bucks for something to eat. What do you serve them to turn a profit? Better yet: what do you serve them so they come back next week and give you another two bucks? And bring their aunts? Their cousins?"

And so Solange's vocation began. From that moment on, with Madeleine high on pregnancy hormones, she officially became Madeleine's assistant. Zucker looked on at his handiwork and rarely interfered. His benevolence stopped where Madeleine's zeal began. He was even surprised when, two days before Mado's opened in May 1969, the girls offered to buy back the restaurant from him.

"But you don't have the money."

"How much is it?"

"No, it's not for sale. You work. I pay you a salary. Everybody's happy."

"How much?"

Zucker didn't know whether to be annoyed or amused by Madeleine's stubborn tone. Truth was, he didn't need the restaurant. Blessed with an extraordinary nose for business, the Austrian could have sold sugar to Fidel Castro. His food distribution business was thriving; the restaurant would bring him no more than the satisfaction of knowing he'd lifted Louis Lamontagne's daughter out of a life of poverty and degradation. If he was reluctant to sell them the restaurant, it was largely because he feared their ruin in a city where they didn't know a soul. Where would they have gotten the down payment anyway? When Louis died, he'd left behind nothing more than the family home where Irene was steeping in her gin.

"Papa Louis had an insurance policy."

Insurance? In Zucker's eyes, the idea of Louis Lamontagne taking out an insurance policy seemed unlikely. It must have been Irene's idea. She was the only one in the family who had a head for figures. Irene and her daughter, by the looks of things.

"You're too young and it's too much."

"How much?"

Madeleine's determination amused him. Solange, standing behind her, stared at him as though begging him to comply. He almost laughed.

"*Ach! Mädels!*"

"I'll give you three thousand."

The Austrian burst out laughing.

"But I paid much more than that!"

Madeleine didn't turn a hair.

"Three thousand now and we'll owe you the rest."

Zucker thought it over. Barely eighteen and already a nose for business? He felt like having a little fun with them, even if just to see how Solange, a woman in man's clothing, would be transformed into a smiling, gracious hostess. What did he have to lose? Worst case, the restaurant would fall back into his hands. He spared a thought for his mother, a girl the Austrian countryside had catapulted off to Linz at age nineteen, pregnant by her own brother. She'd been taken on by an innkeeper, Ferdinand Zucker, the man she'd married. The eastern front had widowed her in 1943, only twenty years old and in charge of a forty-bed *Gasthaus*, with a rambunctious child running around her feet. *Zum Hirsch* was the name of the inn that had miraculously survived the Allied bombing. He'd grown up there on *Schnitzel* and *Strudel*, on *Knödel* and *Linzertorten*. He wiped a tear from his eye.

"I think we should see a notary."

Madeleine leaped into his arms, shed a few pregnant woman's tears, and went back to her rags and broom. On May 2, 1969, the first Mado's restaurant opened its doors. A monster was born. The restaurant, which had no more than thirty seats at the opening, six of them at the counter, was a surprise success from the get-go. Madeleine, who everyone presumed to be Zucker's daughter, amused the customers, most of them storekeepers on Rue Saint-Hubert. They looked on in astonishment as the pregnant girl flipped pancakes and fried bacon from dawn. Solange learned to smile. Mado's became their life, their *raison d'être*, their one and only thought, right up to the morning of June 15, when Madeleine had to shut up shop. Her child had stopped kicking two days earlier. Zucker was not going to hand her over to the Misericordia Sisters, not since he'd heard that the nuns, intent on teaching unwed mothers a lesson, refused to administer drugs to ease the pain of childbirth.

"Let that be a lesson to you, girl!"

Madeleine had imagined she'd bring her child into the world in the apartment she shared with Solange above the restaurant. But Zucker was having none of it: too dangerous. Instead, he left her in the hands of the nurses at Hôtel-Dieu Hospital, even though the place was crawling with nuns. Every last one of them refused to give the hysterical Madeleine anything to relieve the pain. In the hallways that echoed with her cries for help, Solange tore her hair out by the fistful. The shouts were heard all the way to Alberta. Solange was not allowed into the delivery room.

"Are you the father?" a nurse inquired sarcastically.

The hospital agreed, following a generous donation from Zucker, not to press charges for assault. The doctor had decided not to intervene and let the nun deal with that Amazon woman from the Lower St. Lawrence. He was much more concerned with the position the baby was in and the sounds his stethoscope was sending him.

"Get out of the way, you stupid cow."

The nun opted to stand down. While the doctor went looking for help Madeleine begged Solange to look in her bag.

"Take out Dr. Beck's vial."

"Are you sure, Madeleine?"

"Do what I say or I'll bite your nose off!"

The doctor returned to find Madeleine calm and dangerously dilated.

"You have a bass clef on your inner thigh. Your baby'll be a musician!" he joked.

Madeleine let out a morphinated laugh. Solange smiled grimly. The child, an enormous creature, was breech, as though intent on killing its mother. As it slipped out into the world, the city of Montreal was rent asunder by a cry for the ages. It was almost too much for Madeleine, just as it had been for The American. It was the doctor who helped her survive Gabriel's birth— and for a long, long time Gabriel remained the biggest baby ever seen at the hospital. When Madeleine expelled him from her body with one last push, the doctor picked him up and began to laugh.

"You sure don't do things by halves! But it's not over yet, Madeleine. There's another on its way."

Madeleine began to sing a hymn from her convent days.

"What do you mean, another one?" Solange yelped.

"Do you mean to say your friend didn't go to a doctor during the whole pregnancy?"

"Uh... no, I don't think so. At the start, yes. Dr. Panneton."

"Panneton? And where is his office?"

"Rivière-du-Loup."

"I clearly heard two hearts. Twins in separate sacs."

"Sacs?"

"They won't look like each other. The other might even be a girl."

The nun had taken the baby away as soon as Madeleine pushed it out and the umbilical cord had been cut. She mustn't become attached to it, the doctor said. Solange had seen the huge bloodied child—it was almost blue—pass from the doctor's hands to the nun, who stared daggers at her every now and again. She left Madeleine's side for a moment as her friend was swept up in a voluptuous bout of delirium featuring teal-eyed angels. She walked over to the child while the nun washed him. Solange smiled. She'd never seen anything so beautiful. A miniature Louis Lamontagne, his eyes still closed.

"He looks like Papa Louis, Madeleine!"

"Henceforth all generations shall call me blessed…"

Madeleine had moved on to the Magnificat. Gabriel had cleared the way so well that she almost didn't notice when she gave birth to Michel a half hour later. The nun, who still hadn't gotten over Solange's violent entrance, was now ready to take a bite out of her to defend herself.

"Don't look at them. You mustn't grow attached. It's better for you, and for your sister."

"She's not my sister."

"What are you doing here then?"

"What are *you* doing here?"

They would have come to blows again, had it not been for little Michel, who began to charm everyone around him from the moment he came into the world. The boys were laid side by side in the same bassinet.

"The second's smaller than the first, much smaller! You have to keep them, eh, Madeleine? You can't give them up! I'll help you! At least keep the first one, Madeleine!"

Madeleine fainted. Gabriel waved an arm in Solange's direction. Fascinated by how perfect his little fingers were, she slid her index finger into Gabriel's hand. He held it surprisingly tightly, even for a newborn. He was definitely The Horse's grandson, Solange thought. She was under his spell, always would be. Nothing else mattered. And that was the day, she'd later say, when she herself came into this world, after eighteen years of futile, aimless existence. God had sent her this gift to make up for all the rest, and she never dared admit to anyone that she was convinced she'd come out of the deal better off than before.

"Madeleine, you have to call him Gabriel, like the archangel! You've made two little angels!"

The nun clenched her teeth, spluttering with rage, and envy. In a move that was pure Lamontagne, Madeleine was back on her feet three days later. She gathered her things together and demanded to go home.

Zucker had tried to talk them out of keeping the babies. What's going to happen to the restaurant? What about their father? Who'll be their father? Solange smiled at the question. Crazy. She and Madeleine were both absolutely crazy. Zucker considered alerting the authorities, then, in true Austrian fashion, decided to mind his own business and let events run their course. They would have their fun. He would keep an eye on things, and when they were at their wits' end, the children would be handed over to the state. At least they'll have tried, he thought.

It was late June in Montreal. The streets of La Petite-Patrie were fragrant with the scent of roses; schoolchildren singing odes to freedom. A wind blew across town, rolling up skirts and ruffling men's hair. Hair was getting longer; churches were emptying. The two newborns were settled in a room in the four-room apartment Solange and Madeleine lived in above the restaurant, the same apartment they'd point at only a few years later, saying: "There it is. That was your first home." To help her survive her role as a new mother, Madeleine had decided Solange would take care of one of the boys. And so it was that in June 1969, Madeleine pushed Gabriel into the arms of her friend, paving the way, although she had no way of knowing it at the time, to years of pointless suffering.

"He reminds me too much of Papa Louis. You can take him."

She kept little Michel for herself. He was more fragile, his body always a year behind his brother's. Madeleine was clear: the boys could never know. Ever. She would tell them how they came to be when the time came. There was to be no talk of Rivière-du-Loup, the nuns, Irene, or of those other people who, at any rate, had wanted nothing to do with them. Zucker was instructed to be discreet and never to mention Louis Lamontagne, him drinking himself to death, or anything else that might make him tangible in the boys' minds. They would be Montrealers. Irene's resentment had made it so. Of their village on the shores of the St. Lawrence, the girls would keep their accent, its shortened vowels, its guttural Rs, and an unhealthy obsession with cleanliness and hard work. Their heritage also included a few holy pictures, notably a particularly poignant portrait of St. Cecilia, along with a belief in God and regular attendance at mass, just like they'd promised Sister Mary of the Eucharist, who, no more than any of the other nuns, ever attempted to contact them.

Call Her Venise

Mado's became the neighbourhood's most popular breakfast joint. People would come to watch the two young women bustling about the hotplates. Madeleine did the cooking, while Solange served the customers. Both wore baby blue uniforms, their hair done up in a bun. *Mado's* embroidered in teal-blue handwritten lettering above the left breast. No one, not even Madeleine, had an inkling that this simple outfit was about to become the daily uniform of so many hundreds of young Quebec women. A waitress was hired, then another. Two neighbourhood girls barely older than Madeleine and Solange.

Perhaps things might have turned out differently for the twins and their "moms" if Venise Van Veen had decided to eat elsewhere or to skip breakfast altogether that morning. Until that very moment, the girls' future remained uncertain. Before their fate was to become a story worth telling, they were still lacking the aura lent by celebrity. In short, besides that one small triumph over adversity, they needed something to happen that would propel them even further forward, an event that would cause the media spotlight that swept wildly across the world to stop directly over them and the archangel twins. Years later, Solange must have thought back to the summer of 1969 as the time when she was still in total and absolute control of everything. And if she were asked to freeze a single frame of her life for all eternity, she would choose those summer days in the sunlit diner on Rue Saint-Hubert, with Madeleine busy cooking, her customers sitting in their little red leather booths, a Michèle Richard song playing on the radio, and the till respectably full. The twins sleeping in the apartment upstairs, sometimes needing to be brought down to the restaurant when they cried. Solange sought to recall the particular moment when that perfect balance snapped. She looked back on the journalist coming into their lives the way Americans remember Pearl Harbour. Hard to say what might or might not have been if Venise Van Veen hadn't decided that morning in June 1969 that she wanted to start her day with a pancake. And so it was that a few days before the Saint-Jean-Baptiste holiday, fate once again intervened in Madeleine Lamontagne's life, this time taking the form of a well-known Radio-Canada presenter. It was Solange who spotted her first.

"Don't look now, but I think that's Venise Van Veen... She's coming in..."

Venise Van Veen was the host of the new nightly culture show, *Call Me Venise*, on Radio-Canada. She was the kind of no-nonsense woman who could look a prime minister in the eye and ask, "Are you going to be frank with me, sir?" No shrinking violet, she was used to rubbing shoulders with the who's who of Montreal: artists, politicians, writers, academics. And she was a woman who spoke her mind: at the age of twenty-seven, she had been hired to provide a woman's take on the issues of the day. She came to the restaurant very early that Friday morning, around seven o'clock, sat down at the counter, and ordered a "Solange pancake" in an imperious tone. Solange had watched her walk in slowly, inspecting the diner before she chose a seat in case it was the kind of place where she didn't want to risk being seen. Without a doubt, Solange had thought to herself as she watched her, she would go for the pancake menu. Her father had been born in France and so she spoke with a posh accent that charmed Madeleine and exasperated Solange. As she waited for her meal, Venise gave the Sacred Heart and the picture of Saint Cecilia tacked to the wall a derisive smile. She almost snickered aloud when she caught sight of the palm crosses. Solange came over with her plate and she gobbled it down at once, as though frightened someone might steal her pancake.

"I am a woman of few words," she lied. "But I must say that pancake was especially... how can I put it? Especially *aaairy*! An *American*-style pancake, unless I'm very much mistaken. My compliments, miss," she said to Madeleine, who was bustling between the hotplate and the cutting board, waving her hands in the air like an octopus.

It was Solange who kept the conversation going.

"Thank you, Mrs. Van Veen!"

"You recognize me?"

"Yes, you're on television. We know who you are."

"And *youuuuu* are?"

"Solange Bérubé. And this is Madeleine Lamontagne."

The guest seemed intrigued.

"You both seem very young to be working. Are you *stuuudents*?"

Solange smiled. Venise had a habit of stretching out her vowels, and would do it at least twenty times every show.

"No, we're not students. This is our restaurant."

"I *seeee*. You're working for your parents, like so many young women. So that's it."

"No, no. Mado's belongs to us. She's Mado. This is our restaurant," Solange insisted.

"At your age? But how is that possible?"

"Well, it is. As you can see. More coffee, Mrs. Van Veen?"

"Yes, just a little. But you do *everything*? That seems a lot for two women."

"Mr. Zucker helps us with the accounting, but Madeleine can do most of it on her own now. He's there to help. He gets us everything we need."

"*Zuuucker?*"

"He's from Austria, like Mozart. His name means 'sugar' in his own language."

"Hmm. And Mado's is always this busy?"

"Almost always. It's quieter at the start of the week. We close Mondays and Tuesdays, when it's too quiet."

"A woman needs her rest!"

Their conversation was interrupted by the sound of raised voices from a table behind them. Two shady-looking characters were giving Juliette the waitress a hard time. The men had come in just after Venise, a fat man and a thin one. Laurel and Hardy had sat down and were now harassing the young woman in the lewdest, loudest way. Their degrading insults washed up against the counter, leaving oozing brown stains in the minds of everyone they touched.

"Just one moment, ma'am. I have to deal with this," Solange apologized to Venise.

The two ne'er-do-wells had spent the night out on the town and, come dawn, found themselves famished and with no sweet companions on their arms. For a moment, Solange worried their fetid breath might strip the wild strawberry–print wallpaper from the walls; she'd had a devil of a time putting it up. The scene was brief but effective. A few choice words, a couple of kicks up the ass, and the two stunned rascals were outside on the sidewalk. Solange could be heard proffering further threats from her vast repertoire before they scuttled away. Solange picked up her conversation with a wide-eyed Venise Van Veen without missing a beat. The television personality settled her bill, left Solange an almost embarrassing tip, and announced she would be back at the same time the following day.

"Have you ever been on television?"

"Never."

"See you tomorrow, then, my dear *Solaaange.*"

"See you tomorrow, Mrs. Van Veen."

"Call me Venise."

Venise Van Veen came back to eat the next day and the next and the one after that. Each time, she brought a journalist she worked with, a minor celebrity. In September 1969, she had breakfast at Mado's three times a week. It was in the fall that she put her plan into action. Having gained Madeleine and Solange's confidence, Venise proposed recording *Call Me Venise* in the restaurant, using the opportunity to introduce the province to two women she found fascinating (something she was always telling them).

"I find you both *faaaascinating.*"

Solange turned her down flat. There was no way she was going to take up half of the already too-small restaurant with so many people; people who would go on and on for hours on end while they sipped a coffee or nibbled on a round of toast.

"We only have thirty places, Venise... and overheads," came her curt reply.

Madeleine saw things differently. She remembered her father's business and thought back to the obstacles The Horse had faced. There was no shortage of dead bodies, but they didn't all want to be embalmed by him. How come? As Madeleine told it, it all boiled down to gossip and perception. And now someone was giving her the chance to feed the gossip mill, to have it work in her favour for once. She eventually convinced Solange, who managed to squeeze one concession out of Venise: she would never appear on camera. She couldn't have cared less what the people of Rivière-du-Loup might think; no, her concern lay elsewhere. Solange quite simply didn't want to be around for all eternity. She already had everything she'd always wanted. The rest was no more than "window dressing," as she liked to say.

And so the program was recorded one October morning just after the breakfast rush. The production team had come a few days ahead of time to move this and arrange that, to fiddle with the lighting and gussy up the place. Venise insisted on opening the show with a body shot of herself outside the restaurant on the corner of Saint-Hubert and Beaubien. After a few words of welcome explaining the change of décor to an audience more used to seeing Venise inside a studio, Madeleine was to walk into the shot, coffee pot in hand. Interviews would follow with that morning's guests sitting around a table. The lineup included a French philosopher, a Canadian opera singer, a federal government minister, and, naturally, a "Solange pancake" or two. The introduction was short, and Madeleine entirely charming. Her resemblance to French singer Mireille Mathieu was not lost on a single viewer, and her smile, which she had inherited from her American grandmother, outshone all the guests. She only had to come into shot and suddenly the whole world revolved around her.

Solange managed to keep the boys away from the media circus for a time, but destiny decided otherwise. They shared the same blood as Louis Lamontagne, after all. Venise ended her show with a short interview with Madeleine, asking her to explain, among other things, her menu.

"They're recipes handed down to me by my grandmother."

"Oh *reaaaally*. And was she a cook?"

"Uh… yes. I guess so."

Earlier, the cameraman had also filmed Madeleine lifting cast-iron pans and sacks of flour.

"Madeleine, we saw you lifting heavy pans and the like earlier. Wherever did you get your strength?"

"Oh, you know. That just comes with working in the kitchen!"

Off in a corner by herself, Solange almost choked.

"And tell me, Madeleine, your parents… you told me you lost your parents. Where do you get your inspiration from? To whom do you turn for advice?"

"First, to God. Then to Mr. Zucker, who helped me open my restaurant. He's always there when I need him."

"Siegfried Zucker of Zucker Food?"

"Yes, he's a real gentleman."

"And do you always wear your little cross?"

"Yes, it keeps me safe."

"Well, thank you once again, Madeleine, for such a warm welcome. May God protect you and your restaurant and all those you *looove*."

To thank Madeleine for allowing her to bring her show to the restaurant, Venise presented her on camera with a little pendant, a piece of jewellery beyond the young woman's means. For a moment, the entire province looked on as her gaze fell upon the twinkling object, her lips parted, her fingers took it, her face momentarily hypnotized by the comforting glow of gold and precious metals. Venise had to snap her fingers to rouse Madeleine from her reverie. Laughter rang out. Venise turned to the camera to wrap up the show.

"That's all for today, ladies and gentlemen. Thank you for joining us for this special edition of *Call Me Venise*, brought to you from the restaurant of this exceptional young woman, Madeleine Lamontagne. And if you have a chance to drop by Saint-Hubert and Beaubien, you too will be able to admire Madeleine's eyes. What colour are they, Madeleine. Turquoise?"

"Teal," Madeleine replied.

"*Teaaal*. Charming! And, by the way, life will never be the same again without a 'Solange pancake' for breakfast. Enjoy your weekend. And remember: dare to dream, ladies!"

"And... cut!"

The program was broadcast the following evening, a Friday. In the homes of French Canada, Madeleine's accent was welcomed like the song of an angel. Her ingenuousness, her youth, and her smile melted even the most cynical hearts. Reaction, however, was mixed in Rivière-du-Loup. On the one hand, people were proud to see Louis' girl bring her local charm as far as the big city. But why hadn't she taken the opportunity to honour her father's memory? Some took this to mean Madeleine had disowned them, as though she were turning her back on her roots, which wasn't entirely unfounded.

The morning following Venise's show, Solange and Madeleine woke up from two hours' sleep. The twins were teething. Solange was the first to go downstairs, at six o'clock, Gabriel still screaming in her arms. The staircase led from the apartment right into the restaurant.

"It's more *praktisch* in winter," Zucker had told them.

Solange warmed the hotplates, turned on the taps, set Gabriel down on the counter, switched on the radio, then froze. She had a feeling she was being watched. Someone or something was staring at her. Shadows milled around on the other side of the big windows. People were smiling and waving in at her. Solange took fright and went to get Madeleine, who came down with Michel in her arms.

"What do they want?" Solange hissed.

"Pancakes, dear Solange. They want pancakes. Call Mr. Zucker and Juliette, and tell Juliette to bring her sister."

"She's fourteen!"

"Well, today she's sixteen. That's old enough to work. Now come on. We can do this!"

"But Madeleine..."

By the time Zucker arrived at the restaurant, the girls had already served dozens of customers. A line had formed down the street.

"*Jo, Mädels*, that television show sure was a great idea!"

Madeleine and Solange were up to the job. In March 1970, they opened a second restaurant on the corner of Papineau and Beaubien. Zucker was a big help. It was he who got the servers and the new cooks trained and who took care of the accounting, all while keeping the restaurants well stocked. Months of hard work followed, along with a third restaurant in 1972 (at Saint-Denis and Jarry), then a fourth in 1973 (Mont-Royal and Chabot). The Mado's restaurant chain would never have enjoyed such a meteoric rise had it not been for the administrative clout provided by Zucker Food. Zucker taught Madeleine the joys of vertical integration and the subtleties of running a business. New restaurants popped up like mushrooms across the province, each welcomed with open arms. Having your own local Mado's was a gauge of civilization. Each time they opened a restaurant, Solange and Madeleine gave a town new proof of its existence. Soon the huge egg supported by three roses that Madeleine had chosen as their logo became a familiar part of the landscape in every town or city of more than twenty thousand souls.

Solange remained a staunch ally, through thick and thin. It was she who took care of the buildings and anything with an engine or a mechanism: refrigerators, freezers, stoves, delivery vans. A nanny was taken on to look after the boys, who were growing up in each other's slobbering company, two adorable little youngsters with round faces—the best-fed babies in town. In 1974 (grand opening on Sainte-Catherine and Pie-IX), Solange declared it was time for them to start sleeping in separate beds. Madeleine, who didn't believe in credit, decided she wouldn't move out of the apartment above the first restaurant until she was able to pay for someplace else outright. Gabriel, a sound sleeper, was only too happy to find himself in a little bed of his own, free at last from a nuisance of a brother who was of a nervous disposition and prone to nightmares. Michel wasn't so accepting. The first night, when the boys were put down in their little beds no more than six feet apart from each other, Michel began to howl.

"Nooo! Me want Gabriel! Waah!"

When they were older, Solange would tell them that Michel had thrown such a fit that night that they'd had to lie him down next to his brother. And Gabriel had somehow managed to sleep through it all, as soundly as The Horse ever did. Snuggled up against his brother, Michel had calmed down. Clutching a plush green frog under his left arm, Gabriel snored away, his head on the pillow. He was, and would always be, the first to fall asleep. Clinging to him like a bad smell, Michel, a whimperer and cougher by nature, held his brother by the penis, something he always needed to do to relax.

"It's strange, all the same," Solange remarked to Madeleine, who had found the sight of the pair of them as cute as could be.

"There's no harm in it at all. My brothers Luc and Marc used to do the same thing at that age. If it helps him fall asleep…"

Solange wasn't convinced, but she let this whim of Michel's pass, like many more to come. When he began to talk, instead of pronouncing "Mama" like a good French Canadian, like his brother, like Madeleine, and like everyone else, inexplicably it came out with a posh Parisian accent instead. Madeleine laughed; Solange bit her top lip. "My God, anything but that. Not that pain-in-the-ass accent," she howled inwardly.

"He's already talking like one of those well-dressed gentlemen on the news. He'll be a minister some day!"

Madeleine couldn't get over it. Gabriel, a child who didn't talk much but was plenty physical, required Solange's full attention. She raised him with a virile hand that few men would have been capable of. It was what he needed. Too big and strong for his age, he needed someone to keep a very close eye on him.

In 1975 (Longueuil, then Laval), the boys were packed off to school, where a teacher discovered Michel had a gift for music.

"I think he has absolute pitch, Mrs. Lamontagne."

"What does that mean?"

"He sings perfectly in tune. He can tell the notes apart."

"Is there any money in it?"

So Michel, a docile child who was always keen to please, was sent to a singing instructor, who found him adorable. Gabriel refused to go with his brother. He preferred being out on the motorbike with Solange. He even took to calling her Suzuki in honour of the bike they hopped on every Sunday afternoon while Michel took his singing lessons. Solange had bought it from one of Zucker's customers, who found it too "skittish." In 1977 (Sainte-Foy), Solange and Madeleine managed to buy a lovely home in the upscale Outremont neighbourhood of Montreal as English-speakers were fleeing the province in droves following the Parti Québécois' election. And so the boys played with middle-class Outremont children who had never heard tell of strongmen, funeral parlours in family homes, nuns who lived forever, or Saint-Jean-Baptiste and Corpus Christi parades.

In September 1980 (Rimouski), Siegfried Zucker was diagnosed with pancreatic cancer. Six weeks later, he was down to his last few painful hours in hospital, with Madeleine and Solange praying by his bedside.

"Are you in pain, Mr. Zucker?"

Zucker was in that place, shortly before death, where reason abandons the body.

"Be nice to the boys, Madeleine."

"Why do you say that, Mr. Zucker?"

"Because you're not always nice."

"You're suffering, Mr. Zucker. Would you like more morphine?"

"No, I want to die. Don't forget about The Horse, Madeleine."

Those were the Austrian's last words. Solange reminded Madeleine of them at the cemetery. Madeleine pursed her lips.

"The Horse is dead, Solange. We're on our own now."

Madeleine inherited Zucker's business affairs, including packing facilities, a slaughterhouse, a fleet of thirty-two refrigerated trucks, a warehouse, business premises in Pointe-Saint-Charles, and stock market shares and property assets worth more than every home and plot of land in Rivière-du-Loup put together. On Zucker's desk they found an envelope containing five tickets to *Tosca*, which the Montreal Opera had decided to put on as its very first performance that October. Madeleine looked intrigued.

"He probably wanted to take us. He often said he'd always wanted to go to the opera. Europeans are into that kind of thing… We should go with the boys."

"Aren't they a little young? Someone gets murdered," Solange said skeptically.

"If they're old enough to watch *The Passion of Christ* on TV on Good Friday, they're old enough for *Tosca*."

"How can you compare an opera to the suffering of Our Lord, Madeleine? *The Passion of Christ* teaches us something. It changes our hearts. It's more than mere entertainment."

"The same goes for *Tosca*, I think. They aren't just in it to get dressed up and sing in front of everybody. We're going. I'm sure it'll be good."

"And the fifth ticket?"

"What about the little Haitian girl who takes singing lessons from Madame Lenoir with Michel. What's her name again? The one he invited to his birthday party."

"Anamaria di Napoli?"

"Give her mom a call."

The Book Thief

Dear Michel,

You've been waiting for a while now for this reply to the letter you sent me at Easter. Phoned dear Suzuki last Sunday night to see if you were home, to speak to you. It was still afternoon in Montreal, so I was sure Mother Superior wouldn't answer since she's always at her office then. She was surprised to hear my voice. She told me the big news about you and Anamaria. Am so proud of you both. So you're in Rome? On a big movie shoot, Suzuki tells me. *Tosca*. Funny, it's the first opera we went to see, right after Mr. Zucker's funeral. Do you remember him and the barley sugar lollipops in the shape of a teddy bear he used to give you when he passed by the restaurant on Rue Saint-Hubert on Saturdays? You know, the ones you tried to sell to me, you little devil!

Your letter is full of questions. But where should I start after ten years away? Will try to bring you up to speed as best I can. First you should know I haven't gone mad. I have indeed, as you implied in your letter, the b(lond)est of reasons to be here in Berlin. All in good time. Her name's Claudia. No, not Schiffer; even better than that. Am sitting comfortably on the S-Bahn—it's a commuter train—as I write. It's still the best way to see Berlin, from the S-Bahn.

You ask why I haven't been in touch since suddenly leaving home in 1990. Had to reread your question several times. It's quite simple, Michel: I was sick and tired of being the butt of every joke. *Voilà*. Do I really have to spell it out?

Back when we were kids, you already showed a disturbing proclivity for torturing me. Need I remind you of the day at school when—we must have been ten—that crazy teacher wanted to put on a play about the colonization of Canada? You said I should be an Indian. You, of course, you got to play a French navigator, a role that fit you like a glove. The teacher dressed me up in some sort of loincloth, made from who knows what dead animal, and coated me with red powder. We performed the play in front of the younger kids one afternoon.

Then, when it was over, I couldn't find my clothes. I'd put them in a bag, but they were nowhere to be found. Not in the classroom, not in the theatre. Someone had taken them. And you, you little asshole, you came rushing in, saying Suzuki couldn't come pick us up, you'd spoken with her, she was too busy, we'd have to walk home. You made me walk halfway across Outremont, practically naked while you laughed. People driving by kept pointing at me and grinning. Needless to say, you hid when we got home so you wouldn't be around when I found out about your dumb joke. Claudia thought it was funny. That's because she doesn't know you. "Still so bitter about a cruel childhood prank?" you'll say. That was only one of the first symptoms of your illness.

You don't slam the door on the family nest over something so trivial, you'll say. Do you really think a simple discussion could have put everything right? Reason with Madeleine Lamontagne? You'd be wasting your time, unless your arguments will turn her a profit in the short to medium term.

Then you started winning competitions. When you were eighteen, you were already singing in recitals alongside established names. I think it was the day Mom bought that TV appearance for you (yes, I know it's news to you, but Suzuki told me: the whole thing was bought; the piece they asked you to sing, it was Mom who chose it. She knew that having you sing *La donna è mobile* at five o'clock in the afternoon would boost Mado Group Inc.'s presence in households across Quebec. First, the pancake mix, the cretons, and the frozen meals. Now, the tenor! That's all that was missing…). I'll never forget the day your singing teacher asked to speak to Mom: you absolutely *had* to study music, never had she seen such a precocious talent. To hear her, you would have thought you were the new Pavarotti. "Doesn't his voice remind you of Fritz Wunderlich?" she asked Mom. Do you remember? You can imagine the look on Madeleine's face! She hadn't the faintest idea who this Fritz-what's-his-name might be. But she replied: "Yes, I think so too." I almost burst out laughing in our Outremont kitchen. Already, when your name was still Michel Lamontagne, I barely existed in Mom's eyes; but as soon as you became Michel *de la* Montagne, I was forever condemned to the shadows.

In 1990, it took her a week to realize I was gone, Michel. After that, she had someone track me down. I hung up on her when she called. Our mom's crazy, Michel. Raving mad. Certifiable! For now, this works in your favour; she mollycoddles you, she spoils you, and even buys you a career as a tenor, but one day things are going to change. Once you've dishonoured Mado Group Inc.'s reputation for one reason or another, once you've blackened your name with scandal, that same craziness that made you will turn against you. There'll be nothing for it but to beg Mom for mercy. And to keep your trap shut.

There is still so much more I could tell you, but I know I'll only get carried away and end up writing a bunch of stuff I'll have to cross out afterward so as not to offend you, which isn't at all my intention. My S-Bahn is just coming into Westend anyhow. I'll write again tomorrow. So happy to be back in touch with you, brother.

Gabriel

～◌

Straußberg Nord – Westkreuz

April 30, 1999

Dearest Michel,

I reread the letter I wrote you the day before yesterday. Reading it over again, I realize it skirts the question you're not asking, namely what has become of me since 1990. In metric or imperial? Weighed myself at the gym this morning—I've found somewhere to work out on Landsberger Allee, the SEZ. It's good, almost better than the place I went to in Toronto—I'm almost ninety kilos! I weighed myself again on the S-Bahn scales. The Germans have scales on their railway platforms. It's handy: you can check to see if you've put on weight as you wait for the train. That's another reason I left you all. That crappy food all the time. All your body needs, Michel, is two cups of yogurt, a few pieces of fruit, an egg or two, and some lean meat every other day. The rest of the time, you drink water. Period.

When I left Outremont, I wound up, as you probably heard, at Chantal Villeneuve's, our old French teacher at Brébeuf College. I can hear you laughing. We'd been seeing each other for a few years already, but never openly. When I met her, she was thirty-three and married. Remember? We were finishing high school. It doesn't take long to realize you're good-looking, you know. If schools weren't run mostly by women and staffed by so many gay men, it might take a little longer. At Lajoie elementary school, for instance, I soon noticed the women teachers looking at me differently.

No matter how I misbehaved, I always got away with a reprimand, while the others were suspended for a day or two.

But there's something I have to tell you.

Remember the girl who taught us English at Lajoie before Mom ruined our lives and packed us off to Brébeuf? Her name was Caroline; she was from Saskatchewan. You were sitting up front, as usual, so the teacher could get a good look at you. I was at the back because I really, truly, couldn't have cared less about learning English; right up until the moment Caroline turned up. We were twelve. She was twenty. Long, straight red hair. Less makeup than most of our teachers. Often came to school in jeans and a long white blouse we could see her dark nipples through. A gap between her two front teeth, a little like Madonna. Difficult-to-understand French, but it didn't matter because she was there to speak English to us. Big dangling breasts.

The day she arrived, in September, the English teacher put her in charge of the weakest students, namely me and five other boys who didn't give a shit. You stayed behind in the classroom to keep up your a-do-ra-ble shtick. She led us into an empty classroom with a guitar, had us sit on the floor with our legs crossed.

"So guys, do you know any songs in English?"

She had a slight lisp. One of the boys started bellowing *I Was Made For Lovin' You* at the top of his lungs, making obscene gestures and clutching his balls. Caroline may have looked like a bit of an idiot from a distance, but she just looked him in the eye and said:

"Are you sure you have what it takes, little fucker?"

We weren't sure we'd heard right. I mean, I knew what I'd heard, my English wasn't all that bad, but the others weren't sure. So I laughed and laughed until tears ran down my cheeks. The others couldn't believe it. Caroline didn't even seem worried we might tell someone what she'd said; she was convinced our English was that bad. She gave me a half smile. The moron asked us to translate for him.

"She wants to know if you've got what it takes, asshole!" I said.

I think I heard part of him dying inside. It was the big fat French guy who couldn't skate and had been kicked out of Stanislas lycée for "gross indecency." Guillaume was his name. Anyways. He didn't say a word for the rest of the class and asked to stay behind with the teacher the following day. Lovely Caroline picked up the guitar she'd set down beside her and ran her fingers through her long auburn hair. I can still see her, the colour of her hair... And that's when it happened. She used the same shampoo as Suzuki did back then. It smelled of citrus. The scent hit me like a bucket of ice-cold water to the face. It felt like I was being born, discovering America, walking on the moon, piloting *Apollo 11*, bringing down King Kong, shooting Adolf Hitler between the eyes, occupying my own body at last. Caroline rested her guitar against her breasts, and I imagined I was the instrument, keening at her every touch.

"So, you guys don't know any songs in English?"

The others fiddled with their shoelaces, mouths open, gaping at her like monkeys staring at the moon. I could only think of Suzuki and her disapproving look, of Caroline's hair, and again of Suzuki's voice as she sang "Will you love me all the time...?" you know, the song she said she learned from our grandfather.

"Oh Lord! Where did you learn that?" she asked with her wheaty accent.

I didn't know how to tell her about Suzuki. I've never really known how to talk to anyone about Suzuki, how to define her to other people, how to justify her existence in our lives. So I just said:

"My mother."

"Your mother knows some very old songs! Is she American?" she asked.

Well, it's true. Suzuki was the closest thing I had to a mother. After, she had us sing Suzuki's song. At that moment, I fell head over heels in love with her.

When she wasn't wearing her see-through white blouse, Caroline was fond of tight turtlenecks. She came from North Battleford, a little town in Saskatchewan, she told us, and her father was a music teacher. At any rate, she was in charge of the library Tuesday lunchtimes while the librarian took her break. I suddenly discovered a passion for reading. The school library was usually empty over lunchtime, so Caroline was left to read in peace. I remember, because it's forever etched in my memory, her reading *The Apprenticeship of Duddy Kravitz*. She gave me a half smile as she watched me approach.

"What do you read?" I stuttered.

"A book about a boy who tries to remain honest in a corrupt world. Are you an honest boy, Gabriel?"

"Not always, but I go to confession."

And it was true. Back then, Mom would still drag us off to church in Rosemont so we could confess our sins to Father Huot two or three times a year. I think it was around then that Father Huot started reacting to what I confided in him. I could tell he was nervous when I confessed the episode with Caroline to him, and sometimes I even thought I heard him cry. What a big softy he was! Caroline laughed when she heard I went to confession. A lovely unwavering laugh, not too shrill, just enough to leave you under its spell.

"Really? What do you confess? I mean, what can you possibly be guilty of?"

"I can't tell you. It's a secret between me and God."

"Catholics are adorable!" she said, shaking her head. Her smell wafted over me. She really had a hold on me.

I sat down at a table to hide my erection. She had started touching up her eyeshadow. I was the only other person in the library, there was no reason for her to be redoing her makeup. She looked at me. Then she came over to see what I was reading. Back then I was finishing *Vingt mille lieues sous les mers*. I'd just got to the bit where Captain Nemo comes face to face with the giant squid for the very first time. Right before heroically fighting off a school of giant squid, when he saves a character known as "the Canadian" from their tentacles. The book was very nicely illustrated. She glanced down at the page.

"Squid? You never read in English, Gabriel?" she reproached me gently.

I admitted I didn't enjoy reading in English; it was too difficult. She asked if she could help with my reading and sat down beside me. She wore a little gold cross around her neck, exactly like Mom's. I still don't know how she was brazen enough to come teach in an elementary school dressed like that. She put her hand on my thigh. I immediately went rock hard, and of course she noticed.

"You have such lovely, curly black hair, Gabriel."

Then she ran her fingers through my hair. I thought she was funny. I didn't really feel like I was doing anything wrong. Slowly, she moved closer to me and pressed her lips against mine. She asked me to follow her into a tiny office she had the key to. There, she pulled down my pants and knelt before me. She held my hand in hers and squeezed it when my moans got too loud, as if to hush me. Hiroshima came and went. I was glistening with sweat. Afterward, she kissed me on the mouth.

"You're quite a big boy, Gabriel!"

Back then, I didn't understand. I thought she meant I'd just been through a rite of passage.

"Make good use of it!" she concluded.

It took me years to understand what she'd meant. I found myself outside in the hallway with the other boys, a little shaken. What had happened to Captain Nemo? I ask you. On my way out of the library, I felt like she owed me something all the same. I slipped her book, *The Apprenticeship of Duddy Kravitz*, into my school bag. I've kept it ever since. You should read it. It's very well done.

Caroline didn't stop there. I went to see her in the library every Tuesday. It must have been November. As soon as I came in, she'd start her little game again and come over and touch me. I noticed she'd lock the door behind me so we wouldn't be disturbed. And always in the librarian's little office. The librarian's name was Florence Bilodeau. There were photos of her two children and her mother on her desk. The two little boys stared up at me while Caroline was on her knees. I remember one of them was dressed in an old-fashioned maroon turtleneck that his mother must have made him wear for the photo and that he'd probably taken off right away. My biggest fear was Mrs. Bilodeau coming back from lunch earlier than usual. We must have kept it up until December. And then it was exam time. It was Caroline who gave the English oral exams. Do you remember the grade I got? Mom couldn't believe it.

"For once you get 100% and it has to be in English!"

For Madeleine, of course, math was all that counted. Caroline went back to Saskatchewan in January. I never saw her again. Then there was the woman who worked in the school cafeteria. Diane, wasn't it? Half Italian, I think. Since I always waited until the others had finished before going to get something to eat, she'd noticed me. "My little straggler," she called me. I was always nice to her. She must have been at least thirty-five. One afternoon, it was just after Caroline left, she put her hand on mine as she gave me my change. Nothing happened with her. Nothing more than the confirmation of what Caroline had taught me. It was my last year of elementary school and Mom and Suzuki wanted us to go to Brébeuf. You needed good grades to get in. Caroline had shown me how to get them. Besides her, there were other teachers with grades to hand out. Do you remember Mr. McIntyre, the Irishman? Gay Jesus, we called him. You know, the one who used to turn up with his Vietnamese lover at Christmas? He taught music. And he *worshipped* you! He wouldn't even look me in the eye I made him so uncomfortable. He was a skinny guy… you know the one I mean? He used to lead the choir and he played the trumpet so often his lips were always puffy.

The day of our music exam, I wore the tightest pair of jeans I owned. Mr. McIntyre was very much "peace and love." He really did look a little like Jesus with that beard. He let us choose when we would take our exam.

"I have the utmost respect for you all," he'd say before every class.

He'd set a date—which he would arrange with us—for the performance part of our exam. Since he refused to subject us to the "cruel stares of our peers," as he put it while turning to the louts in our class, the ones who'd openly insult him, he allowed us to play the piece we'd learned with no one but him for an audience.

He'd left the door open, but I closed it, claiming I was embarrassed that the others might hear me playing out of tune. There wasn't much to it. I played my piece on the tuba with an erection I'd given myself by turning my thoughts to Caroline, then I "rearranged" myself to be sure it'd have the desired effect. His forehead began to glisten. I think I could have made him cry if I'd unzipped my fly. At any rate, he gave me a grade well beyond what I'd hoped for, with the tacit assurance that he'd never breathe a word of it to anyone, to boot.

"Thank you, Gabriel. I... I think that's enough."

"You don't want me to play *Scotland the Brave*?"

"No, no. I can hear quite clearly that you're in complete control of your, uh, instrument."

"But I practiced so hard!"

"OK then. Go ahead. But are there other students waiting outside?"

"No, there's no one left, I'm the last one," I replied, not sure if that was true or not.

"OK then. I'd like to hear *Scotland the Brave*."

The main thing was to make sure he felt safe, that he understood it would stay between us. Caroline had made that clear to me. So I played him the second tune, maintaining my erection the whole time. I saw his lips lift into a smile. I haven't touched the tuba since. The last one was my homeroom teacher, you know, Mrs. Boulay, the one Mom always sent the restaurant coupons to? Things almost went south with her. I stayed behind one afternoon to clean the blackboards. The other teachers were in their empty classrooms, doing the same thing. Then I asked Mrs. Boulay if she was married. She laughed.

"Oh, I was once. But things change."

"Was he older or younger than you?"

The question unsettled her.

"Uh, a little younger. Seven years younger," she admitted.

I'd got it in one.

"He left you?"

"No, I left him. But aren't you full of questions, young man!"

"He must have been so sad when you left," I was bold enough to reply, with the conviction of a newsreader.

She looked at me for a moment, her pen hovering in the air, her mouth open. Mrs. Boulay was forty-two, she'd told us before. She lived on Avenue Van Horne. We'd see her grocery shopping on Saturdays and sometimes we'd run into her at Le Bilboquet when Suzuki took us there for ice cream. She was an attractive woman, she'd taken good care of herself and did cardio workouts three times a week. I know because I'd seen her jumping up and down with the other women through the windows of the sports centre on Avenue du Parc.

She took her sweet time; it took me three goes. So I decided to use my way with women.

"You're crying, Gabriel?"

"Y-y-yes," I whimpered.

"A good-looking young thing like you. Why on earth are you crying?"

"I don't have a girlfriend."

We were all alone in the classroom. She came over to me.

"Let me give you a hug, my little Gabriel. I'm your girl friend," she said, and to this day I still don't know exactly what she meant by that. As she held me in her arms I slipped my hand between her thighs. She froze, then stared hard at me, stunned. She went over to grab her bag and left the school as fast as she could. I was still in the classroom while she scurried off toward Avenue Van Horne. I watched her from the window. I'd been sure she'd head straight to the principal's office to file a complaint. I could already picture Mom and Suzuki looking distraught, the inevitable visit to Father Huot, and probably to a psychologist or two. But it didn't go any further than that. I didn't have much time before Mrs. Boulay would hand out the grades that would be used to apply to Brébeuf. She made sure she didn't find herself alone with me, kicked me out of the classroom at every opportunity: "Gabriel, I think it'll be quieter for you in the library." Since Caroline had left, the library had become very quiet indeed, its silence interrupted only by the librarian, Mrs. Bilodeau, humming to herself as she tidied up shelves full of books that no one other than me would ever read.

I was still reading *Twenty Thousand Leagues Under The Sea* when a heaven-sent window opened for me. Mrs. Boulay couldn't come to work one day that winter. I happened to be in the secretary's office when she called, something about papers she had to correct and couldn't come in for because she didn't have the time. The secretary—you remember Laura, don't you?—reassured her.

"I'll bring them over to you, darling. You take care of yourself. Don't you worry."

Then she hung up. The principal came charging in just then, yanking some poor brat by the ear. It was Fat Guillaume, who'd once again been caught feeling up a little Mexican girl, now outside crying in the hallway.

"Laura, I need you right now. I need you to call Guillaume's parents for me."

I was often to be found in the secretary's office for all sorts of reasons. Top of the list had to be Laura's bosom of apocalyptic proportions, and she didn't seem to have any objections to me coming to sit beside her once a week. She would always ask me about Mom's restaurants. I think she was also a bit too curious for her own good.

"My cousin's a waitress at Mado's in Trois-Rivières!" she told me proudly.

"There's two. Which one?"

"Uh... It's on the west side."

"Ah."

"And your mom?"

"Yeah?"

"I mean... you boys live with the woman who comes to pick you up sometimes, right?"

"Suzuki?"

"She's called Suzuki?"

"No. Her real name's Solange, but Michel and I call her that because she likes Japanese motorbikes."

"Ah, so she rides motorbikes..."

She didn't ask me about Mom and Suzuki again after that. She had the satisfied look of someone who's just solved an especially tough equation. People are simple, Michel. Too simple. At any rate, once she snapped to attention to deal with Guillaume, she suddenly realized she wouldn't be able to run over to Avenue Van Horne with Mrs. Boulay's exam papers. And that, my dear Michel, is precisely the moment I decided to make myself useful.

"I can bring the papers over to Mrs. Boulay, if you give me her address."

"Oh! You'd do that for me, my little Gabriel? You're not just a pretty face. You're a sweetheart!"

"It's not far, it's on my way home," I lied.

"Hang on. Her address is… 1272 Van Horne. Thanks so much! And be sure to tell your Mom her cretons are to die for!"

She handed me the exam papers in a plastic bag. It must have been twenty-five below outside, a frigid January day. I distinctly recall it wasn't a Friday afternoon, because there were Orthodox Jews everywhere on Van Horne, their black silhouettes cut out against the white snow like granite tombstones in a wintry graveyard. Clouds of steam escaped from their mouths. Do you remember when Mom took us to the synagogue once to talk to the rabbi? I've always wondered why. She who's never shown an interest in anything other than running a restaurant… I saw you that night on Avenue Van Horne. You must have left school just before me, and you were about to take the bus to your singing lesson in Villeray. You were getting onto the bus when I saw you. It was too late to shout out and you wouldn't have heard me anyway, not over the noise of the snowblowers. That winter we were calf deep in snow until the end of March. Now that it's all far behind us, it seems I can still hear the noise Montreal makes in winter. It's hard to describe. Sounds are at once clearer and more infrequent. Fewer people venture outdoors, and the sounds are muffled by the snow. And it must have been snowing, because I could hear something being dropped into an empty dump truck. I'd recognize that sound anywhere. Like a giant bag of potatoes being emptied onto a tin rooftop. My boots had a hole in them, but I didn't want to ask Mom for a new pair because I was boycotting her that particular week; I'd only talk to Suzuki. If I hurried, I might have time to make it home, go for a skate at the rink, and hit the weight room before supper. As I walked, I thought to myself that Mrs. Boulay couldn't be sick. She must be depressed, or simply hiding away from the cold.

She lived above a dry cleaner's. I rang and she opened the door. She must have been expecting Laura to deliver the exams in person because her apartment door was open at the top of a wooden staircase painted a greyish shade of blue. She had left her shoes and boots outside the door on the landing. There were women's boots and boots belonging to a boy who would have been about our age. I didn't know Mrs. Boulay had any children. Perhaps he went to a different school. Do you remember? Did she ever mention a son?

"Come in, Laura. I'm in the kitchen."

I hoped and prayed I'd find her alone. God heard me. But she almost fainted when she saw me. She stubbed out the cigarette she'd just lit and scowled at me.

"What are *you* doing here?"

"Miss Laura asked me to bring you the exam papers. She was too busy to come."

Mrs. Boulay was wearing only pants and some sort of satin tunic that went almost all the way down to her knees. She didn't look remotely ill. I must have been rosy-cheeked with the cold. She looked me up and down for a good thirty seconds, not sure what was going to happen next. Then she pulled herself together.

"Are you cold?"

"Yes," I told her, hoping she'd feel sorry for me.

"Would you like some tea? I just made some."

"Yes, please."

She sat me down in the living room at the other end of the apartment. I looked at the walls while she made the tea. They were covered in floral wallpaper and framed family photos, some of them very old. She'd put a china vase of dried red roses on a pedestal table and the pattern on the vase went with the cup, saucer, and teapot. There were lace doilies everywhere. She had a bird in a cage. Not a budgie or a parrot, but a much smaller bird, a beautiful creature with brightly coloured plumage, a red head and a pale purple and yellow body. I'd never seen anything so lovely.

"That's Scarpia," she told me.

"What type of bird is it?"

"A Gouldian finch."

"Where's it from?"

"Queensland, Australia."

Mrs. Boulay knew Australia's states and the birds that lived there. I was beginning to find her quite cool. The exotic bird and the overdone, old-fashioned décor made everything a little unreal. I remember wondering if Captain Nemo had been to the Southern Ocean. Probably. Almost certainly.

"Do you like bread pudding, Gabriel?"

"I love it."

She went back into the kitchen, at the other end of the very long apartment so typical of Montreal, and came back with a gigantic helping of bread pudding in a china bowl with a floral pattern on it. I didn't think I'd be able to finish it. She motioned me to sit beside her on the big red sofa. I'd underestimated my appetite. As I ate, she told me about her sister who lived in Gaspé, "where your mother has another one of her restaurants." Of course she did. There was no getting away from them. Then she started asking about our dad.

"Your father never comes to pick up your report cards, Gabriel. It's always that other lady... What's her name?"

"Suzuki. Solange, I mean."

"Yes, Solange. Is she your aunt?"

"No."

"And your father?"

"We didn't know him. We never saw him. He died before we were born."

She looked sad. While it didn't help answer her questions about Suzuki, at least now she knew about our father. She suddenly looked as though she pitied me. To make the most of the melancholic pause my reference to our father's death had triggered, I asked about her father.

"Oh, he's dead too! He was very ill."

Her bread pudding was almost as spongy as Suzuki's. For some reason or other, she'd brought me a silver soup spoon to eat it with, not a teaspoon.

"A big spoon for a big boy," she'd said, holding it out to me.

She'd warmed the dessert for a few seconds in the microwave, and there was a pungent smell of sugar hanging over the room. The smell almost took on a form of its own, barking orders and controlling my senses. The warm caramel oozed down into my belly. I think she must have added maple sugar to the recipe. I winced at the contrast between the cold ice cream and the warm caramel, but continued to gobble up the huge portion she'd served me. Scarpia cheeped plaintively, as though, all alone in his cage, he envied our human treat. Outside, just below the living-room window, I could hear the tires scrunching across the packed snow on Avenue Van Horne. Evening had come. I heard someone shout, "Mordecai! Mordecai!" then a car horn moaned three times. A bus passed by, shaking the floor and drawing a sigh from Mrs. Boulay. The more I stuffed myself, the more apparent her talents in the kitchen became. She had plenty of experience; my taste buds weren't deceiving me. I tried not to seem overly impressed or intimidated by the dessert. I'd downed the ice cream a little too quickly and was now clutching my forehead. While I gamely scooped away with my big spoon at her soft, sticky pudding, I couldn't get the image of Captain Nemo out of my mind, battling giant squid with his harpoon. I wolfed down another huge mouthful. Mrs. Boulay let out a cry:

"Gabriel, you'll choke!"

She put her hand on mine to slow me down, to stop me finishing too quickly.

"Let it melt in your mouth. Take your time. That way it doesn't hurt," she murmured.

I took her advice and scraped my oversized spoon against the sides of the handpainted Moonlight Rose china bowl—when I'd turned it over, I'd seen it said *Royal Albert, England* on the bottom—before plunging into the heart of the matter. The dessert's fleshy plumpness was no match for my appetite; I was always starving after school, like all boys. You know what it's like, Michel: at that age, you don't eat, you just shovel it down!

"You were hungry, Gabriel! Now have your tea. Slowly, gently. Don't burn yourself."

She had tea, too. I had practically licked the china bowl clean. Mrs. Boulay's face was lit up with happiness; I'd never seen her like that. She lit a cigarette.

"Mind if I smoke?"

"No."

"I won't offer you one. You're too young."

"I know. And it's not good for the lungs."

"How right you are, Gabriel."

"And Mom wouldn't approve."

Her face clouded over again at the mention of Mom. I wanted to reassure her: everyone reacted the same way every time her name was brought up.

"So what school do you want to go to next year, Gabriel?"

"Mom wants me to go to Brébeuf."

"Brébeuf? But you need excellent grades to get in there!"

"I know..."

I knew exactly what Mrs. Boulay was thinking at that very moment. "Brébeuf, here I come!" I wanted to cry, but it was mainly so that Mom wouldn't disown me that I wanted to get in. And I had to follow in your footsteps to protect you, Michel. I frankly couldn't care one way or the other about Brébeuf. Honestly, I considered myself tough enough to survive public school. But you were another story: they'd have eaten you alive. A tenor! A little on the pudgy side! With a lisp! Who walked like a turkey!

Poor old Michel, the gods weren't kind to you, were they! What you needed was a private college away from the plebs. Somewhere to go unnoticed. Mrs. Boulay stubbed out her cigarette. Her phone rang. She went into the kitchen to answer it. The conversation was muffled; the kitchen was too far away. I took the chance to look through her bookcase.

By the looks of things, Mrs. Boulay had studied literature before resigning herself to a career as an elementary school teacher. There were lots of classics, books from the same authors Mom had bought in Pléiade editions by the yard to decorate the winter lounge with. There was an old paperback, *Le Grand Meaulnes* by Alain-Fournier, at nose height, on its cover a picture of a beautiful stately home with a blue roof, surrounded by an inviting forest. There was something very French about the picture, like a postcard sent from the old country. Without knowing why, I grabbed the book. Mrs. Boulay had written her name on the first page: *Lucie Boulay, Chicoutimi, 1963*. I felt like I was holding an antique, a saintly relic. I stuffed it into my bag. It was the second in a whole bookcase of stolen books. You'd be impressed by their number, dear brother. All acquired in similar circumstances. Nothing is free. Mrs. Boulay came back from the kitchen smiling.

"My dear Gabriel, I have to go. I'm going to have to show you the door, and it's so cold outside… Would you like me to call you a taxi?"

"No thank you. I only live ten minutes away."

As she walked me to the door, Mrs. Boulay grew more serious.

"It's almost five o'clock and I've ruined your appetite. You won't be hungry for supper. What will your mother think?"

"I don't have to tell her. I'll still be able to eat."

"It's true. At your age, you don't eat, you just shovel it down! The bread pudding will be our little secret. I don't want to be competing with Mado's! Haha!"

"I promise I won't say a word to Mom."

"Or anyone else, my little pet. Otherwise all the boys from school will be turning up here for a helping of bread pudding!"

"It will be our secret."

"You have to promise me, Gabriel."

And I made my first real promise. May God forgive me for breaking it now, Michel.

She kissed me on the cheek and closed the door. Outside, thick snow had begun to fall. The Hassidic Jews walking in tight clusters along Avenue

Van Horne hurried home. The cold had eased a bit, so I took off my gloves with my teeth. My gloves, like my fingers, were imbued with Mrs. Boulay's sweet smell. I couldn't wait to get home to wash them.

Only Suzuki was home. You were still at your music lesson and Mom was out opening one of her restaurants in who knows what godforsaken hole. Suzuki was in the kitchen. I think she must have smelled the bread pudding.

"Pasta for dinner, Gabriel," she snapped. Go wash your hands. It'll be ready in five minutes."

We ate without either of us saying a word. Then, I'm not sure why, and this is to remain between us, I saw Suzuki shed a tear. It was the only time. You mustn't breathe a word. You know how proud she is of the thick shell she's built around herself.

There was no dessert.

You came home late that night. After your lesson with your teacher in Villeray. Do you remember? The one who lived near Jean Talon market? She had you sing Schubert's *Ständchen* at your first recital. I was all alone, lying on my bed after supper. Still reading *Twenty Thousand Leagues Under The Sea*. I was just at the bit where "red with blood, motionless by the beacon, Captain Nemo stared at the sea that had swallowed one of his companions, and large tears streamed from his eyes." We both achieve the same end, Michel. You, with money. Me, with what God gave me.

Before I get to Westkreuz, I have to tell you about something funny that happened on the way back from the gym last night. I took the elevator in my building. It only goes up to the ninth floor and I live on the tenth. To get to the tenth, I have to pass by a door belonging to someone by the name of Berg. Here, everyone has their name on a neatly polished plate. The thing is, I could feel someone watching me through the peephole. And I was sure I heard a noise. So I looked at the Berg door. I could no longer hear a thing, proof positive that there was an eye pressed against the door and spying on me. I wanted to knock, but what would I have said. "Excuse me, but are you watching me?" I would have looked like an idiot. So I just smiled. I've only been here a few months and I still don't know the neighbours. I mean, I met two of them downstairs, two women from East Germany. They're very funny. I think they've decided to adopt me. They insist on doing my washing and are always offering me butter, milk, things one of their nephews brings back from the dairy where he works. You'd think it was still the age of socialism, with people swiping what they could, wherever they could, to survive. This Mr. Berg frightens me a little. We'll have to wait and see.

I have to go now, Michel.

Gabriel

～⌒

Dear Michel,

On my way home, I reread the letter I wrote you on the 30th. Fear not: I'm capable of love. And since last fall I can even prove it. You'll have noticed that I can't resist a teacher's charms. No surprise then that I met Claudia in a classroom a little over two years ago. I've never been so happy, so free.

You might think, like Mom does, that not seeing you all is torture, that I stay away from you as some kind of mortification. But you'd be wrong. I've never felt better than these past ten years when I haven't had you all right there every day reminding me how useless I am and how great you are. You mentioned your singing career has finally taken off. So there isn't even a tiny bit of Mado gas in your engine? Are you absolutely sure?

But first, let me reassure you. In your letter, you call me out for being cold toward Mom. You've got some nerve! Come on, Michel. Mom can go to hell! She doesn't need any help opening her restaurants. All of them look like convent canteens anyway. Maybe she should go confess her past sins. Did you ever notice that every time she brought us to confession in Rosemont, she never spent more than two minutes in the confessional with Father Huot? As though she'd nothing to tell him! I could have dictated a confession worthy of the name, starting with the sin of pride. She's been guilty of that one more times than there are fir trees in Canada. And it was she that insisted:

"Gabriel and Michel, I don't want to see you come out of there before fifteen minutes are up. Get everything off your chests! You especially, Gabriel!"

Me especially! That's what she'd say every time, and you're calling me out for being mad at her? And do you remember her catechism lessons? We'd be treated to them every time we got in the car to go to mass. Mom would have us reel off the responses. Come on! Try the one that's forever etched in my mind. You'll have to imagine for yourself the "I missed my vocation as a nun" voice!

"'Which sins need to be confessed in the sacrament of Penance?' Gabriel? Michel? Which sins must you confess?"

And you, you smarmy little angel, you'd come back with, "We must confess all our mortal sins, but it's also good to confess our venial sins."

Well, here's a venial sin I want to confess to you, Michel: back then, I could have ripped your nose off. She'd smile at you. I wanted to open the door and throw myself under the wheels of an oncoming bus and be done with it all. And allow me to be so callous as to remind you of another well-known question.

"This one's for you, Gabriel: 'What must one do who cannot remember the exact number of his sins?'"

You could have searched me. She must have told me ten times already, but I could never remember. Who gives a fuck? That was the only real answer to her question.

"Gabriel, Mommy asked you a question," she would insist.

I didn't know. Round it up? Work out the square root? Give an even number for luck? You were chomping at the bit to answer. She kept on glaring at me from behind her catechism book.

"Answer me, Gabriel! What do you do when you can't remember the exact number of sins?"

I didn't speak. She lost patience. Then she made me repeat after her: "If we cannot remember the exact number of our mortal sins, we should tell the number as nearly as possible, or say how often we have committed the sins in a day, a week, a month, or a year."

The Church, you'll notice, was very flexible when it came to selecting the unit of time. The rest was basic multiplication. If I calculate that Mom took us to confession three times a year from the age of six for at least twelve years, I make that thirty-six times. Now *there*'s a number she should keep in mind the next time she goes to confession.

Remember the time you threw a tantrum in the car and she whacked you to get you to shut up? Remember what she said? I don't want to bad-mouth her behind her back, but if ever you're looking for an explanation for your neurosis, remember these words: "Michel Lamontagne, stop snivelling. You're going to confession. Period. It's not a choice, it's a duty. If you don't go, I'll have you adopted. Do I make myself clear?"

Perhaps your shrink will find the answers to a few nagging questions in this little anecdote...

You make me laugh, by the way. I know how hard things are for you, but you make me laugh all the same. If you weren't my brother, if I didn't know you so well, I don't think I'd be laughing. But every time I read you, I hear your voice and see every twitch. When you write, for example: "The way Suzuki looks at me pierces me like a sword. Thankfully, Mom is there to calm her down. Otherwise she'd have carved me up into little marinated cubes and served me on caraway crackers a long time ago..." No, Michel. Suzuki's look is nothing like a sword. It's the only human presence I knew in that Outremont home. She doesn't wish you any harm. Leave her alone.

Am sitting comfortably on the Blankenfelde–Bernau S-Bahn writing my letter, far from Father Huot's confessional. It's strange. I used to be content with reading on the S-Bahn; now I write there too. The seats are comfortable, I find. The first time, like everyone, I was amazed to see these little trains—so efficient, so fast, so punctual!—transporting people from one side of this huge city to the other, without having to dive into the bowels of the earth like our subways in Toronto and Montreal. At the start, it was nice: the S-Bahn helped me see a little of the city. Now I sit there more out of resignation than anything. But it's the only place where I still feel like I'm moving forward. And, even though people get on and off every five minutes, you're left alone. Here in Germany, no one ever speaks to someone they don't know—unless it's to point out a by-law they've broken or a faux pas they've just unwittingly made. *Das ist verboten...* And since it's not *verboten* for a young man to sit quietly reading or writing on an S-Bahn seat, they don't speak to me. If only they knew how I revel in their coldness! You with your ear for music, you'll understand the next bit. Wherever you are in Berlin, you can always hear the wheels of the S-Bahn grating against the steel tracks. The sound of German efficiency. You hear it all night on weekends. Every time you close your eyes, it's impossible not to picture a whole people travelling by rail, inexorably driven forward, from Grunewald to Anhalter Bahnhof, from Oranienburg to Ostbahnhof. Tracks are to Berlin what canals are to Venice. People get on at each station by the dozen, looking a little dazed. Young men can even be seen swigging, quite legally, from big bottles of beer. Nothing is more fascinating than these German trains, dear brother. Berlin life is set to the screech of the S-Bahn, the voices of the platform ticket collectors who shout "*Zurückbleiben!*" at the tardy passengers who've just run flat out and are now trying to pry open the doors of the train that's just about to leave, as though it's the last train ever, as though there will never be another. But there always is. For as long as there are people in Berlin, there will be trains.

To answer your more practical questions, I've been living since January in one of the buildings they call *Plattenbauten*, in the Lichtenberg district of former East Berlin, where these tall, narrow apartment blocks stretch as far as the eye can see, looking for all the world like they were built from pastel Lego blocks. The first thing that comes to mind when you see them is: "The wind's going to knock them over like dominos." But they hold up. It's not much to look at, but it's comfortable enough. What am I doing in Germany? It's simple enough: I followed a woman here. Love brought me here. I can hear you grinding your teeth. Rest assured: Claudia and I aren't living together.

When she left Toronto last year after defending her thesis on medieval literature—she's into *Minnesang*, the German version of courtly love—I watched her go and, I don't know if you can wrap your head around this, you who are so much like Mom, but I felt alone for the first time. Do you want to hear where I met her? Are you interested in your brother's love life? Or, in telling you about the woman I love, am I running the risk that you'll jump on the first Alitalia flight to Berlin to murder her in her sleep?

I have to go. The train's pulling into Bernau. I'll write more tomorrow, or another day.

Gabriel

⌇

Teltow Stadt – Hennigsdorf
May 5, 1999

Dear little Michel,

I've even found an S-Bahn route called the Ring. It runs clockwise around Berlin. You can get on at any station along the circle and spend the day on the train without ever having to get off. It's on the Ring that I find the most time to write since the scenery is unremarkable. Industrial estates. East, then West, then East again, in a never-ending circle, a spiral of Berlin's own. *Perpetuum mobile*. Here, far from the centre, the East still looks like the East, and the West still looks like the West. In the distance, the Mercedes logo, that Germanic deity forever twirling in the Berlin sky. You can also travel counterclockwise around the Ring, but I avoid that. For reasons I can't explain, going in the opposite direction makes me nauseous.

Remember when I told you I felt like I was being spied on by a man called Berg while I waited for the elevator in my building? I think I was right, you know. When I came home last night, I could feel someone watching again from behind the same door. This time, I just waved at the person spying on me, as though to invite them to come out of their hiding place. I didn't have long to wait. I went up to my apartment. My door had been closed for no more than twenty minutes when someone knocked on it. Three brisk knocks. I didn't even look before I opened it. There in front of the door was an elderly woman who said she lived just below my apartment. She'd come to ask me to thread a needle for her.

"My name is Magdalena Berg, I'm almost eighty years old, and I'm your neighbour on the ninth floor. Where are you from?" she asked me in war-like German.

"Gabriel Lamontagne, I'm from Montreal."

"*Ach! Kanada!* I thought you were Italian with that wavy dark hair. Or Slavic. How come you speak German?"

Germans are always surprised to find you speak their language, and they often inquire a touch suspiciously, as though they take you to be some sort of spy. I'd started studying German seriously, I explained. I'd been in Berlin for five months, although naturally I didn't tell her I'd learned German for a girl called Claudia who I wasn't even living with. She was a little insistent, as though wary of my reasons for being there. She wanted to know how I'd found the apartment. I think I must have been the first Quebecer to ever live in Lichtenberg. How should I describe her? She's quite a solid woman, the type who could derail a moving tram with a thrust of her shoulder. Five foot seven, I'd say. Heavier than me. She was wearing a sort of maroon velvet dress tied around the waist—or around her equator, should I say—with a rust-coloured leather belt. Her grey hair was cut in a style that was no doubt the height of fashion in 1935, slightly wavy on the sides. She was holding a needle in her right hand and a length of yellow thread in her left.

"Here. I can't see a thing. Give me hand, will you?" she said, thrusting them under my nose.

She wanted me to thread the needle. It was a very fine sewing needle and the hole was so small I could barely see it. I stuck out my tongue as

I concentrated. I'm not used to having to be so precise. She looked me up and down while I threaded the needle. I'd already taken off my shirt and there I was standing before her in my white tank undershirt. She must have noticed my arms and pecs.

"Do you like Riesling?" she asked.

"Yes, but I have to get up early tomorrow," I replied. I found her a little frightening.

"I'm not after your life story, I'm just asking if you like Riesling," she sniffed.

"Ah, uh, yes. Riesling's nice."

"That's all I wanted to know. Thank you. *Gute Nacht.*"

Have you ever heard the like of it? She took the threaded needle from me and repeated my name in her German accent. *"Kapriel Lamontagne aus Kanada…"* Then she went back downstairs. I just stood there, dazed.

Have rehearsals started? If I understood correctly, you're making a new movie version of *Tosca*, like the DVD you sent me? So you're following in the footsteps of Placido Domingo, are you? He's a tough act to follow. Did you know that Bruno-Karl d'Ambrosio was born Marcel Truchon? I kid you not. He comes from La Malbaie, in the Charlevoix region of Quebec. I read that somewhere. He changed his name when he moved to Montreal.

He's the same D'Ambrosio who caused a stir here in Berlin last year with a trashy production of a Wagner opera. *The Flying Dutchman*, is that what it's called? I only know the German title. It was in the newspapers a lot. Apparently one of the characters—Erik, I think it was—shoots a woman dead at point blank range at the end and rapes her corpse in a necrophilic scene that raised eyebrows, and that's saying something for Berlin. It was also him, I think, who had Werner Oberhuber and Andrea Apfelbaum sing *Madame Butterfly*, the pair of them stark naked, in some Austrian or German town or other. Bregenz? Munich? I'd have to ask Claudia. They say that Werner Oberhuber had a bit of a boner going at the premiere. D'Ambrosio explained that the nudity was supposed to represent the purity and innocence of the love between Pinkerton and Cio-Cio San. I can't wait to see your film, dear Michel… You're sure you don't want to start getting in shape for it now?

I'd started telling you a little of what happened to me after I left Outremont. As I was saying, already back at Brébeuf, I was going out with our French teacher, Chantal Villeneuve, who asked me to move in with her when her husband left her for a boy barely older than the two of us. I'll never know if all she wanted was to get her own back by taking a younger lover herself. I had to wait until I'd finished school before moving in. The morning you were crying in your bed, that's when I left. I took the photo of Papa Louis with me, the one Suzuki gave me. I took the metro from Outremont down to Jean-Talon, where Chantal lived. I caught her just as she was leaving. She agreed to let me stay for no more than a few weeks, but I ended up staying a year. Time to find my feet again and become someone.

The rest is pretty straightforward. I enrolled in phys ed at McGill and did a teaching certificate. The chances of running into you at the gym building at McGill were slim. I can hear your mocking tone: Big deal, you'll tell me, phys ed programs will accept just about anyone these days. And you wouldn't be entirely wrong. I'd be lying if I said the education faculty was the most intellectually stimulating place in the world. But I do have a teaching certificate that allowed me to make an honest living in Toronto for six years, which is more than you can say. When you have no one but yourself to rely on, sometimes you have to do whatever it takes to survive. Remember Cyrano: "To be content if neither oak nor elm. Not to mount high, perchance, but mount alone!" We read it with Chantal Villeneuve at Brébeuf; you even enjoyed it. But like most actors and opera singers, you seldom apply the valuable lessons your characters teach you.

In 1994, I applied for a job as a phys ed teacher at a Catholic school in Toronto. I had to take an English test and provide a reference from a priest who'd known me for a while, just to prove that I was a good Catholic and had no intentions of encouraging the students to sin. A brief interview with the principal and the vice principal and that was that. Once that's out of the way, it's pretty much in the bag. Toronto had one big thing going for it: Mom didn't have any restaurants there yet. That changed quickly, but for the first few years at least, I was happy to live in a city where there wasn't a reminder of her on every corner.

I was to replace a teacher the school board had forced to resign because he'd admitted he was gay to one of the girls, and she'd brought his confession home to her mother. The news spread by phone until one of the more pernickety parents pointed out to the principal that Ontario teachers are obliged by law to lead a life *in line with Christian values*. In Quebec or in any public school in Ontario, no one would have gotten hung up about the poor guy's sexual orientation, but not at Holy Canadian Martyrs Catholic

Secondary School. The hysterical mother ended up making a fuss to the archbishop, then they started making it clear to the guy that he'd have to go, which he did, but not before kicking up a stink. He'd have his day in court. Everyone said he was going to win his case and come back to work, but I had his job in the meantime.

On my first day at the school, September 2, the principal, Mrs. Delvecchio, had a word with me "in private" about the teacher. Gerald Lemon was his name. My God, how his students must have teased him with a name like that! She seemed quite fond of him and was still frustrated at being forced by her superiors to let such a good teacher go. They'd even taken down the photos he appeared in with the students in the hallway. You know, the "coach with team" photos? He'd been there four years, and there were pale rectangles everywhere they'd taken away the frames.

"Honestly, Gabriel, if they had to fire every gay teacher in the province of Ontario, there'd be nobody left to teach French, drama, or music! Please don't quote me on that…"

She pronounced my name the English way, as in Peter Gabriel. She chortled at her joke. Then she wanted to know if I was the son of Madeleine Lamontagne, Queen of the Eggs.

"You know, the breakfast restaurants… Mado's." She pronounced it "Maydo's."

For the first time in my life, I lied about it. And so I began my life as a phys ed teacher at the oh-so Holy Canadian Martyrs Catholic Secondary School. Compared to Brébeuf College in Montreal—named in honour of a Holy Canadian martyr though it may be—the school in Toronto was more like a convent. Prayers and the national anthem over the P.A. system every morning. The national anthem, to be like the Americans; the prayers to remind us we were in a Catholic school.

On my first morning at Holy Canadian Martyrs, I didn't have any classes. I was in the gym untangling the volleyball nets when *O Canada* came on over the intercom at half past eight on the dot. I went out into the hallway to see what was going on. There I found a handful of teachers and students standing stock still, as though petrified. Innocently, I walked over to the secretary's office, unaware that I was committing the unthinkable. "Stand still for the national anthem!" a teacher I didn't know barked at me. It was Mrs. Robinson, a crotchety old Irishwoman, who promptly filed a complaint with Mrs. Delvecchio. "The man's a separatist! He was walking around during *O Canada!*" This earned me a dressing-down from the principal. How could I have known? It was all so obsequious! You would have thought we were in the United States.

Nonetheless, this incident was enough to focus the entire school's attention on me. A separatist terrorist from Quebec had taken over from Lemon the Queer! What a kerfuffle! I went back to my gym. But the P.A. system wasn't done yet: the national anthem was followed by a heartfelt Lord's Prayer, read by the English teacher, then by a Hail Mary, delivered in French with charming conviction and emotion by an immersion student with a syrupy voice. Her accent was terribly sexy, somewhere between English and Italian. When she got to "*le fruit de vos entrailles*," I knew she was different. Confirmation of that would arrive soon enough.

The students at Holy Canadian Martyrs had to wear a uniform. The boys wore charcoal-grey pants and a white shirt with a claret-and-grey tie they left at home or in their locker more often than not. Their way of rebelling. Much of our interaction boiled down to reminding them to tuck their shirts in and do up their ties. The girls, meanwhile, wore long-sleeved white blouses in winter and short-sleeved ones from the first day of May. They were allowed to wear pants, but most wore the school's claret and charcoal tartan skirt. In their case, the challenge consisted of stopping them shortening their skirts, which school rules maintained had to be at least knee length. Keeping their hems as close as possible to their patellas amounted to a somewhat Sisyphean task. Some turned the hems of the skirts up, fastening them with a safety pin, ready to be released at the first sign of a teacher or the principal. But there were always exceptions to the rule… Most skirts didn't come tumbling back down when it was me or the young math teacher—an absolute moron by the name of Zbornak—who came into view.

After the national anthem incident, I went back to the gym to get ready for my classes that afternoon. Hardly any students had signed up, and most of those were boys. Past Grade 9, I should point out, phys ed was optional at Holy Canadian Martyrs. I think Mr. Lemon had found himself a nice cushy job! One glance at his notes was enough to convince me that he didn't exactly overexert himself when it came to coming up with ideas for his classes. He was more the type who would string up a volleyball net in September and take it down again before Christmas. Then it was basketball from January to May. In the summer, he'd take the kids outside to play baseball. No surprise the students had no interest in sport. It also fell to the phys ed teacher to teach the students, both boys and girls, about a healthy diet, lifestyles in keeping with sound mental health, drugs and alcohol, safe driving—above all, the dangers of drunk driving—and, last but not least, sex ed. In Toronto, that was all up to the phys ed teacher. Judging by Lemon's empty binders, it had been a long time since the board of governors had shown any interest in evaluating the teachers... As far as I could tell, there were plenty more valid reasons to let him go than his homosexuality, but who was I to pass judgment on Mrs. Delvecchio's decisions? Instead, I set about putting a whole program together from scratch.

What I didn't know, and what a student named Melikah told me later, was that my arrival had caused quite a stir at the school. None of the girls had ever taken phys ed past Grade 9. Sitting in the cafeteria, one of them had wondered out loud if they shouldn't check out the new phys ed teacher, that it might make a change from Mrs. Robinson's drama class—the same Mrs. Robinson from Northern Ireland who had caught me blatantly ignoring my patriotic duty that morning.

Since she'd wanted to be the first to spread the news, young Melikah—she must have been sixteen or so—went off on a scouting mission for the others. It was quite normal for students at Holy Canadian Martyrs to look a teacher over before deciding on a class. Usually, a report from the older students was enough for the new girls to make up their minds. "Don't take drama whatever you do. Robinson's lost it ever since her husband left her." Or "Grade 13 French is Mr. Loser." His name wasn't Loser, but Moser, a Swiss German who came to Canada in 1967 and was still teaching, as he had in 1967, French authors like Nathalie Sarraute whom he considered the height of modernity. They nicknamed him "Sleeping Pill." Melikah, and she was the one who told me this later—what a gossip!—had tiptoed up to the gym door and opened it as quietly as she could. I'd taken off my sweater, thinking there was no one around. So there I was, standing there in nothing but an undershirt and a pair of jeans, unpicking the knots in the volleyball net that had been flung into a corner. Despite the unflattering fluorescent lighting, I must have seemed very different to her other teachers. I'd been working out a lot the summer before I left Montreal and my biceps were like a couple of cantaloupes. Even I was beginning to think it might be a bit much. Melikah held her breath behind the door. She must have watched me for a minute or two, then I heard the door close, without knowing who had opened it in the first place. Quick footsteps echoed along the hallway.

Melikah sprinted back to the cafeteria to report everything she'd just seen to her classmates. By the sound of things, it was a demigod she described—or so she told me later, it's not just me being vain—and so the twenty girls immediately raced to the secretary's office to sign up for my phys ed class. Two of them—Kayla and Candice—stopped by the gym on the way to have a look for themselves. They were bolder than Melikah and marched right in, claiming to be looking for someone or something, then, feigning surprise at seeing me there, they giggled—I love the sound of sixteen-year-old girls giggling—and apologized, chirping all the while on their way out. Their little detour had caused them to fall behind the other girls, who had dashed toward the secretary's office like lionesses pursuing a herd of antelope.

The secretary was behind the counter. She was a homely old spinster who was always in a foul mood. Her ears stuck out and she'd been unkindly nicknamed "Zira" from *Planet of the Apes*—which is what everyone called the secretary's office. Twenty girls were crammed in there now, along with a few boys who'd been alerted by the ruckus. All were clamouring to sign up for the optional phys ed class, which was to begin that same afternoon. They were eager for the man Melikah had described to teach them all about shameful diseases, lost virginities, drinking, soft drugs, and God knows whatever else might feed their sixteen-year-old aspirations. They jostled and elbowed each other out of the way. A girl by the name of Anderson suggested the girls line up in alphabetical order. Another, Ziegler, told her where she could shove that idea. Zira the secretary did her best to restore order amid the chaos, reminding the students of the school's zero tolerance policy on foul language. She grumbled as she rummaged through the class lists she'd put together over the summer and that she'd now have to change.

"So you *all* want to take phys ed? Now that's a first! There won't be room for everyone!" she protested, glaring at the undisciplined rabble.

She handed out the forms the twenty-six girls and two boys would need to change classes as they huddled around the counter. The forms were filled out in record time and in absolute silence, the girls writing on each other's backs, sharing pens, one holding back her bangs with her right hand to see what her left hand was writing. The forms were passed along to Zira, who stamped her feet and raised her voice in an attempt to calm the overexcited schoolgirls. The two boys who had filled out the form slunk off as though they had just committed an obscene, unmentionable act.

"Single file!" Zira barked. She was beside herself now and flung the pile of forms over their heads. The girls suddenly realized they were in trouble. The ape-like secretary made it clear that she would be accepting no forms until the girls had formed an orderly queue, something of a feat in itself given the cramped surroundings. A swaying, Soviet-style line formed almost organically, as though the ability to quickly form a queue was something that came naturally to any student at Holy Canadian Martyrs. One by one the girls smiled and set down their forms in front of the secretary as she counted them aloud. Candice was the last girl but one to put down her form. The secretary gave Kayla a pitiful look.

"Twenty-five!" she announced a touch theatrically. "No room for you, Kayla!"

Kayla shook her head in disbelief. How could there be no room left for her? Who did they think they were? They would just have to make room! She brought her fist down on the secretary's counter to drive her point home. The other girls looked on helplessly at the sad spectacle of a teenage girl being cruelly alienated from her peers by an arbitrary bureaucratic slight. Kayla was beside herself. If there was room for twenty-five, there must be room for twenty-six. But Zira wouldn't be moved and simply shook her head with a smirk, revelling in her power. To be honest, Michel, I think she hated every last one of those girls. Kayla couldn't stand the thought of that frustrated hag of a woman preventing her from signing up for my class, and she lost it.

"I want to take gym with Mr. Lamontagne!" she shrieked, by now quite hysterical.

The shouting roused the principal, Mrs. Delvecchio, who was dozing at her desk. Whatever was going on in the secretary's office? First, she'd had to spend part of the morning calming poor Mrs. Robinson, who'd been thrown into a panic at the thought of having a bloodthirsty separatist as a colleague. Then she'd had to deal with a couple of dissatisfied parents, and now it sounded very much as though the raised voices coming from the secretary's office were again about me! Apparently it was just as Mrs. Delvecchio suddenly appeared on the scene that Kayla really lost her temper.

"Let me sign up for gym class or I'll fucking kill you, ape woman!"

Honestly, dear brother, I should never have taken off my shirt while I was getting the gym ready. I was perhaps partly to blame.

The incident tore through the school like a nuclear bomb. Little Kayla Evangelista had been a model student until I showed up, regularly collecting awards and honours since her first year of elementary school. But now her reputation was permanently tarnished. They didn't let her off lightly: a three-day suspension, a formal written apology to Zira—forgive me, I can't remember her real name—and banned from going to the secretary's office unless summoned *by the principal herself.* Zira had squeezed this final concession from her union, having threatened to sue Kayla's parents if she didn't get her way. When she saw the principal suddenly appear from nowhere, Kayla stopped breathing then, realizing the extent of the catastrophe, burst into tears.

"I'm so sorry," she sniffed.

Naturally I heard the story more than once, first from Zira, then Mrs. Delvecchio, and then the girls in my afternoon class. So this was the atmosphere in which I began my career at Holy Canadian Martyrs Catholic Secondary School in the fall of 1994. Little did I know I was just about to meet the weirdest girl in the world.

But my S-Bahn is reaching the end of its route. I'll try to write tomorrow.
Gabriel

～⌒

Erkner – Spandau
May 8, 1999

Dear Michel,

I haven't written in three days now; I feel a little guilty. The neighbour from downstairs put in another appearance. Something suddenly occurred to me: her name's Magdalena Berg, which is more or less the German equivalent of Madeleine Lamontagne. Don't you find that strange? Especially since the Lamontagnes of Rivière-du-Loup are of German extraction. Their name was Frenchified in the eighteenth century, or so Suzuki told me. But Berg is such a common name in Germany, almost as common as Schmit, Schmidt, and Schmitt! Anyway, the old lady knocked on my door again last night. I was reading a book I'd swiped from Delphine, a French student in my Goethe class. She'd been eyeing me discreetly right from the start of class in January. By the end of the month, I was back at her place. The people she lives with in Kreuzberg were in the other room so we had to be quiet. It was strange: the couple, both in their fifties, were having a real shouting match. About money, I think. There they were insulting each other in German while we did just the opposite. *"Du Dreckstück!"* and he'd come back with *"Du unverschämte Kuh!"* One slapped the other, then we heard a piece of furniture toppling over. We made sure to come during the crying fit. When Delphine slipped out to go to the bathroom, I took my chance and swiped *The Hotel New Hampshire* by John Irving. I hadn't read it. Last night I got to the part where the plane carrying the mother and the little brother Egg is crashing into the Atlantic. "No! No! No!" I thought. "It can't be! He's not going to kill her off now! Not her! Not now!" And then the neighbour knocked on the door. She was wearing a psychedelic-print cotton dress (very German Democratic Republic), the type of design you'd see on wallpaper in the 1970s. Brown, orange, and yellow circles... It looked as though she'd dressed up before coming to knock at my door. She was holding another thread, green this time, and a needle she wanted me to thread for her.

"I can't see the hole! It's too small!"

While I lent a hand, she took a deep breath.

"Would you have a glass of Riesling with me tomorrow evening? Around eight? At my place."

Since I had no plans and had already admitted to my fondness for Riesling, I agreed. And so tonight I'm having a glass of German Riesling at Magdalena Berg's. She seemed pleased when I accepted her invitation. She told me she'd be able to tell me about Potsdam and the former GDR. My downstairs neighbours have already told me a little about her. She never married and has lived in our block since the 1970s. She worked for the GDR's national monuments commission. Since the wall came down, she's been collecting a small state pension. Her neighbours don't seem to like her very much. "She has a foul temper," Germana on the seventh floor told me one day. Hilde, who lives on the third, has fallen out with her altogether. Mind you, Hilde, back in the days of the GDR, was a party member and responsible for reporting on the goings-on of everyone who lived here. I don't think she turned anyone over, but you get the impression the others hold a grudge against her; there are still a few old scores to settle. Magdalena Berg will tell me all about it this evening, I suppose.

You wouldn't believe just how big this city is. There aren't that many people, but it just goes on and on. It would take you more than a day to walk from one end to the other. The wonderful S-Bahn sure comes in handy.

Before I came here, I used to wonder if you could still see a clear dividing line between East and West, even in 1999. Of course you can. The wall has come down, but you only have to look out the S-Bahn window to see if you're in what used to be East Berlin. The people are still very different too. I've met girls who sometimes try to cover up the fact they're from the East. Twice I've met a girl who claimed to be from West Berlin and it turned out not to be true. But there's one way to find out the truth: you just have to undress them. East Germans our age always have a scar on their arm left by a vaccination—polio, I think. Back home in Canada, and in West Germany, only people Suzuki's age have one. They must have stopped doing it shortly before we were born. It's as if a whole people has been scarred by communism. I don't even understand why they don't want to admit they're from the East. *Deutsch ist Deutsch*, if you ask me!

As the train makes its way to Warschauer Straße, I remember there were hardly any Germans at Holy Canadian Martyrs. Since it was a Catholic school, the children were mostly Italian and Polish immigrants, or of Irish descent. An altogether Roman mix. My class lists must have resembled the list of names gathering dust somewhere in the Vatican cellars: Pantalone, di Franco, Kubica, Murray... Quite the synod! On the first day of school, right after the incident that seriously jeopardized young Kayla's chances of leaving one day with a high school diploma, Zira the secretary came to see me during lunch.

"Your classes are full!"

She gave me the lists and I looked them over carefully to give me an idea of what lay in store. Students began streaming into the gym well before the start of class. Most of them girls who had signed up that morning. A few of the boys asked if I was on steroids and if I could get some for them. It's all about hard work, I told them. They wanted to know if we'd be working out, if they'd have pecs like mine by June. They were funny.

A few seconds before the bell rang, a girl came in by herself. The other girls giggled when she walked in, and no wonder. She might have been wearing a school uniform like everyone else, but she looked totally out of place. She was short and plump and wore thick black glasses. Two godawful braids framed her face, which was more of a baby face than the other girls'. I thought for a second she might be wearing a different skirt to the others, but then I realized she was the only one not to have turned hers up. I asked her what her name was.

"Stella Thanatopoulos, sir," she said, staring at the floor.

"Saint Stella!" some comedian chimed in.

I'd recognized Stella's voice right away. That morning, just after the national anthem and the Our Father, she was the girl who'd said the Hail Mary in French to welcome the new teacher from Quebec. She lived alone with her mother, who'd sent her to Catholic school since she hadn't been able to get her into an Orthodox one. Stella sang at mass on the first Friday of every month. The girls who'd signed up for class that morning had raced home for their sports gear, lending clothes to the girls who lived too far away. The students went off to the locker rooms to get changed. All except Stella, that is, who just sat there looking sheepish on the bench. Later I found out that Stella's mother had made her sign up for phys ed before I was even hired.

"Aren't you going to get changed?"

"I forgot my gym clothes."

We spoke in French, and Stella spoke it quite well, better than the other girls in her class at any rate. She would never look me in the eye, which annoyed me no end at the start. When the others came back from getting changed, I had them warm up and then we organized a volleyball game. Little Stella stood beside the net like a martyr in a Roman arena. She showed absolutely no interest in the ball, instead doing her best to avoid it at all costs. The others rolled their eyes every time she failed to send the ball back. When it was her turn to serve, another girl shouted: "She won't be able to, Mr. Lamontagne. She's too much of a klutz!" And wasn't that the truth. Stella only managed to make contact with the ball about half the time, grunting and groaning as she did, much to her teammates' despair. Eventually she went to sit back down on the bench, looking glum. I told her to come back, but she just stared at the floor. "Never mind her, sir," the other girls said. "She's always like that." So the game went on without Stella. One of the stronger girls then launched a rocket of a serve. There was no way to tell if she meant to or not, but the ball shot across the court, striking Stella right between the eyes. The little Greek girl tumbled backward off the bench, where she'd been busily gnawing her nails. As she fell, her checked skirt rode up over her belly, revealing a pair of immaculate white panties. The others laughed themselves silly, then, realizing she was unconscious, began to look frightened. Their concern spoke volumes about Stella's importance to Holy Canadian Martyrs.

I ran over to her. Fortunately she was still breathing. The ball had knocked her senseless, that was all. She lay there on the floor, arms splayed and eyes closed.

"Stella! Stella! Are you OK?" I asked, pinching her cheeks.

Slowly, she opened her eyes. She looked at me as though the Virgin Mary herself had suddenly appeared before her.

"The Archangel!" she gasped.

The others sighed with relief. It was then that I realized that Stella held a special place at the school, perhaps even in their hearts.

"I'll take you to the secretary's office, Stella."

"I can't get up."

I had to carry her like a child. Despite her chubbiness, she wasn't especially heavy, not to me anyway.

Zira almost fainted when I came into the secretary's office with a dazed-looking Stella in my arms.

"Oh my God! What happened to Stella?"

She called an ambulance right away, along with Stella's mom. At the hospital, they realized she was more shaken up than hurt. She'd come out of it with no more than a bump on her forehead and the shame of having flashed her underwear at her classmates. That was the day I met Mrs. Thanatopoulos. Just to give things a more solemn turn, let's just say I could tell you the exact time we met, the way women remember precisely at what time they gave birth to their first child. After class, Zira called me to the secretary's office over the P.A. system. Mrs. Delvecchio and Mrs. Thanatopoulos were waiting for me there. Stella's mother was a tiny little woman. She looked like a plumper version of Nana Mouskouri and wore the same glasses. Carefully and impeccably made-up. A classic yet modern hairstyle. The anachronistic, enticing elegance of the Old World, with a dash of Asia Minor. Her daughter's antonym—or perhaps her future?

"Mrs. Thanatopoulos would like to talk to you," the principal told me, before leaving us alone in a small room next to the secretary's office.

I expected her to tear a strip off me, threaten to sue me, have me fired, decapitate me with a shovel, roast me on a spit for Orthodox Easter. She sat opposite me, her handbag on her lap. Judging by the way she was dressed, I could tell Mrs. Thanatopoulos wasn't short of money. Everything about her exuded money, old money, the type that can't be hidden. The way she carried herself made it clear that, before coming to Toronto, her parents hadn't exactly been herding goats on Mount Olympus. They'd come to Canada through the main door and had a grand old time of things there. Her husband, she explained, was a successful businessman who'd died of a heart attack when little Stella was only five. Overweight. "A Greek disease," by her own admission. The child had barely any memories of her father since he'd split most of his time between London and New York, where he worked in banking. He'd settled his wife and daughter in Canada because he found American cities, especially New York, overly vulgar and overly dangerous. He'd been won over by Toronto's good manners in the 1970s. When he died, his wife decided to stay in Canada so that her daughter could learn English and finish school. After that she was set on returning to Athens, where she'd grown up. Mrs. Thanatopoulos spoke almost flawless English, with the accent of Melina Mercouri. She had never managed, for example, to bring her *r*'s under control, or perhaps she had and pretended otherwise to make herself adorable. She'd understood that displaying her imperfections was the way to win me over.

"Bless your soul, Meesterrr Lamontagne. God bless you for coming to this school!"

I was a little taken aback, still expecting to be in serious trouble for having almost allowed her daughter to be murdered in gym glass, and here she was blessing me!

"I am really very sorry about this afternoon. How's Stella?"

"Stella's fine, thank God! I left her at home. A little ice on her forehead and she'll be fine by tomorrow. She's told me a lot about you."

I wondered what she might have said. We'd seen each other for an hour at most.

"She says you're verrry nice, verrry polite to her. My little Stella is a very particular child, you know."

So I'd already noticed. And I would have liked to ask her mother why she let her daughter go to school with those dreadful braids and stupid glasses.

"My little Stella works verrry hard. She has her nose buried in a book morning, noon, and night, only taking a break for her music lessons. Her dictionary is her pillow."

"She plays piano?"

"No, she sings. You'll be able to hear her soon enough. She sings at everrry school mass, but I have higher hopes for her."

As soon as she said she sang, I almost mentioned you, but then I thought better of it. I'm not exactly dying for everyone to find out I'm Madeleine Lamontagne's son. She shut her own parents out of her own life; I don't see why I should keep her in mine.

"The Good Lord has given my daughter a most wonderrrful gift: the voice of an angel. But as you perhaps already know, it takes more than that to make a careerrr of it."

"Yes. It takes discipline and a good deal of patience."

"Those she has already. I mean something else."

"And what's that?"

"You've surrrely noticed that Stella is still... umm... how to put it... a little girl."

"She'll grow up."

"I'd like her to slim down," she replied, pursing her lips.

"But why? What's that got to do with singing?"

Mrs. Thanatopoulos took a deep breath.

"Meesterrrrr Lamontagne, the Lord has blessed you with the body of a god. Just take a look at yourself!"

"Thank you," I said, refraining from adding that it was actually more thanks to the many hours I spent in the gym. It would have been impolite to correct a student's mother.

"I think my little Stella has everything it takes to become a diva, a diva who will redefine the verrry notion of stardom. But first she must understand that she has to sing with her whole body, and that body must be appealing to the audience. She must be desirable, other women must want to be her and men must want to have her. Right now she's still an ugly duckling. I am humbly begging you to help me make a woman of her."

I almost fell off my chair. Make a woman of Stella?

"I might be rrreligious, but I'm not too naive to realize that Stella isn't fully in possession of her own body. She needs to lose weight and learn how to love herself. You seem so comfortable with your own body, Meesterrr Lamontagne. You can help her. She already admires you. She told me so. 'Momma, he's the handsomest man on the face of the earth,' she said. 'He has the charm of an angel and the body of a god.' What do you say, Meesterrr Lamontagne?"

"Mrs. Thanatopoulos. I'm a gym teacher, not a private trainer. Your daughter can join a swim club or take up jogging. I can give her advice, but the will to change has to come from within. And, to be honest, I'm not sure you're going about it the right way..."

Mrs. Thanatopoulos took a thick brown envelope out of her purse.

"We can start off like thees. There will be other envelopes, God willing. One for every kilo you help Stella lose."

I couldn't believe my eyes. I'm all for singers—especially you—losing a few pounds to look better, but it has to come from them. Mrs. Thanatopoulos set the envelope on the table, stood up, and walked out, leaving behind her address on a scrap of paper.

"Come over Saturday morning at ten. Thank you for your time. Have a good day, Meesterrr Lamontagne."

I went back to the staff room in a daze. There was a thousand dollars in the envelope. In spite of myself, I started working out just how many kilos Stella would have to lose to be transformed into a graceful diva. Ten? No, fifteen! Maybe even twenty thousand dollars if I really helped her shed the pounds. Enough to pay off my student loan.

A week passed. I'd become friends with the school librarian, Jodi, who was from Thunder Bay. She was a tall and charming blonde who bore a passing resemblance to Jodie Foster. I told her about Stella.

"I'd go for it if I were you. You don't have much choice anyways."

"How come?"

"Holy Canadian Martyrs isn't like other schools. It's funded by the government, sure, just like every other Catholic school in Ontario, but it also relies on private donations, including from Mrs. Thanatopoulos."

"You mean that if I refuse to play ball, she might stop giving the school money?"

"No, that's not it. She'll keep giving the school money, but with *certain conditions* attached."

"Such as...?"

"It wouldn't be the first time. Didn't you ever wonder why your predecessor left?"

"He was gay and a good Catholic school was having none of it, right?"

"Nope. Lemon was gay, sure, and everyone knew it. But as long as he kept quiet about it, nobody cared. He was just fine until the day he refused Mrs. Thanatopoulos a favour."

"What sort of favour?"

"Exactly the same thing she asked you! To help her little piglet lose a few pounds!"

"That's why he was fired?"

"Not exactly, but let's just say that Mrs. Thanatopoulos went out of her way to make sure everyone knew he was gay. I think she might also have had her eye on him, and he refused her advances. It was crazy... Listen,

Gabriel, you need to be careful at Holy Canadian Martyrs. People here can be too Catholic for their own good. If I were you, I'd go jogging with her little bundle of lard three times a week and be done with it. She's paying you a bundle, too! Ha! Ha! See what I did there? Everyone's a winner. Do you know what it's like being fat in high school? The girl's going through hell!"

"Who else should I keep an eye on, Jodi?"

"Robinson, the Irishwoman. She's nuts! Northern Irish Catholics are the worst. After the Poles, that is. Then there's the old Swiss guy who teaches French. Stay well clear of him. He's a real stinker. Delvecchio, the principal, might appear to go at everything like a tank, but she's got more common sense than she lets on. Rumour has it she's gay, so you're out of luck there! Oh yeah, and Zbornak, the math teacher. I'm not sure about him either. Just keep in mind that Zira is probably the most genuine of the whole bunch. After me, of course. That goes without saying."

"Thanks for the advice."

"One more thing, my little Angel Gabriel: anything goes in Ontario's Catholic schools, as long as you don't get caught. Don't mention abortion, homosexuality, common-law unions, soft drugs, sex, or alcohol and you'll be fine."

"But they all drink, even Robinson! I'm sure of it!"

"You still don't get it. Every teacher hired by a Catholic school has to provide a letter of recommendation from a priest. You've got one, right? You know, a letter proving you're a good Catholic and all."

"Of course."

"Good. Keep it safe. That's your passport. Everyone here has a letter like that. Some of them are forged, like mine. I'm not even Catholic, but I needed the work. So I dreamed up a priest in Manitoba and my letter passed muster. Don't breathe a word of it to anyone or they'll fire me on the spot! Just imagine! A Protestant! An anti-papist wretch making reading suggestions to pure Catholic souls. Even the janitor has to be Catholic! If ever he wasn't and the parents were to find out…"

"That's not even legal!"

"But that's the thing. It's all perfectly legal. It's like living under a pain-in-the-ass political regime: it has its pros and cons. At least we have a job, it's a good school, we're left to get on with things. As long as everything seems above board, no one's going to go around accusing anyone of being a bad teacher or being incompetent. Being Catholic is enough. But the regime has its downsides, too. Woe betide anyone who isn't careful to hide the things that must always remain out of sight. In other words, Gabriel, if ever you're tempted to go pay the boys of Church Street a visit and have a bit too much of a good time, I'd advise you to keep your mouth shut. Fuck all the women you like, but keep your hands off the boys. You don't want the priests giving you a hard time, believe me! Forget Montreal, you're in Ontario now! This is God's country! Oh and one last thing, just imagine one of our little idiots comes up to you. She's distraught. Turns out she's pregnant. She's eighteen and wants your advice. What do you do?"

"Uh, send her to see the psychologist?"

"Right answer: two points! Now, the girl asks if you know a doctor who might be able to help. What do you say?"

"Look in the Yellow Pages?"

"Bang, bang, you're dead! You cross yourself, you tell her you don't know a soul, and you turn and run! And when they give you the Gestapo treatment to find out what you told her, you say you never met her. That's what you do. Got it?"

"I run off to Church Street?"

"You really are an idiot, aren't you? Now, care for a little hashish?"

Jodi was cool, all the same. She invited me over. I figured it was to encourage me to stay on the straight and narrow and help me survive Ontario's Catholic school system.

"I'm cooking chicken tonight, if you're up for a bit of thigh. I live on Bloor Street, not far from your place."

Jodi had a twisted sense of humour. She lived in the Annex, one of Toronto's swankiest neighbourhoods. She shared a small apartment with a girl from British Columbia. They lived on the second floor of a house, above a Chinese family. Her apartment permanently smelled of garlic and ginger. I went over a few times, then one morning she got up and announced we should just be friends. I was all in favour, to be honest. They do say you shouldn't sleep with colleagues. "Dogs don't eat where they shit," was how she put it. I agreed, especially since she didn't have the talents of my first English teacher, Caroline from Saskatchewan.

"So Gabriel, why don't I make you eggs, then you can fuck off," she said to me that last morning.

While she was cooking the eggs, I swiped Jeannette Winterson's *Oranges Are Not The Only Fruit*. It's not bad, just a little sad. It's the story of an

English girl growing up in a Christian fundamentalist family. The thing is she becomes a lesbian and her mother decides she's possessed. She even has her exorcised. It reminded me of Mom having us go to confession three times a year. Maybe you think I'm always banging the same drum, but in my defence I've never seen the like of it anywhere else. Maybe among particularly devout immigrant families. Perhaps Stella had a confessor to turn to? I'd soon find out for myself.

That Saturday, I got up early to work out before going over to Mrs. Thanatopoulos's. She lived pretty far away, in a big, fancy house in Don Mills. A BMW in the open garage. It was Mrs. Thanatopoulos who met me at the door.

"Ah! Meesterrr Lamontagne... I knew you'd be on time. Stella is waiting for you."

I was expecting to find her still in her pyjamas, still half asleep after a typical teenager's long night in bed. As it turned out, she'd just finished two hours of music theory with her teacher, who was still sitting before a gleaming Bösendorfer. Stella was delighted to see me. She was still wearing her huge black glasses and those awful braids of hers. The music teacher was a little bald man. He said hello politely and left, humming the melody that Stella had just been practicing. Mrs. Thanatopoulos was keen to sit in on our first meeting, which involved going through Stella's diet. Sweeping changes were in order. As I talked to the mother and daughter, I realized that Stella had been fattened up on Greek cooking: greasy meats, all-you-can-eat baklavas, full fat yogurt, and what have you. I put together a more spartan diet for her there and then. Her mother didn't bat an eyelid. I think if I'd ordered her to feed her daughter nothing but spinach and water for three months, she wouldn't have asked any questions. Then I asked Stella to change into her gym clothes. She disappeared for a few minutes. Alone with her mother, I put her determination to the test.

"Are you sure you want to go through with this?"

By way of reply, Mrs. Thanatopoulos took a thick album out of the drawer of an antique cabinet. It was full of photos of her youth in Greece. She'd been very pretty. I mean it when I say she looked like Nana Mouskouri. You just have to imagine Nana Mouskouri a little rounder, more jolly, and a lot more padded out. There were photos of her on stage. She'd sung in opera productions in Athens and even Italy. Always minor parts, nothing very serious.

"I was too lazy to slim down. I was never able to make a career of it."

"But lots of voluptuous opera singers have enjoyed great careers."

"Like Montserrat Caballé? I saw her in *Tosca*. London, 1976. What a voice, but she could hardly move around the stage! It was laughable when Scarpia wanted to have his way with her in Act II. She might have smothered him between her thighs! Wait a second, I want you to hear her."

She took out a *Tosca* CD so that I could hear Montserrat Caballé. I wanted to tell her that if God had given her daughter even a quarter of the beauty in that woman's voice, then no one would give a damn what she looked like. She could go on stage looking like an orangutan and she'd still win everyone over.

Stella came back dressed in a fashionable sports outfit that must have cost a fortune.

"I'm ready, Mr. Lamontagne!"

We began with a few stretches, then I took her out for a jog in the park, with her mother still tagging along. Here, it's important for me to stress, dear brother, to give you a proper idea of the creature who was handed over to me by her own mother, that Stella never shed a single tear. I've seen men bawl in agony after going through half of what I subjected her to. When he was programming her, the great I.T. guy in the sky must have forgotten to activate the self-pity function. People looked on in disbelief. Stella was breathing harder and harder, panting for breath, labouring like a worn-out mare. She did everything I told her, her face wracked with pain. Her mother watched us, arms folded, from the side of the running track. I took pity on the girl after an hour.

"That's enough for today, Stella. We'll get back at it Monday after school."

And so it went for three months. Cycling. Swimming. Weightlifting. Aerobics. The diet I prescribed was followed to the letter. And on the second Sunday of Advent, Mrs. Thanatopoulos handed me an envelope containing ten thousand dollars. I'd helped her daughter lose ten kilos.

"Come back after Christmas. There's still work to be done."

Honestly, I would happily have stopped there. At school, the other girls had of course noticed that Stella was getting thinner by the minute. The poor girl had lost so much weight she'd had to buy a new school uniform. Candice, Kayla, and Melikah, the inseparable Grade 11 trio, would often stay behind with me in the gym for a chat after school. I think they had a bit of a crush on me. But I remembered Jodi and what she'd said about dogs not doing it where they ate. Especially not in a Catholic school of all places.

"Mr. Lamontagne, Stella has gone nuts since you've been here!" Melikah told me one December evening as I graded tests in the gym.

"What do you mean?" I asked, looking up from my papers.

The others didn't know I'd been training Stella. Even Mrs. Delvecchio had no idea. She'd thought, the day Mrs. Thanatopoulos had wanted to speak to me in private, that it was to remind me about the basics of gym safety. Mrs. Thanatopoulos didn't want anyone to know. She'd been very clear about that.

"In English class, we had to read out a poem we'd written," Melikah continued. "Stella's was called 'The Archangel!'"

"So what? You all know how religious Stella is. Why shouldn't she be interested in angels?"

I tried to distract them.

"You don't understand. It was so *steamy*! You remember, don't you, Candice?" she insisted.

"In your arms of steel, all truth is above
In your eyes of teal, I'm waiting for love," Candice recited, pretending to swoon.

The girls burst out laughing.

"And that's not all! The rest of the poem goes on about the Annunciation and all kinds of shit. But that's only two verses. There are another twenty and they're even more juicy!"

"Whatever," I replied, irritated now.

"Mr. Lamontagne, haven't you noticed how much weight she's lost since you showed up?"

"Yes, but there's nothing unusual about losing weight quickly at your age."

"You don't want to see the truth, do you?" Melikah teased.

"Truth is, you should all leave poor Stella alone and worry about other things."

"Such as?"

"I don't know. Things that are more important than how much your classmates weigh."

"And what about you, Mr. Lamontagne. Do you like Stella's new look? Do you think she's *purrdy*?"

I shooed them out of the gym so that I could finish my work in peace. To be honest, Michel, even though pretty much all of my colleagues were nutcases, especially the old Irishwoman, I was very happy in Toronto. I had all the girls I wanted, and every time Stella lost a gram, I earned a dollar. I had my little twenty-first floor apartment on the corner of Spadina and Harbord, complete with views of the CN Tower. I could have lived like that for another twenty years. Then Claudia showed up like a miracle, like the springtime. You've got to hear how it happened.

The school had a history and geography teacher by the name of Véronique Poisson. Another Quebecer who, like me, taught her subjects in French as part of the Holy Canadian Martyrs French immersion program. She'd been there four years. The students called her Miss Fish. I never found out what they called me behind my back. Melikah and Candice told me once that the boys had nicknamed me Arnold Physedteacher, but they never said it to my face. I would have taken it as a compliment in any case. Thing is, around Christmas 1994 I very briefly hooked up with Miss Fish. She was one of those women who spend their whole lives taking evening classes. Spanish, Italian, Thai cooking; anything to stave off boredom. In January 1995, she persuaded me to take a German class with her at the Goethe-Institut. I told her right from the start I'd no interest in German.

"I'd forgotten. Phys ed teachers need to be doing things with their hands. Culture isn't your forte."

You see, Michel? Now that's exactly the sort of condescending remark you might have come up with. What Véronique meant is that a phys ed teacher is some kind of gorilla who can't count higher than one hundred, a hulking great philistine who likes to belch at the back of his gym. Granted, maybe most phys ed teachers don't read beyond the sports section in the tabloids, but there are also French teachers who've never picked up Molière. So I followed Véronique along to the Goethe-Institut one evening, just to show her that I was more than capable of taking a German class.

I'd swiped Véronique's copy of *The Thorn Birds*. The novel the TV series was based on, you know the schmaltzy one that makes grannies cry. It's set in Australia. It doesn't get any cornier than that. Véronique had only that type of thing on her bookshelf. And she was the one lecturing me about culture?

At any rate, at the first German class I found myself sitting between Véronique Poisson and a Polish guy who was studying philosophy at the University of Toronto. It doesn't get more eclectic than a group of students learning German at the Goethe-Institut, I thought to myself as I ran my gaze over the twenty people gathered around the table, busily flipping through their German workbooks. The reasons for learning German are as difficult to grasp as the language itself, and as a result such groups are a real mixed bag. First off, there are those who have to learn German: Air Canada flight attendants, businesspeople whose work often takes them to Germany, diplomats and their families. This group shows the least interest, resigned to its fate. Most of the time, their boss is paying for the class and their attention appears to be directly proportional to the amount paid out of their own pocket. While they may be lacking in motivation, these students condemned to learn German tend to keep a low profile: they regularly skip class, ask no questions, and manage to get a passing grade to keep their employers off their backs. All Germans speak English anyway, they say, so what's the point? Then there are the students who are doing a PhD in philosophy, comparative literature, or the differential history of Medieval Yiddish. They likely chose their field of study to set themselves apart from their roommate, who's hard at work on a dissertation on Toltec culture. They're pretty much guaranteed to be assholes. Not five minutes goes by without one of them—usually some scrawny type who hasn't touched a dumbbell in his life or a completely unfuckable fatty who speaks in a falsetto—raising a hand to ask the teacher a question clearly designed to catch them out, things no one could care less about, like "Do you mean *Vorstellung* in the Heideggerian sense?" They're insufferable and conceited, and carry around German copies of Nietzsche in their worn leather satchels, nonchalantly leaving them out on the table to make it clear they're interested in all kinds of things that sail right over your head. Then there are the retirees who have nothing better to do and are making good on the dreams of their youth. These students come in two flavours: there's the quiet gramps who diligently does his homework, then there are the old grannies who never shut up, always bringing everything back to themselves, rabbiting on about their children and the grandkids, thinking they're ever so funny. Sometimes they bring homemade muffins to class and go on about how they got the recipe from their mother. And then there are what I like to call the "old Germans," people with some connection or other to the motherland but whose family forgot the language a generation after stepping foot in America. They never last long. It only takes a few grammar exercises for them to work out why their granny from Hannover always refused to speak German at home. And there are always one or two Jews that I lump together with the old Germans, because they never stick around very long either. I don't know what they were expecting to get out of the Goethe-Institut. If I were a Jew, it's the last place I'd go to take a class. I'd learn Chinese, jazz ballet, or Cambodian cooking, but not German. This hodgepodge of students invariably includes a few lost souls like me and Véronique Poisson, who have no good reason for being there. And when I spied a philosophy student with a particularly filthy and matted head of hair, I immediately resolved to sneak out at the break. Maybe I could make it to the pool before closing time.

Then Claudia walked in.

First from the side, then from the front.

How best to describe her? Imagine that Claudia Schiffer had a prettier older sister. Imagine a woman born five years before us, in 1964, in Cologne, Germany. Imagine a German-as-a-foreign-language teacher giving her first class one freezing Monday night at the Goethe-Institut on Yonge Street in Toronto in an old red-brick house. Imagine the piercing gaze of Marlene Dietrich and the figure of Brigitte Bardot. Now imagine she has a slight lisp. That's Claudia. One other thing: I'm pretty sure she was at least five foot eight or five foot nine. Blonde hair held in place on the left side by an opal-blue barrette, somewhere between Marlene Dietrich and Claudia Schiffer. Eyes the colour of a blue sky in May. Ample but disciplined bosom. Gap chinos, suede belt, lavender blouse with a stand-up collar. Pumps that clicked with every step as the wooden heels struck the Goethe-Institut's worn-out floorboards. Opal-blue socks that matched her barrette. Understated gold-rimmed glasses balanced on the bridge of her nose by some unseen angel. A golden chain and a little cross against her cream-coloured skin. An inch east of the cross, a beauty spot around which the entire world revolved. And to ward off the drafts in that old building, a pullover draped over her shoulders. Handknit. Chunky stitch. Baltic blue. She set down the pile of workbooks she'd been holding under her right arm, produced a sheet of paper from a binder, and made a show of studying it, a blue Bic pen held up to her lips. Then she looked up.

"Guten Abend!"

When she looked at us, the first thing I wondered was which book I was going to swipe from her. Something big. Günther Grass's *Tin Drum* or Thomas Mann's *Magic Mountain* perhaps. Something I'd read in the original for years without ever tiring of it. I didn't miss a single class. I went about my homework with the zeal of a Carmelite nun and the conscientiousness of a Jesuit. I bitterly regretted the shelves of stolen books and prayed that I would never have to explain where all those books had come from, books with women's names written on the inside of the front cover.

Claudia ticked every German beauty box. She had class, education, great posture, good manners; everything about her exuded perfection. The staggering beauty of a secret weapon. The promise of a brighter future. The Kaiser's revenge. Know what I mean? I didn't dare approach her, of course. I felt as though I sullied her every time I looked at her, and still feel that way even today. I don't think I slept for three straight nights. Needless to say, I learned German faster than you can imagine. By the end of the term, in April, I'd plucked up enough courage to speak to her in private after class. A Pole—Wlad, I think his name was—had also taken the opportunity to talk to her. For as long as we were taking the class, I think we both followed the unwritten rule of not chatting up your teacher. But once it was over... The Pole was built like a string bean; he just didn't measure up. I let him play out his pathetic little routine. Claudia spoke a few words of Polish, probably just to make him happy. She's incredibly well mannered. Then the asshole gave her his card and cleared off without so much as a glance in my direction. Someone needed to teach *him* some manners. I thought to myself that Jodi had been right about the Poles: they were hysterical Catholics who were best avoided. Now all alone in the classroom with Claudia, I felt both completely naked and in my element. I tried to speak to her in German, but there was a tremor in my voice.

"*Ich, Ich... Sie... Es... Vielleicht... Möchten Sie mit mir Freitag Abend essen?*"

I couldn't believe my own nerve. Claudia smiled, then replied in English.

"Perhaps not dinner, Gabriel, but you can come with me to church this Sunday, if you like."

Church? I couldn't believe it. I hadn't even meant to ask the question and now that was her answer. Church? So she went to church. Well, it was that or nothing.

That Sunday, I went along to the church where she'd agreed to meet. I hadn't even asked if she was Catholic or Protestant; you never know in Germany. It was a Lutheran church downtown on Bond Street. A pastor led the service in German. One thing about Lutheran services: they might not know how to decorate their churches, but they sure know how to sing. Never have I heard a choir in such perfect harmony.

Afterward, I invited Claudia to have a cup of tea with me on Yonge Street. It was a Quebec café. Maybe you've heard of it? Le Kilo? Anyway, there's one in Toronto. She told me a little about herself, how much the Lutheran Church meant to her, and gave me the third degree about my religious practices. I told her about our confessions to Father Huot, of course. She seemed impressed. Apparently in the Lutheran Church, the pastor absolves everyone of their sins at once. No one is expected to list their transgressions against God and their neighbour one by one. And, according to Claudia, Lutherans believe that it's not possible, indeed that it's pointless, to set out all one's sins. Now that would have really shut up you-know-who. It's all about faith. I timidly asked about her love life. Just like that. She replied that, at age twenty-four, she still hadn't met a man worth getting involved with. My dear Michel, I found her answer so delightfully pure. I felt as though I was sitting in a café with a talking white lily. She was polite enough not to inquire about my own love life. I would have denied it all anyway. We continued to get together every other Sunday.

Mom would go mad if she found out I went to a Lutheran church for three years. But would anyone notice the difference? Just saying.

So that's how I met the woman. That's why I'm in Berlin.

I'm in love, Michel. And it's killing me.

Gabriel

P.S. Véronique Poisson dropped out of German For Beginners. She couldn't get her head around the grammar.

～⌒

Zeuthen/Grünau – Hohen Neuendorf

May 9, 1999

Dear Michel,

It's noon and I've only just crawled out of bed. A word of advice, dear brother: when your career as a tenor brings you to Germany one day and you find yourself living in an apartment block, perhaps a *sozialistischer Plattenbau*, an old lady might well ask you to share a bottle of Riesling one evening, eager to learn more about the strange creature that's moved into the apartment upstairs. Whatever the circumstances, whatever the inhuman demands of your rehearsal schedule, say yes. When I got home yesterday after a long day admiring the sheer immensity of Berlin from the S-Bahn, it was already eight o'clock. I'd almost forgotten my appointment with Magdalena Berg, and it wasn't until I passed by her door that

I remembered her curious invitation. I got changed at top speed so as not to be late: nothing distresses a Prussian more than tardiness. As I waited for her to come to the door, I could clearly sense someone peering out from behind one of the other doors on the landing, come to see who had rung Magdalena Berg's bell.

"Kapriel! How are you? Come in!"

Magda Berg's apartment was bigger than mine. As well as a living room, there was also a bedroom and a little corridor that linked all the rooms. A large bookcase stood in the corridor, overflowing with books, new and old. DDR deco; wallpaper in the same pattern as her dress, appliances with brand names unknown in West Germany, orange carpet that swallowed the sound of every footstep. She led me to the living room, where a sofa took up much of the space. There was a bottle of Riesling from the Rhine Valley on a coffee table, left to chill in a bucket of ice. She'd set out a bowl with those crunchy little fish you nibble on while you drink, like peanuts.

"Sit, Kapriel."

Magda Berg's German separated each word with perfect diction. It was easy for a foreigner to understand her, easier at any rate than Germans from the south, who have an accent that's more difficult to decode to an outsider's ears. She sat in a large armchair to my right. Her window had brown and orange velvet drapes—and the same view I had, looking out over the buildings of Lichtenberg.

"It's a nice little Riesling from the Rhine Valley," she told me. "I have it sent by the case. It's cheaper that way."

Magda has only a very modest pension to live on. She told me the amount. It's enough to make you wonder how she manages to survive on so little. And yet Magda seems to be well fed: you'd think she ate at Mom's every morning and ordered the Louis Cyr special with ham, bacon, and sausage. If I had to guess, I'd say she weighed one hundred and twenty kilos. She was big boned and had plenty of meat on her. A far cry from Claudia, my little mermaid. Magda liked to tell jokes.

"Do you like jokes?"

"Uh, yes. Do you have one for me?"

"Yes. It's very funny. I heard it a long time ago, but I still tell it because it makes me laugh every time. Would you like to hear it?"

"Sure. Go ahead."

"So, Kapriel, there once was an old woman who liked to read in the park. One day, she sat down on her favourite bench in the park near her home. Suddenly a pigeon arrived and she had a very pleasant conversation with it. The two got on famously. But time passed. The old lady asked the pigeon to come round the following afternoon at four o'clock for tea. The pigeon agreed."

"That's very funny," I lied.

"Wait, that's not all! The following afternoon at four o'clock, the lady waited for the pigeon to arrive but it never came. Twenty minutes past four and it still hadn't shown up. The lady was bitterly disappointed. At four thirty, the pigeon rang the doorbell at last. The lady rushed to open it. 'Ah, there you are! Wherever were you?' she asked the tardy pigeon. 'I'm terribly sorry, ma'am,' the pigeon told her. 'It was such a nice day I decided to walk.' Hahaha! Isn't that charming? It was a doctor who told me it. I was sad and he wanted to make me laugh. What was his name again? Beck! Yes, that's it! His name was Beck."

Magda laughed at her own joke for a couple of minutes more. It wasn't every day that someone took such pleasure in telling such a lame joke.

"You see? If the pigeon had flown, he'd have been on time! Hahaha!"

I laughed, even though I knew Magda and I weren't laughing for the same reason.

"Do you know any jokes?" she asked me.

She'd caught me a little off guard. The only jokes I knew weren't the type you could tell to old ladies. So I told her the one about the frog with the big mouth that goes to the photographer's. There's no point repeating it here, you know it already. It was Suzuki who told us it. Magda thought it was very funny.

"I love animal jokes, don't you, Kapriel?"

Then she told me she'd been born in Königsberg in 1920 and had grown up in Berlin. She's a very interesting woman, the kind who doesn't think twice about opening a second bottle of Riesling. She asked me all about my life and about Canada, too. Magda is, like many Germans, very curious. Unlike the French, who always seem to have an answer to the questions they haven't even asked yet, the Germans are full of *wann? wie? wo? warum? wer?* and don't live in fear of one day having to admit: "I don't know." She positively devours books and listens to nothing but classical music. I think that's what I like most about Germans, particularly East Germans: their almost childlike curiosity for all things foreign. Ever since the wall came down, Magda has been visiting ruins all across Europe.

"Ruins don't change. They always stay the same. Look, this is a photograph of me in Athens last summer. How wonderful to be able to travel at last! You know, East Germans weren't allowed to travel before the wall came down. We could go to Poland or Romania, but I'm only interested in Greco-Roman ruins, so, Bucharest and Cracow, well, they're not for me..."

I wondered how a seventy-nine-year-old pensioner could afford to fly. (The downstairs neighbours later told me that Magda would regularly borrow small sums of money and never pay them back. Since they'd known her for a long time and there was something akin to friendship between them, they agreed to lend her the money, knowing full well they'd probably seen the last of it.) She also showed me some lovely photos of herself. They were from during the war, back in Königsberg in East Prussia. She'd had her photo taken in a zoo with a group of children in front of the zebra pen. In another picture, she was on the beach at the Baltic Sea with two or three of the same kids in their swimsuits. In those old sepia photos, Magda wasn't at all fat. She reminded me of one of the sixteen-year-old boys at Holy Canadian Martyrs.

"That's me in Cranz on the Baltic Sea. And there in Königsberg, with the zebras at the zoo. Are you familiar with *Ostpreußen*? It was still Germany back then..."

She fell silent for a moment, almost as a sign of respect. Have you ever heard of East Prussia, Michel? I knew there was Prussia, but not East Prussia. At any rate, Magda went there during the war and had her photo taken. We went on drinking and talking about books we'd read.

She promised to show me around Potsdam, which she knows like the back of her hand. Next Sunday, she wants to bring me for a walk through the *Schrebergärten* near here. I don't know what the word means, but it seems there's a *Biergarten* there, where Berliners like to spend their summer afternoons. I left Magda's apartment at midnight, a little drunk. I hardly ever drink, so I pretty much passed out. This afternoon, I took to the S-Bahn to write to you. What else can I say about Magda other than I feel as though I've always known her? When I'm with her, it's almost enough to make me forget that Claudia's been gone from Berlin for close to six weeks.

She asked if I liked opera, so of course I had to tell her about you. Her eyes lit up when she heard my brother was an opera singer. I didn't dare tell her *Tosca* wasn't at all my scene. She explained to me the meaning behind "Tosca's black eyes." I must admit I'd completely forgotten. I hadn't exactly been paying attention, mind you. The first time, in 1980, I fell asleep. The second time, I was too busy reading the surtitles. In Act I, Magda reminded me, Tosca walks into the church, where her lover Cavaradossi is painting a portrait of Mary Magdalene. He's using a blue-eyed woman he saw praying in the church as a model. Tosca, who has black eyes, recognizes the woman and flies into a jealous rage. She can't bear to see Cavaradossi painting another woman. On her way out of the church, she makes him promise to paint Mary Magdalene's eyes black. Such a jealous woman! Can you believe it! And all over a portrait.

Even though I saw Claudia every other Sunday for three years, I kept on flitting from one woman to another while I was in Toronto. There were a few substitute teachers, then the parent-teacher evenings, where the moms always outnumber the dads four to one. At the parent-teacher evening in October 1996, there was a long line in front of my desk, mostly moms come to see with their own eyes the man their daughters had told them all about. Mrs. Thanatopoulos was there, too. She'd eased up on her daughter's training sessions to force her to concentrate on music instead. Stella had already lost fifteen kilos.

"Another ten and she'll be ready," Mrs. Thanatopoulos said.

On her singing teacher's advice, Stella had also stopped performing at school mass, much to the despair of Mrs. Delvecchio, who loved her rendition of *Ave Maria*. Stella was as shy and reserved as ever with me. She was only fifteen when I came to Holy Canadian Martyrs. They'd had her skip a year of elementary school. She'd been just too smart—and Mrs. Thanatopoulos had apparently made a generous contribution to the school's coffers, which meant that Stella had started high school a year before the other girls her age. But a year can make a big difference in phys ed class. Not only was she younger than her classmates, she was obese, shy, and short-sighted, too. Little Stella would need her peers to go easy on her if she was to survive. It would be wrong to say they bullied her; let's just say she frightened them, and their gibes were a sort of defence mechanism against the authority they felt she represented. I think I'm safe in saying we were all a little afraid of her, afraid of running into her in the hallway. A little like you might be afraid of seeing an apparition of the Virgin Mary, something that would force you to change the course of your existence, to start building a cathedral or converting heretics or something. In other words, to no longer be in control of your own life. To no longer belong to yourself. To be like Mom and her restaurants. I still have trouble explaining the almost religious impact that Stella had on everyone she met.

First, she displayed a degree of piety that bordered on the grotesque, even for a school like Holy Canadian Martyrs. On top of the prayers she read to the entire school every morning, Stella also played an active part in every religious ceremony at the school, first as a singer, then as an altar girl. She fasted for Advent *and* Lent and was regularly absent on the Orthodox saints' days, which fell a few days after the Catholic holy days. Sure she was harmless enough and wouldn't have hurt a fly, but Stella still earned all kinds of unflattering nicknames, from Saint Stella and The Immaculate Conception to Mary Mother of the Poor, and, least flattering of all, The Nun. Regularly—and by that I mean at least once a month—Stella would ask the staff and other students to donate to whatever charity tickled her fancy. In June 1995, for example, she organized a fundraiser for children in Haiti. Armed with a little plastic bucket like the ones kids take to the beach, she went around every classroom and the staff room where the teachers were holed up. Stella stuck to her guns. For instance, in December 1996, by which time I was no longer her secret personal trainer, she walked in on one of my classes. I'd just finished drawing a uterus and two ovaries as an introduction to a class on sexually transmitted infections. Stella knocked discreetly.

She stood in front of the giant uterus complete with pelvic opening on the blackboard, holding up her little green plastic bucket. The Fallopian tubes seemed to be coming out of her ears.

"It's for the Hospital for Sick Children!" she said, her face beatific.

The others had a good laugh at the sight of Poor Stella With Uterus. Despite my best efforts, she'd still managed to put back on half of the weight I'd helped her lose, ever since her mom had put an end to our meetings. The students produced a handful of coins from their pockets. Stella was radiant.

"And what about you, Mr. Lamontagne?"

I took my wallet out of my pocket and slipped the last five dollars it contained into her little bucket. She was still staring at me with the wide eyes of a spaced-out nanny-goat. She gave the bucket a little shake, to indicate that it wasn't enough.

"It's for sick *children*, sir," she repeated, stressing the word as though I hadn't understood her pitch.

It seemed sick children were a cause close to her heart. I apologized and promised to give her more money at lunchtime. I'd have to borrow from Jodi or Zira, but there was no point trying to explain the notion of liquidity shortfall to her. My gifts as a teacher had their limits.

"Mrs. Robinson gave me ten dollars," she prodded, trying to get me to double my contribution.

She walked out of the classroom as quietly as she'd come in. The other students sighed with relief.

"She's so annoying, sir," said Candice, who'd had enough of the braided saint taking her pocket money.

"I know it's irritating," I said, "but she's doing it to help others."

"So she can just bug the hell out of us because she's trying to help people?"

"Candice, watch your language! Yes, as it happens I think it's sometimes OK to bend the rules if it's for the good of others."

"Really? Which rules?"

"The rules of common courtesy."

"I'm going to take you at your word, Mr. Lamontagne."

And so Stella went about rattling her bucket for all kinds of causes no one could possibly be against: sick children, poverty in Haiti, and all the hard times people fall on in spite of themselves. It would never have crossed Stella's mind to ask for money for a sports team or a cause of more dubious morality like AIDS. Each of her causes had to be entirely beyond reproach; absolutely impossible to refuse, at the risk of looking like a heartless brute. I borrowed five dollars from Jodi at lunchtime in the staff room and handed them over to poor Stella with a smile.

"Oh! Thank you, Mr. Lamontagne! That's so generous of you!"

It was that day that a crack opened in the wall of saintliness surrounding young Stella. I was in the room beside the secretary's office, where Zira and Mrs. Robinson were jabbering away, waiting for the bell to ring. Mrs. Robinson was complaining at once again having to face Stella and her little plastic bucket. Zira agreed, admitting that she'd given a dollar to get rid of her.

"I didn't give her a cent this time," came the reply. "She can go ask her mother, so she can!"

Mrs. Robinson wasn't the type of woman to lie or go around making a show of her own nastiness. She no doubt hadn't given Stella a cent, and then Stella had lied to me in front of the other students to get me to cough up. The incident amused me and brought me no small amount of comfort. So Stella Thanatopoulos wasn't a saint after all; she was able to lie and manipulate with the best of them.

Stella's thirst for philanthropy didn't start at Holy Canadian Martyrs. She had already showed interest in worthy causes as a child. But of all the tales of good deeds and charity work, the Eaton Centre story takes some beating. Wait till you hear this: it really sums her up. Jodi the librarian told me all about it. She'd even kept the press cuttings: Stella's stunt made every Toronto daily.

It happened a year before I arrived at Holy Canadian Martyrs. No one talks about it anymore; it seems that all there was to say about it was said in the days following the incident. If you ask me, I think Stella's antics were a pivotal moment for her future, a foreshadowing of what might become of her. Jodi told me the story while rolling a joint in her Annex apartment after supper. It's a good one, you'll see. Just picture a slightly tipsy librarian smoking weed as she tells you a cockamamie story of epic proportions.

It was the fall of 1993, and Stella had found a new cause to obsess over: animal rights. She was raising money for a cat shelter, handing out leaflets exposing the treatment of lab animals, and haranguing teachers who wore makeup:

"Do you know whether your lipstick was tested on animals, Madame Poisson?"

"I... uh... I don't think so, Stella."

"You don't think so or you don't *know*?"

"Well, I hope not. I'll look into it."

You get the picture, right? So anyway, one fall day in 1993, Mrs. Thanatopoulos decides to go spend a small fortune at the Eaton Centre, on the floor where the chic fashion boutiques are. Our Stella goes along with a Greek friend to the mall's huge pet store, where she badgers the staff about the animals' living conditions. Why do they keep them in such tiny cages? Why do they clip the parrots' wings? Picture the scene: it's an enormous store, as big as any supermarket. It has anything you could ever want: poodles, Siamese cats, cockatoos, tarantulas, rabbits, ferrets, and everything you'd need to look after them. Big business, American-style. A hulking great Noah's Ark. The employees end up tuning her out and she eventually leaves—but it proves to be no more than a strategic withdrawal! The following weekend, she tells her mother she's sleeping over at a friend's, a poor girl she's brainwashed with all her nonsense. So the two little nutbars take the subway downtown, all alone one Saturday afternoon—they're only fourteen, remember—while the friend's parents think they're playing in her room. They both show up at the Eaton Centre, their faces covered by black scarfs, and slip quietly in behind a cat litter display fifteen minutes before closing time, where they patiently wait for the employees to go home. Once the Eaton Centre is deserted and the security guard's footsteps fall silent, they open the cages one by one! The store is soon crawling with snakes, rats, lizards, dogs... hundreds of them. They even free the cockroaches that were to be fed to the reptiles, which were apparently all on special that day. As you might imagine, none of the animals were used to being able to move around as they pleased and so they panicked. There were dogs running about with dead hamsters in their mouths, cats ripping lizards to shreds. It was a bloodbath. The two girls took fright at the carnage, but were still too daft to understand there was no way out of the jungle. Terrified by the screeching birds, howling dogs, and the high-pitched shrieks of a ferret being disembowelled by a particularly aggressive cat, the panicked girls banged on the doors for all they were worth. They were out of luck: the security guard was on a different floor and didn't hear the ruckus. They finally took their courage—and a cash register—in both hands and smashed one of the glass doors. They scrambled out, the animals in hot pursuit, to the deafening sound of the alarm they had set off in the process. The Toronto police were first on the scene. Then came the journalists. Since the girls were both minors, the media weren't allowed to reveal their identities or disclose the names of their parents. Every newspaper picked up on the story. It was on TV and radio; it even led the six o'clock news on CBC. The journalists dubbed them, appropriately enough, the Pet Shop Girls.

Most of the bigger animals were rounded up the next day from all four corners of the Eaton Centre. But for a good month after the break-in, the pet store employees and people working in the other shops were still finding tarantulas, lizards, and snakes, both dead and alive, in the mall. They never knew when they would stumble across a cadaverous chameleon, a lifeless finch, or—worse—a very much alive snake. Of course, Mrs. Thanatopoulos had to hire a lawyer to defend her daughter. And a psychologist, too, for a while, at least until she'd gotten over the trauma. The subject was best avoided at school, Jodi said.

"It might get you into trouble. Nobody talks about it anymore."

So everyone at Holy Canadian Martyrs knew the real identity of the Pet Shop Girls. Isn't that terrible? Do you see now why I keep mentioning Stella? You end up forgetting the names of most of the students who pass through your class, you know. But how could I ever forget Stella Thanatopoulos? Her name is forever etched in my memory.

Three years went by at Holy Canadian Martyrs. My shelf picked up a new book or two every week, although I still hadn't managed to get my hands on one of Claudia's. One Sunday in August 1998, she told me her contract at the Toronto Goethe-Institut wasn't being renewed. She'd have to return to Germany that September. She told me this just before the Lutheran service began. It felt like a funeral. The pastor spoke of the Lord's miracles that day. I prayed that Claudia would opt to stay in Toronto. I asked her later what future she saw for us. This led to a slight misunderstanding.

"I'm wondering, what do I mean to you?" I asked her as we walked to the subway.

"What a funny question! You're my friend. That's what you mean to me."

"But we both have tons of friends."

"You Americans do, yes, but we Europeans have fewer friends. Two or three in a lifetime, no more."

"And am I an American friend or a European friend in your eyes?"

"You're a citizen of the world, Gabriel."

She went on to assure me she loved me with all her heart, but she had to go back to Germany, where she had hope of finding a better job than working as a language teacher. Claudia had written her thesis on courtly love in the literature of the Middle Ages. She hoped to teach at Humboldt or the Freie one day, but they're hard to get into.

When Claudia left Toronto in August 1999, I knew I wouldn't last long; it was only a matter of time. I knew it as soon as I saw her: we were made for each other. I could either accept an apathetic but peaceful existence at Holy Canadian Martyrs, or risk everything. It didn't take me long to come to a decision. I would have to keep working on my German, its irregular verbs, its strange syntax, its devilish declensions, and, of course, the incomprehensible existence of a third gender, neither masculine nor feminine, the intriguing *das*.

I read in the *Berliner Morgenpost* this morning that people are eagerly awaiting the latest version of *Tosca* that Bruno-Karl d'Ambrosio is getting ready to film in Rome. It must be said he left—how should I put this?—a whiff of controversy behind him here in Berlin. I think that's the right expression. He produced Wagner's *Rienzi*. That was Adolf Hitler's favourite opera, did you know that? It's hardly ever performed nowadays. Not even the Bayreuth Festival will touch it: it's too hot to handle. But D'Ambrosio is up for anything. To get the audience warmed up, he dressed all the singers and walk-on parts as Nazis. A third of the audience left as soon as the curtain went up, some of them spitting on the floor in disgust on their way out. But D'Ambrosio wasn't done yet. He was determined to make sure all of Berlin could smell his shit, so he decided to include a gas chamber as part of the stage set. There was only one performance. I'm happy and proud, you know, that at last you've been given a role equal to your talents. But are you absolutely sure you want to be in a D'Ambrosio film? What should we expect? Are you sure Puccini wouldn't be better served by a more conventional production? I'm a little worried for you, to be honest. And for Anamaria. I've always had a lot of respect for her.

My train's pulling into the station. I've already travelled the length of the line two or three times both ways.

Gabriel

❧

Blankenfelde – Bernau
May 17, 1999

Dear Michel,

It's been a week since I last wrote, but I've been very busy with my German homework. You'd be surprised by my patience and tenacity, dear brother. I waited until March before I told Claudia I was in Berlin, just a note I mailed to at least let her know I was there. I was afraid of bumping into her, you see. I didn't want her to say, "Gabriel, the swine, was in Berlin all this time and he didn't even tell me!" I always pretended I was still in Toronto in our emails. She must have been astonished to get a letter from Lichtenberg with a photo of me in front of the Brandenburg Gate. I don't dare call her.

She took two weeks to get back to me. Her reply didn't reach me until Easter. She said she was very happy to hear I was in Berlin, but it was all very restrained, very German. And that's what I like about them. They never go overboard; their actions and feelings are pure. They don't go in for all that Latin playacting. And the short letter she wrote me—no more than a page—evoked in its simplicity the spartan nature of the Lutheran Church, the very image of the purity of faith: "Gabriel, I am very happy to hear you are in Berlin. Of course, I would be more than willing to meet up with you as soon as possible. Unfortunately, I am leaving for Egypt with my sister in three days. We'll be spending six weeks in Cairo. The pyramids, the Sphinx, the tombs of the pharaohs... Ah! If only I'd known, I could have booked a ticket for you too. I'll be back in Berlin on Saturday, May 22. I'll probably need a little while to recover from such a long trip. I'll write to you when I get back. Fondly, Claudia." You might think me discouraged by the wait, Michel, but you couldn't be more mistaken. The wait has only stirred my passion, especially since it gives me a little longer to work on my German, my secret weapon. I've found my neighbour Magda to be a valuable ally. She speaks clearly and is always correcting me. It's really helping.

Speaking of Magda, I've just spent a very strange weekend with her. But first, to give you a feel for my neighbourhood, Lichtenberg, I must tell you what happened to me yesterday. I live a stone's throw from the corner of two streets that were known until very recently as Ho-Chi-Minh-Straße and Leninallee. Today they've reverted to their old names: Weißenseer Weg and Landsberger Allee. Magda tells me that no one used the names imposed by the regime anyway; everyone went on using the pre-GDR names. It's a neighbourhood where there is nothing but the *Plattenbauten* I've already told you about, the long buildings that go on forever and all seem to be about ten stories tall. Just imagine the Soviet satellite towns, only in Germany. The socialists were very pragmatic and very broke. They built these *Plattenbauten* at a feverish pace all through the 1970s, with East Germans lining up to move into them. Couples were given one-room apartments like mine. Those with children were given larger apartments like Magda's. I don't know how she managed to get her hands on such a big apartment just for her. I'd have to ask her, but I don't dare. There's a small square at the end of the street, near the tram stop. There's a post office, too, a florist, a Turk who sells spit-roasted chicken, and a supermarket that used to be a Konsum but today goes by another name, just like the streets. That's where I buy my groceries. Yesterday, Saturday, was a bit of an adventure. It was a beautiful day and I rushed to the supermarket. It closes at noon and after that you'd have a hard time finding so much as a pack of dry biscuits.

I ran into Magda. She seemed to be waiting for someone outside the supermarket. I've no idea why, but she pretended not to see me when I walked up to her. I had to call her name two or three times before she reacted with feigned surprise.

"*Ach*, Kapriel! It's you! I didn't recognize you with the sun. What lovely weather. I hope it holds for our outing tomorrow."

We spoke for a few minutes. She must have left our building just before me. She asked if I'd come to buy groceries. I said yes. Since German supermarkets are always packed on Saturdays, I offered to do her shopping at the same time.

"Would you like me to pick anything up for you?"

"*Ach!* You're so kind. I was just enjoying this wonderful spring sunshine, and I couldn't face the thought of having to wait at the cash register. You're such a gentleman, Kapriel. Here, take this and pick me up 250 grams of thinly sliced ham, a tube of Bavarian mustard, some black bread, a small pot of pickles, some cookies, two packs of powdered soup, six bottles of water, and… umm… *ja!* Eggs! I need some eggs, too! I'll wait for you out here in the sunshine."

I took her fifty marks and went grocery shopping for both of us. I found her outside. I gave her the food and her change. She didn't look happy as she peered into the bag. She didn't like the cookies I'd chosen, she explained. How could I have known? Germans make all kinds of cookies. Bahlsen alone must have a dozen sorts. Cookies are to Germany what sushi is to Japan. And since I don't even eat them, don't ask me which ones are the best.

"These ones are a little hard to chew…"

She could always dunk them in tea or coffee, I explained. I really didn't want to have to go line up all over again. She gave me a sad look, sighed, and took the bag. I felt a little sorry for her. I imagined Suzuki at that age, all alone in Outremont, her eyesight too bad for her to go to the supermarket, and I hoped someone would take pity on her in thirty years' time and buy her cookies that were easier to chew. So back I went into the supermarket to get her some softer cookies. As luck would have it, I didn't have to wait too long to pay. Magda was still there when I came out, waiting for me outside. She'd been rummaging around in my bags and was eating one of my bananas.

"Those are my bananas, Magda!"

She almost choked. She hadn't thought I'd be back so quickly.

"Yes, they looked so tasty. You know, since we couldn't afford them for forty years in the GDR, I still consider them a luxury. I'm sorry. I'll pay you back, of course."

"Not at all. My treat."

"Did you find me some softer cookies? You really are an angel, Kapriel."

And all this in German, dear brother! No one is more surprised than me at the progress I've made. Magda wanted to take my arm on the way back. She made a point of calling out "hello!" to each of the neighbours we met.

"Look, Kapriel. That man with the wooden leg. His wife ran off to the West in 1985. The regime made things so hard for him because of her that he tried to end his days by throwing himself in front of the tram. The doctors saved him, but not the leg. Say hello to the poor devil."

Magda knows everyone. I think she only said hello because we were walking arm in arm.

"Let's stop here at the snack bar."

It was a stand that sold waffles in winter and grilled sausages in summer. They also had cigarettes and cheap booze by the bottle. Magda wanted to buy a small bottle of Chantré, a type of brandy, the cheapest there is, I think. She drank a glass or two before we moved on. She chatted away to the woman who worked there.

"Look, the wall comes down and here I am getting married to a handsome Canadian! Charming, isn't he?"

She was a little drunk. I had to walk her home, at a snail's pace. She was unsteady on her feet and clung to me like a life preserver. The children belonging to the woman back at the stand had gone over to the West before the wall came down, she told me. She had a daughter in Cologne and a son in Munich, but they never visited.

It took us a good twenty minutes to cover the three hundred metres that separated the supermarket from the door to her apartment. She asked me in, but I didn't dare. To be honest, I was glad to be rid of her. I left her there with her shopping. That afternoon I went to the gym and when I came back I bumped into Hilde from the third floor, who had something to tell me.

"The TV people will be coming by for their money."

"What money?"

"Money for state television. You have a television in your apartment, don't you?"

"Of course."

"Then you'll have to pay."

"That's funny. Magda never mentioned it."

"Magda doesn't pay!" she laughed. "She stays clear of the inspectors. She pretends to be dead when they get to the ninth floor."

"Well, she's very much alive. I'm just back from the supermarket with her."

"What?"

"From the supermarket."

"They let her in?"

Hilde was about to let me in on a good one.

"No, I went in. I saw her outside and offered to buy her groceries for her."

"Ah, that doesn't surprise me."

"How come?"

"They caught her red-handed. Twice! Since then she's not been allowed in."

"But how does she do her shopping?"

"She waits for someone to do it for her."

"She was shoplifting?"

"How do you expect her to live on what they give her every month? It's enough for wine and beer, but not luxuries. Twice they caught her with smoked salmon in her bag. Once she even had cheese hidden away in her brassiere. Not bad, eh? When you think of all she got away with, to only get caught twice! She's not the only one either. There are always two of them waiting outside for someone to get their groceries for them. Sometimes I do it for her. She's my neighbour after all. But I'm not always in Berlin. I tried having a word with the manager, but he didn't want to hear it. The worst possible kind of *Wessi*. Lots of elderly women just can't get used to life in a unified Germany. It's hard. I work, so it's different for me."

So Magda was stealing cheese and smoked salmon. At least she had taste. I told Hilde I was going to the *Schrebergärten* with Magda the next day, and that I was to be ready at noon.

"She loves going there. She'll want to show you off. Be careful with Magda. She'll get too attached to you."

"But she's almost eighty and I've just turned thirty."

"So what?"

That evening I watched a little *Tosca* with Placido Domingo and Kabaivanska on the DVD you sent. I'm starting to realize something, Michel. It's actually the story of an honest, innocent woman who comes up against the forces of evil, who's caught in the vice-like grip of history. Isn't that it?

The next day Magda rang my bell at eleven forty-five. She was wearing a summer dress with flowers on it and a little makeup. She had an apple-green barrette in her hair. She looked radiant. I felt like I was going to a wedding with her.

"Ready, Kapriel?"

Truth is, I wasn't quite ready, but she seemed so excited to be spending the afternoon with me in the *Schrebergärten* that I didn't dare make her wait. She had her Sunday cane with her, the one with the wooden knob.

"A Saxon artisan carved it," she told me proudly.

The cane was a real work of art. I thought to myself that one day, when Suzuki was getting on in years, I'd give her one just like it. Fortunately, the *Schrebergärten* weren't far. There were community gardens just like them in every city in Germany, Magda explained. Little pockets of greenery, small plots with fences between them, where Germans built tiny homes they only used in the summer. They planted flowers and vegetables and spent entire weekends contemplating the sun. The avenues of lilacs and peonies gave way to a *Biergarten*, where a few old folk were having a bite to eat.

"Here we are!" Magda announced.

I could tell by the sound of her voice that we'd arrived somewhere she was very fond of. She seemed to know everyone sitting at the tables. They said hello. *"Das ist mein Kanadier, Kapriel Lamontagne,"* she replied to anyone who asked who she was with. *Her* Canadian! As though she'd caught me with a net! Magda ordered us beer and food. Some kind of bitter-tasting wheat beer that had been dyed green.

"Such a lovely place. Best to enjoy it now before it's overrun with *Wessis*. *Prosit*, Kapriel!"

Wessis are West Germans. I got the impression Magda didn't especially enjoy their company. She took a swig of the green beer and brought her glass down hard on the wooden table.

"Decent folk can't even go out in Berlin anymore. Ever since the wall fell, we've been allowed to travel, sure, but the problem is the whole city is overrun with *Wessis*. Not even *Wessis* from West Berlin, from Kreuzberg or Charlottenburg where I went to school: people from the Rhine Valley, from Bremen, from all across the Federal Republic! Bavarians! *Pfui Teufel!* They buy up all the apartments and ruin the scenery just by being here. A real scourge!"

A couple in their sixties were sitting nearby. They smiled at Magda's rant. I asked Magda if she might be exaggerating a touch.

"You don't know them! Ignoramuses, frightful barbarians. Money is the only language they understand. I won't hear otherwise. They come over here like they just conquered the place, they look down their noses at us and belittle everything that happened before they got here. A plague, I'm telling you. What I'd give to have my wall back!"

Those sitting nearby raised their glasses in agreement.

"And don't try to talk culture with them! All they know is American pop, if that! Stomachs filled with Big Macs and heads with Michael Jackson. Cretins, the lot of them. Won't you have another beer, Kapriel? It's my round!"

Magda had already finished her glass. The sun shone high in the sky, the birds were singing, and Claudia would be back from Egypt in less than a week. There were plenty of reasons to celebrate. I never drink more than one beer, but I let Magda lead me down a path of decadence that Sunday afternoon in Lichtenberg. Our food arrived and Magda ordered two more green beers. Feeling a little tipsy myself, I told her what I was really doing in Berlin. Until then, I'd always said it was to learn German, which wasn't that far from the truth. I'd never have mentioned Claudia if she hadn't asked me directly.

"But why a Canadian does he to learn German want? They don't speak German in Canada. Did your ancestors speak German?"

"As it happens, yes. The Lamontagnes had the same name as you: Berg. Strange, isn't it? Their name was Gallicized in the eighteenth century."

"Germans. Really? Do you know where they came from?".

"Not really, no. I know virtually nothing about them. Thing is, there's another reason I'm learning German. It's less about the past than the future."

The beer was going to my head. I noticed the dye had turned Magda's lips and tongue green. You could see how green her tongue was every time she laughed, which made her look a little like an iguana. Don't ask me why, but I told her about meeting Claudia in Toronto. I told her the lot: the courtly love, the gallant knight in shining armour who performed amazing feats so that his sweetheart would find him desirable. And my feat was learning German, so that I might win over Claudia's heart and become her German-speaking lover.

The people sitting at the other tables lowered their voices or stopped speaking altogether as we chatted, not wanting to miss any of our conversation. But I was too drunk to care what these *Ossis* might think as they listened on from the neighbouring tables while a Canadian poured his heart out in his bad German.

"What's her name?" Magda, now on her third green beer, asked me brusquely.

"Uh, Claudia, she's called Claudia," I stammered.

"Claudia. A Berliner. Well, I suppose we should be grateful for small mercies," she hissed.

"She's actually from Cologne," I said without thinking.

"From Cologne! *Eine Wessi-Tante! Ach! Scheußlich!*" she raged.

The other people in the *Biergarten* chuckled quietly. *Eine Wessi-Tante* was perhaps the worst thing she could have called her, Michel. Such contempt. It means some bird, some chick from the West, but it's more insulting than that. The same way Quebecers would say "A *maudite Anglaise* from Westmount!"

I didn't speak for a second, taken aback. How dare this crazy old woman insult the woman I considered to be my future, my dreams, my Holy Grail, the solution to all my problems? But I kept my cool. I tried to get Magda to understand that Claudia had in fact defended her PhD thesis on *Das Nibelungenlied* in Toronto. She must have something between her ears.

"In Toronto? On something so German? She can't have been good enough for our universities. There you have it. And you're in love with her, Kapriel? You can do much better than that, a handsome young man like you! I would almost rather you had told me it was boys you were into. *Eine Wessi-Tante! Na, was soll's!* That's really asking for trouble..."

"Magda, now you're being nasty..."

"I only want what's good for you! Don't say I never warned you. You don't know what you're letting yourself in for. She'll have you under her thumb before you know it. Vixens, the lot of them! And from Cologne to boot!"

"She's absolutely right. And I speak from experience!" a man in his sixties piped up, having followed the conversation from the beginning. His wife promptly emptied her beer over his head, much to everyone's amusement.

"I married her two years after the wall came down. From Hamburg, she was. And look at me now! Here she is pouring beer over my head. Watch yourself, *Kanadier!*" he warned me, patting his face dry with a napkin while his wife stormed out of the *Biergarten*.

The laughter took a full minute to die down, by which time the man had gone after his *Wessi-Tante*, no doubt to try to patch things up before she emerged from the kitchen wielding a knife. Magda realized she'd gone too far. She tried to change the subject.

"Did you know, Kapriel, that I used to sing? It was a long time ago," she said.

"Opera?"

"Everything. Schubert, Mozart. I was a soprano."

The thought of this woman singing made me smile.

"You don't believe me?" she asked. It was as though she'd read my mind. "I loved Italian opera best, Puccini."

"*Tosca?*"

"Yes, *Tosca.*"

More beer arrived. Magda began telling me about Puccini.

"In Berlin in the 1930s, I went to the opera twice a week. I must have seen *Tosca* at least twenty times. No, more! At the Deutsches Opernhaus in Charlottenburg and at Unter den Linden too. It was my favourite Puccini opera. People tend to prefer *Madame Butterfly*, but I always preferred *Tosca*," she confessed, now seriously inebriated. "Whenever I think of that idiot Cio-Cio San waiting in vain for her Pinkerton to come back! And the other one, Suzuki! Completely under that crazy woman's spell. When you stop to think about it, *Madame Butterfly* is nothing but a defence of slavery!"

She stood up. And there, in the middle of the *Biergarten*, leaning on her cane, she began to sing. People pretended not to notice, but she sang so loudly that soon all eyes were on her. The funny thing is, she sang really well. She projected her voice just like Anamaria di Napoli does, and she knew every word of *Tosca*, only in German! Michel, she sings every bit as well as Montserrat Caballé! Such a pure voice! I recognized the part from Act I when Tosca surprises Cavaradossi painting Attavanti's face in the church. You must know it by heart.

Von unserem Häuschen mit mir sollst du träumen,
Es hängt versteckt hinter blühenden Bäumen,
Fern von der Neugier, vom Geräusch der Welt
Nur dem Liebesglück geweiht.

It sounded even more beautiful in German, the kind of thing I'd like to come up with for Claudia. The others stared at her in admiration as she sang. She went on for at least a minute, a song about stars, about the wind rustling the leaves, about a place where Tosca might be safe and loved. I would have given anything for you to be there to sing back. She looked at me like

Kabaivanska looks at Placido Domingo in the film, her gaze just as heavy with meaning. Then, people began to applaud. Someone shouted, "Bravo, Magda!" which only went to prove that everyone in the *Biergarten* knew her. She was too drunk to go on, but still she clenched her fist and shouted: *"Ah diese Kokotte!"* I had no way of telling if it was Tosca calling Attavanti a tart, or Magda cursing Claudia, my *Wessi-Tante*. Magda could barely stand.

"Time to go home, Magda. I'm tired too."

"Help me. I can't walk anymore."

I walked her home as best I could, stopping a hundred times along the way. She had to concentrate hard on every step so as not to topple over. A combination of her cane and my arm helped her keep her balance. When we got to her door, she rummaged for her keys in her bag, grumbling all the while, and eventually unlocked it.

"Carry me to my bed, Kapriel," she implored me.

I sat on her bed with her for two minutes, just to make sure she didn't choke on her own vomit. She seemed OK. Her eyes were open and she was getting her breath back. She began to talk, but clearly not to me. She kept saying the same thing, over and over. "I left her by the side of the road, there was nothing else for it. She was just too cold. My little Helga... My little Helga." She was delirious. I went back to my apartment, a little worse for wear after my afternoon in the *Schrebergärten*. It never crossed my mind that Magda might have taken a shine to me, but I swear for a second I wondered whether she was jealous, as jealous as Tosca. Why attack Claudia like that? She doesn't even know her. And that voice! I'm no expert, Michel, but she's quite the opera singer, a real diva! What a surprise to hear a voice like that coming out of such an old, clapped-out body. I didn't even know there were German lyrics for *Tosca*. Isn't it always sung in Italian? You'd know better than me.

Since I was still a little tipsy, I hopped on a tram and went out to a bar in Prenzlauer Berg. I couldn't stop thinking about Claudia. It was a singles bar. I kept on drinking and struck up a conversation with a blonde who vaguely resembled Claudia. From a distance. She took me home to her place. The whole thing was done and dusted in under an hour. I swiped her copy of *Harold and Maude* and by the time I got back to Lichtenberg in the early hours of the morning, the stars were shining in the sky, Michel. The stars were shining...

Gabriel

Dear little brother,
Time flies. Only four days before Claudia gets back to Berlin. May 22.
Mark the date on your calendar. Declare a national holiday in every country
around the world. Another four days and I'll be free. Another four days
and my life will begin at last.

Today I sat in the S-Bahn that goes around the Ring, the circle line around
Berlin that leaves from Westkreuz and goes to Ostkreuz before returning
to Westkreuz via Südkreuz *und zurück*. I was sitting opposite a very elegant lady, very German, probably what Claudia will look like twenty-five
years from now, perhaps how Suzuki would have looked if she'd been born
in Lichtenberg or Charlottenburg. I try to steal a glance or two: German
women, Prussians especially, don't like being looked up and down like
cuts of meat. In that respect, they're a lot like women in Quebec. She was
wearing a salmon-pink summer dress, an off-white cotton knit shawl over
her shoulders. Her red lipstick went perfectly with her purse, itself half a
shade darker than her dress. Like Claudia, she too had a Marlene Dietrich
hairdo, and she wore a small amber necklace. Did you know that amber
comes from East Prussia, Michel?

The lady in the S-Bahn must have sensed I was watching her because she
started fingering her amber necklace, just like Mom would often do with the
little cross she wore around her neck. Was she afraid I might steal it? I looked
away as the train stopped at Jungfernheide. The doors opened, then closed
again. The conductor had already shouted "*Zurückbleiben!*" to make sure any
latecomers kept well back when a man dressed in a 1960s black suit appeared on
the platform, striding along as quickly as he could. He leaned on an umbrella
as he walked; it too was black. We were all sure the train was just about to
leave, but sometimes a kindly conductor will let you open the doors at the
very last moment and slip inside. This is probably what the man was counting on as he tried, in vain, to open one of the doors right as the train lurched
off. My neighbour and I moved our heads imperceptibly to see his reaction:
a mixture of disgust, disappointment, and resignation. For a split second, we
both believed we alone had secretly witnessed the poor man's despair. He now
bowed his head in submission, no doubt because the worst calamity of all had
just befallen him: he was going to be late. He must have been too caught up

working out the minutes and seconds to realize we were watching him from our seats on the other side of the window. Then it happened. I looked over at my neighbour, the ever-so-sophisticated lady, and realized that she was wearing an expression of sympathy for the gentleman in black. She was genuinely sorry to see the poor man miss his S-Bahn. But it's not this clandestine compassion that's the most profoundly German thing about this story, Michel: it's the fact that as soon as she realized I was looking at her, she immediately pulled herself together and her face regained the neutral, sophisticated expression it had had since leaving Westkreuz. You see, it was that brief moment of weakness when the lady had thought: "This stranger is watching me while I experience emotion. Quick, let's put an end to this shameful spectacle." For me, that's such a German reaction. The moment you regain your self-control and get the better of yourself. Needless to say, I began to lust after the woman.

The Germans say *sich zusammenreißen*, to pull oneself together. And watching them get a hold of themselves is the most moving sight in the world.

I rang Hilde's doorbell. I wanted to print out a document to hand in to my German teacher at the Goethe-Institut on Tuesday. She was home, thank God. I spoke to her a little about Magda, asked if she knew anything about a little girl called Helga by the side of the road. "You know, Kapriel," she said. "Magda's washed with every water, she's been around, you know. She might have been talking about East Prussia. I know she was in Königsberg during the war. That might have something to do with it. Times were tough in Königsberg with the Red Army, especially for... Do you know much about East Prussia?"

East Prussia, she told me, was a German province. Its capital was Königsberg, Immanuel Kant's hometown. (It's funny: Königsberg means the king's mountain, just like Montreal is the royal mountain. They both basically mean the same thing.) It was a German province for centuries, until the Red Army rolled in with their tanks in 1945. The three million or so Germans who lived there had to flee. It was total chaos, in the middle of winter. Hilde told me that Magda had been there in January 1945 when Germany fell. She showed me a pair of earrings. "*Das ist Bernstein.*" Amber. East Prussia is on the shores of the Baltic Sea, where amber comes from. It's petrified pine resin, apparently.

I think it must look like the Gaspé Peninsula or Rivière-du-Loup. Like where Suzuki grew up, I mean. Hilde told me about the gorgeous sunsets over the sea. At any rate, the woman sitting opposite me on the S-Bahn, on the circle line that travels clockwise around Berlin, she's wearing a yellow amber necklace that's the same shade as Hilde's earrings. It's the amber that made me think of all that. Amber's lovely. It appeals to the gentler side of our nature.

Yesterday's operatic incident in the *Schrebergärten* for some reason or other reminded me of my final few months at Holy Canadian Martyrs. As I mentioned already, young Stella stopped singing for two years, at least in front of her classmates and teachers, on the orders of her singing teachers, who wanted her to rest her voice. It seems she had two singing teachers as well as a music theory teacher, the one I met that Saturday when I went over to the Thanatopoulos house for the first time. In early January 1998, the girls I'd first taught in Grade 10 were finishing high school. Most had already chosen a university. My three favourites—Melikah, Candice, and Kayla—had grown into glorious young women who had moved on from experimenting with makeup and short skirts. They had taken every phys ed class up to Grade 13, even poor Kayla (Zira the secretary let her sign up for my classes for her last two years of high school to show that all was forgiven). They were my informers, almost my girlfriends. They would always come sit with me in the gym after school, chattering away while the boys played basketball. This closeness brought with it an unhealthy curiosity about the state of my love life.

"Is it true that you slept with the librarian?"

Melikah wasn't the type to beat about the bush. I managed to dodge their questions most of the time, telling them that wasn't the type of thing you asked your teacher.

"Mrs. Robinson says we should watch ourselves around Mr. Lamontagne, is she right?"

I don't know what Candice meant by that. Had Mrs. Robinson really told the students to be wary of me? The poor woman...

"And what about Mrs. Robinson, did you have your way with her too?"

Of the three, Kayla had the sharpest sense of humour. We laughed for ages. The very thought of Mrs. Robinson at the height of passion would have left a dead man in hysterics. Melikah did an impression of her climaxing in her Northern Irish accent...

"Oh Lord! Oh Lord! Oh! Jesus, Mary, and Joseph. Yes, yes, yes. Glory!"

We were crying with laughter. I think it's my time with the girls at Holy Canadian Martyrs that I miss the most. Their youthfulness, the laughter of eighteen-year-old girls. They weren't going to let it go.

"You know, Mr. Lamontagne, we're eighteen now!"

"Put a sock in it, Candice."

"Do you want to have a beer with us?"

A beer. In Ontario they could lawfully have sex with a twenty-nine-year-old man, I reminded her, but she'd have to wait another year for a beer. I don't know what young Ontarians find so fascinating about having a beer with their teachers anyway. It seems to be a rite of passage, as important to them as being baptized or circumcised is to others. And yet every year, some dumb, greenhorn teacher gets caught raising a glass with his underage students. Complaints are filed; names are printed in the newspaper. All hell breaks loose. This is Ontario.

"So, yes?"

"So, no."

They seemed disappointed. But they still managed to convince me to take them to the University of Toronto pool on Harbord Street, just opposite where I lived. I'd been training at the weight room there ever since moving to Toronto. I think they were keen to lift the veil on my mysterious private life, to see where I went outside the world of prayers at Holy Canadian Martyrs. Part of them probably also wanted to explore the bowels of the university all three had chosen to continue their studies. As good little girls from Toronto's well-to-do suburbs, they were seldom allowed to venture downtown alone. Never at night. They were to be home for supper and never so much as mention the streets they walked like voyeurs: Queen Street, where junkies staggered about in broad daylight; Church Street, where the gays strutted; Spadina Avenue, positively crawling with Chinese. They said they were going to see a show. Which, strictly speaking, wasn't entirely untrue. And so it was agreed we would go swim lengths at the university pool the following Sunday.

It was unbelievably cold that day. The girls found me half frozen by the door to the university sports centre. They'd swapped their Holy Canadian Martyrs uniforms for outfits that were much too sexy for a wintry Sunday afternoon in Toronto. Candice was shivering. They took forever to come out of the locker room. When they finally appeared poolside, I thought I was going to have a heart attack. They were all wearing microscopic fluorescent bikinis, the kind Brazilian girls strut around in at Copacabana. And since they squealed with every step, their entrance did not go unnoticed. They were quite strong swimmers, Candice especially. By way of retribution,

I challenged them to swim eighty lengths, which I do every Sunday. They managed forty without batting an eyelid, swimming front crawl and breast-stroke. Melikah stopped at sixty, half dead. Kayla, out to impress, made it to seventy-three. Only Candice kept up with me right to the end. It took two of us to help her out of the water. They were much more subdued after that, slinking back to get changed in silence.

I had to wait a good twenty minutes for them by the entrance. None of them had dried their shoulder-length hair. They wore it like agent Dana Scully from *The X-Files*, apart from Melikah, that is. Her curly hair was a little longer. Three drowned cats on a freezing Sunday afternoon.

"Are you nuts! You'll catch your death! It's minus ten out!"

"The dryers weren't working. This place is a dump," Kayla complained.

"What do you mean the dryers weren't working? None of them?"

"None of them," Kayla replied. "Do you have a hair dryer at your place, Mr. Lamontagne?"

It was always the same every time my three princesses had done something wrong or were trying to wheedle something out of me. I knew the locker room dryers were no doubt in perfect working order, that they were only looking for an excuse to come back to my apartment. They must have looked me up in the phone book and seen that I lived in the block right beside the pool, on Spadina. Poor Kayla gave herself away as she asked me, nodding over to where I lived. They were all so flawed, so adorable. And there I was, torn between leaving them to wander the streets of Toronto with wet hair and the risk they would tell their parents they had spent Sunday afternoon at their gym teacher's place.

"We won't tell a soul," simpered Melikah.

I should have let them catch pneumonia instead of giving in to their mewling. And yet they meant no harm. They just wanted to see a bachelor's apartment with their own eyes. In the hopes of spotting a stray bra, a pack of condoms by the bed, perhaps a lover still fast asleep… But they would see none of that because I never bring anyone back to my place, except Claudia once in 1995 and that was only for a cup of tea. I'm more the "don't stay the night, leave with a book" type. My bookshelf wasn't going to get any heavier if I began bringing girls home.

"Dry your hair and get out!" I said, a little irritated.

The girls went all quiet and solemn when we reached my twentieth-floor apartment, like archaeologists who have just uncovered a lost tomb in the sand

and knocked down the last remaining slab that stands between them and the mummy they've spent the past fifty years searching for. They walked into my three-room apartment, their hair still dripping wet, in tomb-like silence.

"Wow! What a great view of the CN Tower!"

"You can even see the SkyDome!"

They sat quietly on the sofa while I rummaged around for my hair dryer in the bathroom. I could hear them laughing. Kayla was holding a framed photo of Claudia.

"Who's this? Mrs. Lamontagne?"

I snatched it from her and set it back on the bookshelf.

"A German friend."

"That's why you've so many German books?" Melikah inquired.

They flipped through the textbooks from the Goethe-Institut, trying to read the German words out loud. They were so cute!

"She's pretty, your *Fräulein*. She's lucky," Melikah sighed.

Candice was the first to use the hair dryer. Don't ask me why but she'd taken off her blouse to dry her hair in front of the bathroom mirror. Meanwhile, I tried to get Melikah and Kayla interested in German grammar. I told them about courtly love, Claudia, the adversity we must put ourselves through to earn our sweetheart's love. They were enthralled by the idea.

"She won't believe you've gone and learned German just for her, Mr. Lamontagne," Melikah said.

"She'll fall into your arms just like Stella Thanatopoulos did!" Kayla teased.

"Leave Stella out of this, Kayla."

"But she's such an idiot. And her mom—"

It was at that very moment, dear brother, that the phone rang twice to let me know someone was downstairs and wanted to come up. Who could it be on a Sunday? A woman's voice told me it was a delivery. But I hadn't ordered anything. Flowers? I began to shake like a leaf. Who was about to knock on my door and find me with three eighteen-year-old students, one of them drying her hair in her bra in my bathroom, the other two still dripping wet and giggling on my sofa? My throat went dry. A century went by. The elevator must have been full of people coming back from mass or from walking their dog in Queen's Park. The girls didn't seem to grasp the seriousness of the situation. Three knocks on the door. Like Louis XVI walking to the scaffold, I opened up, my head held high. Horror of horrors! It was Mrs. Thanatopoulos! She was wearing a long, Arctic fox fur coat and hat. She stepped forward and thrust a Pyrex dish under my nose. Imagine, Michel, that Nana Mouskouri in Furs shows up at your door one January afternoon, bearing a Greek dessert.

"Do you like galaktoboureko, Meesterrr Lamontagne?"

I thought I might faint. The girls had bounded up off the sofa, electrified. They said hello to Mrs. Thanatopoulos and of course she recognized them. They tried to look calm. And that's when Candice decided to saunter out of the bathroom, blouse unbuttoned, her black bra on display for all to see. With the hair dryer on, she hadn't heard what was happening in the living room. Not realizing Mrs. Thanatopoulos was there, she called out:

"Girls, you *have* to see it, Mr. Lamontagne's thing is absolutely enormous," she told her friends. "You practically have to hold it with both hands—but does it ever get the job done! You won't be disappointed. I don't know about you girls, but I'm *exhausted*! My thighs are on fire!"

Mrs. Thanatopoulos cleared her throat and looked irritated.

"I can come back later, Meesterrr Lamontagne, if you prefer. You seem a little busy," she said, pursing her lips.

"No, no, the girls were just leaving. Please, stay," I stammered.

Realizing that all four of us were well and truly up shit creek without a paddle, the girls quickly gathered together their things. Candice had buttoned up her blouse faster than you can say "corruption of a minor." They put their winter boots on without saying a word. The little hussies could barely say goodbye with a straight face. The door closed. Mrs. Thanatopoulos waited for me to ask her to take off her coat, still holding the dish of galaktoboureko.

"I… I took them to the pool and they came back to dry their hair."

"Yes, of course. Please take the dish, it's verrry heavy."

"Would you like a cup of tea?"

"Please. I made you a Greek dessert. It's full of protein. It should help you get your strength back."

I helped her with her coat, wondering why she'd decided to drop by unannounced and how she managed to find me in such a huge city. Probably the same way as Melikah and her friends. There and then, I made up my mind to never again have my name in the phone book. Beneath her Arctic fox coat, she was wearing a figure-hugging purple dress with a plunging neckline and an amber necklace. It wasn't like the one worn by the woman in the S-Bahn. This one must have cost thousands of dollars, and was made with big chunks of amber of all shades, from off-white and rusty red to ebony and caramel. She sat down on the sofa without me asking her to. Luckily I'd put Claudia's photo face down on a shelf after I'd taken it off the girls. I didn't want Mrs. Thanatopoulos staring at her.

"Give me a plate too, would you? I'll have some with you. I make a good galaktoboureko."

Truth is I was hungry after eighty lengths at the pool, but I would rather have eaten something healthier and on my own. Mrs. Thanatopoulos motioned for me to sit beside her. She served me a huge portion of the flan. It must have been at least twenty inches by eight. There had to have been a dozen eggs in it. The type of thing I don't ever want to see you eating again, Michel. It wasn't just a social call. Mrs. Thanatopoulos had something important to ask me. First she inquired what I'd been up to over the Christmas holidays. I made up a trip back to see my family in Montreal. I couldn't very well tell her I'd spent the two weeks cruising women, piling up novels, poetry collections, and history books right, left, and centre. As it happens, she was overjoyed to see my well-stocked bookcase.

"They were right, I see, Meesterrr Lamontagne. You *are* an avid rrreader."

Her remark wasn't without irony. She was making it clear she knew exactly where the books had come from.

"I'm sure the same can't be said of every gym teacher. Have you read them all?"

Perhaps she was expecting a summary of each.

"Of course," I assured her.

Which is true. I never swipe a book unless I intend to read the whole thing. Ill-gotten gains seldom prosper, as they say. But my books weren't ill gotten, and they're still prospering away. I'd wager, in fact, that most of the girls I took a book from never even noticed. And if they did, they were probably grateful for me freeing them of a burden. People are always reluctant to get rid of their books; they enjoy a strange sort of relationship with them. Once they've read a book, they let it clutter up their tiny apartment for years until they suddenly realize, when moving day comes around, just how heavy paper can be. And they swear as they carry their boxes down the stairs, cursing Simone de Beauvoir, telling Thomas Bernhard he can go to hell. But as soon as they get to their new place, there they are, patiently putting up their bookcases again, more often than not arranging the books in alphabetical order, like beavers rebuilding a dam after a flood. Truth be told, I'm doing these girls a favour.

Mrs. Thanatopoulos definitely had a mean streak; I think Jodi the librarian was right and I was about to see for myself. While I poured her a cup of tea, she explained that her daughter Stella was to go to a make-or-break audition at a music school in New York in the fall of 1998.

"The problem, Gabriel, is that I'm not at all happy with her figure."

"What about her voice?"

"Her voice? Her voice is tremendous. But she'll go nowhere if she keeps putting on weight. When you first came to Holy Canadian Martyrs, you were a big help to us. She lost ten kilos. But the poor darrrling has put five of them back on. We need you again, my dear Gabriel."

"Mrs. Thanatopoulos, I understand you'd rather your daughter's body was different, but have you ever asked her what she thinks?"

The eternal fire of the Olympic flame flared up in Mrs. Thanatopoulos's pupils. For a second I thought she might be about to slit my carotid artery with the pie server she was holding in her right hand. I'd gone too far. You don't want to upset the kind of woman who walks around Toronto draped in dead foxes on a Sunday afternoon.

"Our agreement stands. A thousand dollars for every kilo."

"I won't do it. Stella knows how to lose weight now. The rest has to come from her."

"Oh, so you feel sorry for her. You're a kind soul, Gabriel. A man who likes to read, too."

"I read enough to know that your daughter has rights."

"*Rrrights?*"

"It's her body. That's what I mean. She might not be an adult yet, but she should have the right to decide whether or not to lose weight."

She pursed her lips.

"It's strange to see a gym teacher who's only starting out turn down easy money. Especially since you don't seem to come from a particularly well-to-do family, judging by the way you talk. I mean it's perfectly *nice* and everything, but…"

"Now you're being nasty, Mrs. Thanatopoulos."

"As nasty as the CEO of Mado Group Inc., Gabriel?"

My heart stopped beating. How could this harpy from hell have found out I was Madeleine Lamontagne's son?

"And yet she's got plenty of money. Why doesn't she help you find a better place to live? Does she know you're in this miserable tower block? Oh, I'm so sorry! It's probably none of my business! I talk too much. It's a bad habit of mine. I just don't know when to keep quiet. And people take me for an idiot. But not you, Gabriel, isn't that rrright?"

"I…"

"I just can't keep my mouth shut! But I'm working on it. We Greeks, we just go on and on and on, you know. We're almost as bad as the Northern Irish! I happen to know the young girl's parents. What's her name again? Candice? The one in the black bra. Do you remember? The one that thinks you have an absolutely enorrrmous thingamijig."

"It's not what you think. She was just drrrying… errr… drying her hair."

"Gabriel," she concluded, her voice ice-cold now. "Tell that to the crown prosecutor. I'm sure the Ontario courts will even let you defend yourself in French. Even in prison, I'm sure they'll find someone to do the body search in French. That, too, I believe is one of your… *rrrights*. Another slice?"

I was speechless. God had just provided me with irrefutable proof that there is in this world a thing, an entity, a force more wicked than our mother. But I wasn't out of the woods yet, dear brother.

"You seem rather fond of unrrripened fruit, Gabriel, but I intend to show you that fruit tastes even better once it's been given time to mature."

"You really are a horrible woman."

"Go on… Won't you have a little? Eat it all up now."

She handed me a huge slice of flan.

Galaktoboureko is a milky dessert, a more generous version of Portuguese nata tarts. It's made with filo pastry like the kind they use in those spinach appetizers, only stuffed with a denser version of custard. They serve it cold. Mrs. Thanatopoulos's had been made that morning. If I hadn't spent two hours swimming with the girls before Stella's mother showed up, I wouldn't have managed a single bite. But the Gorgon insisted. "Go on, just a little more!" she murmured. She took forever to finish her serving. "Isn't it delicious, Gabriel? Tell me it's delicious!" And I had to tell her I'd never had such a creamy dessert, that the pastry was at once light and firm, that it was a meal for the gods. I had to have three more helpings. "Go on, you can do it. You're so big and strrrong!" I was going to vomit any minute. As I sunk my fork into the pastry, I thought about poor Lemon, the gym teacher Mrs. Thanatopoulos had sent packing from Holy Canadian Martyrs. The poor guy must have turned down her galaktoboureko and was now reduced to standing up for his *rrrights*. She wouldn't think twice, I was sure of it, about turning me over to the police. She might well even have filmed me coming home with the girls. What with Mrs. Robinson spreading rumours about me too, I'd be lucky to get away with a reprimand. I'd have my teaching license revoked and nothing short of divine intervention would spare me a dreadful trial. Mrs. Thanatopoulos sighed with pleasure as she swallowed the last of the custard. She slammed her plate down hard on the living-room coffee table then disappeared into the bathroom. I heard running water then the hair dryer. She was in there for at least ten minutes. I poured myself a scotch.

"It really is enorrrmous, but oh so effective. The young girl was rrright! It's important to have the rrright tool for the job. We're back to getting along famously, I see, Gabriel. I'm so happy. As proof of my good intentions, I brought you a little gift. Open it! Ah, what a beautiful Sunday! I feel like I'm twenty again! I don't suppose an athlete like yourself would happen to have a little packet of cigarettes lying around?"

I was onto my second scotch by now, desperate to wash down the custard that was sticking to the walls of my oesophagus like glue. She passed me a book wrapped up in the paper Mado's serves its cakes in. The pink tissue paper with the egg logo, you know the one I mean? I grabbed it and unwrapped it. It was *Maria Callas. Portrait of a Diva*. A biography. A Greek gift. As I put my hand on the book, I swore I would never read a word of it. Books are to be taken, not given. I thanked Mrs. Thanatopoulos, then she put on her coat and hat made of dead animals. Before she left, she took a brown envelope out of her bag and flung it on the coffee table beside the empty Pyrex dish.

"I'll be expecting you next Saturday at 8 a.m. Now you understand the stakes. *Yia sas*, Gabriel."

I ran a bath when she left and poured in a half bottle of bleach. I wept. I dreamed that Suzuki, dressed up as a geisha, had come to scrub my back.

The next day, the three girls stayed home from Holy Canadian Martyrs. Two claimed to have pneumonia, the third was apparently suffering from exhaustion. Stella recited her Hail Mary with fervour. In the gym, I kept having flashbacks of the day before as I struggled to explain the rules of handball to the Grade 9 boys. They kept giving me strange looks. I eventually cut my lesson short, strung up the volleyball net like Lemon would have done, and went to sit in the corner while the students played their game. I was worn out, Michel. That week, whenever I fell asleep at night, I'd dream that you and I were Arctic foxes, curled up and fast asleep in a den together in Ungava, far from Toronto. In the same dream, Claudia, a resplendent Ice Queen, found us, tamed us, and took us home as pets. Invariably, the dream turned into a nightmare when a furious Mrs. Thanatopoulos arrived on a sled pulled by a breathless Stella, her eyes rolled back in her head. She would attack Claudia and catch us in a net. That was when I would wake up screaming. I would shout out for Suzuki, just like before, when we were sick and had a fever.

The girls came back to school. They were more distant, as though ashamed of their behaviour at the pool. Candice came to apologize to me, then Melikah brought me an old LP of German songs. "It's been lying around our place for years. Perhaps you'll put it to good use." It was an old Mireille Mathieu record. She sang *Acropolis Adieu* and *Santa Maria de la Mer*. It was funny hearing German versions of songs we know by heart in French. Do you remember Suzuki would play records when we were little? It's almost as strange as hearing *Tosca* in German. I had to use Jodi's old record player in the library to listen to it. Stella caught me red-handed, nostalgic as can be.

"What is that?"

"Mireille Mathieu."

I had to tell her all about the Avignon sparrow, that Mireille Mathieu was a huge hit in France and even in Germany, where she sang in German. Because, you know, if it's not on American TV, then young people in Ontario have never heard of it.

"She needs to work on her accent," Stella said as she listened to her pronounce *was ist geschehen*.

Stella must have taken pronunciation classes for her singing. Mireille Mathieu brought a smile to her lips. I can't quite put my finger on it, but there was some sort of bond between Stella Thanatopoulos and Mireille Mathieu, a line leading straight from one to the other, but I couldn't tell you how or why.

"I think the Germans liked her accent," I reminded my little diva.

In French, the song begins with "*Ce soir le vent vient de la mer.*" Tonight, the wind comes in from the sea. In German, the opening line is "*Es war September in Athen...*" September in Athens.

Stella was back in training from January to September. Her mother greeted me as though nothing had happened the previous Sunday. This time there was no dessert, no threats. Just aerobics, weights, and a strict training regimen with Stella three times a week. Her mom had signed us up to the local fitness club, a sort of high-tech torture chamber for Toronto's well-to-do.

Some woman or other would try to pick me up every time I set foot in the place. Surprisingly enough, Stella threw herself into her training. She told me, between two stints on the stationary bike, that her mom had decided she'd sing *Vissi d'arte* from *Tosca* for her Juilliard audition that September. I was surprised by her choice. That's not the type of thing people would usually choose. I'm no expert, but you need to be a first-rate singer to tackle such a difficult piece, if you ask me.

"Maria Callas sang it, Mr. Lamontagne," Stella explained.

"But don't you want to go with something a little simpler? You can't afford to be average at a Juilliard audition."

"No, Mom wants me to knock their socks off. And I think she's right. I need to work really hard! Did you know that *Tosca* was the last opera Callas ever sang? It was in 1965, at Covent Garden in London. She'd pulled out, but the Queen of England was coming to see her sing, and the opera director begged Callas to change her mind. Which she did.

"That's the thing. Callas must have sung plenty of other operas before *Tosca*. She knew what she was doing by then. I'm sure she didn't start out singing *Tosca*."

"But you should know, Mr. Lamontagne. Mom gave you her biography, after all!"

I almost fell over. Just how much did Stella know about her mother's visit to my apartment? I pointed to the clock on the wall and motioned to the bike. It was time to get to it, *vivace allegro*.

Stella had lost a little over fifteen kilos by June. My three princesses at Holy Canadian Martyrs couldn't believe it. But I took no pride in her transformation. Maybe Stella was overdoing things, I tried to tell them.

"She'll only put it all back on when she lets herself go."

"But word is she's working out with you," Melikah said.

So they knew. Later I found out that everyone knew. I don't think Mrs. Thanatopoulos would ever have come clean about the terms of our agreement, but people must have guessed I wasn't doing it out of the goodness of my heart. And yet little Stella was a docile student, hard-working and obedient. But it was clear to see that she was behind none of it: not the music, not the working out. If you asked her to sing, then she sang, just like she would take to the gymnastics mat if you told her to. She toed the line. In Mrs. Thanatopoulos's eyes, Stella was still too fat. She wanted me to spend the summer having her run around the Toronto Islands. I must admit I'd started to enjoy Stella's company. When she wasn't banging on about the gospel or the saints, she could be very funny. She was incredibly cultured for her age. And since you had to take a ferry out to the islands, Mrs. Thanatopoulos left us alone. She suffered from sea sickness, which I thought was strange for a Greek. "Mom is always ill on the boat." I was hardly chomping at the bit at the prospect of finding myself all alone with Stella on the Toronto Islands. If she was even the slightest bit like her mother, God knows what she'd make up to destroy me. I much preferred our workouts at the fitness centre, with the city's divorcees looking on attentively, watching my every move. Any one of them could have testified that my behaviour was entirely beyond reproach. How do I know all those women were divorced? What do you think they were doing at the gym, Michel?

In the summer of 1998—last year, in other words—Mrs. Thanatopoulos would pick me up in the morning in her BMW and drop me and Stella off near Harbourfront. Then she would watch us get on the ferry and wait two hours until we came back. The Toronto Islands are beautiful in a calm but fragile way. Since they're not linked by road to the mainland, only a few hippies live there, in tiny wooden homes that form a charming little village at the eastern tip of the long island. They have a wonderful view of downtown Toronto; in fact, this is the view that's on every postcard of Ontario's capital. Trails run along the island from east to west and that's where I brought Stella jogging. She was no longer fat, not even plump. To be honest, she was already losing too much weight, but that was nothing compared to the pale skeleton she was to become a few months later. Often we wouldn't meet a soul on our morning jogs. Visitors go over mostly on weekends or late in the afternoon. I kept our distance from Hanlan's Point to the west, right beside the airport, where nudists (mainly homosexuals) roamed in all their glory. Stella pretended not to know what went on over on that side, but every Torontonian knows the place.

That July, we'd take the ferry back after training. Stella always stood up front and tried to spot her mother on the wharf. As soon as she found her, she'd take an enormous white handkerchief out of her duffel bag and wave it in the air until her mom saw her and waved back. Stella's love for her mother was boundless, an antiquated respect that would have been admirable if it hadn't been clear to everyone that it would end up killing her. One day in August when we were almost back at the wharf, Stella took out her white handkerchief and told me to wave it to let her mother know we were coming.

I thought her little game was amusing—touching, even—the first few times, but I quickly found it silly and ridiculous, especially once the other passengers began to give us strange looks. What choice did I have, though? The mother still had a hold on me through her daughter.

"Stella, why do you wave your hankie around every time we take the ferry back?"

"Do you know the legend of Theseus? He left Athens to vanquish the Minotaur."

"Refresh my memory."

"After slaying the Minotaur on Crete, Theseus sailed back to Athens. His father Aegeus was waiting for him at the wharf. It had been agreed that if Theseus had been killed by the Minotaur the ship would hoist black sails. And if Theseus returned alive, the sails would be white."

"So it's to show your mom that you're back safe and sound? That you survived the Minotaur?"

"A little, yeah."

The last Friday in August, right before the kids went back to school, Mrs. Thanatopoulos dropped us off at the ferry again. Just before she left us, she looked her daughter hard in the eye with a seriousness I hadn't seen since she came to see me that January. We hadn't been running for more than half an hour when Stella veered off toward a deserted sandy beach. There were a few trees at the end of it and they cast a pleasant shadow.

"Stopping already, Stella? Are you tired?"

"I need to sit for a while. I want to look at the lake."

Lake Ontario is beautiful to look at, it's true. Almost as big as a sea in the middle of the continent. Stella looked serious.

"Mr. Lamontagne, my audition in New York is in less than a month. I'm very nervous."

"I'm sure you'll knock 'em dead, Stella. You have a wonderful voice."

"My singing teacher Mrs. Pantalone isn't so sure. She thinks you need to believe what you sing and sing what you believe."

"What does she mean by that?"

"She doesn't really agree with Mom's choice of song, *Vissi d'arte*. Technically, I'm perfect, she says, but the performance isn't there yet."

"Singing teachers are never happy, Stella."

"It's so nice of you to say so. Mrs. Pantalone says you need to have experienced what you're singing if you want others to believe it."

"I'm sure she's partly right, but it's about acting too. Opera singers haven't been through everything their characters have and we still believe them. You don't have to be a mom who was abandoned by a U.S. Navy lieutenant to play Cio-Cio San in *Madame Butterfly*; you just need to feel what Cio-Cio San feels."

"That's what I tried telling Mrs. Pantalone, too, but she wouldn't listen. She says I'm too young to sing *Vissi d'arte*. She even got into an argument with Mom in June. 'How do you expect the poor girl to feel what Floria Tosca feels?' she said. '*I lived for art, I lived for love…* She's only seventeen! Honestly, I really think we should work on something else, a piece better suited to her age.' Do you think she's right?"

"You're asking the wrong person, Stella. I don't know *Tosca* well enough to answer. What exactly did poor Tosca go through?"

"So, Tosca is an opera singer in real life. In the opera, she's a bit of a diva, *una donna gelosa*. A jealous woman. So we have a singer playing a singer who's being a diva. It's not easy to pull off. When she sings *Vissi d'arte*, it's halfway through Act II."

"And what happens in Act II?"

"It's set in Scarpia's office. He's a monster!"

"And what did this Scarpia guy do?"

I'd touched a nerve, by the look of things. She got up from the piece of driftwood she'd been sitting on and starting explaining *Tosca*'s second act.

"*Scarpia? Bigotto satiro!* He's the police chief in Rome. He has the cavalier Mario Cavaradossi arrested by his henchmen. He has Cavaradossi brought up to his antechamber in Palazzo Farnese and orders his gorillas to torture him, just like Christ Our Lord! He also has Tosca brought up and she can be heard singing at some party or other in another of the palazzo's rooms. Scarpia suspects she knows where Cavaradossi is hiding Angelotti, a fugitive. But Tosca is a real artist, an actress! She stays out of politics and knows when to keep quiet. Then, on dastardly Scarpia's orders the door is opened to the room where Cavaradossi is being tortured. Tosca is horrified to hear his cries of pain, a ring of iron around his temples. Poor Cavaradossi! Tosca begs Scarpia to stop. But the monster only orders his men to torture him even harder, carrying a bloodied Cavaradossi in to Tosca so that she can see what he's done to him with her own eyes, so that she might dip her innocent fingers in his gaping wounds! It's really awful, Mr. Lamontagne! And then the torture starts up again, worse than ever. Scarpia, that awful Scarpia, is about to take advantage of Tosca, because that's what he wants: he wants

Cavaradossi's lover for himself, he even says so! Scarpia wants to have her once, then cast her aside like the stone in a piece of a fruit he's just eaten. But brave Tosca puts up a fight, suggesting she knows more than she's letting on to Scarpia. Tosca offers him money. "Your price?" she asks, wanting to buy her freedom. But that only goes to show how little she knows the ignoble Scarpia. Tosca manages to free herself from her tyrant's clutches. She kneels and begins to sing. *Vissi d'arte*."

Stella struck the poses of the characters as she told the story, driving home every word, and gazing heavenward as though imploring God to spare poor Tosca. I was surprised she knew the word "ignoble." Her mom was right: she must really use her dictionary as a pillow. The whole thing was so over the top, I had to stop myself laughing. I swear to you, dear brother, then she knelt down on the deserted Toronto Island beach and sang the aria from start to finish. *I lived for art, I lived for love, I never harmed a living soul*, she sang. *Why, why, Lord, why do you reward me thus? I donated jewels to the Madonna's mantle...* all the way until *humiliated, defeated, I await your help*. It's a kind of prayer, really, isn't it? She was a convincing singer; it was a moving performance. But aside from that, all I wanted to do was laugh. Now I could see why Stella couldn't play a diva. It was because she *is* a diva. You can't pretend to be something you already are. If her performance didn't ring true, it's because she persisted in playing a role when her regular self would have been enough. I thought back to little Stella barely a few years earlier, the Pet Shop Girl at the Eaton Centre, cowering behind a pile of sacks of cat litter.

"You need to be more natural than that, Stella. You're already Tosca. No point laying it on any thicker."

"You think so?"

"Absolutely."

"But do you also think you need to sing what you believe and believe what you sing?"

"That seems important, yes."

"So how will I ever manage to sing, *I lived for art, I lived for love?*"

"You're an artist, Stella. You've studied music since you were a little girl and you know how to pray too."

"But what about love? How can I sing about love if I've never been loved?"

"There are all kinds of love. There's love thy neighbour, a mother's love for her daughter, love for the work you do... You know love. Do you believe that God loves you?"

"Of course! What are you insinuating?"

"Nothing. Just that you've known love, God's love for you."

"No! You don't understand! That's not the love I'm talking about. Tosca is a woman of flesh and blood."

"Stella, I think you're overestimating the value of experience. I've known the kind of love you're talking about, but that doesn't mean I can sing *Tosca*. If you really don't feel ready, then you need to choose another piece. Why not Schubert's *Ständchen*?"

Stella glared at me with the same look her mother had shot me when I'd tried to stand up to her that day in January. She pursed her lips in exactly the same way. The only thing missing was a dish of galaktoboureko to complete the picture.

"*Ständchen* for a Juilliard audition! You haven't been listening to a word I said. You can't be serious! Besides, it's too late. It's too late to choose something else! Mom wants me to sing *Vissi d'arte*! And that's what I'm going to sing in New York! Do you hear me? I'll be singing *Vissi d'arte*!"

Stella was beside herself. She stomped her foot on the sand, screamed, spat, shouted herself hoarse. Thank God it was just the two of us. Not a soul in sight. Only the gulls echoed the girl's shrieks. Now she was standing knee-deep in Lake Ontario and was holding her face in her hands. I went over to try to calm her. She was sobbing.

"Stella, I'm sure you'll do a fine job with *Vissi d'arte*. If you sing it like you just sung it to me, they'll have to let you in."

"Mr. Lamontagne, love me."

"Excuse me?"

"I want you to love me. Right here, right now."

"What the hell, Stella? I mean, I love you," I lied, "but not like that."

"Stop making fun. I know you don't love me. You might pity me, but you don't love me. You think I'm an idiot, just like everyone else. All I'm asking is for you to do with me what you did with Mrs. Poisson and the librarian and hundreds of other women. Everyone knows you're a real Casanova. Even Mrs. Delvecchio. Even Zira."

"Stella, you're being very unpleasant. I'm not going to touch you. Now let's head back."

"Love me!" she cried, flinging herself into my arms.

She tried to rip my shorts off with her tiny hands. I slapped her.

"Stella, get a hold of yourself!"

She staggered back.

"Listen, Mr. Lamontagne, if you don't take me right now behind these bushes, I'll tell everyone you raped me. I'll start with the school psychologist; he'll have to turn you in. When Mom finds out how disrespectful you were to me, you'll be looking for a good lawyer, believe me. I'm seventeen, in case you've forgotten!"

"Stella, you don't know what you're saying!"

Her arms hung loosely by her side. I was screwed. There was no way out. The ferry would be there in half an hour. If I walked off with my head held high and didn't so much as touch her, she'd tell her mother I'd raped her. She was crazy enough to see her lie through to the end. And her intentions were honest, I realized. She wasn't asking much. All she wanted was to feel a man's body against hers, to feel possessed by someone so that she could sing *Vissi d'arte*. I can't say I found her especially attractive; she was pretty, that's all. Mind you, if that ever stopped me, there would be precious few books on my shelf, no more than five or six. Not between one and two thousand. By the time I turned seventeen, I was already plenty experienced. Weren't all the girls we were friends with in Montreal sleeping with someone when they were seventeen? There was really nothing wrong with it, I said to myself. With her tendency to overdo things, the girl was really all set for a career as an opera singer. Her emotions were completely over the top; it was all or nothing, a nonnegotiable quantity of absolutes that were the polar opposite of restraint and discretion. A monumental failing, a crack so huge it would be pointless trying to paper over it; better to highlight it and build her whole personality around it. Stella was a bad actress, but it was in this duplicity that she was at her most genuine... and a little gauche. You know, Michel, there's nothing more awkward or adorable than youth.

"If you love me, I won't breathe a word. If not... I don't know what I might do."

On the ferry back, Stella had a look on her face I'd never seen before. A peaceful smile, the Mona Lisa's smile. The sun was shining and it was one of those hot and humid summer days you get so often in Toronto. Children raced around the deck. Little blonde girls who reminded me of Claudia. I tried to chat with Stella. I'd forgotten that wasn't her thing. Nothing about her was ordinary or mediocre. Everything had to be taken to the extreme.

"And what happens to Cavaradossi?"

"Cavaradossi? He dies valiantly."

She really had quite the vocabulary. Her English teacher would be proud of her, I thought. The ferry must have been five hundred yards from the dock when, calmly and regally, Stella stood up to move to the bow of the ship, as she always did. Without once looking away from her mother's silhouette on the wharf, she opened her duffel bag and took out a huge black handkerchief, much bigger than the white one she usually had. She raised her arm and, in a precise, feminine movement, waved it over her head like the pennant of a victorious army. Standing behind her, I suddenly felt the full heat of the Toronto summer at my back. She continued to wave the black handkerchief until we docked. Then she tucked it away in her bag.

Mrs. Thanatopoulos walked up to me on the wharf. I kid you not, dear brother: she actually sniffed me. It was discreet, but a sniff all the same. I was speechless. She seemed satisfied. She kissed her daughter on the cheek, sniffing her too, like a sow looking for a truffle. Mother and daughter were silent. They drove me back to Spadina Avenue. I was exhausted. Before she let me out of the car—Mrs. Thanatopoulos controlled the locks on her BMW—she told me that she would no longer be needing my services as a trainer. That she was ever so thankful. That she would be eternally grateful. I stepped out of the car without saying a word. When I got home, I ran myself a bath and poured a full cup of bleach into it.

Then I went out. Since I was heading back to Holy Canadian Martyrs for the last time as a teacher, I decided to do it in style. I walked to Richmond Street West in the Entertainment District. There's a nightclub there, on the corner of Widmer Street, where the women don't take much persuading. In the cruel light of dawn, I staggered back home with *Fall on Your Knees*.

I slept until the Tuesday after Labour Day. I really enjoyed *Fall on Your Knees*. It's a complicated novel that takes place over several decades. Part of the story is about a girl from Cape Breton who leaves to study classical music in New York City just after the First World War. She doesn't stay very long. She comes back home pregnant and dies after her mother gives her a do-it-yourself Caesarean. What a story, eh?

Night has fallen over Berlin. Time for me to head back to Lichtenberg before the last S-Bahn.

Gabriel

My dearest brother,

I'm sitting in the same train as yesterday. Don't panic. I haven't taken to spending my nights at a German railway station. This time I'm going counterclockwise around the Ring. Do you realize, Michel, that I spent the last winter of the century on a German train? A whole winter on a train! Only three days to go before Claudia comes back, and I get the impression I'm in for the spring of my life. Every day I congratulate myself for waiting before I went to see her. Only yesterday, I noticed that I could understand most of the conversations going on around me in the S-Bahn. You just have to keep your ears open. Berliners are talking about the beautiful weather, vacations they're going to take, and little everyday things. I haven't heard from Magda since that afternoon at the *Schrebergärten*. She must feel ashamed about the whole business.

At the thought of Claudia coming back to Berlin, I feel, for the second time in six months, a vast, calm sense of relief washing over my soul. I'm taking advantage of it to write you this long letter, knowing, as I do, that my life begins this Saturday. No more long journeys on the S-Bahn. I've also been thinking about earning a living in Germany. I'll have run out of savings a year from now. There's not much work to be had in Berlin, and my teaching diplomas wouldn't be recognized anyway. *Umso besser!* That's fine with me! I've had enough of being a high school teacher. I'll do anything if it means I can stay here. Two Germans who've been watching me work out for months asked if I'm a private trainer. I think there's potential there. Especially since Germans take great pride in their physique and appearance in general. They seem completely unfazed by nudity, more so than any other people in Europe, I think. Apparently, on Rügen Island, back in the GDR, people would walk around naked. The fall of the wall had a curious effect on them, as if they'd suddenly been stripped of their privacy and were being watched for the very first time. Reunification signalled the end of this earthly paradise in the Naked Republic. And everyone was naked. We're not talking about a handful of rich girls with curves in all the right places who decide to take their tops off one day in Saint-Tropez. I mean whole families at socialist campgrounds playing badminton in the buff, just like God made them. Then capitalism brought the curtain down on their honeymoon with nature. And now the way Germans think of their bodies, as well as training and sport in general, could mean a full-time job for me. Like the Americans, the Germans like to be well built; they've no time for the dainty figures of French actors. God made them strong, and they intend to show it. But all the same it's a weakness wanting to show off how strong you are all the time, and you know the effect weakness has on me.

So you find me at peace today. Claudia in three days. The last time I felt such relief was last fall. It was two weeks after the Toronto Island episode, when I decided to leave for Berlin on January 1, 1999. I would have a year to prepare to ring in the new German millennium. That's when I started to sleep better. I didn't tell a soul: I'd seen how the school board treated teachers who left during the school year. Mrs. Delvecchio asked me into her office.

She was in great form because, she explained, she was buying a brand new motorbike to replace her old Harley Davidson. We talked about Suzuki motorbikes and she was surprised to see I knew so much about them. I strongly recommended she get a VZ 800. Five-speed transmission, two cylinders, burgundy and white. Suzuki loved hers. Do you remember when she'd drive us around the Eastern Townships with one of us sitting on the back? It was usually me, I know. You flat out refused to put your arms around her waist. You don't know what you missed, poor Michel.

Mrs. Delvecchio told me she spent every Christmas vacation in Italy, at her cousins' place in Pescara.

"I have a bike over there too. Another Suzuki! Well, it's actually my cousin's, but he lets me drive it around over the holidays."

Then she announced, proud as could be, there would be a special concert that October, just after the monthly mass.

"Little Stella has her Juilliard audition at the end of October. She's very nervous and her mother thinks she should sing her program at least once in front of a real audience before facing the jury. Since she's a former student, I said she could sing here. Right after mass, accompanied by a pianist. I can't wait to hear her. Such a talented child! And have you seen how she's looking these days? It's a little too much, if you ask me. Women should still have a curve or two: it makes them all the prettier. But her mother has been working her so hard. You'll see for yourself—the weight has just melted off her!"

A concert with Stella after October mass? That was all I needed. I didn't dare mention my imminent departure to Mrs. Delvecchio. I already had my

Lufthansa ticket to Berlin booked, but I knew better than to tell her I'd be taking off halfway through the school year.

"One other thing, Mr. Lamontagne. We have a group of girls in Grade 10 who are quite into sport. I think they should form a softball team. What do you think? Girls tend to get the rough end of our sports program, if you ask me. Can I count on your support?"

I didn't want to let her down. I promised I'd see to it, then went back to my classes.

On the first Friday of October, the monthly mass was cut short by fifteen minutes to make time for Stella's recital. The four hundred students gathered in the school's auditorium. They made a hell of a racket and we had a hard time getting them to quiet down. We'd told them there would be a recital from a former student who wanted to pay tribute to her alma mater before launching her international career. It was hard to say it with a straight face considering everything Stella had been through at Holy Canadian Martyrs, the fun they'd poked at her braids, her weight, her piety. It was like a circus in there. The boys threw paper balls and shouted at each other, while the girls gave strangled little cries and pretended to be divas. Mrs. Delvecchio was incredibly nervous, perhaps even more so than Stella herself. Stella had refused to show herself before the curtain went up, leaving her pianist to come shake the teachers' hands. It was the little bald man I'd seen leaving her house the very first time I'd stepped into Mrs. Thanatopoulos's lair. A handful of parents who didn't have to be at work had made it in that morning.

My three princesses had skipped class to hear the recital. Having known her since elementary school, they were eager to see the new Stella. Melikah, Candice, and Kayla had come into full bloom at the University of Toronto; they were in their element. They now looked like three movie stars, like Charlie's Angels or something. Kayla and Candice were in the phys ed program and Melikah was studying French literature. It's nice to see you can make a difference in young people's lives. Kayla and Candice were planning to finish their studies and open a mega gym in North Toronto.

"We'll be fucking rich, Mr. Lamontagne!"

Melikah, the most sensitive of the three, asked about Claudia. "What about your *Fräulein*?" She wanted to know all about courtly love and confessed to taking a medieval literature class to satisfy the curiosity Claudia had aroused in her. Her professor at the University of Toronto was gay, she complained. "I mean, not that I've anything against that, but what does a fag know about courtly love? It's not hard to respect your fine lady when you've only got eyes for the knight's ass!" The three of them sat down beside me.

Mrs. Delvecchio walked up to the microphone on stage. She could be quite menacing when she put her mind to it. A fine actress, she wore the expression of a Mother Superior with a nasty case of hemorrhoids.

"Be quiet! Now!"

In the eyes of the students, Mrs. Delvecchio was a no-nonsense matron. They were frightened of her. Because she rode a motorbike to school, weather permitting, and because she had no husband or children, as far as they knew. She didn't fit the traditional model, so the students at Holy Canadian Martyrs didn't know what to make of her. At any rate, her carefully tended virago image came in very handy at moments like these. The students fell silent as one.

Mrs. Thanatopoulos appeared on stage. She wore a black evening gown with a single strand of pearls. A nostalgic short-sighted audience member might easily have mistaken her for Nana Mouskouri.

"My dearrr students. Thank you for all being here this morning to listen to my dear Stella's rrrecital. As you know, Stella will soon be leaving us for the United States to study at one of the finest music schools. What you are about to hear is the rrresult of years of hard work. Your ears may not be used to such divine music, but I have no doubt, my little darrrlings, that you will appreciate it for all its worth. Remember the name! Now, without further ado, please welcome the new prima donna, Stella Thanatopoulos! God bless you, my little darrrlings!"

Candice stuck a finger down her throat and pretended to gag. "She's just as annoying as her daughter," she whispered. I had to stop myself from correcting her. No, Mrs. Thanatopoulos wasn't as big a pain in the ass as her daughter: she was ten times worse. But the show was about to begin. Mrs. Thanatopoulos had spared no expense. She'd rented a grand piano, a Yamaha, delivered just for the recital. The little bald man came out first. There were a few titters; he waddled like a duck. He sat down on his stool, carefully arranged his sheet music, then practically went into hibernation while we waited for Stella to make her entrance.

How shall I put this? How can I describe the *thing* we saw trotting onto the stage? "Oh my God!" my three princesses chorused. The students applauded. They weren't so ill-mannered, after all. But the Stella on stage before us was a far cry from the Stella we'd known. I hadn't seen her since that last day on Toronto Island, when she'd already weighed ten kilos less than she should have. She'd lost a lot more weight since then. I wondered how it was even possible. Already sylphlike in late August, now in October, she looked like an Auschwitz survivor. Or someone in one of those awful anorexia awareness campaign photos they show to young girls. Skin and bones, that's what she was. Gone were the braids. She'd had her hair done for the occasion, a hairdo fit for a diva. She wore a diamond necklace and matching earrings. A burgundy velvet gown. Shoes, likely Balmain. Her radiant smile contrasted with the rest of her. You wouldn't have thought someone so thin could still manage to smile. She waited for the applause to die down. I glanced over at Mrs. Delvecchio. She had her hand clapped over her mouth, as though a plane had just crashed right before her eyes. But what we were watching was much worse than a plane crash. A plane crash is an accident; an occurrence no one wants. Dozens of people are hard at work every day in Berlin alone just to keep planes from crashing. What we had before us was no accident. It was something we had all contributed to, none more than me. I kept thinking Stella was going to topple over and fracture her hip at any moment. All that remained of her chubby little face was a gaunt, made-up surface with hollowed-out cheeks. Once round, plump breasts now hung limply like old oranges in a plastic bag. An emaciated mare. Fit for slaughter. Mrs. Thanatopoulos clearly didn't do things by halves.

Stella sang without a microphone, as every self-respecting opera singer should. The recital lasted a half hour, during which it was as though her audience was under the influence of a powerful narcotic. Stella's voice was sublime. It reminded me a little of Teresa Stratas's. You had me listen to her once. The same purity, the same metallic sensibility, clear as crystal, as rich and thunderous as Lake Ontario, as fragile as dew in summer. She started off by seriously embarrassing me.

"First, an old French song for my favourite teacher," she said, looking straight at me. "I'm going to sing it for him in German. He'll know why. *Danke schön*, Monsieur Lamontagne…"

I thought I was going to die when I heard the opening chords of *Acropolis Adieu*. "*Es war September in Athen, der letzte Abend war so leer. Ich fragte ihn, wann kommst du wieder? Da sagte er, vielleicht nie mehr.*"

"September in Athens. The last night was so empty. I asked him: 'When will you return?' 'Perhaps never,' he replied." Then the chorus. "*Akropolis Adieu, Ich muß gehen…*" which says more or less the same as the French version we both know. She'd chosen to say goodbye to me in this strange way, knowing full well that no one other than me would understand the message contained in the song that seemed to go on for three hours. Then Stella returned to her opera pieces. We were treated to Mozart's *Voi che sapete*—honestly, she sings it better than Anamaria—and the inevitable *Habanera*. Once again, she stared down at me while she played an improbably thin Carmen. Never more so than when she sang, "Take gua-ard yourself!" She had no doubt chosen to sing *Habanera* to show off her impressive range.

I'd be lying if I said I wasn't moved by the second-to-last song. I knew the tune. I think Anamaria might have sung it a long, long time ago, back when your singing teacher in Villeray organized those recitals. We must have been eighteen. It's an airy melody, mysterious and a little exotic. It was about a woman called Chloris, I think. I forget the words. Something about "the grace of her eyes" at the end. Stella really touched me with that one. Somewhere very close to the heart. I couldn't stop thinking about Claudia. You have to admit that Chloris sounds a lot like Claudia. But I'm getting off track, dear brother.

Once her strange medley was over, she disappeared backstage to great applause. She was obviously angling for an encore. The students stamped their feet like the Germans do in concert halls, threatening to bring the roof down. Then she was back, looking radiant. The applause died down. Someone whistled. And then, pulling herself together the way a German woman would, she launched into *Vissi d'arte*. What can I say? How can I describe the magic she breathed into that prayer? When she fell to her knees imploring God, we were all sure her kneecaps would shatter as she hit the floor. The piano accompaniment was barely there. She alone bore all the misery and suffering of the aria, as though the words had been written for her. The students were very impressed to see her kneeling there, eyes raised heavenward. They were Catholic, after all. It's the kind of image that always troubles us deeply. When she sang, "*Per che, Per che Signore*," I think Melikah and Candice both shed a tear. She has this vibrato—no, more of a wave in her voice—that has the effect of squeezing her audience's heart valves. After the last notes, the auditorium was silent for a long while. I heard Mrs. Delvecchio sniff, then tissues being passed back and forth. It took a while for the applause to build. I think the students were still in shock at what they'd just heard. I'm sure some of them will remember that performance for the rest of their lives. Stella was given a tumultuous ten-minute standing ovation, complete with feet-stamping, whistles of admiration, sobs, and "*Bravas!*" She never once stepped out of character, not even during the applause, which left us feeling as though we were applauding a true martyr. The only one ever to have walked through our school's doors.

It was impossible to speak to Stella that day, or to her mother. Apparently she had to be whisked back home as quickly as possible to get ready for the trip to New York. I wouldn't have known what to say anyway. She no longer belonged to the mortals of this world. Melikah was in tears after the recital, both charmed by the music and aghast at how sickly her former classmate looked. "You think it might be cancer, Mr. Lamontagne?" I didn't dare tell Melikah that Stella wasn't ill. Her problems ran deeper than that: unlike me, she hadn't managed to ward off that long, painful, and fatal scourge known as "Mom."

The fall semester ended. I kept on writing letters to Claudia. Her replies were guarded; she always kept her emotions in check. Her reserve only made me want her even more. That December, two days before the end of term, I told Mrs. Delvecchio I wouldn't be coming back.

"Oh, I suspected as much! And guess what? Lemon won his trial! We found out yesterday. The court ruled that the school board had no right to fire him just because he's gay. It looks as though the archbishop of Toronto will be protesting. Good Lord! I'm glad. The whole thing was a little too much. As it happens, I was just about to tell you we'd have to find you another school. We were thinking Brebeuf or St. Joseph's—a girls' school! You're so good with the girls! Before you came, none of them did any sports at all. Now they even have teams of their own! It really is a shame you're leaving, but you're still young, you'll be wanting to see the world. I hope Lemon will be equal to the task."

"Did you get your motorbike?"

"Oh yes! In November. You were right, Gabriel. Nothing beats a Suzuki! Elvira loves it!"

I wasn't tactless enough to ask who this mysterious Elvira might be. It was the first time she'd mentioned her. It must have slipped out. She looked away and cleared her throat as soon as she said it. She showed me photos of the bike and wished me good luck in Germany. She was a good egg, Delvecchio. I hope all the Italians you meet are like her.

Before I left Toronto, I needed somewhere to leave my books. I donated them to the school library.

"I can't have *The Diary of Anaïs Nin* on my shelves!" Jodi laughed. "The parents will lynch me!"

I gave the racier novels to my princesses. They were overjoyed, Melikah especially. She was working on a manuscript, she told me, and had started going out with boys.

"I steal a book from every one of them!"

"What do you do when they don't have any?"

"I don't screw 'em!"

You see, Michel? Even a phys ed teacher can make a difference.

My train is pulling into the station. I've gone around Berlin three times counterclockwise. I won't have time to write for a while now. My letters will be less frequent. I'm planning on mailing them all to you just before our birthday in June. Come Saturday, I'll be Claudia's knight in shining armour.

Your brother, on the cusp of happiness.

Gabriel

～っ

Ahrensfelde – Wannsee
May 21, 1999

Before I go, I really must tell you about last night. You're going to fall off your chair. Are you sitting down? I got back to Lichtenberg around five. Then I decided to go for a swim at the sports centre across the boulevard where the tram runs. Magda had told me about the place; she's been going there for years. I still hadn't been. The pool wasn't great, but at least it was close. After my swim, I decided to try out the sauna. I know what you're thinking, but I wasn't looking to hook up! First off, the sauna is very busy, but not with the type of bodies you'd like to see there. Before I went in, a woman who worked there made me take off my towel.

"It's more hygienic," she said.

She had a point. Anyway, it wasn't as if I knew anyone. It hadn't occurred to me that I might run into one of the ladies from my building. Like all good Germans, they love to slowly bake themselves in wooden boxes. And I hadn't realized that some nights the saunas are mixed. Like last night. Gasp! Fortunately, there were only three people inside: an old man who grunted occasionally as he stared at the floor and sweated buckets, a huge man about Suzuki's age, and an old woman sitting on the upper bench. I didn't look up, wanting to preserve her modesty.

The big man nodded at me and went on sweating in silence. Then he said something to the old guy that I didn't understand. Two minutes later, they left. I think the old man might have been the fat guy's father. Finding myself alone with the old woman, I risked a glance in her direction. My heart skipped a beat. It was Magda! Stark naked! She appeared to have dozed off; her eyes were closed. I don't know how she could sleep in such heat. I read somewhere that old people are less sensitive to heat. The air was scorching my lungs. Since I was all alone with her, I couldn't help watching her, especially since she had her eyes closed. She really was sleeping. I've never felt more uncomfortable. My only thought was to get out of there without making a noise so we wouldn't both die of shame and embarrassment. How could I ever look her in the eye again?

She stirred suddenly. Her knee moved. I could see between her legs in the half-light. How could I not look? Well, wait till you hear this: she has a birthmark exactly like yours between her legs, a little bass clef. Only with an old scar running through it. God knows how she managed to hurt herself there. Horseback riding? A car accident? A circus routine gone wrong? Who knows! The scar ran right the way through the bass clef. The doctor had done a good job stitching it back up. I wanted to wake her up and say, "Magda, it's just that, uhh, you have a birthmark just like my brother's, right there, just under your vagina," but a little voice inside my head told me not to move. You can't very well tell a seventy-year-old woman you've been peering between her legs. What would she have thought? And anyway I didn't know how to say "birthmark" in German. Shaken and on the verge of collapsing from the heat, I had to get out of there. It was probably a mirage. I got dressed again after a freezing-cold shower. On my way out of the locker room, I saw her slowly emerge from the sauna and smile at the attendant. I waited a long time to be sure she'd left the sports centre. There was no way I was saying a word to her.

I can't believe they can just walk around stark naked like that. In front of perfect strangers, too. Can you imagine that happening in Montreal? Anyway, I couldn't get the scarred birthmark out of my head, not even after I fell asleep. It's on the inside of your left leg, isn't it? Sorry to bring it up, but it really was exactly the same as yours. I almost wanted to take a photo!

My God! Can you imagine the commotion it would have caused, the flash going off in the sauna like that?

Your traumatized brother,

Gabriel

P.S. Did you get the bass clef from Mom? Do you know?

~

Dear Michel,

I have to pull myself together.

Sich zusammenreißen.

Mich zusammenreißen, that's how you say it. But before I recover my self-control, there's going to be a long, noisy fall.

The firing squad used real bullets.

I died instantly.

And yet this morning, I woke up with all the happiness in the world in my heart. If I'd been you, I'd probably have sung something. Forgive me all the jibes. You know I don't mean half of it. Perhaps, like you, I'm just trying to create a stir. I'm about to lose my footing. Look out the window and you'll see me flying high above Castel Sant'Angelo and into the Tiber.

She was to be back from Egypt today. I had the date and the city she was flying out of (Cairo) but no flight number. My enthusiasm, or a sixth sense, sent me to Tegel Airport before noon. That's where flights from Egypt fly into, I think. Although that would mean flying from Egypt.

I'd circled the date on the calendar in my little Lichtenberg kitchen. The weather was beautiful, there were flowers everywhere. Berlin is pretty in the springtime. See? It *is* like Montreal: winter is so ugly that the first lilacs seem fabulously beautiful. Winter here is not the same, you'll say. And I'll reply that Berlin's winter is worse, precisely because they don't have our snow to brighten the gloom.

It was so painful. I went to the airport and sat down at Arrivals to wait for her. There were two flights from Cairo today: the first landed at 1:15 p.m., the second at 5 p.m. I parked myself outside the doors at Arrivals at a quarter past one. After waiting for an hour, I went back to sit in the café, telling myself it must be the five o'clock flight, that she'd be so pleased to see me she'd come back with me to Lichtenberg and spend the night, without even going home first. Worst case, we'd drive her sister back home and then go to my place. It's hard to be left in peace at Claudia's. She shares an apartment with her sister and two other girls in Kreuzberg. I was a bit fed up with "I'd like to get to know you better" and "Things went so fast in Toronto. Now we can start over in Berlin." That's all I've heard from her since I got here in January. She's always refused to see me, claiming that's how all serious relationships should start. In Toronto, we'd see each other every other Sunday. To go to her Lutheran church, you'll rightly point out, but at least she'd come for a walk in the park with me afterward.

At five o'clock, I took my courage in both hands and told myself this was it: she'd be on this plane. Then the passengers arrived one by one: men travelling alone, families, even a group of German grandmothers, their suitcases no doubt full of little terracotta sphinxes. But no Claudia. It was impossible, I thought to myself. She must have given me the wrong date. I stayed there a while longer, in front of the automatic doors.

I took the subway over to her apartment in Kreuzberg, thinking that maybe she'd flown home via London or Amsterdam instead and I'd been waiting at the wrong arrivals hall. I bought her flowers on the way out of the subway, which was strange because that's not something I ever do. I've always thought that flowers belong to another era but, all things considered, the relationship Claudia was proposing was also something from an earlier era. Outside the Anal Café, just opposite her place on Muskauer Straße, I sensed that this was a decisive moment, that I was going to carry her back to my apartment on my shoulders. I bounded up the stairs four at a time. I had that old song in my head, the one Suzuki would sing sometimes. *Will you love me all the time?* I've never heard anyone else sing it. She'd sing it to me when it was just the two of us. In fact, in the beginning—forgive me, dear brother—I thought that Suzuki must be in love with me. You should take a good listen to the lyrics. I know it's not opera, but it stays in your head. Once you've heard it, you won't forget it.

I bumped into Gudrun, Claudia's sister, in the stairwell. When she spotted me, she froze in her tracks, like a pillar of salt. Actually, I didn't recognize her right away. It wasn't until I'd bumped into her that I realized she had to be Claudia's sister: the same nose, same eyes. I spoke to her. She seemed puzzled. I told her who I was. She smiled when she heard my name, a smile I didn't like at all.

"Gabriel! So you're Gabriel!" she said. She started to rummage around in her bag as if to find something she wanted to show me. She thought better of it and, looking away, rushed down the stairs as if the devil himself were after her. I followed her out onto the sidewalk.

"When did you get back? I waited for you all day at Tegel. Weren't you supposed to come back today?" I asked, grabbing her arm. She tried to get away.

"Come back from where? What are you talking about? Let go of me!"

"You were in Egypt with Claudia. Is she back now too? Don't tell me she stayed!"

Gudrun gave me a terrified look.

"You learned German. Claudia mentioned a guy who didn't speak German very well. You're the Canadian, aren't you? Gabriel Lamontagne."

"Yes. What did she say about me? Where is she?"

"Not much. Just that… Listen, Gabriel. Did Claudia tell you we were in Egypt?"

"Is she up there?"

"Can I tell you something about my sister?"

"Tell me!"

"You can either go up and talk to her or not. It's up to you. Either way, the rest of your life will stay exactly the same. Your visit won't change a thing. Claudia has already given you everything she had to give. If I were you, I'd leave right now. But you can always go up if you need to be clear in your own mind. One last thing: I was in Egypt, not her. I was the one who sent you the postcard. I felt bad about it, but I did it for her. You don't know her. She would have made my life miserable if I hadn't. And, by the way: if you tell her you met me, I'll deny the whole thing. *Leb wohl*, Gabriel. Please, you can still save yourself. But she's my sister and I'm stuck with her until my dying day."

Gudrun was rather weird, I thought. A little unhinged, if you know what I mean. But I should have realized she was trying to tell me something important. She practically ran off, yanking her arm free from my grip. I went back inside and slowly walked up to the second floor. I rang the bell. You'll never guess who opened it. Wlad! Wlad from the German class in Toronto! He looked me up and down like he'd just seen a ghost. He spun around and shouted: "*Claudia, komm schnell! Der Gabriel ist da!*" When I saw Claudia, with not the slightest trace of a suntan, I began to piece it all together. Then the Pole started speaking to Claudia like I didn't understand German. Stuff like "What the hell is this gorilla doing here?"

Claudia had just emerged from the bedroom, still looking rumpled. Then she flew into a rage. "What are you doing here?" Questions, reproaches, and that idiot Wlad with his stupid smirk. I would have been able to hold back if he hadn't opened his big mouth. But instead of keeping quiet, or disappearing off into a corner somewhere to let me talk things over with Claudia, he got the brilliant idea of providing me with that bit of provocation I was waiting for to grab him by the throat. The poor idiot, a gangly string bean of a man, looked me straight in the eye, laughing as he said, "*Tja, du hast schöne Blümchen Gabriel! Sind die für deinen Bruder?*" In other words, "What lovely flowers. Are they for your brother?" But in a tone that implied so much more. I don't know what Claudia must have told him about you. Back in Toronto, she'd often ask me about incest and twin brothers. The way she tells it, all twins are in love with each other.

I didn't hesitate a second. I shut the door behind me so that no one would see us from the landing. It all happened so quickly. I put the little moron in a hold, like what I'd do to you when we were messing about in the yard, only this time I wasn't laughing. I grabbed him by the neck the way you'd grab a nervous bull calf, forcing him down as I leaned into his neck with my knee. As soon as his head was caught between my thighs—by the way, I'm up to 350 lb. squats now, I could have snapped his spinal cord in two just by contracting my abs—he realized he was done for. I grabbed both his flailing hands, then, as Claudia looked on, I gave him the hiding of his life. He tried to kick his way free, but the more he kicked, the tighter I held his head. He got the message. I must have hit him twenty or twenty-five times before releasing the stranglehold. His ass was red; he couldn't even stand up. I helped him up, of course, grabbing him by the scruff of the neck and pinning him to the wall hard enough for him not to forget in a hurry. "*Nein, mein lieber Wlad,*" I replied, "*sie sind für dich!*" The flowers were for him. As I said it, I thought to myself how proud you would have been of my repartee. That took the wind out of his sails, of course. Claudia was standing there in the corner, head in hands, begging me to leave, *geh, geh, bitte geh…* I didn't stick around. If there are two things I can't stand it's sarcasm and last wordism. The only person I tolerate those failings in is you.

Outside, I headed to the subway. All I wanted was to keep going, to run away and not turn back. I got off at Warschauer Straße, then took refuge in the S-Bahn. I began to cry. It was all so very clear. Claudia had never gone to Egypt. She'd never sent me a postcard of the Sphinx. She'd asked her sister to, that's all. She'd made the whole thing up to get me to leave her alone. I know people often think I'm stupid because I'm big and strong, but that was going too far. I'll never know if I was crying because of Claudia or because that was the first time I confronted my own stupidity and realized I was no match for it. I cried, not because of what I'd done to Wlad or because I'd no doubt frightened Claudia. No, I cried at my own weakness in the face of so little, at the realization that I couldn't control myself in a situation as stupid as that one. But the sound of the train consoled me; the people sitting opposite pretended not to see me. The stations scrolled past. I changed trains at Spandau and went back to Erkner. And I took a third train at Erkner. I didn't want to ever have to get off. I must have taken the same trip four times before midnight. I took out my notebook to write to you on the final trip. I don't know why I'm thinking of you. I wish it was just the two of us on this train as it travels counterclockwise around Berlin. We could talk. I miss you, dear brother.

A Japanese lady sitting across from me doesn't dare look.

I think I must be crying.

Sich zusammenreißen.

Gabriel

Lichtenberg
May 24, 1999

My dear brother,

It's noon in Lichtenberg. I'm just back from Magda's, where I spent the night. After the disaster at Claudia's on Saturday night and my never-ending S-Bahn journey, I took the subway to Prenzlauer Berg and made my way to one of the few remaining grotty taverns in the neighbourhood. I drank. Schultheiss. Don't ask me how many litres. All I remember is waking up at Magda's at four o'clock in the morning. The cops who had brought me home were still there. I think I must have let myself go a little, lost control.

I was lying on the long sofa in the living room, while Magda showed the cops out. "I'll take care of him," I heard her say curtly. It felt like my head was in a vice. She brought me a bottle of fizzy water.

"You'll be needing this, you drunkard."

"Where am I?"

"At my place. Prenzlauer Berg's finest brought you back here. Just as well you were still carrying that letter from your *Wessi-Tante*. Otherwise you'd be spending the night down at the station. They saw your address on the envelope. They rang all the buzzers. The whole block came out, ten floors of neighbours. They all laughed as they watched the police haul you up to Hilde's. Your muscles are very heavy, Kapriel. Hilde had her lover with her, so she told them to carry you up to your apartment. When I saw them pass by, I told them to leave you on my sofa. You put on quite a show in Prenzlauer Berg, by the sound of things."

"Magda, please don't embarrass me."

"But it's too funny... They say you drank until your head fell onto the counter. When the bartender asked you to pay up, you tried to start a fight. That's when they called the cops. You owe me thirty marks. Your tab."

"I'm so sorry... I'll go back upstairs."

"And that's not all! When you saw the police, apparently you cried: '*Scarpia, bigoto satiro!*' Excuse me for laughing."

"Oh my God."

Magda helped me out of my clothes to take a shower. I was covered in mud and dust. She passed me a lime green robe and forced me to down some aspirin. She wanted to know. I poured my heart out to her, told her all about Wlad, the beating I'd given him, Claudia.

"It doesn't surprise me one bit. I could have told you that would happen."

"But you didn't?"

"No."

"Why not?"

"Because you had to see for yourself. You wouldn't have believed me. Claudia would have stayed in Toronto if she'd had any feelings for you at all. Plain and simple. You'd have been married long ago. You were very funny at the *Biergarten*, you and your courtly love. You're too cute, Kapriel."

"I... I want to go upstairs."

"No, you'll stay right here. I need to talk to you. I was waiting for you to see your Claudia again before I spoke to you. The time has come. Stay here. Don't move. You have a bad case of jealousy! Whoever do you get that from? Did you know that jealousy will destroy you in the end? Jealousy is a poison that kills slowly. It makes no distinction between executioner and victim. You're becoming a danger to yourself and others. I'll let you sleep for a few hours. You'll be able to see straighter after that."

As it happens, I slept for at least another eight hours. I think Magda went out. She must have come back that afternoon. I was sitting on the sofa in tears.

"Dry your eyes, poor knight!"

"Don't make fun of me."

"But you're hilarious. I'm sorry."

"Can I go home now?"

"Not until I talk to you. Wait, I'll pour myself some Riesling. Would you like a glass too?"

"No, no… definitely not."

"Pull yourself together, Kapriel!"

"I can't. I'm finished."

"*Ach!* Horsefeathers! Wait till you hear my story! Then you'll be *kaputt!* Poor little angel!"

"What's your story? Another pigeon joke?"

"No. A tale of jealousy. Or rather, the tale of a fit of jealousy that destroyed two lives. I think you could learn from it before something terrible happens to you."

"Jealous pigeons?"

"Be quiet, you little clown. No one thinks you're funny. I'm trying to warn you about your jealous side. It'll get you into trouble."

"And today's the day to warn me?"

"*Ja*, today. No better day for it. The sun is shining, the sky above Berlin is bursting with springtime, your birthday is coming up, you think you're unhappy. There's no better time. You'll feel better afterward. You'll realize that things could be worse, after all."

At that, I stood up and rummaged around in my jeans for my key. It wasn't there.

"They said you lost it in the bathroom back at the tavern. The locksmith can't come until tomorrow. It's either my sofa or Hilde's, but her lover's coming over tonight and I've never heard her expressing any interest in a *ménage à trois*."

"Be quiet and give me back my key."

"I'm telling you, it's at the bottom of a Prenzlauer Berg sewer, Kapriel. Go on, have a glass of Riesling. It will help you get a hold of yourself."

My dear brother, Magda went on to tell me the story you'll find in the two notebooks I've put in with these letters. I'm still in shock. I tried to stay as faithful as I could to everything Magda told me. That way you'll be able to feel the full force of the story for yourself.

I'm sending it to you because I want to share a very moving story with you. This woman is a bit like your reflection. You have the same interests, you're both into Puccini, and as I've seen for myself, you both have a bass clef birthmark in exactly the same spot. She's like a lost sister of yours, Michel. Closer to you than to me, that much is clear. I'm taking the time to write down her story and send it to you because I'm quite sure it contains some sort of warning for us.

She was wrong anyway. I've never been so consumed by Claudia than since I heard her story.

Gabriel

Magdalena Berg's First Notebook

I haven't told you about my parents, Kapriel. They loved me for the longest time. They still love me from where they are now, no doubt about it. You don't know the first thing about my hometown, I'm sure. I'm from Königsberg. In East Prussia. Just try talking about East Prussia with a German, Kapriel. They know precious little about it. "It used to be part of Germany," is about the best you'll get. Most will tell you all they know about Königsberg is the meatballs, *Königsberger Klopse*. My father was from over there, from Cranz, on the shores of the Curonian Spit. Do you know of it? He was the one who wanted me to be called Magdalena. It was a common name in our family, he said. The Bergs always had to have at least one living Magdalena. But I can tell by your eyes that you couldn't even place East Prussia on a map. The Baltic Sea? Lithuania? Ring any bells? Poland? Whatever do they teach you at school in Canada? Do you at least know where you are today? I'm talking about old Poland, not the country that the Russian tanks pushed westward in 1945. East Prussia was Germany on the Baltic Sea. Today it's Russia. Three million Germans lived in that little country for centuries, beside the Masurian Lakes, in Königsberg, and on the shores of the Baltic Sea. Perhaps it looks like a country you already know beside the sea. To the north. In East Prussia, Kapriel, it's one beautiful beach after another. Two long strips of land jut out into the Baltic: the Curonian Spit to the east and the Vistula Spit to the west. The two strips of sand are three hundred metres wide and at least one hundred kilometres long; between them there are two narrow stretches of fresh water that freeze over in winter. The peninsula's sand dunes are like mountains. They shift slowly in the wind. Between those two enormous sand dunes, Kapriel, there are wonderful pine forests, where deer run wild. I saw them when I was small! My mother came from Königsberg. She was a real Prussian and learned French at school. "Every young girl should be able to speak French," she'd tell me. I think she must have met the Kaiser himself when she was a child. The Prussian emperors were crowned in Königsberg, did you know that? That's where I was born. On Schrötterstraße, not too far from the zoo. I remember the old city of

Königsberg well. My father helped run a theatre there. He was an entrepreneur, too, and he owned two cinemas. When I was fourteen, in 1934, he announced to my mother he'd been transferred to the Reich's capital in Berlin. Well, not exactly transferred… He'd been taken on by Kraft durch Freude, ever heard of it? No? Kraft durch Freude was a big group of German workers from the *Deutsche Arbeitsfront*. Kraft durch Freude, or Strength through Joy, became the world's biggest entertainment provider in the 1930s. The *world's* biggest, Kapriel. We like to say that all the time in Germany: the world's biggest. We love excess. The world's biggest book fair, the best beer in the universe, the most terrifying dictator in history, the mother of all orchestras, the war to end all wars. German excess, all of it. Kraft durch Freude. The Germans called it KdF, three letters that were synonymous with vacations, theatre, music, and Mediterranean cruises. Every worker in Germany could pay in each month, and in return enjoy discount travel across the Reich. Prussians would travel by train to the Alps, while Bavarians went to swim in the Baltic Sea. It was Germany's first organized vacations. But KdF was much more too… My father, for example, was one of the first Prussians from Königsberg to travel thanks to KdF: he was sent to the Salzburg Festival in 1934. It was a dream come true for a man who loved music like he did. I also travelled a lot thanks to Strength through Joy, but first I have to tell you how we arrived in Berlin. My mother was far from enamoured with the city. I think it frightened her a little. She found the people impolite and poorly educated, and she had no patience for the communist plebs running loose in the streets. My father had a hard time persuading her to move there. She had her conditions. Funnily enough, it wasn't the promise of a huge apartment or nights out at the opera that made Mama change her mind, it was the assassination of Röhm in 1934. Nothing disgusted or frightened her more than disorder. Even though she was far from a fan of Adolf Hitler, to her mind Röhm's death brought an end to the chaos. And Berlin was such a violent city that Mama was frightened for herself and for me. "I don't want to go to Berlin, it's full of communists," she'd told Papa. Most people in Königsberg, it must be said, backed the Führer. I was fourteen and didn't know much about what was going on. Papa had told me, with a gleam in his eye, about the Reich's capital, its three opera houses, its theatres, its cabarets, and the Berlin lifestyle. But Mama wouldn't hear of it. "You won't have me living among Bolsheviks, Alfred!" Then came the Night of the Long Knives in summer 1934. Ever hear of it? No? *Ach... Gott!* And you were planning on marrying a German girl, Kapriel?

I'll spare you the details. Back then, I knew nothing at all about the Night of the Long Knives; that kind of thing didn't interest me in the slightest. All I know is that in September 1934, my mother agreed to move to Berlin. Papa was overjoyed. "You'll love it, you'll see," he told me. Because I was a little afraid. Afraid for Mama, because she didn't have a strong constitution. She became diabetic after I was born. She always needed looking after. As a very little girl, I learned to read her blood sugar level just by looking at her face. You can laugh, but it works! It was obvious: a little too much sugar would have killed her. Papa told me early on all the food we weren't allowed to keep at home: diabetics sometimes wake up starving and will wolf down anything they can get their hands on, only to fall into a coma! It's awfully dangerous. We never had desserts or candy in the house, in Königsberg or in Berlin.

A week before the move, Mama asked how I planned to say my goodbyes to Königsberg. All I wanted was to visit the zoo one last time. It was right beside where we lived. So Mama and her sister, my Tante Clara, took me to the zoo one last time one Saturday morning in October. Königsberg Zoo was one of the best in Europe. I could spend hours gazing at the zebras, passing them cabbage leaves through the bars. They were right beside the giraffes. Tante Clara was sad. She only had the one sister; in fact, I think we were all she had. And we were leaving. She had been a music teacher at a school.

"My little Magda, come back and see me during the holidays. We'll go to the beach in Cranz every day, if you like," she told me at Königsberg station before kissing me for the last time. Tante Clara wasn't married yet. She met Wolfgang later. We called him Onkel Wolfie. I think they got married about a year after we left Königsberg. It wasn't before, I'm sure of that. I was to meet the bastard soon enough. Poor Tante Clara! She deserved better than that disgusting animal, that bigot, that satyr! Forgive me, Kapriel, I'm getting carried away. You're an uncomplicated soul: you like your stories in chronological order. I should really tell you things as they happened. It's easier that way. But I can't help myself: Wolfgang Hinz was a pig!

As I was saying, before we left for Berlin, Mama had set out her conditions. First, we were to live in Charlottenburg, nowhere else. "It's Charlottenburg or nothing, Alfred," she told Papa. Mama was a real Königsberg *bourgeoise*. My grandparents owned a shipyard and they were distinctly unimpressed when their daughter married the son of a forester from Cranz, even if he had studied literature and music.

Mama also wanted me to go to the finest schools in Berlin, and those schools were in Charlottenburg. "I want her to learn French and English. A respectable young lady must speak French." Mama got her every wish. I even learned French. But what made her happiest of all, I think, was the apartment Papa found in Charlottenburg. When he came to pick us up at the railway station in the car—he already had a car—Mama looked out at the noisy, filthy streets of Berlin, completely discouraged. I'm quite sure that Papa made a point of taking the Kurfürstendamm so that Mama could see our new neighbourhood in all its glory. The apartment was in a big house on Schillerstraße, not too far from the new opera, the Deutsches Opernhaus, which had been the Charlottenburger Opernhaus before that. "See? You're right beside the opera house, Waldtraut. It couldn't be better." We drove past the opera house so that Mama could see. She didn't even look, she was so exhausted from the trip. Papa had bought an enormous bourgeois apartment. Eight big rooms and some furniture left behind by the previous owners. They must have left in a hurry: they hadn't even taken the piano. It wasn't until much later that a neighbour told me the apartment we lived in had been confiscated from a Jewish family that had had to flee Germany. Papa must have known. Mama, too, but they didn't tell me a thing. I wouldn't have understood anyway.

Mama was enchanted. "Why Alfred, an apartment like this must have cost you millions!" Papa had got a very good price, he said. "It's unbelievable," Mama laughed. "We should have come to live here sooner!"

It's true that the little house in Königsberg was no match for the palace Papa had just bought. We weren't the only newcomers to the building. There were three other apartments with new owners, one of them a colleague of Papa's at Kraft durch Freude, a man by the name of Nowak. I was a little sad all the same. In Königsberg, we'd had a yard with a little shed, where I raised animals. I'd had a little dog, rabbits, and even three ducks one summer. In Charlottenburg, we were on the second floor: there was no way we could have rabbits, not even a cat. Mama found me a place at Sophie-Charlotte-Schule the first week. She didn't want to send me anywhere else than a school for girls that taught foreign languages, Latin, Greek, and all the humanities. The principal gave me a funny look, I remember, because I still had my East Prussian accent. It must have been quite strong: she said something about how important it was to speak good German. And it was there on that October day in 1934 that I first encountered the idea of being in love.

The principal escorted me to the classroom when Mama left.

"Your group has a French class now. Do you speak French, Magdalena?"

"*Naturellement*," I replied.

It was true. I'd taken French lessons in Königsberg, but Sophie-Charlotte-Schule catered to the daughters of Berlin's finest families. Some spoke French fluently. I got there before the class started. It took less than two minutes for the other students to begin tormenting me. "So are you a boy or a girl then?" "Looks like a boy with long hair." Those Berlin girls were unbearable. Yes, I looked like a boy. A real tomboy. Not ugly, but very masculine. And I wasn't blonde. Not being blonde at fourteen was a calamity! Then it happened. She walked in: Mademoiselle Jacques. As she came in, the students rose as one until she told us to sit back down. It came as a complete surprise to me. Teachers in Königsberg would all bark "Heil Hitler!" as they came in, but Mademoiselle Jacques made do with a simple "Bonjour Mesdemoiselles." Until that point, I'd had German teachers teaching me French. They would cut up their consonants into little cubes, *iff you know vat I mean*. Mademoiselle Jacques pronounced every word the way I'd imagined the French must speak. She was a real lady. For the longest time, I thought she was French. She was, in fact, German, descended from the Huguenots, but given her name and occupation I took her to be French.

The word *Mesdemoiselles* hadn't finished rolling off her tongue and I already knew she'd land me in all kinds of trouble. With the first consonant of *Mesdemoiselles*, when Mademoiselle Jacques' lips came together to send the rest of the word off on its delightful way, angels hidden I don't know where in the classroom fell silent. Her *-elles* struck me square in the face like a summer breeze coming in off the Baltic Sea. Yes, Kapriel, the charm of foreign-language teachers is as innocent as it is apocalyptic. And don't they know it!

Mademoiselle Jacques—I'll remember to my dying day, and even beyond—was wearing a long grey skirt, an ivory blouse, and a navy blue jacket made of the same material as her skirt. Her thick head of hair was tied back in a bun, just above which she wore an amber barrette. When I saw it, I thought she must be from Königsberg, because when I was that age I thought all the world's amber came from Königsberg. The tiny piece of my homeland she was wearing in her hair might as well have been a tiara.

When she turned around to write on the board, my gaze got lost in the spiral of her chignon. I fell straight into it that day in October 1934, never to re-emerge. I'm still trapped in there to this day. The other day, while you were telling me you'd fallen head over heels at the Goethe-Institut in Toronto the moment Claudia opened her mouth, the same wave of dumbfounded joy washed over me again. I couldn't even hear what you were saying. It was as if I was fourteen again. Then Mademoiselle Jacques asked me to stand up and introduce myself to the class in French. A few hurtful girls laughed at my faltering French.

Mademoiselle Jacques smiled. "You can sit down, Mademoiselle Berg. Welcome to Berlin. Can you tell us which part of the Reich you're from?"

She must have known already and just wanted to hear my French. And there I was, standing like Marie Antoinette before the people of France, about to lose my head.

"My name is Magdalena Berg. I'm from East Prussia, from Königsberg. Königsberg is a German city by the Baltic Sea. The Pregel River runs through it…"

Tante Clara had taught me how to say that much in French. Then I fainted. I fell hard, like a sack of potatoes. When I woke up, Mademoiselle Jacques was on the floor beside me. My head was on her lap. She was touching me, Kapriel! The angel was actually touching me! Other teachers came in to help, along with the principal.

"*Ach!* It's the little girl from Königsberg. What's gotten into her?" I heard. They called my mother since we had a telephone at home. My father was high up in Kraft durch Freude, you see. Mama arrived with the maid to bring me home.

"She must be exhausted!" Mama declared.

She thought the 500-kilometre train journey from Königsberg must have taken its toll on me, or maybe the noise of the city was driving me crazy, or I don't know what else. But the beautiful Mademoiselle Jacques had quite simply knocked me on my back. But what could I say? How could I explain such a thing? It had never happened to me before, it was like no symptom I'd ever had, it was at once menacing, marvellous, and lethal. At any rate, Mama ordered complete rest for one week, which seemed like an eternity. I had to put up a fight to be allowed to open the French books we had at home. That's when I became truly infected, that's when, in the half-light of my bedroom, I began to daydream about Mademoiselle Jacques, her bun, and her—at least to my mind—oh-so-French lips.

Mama had kept all her French schoolbooks from Königsberg. The moving crates were barely emptied and I already had my nose buried in books on French literature. In bed, I'd fill my head with subjunctives, perfect tenses, and past participle agreements. I went about it methodically, but I still allowed myself flights of fancy into books that were too advanced for me. I was like a smooth-cheeked cabin boy at the helm of a ship that was too big for him.

"You'll kill yourself studying," Mama shouted. "You need your rest!"

Mama was always shouting. Papa was always off with KdF. In the Alps, by the sea, Munich. He used to travel all around the Reich with Germans on holiday.

For me, it was clear that happiness could only come through learning French. Mama was overjoyed by this sudden enthusiasm for foreign languages. I had been a mediocre student in Königsberg, a tad undisciplined, more interested in trips out to sea and along the Curonian Spit with Papa Alfred than mathematics and subjunctives.

"It's the Charlottenburg air," Mama would say, seeing me go over my French conjugations again and again.

Mama had played the piano since she was little. When orders dried up and her parents were forced to sell the shipyard in 1930, it fell to Papa to indulge her fondness for grand pianos and music teachers. Music costs a fortune, Kapriel. You should know.

One night in December 1934 when Papa was off travelling and Mama was feeling unwell, I used the time to myself to plaster the apartment in pieces of paper, labelling every piece of furniture, every item, in French. There were dozens of them: *la table, la chaise, la fenêtre, la fourchette, le plancher, le portrait, le téléphone, le piano...* Everything got its own piece of paper. The following morning at breakfast, Mama thought she'd lost her mind.

"What are these French words doing all over the house?"

"They're for Mademoiselle Jacques."

Mama had a good sense of humour. She cut out a piece of paper, wrote something on it, and put it on my head: *die Gans.* The goose! When she wasn't feeling poorly, Mama could be very funny. Because of Mademoiselle Jacques—or thanks to her, I'm not sure which—I quickly became the hardest-working student in French class. You see, Kapriel, French to me was not a language that was spoken by real people. Sure, I knew it was spoken in France, but France was a distant, abstract idea. French was the language Mademoiselle Jacques spoke. If she had taught Sanskrit, I'd have learned

Sanskrit. But Mademoiselle Jacques was only the beginning of my "emotional" problems. Much worse was to come.

When she realized my infatuation with the French language, Mama imagined I might also have a talent for music. At last I was beginning to take an interest in things proper young girls should enjoy. In her mind, I should work on my gifts. In December 1934, Mama told me she had come to a decision.

"Have you noticed, Magda, that nearly all the girls in your class play an instrument?"

"No."

Which was true. I hadn't noticed. Did Mademoiselle Jacques play an instrument? That was the question she should have asked.

"They do, Magda. They all take piano lessons."

"I don't like the piano."

"I know, darling. But you'll have to either choose another instrument or learn to sing. I don't want you to get left behind. Music is good for a girl: it shows her feminine side. And Papa can well afford it."

"Can you sing in French?"

"Ah! It's clearly an obsession with you! Of course! It's more difficult than in German, but there are songs in French, lots of them. Wait a moment... What's he called? I've forgotten his name, but I still have the book in the piano bench..."

"Will you teach me to sing?"

"No, no. We'll find you a nice singing teacher right here in Charlottenburg, and you'll learn all about singing. It will change your life, believe me!"

"Change my life how?"

"You'll see the world differently. And the world will see you differently too. People adore people who can sing. Everyone knows that. It's so easy to fall in love with a beautiful voice that hits all the right notes."

She didn't need to say another word.

"Can we go now? Before lunch?"

Mama laughed. Back in 1934, she still laughed a little. Much less than in Königsberg, but still every now and then, whenever I said something like that. She hadn't started to hide herself away in her bedroom yet.

She began looking for a singing teacher there and then. It wasn't hard. Papa was an important man at KdF, and KdF was an extraordinary outlet for artists, musicians especially. One of the things my father did was manage all the shows put on by KdF. They didn't just organize trips, oh no! They put on operas and sold cut-price concert tickets to Germans. So all he had to do was ask at the opera. Three days later, Mama came to pick me up outside Sophie-Charlotte-Schule. I was still woozy after French class.

"I found you a singing teacher! We're going right away! You'll see. She's very nice. I met her this morning."

We had to take the subway from the Deutsches Opernhaus to Nollendorfplatz. I'd never taken the subway before. The train went in and out of the ground, showing me flashes of Berlin, fascinating places I was about to discover. Remember that at that age I wasn't allowed to walk around as I pleased. Mama would never have agreed. Plus, I would have been scared to, and with good reason. Berlin wasn't safe.

Bülowstraße. That's where my singing teacher lived. As I rode the subway, my mind was filled with daydreams, nothing unusual for a fourteen-year-old girl. They came in three main flavours, with the occasional variation. But they were always more or less the same. Those images haunted me in my sleep and in my every waking moment too.

First dream: I'm walking with Mademoiselle Jacques at Königsberg Zoo. We're the only visitors. I bribe the zookeeper to get my hands on the key to the zebra pen. Mademoiselle Jacques and I walk up to the animals and they're not at all frightened. Mademoiselle Jacques is astounded to see what a talented animal trainer I am. I whisper into a zebra's ear. After a few minutes, it lets Mademoiselle Jacques climb onto its back. The two prance about, Mademoiselle Jacques' laughter echoing around the zebra pen. Later she and I gallop through the streets of Königsberg as people wave at us. End of the first dream.

Second dream: A concert hall. Mama is on stage, sitting at a piano. I'm in a blue dress, standing before the audience. Mama launches into the opening bars. The French words flow out of my mouth like caresses, straight into the third row, where Mademoiselle Jacques sits smiling up at me blissfully. The finale is grandiose, ethereal. Before Mama even gets to the final bars, the applause brings the house down. Mademoiselle Jacques is crying with joy. End of the second dream.

Third dream: A boat. Mademoiselle Jacques and I are sailing silently along the Curonian Spit. An elk watches us from the shore. She talks about Goethe and explains the subjunctive to me. I reply by citing an excerpt from *Werther*: "A wonderful serenity has taken possession of my entire soul, like these sweet mornings of spring which I enjoy with my whole heart." Mademoiselle Jacques looks delighted and shields her eyes from the sun as it sets over the Baltic Sea. End of the third dream.

What I didn't know that afternoon, as Mama told me to hurry along Bülowstraße, was that two new characters were about to join the cast of my daydreams.

"Here it is!" Mama announced, pointing to a big door. "Her name is Terese Bleibtreu!"

(Michel, Bleibtreu means "stay true"—a funny name for a singing teacher.)

We went up three floors. Mama was out of breath. Behind the door, we could hear someone playing the piano, then a boy singing *Semplicetta tortorella*, the Nicolai Vaccai ariettas. No one came to open the door so we walked on in. There was a long hallway with a few chairs obviously set out for visitors. The boy's voice now reached us more clearly.

"I think he's a baritone. Nice isn't it, Magda?"

"Yes, very nice."

It's difficult to describe a voice, Kapriel; it's easier to explain the impact it has, the images it evokes within us. The boy's voice entered my head right at the moment the image of the zebra at Königsberg Zoo was passing through for the thousandth time. It was a well-rounded sound, big as the sea, but as fragile as the breeze. The boy was only a beginner, even I could tell. We heard Frau Bleibtreu interrupt him: "Watch the note, Ludwig!" His name was Ludwig. Mama smiled a little. To Prussians like us, the name "Ludwig" is a little... how should I put this? Bavarian. He started singing again. A very simple arietta about a turtledove, Mama explained. "Tante Clara used to sing it too, in the early days." Ludwig's disembodied voice swept through the hallway.

"Per fuggir dal crudo artiglio vola in grembo al cacciator..."

Then something strange happened, a phenomenon that I still can't explain to this day, Kapriel. My mind took flight, at the sound of Ludwig's voice, from Königsberg Zoo to the concert hall and on to the Curonian Spit, and soon all three scenes were overwhelmed by the warm, round voice of a boy I hadn't even set eyes on. His voice became a character in my waking dreams, a sonorous entity that permeated every last corner of my conscience. That voice was almost blue in colour; it quieted all the other sounds in my dreams. All I could hear now was Ludwig singing *Semplicetta tortorella*. And the voice enchanted Mademoiselle Jacques every bit as much as the galloping zebra and the sun setting over the Baltic Sea. "How beautiful, Magda," she said in my dream. "How delightful."

Ludwig's lesson was almost over. Terese Bleibtreu reminded him what he was to prepare for their next lesson, then the door to the studio opened. It was Ludwig who saw us first.

"Heil Hitler!" he simpered, giving the Führer's salute.

Mama rolled her eyes. "Heil Hitler," she replied. Mama never said "Heil Hitler." She repeated it if someone said it to her, but she never said it first.

Ludwig was out in the hallway now. Terese made the introductions. Ludwig was a... how should I put this? A very ethereal boy. If he hadn't been wearing his Hitler Youth uniform and his hair had been longer, I might have taken him for a girl.

"Ludwig Bleibtreu," he said by way of introduction.

He was her little brother! I'm not sure I could have put up with my own sister as a music teacher, but Ludwig and Terese seemed to get on like the very best of friends. My God, such Catholic names they both had now that I think about it. Not Berlin names at all! She must have been ten or twelve years older than him. You know, Kapriel, even if I'd met Ludwig on the sidewalk on my way out of the building, I'd still have known he was Terese's brother. The boy was an exact, only slightly more masculine, version of his older sister. The world had just shifted beneath me. The boat Mademoiselle Jacques was sitting in began to take on water and sank to the bottom of the Baltic Sea. After his Hitler salute, he walked forward and peered at me hard, as though he thought he recognized me. Terese sensed her brother's uneasiness.

"Ludwig is very tired. He didn't hear you come in," she said in a singsong voice. Ludwig excused himself and left. Mama left me alone with the teacher and took her seat again in the hallway. Terese sat down at her grand piano. The room was a timeless place. The window looked out onto Bülowstraße, with distant conversations, the sound of traffic, and children's cries occasionally drifting up. There were photographs on the walls of Terese on stage, in roles I didn't recognize. In one corner, a mannequin dressed in feathers and a little bird, a real one this time, in a cage. Perhaps it had been caught by the man wearing the Papageno outfit, who knows?

"That's Amadeus," she said.

"What type of bird is it?"

"A Gouldian finch."

"Where does it come from?"

"Australia. Queensland, I think. I can't remember," she tittered.

Terese Bleibtreu knew the provinces of Australia and the birds that lived in them. I was beginning to find her a bit odd. The exotic bird and the outdated surroundings created the impression that nothing was quite real. I remember wondering if you could travel to Australia with KdF. Probably. No doubt. I'd have to ask Papa. But why that look, Kapriel! Plenty of people used to have birds in their Berlin apartments. In fact... oh yes, I remember now.

"I have a bird!" Terese said, catching me staring at it. "But only a little one. Don't worry, Magda..."

Don't you find that funny, Kapriel? In German, when you say, "She has a bird" that means "She's crazy." That's why it was funny. She meant she was only a little crazy. And soon I'd have proof.

Ludwig, the boy who had just left, was also a new student, she explained. He'd only been coming for three weeks.

"Ludwig is my little brother. He's very talented! Perhaps you could sing a duet together."

For the first lesson, Terese had me reproduce the notes she played on the piano, just to make sure I wasn't tone-deaf. "*Sehr gut!*" she said each time. Then she had me lie on the floor to show me where the sound a singer produces comes from: the muscles down there that do all the work. She had me spend fifteen minutes doing arpeggios. She would sing a series of notes and I had to repeat them as accurately as possible. Sometimes she'd say "*Nein! Hören Sie genau zu!*" or "*Jaaaaa! Genau!*" depending on whether I managed it or not. Standing up, sitting down. A real workout. She touched me a lot, too. After an hour of that I was exhausted. Then Terese had Mama come in.

"I think we'll be able to work together. She has an ear. Although, of course, we are starting from scratch, so..."

I stared at the Australian bird while Terese and Mama ironed out the details of my musical education. They decided on an hour's singing lesson every Tuesday after school.

"But she can come and practice whenever she likes. My door is always open!"

I asked if I could have my lesson with Terese right after her brother Ludwig's.

"Of course, but why, darling?" she asked. (She always called me darling.)

"Because I want to hear him sing before I start my lesson."

Mama and Terese were tickled by my ingenuousness. They couldn't begin to imagine the effect Ludwig's voice had had on me. They didn't realize I was still reeling from its timbre, and from the blue colour it seemed to give off.

From that moment on, Ludwig Bleibtreu invited himself into my daydreams. A dejected Mademoiselle Jacques upped and left for someone else's. Ludwig took her place on the back of the Königsberg zebra. It was he who rowed the boat across the Baltic Sea, who waved to the elk watching us from the shore. On stage, it was the two of us who faced the audience side by side. Mademoiselle Jacques stormed out in a jealous rage and slammed the door behind her. His voice was the soundtrack to my every reverie.

Mama decided to walk home since we were in no rush. She was in fine form.

"And you've made such a nice little friend! You'll have to start going to the opera. Papa will find us tickets. You'll be able to sing Schubert with Tante Clara. She adores Schubert! *Ach!* Magda! You'll also be able to sign up to…"

She was practically *hysterisch* now. She even insisted on taking me for tea on the Ku'Damm. It was December and cold after all. There were stars of David painted white on some of the store windows. I remember asking Mama about them.

"They're all mad, Magda. But don't repeat that to anyone. Papa could get into trouble."

Until that moment, Kapriel, I hadn't the faintest idea what was happening to Germany. I hadn't paid much attention to it. But I've run out of Riesling. Hold on a second, there's some in the kitchen.

(At this point, Michel, she got up to look for another bottle of Riesling in the kitchen. I think I heard her sobbing, but I'm not sure. It might have been the faucet or the plumbing. She came back with an open bottle of Riesling.)

Ach! There were some very nice people in Berlin, let me tell you, Kapriel. The following Tuesday I took the subway by myself to my music lesson, running the rest of the way so as to be sure I'd hear Ludwig singing as I waited in the hallway. Memory does a poor job of recording voices. We forget their pitch, their colour. Words we remember, but memory never manages to bring a voice back to life. A voice needs to be there for us to pick it out among others. Voices are as tricky to describe as the taste of nutmeg or the feel of sand between your toes. All I can say is that that desire to hear Ludwig Bleibtreu's voice again made every hour at Sophie-Charlotte-Schule interminable. Worried that he might finish early, I'd tear down the stairs at the Nollendorfplatz subway station and run flat out along Bülowstraße. You'll never know Ludwig Bleibtreu's voice, Kapriel. That is your misfortune, your tragedy, Kapriel.

I must have arrived an hour early. I didn't want to miss a thing. I raced up the stairs to Terese Bleibtreu's four at a time, on the tips of my toes so they wouldn't hear me, frightened he'd stop singing at the sound of my footsteps. In my mind, I sung the arietta I'd practiced with Mama. "*Semplicetta tortorella, che non vede il suo periglio…*" Poor turtledove doesn't see the danger… Truer words were never spoken!

I walked silently into Terese Bleibtreu's hallway, hearing only Terese explaining something about the diaphragm. Then he sang, something different that time, another of Vaccai's ariettas, the one they use to teach intervals of a fourth. "*Lascia il lido, e il mare infido…*" I closed my eyes and let Ludwig's voice awaken dreams of being on a zebra's back, in a rowboat, in a concert hall. Then Terese and Ludwig began laughing. I didn't dare budge in case they realized I was there. I was an only child, you see. I didn't know what having a brother or sister was like. To me, listening to Ludwig and Terese Bleibtreu giggling after singing class was akin to voyeurism. I hung on their every word. They were looking for a score. They sang a completely moronic song I didn't know. Marlene Dietrich once sang it as a duet with a singer by the name of Claire Waldoff, *Wenn die beste Freundin*. They sang in unison; the words were very funny. Then Terese opened the door to find me there, waiting in the hallway.

"Whatever are you doing there? Why didn't you knock?"

Terese was a little annoyed, as though I'd caught them red-handed. She reminded me I wasn't to go around listening at doors. She even asked what I'd overheard. I didn't know she'd been singing what the Nazis called "degenerate" music. I promised not to tell a soul, not so much to reassure her as to bring the three of us closer together. The pair of them fascinated me. I wanted to belong to them, to be their sister. And what can I say? Ludwig made me laugh! He was wearing his Hitler Youth uniform again.

Terese said goodbye to him and invited me in. Like the week before, he gave me the Hitler salute and stared hard at me. He didn't say much. Then my lesson started.

"Magda, darling, let's go!"

Terese was dangerously on form. After the warm-up, she asked me to sing *Semplicetta tortorella* at least fifteen times. Like all singing teachers, Terese was never satisfied. "Your tongue should be doing all the work, not your jaw!" and she held my jaw while I sang. It wasn't easy. Then she had me say the Italian words with a cork between my teeth. Like this! Phew! At any rate...

"You're as big as a barrel, Magda. You're getting bigger like a toad. You're a Zeppelin over Berlin. Big as the Reichstag! *Ja...* There you go."

Then she suddenly stopped playing.

"What do you like to eat, Magda? What's your favourite dish?"

"Caramel pudding!"

"*Ach!* The Führer loves that too! When you're singing, think of caramel pudding. You're a caramel pudding, Magda! Come on! And stop wagging your jaw, for heaven's sake!"

At the end of the lesson, I opened the door to find Ludwig in the hallway. He'd been waiting there the whole lesson. He looked like someone who'd been caught stealing bread.

"*Ach!* You're still there, my little Ludwig! You stayed behind to listen to Magda. You're so charming, the two of you. You know my house is always open. You can come and go as you please. You can practice anytime I'm not giving a lesson."

Listening to Terese Bleibtreu bless our union like that, I felt as though I was being admitted to an inner sanctum, being initiated into a mystery religion, joining a new family that was a far cry from my depressed mother, absent father, and the little brats at Sophie-Charlotte-Schule. It seemed as though I'd found my real family, the one I'd clearly been separated from at birth. As for Ludwig, I already knew from hearing his voice that, were he ever to die, my life on this earth would become one long painful, pitiful tale of woe, a gaping crater of solitude, a futile, sorrowful journey.

Ludwig followed me down the stairs.

"You have a lovely voice," the little charmer told me.

No one but Tante Clara and Mama had ever complimented me. Oh, there was Mademoiselle Jacques who, even though she officially took me to be an idiot, would congratulate me on the progress I was making in French, but no boy had never praised me before. Ludwig and I decided to walk together. He lived near Nollendorfplatz. His sister Terese no longer lived with her parents and was now staying with an aunt, a woman who could sometimes be seen wandering around the apartment, interrupting lessons with her applause or an admiring "*Schön!*". Like the idiot I was, I followed him, even though Mama was to pick me up from Terese's.

"I have to go to my Hitler Youth meeting. It's Tuesday."

Standing outside the subway station, Ludwig told me he'd been allowed to take singing lessons only after striking a deal with his father. Ludwig didn't like the other boys. His father had agreed to pay for the singing lessons, provided he join the Hitler Youth. His father must have been a real bundle of laughs.

"The other boys are as thick as two short planks," Ludwig said.

"The girls aren't any better," I replied. "I go on Sundays and it's to make Papa happy too. But it's awful! A bunch of nincompoops. And those idiotic songs they make us sing!"

"I know, I know. We have the same ones. I prefer Schubert any day. What about you?"

"I don't know much Schubert."

"I want to learn *Ständchen*, that's what I told Terese. Look, she gave me the score."

"'*Leise flehen meine Lieder durch die Nacht zu dir.*' You're going to sing it to a girl?"

"It's written to a girl?"

"I think so. '*...fürchte Holde nicht.*' *Holde* is his sweetheart."

"I hadn't thought about that."

The words on the score seemed to be written for me. For me to sing them in Ludwig's voice to Mademoiselle Jacques on a zebra. Although I didn't really know anymore. I think Ludwig's voice might have sent poor Mademoiselle Jacques packing for good. She hadn't cut the mustard; I almost felt sorry for her.

We stayed outside the subway station for a good while, then Ludwig suddenly began to panic.

"Quick! Hide! Here come the baboons from my group!"

He dragged me behind a wall just as four young men came out of the station, all wearing the same uniform.

"It's my *Oberkameradschaftsführer*, Kranz! He's a real moron, but he might recognize me! They almost saw me! Quick, let's get out of here!"

And so began my life with Ludwig Bleibtreu. Five years of poetry in motion. Five years of *folie à deux*. Five years of dizzying promises. We went to hide with the zebras at the zoo. Ludwig was achingly funny. He would get up on the benches and mimic Terese's coloratura soprano, dishing out singing advice to passersby. "You over there! Stop moving your jaw! And you, sir! Your posture! Stand up straight like you're hanging from a thread! And, remember, that's a D on *vola*!"

I rolled about laughing. Then he sang *Semplicetta tortorella* to the zebras, like in my dream. Do you know Max Raabe, the singer? No? Well, he looked like him. A graceful blond cherub who wouldn't hurt a fly but had cutthroat charm.

Ludwig wore a little cross on a gold chain around his neck. His aunt, the very devout Bavarian that Terese lived with, had given it to him the day his father forced him to join the Hitler Youth. "At last have that under your uniform," she'd said. No one has ever made me laugh as much as Ludwig Bleibtreu. No one will ever pay me more attention than Ludwig Bleibtreu did. No one will ever look at me the way Ludwig Bleibtreu looked at me. My little angel in a uniform that was too big for him. As blond as the wheat in East Prussia. A true German, I'm telling you: wearing an idiotic uniform, his auntie's cross around his neck, but give him the choice and all he wanted to do was sing. A true German. A Bleibtreu. And he moved with all the grace of Mademoiselle Jacques. *Ach!* That boy! Forgive me, Kapriel. I need a tissue.

I got home at six thirty that evening, lips blue with cold. Papa and Mama were frightened half to death.

"Where on earth were you? We looked for you everywhere, you little nitwit!" Papa roared, slapping me twice. Papa Alfred hit me twice a year. Since it was already December and he'd spared me on account of the move to Berlin, he gave me two good slaps I wouldn't forget in a hurry, once with the palm, once with the back of his hand. But he wasn't angry for long. I was even allowed to have supper with them once Mama had calmed him down. Ludwig got a thrashing from his father; Kranz the baboon had told him his son hadn't been at Hitler Youth. They had no way of knowing that by beating us, our fathers helped forge a bond stronger than steel between the two of us. Ludwig and I understood with each blow just how much we meant to each other. The first six months of 1935 we spent almost entirely at Terese Bleibtreu's. By then we were having our lessons together. Two hours straight. Ludwig's sister had no objections, but Mama couldn't find out.

"As long as you keep applying yourselves! You're here to work!"

I celebrated my fifteenth birthday at Terese Bleibtreu's. Ludwig too, two weeks later. We told our parents we wanted to practice our singing.

"But you can practice here. We have a piano, after all. I can even accompany you!" Mama protested.

"It's better at Terese's. She helps us."

It was a terrible lie. Terese let us hide in the next room while her students practiced. The little room had two armchairs and a table with framed photographs on it. Photos of Terese. One big photograph, I remember, showed her with a gentleman sitting at a piano. He was in five of the photos.

"Her fiancé," Ludwig whispered.

It felt as though Terese was committing adultery.

To my mind, Terese, Ludwig, and I formed a single emotional entity with no room for a fourth person.

Hidden away behind the door in our little boudoir, Ludwig and I listened to Terese give her lessons. All kinds of people came and went, from professional singers at the Deutsches Opernhaus in search of technical advice and amateur chorists from the Reich's railway choirs to beginners like us and men in their thirties who would sometimes forget their manners between two scales. I remember one particular gentleman from Wittenbergplatz… The poor man would begin to stutter every time he walked into Terese's parlour. I couldn't look at Ludwig the whole time he was there, otherwise I'd have burst out laughing.

"T… Te… Ter… Teres… Terese… You are th-th-the v-v-very p-p-picture of r-r-radiance it-itself," the poor man would stutter. Shurbaum, I think his name was.

"Don't make me blush, Herr Schurbaum," she tittered. "Shall we begin?"

Herr Schurbaum had a very pleasant *basso cantante*. Like the sacristan in *Tosca*. Or Sarastro in *The Magic Flute*. Terese was radiant, it was true. And Ludwig and I would hear all those voices, all the advice she gave. Terese would come see us after every lesson. We'd talk technique, colour, timbre, the pieces that her students were singing. I remember the tenor who sang Cavaradossi at the Deutsches Opernhaus. He'd also come to see her. We called him "the goat" because he'd put tremors and vibratos absolutely everywhere.

"*Nein! Nein! Kein Vibrato!*" Terese would shout, enraged.

I think it was there in Terese Bleibtreu's boudoir that the first challenge was laid down. The first tests, I should say. I think I mentioned, Kapriel, that Ludwig wore a little cross around his neck. The gold shone in the half-light where we were hidden. Sometimes I'd take it between my fingers and caress the smooth metal. His date of birth was engraved on the back, along with his initials. *L. B. 13.12.20.*

Gold has always fascinated me, Kapriel. "Solidified light raised from a subterranean world," that's what Karl Marx wrote! It was October 1935. Ludwig set me my first mission. Kapriel, you must promise me you'll tell no one. The missions... *Ach!*

"Do you like my cross, Magda?"

"Yes, it's pretty."

"Do you want it?"

"No! It's yours!"

"Admit it. You want it."

"I do, but it's yours. It even has your initials engraved on the back."

"It's yours."

"But I don't want it." (I was lying. I wanted that cross as badly as Hitler wanted war.)

Ludwig had taken off the chain and was dangling the little cross in front of me. We had to whisper while the tenor wailed *Und es blitzten die Sterne*. Like your brother, only in German. That's right: he was singing *Tosca* in German. Ludwig waved his little cross under my nose.

"I'll give it to you on one condition."

"What condition?" (I was curious.)

"You'll have to pass a test."

That's when the missions started. Childish games that quickly spiralled out of control. The first one was simple. I didn't have to bring back the Golden Fleece, just Mademoiselle Jacques' barrette. Ludwig knew all about her, my every feeling for her. He hadn't even met her, but he told me he loved her just as much as I did.

"If you love her, then I love her too," he said.

You have to admit he was good!

Steal Mademoiselle Jacques' barrette. *Gott im Himmel!* A little silver barrette she wore with a long piece of amber on top.

One day, I was with Ludwig on Schillerstraße and we bumped into Mademoiselle Jacques. Well, she didn't see us, but Ludwig had noticed her amber hair clip. I had to wait for the right moment. Don't get me wrong, Kapriel. I've never been a believer and even if I had been, I wouldn't have walked around with a cross hanging from my neck! It was a piece of Ludwig I was after, something that had touched his skin. I don't believe in God, but I do believe that every object has a memory of its own.

It wasn't easy. I had to get Papa's help. And guess how? Thanks to *Tosca*! You'll like this story, Kapriel! You already know that Papa worked for KdF, that he had opera tickets for the workers. In the fall of 1935, that October, he got tickets to *Tosca* at the Berlin Staatsoper for Mama's birthday. Mama had already taken me to *The Magic Flute* and other Mozart operas, but she thought I was too young for Puccini. I remember them arguing about it. Papa insisted I go.

"What harm do you think *Tosca*'s going to do her?"

"All that violence. Come on, Alfred. You know very well what happens in the second act. There's a torture scene, then Tosca stabs Scarpia to death. It's a story for adults. Plus, she'll be bored. Mozart is what she should be listening to at her age. Mozart trains the ear without corrupting the soul! It's nice of you, Alfred, but I won't go. I get nightmares every time I see that jealous woman throwing herself to her death at the end of the opera."

"Do you really want us to go see *The Magic Flute* again?"

"Alfred, you simply cannot take her. I forbid it. Puccini just isn't suitable for a young girl who's studying French and learning to sing like our Magda. She needs stories that are right for her age. I won't even hear of her going to see *Madame Butterfly*!"

"I think I'll leave it up to Magda, darling."

"That's right. You bring her to see *Tosca*. Just don't be surprised if she ends up with blood on her hands!"

"For goodness' sake, Waldtraut! Listening to Puccini won't turn someone into a murderer!"

"Do what you like, Alfred. You always do anyway. All I can do now is keep quiet."

I would often hear them arguing in their bedroom or the living room where I never went to sit with them. From that moment on, seeing that forbidden opera where passions were unleashed seemed to me my sole reason for living. Papa made me wait until Saturday, October 19. The entire Staatsoper had been booked by KdF. Papa even gave some opera tickets to Sophie-Charlotte-Schule, probably to get the principal on his side. The concert hall was almost full. I was in the orchestra seats with Papa. A wonderful place, Kapriel. Prettier than the Königsberg theatre, much prettier. There were speeches by people from Kraft durch Freude then the Hitler salute. The usual blah-blah before a show. The Führer generously ensures you have this and that and the other, the regime is pleased to offer you this performance of *Tosca*... Pfff! They stopped just short of claiming Hitler had written the score himself! Anyway, you'll never guess what I saw no more than three rows in front of me, a familiar sight, glinting in the half-light... Mademoiselle Jacques' barrette, neatly pinned to its owner's hair! She must have been given one of the tickets Papa had left at the school.

The speeches finally ended and the curtain went up. I spent the whole first act thinking this was my chance, it was now or never. I barely paid any attention to what was happening on stage. D'Angelotti arriving, hiding when he sees Cavaradossi, then that sacristan idiot. Tosca at last coming into the church, shouting "Mario! Mario! Mario!" convinced she'll catch him with another woman! You know, Kapriel, it's a woman's jealousy that brings the whole thing crashing down, that's what *Tosca*'s all about. Had Tosca been a bit more sensible, none of it would ever have happened. It was through that flaw that Scarpia managed to worm his way into her heart. That's what Papa told me. I needed to find a way to sidle up next to Mademoiselle Jacques. The first intermission came just after the *Te Deum*. When we came back from the bar, I noticed that the seats behind her were empty. The people sitting there had had enough after the first act!

"Papa, may I sit a little closer?"

"Of course, darling. No one will mind if the people have left."

From that moment on, it all happened very quickly. Mademoiselle Jacques didn't see me in the dark hall, and since Papa didn't know any more about her than what Mama had told him, he had no way of knowing it was her. The barrette glistened in the darkness. But it was far from in the bag, Kapriel. Even if I'd managed to get the barrette out of her hair without attracting her attention, the people behind would have caught me red-handed and turned me in on the spot. Papa would have been disgraced! But it was Tosca who delivered the barrette into my lap, almost literally. Mademoiselle Jacques became more and more agitated during the second act. She jumped in her seat every time Cavaradossi let out a tortured cry. She buried her face in her hands as though it was she or her lover being tortured! She even wept during *Vissi d'arte*. I could have pinched her barrette while she sobbed, but someone would have seen me. Mama was right after all: Puccini does drive people to a life of crime! Ha! Ha! I was getting desperate. The second act was almost over. Tosca grabbed the knife from the table, ready to murder Scarpia, who had been going to rape her. It was the pact they had made: he'd let her leave with her lover Cavaradossi and in exchange she'd give herself to him. The ink on their safe conduct out of Rome was barely dry when she seized the knife and approached him. And that's when the miracle happened. By the look of things, it was a folding knife that refused to give way at the right moment. Poor Scarpia took a knife to the stomach. Everyone thought he was acting; it wasn't until the blood dripped down onto the stage that we understood what was going on.

People stood to get a better look, began to whisper. "He's bleeding! He's going to die," a woman suddenly cried. "Quickly, a doctor!"

Men leaped up from the orchestra to come to Scarpia's aid as he lay moaning in a pool of blood. The poor soprano who played Tosca had buried her head in her hands with shame; the musicians poked their heads up from the pit to watch the drama unfold. People began to shout. That was when she dropped to the floor. Mademoiselle Jacques couldn't bear the sight of blood! She had stood up to look and fell straight back into my arms. She never knew it was me who had caught her.

The barrette was a cinch. It was in my pocket in a second. People were shouting and running about the hall. Someone had the presence of mind to close the curtain. Someone else gathered up Mademoiselle Jacques. "Let me help you, Miss." I already had what I wanted. Papa and I went home. The next morning, it was all over the newspapers and the barrette was in my secret drawer.

"I told you, Alfred. I knew you were going to traumatize her."

If Mama had known what still lay in store for me, she wouldn't have raised so much as an eyebrow.

I couldn't wait for my next singing lesson. When I got to Terese's hallway, I admired the little barrette in the sunlight, then clipped it in my hair. It was the first thing Ludwig saw when I walked into the studio. He was speechless.

"What a pretty barrette, Magda!" Terese said.

Ludwig wore a wry smile, and his eyes were filled with disbelief. After our lesson, we walked along Bülowstraße.

"How did you pull it off?"

I told him everything. I exchanged the barrette for the gold cross and the deal was sealed. He must have told his parents he'd lost the cross. I don't know what he did with the barrette. Maybe he gave it to his sister.

In February 1936, a new version of *Tosca* came to the Deutsches Opernhaus in Charlottenburg. I went to see it at least a dozen times. Three times with Ludwig, who was as intrigued as could be. It was always Papa who got me tickets. I think he did it just to annoy Mama. I can still see her feigning disinterest on her way out of the living room.

"I won't go. Puccini isn't music: it's shouting. It's not for me, thanks all the same, Alfred."

Mama had her own tastes.

Ludwig wanted the cross back. Naturally. I was going to make sure he paid top price for it.

"You'll have to serenade me."

That was my price. And that's what he did, the silly fool. It was one morning in June 1936. I'd had the cross for months. The sun was barely up when I heard Mama knocking at my door.

"Magda! Come at once!"

The living-room window was open. We could hear men grunting and exclaiming loudly. It sounded like they were moving something heavy and unwieldy. Their grunts mingled with shouts from people in our building. "What's all that ruckus at this hour? People are trying to sleep here! I'm going to file a complaint." Mama was all aflutter.

"Alfred, is it the Bolsheviks?"

Papa seemed to find the whole thing quite amusing. On the sidewalk right below our living-room window, three heavy-set men with mustaches were unloading a black, upright piano from a wood-panelled truck.

Who on earth, I wondered, still swimming in the fog of sleep, would have a piano delivered at six o'clock in the morning? The serenade had completely slipped my mind.

Then the truck left, and the three men with it. The piano was all alone on Schillerstraße, like it was waiting for a bus or something. People exchanged looks from their windows on either side of the street.

"I assure you we have nothing to do with this," Papa said, keen to make sure the neighbours understood his mission to entertain the German people only went so far. Birds sang in the linden trees. A crazy woman shouted: "There must be a bomb inside! It's gonna blow!"

"My goodness, Alfred!"

Mama was quivering with fear. But we were quickly reassured. Footsteps could be heard coming from Kaiser- Friedrich-Straße. Slow, deliberate footsteps. Everyone went quiet. From above, we could see a blonde lady making her way toward the piano. She was carrying a folding stool, which she set in front of the instrument. Then, raising her head, she looked up at us.

It was Terese, my singing teacher!

Her smile was sweet and gentle, her skin pale, like Ludwig's. Even from a distance, we could see she had long hands. With a nod to her audience, she sat down on the stool and took a score out of a bag she was carrying on her shoulder.

"Don't tell us you're going to play Schubert!" someone shouted. And that's exactly what she did.

"Alfred, it's Schubert's *Ständchen*!"

Mama still thought Papa was behind it all. It was the kind of thing he would have done. The woman played Schubert's serenade for a minute. It was the piano version, so gentle that you fall in love with it the first time you listen to it. You want to hear it a second time, just to relive its thematic repetitions, just to revisit its nuances. Do you know it? Yes? *Ach!* At last something you know, Kapriel!

The people at the windows began to laugh. A woman sang the song's first words: "*Leise flehen meine Lieder…*" in a faltering voice. Then Terese suddenly stopped playing. At the corner of Kaiser-Friedrich-Straße, exactly where Terese had appeared, stood Ludwig. Of course, I'd suspected from the very beginning that this was one of his schemes. But until the moment he appeared, I was torn between the hope of seeing him and the pain of having to part with the cross. My thoughts hadn't yet turned to what my neighbours and parents might think of the whole thing. Unconsciously, I covered the little cross with my hands, as if to protect it. So, he was prepared to go that far… He stood beside the piano. Mama recognized him.

"Magda, it's your singing teacher and her little brother. What's his name again? Joseph?"

"Ludwig, Mama. His name is Ludwig Bleibtreu."

And so Ludwig Bleibtreu sang *Ständchen*, looking up to my window from time to time. His voice echoed off the walls, rose up to the sky, filled the linden trees with fragrance, and charmed the sparrows who, I swear, Kapriel, went quiet the whole time he was singing. He delivered the second "*jedes weiche Herz*" with a vibrato that I can still hear to this day. They'd clearly been practicing. But who had agreed to deliver the piano to our doorstep so early in the morning and, more importantly, how were they planning on taking it back? He even held a flower in his hand, the silly boy! Every blind on Schillerstraße was open now. The rare drivers on Schillerstraße that morning stopped for a closer look.

Needless to say, fate had it that a journalist lived in the building opposite, a gentleman that Papa knew through KdF. The Arts section of the following day's newspaper featured a photo of Terese on the piano and Ludwig singing beside her. The writer headlined the article *"Bebend harr' ich dir entgegen,"* the words Schubert's song ends on. "Trembling, I shall await thee here." Since then, I've never been able to imagine love other than to that tune and those words. You know you're in love the moment you walk up to someone trembling, I'd think to myself. And since I associated trembling with the freezing cold, having grown up in East Prussia, I associated love, that awful feeling, with the sumptuous winters of my native land. You're the only one in Berlin who could know what I mean, Kapriel. You need to feel all the coldness of that music. I think it's a song for the cold of heart. For people like us, Kapriel. I wait for you, trembling. Words to be sung in despair, one last cry from the heart, a petition of sorts. Do you follow me? It takes someone familiar with the body's tremors, the inexplicable bumps and jolts of the nervous system, to understand Schubert. Did you know he died of syphilis? No, not Ludwig. Schubert. You did? At any rate, Mama was prostrate on the sofa, head in hands.

"Alfred, everyone's watching us. Make him stop!"

"No, no! It's too funny. We have to let him finish."

Papa was helpless with laughter. I was trembling with barely contained anger. Not because the whole street was watching us, not because everyone would sing *Ständchen* as I walked down Schillerstraße for months to come, but because I was going to have to give him back the damned cross. It was out of my hands.

A crowd gathered around the piano below. Germans are morning people, as you know. And since he sang so well, they asked him three times to start over, then he sung a little Mozart until I went down to the sidewalk, after hurriedly getting dressed, my hair still in a state, to accept the stupid red rose with my left hand, slipping the cross into his pocket with my right. That was the rule. The cross had to be handed over as soon as the test was passed. No dithering, no haggling. Just the cross. I was furious. All of Charlottenburg applauded for ten minutes or three centuries, I can't remember which. No more than three quarters of an hour after the show began, the same truck came by with the same strapping men. They loaded up the piano and left, this time with Terese and Ludwig holding on to the side of the truck with one hand and waving goodbye to their Schillerstraße audience with the other. His father no doubt punished him for requisitioning the truck for nothing more than a serenade. He probably beat him, like he did when he missed his Hitler Youth meetings. But it was too late. I'd grown fond of our little game. And if you think, Kapriel, that I'd seen it all with that piano arriving on Schillerstraße at six o'clock in the morning, you've got another think coming. I was about to perform any number of outrageous acts to get my hands on that cross. That was in the summer of 1936 in Berlin.

(At this point, Michel, she got up to go into the kitchen. I heard her turning on the taps to hide the sound of her sobbing. There was no doubt: she was in tears. Until then, I hadn't quite thought her capable of tears, but she was definitely crying. She came back to the living room with a glass of water, keeping up her pretence right through to the end.)

Things with Mama were never the same after the serenade. On the one hand, Ludwig had charmed her beyond belief, probably more than he had charmed even me. On the other hand, she disapproved of such extravagance.

"Whatever will people think of you, Magda?"

"Let them say what they want, Waldtraut…"

Papa, on the other hand, had been moved by the whole incident. For the last few days of school, the girls, who had all heard one version or other of the story, no longer eyed me scornfully. I had become someone. When a boy sings Schubert for you, that makes you someone in other people's eyes. That's why you'll never amount to anything, Kapriel. I'm joking, I'm joking!

August brought with it the Summer Olympics. Papa found a job for me as a hostess because I had a gift for languages. I welcomed foreign visitors and helped them find their way around Berlin, the venues, and Charlottenburg. I spoke French for close to a month with visitors from France and Belgium. If it hadn't been destroyed in the air raids, I'd show you a photo of me in my Bund Deutscher Mädel uniform, Kapriel. The French had all sorts of questions: "Is the regime mistreating you?" or "Are you allowed to speak to Jews?" Questions I had no answer to. No one was mistreating me. I didn't know any Jews. At least… Anyway. Of all the visitors, I think the French had the most questions. And they seemed to always know the answers already. Perhaps that's just the impression I had because I'd mostly learned French and didn't speak much English. I don't know.

I barely saw Papa that summer. KdF had tons of events to organize, entertaining people wherever possible and bringing Germans from across the Reich to the capital and people from the capital to the rest of the Reich.

I was all alone with Mama when I wasn't working for the Olympics. One morning, I found her sitting at her piano in tears. She wanted to talk to me, alone. She asked me to close the window in case the maid heard us.

"Listen, Magda. I'm exhausted. And your father has been invited to a huge party at Schwanenwerder."

"I know. At the Goebbels'. He's spoken of nothing else for a month. Tomorrow, right?"

"It's very important to him, darling. I have to go with him."

"And you don't know what to wear?"

That was when she broke down. I'd never seen her in such a state. I had to sit down beside her on the little piano stool, like I did when I was learning my scales.

"Your father loves society life, he loves everything that shines, everything that sparkles, Magda. It's a curse. And he's going around telling anyone who will listen that the Führer himself will be at this blasted party!"

"But Mama…"

"I won't go. And you're going to help me. Remember these words: women must help one another. Never count on a man!"

Mama's plan was simple: she would make herself sick to get out of the party and instead I would go with Papa. It was unthinkable that he would go alone.

"If you're old enough for someone to sing you *Ständchen*, you're old enough for dinner at the Goebbels'. But promise me you'll behave. And don't count on them showing you how to. Those people have lots of money but precious few manners. Anyway, there'll be thousands of guests: no one will even notice you."

"But Papa will never believe you're ill. He'll be angry."

"That's where you come in, darling. You'll go down to the bakery and get me a sugar pie…"

"But you're not allowed sugar! Papa said it could kill you!"

"A little piece will make me just ill enough not to have to go to this stupid party! I'd rather be sick all night than have to clink glasses with proles who think they belong to the bourgeoisie. Now do what I say or you'll never have another singing lesson again."

I was furious with her. Not because she was throwing me in at the deep end at the Goebbels', not because it hurt me that she would poison herself like that, and with my help, too, but because she'd insulted Magda Goebbels, the Minister of Propaganda's wife, a person I worshipped, like many other

German girls. Do you know her? Not personally? Poor Kapriel! She's not one of your *Wessi-Tanten*! She died in 1945. I'd keep every newspaper cutting, every photograph of her I could find. She was a kind of Nazi saint. She was everything I was supposed to become: a mother. That was it. Women were to have children. The Nazis went on about that a lot, just like your Catholic priests. To set an example, Magda Goebbels had already had three children on top of the one she had from a previous relationship: Harald, Helga, Hilde, and Helmut. The six children she had with Joseph Goebbels all had names beginning with H. H for Hitler. Do you see what they were up to, Kapriel? Onkel Adolf didn't have a wife, you see, so Magda Goebbels became the Reich's First Lady by default since she was married to the Minister of Propaganda. Eva Braun? You're joking, Kapriel. We didn't know that little Bavarian mouse was even in the picture back then. At least *I* didn't. Magda Goebbels was blonde and chic, always elegant and impeccably dressed. They say she spoke French like it was her mother tongue. The thing is, she was born in Belgium and brought up by French-speaking nuns.

I didn't understand why Mama said she had plenty of money but precious few manners. If I'd been older, I would have understood, but at sixteen I didn't see much beyond Magda Goebbels' shockingly blonde hair. To be honest, I secretly wanted to be her. She was beautiful, admired, and elegant. And no one was ever going to ask her, just to be spiteful, just to make fun of her, if she was actually a boy.

So it wasn't so much my willingness to help out Mama than my eagerness to meet Magda Goebbels that led to me accompany Papa to Schwanenwerder. The following morning I gave Mama a slice of *Streuselkuchen*, a sugary cake, her poison of choice. Then I went to meet Ludwig at the zoo. He had been severely punished for the serenade and we were only able to see each other once a week at the zoo, in the hour after my lesson.

"Will you go back to taking singing lessons?"

"If Father lets me."

And then, I don't know what came over me. I asked him what I had to do to get the cross back. He said he'd think about it. A half hour later, still on the same park bench, he set out his conditions.

"You want the cross back."

"Yes."

"What are you prepared to do?"

"I don't know. You tell me. Do you want me to sing outside your window?"

"No, I've had enough of that type of thing. It's something else I'm after."

"I'm listening, Ludwig."

"I'll exchange it for another piece of jewellery."

"I won't steal from Mama to get my hands on your cross."

Ludwig took a newspaper out of the trash. There was a photograph of Magda Goebbels in it.

"You want me to bring you back Magda Goebbels, bound hand and foot?"

"No, just this."

He pointed at the photo of my idol alongside the Führer at an award ceremony.

"You want a medal?"

"No, you idiot! I want her earrings!"

"What do you mean, you want her earrings? What am I supposed to do, just walk up to her and go, 'Oh look, a bird!' and swipe them without her noticing? Have you lost your mind?"

"That's your mission, Magda. Magda Goebbels' earrings and you can have the cross."

What a lunatic. He knew how the Reich's First Lady absolutely fascinated me. Hitler, on the other hand, always left me cold. That ridiculous Austrian accent, Kapriel! But Magda Goebbels, well, I was a little... yes, a little in love, perhaps. That settled that, at any rate. I would never see the little cross again. Ludwig would have it forever. I gazed for a long time at the earrings in the photo. Tiny pearls. How much must they have cost? A gift from Joseph Goebbels himself? Who knows? We went back to see the zebras.

By the time I got home, the *Streuselkuchen* had done its work. Mama was in bed, grey. The maid swore to Papa she hadn't seen sugar anywhere. She was a plump Potsdam girl. What was her name? Marie? No. I don't remember.

"I swear, sir. I didn't bring any with me! No cake, nothing!"

He was livid. There was no way he was going to miss the Schwanenwerder party. No way he was going by himself, at any rate. The invitation was for two.

"Magda, your mother is very ill. Would you come with me to the Goebbels' this evening? They say the Führer will be there. I can't promise he'll speak to you; there will be thousands of us. All you'll have to do is be on your best behaviour. Do you have a dress? A pretty one?"

How could I hide the fact that Mama had prepared the dress I'd be wearing before even biting into the *Streuselkuchen*? It was a purple gown, the kind of thing a vestal virgin would have worn.

"There. You look like a Greek goddess! Very *olympisch*!"

Papa was pleased. On the way to the party, he explained what I was to do, what I was not to do, what I mustn't say.

"Talk about Königsberg. People like that. And don't sing! Even if you're asked!"

Then three minutes later:

"Sing if you get the chance. People like that. But don't mention Königsberg, even if you're asked."

I'd never seen him so worked up. At Schwanenwerder, there were so many cars parked we had to walk for at least fifteen minutes. The Goebbels had made a princely home for themselves on Lake Wannsee, on a private island linked to the mainland by a little bridge.

It was no ordinary party, Kapriel! Everybody who was anybody was there—from all over Europe! We were welcomed by young women dressed in white tunics and holding torches, true to the Olympic spirit. Musicians, dancers, and entertainers were everywhere.

The Goebbels had spared no expense. You had to queue for a quarter of an hour just to be able to say hello to the hostess. Night fell around the Goebbels' mansion. All across the lake there were little butterfly-shaped lights. "Italian Night" was the theme.

We were introduced to Frau Goebbels at last. I still tremble at the memory.

"Herr Alfred Berg of Kraft durch Freude, and his daughter Magdalena."

Genuflect, Kapriel! Proffer a little hand. And you'll never ever guess, Kapriel, what Magda Goebbels said to me! *Ja!* You guessed it!

"You have a very pretty name, *Fräulein* Berg."

I thought I was going to faint. Papa clenched his teeth, which I knew meant: "Say something, you little nitwit!" But what could I possibly say to a woman I only knew from the newspapers? The guests behind us were already growing impatient. I barely had time to stammer an awkward thank you before we were shooed into the garden, where supper was to be served.

It didn't take long for the party to descend into drunken debauchery. Sheer decadence. Nothing less. I had no idea, at sixteen, what the word "decadent" meant. All I knew, looking around me at the way people were behaving, was that I wasn't cut out for a life of decadence, Kapriel! Not like you! *Ach!* Stop being so sensitive! I'm not the one the police just brought home drunk from a bar in Prenzlauer Berg! The earrings? Yes! The earrings! Magda Goebbels was wearing the very same earrings. At once a stroke of luck and misfortune. Luck, because now I knew exactly where I could get my hands on them. How else would I ever have found them in such a huge villa? Can you imagine me rifling through the drawers of the Reich's First Lady? And the misfortune being that they were in her ears. It wouldn't be easy getting up close to the ears of the First Lady of the Reich. It was far from a foregone conclusion.

By eight o'clock, the bushes around the mansion were already crawling with SS, throwing up their lunch and everything else. I can still hear the sound of their vomiting... Papa tried to distract me from the shameful scenes.

"Look, it's George II, the King of Greece."

Everybody who was anybody, I'm telling you, Kapriel! The King of Greece with his whole entourage! A tall man with a nose like... Well, let's just say that if he'd been King of Italy you could have said his nose was shaped not unlike his country. You find that funny, do you? Wait till you hear the rest! Now we could hear other sounds coming from the bushes. The hostesses dressed as vestal virgins had been dragged off by the SS men for a roll in the hay under cover of darkness. Nothing too glorious about it all, but just as Mama had predicted. Magda Goebbels was furious! I watched as she stood up and shouted at her husband, but they were too far away for me to hear what she was saying. *Ach!* I'd love to be able to tell you. What was she so furious about? That her lovely Nazi party had turned into a Roman orgy! But there's something else I should tell you: Papa hadn't been sticking to lemonade... Since he was tipsy, I was able to escape his attention for a moment or two.

What can I say about the garden? It looked a bit like a *Biergarten*, with everyone singing and drinking like there was no tomorrow. Magda Goebbels was still trying to stay on top of things. But the harder she tried to calm the guests, the more they acted like savages, and soon the entire staff was busy trying to control the drunks as they fought, smashed furniture, and pissed on the frightened hostesses. We could see the employees running outside to help their despairing mistress.

In the ensuing chaos, I walked up to the villa door and, without even stopping to consider what I was doing, went inside. There were a few famous faces, ministers, people I didn't know in the sumptuously decorated rooms. It was as though they had no idea what was going on outside. Nobody there was throwing up into the bushes; the moans of pleasure hadn't reached their ears. Most of the men were in tuxedos, there was a tray filled with glasses of champagne on a little pedestal table. I helped myself so as not to look out of place. The muffled clanging of pots and pans could be heard from the kitchens. Nobody seemed to be paying me the slightest attention; the staff had its hands full with what was going on outside.

The villa's main room was decorated ostentatiously: busts, paintings, incredibly kitsch chandeliers. Everything in black, white, and red, of course. All the swastikas you could wish for! Women had taken cover inside, away from the vulgarity of the orgy that was now in full swing in the garden. The women were stiff-lipped and sophisticated. They acted like nothing was out of the ordinary, debating the merits of Verdi and Puccini while the SS sodomized the hostesses outside. It was truly pathetic, Kapriel!

At the end of the room, a hallway led off to an office. I noticed a long pedestal table. I could hear a telephone ringing at the end of the corridor. Seconds later a manservant rushed out shouting: "*Frau Goebbels, schnell! Am Telefon!*" Since Magda Goebbels had gone outside to the garden, I had time to make my way down the hallway to the telephone that awaited her. But I was being reckless. I could have been caught in the empty hallway at any minute. I'd walked into a trap. Any second now, Magda Goebbels was going to walk right into me. I had no choice but to hide in the closet a couple of yards away and wait.

Her quick footsteps came closer. I couldn't see her, but I could hear her. She was telling someone it was a shame they couldn't make it to the party. Who was she talking to? How would I know, Kapriel? To the Führer? Surely not. She wouldn't have been so curt and, besides, I think the Führer must have been in bed by then. But I digress. She hung up, then, much to my relief, walked away from the table and back toward the clamour of the party. God knows she might have opened the closet door and found me hiding there between two coats! I waited a minute then tiptoed out of the closet. On the wooden table next to the telephone, something white shone in the light. It was one of Magda Goebbels' earrings! She must have taken it out to talk on the phone, as women often do! It was the same little pearl stud that Ludwig had pointed to in the newspaper at the zoo. I pocketed it without a second thought and quickly returned to the entrance hall. Magda Goebbels was already on her way back. She passed just behind me. I had to look composed, find a conversation to join.

"It was during the second act," one woman was saying to another, a few steps from me. "Right when she wants to kill him to get her hands on the safe conduct. The knife didn't fold, it seems, and the singer was almost killed."

I reacted instantly.

"I was there! A terrible accident. Poor Scarpia!"

Seconds later, Magda Goebbels came back out of the hallway in a panic, her hand against her left ear. I didn't see her again for the rest of the evening. Papa drove too quickly the whole way home, cursing the people who had ruined the party. I pretended to doze, clutching the little pearl in my right hand. Mama was right: Puccini was making a criminal of me. But *Tosca* was to have me do much worse still.

In September, I was reunited with Ludwig at Terese's. I hadn't been able to see him before that. His father had packed him off to Bavaria to work at his cousins'. His reaction was nothing short of churlish.

"You only have one!"

"And that's a miracle in itself!"

"But I wanted both. What am I supposed to do with one earring?"

"Don't tell me you were planning to wear them for the recital!"

"Why not? Perhaps pearls suit me."

"You're an idiot."

"I don't know, Magda. I can't very well give you half the cross. A cross comes in one piece. Otherwise it's no longer a cross."

"A deal's a deal, Ludwig."

"Mmm…"

He agreed to let me have the cross, all the same. Albeit reluctantly.

His concern was understandable. I think we were both beginning to fear the monster we'd created. What would we do next? Yank off the Führer's mustache? Both of us could see we'd gone too far. Papa would have been in serious hot water if I'd been caught red-handed at Magda Goebbels'.

We calmed down a little. In June 1938, I was eighteen. Ludwig too. We were often together, much to Papa's delight. Mama was always ill. We kept on with our singing lessons, even after our *Abitur* at the end of high school; even when everyone was certain war was set to break out. To celebrate the Austrian Anschluss, we put together a shortened version of *The Magic Flute* with Terese. I was Pamina, and Ludwig was Papageno. Terese's other students were given the other roles, with Terese herself singing the Queen of the Night's part. It was probably the happiest time of my life. Just before everything started to smell real bad. All our practicing for *The Magic Flute* meant that Ludwig and I spent virtually all our time together, so Papa ended up allowing him to stay for supper with us in the evenings. When Mama felt up to it, she would accompany our duet on the piano. *Bei Männern, welche Liebe fühlen.* It was a wonderful show! Papa even wanted us to put it on for the workers in the factories, with the financial support of Kraft durch Freude. But we were all exhausted the day after the show. I wanted to return part of my costume to Terese at her apartment on Bülowstraße. I showed up there with Ludwig only to find her packing, looking absolutely radiant.

"I'm getting married, kids!"

Just like that! She'd waited until after the show to tell us. Her parents knew, but hadn't told Ludwig. He wouldn't have been able to keep it to himself. This meant, of course, that she would no longer be teaching us, that she'd be moving in with her fiancé, a man from Posen who'd come to hear her every time she sang. We knew him from photographs. He was much older than her.

"I didn't want to upset you over nothing while you were rehearsing."

"You're leaving for Posen?"

Ludwig was sad.

"Yes, but it's only a few hours away by train. You'll come to visit with Magda."

Losing a singing teacher is a bit like finding yourself orphaned. That's barely an exaggeration. Terese was married one month later. Not much of an engagement. The couple didn't stay in Posen for long, though. Her husband soon fell ill and needed treatment he could only get in the capital. Terese came back to Berlin in 1940. She was widowed by 1944. I think it was multiple sclerosis he had, that fine husband of hers.

Papa felt sorry for us and bought Ludwig and me season's tickets to the Deutsches Opernhaus, with as many tickets as we liked at the other opera houses! What operas did we go to in the 1938-39 season? *Tosca*, at least ten times. *Madame Butterfly* six or seven times. Verdi until we could take no more! And Wagner's *Flying Dutchman* five times at least.

Ludwig and I spent the months leading up to the war at the opera. Today everyone thinks there was only Wagner playing in Berlin in the 1930s. Wrong! They couldn't be more wrong! Do you know what played most often? Do you know what people couldn't get enough off? What we lined up for? Puccini!

Then came Herr Küchenmeister. What can I say? How can I put it? It was a few weeks before the invasion of Poland. There was one word on everyone's lips: war. And what were my parents doing? Off to Norway on a *Wilhelm Gustloff* cruise! The *Wilhelm Gustloff* was a huge cruise ship the Nazis had built. It belonged to Kraft durch Freude. "Deserving" folks went on cruises to Madeira, Portugal, Italy, even to Africa! Papa had always wanted to take Mama on a cruise. As head of the *Amt für Kultur*, he only had to say the word. I was livid they'd left for Norway without me. Perhaps because they felt guilty, they had asked a couple of Papa's colleagues to look after me, as if I wasn't capable of looking after myself! It was while they were away in Norway that Ludwig came across this idiotic ad. It said:

Singing lessons for all levels
Anatomy technique
Guaranteed results after 1 lesson
Herr Küchenmeister
Berlin Mitte

It was written on a little card. Ludwig wanted us to go over right away. I was still mourning Terese and here he was looking for a new singing teacher! What do you make of the young man, Kapriel? His country is on the brink and all he can think about is vocal technique.

I had no desire to ever set eyes on this Küchenmeister fellow. Besides, his apartment was right beside Alexanderplatz. What's that? No, there was no tower back then! Poor Kapriel! It was the GDR that built the tower. No, before that, Alexanderplatz was no place for a young girl from Charlottenburg. Not so different from today, in fact!

The little devil made me take the subway to Alexanderplatz with him one Thursday in August for our first lesson with Küchenmeister.

"Come on, Maggi. Let's give it a try! He works wonders, I hear! Even singers from the Staatsoper go to him for lessons!"

"Lessons in what? It's Alexanderplatz."

"You're a snob. You disappoint me, Magda."

I was skeptical. The thing is, Kapriel, there's a category of singing teachers known as "anatomists." What does that mean? You couldn't care less? I have to explain it to you anyway. The singer's instrument is his body. His whole body. Not just the pharynx, but everything from the toes to the ears, even the asshole. Yes, you heard me, I said asshole. Tosca, when she sings, doesn't leave her legs or liver behind in the wings. Her whole body is on stage. Same goes for Scarpia and every other singer. And teachers, to get beginners to understand the mechanics of singing, to show them how to produce perfect sound, often use metaphors. Terese often did.

"You're floating in a tube, Magda! Now imagine you have a head cold and the sound has to come out just beyond your nose. There you go. Your nose is blocked! Lean into it! Clench your buttocks! As if you had to carry ten marks between your butt cheeks from here to the Bahnhof Zoo!"

See what I mean? Küchenmeister belonged to the school that doesn't believe in metaphors. No imagery. No comparisons. No poetry. Only organs. Perineum. Diaphragm. Pharynx. Stabilizer muscles. Bone resonators. Hard palate. Soft palate. Breath broken up into fractions, not measured in images and colours depending on force and output. Song is a product of the human body; the rest is gobbledygook!

So there we were at Alexanderplatz, Hirtenstraße, not too far from the Volksbühne. All very proletarian. What a contrast with the Italian night at the Goebbels'! Although some of the passersby looked as strange as Joseph Goebbels. Ludwig held my hand all the way to Herr Küchenmeister's. He lived on the fourth floor. No elevator, of course!

He was shorter than me. I'm a little on the tall side, even for a German from the north, but he was fat too, wearing a black suit with a bowtie. Nothing says "I'm a total cretin" like a bowtie, Kapriel. Never wear one! Everyone will immediately think you're a fool. His blond hair was combed over to the side, washing up in a little wave at the top of his forehead. Bulging little blue eyes. A little piggy. A little blond pig with a bowtie. He invited us in to his studio and launched right into his sales patter. Nonsense like "You're lucky I had an hour left on Thursdays! This will turn your world upside down. You won't believe your ears! My revolutionary anatomy-based approach will show your other singing teachers up for the charlatans they are! Who were you with before?"

"Terese Bleibtreu on Bülowstraße," I answered, curtly.

"Never heard of her! Tessitura?"

"Coloratura soprano. She sings the Queen of the Night."

"Where?"

"What do you mean, where?"

"Which opera house?"

"She doesn't sing at the opera. She sings with us!"

"Ah, I see. Her career's seen better days, so she's making a little money on the side taking on students. That's what they all do! I only teach. I'm in such demand that I wouldn't have time for a career even if I wanted to."

The first hour was devoted to exploring our diaphragm's shape, length, and consistency. Then he set our homework: sing five bars of a Vaccai arietta. I did it right there and then so he'd see we weren't beginners.

"*Ach!* You're trying to impress me! But you've got it all wrong, Miss Burg!"

"Berg!"

"Yes, Berg. I can hear your technique and posture problems as soon as you open your mouth. And that F! You do realize it's off key? Believe me, in a month's time I'll have untaught everything that Bleibweg woman—"

"Bleibtreu!"

"Yes, of course, Bleibtreu. You'll get used to my sense of humour. I like to laugh. One thing you'll come to learn at Küchenmeister's is that I don't go in for those silly images other singing teachers use. No pirouetting angels, no balls balancing on top of a fountain, no barrels, no 'You're as big as a Zeppelin.' No! I am an anatomist! Song is produced by the body, by the organs. Accept the body's implacable reality, its limits and promises, and you will progress. If not, you will continue to sing as you do now. I will see you both next week. Needless to say, you'll be on time."

A tenor, he said he was. What a boor! Have you ever heard the like of it! I'd just been singing Pamina in *The Magic Flute* and this crank from Mitte thought he could teach me a thing or two! Song comes from the heart, Kapriel. "*Sing was du glaubst, und glaub was du singst!*" that's what Terese would always say. Sing what you believe and believe what you sing. Never would she have boiled it all down to anatomy. Never.

I didn't say a word between Küchenmeister's apartment and Alexanderplatz Station. Ludwig must have sensed my frustration. How could he stand for this Alexanderplatz swine mocking his own sister? Why had the idiot not stood up for her? But I didn't have to worry.

Papa and Mama came home two days later. Their cruise had had to turn back. All ships were being requisitioned.

"So that's it then. He's going to have his little war!"

That's all Mama had to say on the matter. Papa was pale green. He wasn't much of a sailor.

On September 1, 1939, a huge ass rose on the German horizon. Like a star, it climbed high into a sky normally filled with pale moons, patches of fog, and the occasional harmless witch. Once it was nice and high in the sky, it began to shit, Kapriel. In your country, it snows. Well here, it shits. Brown sticky, stinking flakes of it began to fall lazily to the ground. They fell on people, on cars, on the Olympic Stadium... First across Germany, then across the rest of Europe. At the start, we managed to shovel away the shit that was falling, but soon it was up to our knees, then our waists. It shat for six years. Even today, we're still shovelling away the shit that began to fall that day. What? You thought it had been shitting for a long time before that in Germany? Yes, but it only began to stink on September 1, 1939. You know the rest. Or do I have to explain that to you, too? Not right away, anyway. Now I'm tired.

We never saw Küchenmeister again, thanks to the war. Ludwig was nineteen that September. He was called up right away. Then came the air raid drills. Just as I was about to start studying medicine. Thank you, *mein Führer!* Ludwig came back to Berlin on leave from time to time, but I had to flee in August 1940, as soon as the first bombs began to rain down on the city. Mama was terrified. She rarely left the house by 1940, but the day after the first bombardment she took me to see a house in Moabit that had been destroyed. It had almost become an attraction for Berliners, going to see the first houses destroyed by the bombs. But soon they wouldn't have to go very far for their entertainment. Soon they'd have shows of their own in their kitchens, bedrooms, and living rooms. Mama packed my bag right after the first Allied attack.

"You're not staying here. I'm sending you back to Tante Clara in Königsberg. You'll live with her and her husband Wolfgang. I've sent your father to the station for your ticket and permission to travel. No, Magda. Not another day. You know that Clara and Wolfgang have three children now and a fourth on the way. Onkel Wolfi has been sent to Poland with the Wehrmacht. Clara will need you... Good Lord, Magda, just for once could you try to act like a young lady? I... You know that Tante Clara isn't the strongest. You'll... you'll need to be patient with her. She's been very ill. My God, I wish this war was over!"

Poor Mama! And so, at the age of twenty, I went back to Königsberg. Adolf Hitler had uprooted me in 1934, only to send me back in 1940. Since Mama was becoming gloomier by the day, since Papa was virtually never at home, and since Terese and Ludwig were no longer in my life, Berlin had lost all meaning for me. I was happy to be going back to Königsberg, where there were no bombs falling from the sky. Mama didn't even come to see me off at the station.

But I'm tired now, Kapriel. Shall I tell you the rest tomorrow? Tell you what, I'll take you to Potsdam, just like I said. I'll tell you the rest in the S-Bahn and in Potsdam. You'll love Potsdam. And the end of my story deserves more inspiring surroundings than this apartment. We'll go to Potsdam. Nothing less than an imperial city for this story of madmen.

Roman Epistles

Go get fucked, Gabriel. Or rather, don't. There's a thought that should leave you sleepless for at least a couple of nights. And then, like a moose in rutting season, you'll be off hunting again in your staid, foggy city in the north. What will you take from your next victim? *The 120 Days of Sodom*? Or will you make do with her innocence, like you did with poor Stella Thanatopoulos?

I had to wash my hands I don't know how many times after reading your letters. I felt so soiled by them I even poured a little bleach into my bathwater. Everything about your letters, from the scandalous content to the awful form, would repel any right-thinking person. I was sorely tempted to burn them and spit on them with the contempt reserved for such sheer wretchedness. Because you are nothing short of wretched. Beyond a shadow of a doubt, Gabriel.

And just so you know, poor Gabriel, Anamaria and I have both lost ten kilos since last winter. As per our contracts. And once the production is over, we fully intend to reacquaint ourselves with the curves we both consider to be perfectly normal. What's the difference? We're doing it for art's sake, while you're driven by vanity and depravity. That's the difference.

I've hidden your letters and notebooks until I'm able to dispose of them someplace where no one will ever find them. The last thing I want is for Anamaria to discover them! And what would happen if Bruno-Karl d'Ambrosio ever read them! It would be enough to bring everything tumbling down. The film is dangling by a thread as it is. Things have only gotten this far thanks to Mom's boundless generosity. And Mom, I should point out, is nothing like the cold and calculating creature you depict in your letters. I hope you deeply regret all those ghastly things you said and that you plan on giving her a sincere, honest, and heartfelt apology. Or perhaps you'll find a Catholic priest in Berlin willing to listen to your confession? Speaking ill of one's mother? A clear violation of the fifth commandment, my poor Gabriel. I'm only half joking. You have a distinct lack of indulgence toward a woman who was, after all, born in 1950. She picked up her habits at the convent and there you go running her down with your smugness and self-importance. You should leave it up to the columnists in the Montreal tabloids to humiliate the Catholic mysteries and hold up science and reason to undermine the sacrament of confession. Leave what is beyond your grasp alone. You will recall, my brother, that confession was the only thing she imposed on us. Not once did she force us to go to mass. She always let us get on with our lives. All she wanted us to know, from the earliest age, was that there is a thing called evil and that, in certain circles, some people like to distinguish it from good. There existed a time when believers felt the need to draw up a list of deeds and acts that corresponded to their notion of evil and to share that list with someone. It's called pouring one's heart out. Showing a modicum of respect for traditions that mean so much to her doesn't seem to be asking a lot. Mom has her age and history as excuses. The contempt in which you hold her values says much more about you than it does about her, my brother. Think of all she's done for us. We've never had to work, Gabriel. We had an extraordinarily protected childhood. We went to the best schools, had the best music lessons. It's your problem if you turned them down. And confessions with Father Huot were never the drama you make them out to be. Even as a child, I saw them as an opportunity to take stock, to speak to someone neutral who wouldn't judge. You'll laugh but it's thanks to Father Huot that I discovered the Vétiver cologne I wear all the time. As a child, my senses never knew greater happiness than that blend of grass and woody notes in the Rosemont church confessional. For the first few years, I couldn't put a name on the fragrance. I thought it was the smell of saintliness given off by all the world's confessionals, until, that is, I realized it was coming from Father Huot. When I was seventeen, the day I first tried to seduce Anamaria, I made my way to the cosmetics counter at The Bay to track down the fragrance. Now I'm never without it; it has become my trademark. Mom disapproved at first, probably for financial reasons—you know how she likes to manage her assets!

"You're not planning on smelling like that all the time, I hope!" she said.

Such a display of vanity was, in her eyes, an unjustifiable expense. Vétiver cologne has become synonymous with me everywhere I go, proof of sorts that I was ever there. That, at least, I owe Father Huot. A man of such fine taste!

At any rate, if I am to believe half of what you say went on during your time in Toronto, many an hour awaits you in the confessional—assuming, of course, you can fit your outsized ego through the door. Do you know who you remind me of? The peacock in Ravel's *Histoires naturelles*, the farmyard fop who keeps telling everyone he's getting married. Thing is, his fiancée never shows up. But the bird doesn't lose hope and keeps on with his daily "Leooon-a" cry, bold as you please. The peacock is not at all displeased with this state of affairs since, as Renard puts it in his delightful poem, he's "so sure of his good looks, he's incapable of resentment." If the Buddhists are right, Gabriel, you might very well come back as a peacock in your next life.

Last night, Anamaria and I tried to count the number of girls we'd seen you with in Montreal, back when you still lived in Outremont. It was like counting sheep: it put us both to sleep. Poor Gabriel. We had fun coming up with a kingdom you could rule. It was an amusing game that distracted us from our exercises for a few hours.

You'd wear a plain toga, revealing the virile charms of your muscles as you strutted around your city. The women would be held back by guards. They'd come up to you and rip out their eyelashes and eyebrows as a sign of devotion. The ground having been declared too dirty to receive your saliva, you'd spit into the hands of a courtesan. Everything you touched would be set aside and burned once a year in a ritual attended by one thousand naked women. Not a single woman less. You'd be accompanied everywhere you went by forty handpicked wives, since you'd marry a consenting virgin every day. That's the kingdom Anamaria and I had fun inventing for you. Yes, we had a good laugh at your expense. Because you are grotesque and disgusting. Don't fool yourself. The proof runs through your letters, starting with the poor women you took advantage of at Lajoie. Please tell me you were joking, that you wrote that only to try and make yourself seem interesting. The episode with our Grade 6 teacher Mrs. Boulay is all the more troubling because, unless I'm mistaken, your visit to her home—I think it's fair to call it rape—dates back to the saddest time in her life. That either you don't remember, or you chose to gloss over this point, just goes to show how selfish you are.

In spite of myself, I read your account of the time you ate her bread pudding. You do realize she could have been in real trouble if you'd told anyone. Your anecdote, as touching and illuminating as it may be with regard to the origins of your life as a libertine, also sheds light on an aspect of your personality that you'd rather keep quiet about, a flaw you'd rather accuse me of than accept as your own. My poor Gabriel, you asked if Mrs. Boulay had a son. Allow me to refresh your selective memory for you. That January, when we were twelve years old and in Mrs. Boulay's Grade 6 class, her little boy, who was called Patrick, died suddenly. He'd been born with a heart defect and his days were numbered. He went to our school, but before our time. Mrs. Boulay sometimes brought him to class with her when the other teachers had had enough. That you've forgotten all about him when you can remember the colour of the stairs leading up to Mrs. Boulay's apartment in January 1982 says more about you than the pile of letters cluttering up my coffee table in Rome.

Little Patrick, on top of his heart murmur, also suffered—and I mean *suffered*—from a serious learning disability and behavioural problems too. He had to repeat a year of elementary school, which meant that he was thirteen and head and shoulders above everyone by the time he got to Grade 6, making him even harder to ignore. Are you quite sure you don't remember him? Patrick was incredibly sensitive, a real mama's boy. I can already hear you and that wicked tongue of yours trying to compare his emotional dependence to my profound and completely natural affection for Mom, a woman who, I'd like to point out to you at least once in my life, never shut you out of her heart. She took more of an interest in me; that's all there is to it. One day you'll really have to learn there's no dignity in resentment. But for Patrick it was pathological. The first day his mother dropped him off at school (and only on the school board's orders—she'd been feeding his pathology by refusing to send him to school for fear of traumatizing him) he threw a fit. He bit one of the other boys so hard he drew blood and, when the caretaker was called to bring him under control, he gave him a black eye. I think the kid ended up realizing he'd have to go to school, but only after Mrs. Boulay had begged the principal to accept him, so he'd at least have the comfort of knowing his mother was in the same building. Before she lived in Outremont, Mrs. Boulay was in Villeray, where her teacher's salary allowed her to rent a nice big apartment. At first, she'd had to send Patrick to the school closest to home, while continuing to teach in Outremont. When the principal at Lajoie refused to accept Patrick, Mrs. Boulay had moved to Outremont so that she could send her son to the school where she taught. It won't be lost on you that she lived in the cheapest part of the Outremont neighbourhood—not the Jewish part, and certainly not the most expensive part like we did—right above a laundry on Van Horne. In summer, the poor woman could never open her windows with all the noise. Ah, the things normal people are prepared to go through just to share a postal code with people like us! What was her furniture like? Did you sit down in her living room before coming back home? If Mom and Suzuki had known you were hanging about an apartment above a laundry on Van Horne, they'd have made you take your clothes off before you came into the house. They'd have burned them with gasoline, smothered you with lanolin, and scrubbed you head to toe with quick, precise, purifying movements. Admit it, impure soul that you are, you'd have let Suzuki do it twice. You don't fool me…

At any rate, the little boy eventually won and Mrs. Boulay let him go to Lajoie until Grade 6, which he spent sitting just in front of her desk. You don't remember? But wait: it gets better. Patrick would spend every recess with his mother, reunited with her at last, as though he'd thought he'd never see her again. He burst into tears at least once a day. At lunchtime, Mrs. Boulay dressed her abnormal son and took him back to their apartment for something to eat. We'd see them walking hand in hand, and the taller the boy got, the more unhealthy their relationship appeared to be. It was almost impossible, for example, to find yourself alone with Mrs. Boulay. Patrick was always around, practically standing guard. One day, the other boys in Grade 6 decided to play a trick on Patrick, who by that time was thirteen, a year older than they were. They broke into his locker, where they found a pair of women's underwear that belonged to his mother, of course. The boldest boy of the bunch took off with the matronly rose-print drawers—and flew them from the school's mast, just below the Quebec flag.

Patrick and his mom were well and truly humiliated. News spread through the grapevine so efficiently that it reached even the normally closed quarters of the kindergarten. Everyone but the principal knew. And there wasn't a thing Mrs. Boulay could do to the little hoodlums. Remember the fat French guy who used to get his kicks feeling up little girls? It was him, I seem to remember, who hoisted the underwear to the top of the flagpole under cover of darkness.

And you don't remember any of it? Or are you just setting it to one side? Well, the fact remains, my dear licentious brother who now seems to be suffering from amnesia, that the year after that sad spectacle, you and I wound up in Mrs. Boulay's class, along with some of the Underpants Gang, Fat Guillaume included. Patrick had ended up leaving Lajoie and was now at the public high school in Outremont, where he was, by all accounts, deeply unhappy. In January 1982, Patrick died suddenly at school one morning, running after one of his tormentors, who'd stolen his gloves. He knew he wasn't allowed to run, he knew he wasn't allowed to get short of breath, but he wouldn't listen. He died with his classmates looking on. It was a very cold day. The next morning, Mrs. Boulay didn't come in to teach. That was the day she was absent, the day you brought her the exams she was supposed to mark. When you walked up into her apartment, her son Patrick had been dead for a day. Poor Gabriel, you ate Patrick's pudding. Mind you, we often end up with someone else's dessert. That's just how life is.

I've tried in vain to remember a time when there was still some getting through to you, a time when you weren't completely obsessed with mirrors. Once again, Suzuki is back in the dock. Because it's all her fault. It's her pictures that made you the way you are. It was our birthday in 1981. We'd just moved into the house on Rue Davaar in Outremont. We kept finding stuff in the closets, things left behind by the previous owners, an English-speaking couple who'd moved to Ontario just before the first referendum. Mom had bought the house for a song, and I'd been stupid enough to believe Suzuki wouldn't be coming with us. Until then, I'd always kind of thought that she just worked for Mom, a tomboyish nanny who helped her open restaurants. Someone Mom would let go when we moved. Imagine my surprise to see her organizing the move, choosing colour schemes, telling the workers what to do. And why, oh why, Gabriel, did she insist on speaking in that country bumpkin accent of hers, like she was back in Rivière-du-Loup and it was still 1968? It really grated on the nerves. When she showed up at our parent-teacher meetings, I would rather have been eaten alive by fire ants than admit she was there to pick up my report card with those stubby, hairy fingers of hers. Mom at least made an effort to speak correctly, to be understood by everyone while remaining true to her roots.

We were twelve at the time. Mom was away in the Laurentians, in that home where overworked people went to convalesce. She gave everything to Mado Group Inc., you know. It's not her dedication I'm criticizing or calling into question. But every time she went away, either to open a new restaurant in some other godforsaken hole (back then, she was opening branches in New Brunswick) or to recharge her batteries after pushing herself too hard, she would leave us with Suzuki, whose very smell made me feel ill. When I think back on those mannish hands, how her voice would fall back into its working-class ways. Do you remember when she'd say hello to people? You'd have thought it was a plumber speaking. No class at all. She'd organized a little party for our twelfth birthday. A handful of friends from school were there, even Father Huot. I'm quite certain she'd never have given you that photo if Mom had been there. And you didn't see the expression on Father Huot's face when you took the picture out of the birthday card. She might have been more discreet, waited for us to be alone. But anyone who knows her knows she likes nothing more than wrecking other people's dreams. Suzuki's sly smile told me she'd set the two of us at loggerheads with no more than a photo. She was the one who pushed you away from me. And you know it.

"Your grandfather gave me the photo. The first time I went to eat at the Lamontagnes' in November 1960. That's the archbishop of Rimouski beside him."

I can still hear her telling that embarrassing story to our friends in Outremont in that lumberjack accent of hers. Some memories should stay buried. God, I can see why Mom never wanted to impose that world on us, a world she extricated herself from through sheer determination. You'll recall the hint of nostalgia she had in her voice every time she mentioned our grandfather, no doubt a manual labourer, a bit of a simpleton who did his best given the circumstances. At any rate, I think it was that particular day that the picture of our grandfather in a ridiculously tight-fitting leotard cleaved the rock of our fraternity. And you, poor boy, you were absolutely fascinated by the photo; you stared at it for days. How furious Mom was— and rightly so—when she realized Suzuki had betrayed her! I can still hear them screaming at each other in the living room.

"You just had to go and give him the photo of Papa Louis! You can be so damned thick when you want to be, Solange!"

"They need to know, Madeleine!"

"Need to know what, Solange?"

Mom flew up to her room in a rage, and Suzuki into hers. Two doors slammed. I trembled for both of us. A week later, you disappeared after school. We couldn't find you anywhere. It took Mom a month to work out why you stopped coming home for supper. You'd started going to that filthy gym. It was crawling with old Greeks and Ukrainians, stinking hairy animals that lifted weights all day. A reassuring fatherly presence. Each to his own IQ… Meanwhile *I* found peace among music teachers. Mom wanted to forbid you from going, but Suzuki stood up for you again.

"Let him go, Madeleine. It'll do him good. I spoke to the guys down at the gym. They're looking after him. They'll make sure he doesn't hurt himself. They think it's hilarious, having a young guy in there with all the old fellas! He's like their mascot or something. It's nothing more than a few harmless old men pumping iron."

That's right. Let him go, Madeleine. Let him become a brute like his grandfather. Poor Mom! She worked so hard to pull herself out of that mess, only to have her own son throw it all back in her face. It's enough to make you think Suzuki was beginning to miss the days she'd spent packed in there with her brothers and sisters, the house teeming with lice, coming down with dirty laundry, reeking of that night's broth. I hate her, Gabriel. For everything that leech did to us, and might still. She's totally nuts!

All this reminds me of an article I read in one of the Rome newspapers today. It was about an old woman in her nineties who lived not far from the Coliseum. She left her fortune to a cat she found there, at the foot of the tower where we live. It's the talk of the town. That's how I picture Suzuki forty years from now: old (viragos never die) and completely senile. It would be just like her to find a way to disinherit us and leave Mom's fortune to a cat or, more likely, a snake, her genetic cousin. So please spare me any kind words you might have for Suzuki in future letters. For me, the matter is now closed and I'm looking to the future.

Bruno-Karl d'Ambrosio will be here in fifteen minutes, Anamaria tells me. I'll write more tomorrow.

Ciao!

M.

P.S. My bass clef is about an inch below my left testicle. Does that answer your question?

Rome, October 2, 1999

Dear Gabriel,

I'm reading over the letter I wrote you yesterday. I owe you an apology. It's difficult for me to accept how little Mom and I matter to you. Yesterday's letter—so curt, so harsh—only goes to show how deeply hurt I was when you walked out of our lives. I'm enclosing it, all the same. I know you'll be able to read between the lines. Don't be angry with me. I know that I was

Mom's favourite. That's never been a secret to anyone. You know that you were Suzuki's favourite. That was an open secret, too. As for the nature of their relationship, I'm not sure they wish to dwell on it. Remember what things were like when they were growing up. They left the convent, but the convent never left them.

I've been thinking a lot about this Magda woman you've been telling me all about. Are you sure it really was a bass clef you saw? You were in a sauna, after all. The lighting's often not the best. If I could, I'd take the next flight to Berlin to have a look for myself. But I have to stay here for rehearsals. Besides, I don't think that Magda of yours would be too keen on me pulling up her skirt. Her story is very touching. It inspires me, Gabriel. A memory has just resurfaced. I have to share it with you.

We were seven years old, still living in the apartment on Saint-Hubert. We were old enough to be with Mom and Suzuki in the restaurant, but most of the time we were with the nanny Mr. Zucker had hired. One day, you came home with chickenpox. Mom insisted we sleep in the same bed, so I'd catch it too. You recovered much quicker than I did; you were back at school within days, while I was stuck at home, ill and alone. Mom and Suzuki took turns looking after me. The nanny—she lived on Avenue Christophe-Colomb, I can't remember her first name, Francine? Lorraine?—had never had chickenpox and was terrified she might catch it. Chickenpox can be fatal if you're old enough! Thank heavens Mom was smart enough to spare us that particular ordeal. Anyhow, Mom was in the living room with me. She was wearing her baby blue uniform with the little white collar and the restaurant logo on it. You know the kind: shirtwaist dresses that were beginning to fall out of fashion. I was playing on the floor with my toy cars. Mom was lying asleep on the sofa, flat on her back. Her knees were bent and her skirt had slid up over her hips, revealing her inner thigh. What would you have done? I couldn't help but notice the white rise of her panties. The little bass clef was just to the left. Exactly. The same one as I have you know where. Back then, I didn't know it was a bass clef. I thought everyone had one. Mom snored her way through my anatomy lesson. I can still recall the creamy white of her underwear, the perfectly smooth mound.

Of course, Mom wasn't the type to take her bath with us. From that moment on, I began to believe that everyone but you had the birthmark, that you weren't normal. The following day, I was still too ill to go to school. This time it was Suzuki who came upstairs to look after me. She too fell asleep on the sofa during her break, only she slept on her side, as though to better keep an eye on me. Don't ask me why, but I decided to find out if Suzuki's bass clef was on her left or her right side, genetics being a concept still as yet unknown to me. And so I went over to her. I slowly pulled her dress up as she dozed. First of all, I was surprised to discover that Suzuki's underwear was black, then disappointed to see that the way she was lying meant I couldn't see the spot where I imagined her bass clef to be. Far from delightful, her privates were slightly ovoid, like a nun's chin, an ant's ass.

My face, paying no heed to my brain, came within an inch or two of her crotch, eager to make out the slightest trace of her bass clef. That's how she found me when she opened an eye. A monumental slap. I can still feel the aftershocks today.

"What do you think you're doing, you filthy little pig?"

My head must have spun around at least three times; I fell over backward. My tears and cries barely had any effect. She didn't apologize.

"Do that again and you'll be sorry, you little pervert!"

Hysterical, she was. How can anyone hit a child? That woman is dangerous, Gabriel. It's just as well she didn't do any permanent damage, mental or physical. It took me years to realize Mom and I were the only ones to have the birthmark. She never dared raise a hand to me again. I'd have gone straight to Mom! I told myself I'd get over it sooner or later, but here I am, still consumed by bitterness, all these years later. What are we made of, dear brother, if not bitterness?

I swore I'd take that story to the grave, but I was too intrigued by what you told me. Telling Magda about my birthmark might get her to confide in you... But I don't recommend telling her you were checking it out in the sauna. She might not take it well.

I'm pleased you've found a place that suits you, despite your romantic setbacks. You seem to be enjoying Germany, a country I barely know. Its music is sublime. And you're quite right: if I'd been thinking more about you and less about myself, I would have given you some Bach or Wagner for our birthday. Something to go with your new life. Instead, I weigh you down with my Puccinian preoccupations. To answer your question, it's quite normal for Magda to have sung that piece of *Tosca* in German. The Germans performed Puccini in their own language up until the 1950s.

Yes, I'm delighted to hear you're enjoying Germany, that you've found a passion for something that doesn't involve working out a deltoid or your triceps. But must you really criticize France in every sentence? You'd think it was Suzuki talking. The worst of it is that the venom that oozes from her narrow, hateful little mind has ended up polluting your own thoughts. Nothing puts her nose more squarely out of joint than that French accent and the ways of the "old country," as she puts it. Rise above the swamplands of xenophobia, dear brother!

If there's one thing Magda's stories should have taught you, it's the dangers that come with that line of thinking. Mom never reduced herself to such pettiness. Far from it. You'll recall the number of black waitresses employed by Mado's in the 1970s. Apparently Mom asked no questions. They were hired on the spot and respected while they went about their work.

"For me, what counts is a willingness to work."

Her first commandment, you no doubt remember. Hating the French because they're French, you got that from Suzuki. That creature of the shadows. And it's in the same perfidious spirit that you suggest Mom played a hand in me getting the Cavaradossi role. You're right: Mom, or rather Mado Group Inc., funded part of D'Ambrosio's film. But she insists on remaining an anonymous sponsor, proof of the purity of her intentions. What you don't know, poor Gabriel, is that I was selected at the end of a long and drawn-out audition process. The selection committee was comprised solely of D'Ambrosio and members of the Kinopera Group, which is co-producing the film. Mom would never be so pretentious—or impertinent—as to impose her will when she knows it's not her place. As for Bruno-Karl d'Ambrosio, the man's a genius. Quebec has never known a more extraordinary creative mind. He is, as surely you must know, our finest cultural ambassador. Every play he's put on, every film he's directed, is nothing short of a masterpiece. I know he has his eccentricities, his pseudonym being first among them. Yes, his real name is Marcel Truchon and he comes from La Malbaie. But, just like Mom, he has worked to succeed; he hasn't let his humble origins condemn him to a life of insignificance in a provincial backwater. Do you know the first project he worked on? It was entirely original and completely free of charge, gaining him a following around the world. Let me explain how genius is born.

When he moved to Montreal to study at the National Theatre School in 1982, D'Ambrosio—that was already his name!—lived in a modest apartment at the end of the No. 27 bus line, at the corner of Saint-Joseph and Pie-IX. His first week of school wasn't yet behind him when, one evening, sitting on the bus home, he began reading *À la recherche du temps perdu* aloud. *"Longtemps je me suis couché de bonne heure…"* not stopping until he got off the bus. Apparently people called him every name under the sun at the start, told him to shut up. Can you imagine? Proust in east-end Montreal in the 1980s? Pearls before swine! But he persevered, and some of the swine begin to develop a taste for pearls. Journalists picked up on his initiative and began reporting from the No. 27 bus. Venise Van Veen, who did so much for Mom, was among them. Little by little, Bruno-Karl d'Ambrosio attracted an audience that was eager to hear Proust read out loud to them—and with the correct accent—with the result that the passengers who had at first resisted this incursion of culture into their daily lives came to accept it. There were even, it seems, people who'd take the 27 just to hear Proust. Now that's what I call passion! Within days, his idea was being copied all over the city. Someone began reading Voltaire on the No. 51. The city's English-speaking population, not wanting to be left behind, decided to subject passengers on the No. 144 to John Updike. People began reading on buses all over Montreal. Soon, the idea was picked up in Toronto and the United States. Just remember that I work on a daily basis with the man who started that cultural movement. He even looks like Marcel Proust. There's the same elegance, the same sophistication in how he holds his head. Bruno-Karl is one of the greats. Working under his guiding hand is a gift from heaven.

What's more, he found us an apartment fit for royalty in Rome, equal to the production's means and to our talents. I'm enclosing a photo of Anamaria and me outside Palazzo del Grillo, which D'Ambrosio rented for us for the four months we'll be in Rome. It's no doubt cozier than a socialist apartment block on the outskirts of East Berlin… The shoot should be over by mid-December. The final shots will be filmed on the ramparts of Castel Sant'Angelo, overlooking the Tiber. From our spacious two-floor apartment, Anamaria and I enjoy views of the archaeological site of the imperial forums. To the far left stand the Coliseum, then the monument to Victor Emmanuel that Romans call the "typewriter," then three eternal cupolas that fill me with inspiration: Sant'Andrea della Valle, St. Peter's Basilica, and St. Mark's. We spend our nights contemplating the lights of the city until it's time to go to bed. There is no finer spectacle. Since we have only a few days until the start of rehearsals, until we get down to "brass tacks," as D'Ambrosio likes to say, Anamaria and I went on a tour of Rome today.

My sole regret was not having you and Mom by my side. In the meantime, Anamaria and I are visiting Rome like tourists. No one recognizes us here.

Which reminds me, I simply must tell you what I saw at the Vatican Pinacoteca. You won't believe it. You'll have to come to Rome to see it with me. But hurry! I'll only be here until January! I'll pay for your ticket, if need be.

I must tell you all about the painting I mean, it's a revelation that hasn't let go of me, that has tormented me since this morning. Upon leaving Palazzo del Grillo, we immediately crossed the Tiber, away from the big squares and the bustling shopping streets. Anamaria was desperate for another glimpse of the Sistine Chapel, which she had seen as a child on a rare visit to Rome with her father. She wanted nothing more than to take me there. Even though it was October and classes had started, we still had to queue for an hour to get into the Vatican museums. But what we saw there was worth every minute of the wait in that motley crowd. Evidently, the Church has always favoured quantity... We are all equal before God and the Vatican museums. And so we were almost trampled underfoot by a group of—staggeringly vulgar—Asian pilgrims, then forced to endure the noisy chatter of the Americans in front of us. It's difficult to keep a straight face when that lot open their mouths. That American accent is like a cross between a hooting owl and a quacking duck. No class whatsoever. The whole world is waiting for the day America will finally shut its trap and take a breath.

Inside, Anamaria insisted on making a beeline for the Sistine Chapel, which she'll never tire of admiring. We agreed to meet beneath a huge green pine cone, some type of sculpture, two hours later.

The Pinacoteca doesn't get the attention it deserves compared to the rest of Vatican City. Most visitors do what Anamaria did and don't linger in a museum they deem to be of little interest. Big mistake. They remind me of those tourists at the Louvre who line up for hours, only to race off to the *Mona Lisa* as soon as they get through the doors. There, they swoon before a painting they've seen a thousand times, without paying the slightest attention to any of the other works, before returning to their hotels, utterly exhausted, to keep the bedbugs company. They've installed a replica of Michelangelo's *Pietà* at the entrance to the Pinacoteca, and visitors frustrated at being unable to get a close-up of the original can photograph it to their heart's content. There is a fascinating history behind the Pinacoteca and the works it is home to. Today's building actually dates back no further than 1932. In the 17th century, works were exhibited in the Capitoline Museums. Then, around 1795, the French occupied the Papal States, forcing Pius VI to give up hundreds of artworks and manuscripts. Bonaparte ended up looting the lot of it, bringing it back to France to fill the new Louvre. It was Pius VII who sent an emissary to France to recover the paintings Napoleon had stolen. The emissary managed to recover 249 of the 506 paintings, while the French kept 248 for themselves. What happened to the other nine, I hear you ask? It's quite simple: no one knows. They were declared lost. With time, and thanks to the generosity of the popes who succeeded Pius VII, the Pinacoteca collection continued to grow. It even boasts a Leonardo da Vinci painting of St. Jerome removing a thorn from a lion's paw. But the painting that intrigued me most—I was practically rooted to the spot—was a small piece by a painter I hadn't heard of, a certain Masolino da Panicale, who died in 1440. It's eight by twenty inches at the very most. *Death of the Virgin*, it's called. It shows the Virgin Mary lying on what appears to be a casket. She's draped in navy blue, her hands crossed over her pubis. Standing around her are the apostles and Jesus with a child in his arms. An angel stands at either end of the casket. Michael and Gabriel, no doubt about it. Each holding a long candle, I imagine, to light up the funeral scene. I asked the nun keeping watch over the room why Jesus had a child in his arms. What could the baby possibly represent? She told me it symbolized the Virgin's soul. I was fascinated by the painting, so much so that I was late getting back to meet Anamaria. Caught up in a mystery. Get this, Gabriel: At the entrance to the museum, there's a replica of Michelangelo's *Pietà*. Need I remind you that the sculpture shows the Virgin holding the dying Christ in her arms, just after he's been taken down from the cross? Barely twenty yards away, the Church offers up the same individuals in an entirely different scene: the son presiding over his mother's funeral. And they say opera's hard to follow!

My Italian is good, but not good enough to strike up a conversation with a nun over the paradoxes of religious art. The enigma continues to swirl around my head, refusing to let up. I fear I may lose sleep over it. The picture upsets me in so many ways. First off, I'd always believed the Gospels said the Virgin ascended into Heaven, body and soul, aboard some sort of virginal elevator. Am I mistaken? Isn't that the version defended by the Church? But if only that was all! I'm asked to accept that the mother buries her son, only for, twenty yards further on, the son to carry his mother to her tomb!

As I left the Pinacoteca, the scene remained imprinted on my mind, the figures sprang to life, imposing their will. It was unbearable, Gabriel! The image of that entombment struck the very core of my being, the place where I harbour my darkest fears. Does this *Death of the Virgin* not propel the two of us, Gabriel, you and me, into the future? Those angels holding a candle over the dead mother, aren't they you and me standing over Mom's grave? The painting allowed me to glimpse the scene that awaits us. I find it at once odious and unbearable. I fear I won't be able to get through it.

I know you're mad at her for all sorts of reasons, but the day will come when it is our turn to light up Madeleine Lamontagne's funeral, dear brother. The scene gave me such chills that neither the October sunshine nor Anamaria's anger at my tardiness managed to dissipate. I'm worried. The thought of it has frozen the very depths of my soul, like ten Montreal winters, like the snow you write about in your letters, like the sound of the German railway. To my mind, the thought of Mom's passing is now inseparable from a terrible, everlasting winter descending over us all.

We returned home in the late afternoon. It was only eleven o'clock in Montreal, I thought to myself. I just wanted to hear Mom's voice, wanted to hear her reassure me. She picked up, began telling me off for calling her from Rome.

"It's going to cost you a fortune!"

I didn't know how to explain the state I found myself in. The painting had left me traumatized. I think she must have heard the despair in my voice. She asked me how Anamaria was doing. And also if I'd heard from you. Your silence is causing a world of hurt.

You're right when you say I'm Mom's favourite. She opens up more easily to me. For example, the time she came back to Montreal after our twelfth birthday, we had a conversation I've never told you about, because I got the impression Mom didn't want me to mention it to you. The photograph of our grandfather with that archbishop intrigued me just as much as it did you, you know, but not in the same way. Your reaction, which was to start hitting the weights the very next week, was merely a little boy wanting to emulate his grandfather. For my part, I was curious to get to know the man. And so I asked Mom one Sunday after my breathing exercises. I didn't know how to bring it up. Since she never mentioned Rivière-du-Loup and had never taken us there, I had long suspected she had a painful past.

"What did Granddad do?"

415

"He drank gin and told stories," she replied curtly.

"But what job did he do?"

"That *was* his job, Michel. He drank and told stories. He didn't know how to do anything else."

I tried to insist, but she really didn't want to talk about it. It took a few months for her to react. I don't know why exactly; she brought it up again while she was decorating a little Christmas tree (the one we had in the dining room).

"You asked me about your grandfather last summer."

I couldn't believe it. She had a memory like an elephant. Then she told me a story. Read it carefully, Gabriel.

"Your grandfather would tell stories. He never tired of himself. He'd tell tall tales in the living room for hours at a time, for as long as the gin lasted. All you had to do was give him a glass and he'd be off. He was fond of the nuns, of Solange too. But what he loved most of all was telling stories. And stories, Michel, they're good for a while. They're good for kids, but then one day you grow up and you've got adult problems. That's what happened to me. When I was eighteen, we were dirt poor in Rivière-du-Loup, my mama had to go work at the Hotel Saint-Louis laundry. I'd sometimes help her late at night, wringing out the hundreds of sheets she had to wash. Did you know your grandfather used to beat her? I heard him throw her to the floor one night. Anyway, in December 1968 Mama lost her mind. That's what not having enough money does to you, Michel. It drives you crazy."

Then, since she'd finished decorating the little tree, she asked me to help her saw the bottom off the big tree we'd had delivered for the living room. It was usually Solange who did that kind of thing, but that day I could tell Mom was looking for a reason to keep me close by. It was a few days before Christmas.

"Your grandfather used to say that in Germany they never decorate the tree before Christmas. On the evening of the 24th, they do it up while the children are asleep, to surprise them on Christmas morning. They get them out of bed and bring them into the living room to see the tree all decorated with real candles."

"How did he know all that?"

"He was in Germany during the war. In Bavaria. Pass me the ornaments."

If I'd not been twelve, if I'd been just a few years older, I'd have poured her a gin myself to loosen her tongue, to find out more, though she almost never drinks. But amid the Christmas decorations, the tinsel, and the glittery birds, her eyes shone like those of someone who liked to drink. You should have seen her kneeling there in front of the huge tree we'd just attached to its pedestal, in among the boxes of baubles, tying the sparkling decorations to the tree and thinking back to Rivière-du-Loup.

I'm sorry I told you. Her words seemed to be directed at me alone. She picked up each decoration and admired the colours in the light before hanging it from a branch. She passed me the things she wanted on the higher branches, and I listened to her as I stood on the stepladder. I was dying to find out what our grandmother had done in December 1968; a woman we'd never seen, not even in photos.

"In December 1968, Mama decided I was to move to the city to earn a living. I had the choice between finding a job, becoming a nun, or getting married."

Getting married. I desperately wanted to ask her about our father. But such is my respect for her that I held back, for fear of offending her. I was anxious not to interrupt the tale she seemed determined to tell me.

"Mama packed me off on a bus to Quebec City with Solange. She wanted us to work in the kitchens at the Château Frontenac. She knew people there. We'd earn more than in Rivière-du-Loup. One night, I came home with Solange to find Mama all alone. She told me I'd be leaving for Quebec City the next day. Solange offered to come with me. Mama said no. I didn't want to go peel potatoes in some kitchen in Quebec City. Mama started shouting. Parents were stricter back then. They told you to do something and you did it. She sent me to bed. I knew that Papa was out drinking at the Ophir, that I'd find him there. As soon as I could hear Mama had fallen asleep on the other side of my bedroom wall, I slipped outside to go find Papa. She'd been drinking, so she didn't hear me go out."

I pictured poor Mom, not knowing where to turn, off to find her father on that freezing December night.

"I found Papa Louis at the Ophir, asleep next to his beer. There was almost nobody in the bar. Have you any idea how awkward I felt in there? I was the only woman. Word gets around a small town quickly. No need for a newspaper. I managed to wake him. I explained my problem. His eyes were lost in the distance somewhere, as if I was talking to him in a language he didn't understand."

"What did he say?"

"I'll never forget. He said: 'My poor little Madeleine, if you knew the things they did. The ones who died beneath the snow were the lucky ones, really. Dying of cold doesn't hurt, they say. You fall asleep; that's it. They packed them onto trains. For days, weeks. They died of fear on those trains.'"

"That's what he said?"

"That's what he said. Then his head fell back down onto the table. It was at that moment, dear Michel, that I realized I was all alone in this world. That all I had was Solange and my own two arms."

It was December 1968, Gabriel. She must have been pregnant with the two of us. Suzuki came in just after that. Mom went quiet. I took her silence to mean she'd just shared a big part of her secret. Never again did I ask her about Rivière-du-Loup, about our father, or about our grandfather. You know the rest of it as well as I do, which is to say you don't have the faintest idea.

Bruno-Karl came by Palazzo del Grillo just before lunch to plan rehearsals with us. A little chihuahua follows him everywhere he goes. Wotan is his name. It's rather cute, more so since D'Ambrosio is quite a short man, thin and wiry, almost always dressed in black. He's a good-looking man. Dark, brooding good looks. The dog doesn't fit with his look at all!

I'm a nervous wreck. My God, I can't believe it! I'm singing Cavaradossi's part in a Bruno-Karl d'Ambrosio film! Never has life seemed more delightful, more beautiful. I mentioned the Pinacoteca to Bruno-Karl. He knows it well. We discussed the nine paintings that Pius VII's emissary never managed to recover in France. People have made all kinds of claims about them. Some say they were accidentally destroyed or that they never existed in the first place, that the Italians inflated the number of paintings that Bonaparte took, to try and get more out of the French. Not bad, as tactics go. Most experts agree that the nine paintings were stolen, plain and simple, either by the soldiers or perhaps even by noblemen, and that they're somewhere in Europe, in some third-rate castle in Spain or Germany. Bruno-Karl is very familiar with this particular depiction of the *Death of the Virgin*. There are, he says, other versions in Padua in the form of altarpiece sculptures. The scene is relatively rare since the Church eventually decided to stop going on about Mary's body decomposing. And guess what? Apparently there's even a depiction of Mary's entombment by Giotto di Bondone in Berlin! But he couldn't tell me which museum. Why don't you ask that Brünnhilde of yours? She could take you there in her Zeppelin!

Bruno-Karl has hired a Brazilian man to guard the apartment block. A man of few words who spends his nights outside the door to make sure no one gets in. We're safe here. Tomorrow, they told us, our holiday is over and it's time for the real work to begin. I'm ready. Let the stars shine!

M.

～⁀〜

Rome, October 4, 1999

Dear Gabriel,

Art does like to take its time. The production has just suffered a major setback. Fortunately, Bruno-Karl was equal to it! I knew something of the sort would happen. This morning, we were all set to meet the German baritone who was supposed to play Scarpia. A guy by the name of Mathias Kroll. You've surely heard of him. He's just come off a remarkable performance of *Werther* in Berlin, at Unter den Linden, if I'm not mistaken. A bit of a dandy. And get this: the gentleman is having artistic differences with Bruno-Karl d'Ambrosio! Does the fool realize he might never play a part like this again? It's none other than the RAI National Symphony Orchestra accompanying us! Judging by what Bruno-Karl told us, Kroll was having none of his stagecraft. Who does he think he is? Since D'Ambrosio had the inspired idea of setting *Tosca* in German-occupied Rome in 1944, Scarpia is supposed to wear a swastika on his arm during filming. He refused and went home to Munich. Can you imagine? Scarpia as a Nazi. It stands to reason, right? It's certainly a bold move, but clearly Kroll doesn't realize he's dealing with one of the most avant-garde creative minds of our time. Venise Van Veen said it herself: "What D'Ambrosio puts on stage today sets the trend for tomorrow." There's not a singer alive who isn't insanely jealous of the lucky few who got to shine in his production of *Macbeth* in Zurich. Yet another stroke of genius there: Lord and Lady Macbeth as dictators. In Act I, Lady Macbeth sings before three thousand pairs of shoes, a clear and brilliant nod to Ferdinand and Imelda Marcos. The rest of the production was equally inspired, with the greatest voices a director can only dream of. And in the theatre, he's just wowed San Francisco with *Romeo and Juliet* set in a Japanese internment camp. No one has ever willingly ended their contract for a Bruno-Karl d'Ambrosio production. I can't get over that Kroll's arrogance.

419

It hurts all the more since Kroll is *the* Scarpia of his generation, as it were. He must have sung the role one hundred and fifty times between Berlin and Rome. And he's the perfect build: he would have made an excellent SS officer. Bruno-Karl, who is now insisting that Anamaria and I call him Bruno, did his best to reassure us. He has more than one trick up his sleeve. As soon as news of Kroll's departure started to spread, Bruno's telephone began ringing. Agents offering him their protégés' services. I have no doubt that Bruno will find a worthy replacement.

And what about you? Still drinking white wine with German pensioners in subsidized housing blocks? Still taking the subway?

Bruno was calm throughout. There's simply nothing to all those rumours about his mood swings, his quick temper, or the tyrannical hand he wields over each production. I've never met a creative talent who's so level headed, down to earth, or more approachable. He reminds me a little of Mom.

He also took the opportunity, since we're getting to know each other, to tell us a little more about that dreadful scandal that erupted last winter in Montreal. You were still living in Toronto, but it's absolutely impossible the news didn't make it that far! He was even defending himself to CNN, the poor man. There's no denying it: you have to watch every word you say in this politically correct age of ours! It happened last January, you'll recall. Auditions for the role of Tosca were underway in New York City when a local radio station asked to interview him. A marvellous opportunity to lay the groundwork for the film coming out in a city every bit enamoured with opera as Vienna or Berlin can be. When the presenter, a cheerful guy not overly concerned with ethics, began the interview, Bruno-Karl was under the impression it was a pre-interview, or so he thought his research assistant had told him. And so there he was on the phone with this guy from New York radio in what he took to be a preparatory discussion, not the interview itself. He didn't even know he was being recorded. The presenter began by talking about the great American Toscas: Leontyne Price and Shirley Verrett, who were both black. They discussed the legendary 1965 season, when Rudolf Bing, then general manager at the Met, had seven Toscas back to back in the same season: Maria Callas, Renata Tebaldi, Leonie Rysanek, Birgit Nilsson, Dorothy Kirsten, Leontyne Price, Régine Crespin. Just imagine! They would each perform twice. A marketer's dream! There were people, it seems, who queued for three days and three nights for standing-room-only tickets to see Callas! Can you imagine?

Then the presenter asked which was his favourite of all the recordings, to which Bruno replied—and I can only nod in agreement—that in terms of voice, the greatest Tosca ever was Montserrat Caballé, the Catalan singer. Anamaria would no doubt have chosen Renata Tebaldi, but we weren't the ones being asked. The discussion then took a dangerous turn when the presenter asked the following question: "Mr. D'Ambrosio, based on the abilities of the various Toscas we've just mentioned, how would you create the ideal Tosca?" Plain sailing until that point, Gabriel. And Bruno did fine. He knows what he's talking about, believe me!

"I must say I find the idea of a single mythical Tosca, of constructing a singer as one would choose the toppings for a pizza, most entertaining! It is my belief that the perfect Tosca would have Montserrat Caballé's vocal prowess, Maria Callas's gift for tragedy, Leontyne Price's deep luminous tones, Leonie Rysanek's power, and the sensuality of a Lisa della Casa."

Isn't that a wonderful answer, Gabriel! But Bruno is one of those great minds who often thinks out loud. Nothing would ever have happened, if he'd stopped there. Since I know the man behind the words over which so much ink has been spilled, I will repeat those exact words with you here because everything you have heard is no doubt false. There are bound to have been errors of translation, exaggerations... His precise words were:

"For my film I'm not looking for a Tosca who contains all these qualities together, but rather a woman the audience will fall in love with, just as Cavaradossi falls in love."

"And what do you mean by that?" the presenter asked.

"I mean that, first and foremost, she must be beautiful, sensual, attractive."

"Which is to say that how she looks is more important than how she sounds?"

"I'm prepared to compromise, if need be. Filmmaking, like opera, is the art of visual seduction. You catch more flies with honey than with vinegar. My Tosca would have to be a slim, beautiful woman. No one's going to fall in love with a fat cow!"

There was, it seems, a long silence, followed by a few questions about how the auditions were going. The interview was broadcast that very same afternoon! Since Bruno isn't as well known in New York as in Montreal, no one picked up on his comments. It should also be said that he was speaking to WNYC, a public radio station that has a somewhat limited following. But some people's ears pricked up! You know, Gabriel, some terrible things are said in newsrooms and behind the scenes at the theatre or the opera, and they're never revealed. But in this case it was Bruno, and, obviously, we always want to see the mighty fall, that's how Quebec is! A two-bit place driven by envy and resentment! And I'd like to point out, Gabriel—because, knowing you, you're doubtless judging him as we speak—you didn't treat your little Stella any better! Is that the first stone you're about to cast? A thousand dollars to help you get over your guilty conscience, dear brother? That's your price?

A few hours later, Bruno's words reached Venise Van Veen's ears in Montreal, which led to her kicking up a royal fuss, as you know. I've always been a big admirer of Venise's, especially since it's partly thanks to her that Mom's restaurants have been so successful, but let's just say that in certain areas, she can sometimes be lacking in judgment. Ever since the incident I've only been able to take her in small doses. The story was all it took to bring her back out of retirement. She was the one who gave Bruno-Karl the third degree on the news.

"Mr. D'Ambrosio, today you are joining me on my show in the most unfortunate circumstances. Just to remind viewers of the facts, in an interview you gave to WNYC Radio, you said you hoped to find a singer to play Tosca in your new film, *A Century with Tosca*, who was not, and I quote: 'a fat cow.' As you can well imagine, your insulting comments have caused no amount of distress to the women of Quebec, Canada, and indeed the entire world. Since I know you and have been a fan of your scenography for many years, this evening I would like to give you the opportunity to explain yourself, Monsieur D'Ambrosio…"

She'd always called him Bruno-Karl up until that point. Even on air. He'd already apologized to the former presenter of *Call Me Venise* (now he refers to it as *See Venise and Die*). You have to admit he has a sense of humour! He told Anamaria and I he actually contemplated suicide when he returned to Montreal the following day. The poor man! Crucified for having dared to say out loud what so many were thinking to themselves! And his words were misinterpreted! He wasn't pointing the finger at full-figured women with elegant curves, like Anamaria. No, he was talking about the ones who are absolutely enormous—who could crush Scarpia between their thighs! The whole thing is a tempest in a teacup. And the auditions were to prove Bruno innocent of the accusations brought against him! It was Anamaria and I that he chose. Shapely Anamaria with her voluptuous curves! And

I, no beanpole, a man who has always remained faithful to the picture of the little boy who appears on the packaging of Mado's frozen meat pies. You see, Gabriel, opera is all about the music. All that stuff you say about going on a diet before I get on stage, all that comes from your obsession with appearance. Bodybuilding is also a form of anorexia, you know. Did you ever consider that? What you're advocating for opera singers is nothing short of esthetical fascism. Bruno was caught out by an underhanded line of questioning. You have no excuse. Perhaps the time has come for a little soul searching... I refer you back to that photograph, the poisoned gift from your dear Suzuki. That is the source of your ills. You need to rid yourself of it, dear brother.

Needless to say, the Quebec media were all over the story. D'Ambrosio the Sexist! D'Ambrosio the Barbarian! D'Ambrosio the Wretch! D'Ambrosio the Holocaust Denier! D'Ambrosio the Murderer! Whatever! Bruno-Karl d'Ambrosio is quite simply Canada's most brilliant director and filmmaker in decades—that's what the public just doesn't get! And they didn't stop there! Soon rumours were swirling about Bruno's sexual orientation. It's true there's no wife or girlfriend in the picture, but what does that prove? Not a thing! You've been single for I don't know how long, and half the women in Toronto could vouch for your heterosexuality, if your letters are to be believed! I'd like to silence the rumormongers by pointing out he's never been seen with a lover or boyfriend either. Rumours are given more credence when they happen to concern a man of D'Ambrosio's standing. Envy is an illness and its first symptom is calumny. Never forget that.

I'm quite certain that Bruno is being besieged by hordes of agents as I write these lines, each vying for him to sign up their baritone to take the place of the treacherous Kroll. Anamaria has been playing with Wotan all evening. Such a cute little dog! I think once we're back in Montreal I'll find her a little chihuahua or another little pet... But are we ready to have children, Gabriel? Anamaria and I, I mean. Not you. You're still a child. Children should never have children of their own.

I'll be back in touch soon.

Your brother,

Michel

Rome, October 9, 1999

Wonderful news, Gabriel! Kroll's replacement has been found! We have our Scarpia! Bruno told us this morning. We didn't expect any less from him. He seemed satisfied. You'll never guess who it is! Although, of course, you need to know the opera scene to understand. It's the Polish baritone Mariusz Golub. A big strapping man like you! The directors always find a way to have him take off his shirt at the end of the act. That way, they're sure the audience will come back after the intermission. He's just finished Bizet's *Les Pêcheurs de perles*, which he spent buck naked virtually the whole time. And I won't even mention the *Don Giovanni* production in Augsburg, in the purest *Regietheater* style imaginable, where he wore nothing but a pair of tight fluorescent underpants for all of Act III. Bruno is a big fan of this type of production that pushes art to extremes. He says, and here I really must agree, that the public needs to be shaken out of its set ways and habits. His words are music to my ears. Do you know how many fusty old productions I've had to subject myself to for *The Magic Flute* alone? I won't deny I shone in some of them—Santa Fe and Des Moines spring to mind—but there comes a time when a genius needs to swoop in and shake the music scene out of its torpor! Too bad for the old fuddy-duddies who might be outraged at seeing a swastika on Scarpia's arm!

Golub will be in Rome tomorrow morning. The filming schedule will have be reworked. All his scenes will be done first, five weeks from now. Filming is to officially begin November 21. Six weeks and it will all be over, in time to launch the film in the spring.

I'll keep you posted,
Michel

⁓

Rome, October 10, 1999

My dear brother,
Phew! What a day! Bruno had pledged to make some changes as of this morning and he was true to his word! He arrived at our apartment around eight o'clock, along with Wotan, to explain how the rest of the day was to proceed. We were expecting to be taken to the church, Sant'Andrea della

Valle, which we can see from our apartment block, in order to go through the *mise en place*. Instead, Bruno arrived carrying a set of bathroom scales. We've become so comfortable in each other's company that he just comes on in; no need to knock, just like one of the family. He asked us to weigh ourselves, then wrote down our weights on a big piece of cardboard he put up on the wall. I'm ninety-five kilos; Anamaria is seventy-five.

"There you have it, dear friends. Our goal is to bring Michel down to eighty and you, Anamaria, to sixty before shooting starts in six weeks. I think it's possible if you put your minds to it. You won't be left to your own devices. I have a personal trainer and dietician to help. They'll be here shortly."

We pointed out that we'd already shed a few kilos before leaving Montreal, but he insisted. He takes such good care of us. A real father. The individuals he was referring to arrived a few minutes later, carrying weights and two elliptical machines. The trainer is a Suzuki type woman with an Olympic medal from Lillehammer in the luge. The dietician emptied the cupboards and presented us with a menu for the day. It can't have been more than a thousand calories. Anyone who's overweight dreams of just this, Gabriel: someone coming into their home and showing them exactly what needs to be done, stepping in to stop them being so spineless. Anamaria was a little reluctant. She wasn't sure she wanted to lose any weight. But Bruno is so convincing.

"My entire concept for the film revolves around a victim-executioner relationship that borders on sadism. Your attitude, your appearance, your every movement must scream deprivation and withdrawal. Your curves will prevent the public from believing in your suffering. Catharsis will be impossible. Don't forget the camera adds five kilos! I'm concerned with reality! It's authenticity I need!"

"But the truly great Toscas were never just skin and bone," Anamaria tried to protest. "I—"

"Enough! Anamaria, you have to believe in my vision. Do you believe? Yes or no?"

"Yes, of course, Bruno. It's just—"

"Well, prove it then! As things stand, you're too big to fit the space I've reserved for you in my tableau."

You really must see the determination in the man's eyes when he sets out his ideas, Gabriel. You *want* to believe him! You want to follow him! I had a word with Anamaria to get her to stop tormenting poor Bruno-

Karl. Sometimes when she gets an idea into her head, she can be like a spoiled child. I think Haitian mothers overindulge their children, at least at the table in any case. Anamaria was allowed to eat whatever she wanted at home, whenever she wanted. It's a big change for her. For me, too, but I intend on living up to Bruno-Karl's production. Eventually, she realized this was our golden opportunity.

Bruno left around nine o'clock. He's juggling a number of projects, including stage direction for a French rock singer's show. He's not going to make his fortune with *A Century with Tosca*! He has to accept the bread-and-butter contracts too. Apparently he's in talks with Cirque de la Lune. They're looking to set up shop somewhere in Italy on a permanent basis. Perhaps in Milano. The kind of thing they can't manage in Quebec. The trainer stayed until noon. Forty-five minutes on the elliptical and an hour of weights. By the time she left, I could have gnawed Anamaria's arm off I was so hungry. We had a hard time concentrating on our voice exercises this afternoon. But we'll just have to get used to it. This evening, we rehearsed a few scenes with the pianist Bruno found for us. A very patient man with a permanent smile.

I'm off to bed. All this exercise has me exhausted.

Michel

Rome, October 11, 1999

Dear Gabriel,

We could barely get out of bed this morning. How do you do it? Every muscle in my body aches terribly. Bruno woke us at eight; otherwise we'd have slept until noon. A good thing he's here.

The trainer came back at nine o'clock. It was hard to start exercising again, but if that's what it takes. And once we were into it, we couldn't feel a thing. Endorphins, isn't it? It will hurt less tomorrow. Anamaria isn't saying much. She seems to have courageously accepted her fate. It would be a shame to let all those years of singing lessons go to waste over a simple esthetic detail. She can see that now. My brave little Anamaria. I am as much in love with her today as the very first day we met.

Do you remember that day in 1980? It was winter. On the advice of the music teacher at school, Mom had found me a vocal coach of my own.

Madame Lenoir on Rue Saint-Dominique. How could I ever forget her? You never forget a singing teacher. You ask such idiotic questions, Gabriel! May I remind you that Mom would have paid for your lessons, too, but you dismissed her out of hand, just like you disregarded every other sign of her affection. You preferred debasing yourself, chasing after a ball with those idiots at the sports centre. That Saturday morning when Mom brought me to Madame Lenoir's for the first time... I'll remember it till my dying day. She lived in one of those red-bricked houses in Villeray, on the ground floor. We walked right on in without knocking. There were a bunch of green leather armchairs lining the long hallway. Mom put a finger to her lips so I wouldn't interrupt the lesson that was going on in the studio. I was a little apprehensive. Madame Lenoir had a portrait of Maria Callas on the wall and, on a corkboard, a postcard featuring a quote from the great diva: "An opera begins long before the curtain goes up and ends long after it has come down." Words that were to become gospel for Anamaria and I. We sat. In the studio, Madame Lenoir was giving instructions to someone we couldn't see. I can still remember what she said: "Sing as though you have a cold, Anamaria. The sound must travel beyond the nose as though you had a cold. I'll play the intro and you pick it up..."

And then the miracle happened.

She sang Scarlatti's *Se florindo è fedele*. You could already hear the velvet in the timbre that would have her win all those auditions and competitions. At once strong and fragile, sombre and full of light, Anamaria's voice brought Mom and I back to a preverbal time when words didn't get in the way of the senses. How else can I describe it? Even Mom's jaw dropped in surprise. She who is normally so completely in control of herself. It was the end of Anamaria's lesson and the beginning of our love affair. I already knew that voice would haunt me for days to come. I knew that, for the rest of my life, I would do anything to hear it once again. The studio door had not yet opened to reveal her face to me, but I already knew we were meant to be together. We heard footsteps. Madame Lenoir opened the door and out came Anamaria. She was twelve, the same age as us. Big eyes, warm and deep like her voice. Mom liked her immediately.

"You sing so well! I held my breath for the whole song!"

Good old Mom called it a "song"! Anamaria introduced herself. She said she knew Mom's restaurants. The following week, I arrived well ahead of time to hear much more of her singing.

"You know, Michel, as long as you're here five minutes before the lesson, that's plenty," Madame Lenoir would tell me.

It didn't take long for her to notice my interest in her young student. Anamaria was still a little shy, until Madame Lenoir, who always called us "my little darlings," one day suggested we sing Rossini's cat duet. That was when we really got to know each other. Meowing at each other. Then my voice broke and I had to wait a year until I saw my fair Anamaria again. One year of waiting as a teenager is like ten years of waiting in adulthood. I went back to Madame Lenoir and Anamaria was still there. She'd grown. She lived on Querbes in Outremont, just her, her brother, and her mother. She didn't come from a family of musicians either. Her father, an Italian, had left her mother when she was very young. He went back home. They rarely saw him. She would spend the odd vacation over there with her brother and would each time come back disappointed. Her father lived in a small town south of Rome and everyone stared at her because of the colour of her skin. Everywhere she went, they looked at her like she was from another planet. Then news from the father dried up and he stopped sending money. Anamaria's mother had to work like crazy. The singing lessons were a luxury the family could ill afford, and when she was fifteen her mother regretfully announced that she'd have to give up the thing she loved most of all, the only thing that made her smile. Imagine my dismay. Not only was I going to lose the only friend I had in the world besides my brother, she would also be condemned to a life without music, all over the stupid business of money. You didn't know this Gabriel, but it was Mom who paid for Anamaria's music lessons from the time she was fifteen. Even the one-on-ones and the masterclasses with the top American singers at $200 an hour—that was Mom, too. She always insisted I never mention it; she didn't want Anamaria's mother to feel uncomfortable. I'm telling you this so you might see your mother's true colours at last.

But it's getting late. I think I'm even more exhausted than yesterday, and Anamaria wants to go for a stroll before bedtime. God knows where she gets the energy from! There's no stopping her! Maybe the psychologists are right, after all: we all end up marrying our mothers!

Michel

꩜

My dear Gabriel,

For four days now, Anamaria and I have been subjected to a training regimen that many would find unbearable. But our motivation knows no bounds! It must be said that we're cheating a little, due to Anamaria's fondness for food, what else? In the evenings, when the pianist, the director, the personal trainer, the dietician, and the whole battery of people taking care of us have all left us in peace, sometimes we'll slip out to walk the streets of Monti, one of Rome's historic neighbourhoods. It's teeming with *trattorias*, *gelaterias*, and *pasticcerias* that Anamaria drags me off to, ravenous after all that sport. We have a *carbonara* or a *tiramusu* and *fior di latte* ice cream, then we return to our apartment in silence. With the intense workouts we're doing, I can't imagine these little treats make the slightest difference. Once on our way back from Anamaria's favourite ice cream parlour, we stopped at the foot of Palazzo del Grillo to watch the swifts flit across the Rome skies. Sitting outside a little restaurant in the square, a priest stole a glance at us. For a second, I was tempted to walk up to him and ask him to marry us there and then, as the swifts flew above us, in the splendour of the Rome evening.

We've been learning about the details of the filming in dribs and drabs. We met Golub. He's staying someplace else in Rome, not with us. We'll be starting with scenes from Act II in Palazzo Farnese, from what I've heard. But nothing to worry my head about before late November. I think I'll go lie down. I can barely think straight. I need to go to the post office to mail these letters tomorrow. Keep in touch and don't do anything stupid. Claudia didn't deserve you anyway. What are your plans for Christmas?

Your brother,
Michel

The Königsberg Zebra

Grotesque and disgusting? Why, thank you. Coming from you, that's a compliment. I do try my best.

Your letters arrived last week. Five months to get back to me—you took your time! I was worried, honestly. And there was nothing in them that reassured me. I find everything you say about the whole production completely exasperating. If ever I get my hands on that D'Ambrosio of ill omen, his Proustian moustache had better watch out. I saw his photo in the *Berliner Tageszeitung* when Kroll walked out in October. Apparently he let Kroll rip up his contract under one condition: that he would never reveal his reasons for leaving. Although that's no more than idle speculation, naturally. Kroll, it seems, is using his unplanned holiday to spend some time with his daughters at his chalet in the Bavarian Alps. There were photos of them too. In among the fir trees. Very touching. That's what you're after, isn't it, Michel? Photos of you in the tabloids with the children you'll have with Anamaria? That's sure to sell Mado's frozen meat pies by the thousand. But who am I to poke fun at your dreams, grotesque libertine that I am?

When are you coming to Berlin? My travel budget is somewhat limited. But what till you hear this: I found a job. Or rather the job found me... The sports centre where I work out, the SEZ, asked me if I'd like to be a trainer there. The pay's not great, but I get to meet people. It's helping me get over Claudia. I'll spare you the hoops I had to jump through to get a work permit. Let's just say I'm not sure which I'd rather endure... German bureaucracy or circumcision without anaesthetic.

You really shouldn't get so worked up about Suzuki, you know. I've told you before: she meant you no harm. I was her favourite, that's all. Every parent—yes, I think of her as my mother—has a favourite, especially those who deny it. And the opposite is also true: children have their favourites too, the ones they want to die last! With no father in the picture, let's just say I prefer Suzuki to Mom. I think she's worth more than a father. And you're wrong about that photo of our grandfather. Sure, I found it fascinating, but it was the context more than anything that interested me. Do you know a lot of men who had their photo taken in a leotard alongside the archbishop of Rimouski in the 1950s? I so wish I'd known him! And I think that you, well, both of us really, we've never seen Mom's childhood in Rivière-du-Loup for what it really was. Judging by what you wrote in your letters, you'd think it was something out of Charles Dickens or *The Little Match Girl*. And you wonder why I despise Mom so much? My God! I'm not short of reasons! Let's just say I share the unions' concerns about her. She exploits her employees, she takes on girls who otherwise wouldn't find a job, then has them work like crazy in her restaurants. Didn't you see the documentary? *Waitressing Hell*. Did you know she has them take a vow of cleanliness before she hires them? Has anyone ever told you that? Or about how she greases the politicians' palms to get around zoning by-laws, or the vertical integration that ensures she has absolute control over everything and everyone, from farm to fork.

And people lap it up. A flagship. A national treasure. Just like your D'Ambrosio.

I never told you, but just before I left for Germany I decided to take a trip to Rivière-du-Loup. It was Christmas 1998. Just to see. Because Suzuki had told me I should go one day, and since I had no intention—and still don't—of returning to Canada, I thought it might be the last chance to see where my ancestors were buried. I didn't tell you because I didn't want Mom to find out. It's none of her business. Now you can go running off and tell her everything, just like you've always done. None of that matters anymore. I called Suzuki from Toronto before I left. She didn't want to tell me too much, confirming what I've known to be true all along: she lives in fear of Mom. She was a bit offended, too. I hadn't spoken to her in years.

"What do you want to go there for?"

She didn't want to tell me where our grandmother lived or where our grandparents were buried or where I could talk to people who'd known Papa Louis. Before hanging up, all she told me was that there was a way of the cross worth seeing in one of the churches in Rivière-du-Loup. That even she could still picture it, though she's not one for details.

"But I don't think you'll find a trace of your grandfather. They're all dead anyway, Gabriel. And your mom wouldn't be happy. But if you insist, I can't really stop you. If you go, you have to see the stations of the cross in the church. Take a good look at the figures. Let me know what you think."

It's strange. She was the one who gave me that photo of Grandpa after all. She must have thought she'd gone too far. But I had something else in mind. Mom's right when she says that news travels fast in a small town. And you were right to think she must have been pregnant with us in December 1968. I figured there must have been someone left who remembered her in Rivière-du-Loup. Someone who could tell me more about our father, a man we know nothing about. If you'd mentioned it earlier, I could have dropped by the Ophir. Maybe someone there might have remembered Louis Lamontagne, but it's too late now. I hadn't intended to tell you about the trip, but since you're perfectly fine with running down Rivière-du-Loup without ever setting foot there, let me set you straight. It's a perfectly charming town.

I took the train to Montreal and there I borrowed Chantal Villeneuve's car. Our old teacher at Brébeuf made me feel as welcome as ever.

"By all means, Gabriel. Just keep your paws off my books!"

She's starting to know me. Her car has a stick shift, which didn't make things easy for me in Rivière-du-Loup, where the whole town is built on a slope! You can't stop or you'll never get going again! I stall it every time! Getting there is easy. You drive east along Highway 20 for five hours, then take the Rivière-du-Loup exit onto Rue Lafontaine. It's pretty in all that snow. I'd booked a room at a motel just off the highway, near a place they call the Point. That's where the ferry leaves from, the one that goes to the north shore. It was early afternoon, a Saturday. I watched the ferry break through the ice of the frozen St. Lawrence in the winter sunshine. It skirted Île aux Lièvres, then disappeared. I stayed in the car on the wharf until sunset. Everything turned orange and pink: the houses, the people, the trees. For a moment, my skin was the colour of a clementine. Then the cold came crashing down onto the town. Through the ice you could see that the water was green, the green of lies, Michel. And the sky contained more stars than either Montreal or Toronto. I had chicken for supper and slept in the calm of the deserted motel. The next day was December 27, I think. It was a Sunday in any case, and I got up fairly early. There was a Mado's outside the motel, complete with the egg. Her again! I felt like I was being spied on.

I set out to explore the town's churches. I walked, since I was scared I'd stall the car at the traffic lights. At the foot of the slope, three church steeples glistened in the sunshine, like fingers pointing up to God. The first steeple was at the bottom of Rue Lafontaine. It was Saint-Patrice. OK, OK, I'm well aware you have the domes of Rome at your feet and that you're

435

not going to get excited about a few miserable colonial chapels, but I found the whole thing very moving. More than your visits to St. Peter's in Rome. It's in these humble buildings in our little towns that the humility of the earliest churches is to be found. Not where you are, believe me. Mass was about to begin at Saint-Patrice. I watched the people discreetly. Of course, they looked at me out of the corner of their eye; I'm on the tall side and not from around there. Unfortunately, the way of the cross was nothing to write home about. The same pictures churned out by an assembly line, without the slightest trace of originality. They did what was asked of them and nothing more. I didn't stay for mass. I planned on visiting the three churches while they were open.

After that, I went back up Rue Lafontaine. There were pretty little stores all decked out for Christmas. A florist's in particular. Moisan, I think it was called. It was strange. I felt as though I knew where to go. By the time I reached the top of the hill, my hands and ears were freezing. The wind in Rivière-du-Loup would cut you in two! I wasn't sure which of the churches to inspect next. I decided to go left. To cross the river the town is named after, almost completely covered in ice. Outside the church, I saw I was now in the parish of Saint-Ludger. Mass had already started, so when I walked in, the people sitting in the eight or nine pews at the back all turned around to see who'd interrupted their prayers. They looked me up and down then turned their attention back to the priest, who was droning on in a nasal voice. Only one of the women kept on staring. She looked me right in the eye. She was a plain woman, fifty-five, maybe sixty. She kept looking around every ten seconds to check I was still there. I almost wanted to laugh. Me being there really seemed to amuse her. The collection was taken and a basket was thrust under everyone's nose. When the basket reached her, she acted as though it didn't exist and pretended to be praying. The man holding the basket waved it under her nose three times as if to say, "Come on, it's collection time!" But the woman didn't budge and the man moved on. I felt sorry for him and gave him two dollars, almost feeling obliged to make up for my new admirer's stinginess.

Alas, the way of the cross wasn't worth the visit to Saint-Ludger either. It was just as run-of-the-mill as Saint-Patrice's. I walked up to every station while the people around me wished each other Happy Holidays. The penny-pincher was waiting for me outside. I jumped when I saw her. She remained impassive. She introduced herself. Annette Caron. Ring any bells,

Michel? She didn't give the merest hint of a smile. "I suppose you think you're very funny," she added. Then she was gone. Talk about manners! I watched her go; she lives by the church. I wasn't even dressed strangely. I'd no idea what she meant.

I hurried over to the last church, Saint-François-Xavier. The patron saint of tourism! By this point I was chilled to the bone. Mass was over. There was only a handful of women talking to the priest. I was disappointed for a third time: the way of the cross was nothing more than a series of deathly dull holy pictures. Gloomy, depressing, conventional. Nothing more. Even Mary Magdalene seemed bored by the crucifixion. The women who had been talking to the priest whispered to each other as they passed me. I'm sure I heard them laugh. I caught the priest just before he disappeared off into the sacristy and said hello to him. He turned around and shook my hand. His eyes lit up when I mentioned the stations of the cross that was worth a look.

"You must mean the stations of the cross of 1968! The one the parish had painted. Ah! What a to-do!"

Apparently the parish of Saint-François-Xavier had their way of the cross painted by a professional in 1968. They say it cost a fortune, with every parishioner chipping in.

"A man by the name of Chevalier. No! Lecavalier! Yes, that's it! And can you believe it was the local undertaker who paid for nearly the whole thing! Rossignol, my predecessor, could have told you more, but he's very old now. He doesn't say much these days. I don't think you'd get anything out of him. The Sisters of the Child Jesus would know more. According to Father Rossignol, the pictures were unveiled at the convent. They'd be happy to tell you more, I'm sure. The convent is opposite the hospital, on Rue Saint-Henri."

The church was broken into in 1975, he told me. The pictures were never recovered. It reminds me of your story of the paintings that were stolen from the Vatican Pinacoteca. Where are they now? What were they of? We'll never know. I mentioned it to Magda and she promised to take me to the Gemäldegalerie at Potsdamer Platz to see this *Death of the Virgin*. She knows the painting; it hasn't been there long. It used to be in a museum in Dahlem, in the West. Anyway, the priest showed me out since he was off to get something to eat. As I walked over to the convent, he drove by in an old American car, a Buick or something similar, lighting up a cigarette. He waved at me.

The convent, Michel, is a long yellow-brick building overlooking the town. The nuns have a wonderful view as the sun sets over the Charlevoix mountains. A nun who was getting on in years came to the door. At least I'm guessing she was fairly old since she took a little while to react to my request. I'd come from Toronto, I said, and was wanting to find out about the way of the cross from 1968. She looked like she'd just seen a ghost. She didn't even ask my name! She practically ran out of the parlour. I could hear her footsteps hurrying down the hallway. She was wearing those beige shoes that only a nun would ever wear. With a wooden heel and most probably orthopedic soles. They all wore shoes like that. She was back two minutes later, holding a really, really, really, really old nun by the hand, a nun with a nose as long as a day without bread. She stopped dead in her tracks when she saw me.

"There you are at last! Come in, come in!"

She led me into a living room filled with leather armchairs. There were white poinsettias on a table. The first nun left us alone. On her way out, she asked if she should let the laundry know. That wouldn't be necessary, said the nun with the long nose, she'd take care of it herself. She introduced herself as Sister Mary of the Eucharist.

"You kept your religious name?"

"Yes, me and my sister, Sister Saint Joan of Arc. We're the only ones. The others all went back to their lay clothes and the names they were baptized with. I'm so happy to see you. You have no idea."

It was strange: she wasn't smiling. Rather, she looked like someone who's been told her pregnancy test is positive. The nun who had let me in must have shared the news of my arrival, because from time to time another nun would come down the hallway, glancing curiously in my direction. Sometimes they walked past two at a time! Sister Mary of the Eucharist grew tired of their little game and closed the door.

"They're curious. I knew you'd come one day. You took your time."

"Do you know me?"

"Of course I do! You're Gabriel Lamontagne, son of Madeleine, who's the daughter of Louis, who was the son of Louis-Benjamin, who was Madeleine's son!"

"I know. Suzuki, uh... Solange told me a little about them."

"Ah! Solange... I knew it would come from her. Ah! Lovely little Solange..."

She buried her face in her hands. I felt bad. I got the impression my arrival had upset their peaceful world. I was sorry I'd gotten that far. She told me lots of stuff about Mom, and about Suzuki too. We must have talked for a good hour. Well, she did most of the talking. Naturally enough, she knew all about Mom's business success, she'd seen you on TV. She was very proud of it all.

"You know, Gabriel, you and your brother are like grandsons to us. Tell him he needs to calm himself. You can hear the anxiety in his voice. When he sings you can tell he's afraid. It's as though he's being chased by someone or something. Can you suggest that he seek peace in prayer? There's nothing on this earth he has to fear other than God. Once he understands that, he will fear no man."

I'm telling you this so you don't think I'm making it all up. She really said that! Those exact words, Michel. You see, Madame Lenoir told you the same thing. You can hear the fear in your voice. Even the nuns in Rivière-du-Loup can tell! She held my hand while she spoke. My God, she had a lot to say! And Granddad had an undertaking business. Not bad, eh? He paid for the stations of the cross that was stolen in 1975. And the Caron woman I'd seen earlier that day in Saint-Ludger, well she was one of our cousins! Grandma's name was Irene Caron! She died in the 1980s, in the house where Mom was born. Other people live there now. I didn't dare go. Apparently after Grandpa Louis died, she shut herself away in the house, all alone. Her brothers and sisters rarely visited her. And you have the nerve to ask why I hate that other crazy woman? She stole my grandma from me! I wish I'd known her! And she would have liked that too, I'm sure. Anyway, they say our grandma didn't change a single piece of furniture after Louis died. Even the caskets stayed in the basement. One day, in 1995, she did her hair, put on her makeup and best clothes, like she was going out. She went down into the basement, lay down in one of the caskets, and died in peace, clutching a set of rosary beads. She wasn't found for days, but it was winter and she'd turned off the heat and the lights. She was frozen stiff, blue from the cold. The nuns let Mom and Solange know and they didn't tell us a fucking thing!

Oh, Michel, I've so much to tell you. She told me so much. His name was Louis Lamontagne, and his mother was American! Madeleine, she was called. And her grandmother too! Then the old nun went off for a few minutes and came back with a pile of old photos. She rummaged through them for a long time. Just as she was about to give up, she stopped and shouted: "Here it is!"

You won't believe it. It was a photograph of the Saint-Jean-Baptiste parade in 1948. Grandpa was pulling a float behind him, with little St. John the Baptist and his lamb perched on top. The float had broken away from the harness, the nun explained. Grandpa was just home from the war, still dressed in his G.I. uniform. He pulled the cart all the way to the top of what looks to me like Rue Lafontaine. Just so you know, Michel. They didn't call him The Horse for nothing. I know you're dying to hear the rest. I'll tell you what I know when you come to Berlin. Hurry up and be done with that monster D'Ambrosio and we can talk face to face. Come in January, come with Anamaria! You can stay with Magda. You can sleep on her sofa bed! She can't wait to meet you.

There was another photo of a nun who looked exactly like her. Can nature really screw everything up not once but twice? One face like Sister Mary of the Eucharist's is something, but two! It was her twin, Sister Saint Joan of Arc, also known as Sister Mary of Nagasaki, who was killed by the atomic bomb in 1945. She's standing in the photo, in front of a tree in full bloom, beside a little white Japanese house. I couldn't tell you if she was smiling or if her face was always contorted like that. Sister Mary of the Eucharist asked if I wanted a copy of the photo. It's a very touching picture, especially when you know it was taken no more than two months before the bomb exploded over Nagasaki. I didn't know any Quebecers had died in the bombing. They were all Sisters of the Child Jesus who were on a mission over there.

"I kept all the photos when your grandmother died. Would you like them, Gabriel?"

I'll have to show you the album.

After a time, silence fell over the parlour. The nun was tired.

"I would invite you to eat with us, but our encounter has left me quite exhausted. I really must rest. If you would pass by the cemetery to lay flowers on your grandfather's grave, that would soothe my soul, Gabriel."

She walked me to the door. Before we said goodbye, she asked me when I'd be leaving for the old country. How did she know I was getting ready to go to Germany? Not only did she know all about the past, it was as if she could see the future too! Then she wanted to know—and it seemed important to her—if Mom still had her little gold cross. I told her I'd never seen her without it. She seemed very pleased, practically relieved. I'd almost left the convent when I heard someone inside shouting my name. It was another nun, holding an old Polaroid camera.

"Don't move, Gabriel! Smile!"

Carrying the shoebox full of photos the nun had given me under one arm, I picked up a wreath at Moisan the florist's. The cemetery was just behind the hospital, the gravestones sticking out of the snow like the black notes on a piano. I found them all together at one end. Grandpa, Madeleine the American (it was even written on the tombstone that she was American!), Grandma Irene Caron, our uncles Luc and Marc. Marc died only a year before we were born. I even found Louis-Benjamin Lamontagne's grave just outside the cemetery. He was born in 1900—the same year Tosca was first performed!—and died in 1919. There was no grave belonging to Madeleine Lamontagne, Grandpa's grandmother. It must have been her who raised him, since his own mother, the American, died in 1918. Logic would have it that she'd be buried alongside her husband, just like every other wife back then, but I didn't find her. Strange. And I was too cold to keep looking: the sun was setting over the frozen St. Lawrence. There was just one thing I regretted: that you weren't there. We could have gone looking for the grave together!

I walked back to the motel. I had a boiling-hot bath and my thoughts turned to the road ahead the next day. The weather forecast was bad. The road back to the highway was flat, thank God. I'll really have to practice with the stick shift if I want to drive in Germany. If you gave me a VW right now, I could drive it. But I wouldn't be able to start it on a hill. Shameful, I know! But it will be a while until I can afford a car with the salary I'm on. I'll keep taking the S-Bahn!

I'll write more tomorrow. I have to go to bed now. I'm working early.

G.

P.S. Did you know what Louis Lamontagne had engraved on his headstone? *"Jesu, Joy of Man's Desiring."*

Berlin, November 9, 1999

Dear Michel,

Time goes by like a thief in the night. I haven't had time to write until today. Yesterday I saw the painting you were telling me about, *Death of the Virgin*. Magda agreed to go with me to the Gemäldegalerie at Potsdamer

Platz, even if she was very unpleasant while we were there. Funny, but unpleasant. She makes a scene every time we're in what used to be the western part of the city. People must think she's my grandmother. I take one arm, while she holds her cane with the other. As soon as she hears people from the West, she starts mumbling things like "Numbskull!" She nearly had us thrown out of the museum before we got to see *Death of the Virgin*. We were in front of another painting, a Venus by Cranach. You know the type: pale and almost see-through, so they look like they're drowned. If Magda hadn't been such a complete and utter cow, I would have forgotten the artist's name and remembered nothing more than the pretty girls he painted. Two other women were admiring the Venus at the same time as us. They mustn't have read the little metal plate and seemed to be under the impression it was by someone else.

"It's a Cranach!" Magda barked.

"Oh, are you sure?" the lady replied.

"It's right there in front of you! Written in black and white!"

I should have shut her up.

"You're right, madam. It is indeed by Cranach. Why didn't I see that right away?"

"Because you're an idiot. Anyone can see that."

I swear the two women would have rammed her cane down her throat if I hadn't been there. They went off to complain to the security guard, who didn't want to get involved, good Ossi that he was. Magda seemed delighted she had shocked them. Before we left the museum, she bumped into them again on the way out of the washroom. "I apologize for earlier," she told them. "I said you were stupid. If I'd known it was true, I wouldn't have said it." Sometimes she can go too far. She can't stand Bavarians, she told me. I hadn't even noticed they had an accent.

"But it's so obvious! Open your ears, Kapriel! Austrians, Bavarians, all those Catholics from the south speak the same strange dialect!"

Magda can be a little hard on her compatriots. The Giotto di Bondone you were telling me about was at the far end of the museum. It's a little different to how you described it. First of all, the Virgin Mary's head is leaning to the left, not to the right. Does it matter? Her legs are covered in a pink sort of sheet. At the end of what looks like a bed—I know it's her tomb!—there's a man wearing a purple toga thing. He's leaning over her, as if he's crying. Another man with a beard is laying her down onto the bed.

All around there are dozens of people with, in the centre, Jesus holding a little baby in swaddling clothes. There are angels at either end of the bed. Magda and I stood looking at the picture, Michel, but honestly we didn't feel the same anxiety you did. Magda actually found it reassuring.

"She doesn't die alone. There are dozens of people around her, even her son. I don't see why it frightens your brother, Kapriel. He must be an anxious man."

I didn't dare tell her she was right. She'd be only too happy to die like that, she said, with two angels by her feet. Magda said you should come to Berlin when she dies. That way, we can hold candles to light her deathbed. Magda can be a little morbid. Insolent and morbid. As for Mom's death keeping you up at night, I must confess I don't share your concerns. God always calls the gentlest souls unto him. So we can't rule out Mom living until she's a hundred.

To be honest, when I sent you my letters from Potsdam, I'd been hoping Magda would tell me the rest of what happened in Königsberg. Nothing. Not another word.

"I just wanted to console you with the story about Ludwig. Because of your *Wessi-Tante*. The rest is of no interest."

"Why would the story about Ludwig make me feel any better?"

"I don't know. It might help you understand."

"Understand what?"

"That everyone has had their heart broken. Even me."

That's a load of nonsense, Michel. But I think I know. I need to get her drinking if I want her to talk. Preferably German white wine. I'll have to pick the right moment. In the meantime, Magda's become—how should I put this? You'll laugh!—well, pretty much my best friend! I'm quite fond of the old fool. She always lets you know exactly what she's thinking! She's taken me under her wing. After the museum, we went to eat back at her place. It's too cold for the *Biergarten* now. She made her Broiler Special: a barbecued chicken she buys from the Turk at the end of the street for fourteen marks. We each pay half, like a couple of teenagers! Magda wants me to mend my ways.

"Your reading material, Kapriel? It's all books you've taken from girls, right?"

"Uh, yeah. Apart from a few that people gave me or that I had to read for school."

"So your choice has been limited to your lovers' tastes, right?"

"I've had a lot of lovers."

"All the same. It's a kind of rape."

That hurt. I've never had a woman without her consent. Ever. But to hear Magda, every book we read becomes part of us, an open drawer to our conscience. Every time I steal a book from one of my lovers, I take a little piece of them, of their being. That's a bit of a stretch, if you ask me. She told me something I've known for a long time: I should just ask if I can take a book. Most of them would happily give me one. But you see, Michel, that would mean they'd probably give me their favourite book, and it might bore me to tears. I told her this.

"How would you know? You've never done it, Kapriel."

Maybe Magda's right. My reading habits tend to take a tortuous path; I only have a few seconds to swipe a book while the girl is in the bathroom. The following afternoon, I came back from the sports centre to find a book outside my door with a note from Magda: "Tired of all this rain. Away to visit friends in Magdeburg for a few days. Here's a book from an author who was born in Königsberg. Don't think I'm flirting with you, you little pervert. Since it's probably too difficult for you to read in German, I found you a translation. Hope you enjoy it. Magda."

The book's called *Origins of Totalitarianism*, by Hannah Arendt. Ever heard of it? It's enormous! Looks like philosophy... yuck! But I'll take a look this evening, since Magda gave it to me.

Gabriel

⁓

Berlin, November 20, 1999

Dear Michel,

I tried and tried to read the book Magda left for me. It's a lost cause. I keep having to put it down. It's as dull as could be. All that's managed to stick with me is this sentence from the back cover:

"What totalitarian rule needs to guide the behaviour of its subjects is a preparation to fit each of them equally well for the role of executioner and the role of victim."

I don't get it. I like it better when Magda tells me her stories. I miss her.

At the SEZ, the sports centre where I work, I've become friends with the guy who does the books. He told me that privacy laws are very strict in Germany. In other words, I wouldn't be allowed, as a private citizen, to inquire about the address of someone else living in Germany, whether I know them or not. Although a company would be able to. I immediately thought of surprising Magda. I haven't mentioned it to her, but I've got Bernd—that's the guy's name—trying to track down Terese and Ludwig Bleibtreu. Do you remember them? Provided they're not dead and are living in Germany somewhere, Bernd'll be able to get their address. It will come as such a surprise to Magda! Maybe in time for her birthday on January 30! She'll be eighty. Bernd sent off the information request yesterday. If Magda's remembering things right, Terese would be ninety-two today. Do you think singing teachers live to a ripe old age?

Gabriel

⁓

Berlin, November 23, 1999

Dear Michel,

Magda is back from Magdeburg at last. I was starting to worry. I even went downstairs to ask Hilde about her. She told me not to worry, that Magda regularly disappears to see friends she has all over the former GDR. When she's not in Magdeburg, she's in Leipzig.

"With people like her."

I don't know what she meant by that. At any rate, Magda came straight up to let me know she was back. She wants me to come over tomorrow night for a glass of white wine. I didn't mention I was trying to track the Bleibtreus down. Bernd has found four Terese Bleibtreus in Germany. He gave me their addresses and made me promise never to tell anyone he'd given me them. He could get into trouble. So keep this to yourself. I took out my grammar books and my dictionaries to send off a letter to the four strangers. One of them might be the one. To encourage them to reply, I enclosed a photo of me and Magda that a Swedish tourist had been kind enough to take in front of the rose garden at Sanssouci Palace in Potsdam. No doubt she'll recognize her. I know what you're thinking, and that's fine with me. I'm looking for an answer. Here's what I wrote in German:

Dear Madam,

My name is Gabriel Lamontagne. I am writing to you today because you might be the person I'm looking for. I have been living in Berlin-Lichtenberg for one year and have become friends with a nice woman by the name of Magdalena Berg. She was born in Königsberg in 1920 and spent part of her youth in Berlin-Charlottenburg. Perhaps you might be a friend she has told me about. I would like to prepare a surprise for her eightieth birthday on January 30. If you recognize the woman I'm talking about and happen to be Ludwig Bleibtreu's sister, I would be so grateful if you could reply to me as quickly as possible so that I can organize her birthday. I'm enclosing a recent photo of me with Magda in Potsdam, along with a stamped addressed envelope you can use to reply. If you are not the Terese Bleibtreu I'm looking for, please be kind enough to reply anyway. That way, I'll be able to rule you out.

Yours truly,

Gabriel Lamontagne

Do you think it might work? The German must be full of mistakes, but they'll get the gist of it. I'll put all the letters in the mail tomorrow. I would have at least liked to know how old each Terese was, but there's not much I can do. I think there's a good chance. Perhaps she can tell me what happened to Ludwig, if he's dead already or no longer in Germany. I can just picture Magda's face! She could give her back the little cross she must still have lying around somewhere. My Terese Bleibtreus are scattered all across Germany. There's one in Berlin-Tempelhof (she's probably the one I'm looking for), one in the Münster area, a third in Stralsund, and a fourth in deepest Bavaria, practically in Austria. I can't wait!

Write back to me. I haven't heard from you in a while. I miss your insults, you big fat lump! Give Anamaria a kiss from me!

Gabriel

P. S. This will be my first Christmas in Germany. Down but not out. Still keeping a hold of myself.

Dear Michel,

Ooph! I'll spare you. Or rather, I'll tell you. Everything. Since you want to know. I've just finished writing down everything Magda was able to tell me. My eyes are killing me.

I'm sure you're both well. I heard back from my Terese Bleibtreus! What a disappointment. The one in Berlin-Tempelhof got back to me straight away!

Dear Gabriel,

Unfortunately, I'm not the Terese Bleibtreu you're looking for. I was born in Hamburg in 1966 and don't know any Magdalena Bergs, nor do I recognize the lady in the photograph. I find your efforts very moving. You must be a sensitive man. Feel free to get in touch if you'd like to go out one night in Berlin. I work at the Freie Universität in Dahlem and am single. I'm enclosing a recent photo of me on a trip to Paris. I'd be happy to get to know you. Are you from France?

Terese

A pretty girl. It's funny. The photo was of her standing in front of Notre-Dame, wearing red pumps that must have been brutal to walk around in. I think I'll call her in January when I have more time. I got another reply from Stralsund:

Dear Sir,

I am happy and a little curious to reply to the request you sent to my late wife Terese Bleibtreu. Unfortunately, she left us two years ago now, after a long illness. I very much doubt Terese was the person you are looking for. She spent her whole life in Stralsund and rarely visited Berlin. Moreover, Terese had two older sisters and no brothers. If ever you're passing through our pretty little town, feel free to drop me a line. I'd be delighted to show you around.

Sincerely,

Günther Bleibtreu

I'm not holding out much hope, as you can tell. But I'm not giving up. I'm warning you now. The rest of Magda's story is likely to leave you in tears.

I know she wouldn't want me to tell anyone, but once she's no longer around, people should know what she went through. I think it's important. More important than my little heartbreaks, at any rate. Pulling oneself together takes such a long time, dear brother! I still think of Claudia all the time. The future looms ahead of me like a gaping black hole. Thank God I have work to take my mind off things.

Send me a Christmas card at least!

Gabriel

Magdalena Berg's Second Notebook

And what about the Hannah Arendt book? What did you make of it, Kapriel? Do you agree or not? I don't know. How can you say whether everyone was victim or executioner? How can you tell them apart? There was a time when everyone was both victim and executioner. And what does she mean by "fit for the role of"? Able to become or willing to become? There's a difference.

I thought of you a lot when I was in Magdeburg. I found the time in the countryside to set a few things straight in my head. I had to remember the details, ask many questions of people who had a better memory than I of those years. Anyway. I must've already told the story of what happened in Berlin a hundred times. But never a word about Königsberg. And not because I wasn't asked! Last year, before you came, the television people wanted to make another documentary. As if there aren't enough already. They contact me every time. And every time I say no. Not because I'm shy, you know that. But because I find those people ask the wrong questions. It's always: "What did you do when you heard the artillery fire for the first time?" What idiots! I ran, like everyone! I didn't hang around to get a better look! It's as if talking about it, from one German to another, is not allowed. Don't ask me why. It's as though we've all agreed that we deserved everything we got. And then there are those imbeciles, the skinheads, who look to the stories and demand this or that, who see justification in the suffering, a way of saying that Onkel Adolf was right in the end.

Because you are, for all intents and purposes, ignorant. No, be quiet, calm down. Sit. You are ignorant, Kapriel. It's not an insult, I'm simply stating a fact. You know nothing. I know you well enough to be able to see that. Since you're unbiased when it comes to East Prussia, I can tell my story without you rushing to conclusions. So, since you insist… let me tell you the story about the Königsberg zebra.

You know, Kapriel, travelling one hundred kilometres in 1940 felt like travelling five hundred kilometres today. That's what I thought to myself on the way back from Magdeburg the other day. The world is simply smaller now. I took the train back to Königsberg in the summer of 1940. I was twenty.

Tante Clara didn't meet me at the station. She was too ill. Instead, there was a Polish man by the name of Marion, a servant or, should I say, a slave, at Tante Clara's. Back then, Poles were divided into three or four classes, I'm no longer sure, depending on whether or not they had German ancestry. In East Prussia, many people had some degree of Slavic blood. Marion belonged to the category of Poles we were allowed to talk to, to sit at the table with. He knew a little German. Back then, Kapriel, you needed only to order a Pole and you'd get one. To them, working in a house like Tante Clara's was a much nicer option than being sent to a labour camp, having to work in a factory, or being deported. In Königsberg, they had enough to eat and somewhere warm to sleep. Don't repeat this, but I think he was—how should I put this?—privileged. Yes, that's how it was.

It's funny, Kapriel. In my memories as a little girl, Königsberg was nothing but a theatre, a zoo, and the garden outside our house. As well as the beach at Cranz and the Curonian Lagoon. But the rest of it, which is to say Königsberg's impressive splendour, I'd completely forgotten about. I'd forgotten the castle, the red-brick cathedral, the city's seven gates, the bridges, the stores, the noisy fish merchants, the gigantic railway station, the little lakes dropped down like pearls right into the city itself. I couldn't remember the *Nordbahnhof* at all; no doubt it was built when I was off in Berlin. Since the *Hauptbahnhof* is right on the city's southern edge and my aunt lived in the north of the city, we drove all the way across town. Marion didn't say a word. He must have been my age. Tante Clara lived on Mozartstraße—yes, I know, it just had to be Mozart! I'd never seen it before. It was close to the zoo. She'd gotten married in 1934 to Wolfgang, that turd I was about to meet. Before that, Mama's sister had worked in a school. Up until 1932. I knew she'd fallen very ill, but I had no idea just how badly.

"Frau Hinz is doing better than yesterday."

That's all Marion said.

"What do you mean, better than yesterday?"

"Her fever's down."

Fever at the height of summer? Marion was a young man of few words. He always wore the little black P against a yellow diamond. I never could get used to it. I'd never met any Poles in the capital. And here I was being picked up by a man from the nation we were at war with. I couldn't get my head around it, Kapriel.

We passed by the zoo, then the house came into view. Wolfgang had money, more than I would ever have believed. Mama had said he was rich; and a good thing too for Tante Clara, given her "condition." Here was I thinking she'd meant music teachers weren't well paid. How wrong I was! I hadn't known what I was in for! If Mama had warned me, perhaps I'd have preferred the air raids to East Prussia—so peaceful, so far from the war.

What else can I say about my first impressions? That I felt I'd returned at last to the Promised Land. Tante Clara's house was enormous, a bourgeois villa with a garden and a barn to keep a horse in. There was even a small vegetable garden. She and Wolfgang had servants. Apart from Marion, there was an old East Prussian woman, Frau Meisel, who cooked, and a girl who did the housework, washing, and cleaning.

"You're lucky. Master isn't in."

That's what Marion said when we got there. I'd never met my uncle Wolfgang. All I knew about him was that he worked in the same building as Erich Koch, the *Gauleiter* for East Prussia. What does that mean, you ask? The Nazis divided the Reich up into *Gaue*. Things are no longer that way, of course. The *Gauleiter* were like mini Hitlers. Erich Koch was our mini Hitler for East Prussia. He must have been very efficient indeed because there were swastikas everywhere. The Hitler salute was also more common in Königsberg than Berlin. Of course, looking back now, everyone likes to say that. Say what? That there were more Nazis per square metre in East Prussia than anywhere else in the Reich. Which isn't untrue. But to hear the Bavarians talk... Yes, yes, I know, Kapriel. I'll leave them be...

The cleaning lady—the *Dienstmädchen* we called her—was also from Poland. Anja was her name. Like Marion, she wore a black P on a yellow background every time she left the house, which only happened when she went to do the shopping. Shy. Efficient. Kept a low profile. You couldn't get a word out of her. At any rate, with all the work she had to do... She and Marion would sometimes mumble to each other in Polish, or perhaps it was Masurian, a dialect spoken in East Prussia, I'm not sure. Occasionally I'd catch them in the garden or in the kitchen, talking quietly in their slippery, warbling language. They'd stop talking as soon as they saw me, or switch to German mid-sentence. I realized why the day after I arrived.

Anja showed me my room. It was late. I slept a little while, then went downstairs to look around the grand house. Wonders everywhere! Paintings, the finest furniture, gilded crockery, and even, on the ground floor, a music room with a piano. Tante Clara had been a music teacher, after all! A score from one of Schubert's *Impromptus* lay open. I don't know which one, but one of Schubert's nostalgic, monotonous pieces. What's that you say? All of Schubert is nostalgic and monotonous? No, some of his pieces are romantic and maudlin. And sometimes, all that at once. The sun was setting. A new scene awaited me in the dining room. Three young children were standing beside the table set for dinner. As I came in, the oldest, a little boy, politely said hello. Hans. The second was a little girl: Hannelore. The third could barely stand, and was clinging to his older brother.

"His name is Heinrich," said Hans, helping the little boy into a high chair. A place had been set for me and for another as-yet-unseen guest.

"Madam is on her way," Anja murmured.

Anja was doing her best to spoon-feed little Heinrich, but he kept spitting up his purée. The other two ate more or less on their own. I had to cut Hannelore's fish for her.

"Are you the cousin from Berlin?"

Little Hans, I was about to discover, was a real chatterbox.

"Yes, I just arrived from Charlottenburg. But I'm from here, like you."

I was almost in tears as I listened to the children speak with their Prussian accents. Imagine, Kapriel, that you were cloned at age six, frozen solid, then introduced to your unsuspecting self fourteen years later. That's what it felt like.

The children spoke the way I used to before I left East Prussia, with the same accent, the accent I'd had before Berlin, the same one I'd heard at the station when I got off the train. These children were *me*, I thought to myself. Then Tante Clara came in. She fell into my arms without saying a word. How can I best describe her? White blouse, green skirt, low heels. Do you know the Swedish rock group BABA? No, wait… ABBA? That's the one! Picture the singer. No, the blonde one. With the bangs. That's what Tante Clara looked like. Very Scandinavian. You prefer the brunette? Who cares, Kapriel! She apologized for being late. Anja disappeared off into the kitchen and Tante Clara took over feeding Heinrich.

"My, how you've changed. I'm so glad you're here. You will be a great help, especially with my fevers. Wolfgang is in Poland most of the time. I'm all alone with the three children, but they're sweet, you'll see. And look (she pointed to her belly), this one will be here in time for Christmas."

"Why do all their names begin with H?"

She stopped what she was doing. She set down the spoon, still full of purée, grabbed me by the wrists, and looked me straight in the eye.

"What a strange question, Magda. From you of all people—you've just come from the capital! I'm following Magda Goebbels' example! Her children all have names beginning with H, too. H for Hitler!"

Magda Goebbels. So she admired her, just like I did. I didn't dare tell her about the earring, in case she thought badly of me or flat out didn't believe me.

"I met her during the Olympic Games, thanks to Papa!"

She almost fainted.

"You... I mean... She spoke to you?"

"Yes. She shook my hand and said I had a pretty name."

"Which hand?"

"Uh, the right hand, of course. I didn't give her my left!"

She stared at my hand like a nun contemplating a piece of the actual cross.

"How lucky you are... Wolfgang has promised, when I get better, to take me to Berlin soon. Once the child is born. Tell me about her! What's the house like? The garden at Schwanenwerder? And her children? Did you meet little Helga? I want to know *everything*! Tell me, Magda!"

I told her all about the Schwanenwerder party, leaving out the earring incident, of course. I also didn't mention the people in the bushes who were... Well, you remember, don't you, Kapriel? She listened to me with wide eyes that reminded me of Mama's. But there was something unsteady about her gaze. You know, like the people who rave in the street that the end of the world is nigh? That St. Michael is getting ready to weigh our souls? Her eyes were like that. After supper, she put the children to bed.

"How about a little music, Magda?"

Mama had told her I sang. She took out a collection of Schubert pieces, and we began singing the *Lieder* that I knew. Even *Ständchen*. She played the piano beautifully and caught me every time I stumbled. She smiled at me after each piece.

"I think the two of us are going to get along famously, Magda. I'm almost happy we're at war. Otherwise, God knows if I would ever have seen you again! You sing so beautifully! Waldtraut told me you sing *The Flute*? Is that so?"

I was almost happy too. Tante Clara was sweetness personified. Like Mama, before she'd fallen ill. We sang until midnight... or *I* sang, at least. Her voice wasn't especially good. But we could have held recitals together, she played the piano so well. At midnight, she closed the piano without warning and went up to bed without saying a word. I did the same. I was a little in love, of course. As much as you can be in love with your aunt. You're smiling? Before I fell asleep, I remember thanking Churchill for bombing Berlin! The shame of it! But I was worn out from all the travelling…

The children woke me the following morning. Little Heinrich still clinging to Hans. They'd been waiting beside my bed for me to wake up. The little girl had picked a flower from the garden for me.

"Mama has a fever again. Will you bring us to the zoo?"

Anja explained when I went downstairs. "Madam still fever. Maybe down today, later. She play too much music. Too late." I wasn't brazen enough to tell her to mind her own business. Had we kept her awake? I couldn't believe how insolent she was.

The zoo was a hop, skip, and a jump from the house. We just had to walk around the back to get to the main entrance. We would sometimes hear the elephant trumpeting from our garden. Heinrich was asleep in his baby carriage; Hans and Hannelore bombarded me with questions. "Are you married?", "Who's your papa?", "Why do you always speak so funny?" It must be said, Kapriel, that I'd lost a little of my East Prussian accent in Berlin.

At the zoo, I found the zebras of my childhood in the same enclosure, in the same spot, still munching on cabbage leaves. How long does a zebra live? The zookeeper confirmed that some of them were actually the same ones I'd seen in 1934. Old friends. And, all around me, everyone talked the way I'd talked as a child. The sun was shining. The war had made me so happy!

A surprise was waiting for me when I got back. Wolfgang had returned from Poland. Special permission—surprise! Wolfgang was SS, or at least that's what Mama told me. And she was right. I'd never seen one up close. Or rather, I had. At the Olympics. And they'd been at Schwanenwerder, too. But I was to call this one Onkel Wolfi. He was charming, but cold. At first anyway. He was coming down the staircase as I walked through the door. A tall, handsome man with grey eyes and a ready smile. The children started clamouring "Papa, Papa!" and *presto!* I'd lost them. Once the introductions were over, he sent the children in to see Anja in the dining room, where they were to ask for a piece of the *Streuselkuchen* he'd brought back. It didn't take long for me to learn, just like Pavlov's dogs, to associate *Streuselkuchen* with Onkel Wolfi. He often brought some back with him. I haven't eaten it again since the war. With the little ones off, he looked closely at me, the way you look at a child to try to see how they resemble their parents.

"You look like your father in photos. Twenty, are you? What a fine age! About time you got here! Clara and the Pole had their hands full with the children."

It was true. I'd always looked like Papa. So Onkel Wolfi considered me to be a sort of nanny. A question scalded my lips.

"What's wrong with Tante Clara?"

"Your Mama didn't tell you? Clara has paludic fever."

Paludic fever? That was all I needed! You don't know what it is? Malaria, plain and simple. Don't look at me like that. Malaria was raging in Europe right up until the Second World War. Around the Mediterranean especially. In Sicily, Sardinia, and Corsica, where the mosquitos live. But let's just say it was rather rare in Königsberg. Wolfi explained that Tante Clara had a disease of the soul. That in 1932 she'd been placed in an institution in East Prussia, where she'd been diagnosed with schizophrenia. Back then, insanity was commonly treated by injecting patients with malaria, particularly mental disorders that arose from syphilis. It was fighting fire with fire. Every hospital in Europe had a malaria strain to inject its psychotic patients with. You don't believe me? But it's true! No, no, it has nothing to do with concentration camps. You're a simpleton, Kapriel! It was an Austrian, Dr. Wagner-Jauregg, who discovered the virtues of malarial fever in treating mental disorders. He even won the Nobel Prize for his discovery, in 1926 or 1928, I can't remember which. Of course he lost a few patients to the treatment, but up until 1945 malaria inoculation was used to treat insanity. I don't know what they were thinking. Perhaps that the fevers weakened patients to the point that madness became an extravagance they could no longer keep up. And there's something else you must understand. Diagnosing someone with schizophrenia in 1932 was something of a grey area. Back then, you could still have your wife locked up because she was being a pain in the ass. Oh yes you could! So a doctor at the hospital in Königsberg decided to give malaria therapy a try. It seems—and Clara later told me this herself—that she was delirious at the time, imagining that she was being pursued by monsters.

"Strangers, men with long beards. By popes, mustachioed popes!"

She was convinced she was being persecuted, that she wouldn't survive the dreams. She stopped eating, let herself waste away. Would sometimes doze off only to wake up screaming for help. The attacks left her very weak.

"I would hear voices. Deep, menacing voices announcing the worst."

In January 1933, the day Adolf Hitler came to power, she was injected with malaria. The effects didn't take long to manifest themselves. Two weeks later, she was bedridden with fevers of volcanic proportions. The first attacks were the worst. Then things settled down. They almost lost her. But when she came around, she was almost back to normal. She even played the piano a little in hospital. That's where she met her husband. In the hospital. I never did find out what he was doing there. If he was visiting, a patient himself, or working there. And I was too shy to ask him a question like that.

"Now, fever can be treated with quinine. She was lucky: none of her children got it. We must be very careful. And her attacks are rarer, you'll see. You need to keep an eye on her. See that she takes her quinine, but never when she's pregnant: that would mean she'd lose the baby. Will you promise me you'll keep an eye on her?"

"Yes, Onkel Wolfi."

I didn't know what I was getting myself into. Strangely enough, the whole thing made me happy. At last I had a role to play. I was someone in a world that resembled me: East Prussia. Uncle Wolfgang's true nature wasn't revealed until he came back from the Ukraine. We went into the dining room, where the children were stuffing their faces with *Streuselkuchen*. Anja had just said something to Hannelore in Polish. Wolfi turned bright red and gave her two monumental slaps.

"*Auf Deutsch!* My children speak German!"

Anja ran out while the children swallowed their cake in silence. Don't be angry with me, Kapriel, but I thought he was right. And she never spoke Polish in front of us again.

Tante Clara had quartan fever, which is to say that her attacks were separated by two days of respite. You can read malaria like sheet music, Kapriel.

"It's worse when I'm pregnant."

Wolfgang only stayed for three days. Then he left again for Poland. We didn't see him again for another two months. I quickly settled into a home that was missing a head of the household. Most of the men had been called up, you understand. The only ones left were women, children, and old men. Two weeks later and I was calling the shots: what we'd eat, where we'd go, what we'd sing, when employees would take time off, if a tree should be cut down because it was diseased. I was captain of that particular ship. Onkel Wolfi even called me his little colonel.

At Christmas, Clara gave birth to a little girl. She decided to call her Helga, after Joseph and Magda Goebbels' eldest daughter. The child was healthy: thanks to the doctors, Clara hadn't passed on her malaria. In winter 1941, Clara's condition began to improve. They say that malaria makes pregnancy worse, and vice versa. She came back to life. She reminded me very much of Mama, before she fell ill. By then, Mama would only write now and then, complaining about the air raids over Berlin. Ludwig was off at the front somewhere, I didn't know where. I think he must have been angry with me because I hadn't told him I'd gone to Königsberg. He must have gone back to Berlin on leave and not found me there. But I'd stopped thinking about it. The truth is, Kapriel, the only thing I missed in Königsberg was *Tosca*. There was a smaller theatre that would put on Puccini-Wagner-Verdi in an endless loop, but no *Tosca*. They seemed to be obsessed with *Madame Butterfly*. It's true that perhaps *Butterfly* spoke to all those women waiting for their man to come back from the front, but it's not my cup of tea at all! Ha! Tea! Do you get it? That's Suzuki for you, completely under her mistress's thumb, ready to do anything for her, no matter how crazy she gets. An apology for slavery, that's what it is. Why the face, Kapriel? I've already told you? Am I repeating myself? Forgive me! No, I still prefer Tosca. There's much more pluck in a character like her.

In June 1941, it was decided Tante Clara was up to a little trip. The home belonging to my father's parents in Cranz, on the Baltic Sea, had remained empty. It was only thirty minutes by train from Königsberg. I decided to take Clara and the children, after asking Papa's permission, of course! *Ach!* Cranz! I hadn't seen the Baltic Sea since 1934. It was a little Scandinavian-style wooden villa close to the beach, not far from the Cranz Hotel and the seaside promenade. From our yard, we could see the sun setting over the sea. One day I'll have to tell you all about those sunsets over the Baltic. They have to be seen to be believed. There were only two bedrooms. One for the children, and one for me and Tante Clara, along with little Helga, naturally. We spent the whole summer there.

Onkel Wolfi came to join us. He was unhappy because Hitler had declared war on the Soviet Union and that meant he had to leave for the Ukraine, where he would be further away from us. I was quite fond of him, but when he was around, I turned back into the twenty-year-old Berlin girl who had run away to the provinces to escape the bombs. As soon as he left, Tante Clara would become something approaching my wife. I was the family's father figure.

"Listen, my little colonel. I'm being sent to the Ukraine. You'll look after my little brood for me, won't you?"

I tried my best to look sad. But that evening, I silently thanked the Führer one hundred times. Wolfi trusted me so much that he taught me how to drive the car! An Opel Wanderer. In the whole Reich, there must have been no more than ten or twelve women who could drive and I was one of them! But since we needed to move around and there was still gas available… In the summer of 1941, while the Wehrmacht tore the Ukraine apart, I was taking Clara, Hans, Hannelore, Heinrich, and Helga to visit the Curonian Spit, where immense dunes were whipped up by the wind. How many days did we spend playing in those pine forests? In the village of Neu-Pillkoppen, Clara fainted at the sight of peasants decapitating birds, whooping cranes they'd caught in late summer, I believe. They bit the heads clean off! Absolutely disgusting! In the evenings, we would go to the Cranz Hotel. Anja would look after the children. There we danced and listened to music. We had a great time! You would never have thought we were living in a country on the brink. Not for one minute. We were dancing on the volcano.

We went back to Königsberg in the fall: little Hans had started school. Clara was feeling better and better. Onkel Wolfi had forbidden her to write any more letters to Magda Goebbels, who she continued to idolize. Sometimes she would dress up for dinner as Magda Goebbels. There was still a little craziness inside her, all right. Her malaria hadn't completely healed her… I played along and bought her a pair of earrings that were identical to the ones I'd stolen at Schwanenwerder in 1936. Do you know what she told me?

"Why Magda! How pretty they are! They're identical to the ones Frau Goebbels used to wear. You don't see photos of her wearing the little pearl ones anymore. Maybe she lost them."

"Or maybe she happens to be wearing other earrings when someone takes a photo."

Clara dreamed of receiving the Cross of Honour of the German Mother from the hands of Magda Goebbels. Women were supposed to have children; it was one of Hitler's obsessions. The Nazis came up with a reward system to encourage them. They gave medals to these *Reichsmütter*. When little Helga was born around Christmas 1940, Wolfi had ordered the bronze Cross of Honour of the German Mother. Clara wore it over the holidays.

"Two more children and you'll have the silver cross!"

Women who brought eight or more children into the world were awarded the gold cross. Honestly, those Nazis had completely lost the plot! Can you imagine? One woman, eight children? They'd spend their whole lives pregnant!

Need I point out, Kapriel, that Tante Clara seldom made it through the day? She would usually have to take long afternoon naps. I used the time to go out with the children. When I managed to go out alone with Hans, the eldest child, we'd take the tram into town. The others were still a little too slow for me to be dragging them around the streets. With each visit to the zoo, Hans developed a growing fascination for zebras. He wanted to know everything about them. The ones at the zoo were no longer enough; he demanded books, pictures, and stories all about zebras. The neighbours sent me to the museum to show him the quagga. Do you know what that is? The quagga is a recently extinct species, half-zebra, half-horse, that lived in South Africa. The last of its kind died at the end of the nineteenth century; now all that remains of it are twenty-four stuffed specimens in museums the world over. Well, twenty-three today. It only had stripes on its head and fore end. For a long time people mistakenly believed the quagga to be a subspecies of the zebra. At any rate, Hans adored them. He never wanted to leave the museum, always wanted to go back. The quagga became one of his little-boy obsessions. Do you know what he told me one day?

"Quaggas are a little like you, Magda. They're half-zebra, half-horse."

I didn't know what he was getting at.

"Papa says you're half-girl, half-boy."

Such a plain-spoken young thing! How could I be angry with him? After the war, some of the survivors from East Prussia told me of the sad fate of the Königsberg quagga. Just before the Red Army arrived, the museum moved it to a villa in the hope that the Russians wouldn't get their hands on it. The stuffed animal was standing in a bedroom when the Russian soldiers, drunk to a man, kicked the door in as they took Königsberg. They almost died with fright at the sight of its big eyes gleaming in the darkness. Furious, they flung it out of the window, pissed on it, and burned it in the garden. There you have it. I think that little scene gives you a good idea of the fate of... Well, anyway.

(At this point, Michel, she got up again and went back into the kitchen looking for something. I heard her turn on a radio or something, no doubt to cover her sobs. Crying over a stuffed half-zebra so many years later... you don't see that every day.)

Onkel Wolfgang came back from the Ukraine for Christmas 1942. He came back often, but this time he was a changed man. He didn't speak, just locked himself away in his room. He took no interest in the children. He also seemed to suspect I'd been playing a bigger role in his absence; he had harsh words for me.

"You think you can take over my home just because I showed you how to drive the Opel, Magda?"

His voice was calm, cold, and detached as he ate his supper. Clara stared at her plate. The children didn't say another word.

"I'm not taking over anything, Onkel Wolfi. I'm just keeping an eye on things."

"Well, just remember it's all fun and games until someone loses an eye."

He would ramble on incomprehensibly. Then sit watching the snow fall for hours at a time. He barely showed any interest in Helga, who turned two on December 28. Shortly after the Epiphany, he told us he was leaving. Clara wanted to surprise him by dressing up as Magda Goebbels again!

"You're crazy!" He slapped her. "Will we have to have you locked up again? Get a hold of yourself!"

She'd lost her earrings. She cried all night. I heard her. And I heard him, too. He... Well. You know what I mean? He left the next day and Clara was again gripped in a cycle of fevers for the first time since fall 1940. It took me three months to get the house back to normal. When the two of us sang together it helped Clara keep her sanity. But as soon as we stopped for, say, a week, she would start thinking she was Magda Goebbels again. It was as though music brought order to her mind. Order that came undone every time Onkel Wolfi came home on leave.

Winter 1942 brought with it terrifying news. Stalingrad. Ah, now you know what I'm talking about. That's just like you, isn't it? No head for poetry, but when it comes to human suffering, you're no slouch. A typical man. Calm down, calm down. I'm only joking.

Summer 1943 was magnificent. My little Helga was walking, Heinrich was chattering away, almost as much as his brother Hans, who was already reading. Hannelore had learned to braid my hair. Lazy days on the beach at Cranz, then the world's most beautiful sunsets every evening. We had a little problem that summer. Marion the Pole was requisitioned by the *Arbeitsamt* to go work in a munitions factory in Germany. It was quite unfortunate since he was a good worker. As time passed, there were fewer and fewer men left in Königsberg.

In late August, I decided to bring Hans and Hannelore to see their first opera. A one-off production of Weber's *Freischütz*. Do you know it? No? It's very German. The music is magnificent. Which theatre? Oh, it wasn't in a theatre: it was outside. Yes, indeed. It went with the theme. It was an evening performance, in Heiligenbeil, a small town. The children were dying to go, just the three of us. Some say opera is too complicated for children to understand, that they won't like it, but that couldn't be further from the truth! Nothing fascinates them more than hearing the Queen of the Night!

The stage was set up in the forest, at the foot of huge fir trees that swayed in the twilight. There must have been at least five hundred people there. The *Freischütz* is a *Singspiel*, with singing and spoken dialogue. It's better to start children off with a *Singspiel*; it's often the recitative operas that throw them. The *Freischütz* is the story of a hunter, which is why it's nice to perform it outdoors, in the heart of the German forest. It's a very complicated story. It's basically about a hunter who makes a pact with the devil. Oh yes! Another German specialty! He trades his soul in return for magic bullets that never miss their target. Needless to say, the final bullet belongs to the devil and he'll kill the beautiful Agathe, whom the hunter was all set to marry. It's the kind of opera that makes you jump with every gunshot.

The staging left everyone confused. Just imagine, Kapriel: usually the actors fired shotguns—blanks, of course. But this time, since we were at war, and perhaps because there were children in the audience, the direc-tor had replaced the bullets with arrows. What an idea! *Freischütz* meets the Wild West! It might have made sense for William Tell but not for *Freischütz*! I was scandalized. And as if that wasn't enough, the perform-ance ran into a problem. The last three arrows that were fired off never came back down again from the trees that hung over the stage. I can still see Hans and Hannelore watching the archer's every movement, their eyes trained on each arrow, following their trajectory into the black night sky only to watch them, open-mouthed, disappear into the skies of East Prussia! The children wanted to speak to the singers after the show, as did I. I was curious to know how they'd managed to avoid being called up so they could sing *Freischütz* outdoors. But you couldn't ask that kind of thing. They were very nice, though.

"I lost my three arrows," one of them said. "It's a real mystery. I shot them up into the sky and they should have fallen behind the trees as usual. I looked everywhere, but no luck. Perhaps I'll find them in the daylight."

Hans and Hannelore were jumping about with excitement the whole way home. The only thing they remembered about the whole story was the lost arrows. Nothing could have been more important to them than those damned arrows! They talked about them for two weeks. That evening at Heiligenbeil reminded me just how much I missed opera, or rather the fine productions we used to enjoy in Berlin. Even today, sometimes I too dream of the three arrows streaking across the East Prussian sky. God only knows where the bloody things landed.

It was my last trip in the Opel. One week later, the car was requisitioned for the front. Disturbing letters reached me from Berlin. Bombs were raining down, sometimes in broad daylight. Air raid sirens every night. The letter came that fall. The one I never wanted to get. Fate had it that Tante Clara was the one who opened it. Mama had died in an air raid. Or rather, not in a single air raid but in a series of them. She'd locked herself away in her room with a bottle of German white wine. When the siren sounded, she didn't go down to the bunker with Papa. He tried to force her to come, banged on her door, but she wouldn't open. He could hear the bombs drawing closer to Charlottenburg. To save his own skin, he had to go downstairs. The house was still standing when he came out of the bunker, but Mama had jumped out of the window. Like Tosca. She'd finished the bottle of wine, then written a note and slipped it into the neck of the bottle. The note was for me. Papa sent it to me.

My Little Magda,
I can't go on. I no longer want to live in this world. Try to be happy. Take care of your aunt.
    Mama

I don't know who was more stricken: me or Tante Clara, her sister. Clara immediately slid into a feverish spiral. Wolfgang was far from home in the Ukraine. Up until Christmas 1943, I think I spent most of my time staring into the distance. I was paralyzed by pain. Clara wrote long letters to Magda Goebbels. I think she might even have mailed them. She asked her for help at this difficult time. She never got a reply. We would have heard about it. The whole world would have.

You know, Kapriel, if I hadn't had the children to look after, I would have gone crazy with sadness. Now one thing was certain: I wouldn't be going back to Berlin after the war. I would stay in Königsberg, where I had my roots. In February 1944, Wolfgang came back from the front. He was ill. By some miracle, he had survived typhoid fever, proof that God calls only the pure of heart back to him. He was still weak and had to be taken care of like an invalid. Now I was looking after a woman who was burning up with malaria and a man that typhoid had reduced to skin and bones. I don't think I would have managed without Anja and the cook, Frau Meisel. By June, Wolfgang was doing better, but his illness or his time at the front, or perhaps both, had changed him. He'd become ill-tempered and paranoid. He was convinced I was filling his children's heads with all kinds of lies about him, that Clara and I were plotting to kill him. He was raving mad. And Clara wasn't doing much better. She would sometimes pray for Magda Goebbels for hours at a time. Since she'd heard she was a Buddhist, she made the children meditate in the mornings to strange, disturbing mantras. Anja was afraid of her. One day in the fall of 1944, Wolfgang flew into a rage. I figured he must have raped her; she spent a full day prostrate in her bedroom. It happened while I was at the zoo with the children. Anja was hiding in a closet when I came home. He was still ranting and raving upstairs. I went up to take a look. Tante Clara was lying on the bed in tears; he was standing over her, with no pants on, roaring: "I'll have you locked up. You'll give me another son or I'll have you locked up!" He turned around and saw me standing there. The door slammed shut. Then they fought. More than once. How can I explain it, Kapriel? I wasn't used to that kind of thing.

In July 1944, thank God, Wolfgang was sent to Gotenhafen, near Gdansk. It's only two hundred kilometres from Königsberg, on the Baltic Sea. His illness meant he was no longer any use on the front. He was to be in charge of the ships that docked in the port at Gotenhafen. When, after he left, Clara collapsed into my arms and sobbed "I'm pregnant," I realized he *had* raped her.

It was during a time of absurd calm, given what was happening in the rest of Germany, that the festivities were held to mark Königsberg's four hundredth anniversary that July. There were celebrations everywhere, along with swastikas, the *Reichsmütter* parades, the old men from the *Volkssturm*, and the *Hitlerjugend*—the only men left in East Prussia! I remember singing *Erlkönig* with the children at a country fair, this time with a different pianist since Tante Clara was feverish. It's funny: no one dared say a word about what was going on, no one had the right to doubt a thing. Anyone who voiced his fears was accused of being defeatist and locked up, or worse. And yet that *Lied*, *Erlkönig*, clearly announced what was to come, right down to the tempo, right down to the tragic end when the father gallops back to the castle only to discover his child has died in his arms. And how the people enjoyed our performance as we announced their imminent demise. The women thought Hans was absolutely adorable. He sang the child's part, while I played the father and the Elf King. If I'd known, I'd have chosen something different for the festivities.

Wolfgang came back every two weeks, ever more sombre, ever more unpleasant. I would make sure I was in Cranz when he arrived, leaving poor Clara at his mercy. One day, I came back from Cranz with the children and he was still there. His driver was late picking him up. Clara was almost mad with fever. He gave me that spineless look of his on the way out, then eyed the children. Do you know what he said to Hannelore? I'll never forget it: "Make sure you don't end up a monkey like her!" and he pointed at me. He shoved me against the wall, then went outside to where his lift was waiting. Typhoid is a terrible thing, Kapriel.

In late August 1944, the sky fell on our heads. Literally. Until that point, the air raids had miraculously forgotten Königsberg. Every German town and city was in flames, apart from Königsberg. It was as though there was a problem with the English maps. But on the night of August 26 to 27, the bombs rained down on our city. We weren't spared after all. After two dreadful nights, the house was still standing, but not everyone on Mozartstraße was so fortunate. You have no idea the din it made... You'll never know either, and it's better that way. The first air raid completely razed to the ground the neighbourhood beside ours, Maraunenhof.

During the second air raid, on August 29, Clara became totally hysterical. We were all in the cellar when she got up to run out of the house, looking for Wolfgang. Anja and Frau Meisel tried to stop her, but she was too strong. The noise of the bombs drew nearer. The children were crying. At the height of the bombing, I went outside to find her. The sky over Königsberg was all red; people were running and shouting in the streets. Then, nothing. I made my way toward the zoo, ruins and dead animals to my left and right. It was almost like daylight, the explosions were so bright. Then I came across burned bodies, all shrivelled up. Like little children... The heat of the phosphorus bombs had baked them in seconds. They were like dolls. There was one, Kapriel. My God, how can I explain it? She was dead, shrunken, burned by the phosphorus, holding a cage that had melted onto one of her arms. She was lying on her back, her finger pointing up into the air, with a budgie on the end of it, wrinkled and dried up. Can you imagine?

Then the zebra walked by.

A bomb must have knocked down one of the walls to its enclosure. I'll never forget the sight of it galloping through the burning ruins, gripped by panic. Then my coat caught fire. I had to rip it off before I became a human torch. The zebra ran in my direction; I was terrified, rooted to the spot. I could feel its breath on my neck. It seemed cold compared to the air around me, then it neighed and brushed against me as it raced toward the town. It disappeared into a cloud of smoke. I went on looking for Clara for another half hour as the bombs fell. When I went back to the cellar, she was already there. Out of her mind. Shaking. She looked me in the eye and said (I can still remember what she told me above the children's sobbing):

"There's a zebra running through the streets. Everything's on fire. We're at war, Magda!"

Yes, I slapped her a few times, I admit it. Three slaps. You would have done the same! Five years of sirens, air raids, ration cards, and flattened cities, and it took a zebra running through the burning streets of Königsberg for her to realize that Germany was at war! The poor woman! The children cried until the next morning. They found the zebra, dead from fear and exhaustion, a hundred metres from the house. We had heard it still neighing pitifully at dawn.

We had to take in the Neumann cousins at our house or, I should say, at Wolfgang's house. They'd lost everything in the air raids. They had nothing left but the clothes on their backs. Wolfgang reappeared a few days later, serious and a little more composed this time. We were all in the main living room along with the Neumanns—there were five of them—plus Anja and the cook, old Frau Meisel. Wolfgang explained that the Red Army was at East Prussia's door. Clara sobbed. We'd just have to trust in the Wehrmacht, he said. The final victory was at hand, but we'd need to resist in the meantime. Nobody believed in the final victory anymore, nobody but children and lunatics. Wolfgang tried to sound reassuring:

"The Germans have a secret weapon they'll use to wipe them out at the last moment, just as they're about to strike."

The Neumanns listened politely. They wanted to leave for the West. Not wait for Ivan.

"My father fought in the Great War," Herr Neumann said. "We're better off hanging ourselves before the Russians get their hands on us."

"The Russians won't be getting their hands on anyone!" Wolfgang roared. "Anyone fleeing Königsberg will be accused of treason and will pay the price. *Aus!*"

He went back to Gotenhafen, just west of Gdansk, the following morning, leaving us there. The air raids had destroyed almost all of the city centre, the castle, the cathedral, Königsberg's seven bridges, the shops. Seven hundred years of German history reduced to rubble in two nights of bombing. Most of the streets were cluttered with debris. Long convoys of refugees made their way along the roads in ox-drawn carts, people from the east, from Memel, who preferred to flee rather than fall into Russian hands. Trains passed by, cars loaded with mountains of furniture. But we weren't allowed to flee. Hitler had declared Königsberg an impregnable fortress. Fight to the last. That was our order. The Neumanns were far from convinced. They left in late September, on a cart drawn by two horses. Six hours later, they were back. Frau Neumann was shaking. Along the way, her husband explained, the Wehrmacht had stopped them. The message was clear. Everyone was to stay put.

"I'm going to have a boy, I'm sure of it," Tante Clara told me one day.

She must have been three months' pregnant. Then I remembered what Wolfgang had told me about how quinine could bring on an abortion, that I was to be careful not to give any to Tante Clara while she was pregnant. I had no idea how she could envisage bringing a child into the world given the circumstances. Especially when she wasn't really able to look after the ones she had already… Everywhere, word had it that the Red Army—known to everyone simply as Ivan—was at our door. If we were to flee, would we have to leave Tante Clara behind? I think her doctors must have warned her about the dangers of quinine. So I had to slip it to her. It wasn't easy: quinine has a very bitter taste and there was no sugar to be had in town to mask it. I settled on giving her the poison in tiny doses, in everything she took. In her morning chicory (we'd run out of coffee), her nettle soup at lunchtime (you've never had it? It's a cheap wartime meal.), and sprinkled over the turbot fillet she'd eat in the evenings. Slowly, the poison took effect. She lost the child after three days, toward the end of September. I was trying to dig up the last remaining potatoes and onions before the frost came when Anja ran out into the garden. I made an effort to look horrified.

"Promise me you won't tell Wolfgang I was pregnant. If he knows I lost the baby, he'll say I did it on purpose."

"I promise, Tante Clara."

I kept my promise, Kapriel. And Clara kept her composure. We took the children and a few suitcases to the railway station, with Herr Neumann leading the horse. We'd run out of gas a long time ago. Butter, too. We didn't have much of anything left, to be honest. The station was in complete and utter chaos. The tracks were being cleared of debris, but no one was allowed to travel. *To victory our trains will roll on. No travelling until the war is done.* That was one of the signs at the station. The Nazis were rather fond of inane rhymes. If it rhymes, then it must be true!

So there was to be no taking the train unless authorized by God knows who. Erich Koch? Clara was only just holding it together. She called the railway staff every name under the sun: "I'm a personal friend of Magda Goebbels! You haven't heard the last of this!" We couldn't calm her down. I tried to look on the bright side: Hans and Hannelore had stopped crying. They'd become numb to trauma, a defence mechanism that would soon serve them well.

We had to stay home. Dreadful news reached us that October. The Russians had broken through the frontline, coming into East Prussia through the village of Nemmersdorf, where the Wehrmacht managed to beat them back a few days later. Villagers were found massacred, their bodies mutilated. All the women had been raped, some finished off with bayonets. People were nervous, but nobody dared leave.

The Neumanns didn't hold out much longer. One night in November, they left without saying a word to anyone. Only to come back again three hours later. They had come across three hanged men after a bridge. One had a sign around his neck: "I tried to flee."

Wolfgang didn't come home until Christmas. He assured us that the Wehrmacht was preparing—in the event of an emergency, we shouldn't talk about it—a mass evacuation by way of the Baltic Sea. That if the Russians came, if we heard artillery fire, we should leave for Gotenhafen. The order to evacuate would come eventually. He seemed very calm. All of East Prussia was absurdly calm in December 1944. He even decorated a Christmas tree for the children. He looked relieved. Neumann explained to me later that Wolfgang must have understood that the war was almost at an end, that he would be able to go back to his normal life again, in his own home. Little

Heinrich was already talking. Hans was eight years old. The two eldest were able to sleep, but the youngest would often have nightmares. They would dream of the zebra galloping as the bombs rained down, you see. You're smiling, Kapriel? Do you think it's funny? Would you like me to stop there?

(Here, Michel, she stood up. She went into the kitchen, where I heard her sniff once. She blew her nose, then came back in, standing stiff as a poker.)

Wolfgang left again for Gotenhafen on January 6, the feast of the Three Kings. Before he left, there was of course a scene or two with Clara. I could hear them through the wall shouting at each other. "When it's all over, I'll have you locked up! You'll go back to the institution, you crazy bitch!" And he left, at last. Anja pointed out to me that there were no SS families left in Königsberg. Unlike most, they had been given permission to travel. All people wanted was to find refuge in the Reich, in Berlin or Dresden, not to stay there, waiting to be torn to shreds by the Bolsheviks. Anja found it strange, and I did too, that Wolfgang hadn't wangled us permission to travel. Before he left, he said to me again: "When the Russians come, leave with the Neumanns. Come meet me in Gotenhafen and we'll all leave by sea."

Heavy snow began to fall, Kapriel. A real winter like none East Prussia had seen for a very long time. A Soviet winter. Fifteen, eighteen degrees below zero. What? You're not impressed? On January 12, 1945, the Russians marched across the German border and news spread like wildfire across the city. This time, people openly ignored the travel ban, hitched up their oxen, their horses, put together makeshift carts. An entire people took to the roads.

The Neumanns had prepared a cart. It even had a roof. Frau Neumann was in a particular rush to leave: she had three girls, all younger than I was, who had been sharing the same room, our old living room, with their parents since August. In the meantime, we had had to put other people up, so many homes had been bombarded.

We left on January 22. I led the procession. Two carts and four horses for four families. Just the one man, Herr Neumann, who had never led anything in his life. All these people had become my whole world. My mission was to bring them to Gotenhafen, or further west, ideally as far as Berlin.

"We're not waiting any longer. We'll have to walk to Elbing. There will surely be a train after that."

Clara refused to leave. She clung to her piano, wouldn't hear of leaving the music room. It was too cold, she cried. Herr Neumann had a wooden leg, that's why he was still in Königsberg and not with the Wehrmacht. We had buried the china and silverware in the garden again, not too far from where the Neumanns had buried the zebra, by an apple tree. Because we were sure we would be coming back. It would only be for a while. I put the children in the cart with a suitcase, then went back into the house to tear Clara away from her piano.

"We have to leave right now."

"I'm not going anywhere without my piano."

Then she wanted to bring all her scores. I let her bring just the one book. You know what she wanted to keep? *The Magic Flute.*

"To sing with the children along the way," she said.

We walked alongside the cart toward Elbing. How far? At least one hundred kilometres. The temperature had fallen again to around minus twenty-five. We walked in silence. A long, unending line of people. Only the old, the children, and the sick sat in the carts; the others walked. Shortly after Königsberg, shouts and cries from behind us. "Out of the way!" It was the Wehrmacht, our own army, travelling by truck, fleeing the same danger we were, only they had gas! And they were knocking down the carts, knocking down people to save their own skin. How many kilometres did we walk the first day? Twenty? No. Fewer. We had to find somewhere to sleep. In the homes abandoned by people who must have been further ahead, we even found a few potatoes. The second night, we slept in the home of a countess. I don't remember which one, but she let us sleep in her heated anteroom. Otherwise everyone would have died of cold. She said, I remember:

"We have to get past Elbing as quickly as we can. We need to hurry before they surround us."

That very night, the countess left with her people, in the shadows. We needed to sleep. But the rest proved fatal. There must have been twenty-odd families from Mozartstraße. Some had stayed behind, like Anja, who didn't want to come with us. It's funny, it wasn't until a few days after we left that I started to wonder what had happened to her. What would become of her? What would the Russians do to her? She hadn't wanted to come to Germany. She preferred to try her luck with the Russians. Go figure… To do that, Kapriel, to do that, she really must have thought the Germans were… Anyway… A little more white wine? Where's the corkscrew? How old would Anja be today?

(With that, Michel, she got up again, pretending she couldn't find the corkscrew she had left on the little table beside her. She disappeared into the kitchen. I heard her blow her nose again, once or twice. Then she came back in with another corkscrew.)

This will do the job! Look, Konsum's finest! Made in the GDR! Ha! Ha! Now where was I? Oh, yes! It's so easy to lose all notion of time, you know. I know we left Königsberg on the 22nd, I remember that the countess was the second night and that Clara wanted to play her piano. There must have been a hundred of us watching her play the overture of *The Magic Flute* in the music room of that grand old home.

It would be the last time she would ever play the piano. Then she wanted me to sing *Ach, ich fühl's*. I got through half of it. How they applauded! I had never been applauded like that. Just to please them, I finished the song. The next day, the shit began because, until that point, the heavens had been with us. First, old Meisel, the cook I had been holding by the arm as we walked beside the cart, sat down on the side of the road. She never got back up. She died right there and then, Kapriel. It was cold enough to kill you standing there with your boots on, you can tell them that back in Canada. And that's what happened to her, along with thousands of others who never picked themselves back up again from the side of the road as they tried to flee. Then, just before Elbing—it must have been a little after Heiligenbeil—a Wehrmacht convoy appeared right in front of us.

"Turn back," they shouted. "They're at Elbing!"

"Who is?"

"Ivan!"

There were a million and a half of them, Russians hell bent on revenge, pouring into Germany. They had taken Elbing, which meant that East Prussia had been surrounded. All the carts pulled off to the side and the Wehrmacht trucks raced past. Some were only half full. They didn't think to stop to pick up the sick or the children. We needed to turn around, but to go where? The sea was our only means of escaping Ivan, to the north, beyond the Vistula Lagoon. We had to reach the small strip of land, the Vistula Isthmus, that links Gdansk to East Prussia. Ivan hadn't gotten that far yet. The cold that had taken so many children and old people now gave us the ice that would save us from the Russians. Thousands of families waited, not daring to venture out onto the ice. Far off in the distance, we could hear the artillery. I had to take Clara by the arm; she was liable to collapse at any minute. She climbed onto the cart with the children, then Herr Neumann made the decision.

"We need to cross. Otherwise Ivan will take us here on the shoreline."
And like a colony of ants making its way across the white tiles on a bathroom floor, we advanced. In silence so we could hear the sound the ice made when it cracked. The clanking of the harnesses, the children sobbing in the carts, the wailing of the old folk. Then a cry rang out:

"Planes!"

It was already too late to take cover on the shore. Three times they swooped down at us. Whole families were swallowed up with each explosion. There was nothing we could do for them. We just made our way around the holes and kept on walking and walking. Picture the scene. We were walking across the frozen Vistula Lagoon to reach Gdansk when the planes arrived. We could hear them long before we saw them, the sinister din announcing our imminent death. The whistling sound draws nearer, won't take no for an answer, grabs your attention and won't let go.

But you run, there's no time. The harnesses clank even harder, the horses whinny in fright. Then the planes dive down. You pray to the heavens. Not me! Have pity, not me! I'm a good girl! I went to Sophie-Charlotte-Schule! I learned French! I don't deserve these bombs! And twenty metres ahead of us, the ice opens wide, swallows two carts. An old woman stands at the edge, peering into the icy hole her family has just fallen into. Keep going. Walk on. And the music of Mozart going around and around in your head, because after three nights without sleep, you're starting to go mad. You can hear voices. And the overture to *The Magic Flute* is banging away at your eardrums. *Ach!* When it wasn't the Russian bombs—dropped on civilians, Kapriel!—it was the sometimes too-thin ice that gave way beneath the weight of the carts. Shouts. The sound of the water, lapping. Then nothing. Go on. Walk around the hole. In silence. I remember, on the other side of the lagoon we walked a few kilometres across the ice that covered the land. There was a woman tugging on the arm of an old lady, her mother. People were just dropping dead at the side of the road. No time to bury them, no time to say goodbye. Anyone who sat down stayed down. Frozen in two minutes flat. It wasn't until we got to the other side that we realized: Helga. You know, children don't stand up as well to the cold. We had to leave her by the side of the road, too. Without a word.

Two nights in a stable. Then the road, the long, snow-covered road, the planes screaming down at us, dropping bombs on us. A woman holding an ax, tears in her eyes, cutting off her son's frozen toes while he screams blue murder. Blood on the snow. I still see it. After how many days? Eating snow so as not to die of thirst. The animals dying of exhaustion. The length of the snow-covered trail, the skeletons of horses we slaughtered and ate while the flesh still quivered. Each pushing forward his last possessions on earth. I saw her, Kapriel, and on nights when I don't drink enough I can still see her: that woman dragging a blanket with a gramophone on it, its long copper corolla advancing like a cursed mechanical flower in winter. I remember because two days later I stumbled over her body, lying dead beside her gramophone, and I cursed her in the darkness. And the overture of *The Magic Flute* swirling through the frigid winter air. Then the city, at last. The people hanging by their necks as we approached Gdansk. A city jam-packed with refugees with nothing to offer those of us who wanted for everything.

All of East Prussia converged on Gdansk. Cinemas and schools had been closed; every building was being used to house the waves of refugees.

Some had come from Allenstein, others from Cranz, from Memel. All were fleeing Ivan. The stories circulating about the men—and especially the women—who stayed behind were enough to make your blood run cold. I thought of Anja, and of our neighbours who had preferred to stay. You know, Kapriel, of the three hundred thousand Germans who, for all sorts of reasons, didn't manage to flee East Prussia, the vast majority of them died: from the cold, from hunger, from illness; raped, or shot. The luckier ones got three weeks on a train to Siberia, where they were imprisoned in labour camps.

And so there we were in Gdansk, after five days of walking through the most unbearable cold. We'd lost Helga. And Clara was showing signs of a new round of fever. We were in a classroom. Hannelore was ill too. People tried to sleep, piled in on top of each other. We'd been given tea and blankets by the auxiliaries or some other women in uniform. Clara kept saying: "Our Führer will send us a ship!" or "After the final victory, we'll throw a huge party!" And that was while she was lucid! Clara got increasingly delirious. What else did she used to say? Oh yes, I remember: "Do popes have mustaches, Sister? No! A pope has never had a mustache!" I think when we were on the road, Tante Clara completely lost her mind.

In the morning, people from the Wehrmacht told us that ships were taking aboard refugees in Gotenhafen. That we'd have to walk thirty kilometres and, after that, there would be boats for Denmark and for Kiel or Hamburg, I can't remember which. Clara came around to her senses at the sound of the name "Gotenhafen."

"That's where Wolfgang's waiting for us. We must push on, Magda."

To Gotenhafen, thirty kilometres, still with the Neumanns. Some of the Wehrmacht, moved by the sight of the children, let us climb aboard their truck. The Neumanns' horses had dropped dead from exhaustion just before we got to Gdansk. So we ate them. Gotenhafen was a small port town on the Baltic Sea. In late January 1945, there were 120,000 refugees trying to sail back to the Reich. I welled up when I arrived at the port. Do you remember the *Wilhelm Gustloff*, the boat my parents took in August 1939? Well, it was right there! In Gotenhafen! It had been turned into a floating hospital as part of the war effort. Word had it the *Gustloff* was about to cast off and that she was taking refugees. Thousands were already on board, apparently. People had built makeshift shelters in the streets; they were burning wood they'd ripped from the roofs to keep warm. Scuffles kept breaking out between the homeowners and the refugees. Real battles. The port itself was in total chaos. Everyone wanted to get on the *Gustloff*. Anyone with a ticket was saved. Refugees trying to clamber up onto the gangways were pushed back by the Wehrmacht. I managed to make it that far.

"We're looking for *Obersturmführer* Hinz."

Nobody seemed to know who I was talking about, but one man agreed to have a look on board. A half hour later, the soldier came back to tell me he hadn't found Wolfi on the *Gustloff*. That it would be best to ask the port authorities. I asked him if the children and Clara could board once the boat was ready to leave.

"They need tickets. Ask at the office. No one knows when the boat is leaving. It's already quite full. I don't think there are any tickets left."

We had to be quick. There were so many people crammed into the port that just trying to move turned into hand-to-hand combat. I swear I stumbled over a dead grandmother. She didn't seem to belong to anyone; she'd just been left there. Two hundred metres in front of us, homes and offices were about to be pounded by the Russians. We needed tickets—now. I left Clara and the children by the gangway and threw myself into the mass of bodies. People were jostling and shouting outside the ticket office:

"I've been a party member since 1934! I have six children! I need to get on the *Gustloff*!"

Others produced bundles of cash. Blows were exchanged. Everyone wanted to get on that boat, no matter what. Rumour had it the Russians were no more than twenty kilometres away.

"They're strangling children and raping women!"

That was the type of thing I was hearing from people driven insane with fear. There was a row of ugly concrete buildings beside the ticket office. People from the Wehrmacht were going in and out and I thought to myself that they might know where Wolfi was. I knocked on the first door and a young soldier opened. I explained the situation.

"SS? They're all over there. Not here."

He pointed to the last building. I was just about to knock on the door when Wolfgang himself opened. You should have seen his face. It was like he'd seen a ghost.

"Magda! What are you doing here?"

"I'm keeping an eye on them."

It was obvious: he hadn't expected us to make it, the bastard.

"We're trying to get on the *Gustloff.* Your wife and children are ill. We need tickets. Do you have any? I'll bring them to Papa in Berlin."

He looked around then dragged me inside by the collar. It was a big room with desks and telephones. Four or five men were in conversation, SS, as far as I could tell, but there were also Wehrmacht soldiers, too. Along with a marine auxiliary. I'm quite sure of it. She looked at me, then at Wolfi. There are some things you can tell from a single glance. She seemed to want to know. She opened her mouth, but didn't say a word. I hadn't slept properly in six days. I stank. Those people were looking at me the way you might look at a dead rat, which I imagine was what I looked and smelled like.

He pulled me into his office.

"How did you get here?"

"Like everyone else! We walked across the frozen lagoon."

"What do you want?"

"What do I want? I want tickets for the *Gustloff* for Clara and the children, and for me."

"You're asking a lot, Magda. I don't know who you think you are. You show up from Berlin, set up home in my house, lay down the law, act like you're a governess... You certainly don't let modesty get in your way, Magda."

"You asked me to keep an eye on them. That's what I'm doing."

"What condition is Clara in?"

"She's delirious. Fit to be locked up."

"And the children?"

476

"Funny you should ask, all of a sudden."

He slapped me with his gloved hand.

"Be civil with me, Magda."

"I'm sorry."

"As you can see, you've caught me unawares."

He grabbed a sheet of paper and put it in a typewriter. He typed for a long time, asked me how to spell Papa's name and our address in Berlin—the poor fool couldn't even spell Alfred Berg let alone Schiller—then handed me the letter. It was a safe conduct, a letter explaining to people on the *Gustloff* who we were, that they were to let us board and not give us any trouble. The SS stamp and everything.

"Get out of my sight. You stink, Magda. Get out of here, you and your crazy aunt."

"You're not taking the *Gustloff*?"

I still had enough nerve to ask questions.

"No, I'm not taking the *Gustloff*. I'm staying here. Don't you see all these people? They need to be evacuated."

"Why didn't you send for us earlier?"

"There was no way to, Magda."

"You didn't want to see us here. You were sure we were going to be stuck there with the children, isn't that it?"

Onkel Wolfgang had turned his back to me while he looked about in a large armoire for an envelope to put the letter into. He kept on looking for a long time, even though the envelopes were right under his nose.

"Tell me, Magda. Clara confessed to me over Christmas that she lost a child in September. You didn't know your aunt was pregnant, did you?"

"No," I lied.

He knew.

"You were the only one who knew where I hid the quinine, weren't you?"

"Perhaps."

"I can only hope you brought the rest of it with you. The Reich is running short on just about everything. And quinine can come in very handy. Isn't that right, Magda? Clara had never lost a child before. Ever. She told me the day she miscarried she suddenly felt very ill, as though she'd taken quinine."

For kilometres all around us, there was nothing but fear, fire, and bloodshed, and all he wanted to talk about was the child I'd spared from being born and dying in this hell. That's Nazi logic for you, Kapriel.

He'd left his weapon on the table. My wilder side ran over all the ways I could get my revenge. His war was lost anyway. Who would have missed the boor? Once we were safely in Berlin, I thought foolishly, he'd track us down and try to separate me from Clara and the children. I wouldn't even have needed to shoot—I wouldn't have known how—just hit him over the head with the rifle butt, and keep hitting and hitting until he stopped moving. I must have considered it for two seconds too long. That's my sole regret, Kapriel. You can tell anyone you like. I bitterly regret not killing my uncle that January day in 1945, for not having made a Tosca of myself. If I were Catholic, I'd be consumed with a desire to seek forgiveness. But that's not the case, thank God.

Without insinuating anything else, without saying a word, he turned around, handed me the envelope, slapped me two or three times, told me that I was ugly, that no one would ever want to sleep with me, that I was an idiot, then grabbed me by the ear and, in front of everyone in the other room, dragged me outside.

"Don't hang around, you little bitch," he hissed. "They leave at noon."

I was shaken. Once again, I had to beat a path through the crowd to the bottom of the gangway. There I found Clara and the children. Clara was sitting on the only suitcase we still had, clutching the children. What I had feared was about to happen.

"Magda, I'm freezing cold. It's starting up again."

The malaria was taking hold of her. Hans and Hannelore helped me pull her to her feet. A dense crowd of refugees blocked our path on the gangway; there was no way up. I had to push my way through, bite my way through.

"I have the *Obersturmführer*'s permission!" I shouted to the solider. He began to laugh.

Since I still had the imprint of Wolfgang's hand stamped across both cheeks, my words must have seemed even more ridiculous. I looked more like I'd just popped straight out of the second act of *Tosca*.

"And I have the Führer's mustache in my pocket! That's my safe conduct!"

Everyone on the gangway burst out laughing. That's where the Germans were at. I had to push and shove my way through to him. You should have seen his face when he saw the SS stamp and the signature! He carried the suitcase himself, then took the children in his arms. We were saved.

Aboard the *Gustloff*, we were shown to a cabin on one of the upper decks that were already full of Wehrmacht, only men.

"Unless you'd rather go down to the lower decks. You could ask the auxiliaries to let you into the pool."

"The pool? Is this really the time to go for a swim?"

"There's a pool down there, but it's been emptied to make more room."

"We'll stay here, thanks."

They were kind enough to find a berth for Clara, who was already shaking with fever. She was still delirious: the same old song about the pope with the mustache or some madness about sugar.

"As much sugar as you can find, Magdalena. You need the purest sugar, his favourite kind. You'll give the oven a good clean later..."

Did I mention she kept going on about sugar? It doesn't matter anymore. The past is in the past. It didn't make any sense then; I don't know why I'm trying to make sense out of it almost fifty-five years later. Then she ran her fingers over invisible piano keys. We went out before the children could see.

"Please, keep an eye on her. I need to go with the children. They're hungry."

The *Gustloff* normally held around two thousand passengers. There must have been ten thousand of us on board. Even today, no one is sure precisely how many. In other words, the ship had bathrooms for two thousand people, not ten thousand! The smell invaded every gangway, lounge, and staircase: people had relieved themselves wherever they could. A terrible stench. Some were seriously ill; you could smell it. Old men, children, women, and Wehrmacht officers. I found a place with the children that didn't stink too much of shit. I felt so relieved. First, to know that I was saved. We were going back to Berlin, far from the war, far from Ivan! The auxiliaries daubed the children's chapped cheeks with some sort of ointment. Men on the wharf were casting off. We'd only just made it. Women were throwing their children into the arms of strangers, Kapriel; I swear it. Children's bodies that had missed the deck lay in the water between the *Gustloff* and the wharf.

Hundreds of people were still trying to board. There were shouts and screams, but soon the engines revved and, a little after noon, I think, the *Gustloff* pulled clear of the wharf. The children waved to those left behind, those poor, desperate prisoners of hell.

He was there, on the wharf, with her. The auxiliary I'd seen outside his office. His hand on her shoulder. Behind every man, Kapriel... Always look for the blonde.

I was also elated to be heading out to sea that day because the *Gustloff* was taking me back to Papa, and I hadn't seen him since leaving Berlin. It was, after all, a KdF ship he'd travelled on himself. But the trip meant even more to me than that: Papa had also told me that one of our ancestors had taken to the Baltic Sea one day, never to return. Here I was, taking to the sea, to go back to my Papa in Berlin.

Clara had fallen asleep in the cabin where I left her. I wanted to show the children around the ship. They'd never seen anything so luxurious! Mama had told me that the Führer had his own cabin, the only to be so lavishly furnished. Because there was no first class aboard the *Gustloff*. All the cabins were the same; there was no hierarchy. Everyone had the right to the same luxury. That was another of Onkel Adolf's ideas: every German should have the same odds, even on a cruise! But apparently the Führer had his own cabin on board, finer than all the rest. It was, it seems, never occupied. The sheets were never dirtied; for years it was dusted in the hopes of a visit that never came. But there was no way of showing that to the children: there were too many people on board. Mattresses lined up side by side in the ballrooms, where the sick lay, and those, like us, who'd trudged for days and weeks through the ice and snow. And now we were going back to the west, far from the war, far from the Russians.

We were sitting in a grand room with panelled walls that must have been a lounge or smoking room in better times. There were people everywhere. Every time you moved, you'd bump into an old man or step on a child. People were sitting on the lounge floor. They'd been through hell. Saved at last. "We're going to Kiel!" someone shouted. And in no time at all German hearts were gladdened and people began to sing. Bottles of schnapps appeared out of nowhere. From the end of the gangway, snatches of an East Prussian song reached us. I forget how it went… Someone within earshot was telling dirty jokes. We could smell bread being baked in the galley. There would be food! An auxiliary, a girl from Memel, I think, had become fond of the children. She told them stories since she could see I was just about to keel over. Hours passed. At some stage, a few strapping young men who were hiding who knows where began belting out the hunters' chorus from the *Freischütz*. Hans and Hannelore recognized it right away. I was pleased to see I'd awakened an interest in music in them. And, amazingly, even after days of fleeing through the snow, even after nights without sleep, that song from the *Freischütz* brought them back to the night they'd held my hand at the outdoor opera. Hannelore even asked if I thought they'd find the three arrows one day! She was still thinking about those damned arrows, even as we were aboard the *Gustloff*!

We could hear a radio playing a speech by the Führer: "Today marks the twelfth year of our reign…" And only then, Kapriel, did I realize it was January 30. It had been six days since we'd left Königsberg. For six days, we'd stumbled through ice and snow, been attacked by fighter planes, we'd lost Helga, eaten bark, and fought off death, the *Erlkönig*. I sat down on the lovely hardwood floor. The overture of *The Magic Flute* kept running through my head. The children sat down too. Hans to my right, Hannelore to my left, Heinrich between my legs. We settled ourselves on a spongy bed of life jackets that had been handed out just in case. We fell asleep to the sound of the Führer's voice.

"You're twenty-five, Magda! Happy birthday!"

Those were the last words Hannelore said before she fell asleep. (It was at that moment, Michel, that Magda lost her temper. I had just asked her how long it had taken the *Gustloff* to get to Kiel. Because that's where it was headed. Magda slammed down her glass and stared hard at me. She pinched the bridge of her nose as if she'd never heard anything so stupid. She tsked loudly. It must have been getting late, after eight o'clock. She said she was very tired and asked if we could go on the day after tomorrow. So I left. She seemed exhausted. As well she might be. I cried into my pillow. Poor little Helga; how sad.)

～○

Berlin, November 25, 1999

Dear Michel,

Today's Thursday. I haven't heard from Magda since Tuesday. I knocked last night after work but she wasn't in. You'll have to wait to hear the end of the story. I wonder if Wolfgang's still alive. What a nasty piece of work! Speaking of which… Today I got a strange card in the mail from Bavaria. The fourth Terese Bleibtreu, do you remember? The one I was holding out least hope for? Well, wait till you hear this. She sent me a postcard:

"Dear Sir, Come by whenever you like, but don't wait too long. You never know at my age. Terese."

She'd picked out a postcard of the Alps. Very Heidi. I have to go! I don't dare ask my boss for time off, and that leaves me only Sunday and Monday. But Terese lives in a village called Feldafing, southwest of Munich. The asshole of nowhere, as Magda would say. The train ticket will cost me a fortune, but I'm dying to meet her. The longer I wait, the more complicated the trip will be. Anyway. I'll try Magda again tomorrow and maybe leave Saturday afternoon after work. So exciting—*spannend*, as they say!

Gabriel

~~~

<div align="right">Munich-Berlin train, November 28, 1999</div>

Dear Michel,

It's absolutely unbelievable. I thought I'd seen it all at Holy Canadian Martyrs with that Thanatopoulos woman, I thought relationships didn't get any stranger than the one between Suzuki and Maman, and here I am discovering all kinds of even weirder goings-on in Germany. I've just passed Nuremberg. The Bavarian night is just on the other side of the window. They've hung little Christmas lights around the bar in the restaurant car, where I've come for a well-deserved beer. As you must have guessed by now, I decided to take the quick trip to Bavaria in the hopes of finding Terese Bleibtreu, older sister to Ludwig, the childhood sweetheart of my ninth-floor neighbour, Magda. I haven't seen her since she told me the terrible story about fleeing Königsberg. Well, I think I might have spotted her on the tram on Frankfurter Allee, but I couldn't swear to it. It might have been just another old East German woman. I left her a message and she must have read it: it's no longer in her mailbox. Thank God I didn't mention Terese Bleibtreu. You'll see why. What a funny country Germany is. You think you have all the pieces to the puzzle, and then it all gets mixed up again. Everything goes to hell. There's nothing for it but to pull yourself back together.

And start over.

On the other hand, dear brother of mine, my German is really coming along. I'm still taking classes, but now they're at the Humboldt. *Deutsch für Ausländer.* I took the train to Munich in the early afternoon, just after my shift at the SEZ, and read the wonderful *Die Zeit* newspaper from front to back. We don't have any quality newspapers like that back home; I think they're only in Germany. It took me some time, and I'd only just finished the last article when we pulled into the station. What can I say about Munich, other than it is to Berlin what Toronto is to Montreal. Richer, shinier, cleaner, more moralizing, more religious, more… Bavarian. I got a room in a not-too-expensive hotel beside the Marienplatz, *Die Deutsche Eiche*. The German Oak—the name inspired confidence. Imagine my surprise when I discovered a gay sauna and an equally gay restaurant attached to the hotel. The guy at the front desk told me I could use the steam bath for free since I was staying the night. Very German. I wandered around the old city for hours. Munich is the Germany of second-language textbooks: beer and sausages, old women with grey chignons in loden coats, 400 mark shoes on a crappy bike, S-Bahn trains with floors you could eat your dinner off, the sparkliest of Christmas markets, city hall and its glockenspiel. It's all so charming. It's the clockwork Germany: wind it up and it'll do a little dance. *Ein Prosit, ein Prosit, der Gemütlichkeit…* At the hotel restaurant, the owners heard my accent and put me down as a Quebecer right away. They have friends in Quebec City and go there regularly, they love it, etc., etc. You know the type.

They even know Villa Waldberta, where Terese lives. Don't worry, I'm getting to her. Well, I will just as soon as I manage to sort out everything she told me. It's complicated. Not from a language point of view; I understood every word. But I can't get my head around the whole story.

The guys at the restaurant told me how to get to Feldafing.

"Leave early. It could well start snowing and the S-Bahn can get stuck for ages. It'll take a good hour. I think it's two or three stations after Starnberg. Yeah, Starnberg, Possenhofen, then Feldafing after that. Once you're there, you'll need to walk to the top of the ridge that overlooks the village and the lake."

They know the spot since the villa was apparently a residence for artists up until 1995. After that, it had been turned into a hospice for the elderly. I couldn't wait to see it. This morning I was on the S-Bahn platform at the Marienplatz waiting for my little red train to Tutzing when a train for Dachau passed by. My heart skipped a beat. It's as though a train heading for Auschwitz had just pulled into the station or, I don't know, a train to some other terrible place you don't want to go. Inside, perfectly normal-looking people were off to spend their Sunday morning in Dachau. But Dachau was there before the Nazis and it'll be there long after we're gone. Words take on such importance, and what for?

After Pasing and Westkreuz in the suburbs, you reach the little town of Starnberg, where you can catch a glimpse of the lake that shares its name. At the end of the lake, the snow-covered Alps stretch out in the mid-morning sunshine. I'm telling you, Bavaria has got some picture-postcard scenery! At Feldafing, I was the only one to leave the train, which pulled away from the station in a blizzard of snow. The hill was steep—just as well I was wearing waterproof ankle boots with sheepskin liners and nonslip rubber soles. The village of Feldafing is a discreet community. You can't even see it from the S-Bahn. Since it was Sunday, everything was closed, and I had to walk to the old church to ask the way. I was very early. Terese was expecting me at noon and it was still only eleven. I had an hour to kill in a dead village. I walked around once or twice. There was a luxury hotel—the Kaiserin Elisabeth (it's Sissi, Empress of Austria... she came from this part of Bavaria!)—and a bakery. On the main road, to the left, there was a golf course, or at least what looked like one beneath the snow. Pretty homes. You would have laughed—there was someone playing the piano in one of them. A good-looking young woman, who seemed to be practicing a Christmas piece. Bach, I think. You'd know. Then I came across an old lady and asked her for directions. She was very nice. She was affable in the way that people from the country are, like the nuns in Rivière-du-Loup. She showed me a staircase leading up to the ridge that looked down over the lake.

"Then turn left and you're there!"

It was the first Sunday of Advent and she was carrying a wreath, like the ones Mom used to decorate the kitchen table with, do you remember? The other children would laugh at us because she'd insist on lighting all four candles before Christmas. As I climbed the staircase that made its way up between the homes and gardens, I was almost eaten alive by an enormous guard dog. It was ugly and stupid, trained to frighten people. Up above, there was a little Protestant church where people were singing *Tochter Zion, freue dich*, a hymn that rings out in German churches during Advent. It was so lovely that I stopped to listen. Do you know who composed it? Could you look it up? It's so delightful. It's almost enough to make you want to start going to church again.

Villa Waldberta doesn't look anything like a hospice. It's a large, pale home built in the Bavarian style, with a little onion-shaped dome. Huge grounds overlook the wonderful lake, with trees so tall they must have already been standing in 1945. Idyllic surroundings: a cherry tree serving its buffet of frozen fruit to famished birds and a huge hemlock shaking a little of the previous night's snowfall from its branches. My soul filled with a vast sense of relief. The place was perfectly relaxing.

As I approached the house, a little chihuahua began to bark. He made me think of that Wotan, your D'Ambrosio's dog. A nasty little mutt. I rang the doorbell. The chihuahua was running rings around my legs. Someone had dressed it in a little tartan coat and four little booties so its feet wouldn't freeze. The service entrance opened and a stout little woman was standing there, a broom in her hand.

"Can I help you?"

She looked like she owned the place. I didn't need to say much. A few words and my accent gave me away.

"You're the Canadian from Berlin? Terese is expecting you at noon. Would you like to warm up in the kitchen?"

"I'd love to."

"Be quiet, Merlin! Merlin's the guard dog. He won't bite. I'm Berta."

"You seem a little young to be living here."

"I don't live here. I just look after the house. It's enormous! There are six apartments to clean, the common rooms, shopping to do for the residents! I never stop!"

"Did you change your name to match the villa's?"

"Ha! Nothing gets by you! Listen, knowing Terese, she might have forgotten you're coming. She mentioned it to me yesterday, but given her age, I'd rather go up and see first. Come in, come in, or the damned dog will never stop! It's freezing! Merlin, shut up! And your name is...? Oh, hang on, she told me just this morning at breakfast..."

"Maybe she's at mass."

"Ha! You obviously don't know Terese. No, I'm quite certain she's not at mass. Hee hee! I'll have to tell the gardener that one! At mass! Terese! Please, what's your name again?"

"Lamontagne, Gabriel Lamontagne."

Since she couldn't pronounce Lamontagne and I found her quite charming, I said she should call me Gabriel.

"I won't shake your hand, Kapriel. God only knows what I might catch! People are covered in germs! Just two weeks ago, an electrician came to do some work and gave me the flu. The second since October, I'm telling you. And you have to be careful around the old dears. So try not to touch the door frames or the handles. You took the train, didn't you? Full of germs! A petri dish on rails! Would you mind washing your hands in the sink here before I let you up? You can't be too careful. That's what my mother always said."

It was just like I was back at home, Michel. You'd have sworn it was Mom with her rags and bleach. You know what I mean. And she talked, on and on in that accent from the depths of Bavaria that I barely understand. At least one word in three was lost on me. She showed me into the kitchen and went off to tell Terese that I was there. Inside the villa everything was very Bavarian, with Jugendstil furniture and a forest-green tiled masonry stove. I wondered whose bright idea it was to put a bunch of old people who had trouble walking in a house with so many floors and staircases everywhere you looked. A platform elevator answered part of my question. It clicked on with a dull, electrical sound and Terese came down slowly to the main floor. And as the old German lady descended from her little nest on high down to where the mere mortals roamed, I considered the question that I hadn't asked because I'd been caught up in the moment, without stopping to think what I was going to ask Terese. What exactly did I want from the woman? For her to come visit us in Berlin at the end of January? Would she even be able to? And what did she remember of Magda? For the first time, Michel, I thought about the reasons that had led me to take an eight-hour train journey only to end up in this movie set of a place where suddenly I couldn't understand a word anyone was saying. Would Terese remember anything other than the 1930s? And if they hadn't found each other since the wall fell in 1989, wasn't that a sign that fate had separated them forever? Perhaps each one thought the other was dead. When you hit eighty, are you really going to start looking for your high school friends? The platform moved as slowly as my questions; I still had two seconds left to leap off the sofa and make a run for the exit before Terese saw me. And I should have run, now that I think about it. I should have gotten out of there. The platform stopped two seconds later and at last the woman in the wheelchair was in front of me. Berta was behind her, smiling.

"She hadn't forgotten. Isn't that right, Terese? It's Mr. Montaigne!"

"Lamontagne," I corrected her.

Her back was to the light, so I didn't have a clear view of Terese's face. Berta pushed her wheelchair into a nicely decorated room and left us to it. Through the glass door, I could see her spraying more disinfectant where I'd been sitting on the sofa. Remind you of anyone? Terese was almost exactly as I'd imagined her. She was wearing a long Bavarian-style dress with green flounces. She was fairly well built. Not as fat as Magda, but not far off, and rather barrel-shaped. She smiled. And I swear, dear brother, in her hair—tied up in a nice little braided bun—she was wearing the amber barrette that had once belonged to Mademoiselle Jacques.

"So you're Magda's friend! You've taken me back years and years, Kapriel. May I call you Kapriel? You're so young…"

"If I can call you Terese."

"As you wish."

"Are there many of you in the villa?"

"Ten. There are six apartments. Four couples and two old women like me. It used to be an artists' residence, but the Bavarian government turned it into an old folks' home. I was fortunate enough to get one of the apartments."

"How does a singing teacher from Charlottenburg wind up in Bavaria?"

To my great surprise, Terese got up from her wheelchair before answering my question.

"Relax, it's not a Christmas miracle! I just wanted to play a little joke on you! Ha! You should have seen the look on your face! I only use this wretched chair on the platform, but I can walk otherwise."

I really hadn't seen it coming. She glanced over at the front door. Berta was outside.

"She's gone out. I can light one up. I'm not allowed to, strictly speaking, but it's Sunday. Do you smoke?"

"No, never."

"Very wise. It's very bad for your health. And you don't have the physique of a smoker."

She took out a silver cigarette case with her initials on it—T.B., as in tuberculosis!—and lit a long cigarette. There was something about her, a touch of *La Cage aux folles* that amused me. She reminded me of someone out of an opera, but I can't remember which one. Probably every woman in every opera. That's who Terese Bleibtreu reminded me of. She wanted to hear my story. Then she told me hers. She'd fled the advancing Red Army, too. She'd even made it to Bavaria only days before Berlin fell. She stayed on after the war, in the zone occupied by the Americans.

"In East Germany, under the Russians, they'd nothing to eat for years. Here, very quickly, no one went hungry. And I'm Catholic: it was easy to settle here. I had family on my mother's side in Tutzing, the town at the end of the S-Bahn line. I put down roots here and taught music in college. Then I was a choir mistress for a while."

She'd known the G.I.s, she told me; some had even fallen in love. Right after the war, refugees from the East flocked to Villa Waldberta. Jews, mostly. There and at the Feldafing camp, they waited for visas to America or Argentina.

"Many went to Canada, I recall. They all wanted to go to Canada. Some of the people who lived in this luxury villa were Auschwitz survivors. They were dumped here. They were sick and everything... Many died here. Too weak. After that, the house was used by the planning committee for the 1972 Olympic Games in Munich. Then the artists moved in. Painters, writers, musicians, people from everywhere came to work at the villa. Back then, I remember, I was still in Tutzing; in 1992, I came to hear some Brazilian musicians. Their music was so delightful."

"But nothing beats Schubert's *Ständchen*..."

She stopped, looking a bit put off.

"She told you about the serenade? Magda's never been one to hold her tongue. How is she? No! Wait! I'll get us a scotch, then you can tell me how Magda of Prussia is doing! Ha! I'm going to have a nice afternoon to myself with this handsome young American. Stop blushing—I'm not the first to flirt with you! Sit down so they can see you from the hall. That's it. I want to make absolutely sure Frau Namberger sees you on her way back in from mass with that senile old husband of hers. It'll kill the old cow! Now be a dear and play along..."

She poured two scotches, no ice, then went on with her story, not stopping to listen to mine. She had taught music in Tutzing, then retired like everyone else. After falling in her bathtub, they'd said she should move into a retirement home. She didn't like the people she lived with in Tutzing. She found a place in Starnberg, but this time she didn't like the staff (not clean enough for her liking). Then Villa Waldberta opened its doors and she'd been lucky enough to get her hands on an apartment there.

"It's not for everyone. You have to like peace and quiet. Magda would have died of boredom. She hasn't changed, I expect. She always needed to be in the thick of the action, always moving, always stirring the shit somewhere. Oh, but you'll think I'm still bitter over Ludwig. I take it back."

Already I sensed I'd made a big mistake. I'd opened a German Pandora's box, dreamed up by the craziest producer imaginable.

"She loved *Tosca*. That I know. She and Ludwig, my little brother, must have seen that particular opera dozens of times together."

"Yes, and no doubt having a father who worked for KdF made it easier to get tickets."

"KdF?"

"Yes. Kraft durch Freude. You remember, don't you? The big travel and entertainment agency in the 1930s."

"Ha! Ha! Ha!"

"Did I say something funny?"

"She told you her father worked for Kraft durch Freude? Interesting."

I didn't like the way her tone of voice had changed, as though she was preparing to reveal everything. How was I supposed to know if Magda's father, Alfred, had worked for KdF or not? I'd no idea who my own father even was, I felt like telling her. I don't even know what he did for a living, and that hasn't stopped me from having a life of my own, from doing things... I didn't want to antagonize her, but already I could tell there was something unresolved between Magda and her.

"She also told me you play the piano very well and that your brother Ludwig was a wonderful baritone."

"Light baritone," she corrected me. "His timbre was light. He was light in all things."

"I wanted to surprise her for her birthday. Is your brother Ludwig still alive?"

"Why, of course not! What a strange question! Does she really think he's still alive? Be honest with me, Kapriel: is Magda Berg walking around Berlin saying my brother is still alive? Has she lost her mind like the Nambergers?"

"No! No! She only told me how she loved him, all the stories, the little cross..."

"She told you about the little cross?"

She looked ready to throw her scotch in my face. She lit another cigarette. The air in the little living room began to thicken. We heard Berta's footsteps. She wasn't at all happy that Terese had decided to light up in there.

"Then please, my dear Berta, explain to me what an ashtray's doing in here?"

"It's a decoration. It's an antique."

"Because there's a little swastika on the bottom? That's why we keep it? As a reminder of the days when they made German shepherds out of porcelain?"

"What do you mean, a swastika?"

"I'm joking. I have every right to smoke on the ground floor. My lease couldn't be clearer. Your own mother smoked, Berta. So they tell me. So why are you intent on giving smokers such a hard time?"

"Because it's a filthy habit!"

"Get out of here, Berta."

She slammed the door behind her. Mom really does have a long-lost sister in Germany. No two ways about it. Terese opened a window so that I had some fresh air.

"I have no idea what you do know, young man. I have no idea where you come from or how you stumbled across Magda in Berlin-Lichtenberg. You say 'Canada,' she says, 'Kraft durch Freude' and I'm supposed to believe you, just like you believe her little stories! Why are you even interested in all these stories about… about…?"

"About Germany?"

"Yes. All these stories about Germany."

"I think it's too late to be asking now. Sometimes it's Germany that takes an interest in us."

"Quite."

"Your cigarette's out."

"I know. They go out all the time. Like everything. They only last for so long."

"Could you be more precise?"

"What do you want to know?"

"I don't want to know a thing. All I wanted was to surprise Magda for her birthday on January 30."

"You're very nice. That's a very 'New World' thing to do. Together again for her birthday! It's not very German. Here, what's buried stays buried. We let sleeping dogs lie."

"Terese, if you have something to say to Magda, if you have a gripe with her, I can—"

"A gripe? No, that's not it at all! I won't be going to Berlin. But since you've come so far to see me, I owe you an explanation. Actually, I replied to your letter precisely because of that little gold cross."

"Ludwig's cross?"

"Yes, Ludwig's cross. Does she still wear it?"

"I… Perhaps. I'm not sure."

"But I'm boring you with all this talk of jewellery! You want to know why I won't be going to Berlin. I'd be lying if I said I was too lazy or too ill."

"Don't feel obliged to tell me everything. If you don't want to come, that's fine. I won't be offended. But she's told me so much about Ludwig and the 1930s that I was curious to meet you."

Terese looked out the window. She fell silent. And then, without looking up at me, she began to talk.

"When the Bergs arrived from Königsberg in 1934, Magda just about had a nervous breakdown she missed home so much. In the city, she looked a little like you do here: like a lost lumberjack. She was very masculine. She walked like a Wehrmacht officer. And Ludwig was just the opposite, if you catch my drift. I realized from a very early age that I'd have to protect my little brother. I knew why I'd need to protect him, but not from whom. If I'd known that, he might still be with us today, but I didn't. No more than Magda was able to protect her little sister."

"Her sister? Magda had a sister?"

"Oh... She didn't tell you about her sister Elisabeth? A shame..."

By that point, Michel, I knew it was too late. A dog barked outside. A crow cawed. Two old people came in, probably the Nambergers she'd mentioned earlier. The old woman smiled at me and glanced over at Terese, who gave her a knowing look. The old man looked completely lost. They went up to their apartment.

"That's her, the Namberger woman. Thank you, Kapriel, you're a darling."

"You were saying that Magda had a sister..."

"Are Canadians fond of stories?"

"Canadians love stories. If they didn't tell them, there wouldn't be a Canada today."

"Even ones that end badly?"

"Your stories often end in Canada..."

"You can be quite witty when you put your mind to it. Let me pour you a little more scotch, my dear Mr. Lamontagne. I'm starting to realize that with you, things need to be explained clearly and slowly. And you have the same name as she does!"

Terese finally told me her story. I was starting to see why Magda had never gone off looking for Terese Bleibtreu.

"If I'm to remember everything, I must first think back to my brother Ludwig, to everything he told us about Magda. From 1935 to 1939, they were inseparable. Much of what I know of her, I learned from him. My dealings with her were limited to singing and teaching her music. We music teachers learn more about our students than they ever do about us, even if we're the ones talking the whole time. Because you never learn from someone directly. What you really know about a person, you learn through other people. It sounds cynical, but that's how it is.

"When the Bergs came to Charlottenburg in 1934—yes, that's right—they came from Königsberg and the father was indeed with KdF. Magda's mother was rather bourgeois. Let's just say Berlin wasn't her cup of tea. Too common for her. On that, she and I agreed, but that was as far as it went. The Bergs had two girls. The one you know and a younger daughter who must have been six or seven in 1934. What I heard—again from Ludwig—is that Elisabeth was handicapped. What was wrong with her? I don't know. She couldn't really speak. No, I never saw her. From what Ludwig told me, she must have had Down's syndrome. She lived with her parents at the beginning; they had someone to help with her at home. Then Elisabeth was committed. In 1936, I believe. Her mother didn't want to, but her father's mind was made up. Barely three years later, a letter arrived from the institution. Elisabeth had died from the flu. The doctors hadn't been able to help her. Needless to say, she'd probably been gassed like the other handicapped people in the Third Reich, but the fewer questions you asked, the quicker you climbed the ranks. That was true for KdF too. You find me heartless? Perhaps. But wait till you hear the rest!

"Frau Berg never really got over it, and I'm only assuming she knew how her daughter died. Let's just say there was a particularly nasty strain of the flu going around German institutions in 1939. When Magda was sent back to Königsberg, it was largely because her mother was losing her mind over what had happened to Elisabeth. She wanted to know. She sent letters along the lines of "Where's my child?", as did others who knew the flu was nothing more than a lie. But in a world in which everything is a lie, there are no liars. Do you follow? It's the same for God and money. In order for it to work, everyone or almost everyone has to believe. And it works. For a while.

"When her husband told her to shut up once and for all, Frau Berg locked herself away in her room. She killed herself during an air raid in 1943. I'll never forget the sight. There was no debris in Schillerstraße, only broken windows and, in the middle of the street, Frau Berg's body lying in a pool of blood, right where I'd played *Ständchen*. She'd jumped, like Tosca. A little more scotch? I can hear your soul positively melting away. Poor Kapriel. Buck up, pull yourself together!

"I'm guessing you have a brother or sister. Otherwise you wouldn't be fighting back tears. The rest of it—the singing lessons, the friendship, the cross—Magda told you the truth about all of it. But perhaps not the whole truth. How can I tell? It's simple. First, you don't look like someone one tells the whole truth to. You're too handsome. What's that? You still don't know. The good-looking ones are always fed lies. The others—the ugly ducklings, the just-okays, the five-out-of-tens—they get the truth, the raw truth. The uglier you are, the more people give you the straight goods. How come? Search me. It's as though beauty attracts lies. Do you think people tell Claudia Schiffer the truth? No, they tell her what they think she wants to hear. Perhaps people are trying to hide their ugliness from you, trying to be loved by the good-looking people of this world.

"At the start, when they first met, people thought, I mean my parents thought, things would turn out differently. They would end up getting married, that was for sure. I didn't say a thing. You know, Kapriel, I can remember the day Ludwig was born. There were five of us, growing up. Ludwig was my only brother. Three girls came after him. They're all dead. One from diphtheria in 1945, Maria three years ago, here in Bavaria, from cancer, and another was killed in an Allied air raid. It's pretty, all this snow. It must remind you of Canada. Are you going home for Christmas? No? Ah. It must be beautiful in the forest. Zzzz… Oh! I'm sorry! Where was I? Oh! Yes! My little Ludwig. Ten years my junior. Small from the moment he was born. Fragile. Ethereal. I knew the moment he walked. He took me for his mommy. A slight, blond angel. Too delicate to survive in a world of brutes. As a young teenager, Ludwig was suddenly very expressive. He was funny. Everything Magda told you—his jokes, his scrapes, his pranks—it's all true. He liked to pretend he was that lesbian singer from Berlin. Wait, what was her name again? Waldorf! No! Claire Waldoff!

"Ha! We had such fun on the piano!

"I don't know what Ludwig saw in Magda. Or rather, I know only too well. She was just masculine enough to win his confidence. That's what he liked about her. And she sought the same ambiguity in him. If you stood in front of the pair of them, it was like looking at four different sexes. It was hard to say which of the two was more feminine, which was more masculine. Together, they expressed every possibility. Only Magda was right for Ludwig and vice versa. Magda quickly became all he ever thought about. We'd only ever see him at meals. He'd tell Father he was off to the Hitler Youth, only to come by my place to spend more time with Magda. I think they must have been in love in a way, the absolute love of teenagers, you know, a love that soars high above the pleasures of the flesh. A kind of union of the soul, but in an inexplicable and almost miraculous way, a physical union too.

"In 1939, Ludwig came to me with an advertisement he'd found in the newspaper. A new singing teacher at Alexanderplatz. He was so excited. After a first free lesson, he persuaded Magda to give the man a try. I found the whole thing rather strange, Ludwig going all the way to Alexanderplatz for singing lessons, but well... I went with them to put my mind at ease. The gentleman was very jovial, very methodical, very convinced of his own methods. Always joking. I went along to make sure my little brother hadn't fallen into the clutches of a madman. I wanted to at least be sure before I got married.

"I understood everything when I saw how Ludwig looked at Herr Küchenmeister. 'He says I should call him Peter,' he said on the S-Bahn on the way home. Magda was livid. Küchenmeister had been a little hard on her, it's true, but all music teachers are hard. They have to be. Their profession requires it. Magda was a jealous woman, you know. She must still be. I wouldn't be at all surprised to hear she flies into jealous rages with you.

"And then it happened. One day, Magda came round looking for Ludwig. I told her he was at his singing lesson with Küchenmeister. She saw red. 'Well, he never mentioned it to *me*!' And she stormed off in a temper. I knew it would end badly, I can tell you that right now.

"She rushed over to Küchenmeister's apartment and barged in without knocking. The poor fool didn't lock the door when he was with his students. She went into the studio to find Ludwig sitting on Küchenmeister's lap. The three stood there, stiff as pillars of salt.

"The next day, the *Kriminalpolizei* knocked at my parents' door. Father opened. They took Ludwig away. He was nineteen, Kapriel. They didn't want to say why they'd come for him. Mama was frightened to death. Our sisters were huddled in the corner, crying. I tried to find Magda, but she was nowhere to be found. No one answered at her house. When I managed to track down Herr Berg, he would barely speak to me. 'Magda has left for Königsberg.' That's all we managed to find out. She didn't write, didn't send news, didn't call. Nothing. The last time I saw Magda Berg was when she knocked on my door in 1939 looking for Ludwig. She'd turned him over to the police. No doubt about it. And during the trial, we learned that Ludwig and Küchenmeister had been 'caught in the act.' Who by, if not her?

"Things went downhill very quickly for my little brother after that. We didn't know where they had him locked up. My parents were terrified, given everything else going on in the city: when someone disappeared, it was usually for good. I went to the *Kriminalpolizei* four days after his arrest. I asked them what a poor angel of only nineteen, as frail and slight as a little bird, could possibly have done that was so terrible. Of course, the pleas of a big sister didn't have any effect on them. The trial was held shortly after that. Ludwig and his music teacher weren't tried at the same time. Küchenmeister was sent straight to Sachsenhausen, yes, the concentration camp. His was a repeat offence: he'd already been sentenced two years earlier for homosexuality under Paragraph 175. Ludwig was given two years in a correction centre, which meant that he, too, was shipped off to Sachsenhausen, like Küchenmeister. From that moment, my parents lost virtually all interest in him. To be honest, I'll never know if they were simply frightened or if they agreed that Ludwig deserved to be sent to a concentration camp for being a homosexual. I don't think they thought about it too hard. Did you know that the Nazis created a kind of official agency? The Reich Central Office for the Combatting of Homosexuality and Abortion. Both were considered highly illegal and fought against by the same body. I was able to see Ludwig at the trial, then he disappeared. Six months into his sentence, he sent me a letter from Sachsenhausen. He said he was allowed a visit; he begged me to come. I didn't mention it to my husband.

"He'd lost weight. He was no longer the same boy. He was broken, how else can I put it? I don't know what might have gone on in the camp. What he told me, when he eventually got out in 1941, was that he had sung there. Küchenmeister wasn't released at the same time. I don't know if they were really in love. Ludwig once told me an interesting anecdote. Homosexuals in Sachsenhausen were kept under strict surveillance by the SS and kept apart from the other prisoners. Anyone and everyone was free to hit them, beat them senseless, humiliate them, and worse. Some died from the beatings. Apparently some of the men would sing to summon the strength to get through their gruelling work days. They sang, as Ludwig put it, rubbing their voices together to pleasure each other. Do you understand what he means? No? Me neither, but that's what they did apparently. There were doctors in the camps, real doctors, people who would otherwise have been delivering babies or treating colds, who suggested the homosexual prisoners be castrated in exchange for their release. They were convinced that castration would cure them of their abnormal desires. Isn't that horrible? But it worked, just imagine: some of the prisoners agreed to be castrated in order to survive. Put yourself in their place: anyone sent to a camp knew they had only the slightest chance of ever leaving it alive. So they left their balls behind; they'd caused them nothing but trouble anyway.

"When he got out, my parents didn't want him to live at home. They were too ashamed. He should have been called up but he got caught a second time by the police, this time by a plain-clothes officer he'd approached in the subway. I still saw him, but only rarely. His last letter dates back to May 1942. After that, he probably fell prey to the guards at Sachsenhausen. No one got out. Not anyone wearing a pink triangle anyway. They didn't last long, as a rule. In July 1942, it seems most of them were beaten to death by the guards. Your eyes look like they're about to pop out of your head, dear. Did you notice that you and Berta have the same colour eyes? It's funny. Speak of the devil… What does she want this time?"

(Michel, I didn't catch everything since they spoke in Bavarian dialect. Berta wanted to know if I'd be staying for something to eat, I think. I don't know what Terese Bleibtreu replied. I'm not sure.)

"So, my dear Kapriel, now you see why I probably wouldn't be the best surprise for Magda's birthday. I tried to stand up for my brother, but what could a thirty-year-old woman do against the Nazi judicial system? If you can even speak of justice… You'd do the same if you had a little brother, wouldn't you? If you knew that he was being held by madmen, that his life was at risk, you'd help him, wouldn't you? You're big and strong. They might even listen to you. But Magda's little sister and my little brother couldn't be saved. I'd ask you to say hello to Magda for me, but I'd much rather you didn't mention your visit. There's no point bringing it up with her. But there is one thing you can do for me. It was me who gave Ludwig the little gold cross, the same one Magda was given in exchange for one of Magda Goebbels' earrings. Is that story true? I think so, yes. She was more than capable of such a thing. The cross belonged to my brother. I find it a shame that Magda still has it. *If* she still has it. You never know what that heathen might have swapped it for by now. The Bergs weren't religious at all, you see. She told you? Anyway. If ever you could get your hands on the cross without the long arm of the law getting in the way… Ludwig's initials and date of birth are engraved on the back. December 13, 1920. He would have turned seventy-nine next week. But I'm asking too much… No, forget all about it. What's lost is lost. I'd ask you to stay for the evening, but you said you had a train to catch. You'll be able to find your own way back, won't you?"

She stopped talking, walked me to the door that looked out over a spacious patio and down onto the lake. Beside the door, a little painting above a piano immediately captured my attention. It showed the death of the virgin, the entombment of Mary. I couldn't believe it. It was much smaller than the one in the Gemäldegalerie in Berlin. Twelve inches by eighteen, I'd say, perhaps a little bigger. I smiled and stared at it for a second or two.

"It's a reproduction. The original disappeared at the end of the war, they say. Local legend has it the original was itself a copy of a piece from the Vatican Pinacoteca. The villagers say all kinds of things. Some even say it was an American who took it. Go figure."

"I saw the same picture in a museum in Berlin."

"Do you have an interest in religious art?"

"No, not really. But I have a brother in Rome and he mentioned the painting."

"A brother? How lucky you are to still have a brother. I can't say the same."

It was much colder outside. Only her head poked out through the half-open door.

"I hope I haven't let you down too badly," she said.

"No, I'll just have to rethink my calculations, that's all."

"Calculations? You? No, no more calculations, young man. I can tell you, the craziest calculations are what you call illusions and I can tell by your eyes that calculus is not your forte."

"Illusions?"

"Yes, illusions. We're all stripped of them in the end. That's what's just happened to you."

"I wish I understood what you mean."

"You'd like to understand lots of things, I'm sure, but like I said earlier, you're not the sharpest tool in the box."

"I didn't come here to cause you any harm, Terese. Now you're just being insulting."

"You're an easy target. It can't be the first time."

"How can you be so sure?"

"The truth is, I'm being unfair. You're not stupid, just naive. An easy target for Magda."

"I don't understand."

"You take everything at face value. You must constantly be taken aback, let down by life's little illusions. Your neighbour in East Berlin tells you about her childhood and you take her story as the gospel truth. A woman writes to you from a village in Bavaria, says her name is Terese Bleibtreu, and you come down to meet her, convinced it must be her. If you weren't such a danger to yourself, I'd almost find you sweet."

"If you say you're Terese Bleibtreu, I've no choice but to believe you. And I was the one who contacted you. I don't see who you could be other than Terese Bleibtreu. Even the woman who let me in knows you by that name. Are you forgetting that?"

"Stop it. You're making me giddy you're so fragile right now."

"I don't understand."

"Bring me back my brother's cross and I'll explain what I mean. Have a safe trip home, Kapriel."

As I walked back to the gate, a crow again shouted something in Bavarian. I turned around. She was upstairs already, her face at the window. It reminded me of the old woman's silhouette in Alfred Hitchcock's *Psycho*. Berta was calling after her chihuahua in the villa's garden. It had started to snow.

"Would you like me to give you a ride to the station? If you hurry, you'll catch the next train to Munich. Otherwise you might have to wait a while."

I got into her Volkswagen and we drove off. I tried to strike up a conversation. All I got out of her was that she was born in Villa Waldberta on January 1, 1946, back when her mother worked for the owners and the house was a refugee camp.

"That's why I'm called Berta."

"What if you'd been a boy?"

"My mother says she'd have called me Ludwig. That's Louis in French, isn't it?"

"Yes, it's the same name as Ludwig. Was your father called Ludwig?"

"Seems so. Here comes your train."

I ran to get on the train. German trains are alarmingly punctual. I'd have liked to chat a little longer with Berta, for her to explain to me how and why Terese had become so nasty. So that she could tell me a little more about her father as well, but the train cut short the conversation about her father Ludwig. I was, you'll understand, a little stunned. I hadn't expected our meeting to go like that at all. As I keep telling you, in this country you have to be ready for anything.

I didn't speak or read or write or think on the way back to Munich. But my eyes were open the whole way. At Westkreuz, we passed by neat and tidy *Schrebergärten* that made me think of Magda this summer. S-Bahn stations paraded by like the names of so many concentration camps. At the hotel bar where I'd left my bag, the owner found me a little grumpy. Since I was in no rush, I asked him what he knew about how homosexuals were treated in the Third Reich.

"*Ach!* It was hardly the gayest of times."

Who says the Germans have no sense of humour? He disappeared off into the kitchen. At the Deutsche Eiche bar—which really couldn't be nicer—a guy our age had heard us talking and chimed in. I think he must have been trying to chat me up.

"Homosexuals under the Nazis? It was simple: they were sent to camps. To Dachau, near here, and to Sachsenhausen, further north. Most of those who were caught and sent to camps didn't survive, as a rule. They were beaten to death. The luckier ones—pardon my cynicism—were castrated in return for being allowed out. Some agreed to it. But most died from mistreatment. And after the war, those who'd survived kept their heads down since it was still illegal. Are you in Munich for long? Are you French?"

I thanked him, paid for my beer, then headed to the station. The train is speeding north through the dark German night as I write. I think I'm going to fall asleep. I really have to get some shut-eye. All that effort, only for Terese to turn out to be a confused, bitter, and nasty woman. I know I'm not always very quick on the uptake, but explain something to me and I'll get it eventually. She doesn't seem to understand what it's like living in a foreign language. The Germans are obsessed with always trying to get you to see that you don't understand, and that their lives, their stories, their concerns are far too complicated for your inferior foreign mind to handle. I think that's something they could work on.

Gabriel

Dear Michel,

I'll spare you the details. I saw Magda. She was in Magdeburg again. She came back Saturday. I got another invitation to sit down on her sofa. Now I know the full story. I'm sending it to you along with my latest batch of letters.

Read it carefully. You're blind if you can't see the potential for a book or a film, or an opera. I can't get the scene of the *Gustloff* out of my head. It'll stay with me forever.

I'm spending Christmas here with Magda. Since she's an atheist, she'll be happy enough watching screwball comedies on TV. She loves Leslie Nielsen, you know. She thinks he's hilarious.

Gabriel

Magdalena Berg's Third Notebook

The first torpedo struck just after nine o'clock. I was woken by a deafening clatter, as though a big dresser full of china cups and plates had been tipped from the second floor of a building out onto the sidewalk. Then another, and then a third. People were screaming, crying for help. Almost immediately, the *Gustloff* began listing to the port side. Where do your thoughts turn at times like that? I grabbed the children. I could only find Heinrich and Hannelore. Hans must have gone looking for his mother while I slept. I had the presence of mind to grab the life jackets. We had to get up on deck. And quickly. You know, you don't really think of others in such circumstances. I walked over people's heads. Over dead bodies, I think. Very quickly. I was very strong back when I was twenty-five. Heinrich on my shoulders and Hannelore under my arm. I was holding on to her so tight that I kept turning around, sure that I'd be carrying no more than an arm I'd ripped off. Without a word. Struggling our way up. You can't imagine the screams. Over ten thousand women and children suddenly realizing their best bet has just become a fatal illusion. I can still feel their lifeless bodies giving way beneath my feet. Stumble and you wouldn't get back up.

Despite the panic, I managed to find the gangway leading to Clara's cabin, but a group of men was coming in the opposite direction, blocking my path. One of them recognized me. "Your friend's already out on deck!" I followed them, along with Hannelore and Heinrich. No sign of Hans. The boat was beginning to lurch terribly; people were toppling over.

And the cries, Kapriel. The cries.

(She got up and, for the first time since I've known her, she had to sort of mime her history, as though words had suddenly failed her. But without looking at me, her head turned away, as though she could no longer bear my gaze.)

We eventually made it to the *Sonnendeck*, the sun deck outside. The lifeboats were already full of Wehrmacht officers, along with women and children. Scenes from the end of the world. When they saw that the lifeboats were full, the Wehrmacht soldiers began shooting women and children to save them dying from hypothermia. People clung on to whatever they could.

And the cold, Kapriel. It was as cold as the Germans found God's heart that night. The whole deck was inch-deep in ice. Rafts that should have been put to water were blocked by the ice. I remember one man going at the ice with an ax as he tried to free them... And I saw her. She was being carried off by people, soldiers, to a life vessel. I shouted her name. She didn't hear me. Running as fast as I could across the icy, lurching deck, I caught up with her.

"We need to get into the lifeboats, Magda. The boat's sinking!"

She didn't seem frightened at all. In fact she was calm and still as a summer night. Her fever seemed to have dropped. The lifeboats were already full. Just ahead of us a man was trying to climb into one. But they were for women and children only. He got in all the same. The officer in the lifeboat shot him dead. Right in front of us.

The auxiliary who had taken such good care of the children had managed to follow us. I don't know why. She was holding onto Heinrich.

"Do you know how to swim?"

Clara and I almost had a heart attack. Of course we knew how to swim, but in that water, death was no more than ten minutes away.

"If we don't jump now, we'll be dragged down with the ship. Fasten your life jackets and follow me. We need to go down into the water."

That girl who was just a little bit younger than me, that girl whose name I didn't even know, she saved my life. Her plan was absolute madness. The boat was beginning to pitch dangerously to the left. We were to climb up the highest side, she said. Then step over the guardrail and slide down the side of the ship and into the water.

"It's our only hope. Once you're in the water, swim toward a raft or one of the lifeboats out there. Whatever happens, stay clear of everyone else. Whatever you do, don't cling to me or I'll punch you! Those who hang on to each other will be dragged down. You need to swim!"

"But will anyone come to our rescue?" I asked

"I'm not holding out hope," she said, climbing across the listing deck toward the guardrail.

Clara said the Führer wouldn't let us sink to the bottom of the Baltic; he wouldn't let an SS man's wife and children die. She wanted to know about Hans. It would have taken a good, hard slap to get her to shut up about her Führer. As if that was the time!

Others who'd had the same idea were sliding down the side of the boat. There was a mass of bodies at the bottom. Thousands of people had already jumped and were in the water shouting and screaming. On our way down into the water, we slid past the windows of the *Promenadendeck*, an outdoor deck closed off by unbreakable glass. It was where people went for a stroll on cold days. Thousands of people were now trapped inside. They were beating on the glass; you could heard their muffled shouts. And gunfire, everywhere. The auxiliary, twenty yards before we reached the mass of bodies, pointed to where we should jump. I wanted to live. And so did she. We jumped. She with Heinrich, me with Hannelore. I think Clara must have jumped thirty seconds after us. The water was ice cold.

"Get away from everyone! Now! Quickly! Don't let them grab you!"

You know, Kapriel, the Germans are very fond of swimming. It's one of the things we do well. I followed the auxiliary, who was holding little Heinrich in her arms, but water, Kapriel, water undoes even the best laid plans. Hannelore was lost. All I saw of her were her little feet sticking up out of the water. The life jacket was too big for her; it trapped her upside down, her head underwater. Drowned. The temperature outside was eighteen below. The water was barely above freezing. I kicked away two boys who were grasping at me, having lost their mother.

"It's too late for her. Don't look back!"

The auxiliary swam like a fish in spite of her wool coat. Clara followed behind, gasping for breath. How long did it take us to swim out to the lifeboat? People lifted us out of the water, took Heinrich in their arms. We were freezing and soaked to the skin, but alive. Not long after that, other swimmers clambered into the boat, and others after them, until someone shouted, "That's enough! Another one and we'll sink!" And the men began beating at the frozen fingers that were clinging to the boat. Those still in the water looked at us in disbelief. That man's face, Kapriel. He looked me in the eye as if to say, "What are you *doing*?" Just before he got an oar to the knuckles and disappeared. I can still see him... Every evening.

And suddenly the shouts intensified, if you can imagine! The *Gustloff* lit up like there was a huge party on board. All the lights came on at the same time and the sirens began to wail. Seconds later, the ship slipped into the Baltic. All that remained were thousands of people floating on the surface. Their shouts could be heard for a few minutes longer, then they died of cold, one by one.

There were twenty-five or twenty-six of us in that lifeboat that kept threatening to capsize beneath our weight. We had to wait hours in the freezing cold. The moon was full in the sky above. The wind froze our faces. A first boat came by, a German Navy ship. It turned back when it saw us, for fear of being torpedoed too. We had no notion of time. Very quickly it was too late for Heinrich. Hypothermia takes the children first, you see. We threw his frigid body overboard to lighten the load. People shouted and cried for hours. Every five minutes, a voice would fall silent, taken by the cold. And just like that, little by little, one by one, death came for nearly every person in the lifeboat. We threw their bodies into the water once we realized. The auxiliary, Clara, and I huddled together.

"I think we've lost the war, Magda," Clara said. "The Führer can't do a thing for us now. He's left us here to die."

And then: "Suddenly everything seems so clear... I can see things so clearly now. It's like before... before the fevers..."

And a few minutes after that, the cold silenced her forever. All I could hear was the wind and the three voices the heavens had spared, the auxiliary's body stiff against my back.

Five hours it took for them to rescue us. When they hoisted me up onto the boat, I regained consciousness for a moment or two, then they dragged me over to the furnace with the others. Miraculously the auxiliary was there, too, shivering. They poured cognac into our mouths and we passed out.

They dropped us at Swinemünde; 1,239 survivors out of over 10,000 passengers. The rest are at the bottom of the Baltic Sea. I spent two weeks in a school that had been converted into a hospital. Then I went on alone to Berlin via Stettin. Some people took me by cart as far as Stettin. After that I walked, from farm to farm, from village to village, until I got to Charlottenburg, or what was left of it.

There was no trace of Papa. He must have died in an air raid. Or at least that's what I thought until the Red Cross got in touch to let me know he'd died in Uruguay in 1979. He'd taken refuge over there in the last days of the war. He'd lived under an assumed name, had even married another woman and had two children with her. It was his son who'd insisted the Red Cross contact me. He'd even included a photo. I wasn't hard to find. Everyone was on file in East Berlin. I didn't go around shouting it from the rooftops, naturally. I just thought how history repeats itself. Papa had told me one of our ancestors had left one day, never to return again. How had he known? As part of the hiring process with KdF, he'd had to produce what was known as an ancestor passport, a document that traced his family tree back to 1800. Every civil servant in Germany had to have an approved researcher look into their ancestry. You see, the Nazis wanted to be sure there were no Jews or Slavs or gypsies among their ranks. Do I still have it? Of course not! It was destroyed in an air raid. But Papa showed it to me once. The family tree went all the way back to the late eighteenth century, back to a certain Johann Berg, the son of Christian Berg, a carpenter who left to work as a mercenary in America. After that, we lost all trace of the Berg family. It's strange: that man left to fight in a war, leaving his son behind in East Prussia, while my father was fleeing the war. In both cases, the result was the same: they both abandoned their children. At any rate, knowing he'd felt compelled to flee Germany in 1945 set me straight about a few things.

I took refuge at a convent in Dahlem. And there I waited until the war was over. There you have it, Kapriel.

(She sat back down on the sofa and finished off what was left of the wine.)

After that, I was done with courtly love. I was having none of it. I chose to live in the East because, for me, if you took the "national" out of "national socialism," you ended up with something viable, more or less. Wrong again. I mustn't know what's good for me. Now you know everything. No, wait… In 1948, I contracted tuberculosis, but I recovered. Imagine that!

I've lived in this building since it was built in 1972. Are you crying, Kapriel?

America Forever

At 11:57 a.m. on December 31, 1999, Solange Bérubé climbed the metal staircase to Madeleine Lamontagne's office to deliver the tray of food that she took at that exact time every day. A thin fillet of grilled halibut (it was a Friday) flanked by steamed peas, a boiled potato, a glass of Heinz tomato juice, a plain fat-free yogurt, a maple leaf cookie, and a cup of extra strong Red Rose black tea. Solange knocked three times on the solid oak door. There was no reply. She knocked three more times, this time a little harder and faster: *agitato*. No answer. There was no point calling out; she knew perfectly well that it was impossible for a human voice to penetrate the four inches of solid wood that separated her from Madeleine. Solange set the tray down on the stainless-steel pedestal table that was screwed to the white wall and grabbed the door handle with both hands. She turned it slowly, without making a sound, hoping to find Madeleine deep in concentration over some important file. Instead, Solange discovered the sorry sight of the fifty-year-old woman splayed across a maple coffee table in front of a black leather armchair. Outside, the December wind howled, whistling around Lamontagne Tower. The other buildings around it scraped at the Montreal skyline like so many bodies buried alive clawing at the inside of their caskets.

Madeleine Lamontagne must have fainted in her office on the 61st floor of 456 Rue De La Gauchetière. A large envelope postmarked in Rome a few days earlier lay on the floor. Pages from a school notebook were scattered in front of Madeleine's body as though she had flung them away just before losing consciousness. Her posture suggested she'd been sitting on the edge of the armchair and fallen down onto the table. Solange Bérubé cried out and brought a hand to her mouth. She ran over to Madeleine and tried to bring her round.

"Madeleine, wake up! Madeleine!"

It was clear from Solange's firm grip that she was used to lifting and carrying objects far heavier and more unwieldy than Madeleine Lamontagne's tiny dried-out body. Solange shook Madeleine, slapped her gently, pulled and pinched her earlobes in the hopes of a reaction. No luck. Madeleine's body remained inert. Overcome by panic, Solange rushed to phone for help, her staccato footsteps echoing off the wooden floor. As she explained to the emergency services in her contralto voice that Madeleine Lamontagne had collapsed onto a maple table, the rest of the immediate entourage attending to the president, founder, and principal shareholder of Mado Group Inc., alerted by Solange's cries, had gathered around the still-open door. The deathly silence observed by the small group of some twenty women of varying ages was interrupted only by a few rumbling stomachs, which was perfectly normal for that hour of the day. Outside, in the distance, white icy fog was rising from the St. Lawrence River. A landscape that could have been painted by the hand of death itself. Like a concert of unbridled flutes, the piercing howl of the wind reigned over the sad spectacle.

A secretary helped Solange lay Madeleine out on a leather sofa until the ambulance arrived. A dozen sheets of paper lay on the carpet, each covered in round handwriting, to all appearances a letter sent to the billionaire, its personal nature in stark contrast to the office's sterile surroundings. Raising her eyes heavenward, as though familiar with the letter's contents, Solange picked up the pages one by one and put them out of sight.

"Is she breathing?" someone asked from the doorway, her tone strangely indifferent.

"Barely!" the secretary replied as she felt for the president's pulse.

Solange moved quickly and surreptitiously, scooping up the little brown glass vial that lay by Madeleine's wrist and dropping it into her pocket. If there had been a tiny microphone at the centre of the crowd that had gathered, it would have captured the chatter of the employees who had been forced to work during the final hours of the turn of the new millennium. Torn between the prospect of seeing death carry off the hand that fed them and the hope of finding themselves at last released from their duties, their remarks ranged from neutral to somewhat irritated. They'd just seen her in the elevator, heard her on the telephone, or spoken to her themselves. An intern had given her the mail like she did every day, she said. One hour before noon. In fact, it would have been possible to work out almost to the second exactly when Madeleine had fainted by asking precise questions to the employees gathered in the doorway. All they would have had to do was work out who had been the last to receive an instruction from Madeleine, and at what time, then add on a few minutes. Because it was quite impossible for Madeleine to go more than ten minutes without telling someone what to do. That had never happened, not within living memory. There had once been a time, a far-off, almost forgotten time, when no one had been ordered around by Madeleine Lamontagne, but, aside from Solange Bérubé, none of the employees who worked at Mado Group Inc.'s headquarters could claim to have known it.

In calling the emergency services, Solange Bérubé had made the serious mistake of mentioning that the victim was Madeleine Lamontagne.

"Get a move on. The company president's unconscious," she'd said, to quote her exact words.

The 911 operator had been only too happy to let the ambulance driver know, and he, in turn, had told his girlfriend, who he happened to be talking to when the call came in over the radio. His girlfriend, a gossip if ever there was one, armed with a cell phone and an address book as long as your arm, took a mere ten minutes to rouse enough people for the news to beat a path to the newsroom of a leading Montreal daily, where preparations for the January 1, 2000, edition were in full swing. The editor, Jacques Sanschagrin, was informed by a buxom intern who'd just sent him a touching piece on a toothless old local woman who'd been born on January 1, 1900, and was gearing up to celebrate her 100th birthday. "This might be of interest to you…" she'd said, after announcing that Madeleine Lamontagne, the rich and implacable businesswoman, was on the verge of being stretchered out of the skyscraper that bore her name.

Sanschagrin nearly fainted with pleasure at the news. He threw both arms up in the air, like the patient owl perched on a treetop stretches out its broad wings at the sight of a delicious little field mouse scurrying across the forest humus. This would make a welcome change from the millennium bug and Y2K celebrations. The more quickly a rumour spread, the more likely it was to be true. This was Sanschagrin's guiding principle. Madeleine Lamontagne being unwell appeared about as probable to him as a Martian invasion, but the mere fact that an ambulance had been dispatched to Lamontagne Tower was newsworthy in itself, fit for the front page, or at least the second. At any rate, the information would certainly be of value if gleaned quickly enough. Just to be on the safe side, Sanschagrin let Venise Van Veen in on the news, not wanting to be attacked as a "sad little boor" or a "nasty piece of work" the next time he bumped into her in the softly lit corridors of Radio-Canada or over a steak tartare in a fashionable bistro.

He found her at home.

The news hit Venise hard. Recently retired, she'd kept up only a daily newspaper column, a weekly radio show, the odd TV appearance on current affairs shows, and an occasional panel participation "just to keep her mind active." Since the very beginning of her career, Venise had learned to tick all the right boxes on the questionnaire of public opinion: for abortion, against the death penalty, for secular schools, against sharia law, for the legalization of marijuana, against immigration quotas, for same-sex marriage, against the force-feeding of geese, for outlawing smoking in public places, against the Gulf War, for lacy underwear, against English being taught from the first year of elementary school, for stores opening on Sundays, against compulsory vaccination, for an independent Quebec, against the return of school uniforms, for a more polite society, against GMOs, for an overhaul of the school calendar, against plastic bags, for sanctions on Cuba being lifted, against burkas, for a return to all-boys schools, against uranium enrichment, for new metro lines, against a new gasoline tax, for affordable daycare, against Michael Jackson.

She didn't put a foot wrong.

Five minutes later, without so much as pausing to touch up her makeup, Venise Van Veen sped out of the parking lot beneath her apartment on Peel, heading for Lamontagne Tower. Meanwhile, the ambulance driver who had been dispatched to Madeleine's aid was taking his time. He stopped at red lights, respected the speed limit, and even let a young woman in a fur hat cross the street in front of him (she opened her mouth and let out a cloud of steam by way of thanks). There was no way he was going to hurry to help the woman an editorialist (a sworn enemy of Venise Van Veen's) had just dismissed as "Quebec's very own Margaret Thatcher." The driver's colleague, unaccustomed as he was to such displays of nonchalance, politely pointed out that it was an emergency call, all the same—and a serious, legitimate one at that—to which the driver replied, though only after spitting out the window a toothpick he'd been gnawing on for the last half hour:

"Do you really want that Lamontagne woman to make our lives a misery in the 21st century too?"

"I really want to not get the sack," the worried paramedic replied to his colleague.

Those on the 61st floor eagerly awaited the arrival of the emergency crew. A particularly efficient secretary had already begun cancelling Madeleine Lamontagne's appointments. She'd given the energy minister, the archbishop of Montreal, and the manager of communications at National Bank more or less the same message: *Madame Lamontagne regretfully informs you that she will be unable to attend her meeting with you at Lamontagne Tower this afternoon. Please contact her secretary a week from now to schedule a new appointment. Madeleine Lamontagne is deeply sorry for the inconvenience and hopes you will accept her sincerest apologies.* Nobody on this final afternoon of the year was sad to see their improbably scheduled appointment cancelled, apart perhaps the archbishop's representatives, who had hoped to make the most of the holiday cheer to broach the delicate matter of a new roof for the cathedral. But that, along with the end of the world, would now have to wait until the next millennium. The archbishop would have to address his prayers to the saint whose statue stood atop that very same roof.

The ambulance drivers immediately noticed something out of the ordinary about the skyscraper. First off, everything was impeccably clean. Every surface, especially the glass and metal, gleamed like it had just left the factory. The pale wooden floors appeared to have been sanded and varnished that very morning. The air smelled vaguely like an infirmary: a blend of ether and calla lily. The elevator door opened out onto a spacious room on the top floor. There, lined up as though in a sci-fi movie, were twenty identical wooden desks, ten to the left and ten to the right. A handful of computer screens displayed table after table of complex calculations. And, in the centre, a desk slightly bigger than the others, with a sign: Solange Bérubé, Vice President. The room filled the entire floor, with the skyscraper's huge windows taking the place of office walls and bathing everything in intense sunlight. Aside from the surprisingly spotless surroundings, it was first and foremost the sight of so many people at work on December 31, 1999, that surprised the paramedics. Both just stood there for a moment, long enough for the elevator doors to close on them. The driver pushed the button to open them again and walked straight into what he would later describe to his psychotherapist, a cigarette in his trembling hand, as "a huge dissecting table hanging in the air."

Beside the vice president's desk, they noted a poster resting on an easel, by all appearances a Mado Group Inc. ad campaign. In various shades of metallic blue, the island of Manhattan with its office towers and skyscrapers. In the foreground, the Statue of Liberty with the face and hair of Madeleine Lamontagne; the result being that anyone taking just a quick glance might think that Mireille Mathieu had dressed up as the Statue of Liberty for

Mardi Gras. The picture showed Madeleine Lamontagne wearing a maternal, protective smile, holding a breakfast tray, a cornucopia made up mostly, but not exclusively, of maple syrup pancakes, fried eggs, bacon, orange juice, a steaming cup of coffee, a fresh fruit salad, buttered toast, jam, cretons, beans, ham, ketchup, and sausages. The tray, disproportionately large compared to the tiny woman carrying it, gave the impression that Madeleine Lamontagne had superhuman strength. To the right, in sober, elegant writing:

Mado's
Breakfast from Canada
Opening January 1, 2000
Times Square

It was no doubt at that very moment that the two ambulance drivers began to understand the complexity of the situation fate had just thrust upon them. Along with everyone else, they knew Madeleine Lamontagne as the founding president of the Mado's restaurant chain, with meals served on every continent and its logo (a white egg held up by three roses) plastered across hundreds of buildings around the globe. "An empire upon which the sun never sets," "The jewel of Canada's food industry," "Quebec's embassy abroad," and "*Nostra cosa*"—just a sampling of the platitudes used to describe Madeleine Lamontagne's worldwide business success. In some U.S. business circles, Madeleine was even known as the Queen of Breakfast, a nod to the fact that the market for every meal ingested before noon across North and South America belonged entirely to her. The two dawdlers realized a little too late that by taking their time in coming to Madeleine Lamontagne's aid, they had rendered themselves reprehensible in the eyes of Mado Group Inc., a corporate entity in which God himself seemed to hold shares—which wasn't entirely untrue in a strictly theological sense.

The skyscraper known to all of Montreal as "Lamontagne Tower" was the personal property of Madeleine Lamontagne, who rented out the first sixty floors to various businesses and ministries. Floor 22, for example, was home to the Ministry of Natural Resources and the Brazilian Consulate in Montreal. Dubbed "a lean, mean breakfast machine" by a journalist for *Maclean's* magazine, Mado Group Inc. was known for its pragmatic, efficient business model. And so the company occupied no more than a single floor of the tower with the sixty-foot fibreglass egg on top. At night,

Madeleine's illuminated egg changed colours and could be seen from as far away as the suburbs on the south shore of the St. Lawrence River. The fact that Montreal had been dominated by a giant egg since September 1995 was less down to sheer chance than to Madeleine Lamontagne's determination to prevail over Quebec's largest city. True to form, she had patiently waited for the day 1000 De La Gauchetière opened its doors to unveil, to much fanfare, the plans for her own tower, much to the displeasure of her rivals, whose glory was short-lived.

This was the beast the two ambulance drivers had thumbed their nose at by taking their own sweet time.

Inside the office, Madeleine Lamontagne still lay unconscious on a black leather sofa, surrounded by her all-female entourage. It was this scene— an *Entombment of Mary* fit for this freezing end to the century—that the ambulance drivers discovered as they arrived on the scene. Solange Bérubé was irritated to see that neither man seemed in a hurry and that neither had worked up the slightest sign of a sweat. On the pedestal table to the left of the oak door, Madeleine's cup of tea released its final puff of steam. Solange stared daggers at the men, prodding them into action.

With a few virile and professional movements, they quickly secured Madeleine's little body to the stretcher they'd pushed over to the staircase connecting the mezzanine level to the main room. With the employees looking on, they then headed back to the elevator, closely followed by Solange Bérubé, who'd just given precise instructions as to how the rest of the day was to unfold and grabbed from a drawer in Madeleine's desk a battered, dog-eared book that she stuffed into her bag. Solange motioned to the elevator. By this stage, it was clear to the paramedics that they didn't have a shred of authority in this aseptic women's world. In monastic silence, the ambulance drivers, Solange Bérubé, and Madeleine slowly descended the sixty-one floors of Lamontagne Tower. Solange Bérubé had entered a secret code that meant the elevator wouldn't stop at the other floors, which were empty in any case, as it was a public holiday. They bundled the stretcher into the ambulance in the deserted underground parking lot. Solange sat beside her president and friend. As he was getting ready to start the vehicle, the driver felt Solange Bérubé's bony hand grab him by the shoulder. He jumped. Solange carefully enunciated each of her syllables:

"If anything should happen to our president, I shall personally destroy you and everyone around you."

The driver acknowledged the threat without reply. His colleague swallowed hard. The ambulance sped out of the parking lot and back into the thick of the celebrations, the number of revellers having seemingly doubled within the space of a few minutes.

"We're taking you to Saint-Luc," the ambulance driver said, trying his best to sound reassuring.

"No, to the Jewish General," barked Solange Bérubé.

"But, Ma'am. We're right beside Saint-Luc. It'll take us an hour to get to Côte-des-Neiges in this traffic!"

"To the Jewish General, and stop contradicting me. Use your siren!"

The ambulance driver turned on his flashing lights and siren, and the vehicle took off like a rocket, Mount Royal in its sights. He was too taken aback to argue, and resigned himself to following the madwoman's orders. At 12:31 p.m., the siren's wail could be heard at the corner of Beaver Hall and René-Lévesque, where Venise Van Veen's Volkswagen was heading east.

As the ambulance transporting Madeleine Lamontagne sped by in the other direction, Venise Van Veen thanked God (but under her breath, since she was officially an atheist). The ambulance's siren had brought part of the downtown traffic to a standstill. Without considering the legality of the manoeuvre for even a second, Venise did a U-turn and sped after the ambulance as it turned right onto Guy. She followed it at top speed all the way along Côte-des-Neiges until it reached its destination.

While the sirens wailed their way up Côte-Sainte-Catherine, Madeleine emerged fleetingly from her torpor only to fall back into the depths as though submerged by a wave of tiredness. Solange tried to keep her conscious by reciting Hail Marys to her, which Madeleine would haltingly finish off with "pray for us sinners, now and at the hour of our death." She foundered after the third prayer. Solange, who was holding her head, went on praying alone. The two ambulance technicians had decided to keep quiet. They had been startled by the steel cross hanging over the huge oak door into the office where they had collected their patient, but now these prayers—everyday and innocuous though they were—made their blood run cold. The incantations that had once reassured generations now filled another with terror.

The ambulance was only yards away from the ER when Madeleine was seized by a series of mild convulsions, as though a malevolent spirit was trying to violently extract itself from her body in response to Solange's prayers.

"New York, New York… it's New York, Solange. Or Rome," she muttered faintly.

To which Solange replied: "You're in Montreal, Madeleine. Forget about New York. You won't be going. I leave tomorrow. I'll open the restaurant for you. You won't have to go back there, Madeleine. Would you like me to call Michel and Gabriel?"

Madeleine rolled an unwell eye. She no longer seemed to be of this world. When she heard the names Michel and Gabriel, she turned her head, apparently in acute pain.

"My little angels," she sobbed.

Then she returned to her delirium while the ambulance men opened the rear door to remove the stretcher. The driver offered his hand to help Solange down, but she pushed it away and glared at him for the tenth time that hour.

"Don't touch me, you moron. And you'd better pray our president survives this!" she hissed.

The driver bowed his head, visibly wounded. Madeleine rambled on, without the other passengers paying the slightest heed.

"Berlin is so far… We'll never make it. We'll have to stop at Elbing… The Russians will leave… It's artillery fire… The Russians will come back… Tante Clara, I've lost Hans. He must be on the lower decks…"

Now they were in the parking lot beside the Fannie and David Aberman Atrium, itself a neighbour to the Harriet and Abe Gold Department of Medicine. The ambulance drivers rolled the stretcher into what looked like an aquarium with sliding doors, where an old woman was lying on a gurney. The people in the ER waiting room saw Madeleine's contorted face pass by out of the corner of their eye, followed by the vice president, who now had the look of someone who'd just given up smoking. The hospital staff asked the usual questions. How did it happen? Did she hit her head when she fell? Any relevant medical history? Was she on any medication? Any history of heart disease? Epilepsy? Narcotics?

"Of course not!" Solange protested, tightening her hold on the little brown vial she'd slipped into her pocket.

The president opened and closed her eyes on the stretcher, occasionally went into convulsions, and called weakly for her companion.

"Where is she from?" a doctor asked. He'd something of a poetic bent, and liked to lend an ear to the delirious rambling of his patients.

"Madame Lamontagne is a major donor to your hospital," Solange snapped. "You know very well where's she's from!"

This cast a chill over the room where a battery of nurses, orderlies, and doctors were flitting from patient to patient, coming and going through a set of doors that led goodness knew where, just like in a Feydeau play, where the lover tries to run from the closet he's hiding in and escape out the window, only to end up passing through the kitchen and every other room in the house. The doctor replied in a tone that was nothing short of apocalyptic:

"She's speaking German. 'Die Kinder, die Kinder sind alle tod,' she just said."

"Madeleine doesn't speak German. She has a son who lives in Germany, but she hasn't spoken to him in years."

"Well, it sure sounds like German. Or maybe Yiddish."

"You must have misunderstood. Does it really matter? Can't you just help her instead of worrying about that?"

Solange couldn't see why the emergency room doctor was so preoccupied by what Madeleine was saying. She was delirious, end of story. You don't try to understand delirium; you try to avoid it, to get rid of it. That's how you cure it, not by dwelling on the irrational. Half of what Madeleine was muttering was incomprehensible. It was a stretch to claim it was German. The doctor, a man by the name of David Hirsch, was no crank, however. What he'd heard was too close to Yiddish for him to be mistaken, but if the woman in front of him insisted on denying the obvious, there wasn't much he could do. Madeleine Lamontagne must have heard the words in an opera, he thought to himself. Or some song on the radio. They'd stuck in her memory and chosen to come out at that precise moment. What opera might it be, he wondered. Perhaps Wagner or Strauss. Certainly not Mozart.

A heart attack had already been ruled out, as had an aneurism, and fainting brought about by diabetes. Dr. Hirsch decided to place the patient under observation and wait for her to come around before continuing his examination. For the time being, he suspected low blood pressure or some form of poisoning. Madeleine was moved to a bland little room. It was full of objects whose shape or function made it impossible to forget you were in a hospital. Solange sat down on a chair beside her friend. Once they had the room to themselves, she took out of her bag the little dog-eared book she'd slipped into it earlier and opened it up at a page marked with a bookmark, also dog-eared. The book seemed to be well travelled. Madeleine continued to rave.

"It's the Empire State Building. There it is. It's very high. Right at the top… My name is Madeleine, I'm here for Dr. Beck. I want to see the doctor."

Solange pretended not to hear. She flicked through the little book, looking for the passage she was sure she'd find. "I confess to Almighty God," she began. "And to blessed Mary ever-Virgin, to blessed Michael the Archangel and blessed John the Baptist, and to the holy apostles Peter and Paul, along with all the saints, and you Father, that I have sinned, in my thoughts and in my words." Her voice barely rose above the shouts of pain, the doleful moans coming from the other observation rooms, and the messages over the intercom—"Dr. Hirsch, code blue. Dr. Hirsch, code blue," "Orderly in Cardiology…"—ringing out so sadly less than twelve hours before the year 2000.

Venise Van Veen had blatantly ignored the hospital staff trying to keep her out of the area reserved for patients brought in by ambulance. A bossy nurse had, however, managed to attract her attention.

"There's no way I'm leaving. I've been a personal friend of Madeleine Lamontagne's for years. I really must know where she is."

Only the French-speaking staff recognized Venise. The others took her to be a madwoman. And so it was thanks to Montreal's linguistic divide that Venise's mission proved successful. The domineering nurse realized she was probably the only person in the ER who knew who Venise Van Veen was and the only person who could take her to Madeleine. She also knew that Venise Van Veen and Madeleine Lamontagne really had been friends for years. It was hard not to: for the past week, the national television channel had been advertising a special program to be hosted by Venise on January 1, 2000, with Madeleine Lamontagne, a federal minister, and a host of other celebrities among the guests. The nurse took pity on the journalist she'd always admired.

"This way, Madame Van Veen. Follow me. I hope she'll be OK for tomorrow!"

"What do you mean?"

"For tomorrow's show. With you. Madame Lamontagne is one of the guests, isn't she?"

"Yes, but we recorded it the day before yesterday. I almost never do live television nowadays. It's terribly draining."

"Well, in that case, she can go ahead and die if she likes!" the nurse said without thinking.

"Ahem. Let's hope she makes it until New Year's Day at least!"

Venise remembered an old saying. "If tact were for sale, only those who already have it would buy it." Whoever said that? she wondered. She found Madeleine looking deathly pale and Solange all out of prayers.

"My God, Venise! How'd you find out so quickly?" Solange leaped to her feet, snapping to attention.

"I have sources everywhere. Sanschagrin called."

The two women fell into each other's arms.

"What's wrong with her?"

"I don't know. We found her lying face down on the table in her office. She's been reading letters from Michel the past two days. He's in Rome. He had plenty to say, at any rate! Look, he even sent some notebooks!"

While Madeleine slept, Venise took a look at the envelope, the letters, and the German notebooks. Of Madeleine's two sons, Michel was the one she knew best. She'd often had the young singer on her show to plug his work when the critics had their knives out.

"But the notebooks are from Gabriel."

"What do you mean from Gabriel?"

"Look, Solange: *Magdalena Berg's Notebook, translated from the German by Gabriel Lamontagne.* Has your little Arnold been learning German?"

"He's been living in Berlin for a year."

Madeleine stirred at the sound of Gabriel's name.

"He'll be the death of me, that little ruffian."

A relieved Venise and Solange ran off in search of a doctor.

"She's talking!"

Madeleine spent twenty minutes alone with Dr. Hirsch before being released. He didn't believe her for a second when she explained she'd inadvertently tripped over her brown leather wedge-heel Clarks. Hirsch knew Madeleine, a well-known donor to the hospital. He knew very well that nothing she did was ever inadvertent. Every move was calculated. He'd heard or read it somewhere before. Probably in the *Fortune 100* article about her restaurant chain. The same article where he'd learned she hated anything that took her away from her business. Which explains why she didn't have to work too hard to get released.

"I'd ask that you see your family doctor as quickly as possible. This week, ideally."

"Absolutely."

As she left the Jewish General's Bernice and Morton Brownstein waiting room, Madeleine, flanked by Solange and Venise, didn't make the mistake of walking into the arms of the other journalists who'd had the decency to wait outside the hospital.

"News travels even faster here than in Rivière-du-Loup, eh Solange?"

"Why bring up Rivière-du-Loup all of a sudden?"

"Because a certain someone thought they were doing the right thing by suggesting Gabriel go see the stations of the cross in Rivière-du-Loup. You wouldn't know anything about that, would you?"

The three women passed through the hospital in awkward silence.

"And then handsome young Gabriel went running off to the convent, full of himself, my dear Solange. And looked for all the family graves but couldn't find Old Ma Madeleine's!"

"Madeleine, please..."

Venise got her money's worth. She now had an answer to every question she'd never dared ask. They passed through the Fannie and David Aberman Atrium, turned left, and walked out a door and past the Bloomfield Centre for Research in Aging in the Peter and Edward Bronfman Pavilion. Madeleine glanced distractedly at the gold plates engraved with the names of people who had donated to the hospital. In the column reserved for the most generous donors, those who had given over one million dollars, Madeleine's name was there among the Steinbergs and Rosenblums. She reached out and touched the plate with her right hand.

They then disappeared down a long hallway and came out into a dark room. From there, they went into another building, which brought them out onto De La Peltrie at 1:45 p.m. A strange calm hung over the freezing streets. Madeleine hailed a taxi, paying no heed to Venise as she protested she'd parked her car elsewhere. The Haitian driver immediately recognized Madeleine, a woman he admired devoutly.

"Take me home," Madeleine declared, slumping onto the back seat between Venise and Solange.

There had been so many articles published about her in the previous twenty years that she no longer needed to give her Outremont address when she stepped into a cab, although this happened rarely since she was always driven around by Solange. The taxi driver took her appearance to be a sign from above: the new century would bring him wealth. He felt compelled to tell Madeleine that his daughter waited tables at Mado's on Papineau.

"Which one? There are three."

"Papineau and Bélanger."

"Ah, yes. Marie-Muriel. We took her on last fall after the expansion. She's eighteen, works thirty hours a week. Never Sundays because she goes to church with you. I remember her."

"Oh, that's her all right," the driver replied in amazement.

Madeleine loved surprising people by showing off her astounding memory. She knew every employee by name in each of her 112 restaurants across the province and could name the managers of her 422 restaurants in the rest of Canada and the United States, even the one in charge of the Mado's Express at Atlanta International Airport, a certain Wanda Burns who couldn't have been more than 4'6". The day Wanda Burns took the plane for the first time in her life to fly up to the compulsory Mado Group Inc. managers' convention (the cost of the flight deducted from her monthly salary over the next two years), Madeleine walked up to her at the Palais des congrès in Montreal, shook her hand, and announced in a Quebec accent so thick you could have cut it with a knife:

"'Ello, Wanda Burns, welcome to Montreal. I 'ope you 'ad a nice trip."

But Wanda had heard: "Hello Wanda. Come to Montreal. I hope you and I strip," which had made her smile.

She still laughed about it all these years after that three-hour bilingual talk on "Disinfecting and Cleaning Metallic Surfaces at the Dawn of the 21st Century." Wanda had wondered how on earth that slip of a woman could have remembered her name. She'd only met her once in her life, the day she'd been hired in Atlanta, and her counter had only four employees, all girls from deepest Georgia, none of whom had ever set foot in Canada.

The taxi driver watched the three women in the rearview mirror. Hands shaking, eyes wide: they didn't seem especially happy. A Creole prayer came onto the radio, but Madeleine could only make out the odd word. God... Forgive me... Eternity. She smelled her hands, which still gave off the stomach-churning whiff of the hospital.

"Can't you hurry it up a little, sir?"

"And could you change the station?" asked Venise, who couldn't have cared less about prayers in Creole.

The driver did what he was told and raced well above the speed limit through the residential streets of Outremont. Madeleine bounced three times as they hit a snow-covered speed bump. With his right hand, he searched for a radio station that was to his passengers' liking. He settled on the news.

"Still no word of opera singer Anamaria di Napoli, who disappeared three days ago in Rome while on location for the filming of the latest Bruno-Karl d'Ambrosio movie, A Century With Tosca, *in which she stars. The controversial director says he is certain the soprano will be found and is refusing to cancel shooting of the final act, set to wrap up today at Rome's Castel Sant'Angelo. The director recently caused an uproar with his comments about the size of female opera singers' waistlines and surprised everyone by picking Michel de la Montagne, a virtually unknown Canadian tenor, to star in his new film. De La Montagne is the son of Madeleine Lamontagne, the founding president of Mado Group Inc., who, we have just been told, has taken ill—"*

"Turn it off, please. I've heard enough."

Madeleine raised her eyes to the heavens. The taxi pulled up outside her home, skidding on the icy pavement.

"How much did you give him for his film, Madeleine?" Solange asked politely, trying to wash away the guilt she felt over her indiscretion with Gabriel.

"Solange, this is neither the time nor the place," Madeleine hissed.

"Don't tell me you sponsored that clown's film, Madeleine?"

"I did, Venise. I gave him as much as he needed. And I don't want to hear another word about it. Do I make myself clear?"

Venise followed the two women into their home on Rue Davaar. She knew it well; she had often been there for supper. They deliberated in the living room, by the glistening light of a magnificent Christmas tree. Madeleine had made a full recovery. All three were aware of Anamaria's disappearance. Michel had called two days earlier, to reassure his mother in case she heard the news from someone else, managing to conceal both his concern and the real reasons behind his companion's disappearance. When she'd asked why he'd mailed the letters from Berlin along with his own, there had been a long silence.

"Did you open the envelope, Mom?"

"Of course I did. It was addressed to me."

"No, no. I sent you the Christmas card. The big envelope was for Gabriel. Put it away in my room until I'm back in Montreal, OK?"

He was practically shouting. Madeleine hadn't cared for his tone. She hadn't brought him up to speak to her like that. Given the circumstances, she'd forgiven the slip, but the incident had piqued her curiosity every bit as much as Attavanti's had piqued Tosca's. That very evening, Madeleine had gone back to reading the letters between her sons and Magdalena Berg's story, thereby fulfilling every mother's ambition: to know what her children said about her behind her back.

She got more than she bargained for.

Then it was D'Ambrosio's turn to call. Madeleine had wanted to keep the disappearance quiet, but D'Ambrosio himself had let the Canadian newswires know, much to the despair of Anamaria's mother, who was worried stiff.

"There's no such thing as bad publicity," he'd said.

That wasn't the problem. Nothing could be done from Montreal to find the poor girl. She was probably hiding out in Rome, Michel explained. But Madeleine had other travel plans.

"I never thought I'd say this a second time, Solange, but you need to pack for both of us. We need to leave right now."

"What? Where to? It's twenty below outside! Where do you want to go in this cold?"

"We're going to New York, Solange."

"We agreed I'd go alone. You swore you'd never set foot there again, don't you remember? I am perfectly capable of opening the restaurant by myself. It's not the first time. I went to Calgary on my own. Seattle, too."

Madeleine went up to her bedroom. She came back holding a tin box she'd kept since the 1950s. With her two friends looking on, she took out the contents:

—a wedding band stripped from a dead man's hand at a boisterous wake where the grieving relatives had decided, just before closing the casket for the last time, to settle a few old scores over fisticuffs on Louis Lamontagne's lawn. While Papa Louis separated the men, Madeleine had snuck up to the casket and pocketed the shiny ring that had been calling out to her with every ray it had for the past two days;

—a silver spoon given to her brother Luc and every other child in the Commonwealth who had been born on June 2, 1953, to commemorate the coronation of Her Majesty Queen Elizabeth II;

—a cheap flower-shaped earring her brother Marc had found in the mud in spring 1957;

—a letter mailed from Potsdam, New York, addressed to Louis "The Horse" Lamontagne. Inside, the photo of Penelope Ironstone, the little American girl for whom any reply would now come too late;

—and a dozen little gold crosses stolen from Dr. David Beck in Manhattan, December 1968. The last of her spoils.

Solange and Venise looked on at the strange haul with no small amount of curiosity. Madeleine held up one of the little crosses between her thumb and index finger and handed it to Solange.

"Solange... Can you tell me what's on this one? I don't have my glasses with me."

"*L. B. 13.12.20.* My God, the writing's tiny!"

"Solange, we absolutely need to go to New York. I know who this cross belongs to. It belongs to a gentleman who lives in Berlin, or at least to one of his friends. I think he's dead."

"You took it from Dr. Beck?"

"Yes, and I left him mine by mistake. But now I know who this cross belongs to. You know the corny joke you always tell, the one about the pigeon who arrives late for tea at the old lady's?"

"Uh-huh."

"You heard it from Dr. Beck's daughter in 1968, didn't you? From Rachel."

"Yeah, she told me it. Her father told her, she said. And what about the other crosses? Were they taken by mistake too?"

"Something like that. You'll have to drive me. Please say yes!"

Solange sighed.

"Yes, but it's getting dark. You know I don't like driving at night, Madeleine."

"Solange, I need to be in New York City tomorrow morning. It's too late to charter a jet and I'll never find a flight tonight. It's not the first time. We've done it before."

"More than thirty years ago! And on a coach!"

"Solange..."

"I'm tired, Madeleine."

"Me too, but I have to go to New York. It's important. It's our first restaurant in Manhattan."

"You should have thought of that earlier. You swore you'd never set foot in New York again, remember? You swore the first time we went in 1968. You shouted and stamped your feet: "Solange, I'm never coming back to New York!" then you threw up into a paper bag. People were staring. And now, on December 31, 1999, you suddenly want me to drive you down to Manhattan? I promised you, Madeleine: I can open the Times Square restaurant by myself. Get some rest. You're just out of hospital."

Venise wondered if she shouldn't see herself out.

"Shall I leave you two to talk? Do you still need me, girls?"

"Yes, Venise. The Good Lord sent you to my rescue once again. You're like a guardian angel to me. It's a shame you're an atheist. Otherwise, you'd be certain of your place in heaven."

While Madeleine told Venise what she needed her to do, Solange chewed things over in the corner. Could she really drive her to New York that evening? That hadn't been her plan. She was to take the nine o'clock flight to open the Times Square restaurant alone, and now Madeleine was changing her mind less than twenty-four hours before the opening. All because of a little gold cross that had been left behind in December 1968. Was she really expecting to find Dr. Beck right where she'd left him? Then, amused at the thought of hitting the road again with Madeleine, just like old times, Solange changed her tune. Sure, she could put up with Madeleine being there at the opening of that goddamn Times Square restaurant that had given them no end of trouble. Solange wondered how the boys had managed to be so stupid as to let their mother in on their letters to each other. And she swore at Gabriel's naivety. What had he even found in Rivière-du-Loup? Who had told him what? Solange was beginning to feel the effects of the slow poison of repentance.

Venise had duly noted Madeleine's instructions. She was to do her a tiny favour while she was in New York. Nothing more than throw a few people off the scent and do a little P.R. for her. Her mission? To turn the spotlight away from Mado Group Inc. by any means necessary, keep the journalists' minds off Anamaria's disappearance until Madeleine came up with a solution, write a glowing article about the woman who had just conquered Manhattan with her eggs, pancakes, and toast, and, last but not least, come up with a ruse to lure that little devil, that degenerate Gabriel Lamontagne and his steroid-pumped body, to Rome. If she were to ask him herself, she knew Gabriel would have nothing but a string of expletives in response. Her plan just might work, if Venise Van Veen lent a hand.

"I'm going to settle a few old scores tomorrow, Venise. If ever things don't work out, I'll need someone to speak up for me."

"You can count on me. I've been doing that for years. Are you planning on sorting things out in Berlin yourself?"

"First, we take Manhattan, then we take Rome. We'll see about Berlin after that."

The forest-green Jaguar belonging to Solange Bérubé sprang out of the garage at three o'clock on the dot. Solange was wearing a pair of ivory-coloured driving gloves and a navy suit she liked to call her "travelling suit." Madeleine, sitting beside her, had pulled on a gooseshit-coloured chunky woollen skirt and a black blouse that made her look like a nun.

Since it was a holiday, both women were wearing plain pearl necklaces, a single strand of real pearls fished by real men on the other side of the world from Montreal, in a country where it had never snowed. With a little luck, traffic would be flowing smoothly across the Champlain Bridge and they'd be on the highway to New York State in under twenty minutes. Downtown Montreal lay spread out before them, a spectacle dominated by the huge fibreglass egg atop Lamontagne Tower.

"You have to admit it's a nice-looking egg. I prefer the violet lighting. How about you?" Madeleine asked.

"Sure, but it's a little Easter-eggy. We could maybe keep violet for Holy Week and yellow for the rest of the year."

"Mmm... I suppose. Maybe you're right. I'll have a word with Marie-Claude when I get back. Do we have any music?"

Montreal's radio stations all appeared to be set on a course of decibel one-upmanship to mark the start of the new millennium. Somewhere in the frozen city, an overexcited Céline Dion was going through her warm-up exercises with a singing instructor. Solange's Jaguar stopped at a red light at the corner of Sherbrooke. The pale day lowered its remaining light over a city that had been taken over by noisy clusters of revellers. From the inebriated groups, shouts, cries, and songs about the end of the world rose up in the cold air. A group of McGill University students passed in front of the Jaguar. Two of the boys whistled in admiration, looking Solange in the eye. The drunker of the two took off one of his gloves and began to fondle the metal hood ornament, moaning lustfully all the while, much to the delight of his laughing companions. "Yeah! Jerk it, baby!" they shouted, perhaps hoping the metal jaguar ornament would climax, a miracle for the new millennium.

Solange was still getting used to this kind of reaction whenever she went out in the car. People would stare at the little jaguar on the hood; the more brazen among them would look her right in the eye. Once or twice a day, at least, someone would smile, as though the fact she was behind the wheel of a luxury car made her a woman to be smiled at. But the reaction had never been as vulgar as this. Ever. The two women remained stony faced.

"We should've taken the Suzuki," Solange hissed, trying to pin the blame on Madeleine.

If it weren't for Madeleine wanting to drive around in a Jaguar, Solange would have stuck to the little Japanese cars she was so fond of. Unlike Madeleine who, even under torture, couldn't have told a Volkswagen Golf from a Toyota Tercel, Solange knew her cars, right down to the make and model. She knew it was best to stay clear of Buick drivers and to keep as far away as possible from BMWs, which, in North America at least, are almost always driven by the worst kind of asshole. One glance in the rearview mirror and she could tell by the shape of the car behind everything she needed to know about the driver, his ambitions, his worldview, his dreams, how he smelled, and, very often, what language he spoke. It was her experience with motorbikes that led her to start driving Suzuki cars in the 1980s. Her old motorbikes were still back in the garage at the house in Lac Taureau. The first, an orange Suzuki Hustler 400, still ran like a dream. She'd driven Madeleine to the Thousand Islands on it for the first time, back in July 1973. Needless to say, she didn't have it in her to throw away that pile of junk. Once a year, she'd fire it up and rev the engine, just to relive that trip. Her Suzuki motorbike collection included a 1979 GS1000S (nearly 1,000 horse-power), a 1986 GSX-R1100 (which, Solange liked to boast, she'd driven at 200 km/h between Ottawa and Montreal, proof in the form of a historic speeding ticket that she'd had framed), and her latest acquisition, a 1999 Hayabusa 1300 she'd only been on two or three times late that summer, just to hear the growl of the four-cylinder engine. Nothing in the world helped Solange see and feel things more clearly than a bike ride. She'd made every decision worth mentioning straddling a Suzuki. Her most ardent prayers had all tended to be voiced at speeds over 120 km/h. As a little girl, she'd dreamed of becoming an airline pilot, but the short-sightedness passed down to her from her mother had forced her to reconsider her career path, or so she liked to think. Truth was, Madeleine Lamontagne had become something resembling her one and only career choice. And yet a particularly fastidious analyst could have pointed out—and he wouldn't have been too far wide of the mark—that such devotion can't readily be described as a choice. Solange hadn't chosen to become vice president of Mado Group Inc. The divine forces that had led to her taking up the position were probably the same ones that had arranged the martyrdom of Saint Blandina in a Roman arena and led Mother Teresa to Calcutta. The rest is mere myth. In some cases, *vocation* is the only word that will do, even at the dawn of the 21st century.

And so Solange had proudly taken on the nickname that Madeleine's sons had given her: Solange Suzuki or plain-old Suzuki when they were trying to wheedle something out of her that their mother had already said no to. The nickname went no further: Madeleine had always called Solange by the name she'd been christened with, seeing no reason to burden her best friend with a name normally reserved for noisy, polluting cars and motorbikes. Michel and Gabriel had learned to drive in a manual-transmission Suzuki Swift whose souped-up engine would snarl menacingly every time they so much as touched the stick shift. The two women were in a Jaguar because one day Madeleine had begged Solange to buy a car that reflected her financial success, a car she wouldn't be ashamed to be seen in, a car that would make it clear to all just how thick her purse was. And so Solange had plumped for the 1995 forest-green Jaguar XJR. She only took it out of the garage for longer trips or whenever Madeleine was with her. Otherwise she stayed true to her Suzukis. She hated the big, lazy car; all it did was draw attention, a distraction from the down-to-earth image she wanted to project.

The vehicle, which only had thirty thousand kilometres on the clock, was now pulling onto the Champlain Bridge, heading due south toward the United States. Madeleine was rummaging around for a CD her sons might have left in the car back when they still lived in Montreal. All she found was a box set of *Tosca* that Michel had no doubt bought when he was studying at the conservatory. Rather than subject Suzuki to Puccini after what had already been a long day, Madeleine searched for a radio station that was not completely and utterly devoted to celebrating Céline Dion's career. In vain. Though there was a Leonard Cohen special on the McGill University radio station. The singer's deep voice filled the Jaguar.

"I'm coming now, I'm coming to reward them. First we take Manhattan, then we take Berlin…"

Solange tsked and sighed. Music wasn't her thing, not that type anyway. Madeleine seemed hypnotized by the song.

"What's he going to take?" she asked. "Manhattan and then Berlin? Is that what he says?"

"Yeah, pretty much. Only it's Manhattan we want."

"We don't have any restaurants in Berlin?"

"Not yet. One in Frankfurt and one in Munich, but not Berlin."

"We'll just have to open one then!"

"Are you just saying that because Gabriel's in Berlin? I don't know if he's going to stay there."

"I think we should have one in Berlin just the same."

"There are better, more profitable markets first. Like Florida and the southern U.S. The Americans eat more in the morning than the Germans. You know that."

"The Americans eat more than anyone, whatever time of day it is, Solange. That's why I'm a billionaire."

Solange put this newfound interest in Berlin down to motherly affection. She would have paid a lot of money to see Gabriel's face as he came across a Mado's in the heart of Berlin, having confided in her that he'd chosen the city precisely because it was one of the few places in the western world where he didn't run into constant reminders of his mother around every corner.

"But don't tell her, Suzuki!" Gabriel had implored her, putting his hand on hers. Gabriel's big hand...

Leonard Cohen continued his lament while the Jaguar reached the far side of the Champlain Bridge.

"How many nights I prayed for this, to let my work begin. First we take Manhattan, then we take Berlin."

"My God! It's like he wrote the song for me!" Madeleine gushed in surprise.

"Maybe that's it. Maybe he did write it just for you," Solange joked, overtaking a sluggish black Ford in the right lane.

Silence settled over the Jaguar. Both women stared at the almost-empty frozen road ahead of them. Madeleine picked up *Tosca* again and looked at it. It was the legendary recording featuring Renata Tebaldi as Tosca and Mario del Monaco's unforgettable performance as Cavaradossi. The box clicked as Madeleine opened it. Solange sighed. At that precise moment, she felt as much like listening to the first act of *Tosca* as she did like taking a curare-poisoned arrow between the eyes. She saw the projectile come at her from up the road, pierce the windshield, and bury itself between her eyebrows seconds after Madeleine slid the CD into the CD player. She decided to play for time.

"We could wait until we've crossed the border before we put any music on."

Madeleine hit pause. Solange tried not to sigh with relief. Madeleine had opened the libretto and was trying to make out the microscopic print.

"It's always nice to have the words when you don't understand the language," she said.

"You can't make a word out anyway—even when it's your own language. Do you remember the night Michel took us to see *Faust* at the Place des Arts? They might as well have been singing in Greek," Solange replied, shaking her head.

"But it was lovely, all the same."

"It was *long*, that's what it was," Solange replied, with a roll of her eyes.

"I like opera. It's nice. But the stories just don't hold water."

"What do you mean?"

"The characters are always like caricatures. Take Scarpia, for instance. No one is that awful. It's just not possible. And she's even worse. An opera singer! How are people supposed to identify with that?"

Madeleine pointed to the description she'd just found and read with a little flashlight that had the Jaguar logo on it.

"But of course they're all opera singers once they're on stage!" Solange replied, a touch exasperated.

"No, no. In *Tosca*—it says so right here—the character's an opera singer. The singer's name is Renata Tebaldi and *she's* playing the role of a singer called Floria Tosca."

"I'd forgotten. It's not my forte, you know. It was back in 1980, after all, when Mr. Zucker died."

Solange bit her lip. She hoped what she'd just said wouldn't be taken as a sign she wanted her to play the CD. Three hours listening to people shouting at each other in Italian. And yet she didn't have the strength in her to resist Madeleine. She, like so many others, rarely did. Before Michel had taken an interest in opera, Madeleine hadn't ever given it the slightest bit of attention. But when Michel began to study at the conservatory in Montreal, Madeleine was suddenly fascinated. With every piece her son sang, Madeleine tried to "learn a thing or two," as she put it. When the young tenor had to learn Tamino for *The Magic Flute*, his mother had begun listening to Mozart. The same happened with Bizet and Verdi once he began singing—and quite well, too—some of the arias from *Carmen* and even *La Traviata*. Truth be told, she rarely made it through a recording and had often been seen fast asleep while the singers on stage sang their hearts out. And yes, she'd admitted it herself, she'd fallen asleep the day Michel sang Cavaradossi at the Montreal Opera. "Nice music," was all she managed to say to her son after his *Tosca* premiere. Solange, despite her limited experience in the art of deception, prudently feigned astonishment so as not to hurt Michel's feelings. After Tosca's tragic end, Solange had foolishly thought it was all behind her, that never again would she have to sit through the howling of the second act. And yet here the drama was, threatening to come back for an encore on this New Year's Eve. Solange tried—in vain—to change the subject.

"Gabriel might have at least called over the holidays."

"Perhaps people like seeing an opera singer in trouble, like when the newspapers publish articles about me and my restaurants," replied Madeleine, without registering what Solange had just said.

Or was it no more than Madeleine's usual lack of interest at the slightest mention of Gabriel's name? It didn't matter: Solange's ploy hadn't worked. The Puccinian threat was gathering momentum. She racked her brains for a way to head it off. But Madeleine wasn't for turning.

"Perhaps it's easier for people to identify with a singer rather than a princess, like in *The Magic Flute*. I mean, could *you* identify with a princess?"

"The only opera I could identify with would have to be set in a restaurant."

"There's no mention of restaurants in the libretto. Do you think people would go to see an opera set in a restaurant? Wouldn't it be dull?"

"No, no. I think people like to dream. They go to the opera to dream. It's a little more expensive as dreams go, that's all."

"I remember now. That time we went to see Michel in *Tosca*, what I found hard to swallow was the whole thing between the singer and the head of police. What was his name again?"

"Scarfia?"

"No, Scarpia. I mean, come on. No one's like that in real life. In real life, with real, down-to-earth people, Tosca would still be alive. At least, I don't think she'd've gone that far."

"And what if Tosca had been a manager at Mado's?" Solange asked.

"It's not the same thing. My restaurants are… *real*. They feed real people with real problems."

"Perhaps, Madeleine. Perhaps…"

Solange managed to keep Madeleine talking until they reached the U.S. border. At the customs office, the Jaguar's arrival was an intrusion on another otherwise quiet evening. They sent the young guy out to take care of the two ladies. Nationality? Canadian. Where are you travelling to? New York City. How long do you plan on staying there? Two days, no longer. The purpose of your visit? Solange didn't know what to say. Business? She wasn't sure. Pleasure? They weren't going to be tourists either. Family? They didn't know a soul in New York. How could she tell this man in uniform that they'd suddenly decided out of the blue to go to New York and that Solange didn't really know why. Customs officers like simple answers. And seasoned travellers know better than to reply "It's a long story" or "I don't really know myself," let alone "I got this long letter from Italy. It's right here; I can show you. The contents are so shocking, so surprising, so outrageous, that I had to drop everything and hit the icy roads of New York State. But if you really want to know the whole story, you'll have to hop in. Because right now you're standing outside at a latitude of more or less 45 degrees north on what is probably the coldest night of the year, not dressed especially warmly and wanting nothing more than to go back to your colleagues inside, where it's nice and warm, and, even if I were to recount these adventures in painstaking detail, you wouldn't believe me anyway, and the whole time you'd regret ever stepping inside the Jaguar with me, especially by the time we reached Act II of the Puccini opera that is just about to start blasting inside my luxury car any minute now, so, believe me, for your own sake, and for our sake too, for everyone's sake, I'll just say: to see New York. We're tourists, like all of humanity has been tourists ever since we were kicked out of Eden. We call it tourism so as not to have to call it *deportation* or *aimless wandering*. So there you have it, Mr. Customs Official, we're just two tourists in the American night, come down from the north, not that our point of origin is of any more interest to you than the contents of our handbags. We are hate, we are love, we are poor in spirit and filthy rich, and everyone knows that hearts, rich or poor, can be broken, but that's hardly any of your business. Oh, and we should also point out that just one of our shoes costs more than everything you're wearing right now, that the gloves I put on to drive this outrageously expensive car are worth more than your weekly pay, that we are splendid wanderers, and that we intend to show everyone just how splendid we are tomorrow morning in Manhattan, a place where splendour goes to die." All these thoughts ran through Solange's mind while the border agent waited for an answer to his question. But Solange simply answered: to see the sights. Solange is a pragmatic woman.

Then, at the agent's signal, she steered the Jaguar onto Interstate 87. At that very moment, both women realized that for the second time they were crossing the U.S.-Canada border side by side at exactly the same point, a memory that was at once painful and wonderful. For every Canadian, and probably even more so for every Quebecer, driving across the American border is a solemn, unsettling occasion. They are leaving behind a peaceful, reassuring country they know like the back of their hand to jump into the madness of America, a world they can only ever dip a toe into, hostile territory, the birthplace of every folly, the mould for every vice. All threats come from the south, as every Inuit knows. And America is down below. In temperate climes, as in operas, the strangest events occur and the most uncontrollable passions are unleashed.

Had the women been brought up differently, they would have both burst into tears to underscore the emotion of the moment. Instead of sobbing, there was a heavy silence. Solange almost began to hope that Madeleine would press "play" so that the sound of Puccini would mask the palpable sense of discomfort. Madeleine waited until the signs for the border post disappeared in the rearview mirror before pushing the button. The opening notes of *Tosca* rang out in that ice-cold New Year's Eve. Three chords, ponderous and gloomy, shook the car windows, announcing the end of the world. B flat, A flat, B natural. The Scarpia theme that conveys his brutal menace well before he appears on stage, the music of destiny that draws every soul toward its conclusion. Music to wake the dead. Then a string *decrescendo* introducing the opera's first words. D'Angelotti has escaped from Castel Sant'Angelo, crossed the Tiber in the darkness of the Roman night, and found refuge in the deserted church of Sant'Andrea della Valle. He finds a key a nun has left for him outside the Barberini Chapel. "Ah!" he exclaims. "*Finalmente!*" And Madeleine murmurs to herself, rummaging around in her handbag for the little brown glass vial: "Yes, finally…"

Only one recording of Giaccomo Puccini's voice survives today. It dates back to the afternoon of February 21, 1907, in the New York City offices of the Columbia Phonograph Company as the composer was preparing to take *La Provence*, an ocean liner, back to Europe. In the very short recording, Puccini thanks his New York audience in Italian for their enthusiasm for his operas. He ends on a piece of flattery borrowed from Lieutenant Pinkerton in *Madame Butterfly*:

"America forever!"

Then there is a round of applause, and a few words from his wife. Puccini was to return to New York, this time without Mrs. Puccini—*una dona gelosa*, a jealous woman—to oversee rehearsals for *La fanciulla del West*, an opera inspired by an American play he'd seen during his first stay in the Big Apple. It could be said, without fear of exaggeration, that New York needed Puccini as much as Puccini and Madeleine Lamontagne needed New York. Graced by Puccini's presence, New York could now count itself among the world's foremost opera cities: it could look the likes of Paris, London, and Vienna in the eye.

"Look! He walked our streets! He gave us an opera as a gift! Look at me! Just look at me, will you?"

Puccini went back to Italy and, until his dying day, wore the halo that God gives to Italians who make their mark in America. As for Madeleine, the opening of her Times Square restaurant would make her one of the business world's leading lights.

On the morning of January 1, 2000, Puccini's "America forever" was still echoing among the skyscrapers of Manhattan, travelling along subway tunnels until it was lost in the songs of revellers who couldn't believe they were still alive to see the first dawn of the new millennium. Frank Sinatra was not entirely right when he claimed this was a city that never slept. It drifts off for a few minutes every day—never at the same time—then opens its eyes to see its reflection in the eyes of the tourists come looking for proof that they exist. Because that's all New York City can give you, nothing more, nothing less: irrefutable, everlasting, and intoxicating proof of your own existence. Puccini had worked that out for himself.

Madeleine Lamontagne, too. First in 1968, then again on that morning of January 1, 2000. Which is why, when a journalist from CNN challenged her to lift an enormous tray of plates and glasses of orange juice, she summoned the spirit of Cheval Lamontagne, walked over to the tray, which was resting on a stand, bent her knees, and, all smiles, hoisted it with one hand, even though it must have weighed over fifty pounds. Amid a hail of flashes and applause, she walked to the back of the restaurant, which was bursting at the seams with New York celebrities. An effigy of Good Saint Anne observed the amusing spectacle from its place on the wall. Madeleine's ovation went on for a good while. Then, once she was certain she'd shut the wretched journalist up for good, she handed Solange the microphone and the litany that had been drafted by a New York–based Canada-loving writer friend could begin. The speech lasted a full five minutes. The word *family* came up fourteen times, *work* six times, and *homeland* five. Right on cue, Madeleine shed a tear, which was met with respectful silence.

Since none of the guests of honour had slept the previous night, no one noticed that the travellers were tired. The expression of resigned rage that lit up Solange Bérubé's face as she pulled up to the Radisson in the Jaguar at 5 a.m. was simply thought to be the look of a determined businesswoman. As for Madeleine's pursed lips, New Yorkers took them to be—and they weren't entirely wrong—a reflection of the never-say-die self-assurance that had made her reputation in the restaurant world.

In the 175-seat restaurant, two courses had been prepared for the VIPs. There were politicians, businesspeople, archbishops, mother superiors, and more journalists than you could shake a stick at. Inspired by the substances that had helped him stay up all night, one of the latter had penned the following paragraph for his hundreds of thousands of readers:

"Yesterday morning the first Mado's restaurant in Manhattan opened its doors in Times Square. It has been a long time coming, but at last we have caught up with the rest of North America: we too can now enjoy a breakfast worthy of the name, one that's prepared lovingly and served promptly—with a smile. Having tasted the now legendary Solange pancakes, the end of the world suddenly seems a whole lot less terrifying."

A three-page interview with Solange and Madeleine took up most of the Food section. In it, they set out Mado's business model and the obstacles they'd overcome on their way to opening a restaurant at America's most sought-after location. "Cleanliness is next to godliness," Solange had proclaimed when asked to explain their shared obsession for hygiene. And, to conclude the interview, the journalist had mentioned the rumours that Madeleine Lamontagne might very well have an American grandmother.

"A rumour? Why it's the truth!" Solange had corrected him.

The journalist, tossing the softest of softballs, had then wanted to know if, by opening restaurants across the United States, Madeleine considered it a triumphant return to the homeland of her grandmother. Madeleine, whose son Michel had kept her well-versed in Puccini anecdotes, had simply replied: "America forever."

While the hoi polloi queued outside amid the New Year's detritus, the mountains of confetti, and the portable toilets that were still dotted about the city, Madeleine's waitresses performed their bustling ballet like machines set to "courteous" mode. The restaurant opening had required a great deal of preparation. Given the crowds that had gathered in the area around the restaurant the night before the opening, preparations had to be completed three days ahead of time to avoid deliverymen having to battle through throngs of two million drunk people stretching from Central Park to 42nd Street. Of the two million revellers, plenty stayed out in the cold of night. Beneath the Mado's logo, curious onlookers pointed inside the restaurant, delirious with drink and quite certain that Good Saint Anne had just winked at them!

That day Madeleine smashed the record for the number of breakfasts served in a single day, previously held by the Sydney, Australia, branch during Gay Pride 1997. America forever indeed.

Solange and Madeleine kept it up until noon, then announced they were leaving, utterly exhausted.

"You can go back to the hotel now," the manager, a woman who'd handled the restaurant openings in New Jersey and Connecticut, had reassured them. "It'll all be fine."

"Was the Radisson in the budget?" Madeleine had asked when she saw the room, probably the smallest in the whole hotel.

"I stick to the budget, Madeleine. You weren't supposed to be here. And I was supposed to fly in, not drive up to the door half dead."

"Just don't get too comfortable, Solange. It's time we were going."

Solange pretended not to hear.

"I need to find my cross. Are you coming? I need you."

And so Solange went back to her meditation behind the wheel of the Jaguar. After the incredibly busy morning there were still hours of excitement in store. Madeleine sensed she was close to her goal. The three notebooks Gabriel had filled sat on her lap, the improbable, hopeless story of a German woman. She reread some of the passages, barely moving her lips so as not to disturb her friend while she drove. Madeleine kept a close eye on the words like children watch their manners at the tables of the nouveau riche. They drove down Lexington until 42nd Street. In the Jaguar's rearview mirror, Solange eyed a red Honda Civic in consternation.

"Any closer and it'll be up my ass!" she complained.

At 1:32 p.m., they left the parking lot at the Port Authority Bus Terminal, the orifice through which Manhattan had swallowed them whole the first time, then spat them up later that day in December 1968. Madeleine wanted to do it this way so they could walk back to Dr. Beck's house from there. She remembered the route they'd walked, but couldn't work it out by car—the downside to having a photographic memory. Slowly she'd dragged poor Solange along the filthy, freezing streets, without once taking a wrong turn. Tosca's Diner had gone; a samba school had taken its place. They stood gaping at the plate glass windows.

"First Lesson Free," Solange read out loud.

From there, it took them precisely twenty-three minutes to find the 10th Avenue dry cleaner's that Dr. David Beck worked above, a stone's throw from 56th Street. There was a flashing neon coat hanger in the window, a rather blunt reminder of the services once on offer from the doctor. The gold plate with his name on it had gone. Other names had taken the doctor's place, unknown names of people performing other jobs. But none of this was going to stand in Madeleine's way. She hadn't gone through hell that night to turn back the first time things didn't go her way. All the businesses in the neighbourhood's four- and five-storey buildings were closed for the holiday, except for the Thai restaurant they ventured into. It took Solange a while to explain to the owner what they were looking for. What had happened to the doctor? His office had been next door in 1969. No, no, the brown house. The one above the dry cleaner's. No, we don't need any dry-cleaning done, and we're not sick either. You don't know? The woman agreed to phone the owner of the building. He might know who owned the building next door. She got through to his answering machine and a message that gave his cellphone number. A little irritated by now, she scrawled the number down on the back of a paper placemat and handed it to Solange in a manner that suggested that playing detective wasn't her idea of the best way to spend New Year's Day. Back outside on the sidewalk, Solange turned on the cell phone she'd turned off the day before on their way to the hospital. She ignored the four new messages and called the man who owned the building next door to where Dr. Beck had used to work. With Madeleine looking on anxiously, she managed to get through to a woman with a nasal-sounding voice who explained that the owner, a man by the man of Levi, was vacationing in Florida, that he would be back in four months. Realizing she'd need to be crafty, Solange pretended to be a tenant from the neighbouring building complaining about the noise from next door. The woman with the nasal voice laughed. She'd just have to get used to it. What else could you expect on New Year's Day?

"But," she went on, "if you really are determined to be a pain when everyone around you is enjoying themselves, I can pass your message on to Mr. Levi. He can have a word with your owner, Mr. Ho."

She'd come up empty. Solange wasn't any farther along than before. All she knew now was that the man who owned the brown building was called Ho. Worn out and demoralized, she tried to reason with Madeleine, but she was having none of it. It was now or never. While they wondered what to do next, the door into the building opened and a woman staggered outside, visibly drunk. In a flash, Madeleine jammed her wedge-heel, finest quality leather ankle boot with side zipper and lambskin lining between the door and the frame. The drunk woman, assuming they lived in the building, apologized for not holding the door and turned out onto 56th Avenue.

"Do you recognize the staircase?"

Solange didn't recognize a thing. It was a staircase like any other: no broader, no narrower. The stores inside the building had been converted into apartments, by the looks of things. When they got to the floor where, according to Madeleine's impeccable memory, the doctor's office had been, they stopped outside the door. There was a number on it. Madeleine knocked three times. A dog barked. Then a shadow flickered behind the spyhole.

"Who's there?"

"We're looking for Dr. Beck."

"He doesn't live here."

"We know. But he had his office here in 1968. Do you happen to know where he went?"

"In 1968? I wasn't even born!"

Silence. Then the door opened to reveal a tall girl with brown hair. She was wearing flannel pyjamas, with some kind of apple-green knit beanie on her head. The smell of soup hung in the air. The girl eyed the two women with the smirk of a child who's never had to do the dishes. She was curious now, and let them inside so she could hear their story.

"You don't get that every day. Two ladies going around knocking on people's doors on New Year's Day, hoping to find a doctor they met in 1959!"

"1968," Madeleine corrected her.

"And why are you looking for this Dr. Peck?"

"Beck. He has something that belongs to me, something I want back."

"I hope it wasn't anything that might have gone bad!"

The girl hadn't slept all night, she explained. She'd just got home from a wild party. Time enough to brush her teeth, comb her hair, and pop a pill before heading off to supper with the family.

"You could always call Ho, the guy who owns the building, but you can't make out a word he says. And he wasn't even in the States in 1968. I've been here since 1996. Before that, there was an old Portuguese lady with two sons. My parents rented this apartment from Ho when she died. The Portuguese lady's sons work at a taxi stand right at the other end of the street. Manuel and Pedro Barbosa. Just ask for them. I think that's your best bet. I remember when Mom came to rent the apartment one of the sons mentioned that a doctor used to live here. Maybe he's the one you're looking for. But I'm not sure if they're working today."

She put on warm clothes and insisted on going with Madeleine and Solange to the taxi rank, where a man weighing at least 350 lb. told them that Manuel and Pedro Barbosa both had the day off. Leaning in through the window of his taxi, the girl asked if there was any way to reach them. The man hesitated, looked Madeleine and Solange up and down, and said no. The girl made a face and left the two travellers in front of her building.

"You can always try coming back in a day or two. They'll probably be there then."

Solange thanked the girl again, then gave Madeleine the look of a woman who's done enough.

"Face it: he's gone. You'll have to try something different. Like look him up in the phone book."

"Do you really think I didn't try that already? There must be twenty David Becks! It's the first thing I did when I got to the hotel this morning, while you were in the shower."

They were walking along in silent resignation when Madeleine suddenly turned back. Solange followed after her, now more tired than words could describe. Madeleine marched back to the taxi rank. The obese driver recognized them. Madeleine opened the door, sat down in the back seat, and motioned for Solange to do the same. The driver, who was sucking on an old toothpick, seemed amused. Madeleine opened her bag, rummaged around for a moment, and held up a $100 bill, which she slipped through the crack in the front seat. The driver started the engine before the money had even hit the beige leather seat beside him.

"Manuel or Pedro?"

"Both," Solange replied.

They drove for ten minutes, along streets that became more and more seedy until they stopped outside a run-down building. It didn't escape Solange's attention that the same red Honda Civic that had followed them from the hotel to the Port Authority Bus Terminal was now fifty yards behind. No doubt about it: it was the same car. Solange decided to keep it to herself, not wanting to worry Madeleine.

The driver gave them Manuel Barbosa's apartment number and they thanked him. By some miracle, he was home, but refused to buzz them in. Madeleine had to ring three times before the Portuguese man finally gave in. The women thought they'd seen it all, but they hadn't yet been to Manuel Barbosa's apartment, on the fourth floor of an elevatorless building where, on every landing, you half expected to trip over a still-warm dead body. Solange swore she saw a rat in the shadows. She also swore she'd never set foot inside the place again, but silently, as usual. Barbosa was furious. He was already standing in front of the door, wielding a hammer in one hand. He was maybe thirty-five. He was wearing canvas deck shoes with thermoplastic rubber soles, too-tight Levi 501s, and a green t-shirt with the word COLT spelled out in yellow letters.

"Are you the police?"

It seemed a fair question to Solange. As they explained what had brought them there, a barefoot woman wearing nothing more than a terry bathrobe and way too much makeup appeared in the doorway.

"They're looking for the doctor who used to live in Mama's apartment."

"Your Mama was living with a doctor?"

"No! Before!"

An irritated Manuel Barbosa explained that he knew there used to be a doctor's office in the apartment, but he didn't know when, let alone the guy's name.

"Beck? Yeah, maybe. Pedro would know. But he's in Puerto Vallarta."

"Can you call him?"

Manuel began to laugh. His friend disappeared into the apartment and came back with a copy of *The New York Times*. She waved the photo of Solange and Madeleine under his nose.

"What do you want Dr. Beck for?"

It took fifteen minutes to reach Pedro Barbosa. He was vacationing in Mexico and just coming down off a bad ecstasy trip. He agreed to speak to Solange, although she had to ask four or five times. There was a silence, then Pedro explained that his mama had been the first person to live in the apartment after it was renovated in 1978. Being the eldest, he had a clearer memory of the doctor coming to ask about the mail one day, or rather, it was his daughter.

"But dip me in honey and throw me to the lesbians… I can't remember their name or where they live now!"

Solange imagined Manuel Barbosa dripping with honey and pursed her lips.

"It'll be with Mama's stuff. Tell Manuel to have a look in Mama's old pink notebook."

Manuel grumbled, then went down to the basement, returning with an old suitcase. Left alone with Solange and Madeleine, the woman he lived with—Sandy was her name—told them she'd been a waitress for eight years. Manuel found the pink notebook without too much trouble and, sure enough, there was Dr. Beck's address.

"You're out of luck—he lives in Brooklyn."

Solange buried her head in her hands as the taxi sped toward Brooklyn. Did they really have to find that goddamn cross? Why now? Madeleine, on the other hand, seemed energized by the discovery.

"I just know we'll find him. It's more important than you think, Solange."

The welcome in Brooklyn was less cordial. The address belonged to the last in a row of red-brick houses that had probably been built just after the war. There they surprised a man, who lived alone with his black Labrador, dancing the bamboula. He didn't want to talk about Beck and refused to turn down the techno music that was about to rupture Solange's eardrums. Madeleine managed to loosen his tongue by once again digging deep in her purse.

"He sold this house to my father in 1989. Then my sister lived here, then I moved in when she left for New Haven. Beck moved into an old folks' home. Dad could tell you where, but he's gone now. Now hang on a minute… give Concord Nursing Home a try. Or Buena Vida, one of the two. One of those places where old Jews go to retire. He had a daughter, I think. Used to live with him. That's all I know."

The door closed, much to Solange's relief. Madeleine clenched her fists.

"Now, before you go asking me to traipse around every old folks' home in Brooklyn with you, have you seen the time, Madeleine?"

"It's almost three o'clock, dear."

"I know. And I barely got a wink of sleep!"

"Just a little longer. If we've no luck at the homes, we'll go back to the hotel."

New taxi, new driver, still no luck. At the front desk at Concord Nursing Home on Madison Street, they waited for twelve minutes before the receptionist finally told them that only a pre-approved list of people were allowed to ask questions about the residents. Madeleine produced more money from her bag; the receptionist threatened to call the police. Madeleine gave her an imploring look; the woman remained impassive.

"Get out or I'm calling for help."

Madeleine put her money away and Solange thanked God. For the first time in twenty-four hours, she could see Madeleine's resolve beginning to waiver. Maybe now she might be able to go back to the hotel, lie down, and sleep for a thousand years. But her dream went up in smoke at the sound of a woman's voice behind them.

"Madeleine Lamontagne? I think I have what you're looking for."

Solange and Madeleine whirled around. There stood Dr. Rachel Beck. Their surprise was suddenly interrupted by the sound of Solange's cell phone ringing. Her assistant Marie-Claude had been trying to get hold of her all morning. Madeleine or Solange was to phone the Sisters of the Child Jesus in Rivière-du-Loup immediately. Sister Saint Alphonse had called three times. And she didn't seem to understand the meaning of the words "I don't know where they are." Bruno-Karl d'Ambrosio had also called goodness knew how many times and, after verbally abusing everyone he spoke to, after calling every woman in the building a whore, stupid bitch, or incurable philistine, had demanded that Madeleine Lamontagne call him back urgently, wherever she was, whatever the hour. Marie-Claude had thought it worth pointing out to the director that, given the financial ties between his movie and Mado Group Inc., he should perhaps rethink his communications plan and watch his mouth. All this Marie-Claude explained patiently to Solange while Rachel pointed at her red Honda Civic, parked just outside the home. She didn't hang up until the car was pulling onto the Brooklyn Bridge, bringing them back to the centre of the universe: Manhattan. Madeleine didn't say a word the whole time. An indefinable smile seemed to be playing at her lips. Rachel was in high spirits.

"How Daddy would have loved it!"

Rachel Beck lived in an apartment block on the Lower East Side, on one of the nicer floors. A small apartment for an on-call doctor, with just the odd piece of furniture.

"It's not much, but with Daddy gone, I don't need as much room as I used to. I kept the cabin in the Catskills. I rarely go more than three days a year! I'll really have to consider getting rid of it. Can I make you a coffee? I'm dying for one. I'm just home from the worst nightshift ever!"

Solange and Madeleine sat on a leather loveseat. They looked out from the 22nd floor at the dull greys that make up Manhattan's palette. Rachel Beck's apartment had no more than three rooms, plus a bathroom. The kitchen opened out onto the living room and looked so much like something straight out of a 1970s American sitcom that it would have come as no surprise had Mary Tyler Moore popped out, grinning from ear to ear. Solange was nervous now after Marie-Claude's call for help and asked if she could use Rachel's office to work out one or two things. Alone in the tiny room, surrounded by German, French, and English books, Solange sat down on a wooden stool and called the convent. On the wall, a poster from the Metropolitan Opera announced Maria Callas's much-awaited return as Tosca. She let the phone ring eight times. A voice as old as time answered. No sooner had she given her name than Solange heard the receiver drop and rapid footsteps disappear down a hallway. "Sister Saint Alphonse! She called! Come quickly!"

The atmosphere at the convent was heavy. Sister Saint Alphonse (who had reverted to her given name—Antoinette—in 1969), Sister Fatty who had terrorized the girls of class 4A, had some gruesome news indeed for Solange on that first day of the new century. It had happened during the night. Some of the nuns had gone over to Rue Lafontaine to watch the fireworks at midnight. The good people of Rivière-du-Loup had waited patiently in the Arctic conditions, some warming themselves in the shops that had stayed open for the occasion. Shortly before the first stroke of midnight, a bat had been startled by a firecracker going off and had flown low over the crowd. The sight of the terrified creature had frozen the blood in the nuns' veins and they'd gone back to the convent as soon as the fireworks were over. Sister Saint Alphonse pointed out that she hadn't gone herself, that only the nuns who were still steady on their feet had gone. She'd stayed behind at the convent with the others, notably Sister Mary of the Eucharist and Old Ma Madeleine, who'd agreed to come out of the laundry for the evening. All night long, Sister Antoinette explained, both women, who'd become inseparable over the years, had behaved more than a little oddly. Both had been in unusually high spirits at supper. They'd already polished off the bottle of wine they'd recklessly uncorked for the occasion before Old Ma Madeleine had even finished her meat pie. The three had, in fact, in a manner that could almost have been considered impolite, insisted on eating alone at a table in the dining room. Sister Mary of the Eucharist, aware of the malaise they were causing, had stood to explain herself:

"Sisters, my very dear sisters," she began, clearly already a little tipsy. "You know that I love each and every one of you like my very own sisters. I love *everybody*… But tonight is a very special night for the three of us. Please don't see our celebration as us turning our backs on the community. We have long since proven our affection for you, for the children of Rivière-du-Loup, and for the whole world, but tonight Old Ma Madeleine and I would like to raise a toast (here she had to hold on to the table) to life, to Baby Jesus, and to all our sisters suffering in silence around the world. Tonight let us celebrate life, life lived to the fullest, life that comes through loving! Blessed are those who rise to the call! Blessed are those who laugh! To you, dear sisters! Hahaha!"

The other nuns were dumbfounded, but polite enough to find the whole display rather amusing. Over the past thirty years, the two nuns had distanced themselves from the others; that was clear to all. They would often be seen walking through the forest together on winter evenings, peering up at the sky as though trying to make out the shape of the Blessed Virgin in a constellation.

Sister Mary of the Eucharist had asked for a double helping of upside-down pineapple cake, her favourite dessert. Then they had looked through some old black and white photographs that Sister Mary of the Eucharist has produced from her room. Photos of people who were dead and buried, Papa Louis and his children, construction work on the new convent. The photo of Father Lecavalier had them giggling like novices.

"There was even a photo of you, Solange. On your first motorbike, with Madeleine's little brother. You know, the one who died in the casket?"

From her end in Manhattan, Solange listened to the nun's story, completely captivated. Outside, the wind whistled the murderous weather's lament. She had to lean forward to catch her breath. All those people had stuck in her throat. Sister Saint Alphonse went on with her story. Around eleven o'clock, half of the nuns left to see the fireworks at the waterfalls while the others chose to watch the celebrations on television. No prizes for guessing that the three delinquents turned down the invitation to watch the cursed screen.

"You know very well I can't abide it," Old Ma Madeleine huffed.

Twenty minutes before midnight, to everyone's surprise, the two women got dressed to go for a stroll in the forest. Sister Antoinette was so intrigued she decided to follow them, after waiting five minutes.

"You can't imagine how cold it is here, Solange!"

Out in the forest, Sister Mary of the Eucharist kept up the jokes with Old Ma Madeleine. They were having a grand old time, as if they were at the Saint-Jean-Baptiste parade. Sister Saint Alphonse swore she heard them say this:

"Are you sure it's tonight?" Old Ma Madeleine had asked.

"Absolutely. No two ways about it. The handsome young fella came and went. All that's left now is for Madeleine to make the trip and it's in the bag!"

"I wonder if your little sister in Nagasaki could feel things coming the way you do, Sister Mary of the Eucharist."

"There's no way. There's no way to predict what man will do. Only God's intentions can be foreseen. And even then you need to know where to look! How pure the cold is! Feel the snow melt in your hands one last time! Take in the stars! So beautiful, so many of them! There are as many stars as there are dreams in the world! Breathe in the air of this beautiful land of ours!"

Then Sister Saint Alphonse heard a whistling sound shoot down from the heavens. Like the sound of a mortar shell falling, the noise started off quietly then got louder. Next she heard what sounded like a knife going through meat. Twice. Schlick! Schlack! And not a sound after that. Nothing but the wind in the trees. Sister Antoinette came out of her hiding place, numb with fear and cold, and her eyes fell on a scene that would haunt her until her dying day. Both women lay on their backs in the snow, arms splayed wide. In each of their hearts, firmly planted, a wooden arrow come out of nowhere. On their faces, a mysterious smile, a look of great relief, a grimace that made one wonder what pale-blue fantasy they'd swallowed.

"Like an Indian arrow, Solange! They were dead! The arrows just fell from the sky! You have to pray, Solange! You have to tell Madeleine too!"

Alerted by a breathless Sister Saint Alphonse, the Mother Superior had managed to cover the whole thing up. It hadn't been easy. The pair of them had carried the bodies to an unheated room before the other nuns came back from the fireworks. (The other nuns who'd stayed behind at the convent were either by then fast asleep or secretly glued to the Céline Dion performance on TV and didn't notice a thing.) The next morning, while Rivière-du-Loup was still belching away the night before, they managed to move the bodies to the charnel house by the graveyard, where they would stay until the ground had thawed. The nuns, being independent and self-reliant creatures, alerted neither police nor doctor. The two women, they explained to the other nuns, had been a bit tipsy and died of hypothermia in the forest.

"They'd been wanting to go for so long, Solange. Speaking of which, Madeleine will have to give us their dates of birth for the gravestones. Do you have any idea how old they were?"

Solange didn't say a word. How old they were? What a strange question! Like putting a price on freedom! Sister Saint Alphonse was obviously still as out to lunch as ever, she thought. She promised to speak to Madeleine as soon as possible and thanked the nun for calling.

"One last thing, Solange. Old Ma Madeleine wasn't a nun. She lived with us, but she never took her vows."

"I know all that..."

"Well, now it's become a bit of a problem, what with the picture and all..."

"What picture?"

"You know, the painting that Papa Louis gave her. He brought it back from Germany."

"I remember it vaguely. What's the problem?"

"Well, since she wasn't really a nun, her things don't belong to us. We have to work out who to give the picture to. That old thing can't be worth very much. And it's so poorly painted! You know, the one with the apostles gathered around the Virgin Mary lying on a cement slab? Used to be in the dining room. Not the Virgin Mary, the picture, I mean."

Solange smiled at the predicament. What was to be done? She immediately knew who might like it. She looked up Gabriel's Berlin address in her address book. She asked Sister Saint Alphonse if she would be kind enough to mail the painting to Gabriel Lamontagne in Germany. She would send her a cheque for her trouble as soon as she got back to Montreal. The nun wrote down the address, with Solange spelling out the complicated, rough-sounding German words, and again wished her a Happy New Year.

"I hope the two of you are well."

"Everything's fine, Sister. Couldn't be better."

Meanwhile, Rachel and Madeleine were having a very different conversation. Rachel was small, with the voluptuous hips of a woman who'd hit her fifties. She offered Madeleine a slice of carrot cake, which she declined.

"Do you take sugar, Madeleine?"

"No, never. Thank you."

"Well, I do. I must say you haven't changed much. Five years ago, when I saw your photo for the first time in the newspaper, I recognized you right away. The name, too. I was sure you'd be back in New York one day."

Madeleine wrung her hands nervously. She was about to open her mouth to speak, but Rachel was saying something, the combination of coffee and fatigue making her more talkative.

"Did you know, Madeleine, I've waited for you for a long while. Believe me, I wanted nothing more than to be there when you opened your restaurant in Times Square, but I was on duty, as I said. By the time I got there, they said you'd already left. A server told me you were staying at the Radisson and I saw you come out around 1:30. I knew exactly where you were going, the route you were going to take. You've got guts! Going into the building like that. Those odd people. You weren't the first patient to try to look for Daddy, but you were the first who didn't take no for an answer. That article in *Business Week* was right: it's all about determination with you.

"Once a week, I work in the ER at Mount Sinai Hospital just over there. You won't believe what came in just before I left. How can I explain it? I'm exhausted, forgive me. And I'm talking to you like we're old friends. But I have to tell you. The poor girl... How does anyone wind up like that? I was about to leave. The ambulance brought her in, around 5:45. At first I thought it was another case of New Year's Day alcohol poisoning or another gunshot victim. You know what it's like here. But no, it was a young girl. She can't have been more than twenty, I'm sure.

"When they lifted the sheet, I— My God, why am I telling you all this? I thought of Daddy and those photos from Auschwitz, even though Daddy didn't go to Auschwitz, he hid in Berlin the whole time. But her body was... do you know what I mean? Have you seen photos of people like her?"

"I think so, yes. Just skin and bone. Yes, I know."

"She'd obviously starved herself to death. We already had her on file. A colleague at the Eating Disorders clinic had already treated her a year ago. She was still able to talk. All she would say was, 'I have to work, I have to work...' Then, even after we pumped her stomach, she went and died on us.

She'd taken pills. It's not the first time, but anything to do with anorexia cuts me to the quick. It kills me. A little girl from your part of the world, too! A Canadian. A student at the Juilliard School of Music! Can you imagine? I'll never forget her name. Stella, Stella Thanatopoulos. A young woman from Toronto. We had to call her mom. And—get this—she was livid! Can you imagine? She shouted at me like I'd strangled her daughter with my own hands! People are crazy, Madeleine. Raving mad! The older I get, the more I agree with Daddy."

Both women fell silent. The wind howling outside the skyscraper lent the scene a funereal feel.

"I knew you'd come back for your cross," Rachel continued. "You're not the first. But you're the only girl to leave with crosses that weren't yours! Daddy and I thought we'd seen it all! When you both ran off like a couple of thieves, he raced into his office to find out what you'd taken. He wanted to give you back your cross, but he couldn't catch you. At one point on 10th Street, he almost had your friend by the collar, but then a blizzard suddenly blew in, thick snow that stopped us in our tracks. But Daddy knew the French girls that came to see us always left from the Port Authority Bus Terminal. He also knew that almost none of them could afford a night in a hotel. They always left the same day, even if that meant travelling overnight. So that's where we waited for you. And that damn flower that fell out of your hair! Daddy fractured his kneecap on the floor! You didn't even stop. But no doubt you had your reasons…"

Madeleine squirmed on the loveseat, stared at the floor, breathed heavily. Rachel went on.

"Did you think we were angry with you, Madeleine?"

"I… I…"

"At first, yes. At first, we wondered: what did she do that for? What did we ever do to her? We wanted to help her get her life back on track, like we'd done with other girls, putting ourselves on the line, and she pulls that on us! You had a nerve!"

"When I was getting dressed, I noticed your father hadn't closed his desk drawer. You have to understand: I was distraught, I didn't know what would become of me."

"But we knew all that, Madeleine. All the French girls who came to see us were in your situation. But none of them has done as well as you have, I'm sure. I'm even sure that Daddy would have been amused to see his money led to so much more. Believe me, he'd only have spent it on a woman with a twinkle in her eye or on opera tickets."

Madeleine reached into her bag and handed Rachel a sealed envelope.

"There's the money I took. $3,100, plus compound interest."

"Plus what?"

"Compound interest. I calculated it as though you'd invested the money in 1968 U.S. treasury bonds. Here's your return. It's quite a tidy sum."

"You're really something! There must be over $200,000 in here! Guilt can sometimes be a good thing! But I don't want the money."

"Take it. Please."

"No really. I must have told Daddy a thousand times not to keep his money in his desk drawer. Anyone might have opened it! It was a busy week; he hadn't been to the bank. He didn't notice the money was missing until he got back, his knee all in a mess. But he wasn't exactly going to go running to the police, not considering the line of work he was in. You cleaned us out! If you'd just taken your envelope, I'd have understood, but you ran off with everything in the drawer..."

"Why run after us then?"

"To give you back your cross! He noticed right away that you'd left it behind."

Rachel stood up, disappeared off into the bedroom and came out after a minute with a small metal box that had once held jasmine tea. She handed it to Madeleine, who opened it. In it was a pile of little, glittering gold crosses. Madeleine shook the container to shift the contents. When she saw the cross initialled M.L., she froze. Slowly, she removed it from the container, held it up, then slipped it into her purse.

"Aren't you going to return the one you're wearing, the one initialled L.B.?"

"How? How did you know I took that one?"

Rachel crossed her legs, yawned, and looked outside.

"Do you believe in God?" she asked, sounding more serious.

"Of course! I've just travelled all night to get my cross back!"

"That doesn't mean a thing. Would you like to hear an incredible story, Madeleine?"

"Go ahead. I owe you that, at least."

Just as Rachel was about to speak, Solange came out of the little office and sat down beside Madeleine on the loveseat. She looked shaken. Hearing her come out of the office, Madeleine had quickly slid the envelope full of money back into her bag. Rachel could see in Madeleine's eyes that the matter was now closed. She smiled inwardly and felt a little sorrier for the woman who was at once so rich and so poor. She gave Madeleine a knowing wink, and Madeleine began to breathe easier right away. Rachel had seen in her eyes what she'd always known: Solange didn't know about the money. When Rachel had read the 1995 *Business Week* article about the phenomenal success of the restaurant chain, she'd recognized Madeleine right away. The article and accompanying interview had overjoyed her in a way that was hard to describe. Madeleine had candidly admitted to the reporter that she'd built her empire by investing an inheritance of $3,100, the exact amount she'd taken from Dr. Beck. Rachel had spared a thought for her father. He'd never been good with money, had never been able to say how much he earned, let alone how much he spent. His only extravagance had been to take a lover from time to time and treat her to a night at the opera.

For the rest of Rachel's story, Solange and Madeleine didn't say a word.

"Daddy was German. Born in Berlin-Charlottenburg in 1908 to a Jewish father and a Christian mother. In 1930, he was twenty-two and already practicing medicine with one of his uncles in Charlottenburg. Daddy always, right up until his death, considered himself to be German. Nobody could have convinced him otherwise. Shortly after Hitler came to power, he lost the right to practice medicine, like all the other Jews in Germany. But like a lot of half-Jews, he said the Nazis weren't out to get him, just all the proper Jews. Daddy came from a well-off family. He learned French at the Berlin *lycée*, spoke it fluently. That's why he forced me—and I do mean *forced*—to learn French. When I was twenty-one, he sent me to live with a family in Lyon. I came back plump and have stayed that way ever since, a tribute to my days in Lyon. What bliss life in France was... In any case, he didn't follow the huge tide of people like him who could smell trouble brewing. Since he was getting by in Berlin, that's where he stayed, even when he had the chance to flee to Palestine in 1938. He'd put a little money aside, and he didn't want to leave his mother, who was ill. When the deportations started, he realized he'd have to hide if he was to survive. It didn't take people long to find out about the camps. Everyone knew. You needed forged papers to survive, but even that was risky. Daddy told me one rather funny thing. In 1942 in Berlin, the queue for tickets at concert halls was one of the safest places for those who were persecuted. The Nazis insisted the Germans carry on as before. That they go on living even though bombs were falling on their heads. And so they were encouraged to go to the opera, to go to concerts. The police didn't check papers in the lineups; they didn't want to put people on edge. Music lovers were left alone. And so Daddy would line up for the opera for hours at a time, pretending he was going to buy a ticket. Sometimes he would, but not often: he had very little money left by the end. The last show he went to see was *Tosca*. In 1942. A few months before the opera house was bombed. Then, in fall 1944, he was arrested. He wound up in Sachsenhausen, a camp near Berlin. Luckily for him, the Russians had already liberated Auschwitz late that January, so he was never sent there. When the Red Army marched into Berlin, he was released. He found himself in a camp for deportees at Tempelhof and, since he was a young doctor who still had his health, he was asked to help out. The stories he told me about the camps! Typhoid, diphtheria, even dysentery. The horrors. And then there was everything that happened to the German women.

"When the Russians invaded Germany, you see, they were out for one thing and one thing only: revenge. Daddy told me the German women were raped, often gang-raped by groups of soldiers. Whenever a German woman was caught, no matter her age, no matter her looks, she was often raped by four or five men, one after the other. The kinder ones refrained from finishing her off with a bayonet. In many cases, the women committed suicide, or fell ill and died. But in other cases, some got pregnant, naturally enough. There was no way they were going to bring those children into the world, children of blood and violence, sired by men they considered monsters. They were desperate to abort them, but doctors were few and far between. Daddy said he helped perform at least twenty abortions on German women. None of them had the money to pay. Sometimes the patient would give him a piece of jewellery she'd managed to hide from the Russians, who looted everything in sight. He forgot all of those women, or most of them, he told me; their faces, their stories. At the end of his life, he was no longer even sure if he'd helped twenty or thirty. But there was one he never forgot.

"She was twenty-five. He never knew her name. One day at the Tempelhof camp, someone asked him if he could help a poor girl who'd been raped hours after the fall of Berlin. She'd taken refuge in a convent in Dahlem, where the Russians had found her and left her very much the worse for wear, her and the rest of the nuns. She was three months' pregnant. Now you'll understand why Daddy ran after you. You see, when he performed the abortion on the woman, he noticed that she had a strange birthmark on her inner thigh, shaped like a bass clef. Imagine his astonishment when he examined you on his table on 10th Avenue and saw that you had the very same birthmark between your legs! That's why he gave such a start! He told me all about it later. I hope you're not upset that I've brought it up. The soldiers who raped that particular woman had then taken a bayonet to her genitals. Daddy had to sew her up in three different places. It was ghastly.

"He knew very little about the German woman. Only that she'd survived a shipwreck in the Baltic Sea and that she was from Charlottenburg. She cried the whole time; it was enough to break Daddy's heart. In the end, she insisted on paying him with the little cross, the one with L.B. initialled on it. Her name was probably Louise or Leonore, who knows. A Catholic first name at any rate. Daddy refused, but she insisted. Over the years, do you know how many girls gave my father a little gold cross they'd gotten from an aunt or perhaps from their mother? Daddy kept them all in case they ever came back. Three did, including one from up your way. Péloquin? Poliquin? I'm not sure anymore. It was shame that brought them to us in the first place, and regret that brought them back. Anyways. He kept the crosses his whole life, a man who didn't have a religious bone in his body! He had no time for Orthodox Jews or priests.

"Do you know what he told me? In Germany in the 1930s, the Nazis set up a special ministry to fight abortion and homosexuality. Different sides to the same coin, in their eyes. Daddy always said that every time an American bishop would say something stupid about abortion or gays here in the States, it reminded him of that Nazi ministry. He was exaggerating a little, but even so… He had every right to say that kind of stuff. I tend to agree with him, at least in part. When an outside force takes control of your body, it's fascism. Or its toned-down version: Catholicism."

"I think you're perhaps exaggerating just a little," Solange interrupted, irritated.

"Yeah, you're right. What do I know? I'm lucky enough not to have known either. You should give me L.B.'s cross back now—you never know! Perhaps she'll manage to track me down like you did."

"Miss Beck, what would you say if I asked you to leave the German woman's cross with me?"

"What would I say? What do you want me to say! The crosses are no use to anyone! They're only worth something in the eyes of the person wearing them. Are you going to tell me you've become attached to the cross you're wearing? It's the one you're wearing right now, isn't it?"

"Yes, this is the one. May I keep it? I'll give you back all the others. Here you go."

Rachel's draw dropped. Then she smiled.

"I'll never get my head around you Catholics. Listen, if you really want it, then sure, it's yours. But promise me one thing: if L.B. ever pops up—which is highly unlikely, I grant you—I'll find you and ask you to give it back, OK?"

"OK. I give you my word."

"Ah! I almost forgot! When you ran off, you also left a white silk scarf behind. Daddy kept it all these years." She went off to find it.

"It's incredible. A woman we met in the bus gave it to me. I can't believe it."

Solange fingered the little gold cross they'd been reunited with. Her phone rang, but no one paid it the slightest bit of attention. Then it rang again, and again. When it rang for a fifth time, Solange swore and fished it out of her bag. A familiar voice immediately began babbling a mile a minute. The words shot across the room like arrows across the northern sky. It was Anamaria, desperate, on the verge of a breakdown, demanding to speak to Madeleine. It was Madeleine's turn to disappear into Rachel's office to talk. Rachel used the opportunity to worm a little information out of Solange.

"So, are you lesbians?"

Solange didn't reply.

"I'm sorry. It's none of my business. It's just that since I'm a lesbian too, I thought—"

"You don't have to bring it up."

"OK. Tell me Solange, did Madeleine also take a few vials of morphine with her that day in 1968?"

"Yes. She stole three of them."

"I hope it didn't get her into hot water."

"More than you could ever imagine. But everything's under control now. As long as she doesn't get too stressed. Sometimes she goes off the rails, but I'm there to catch her. She's been for treatment a few times."

"I'm very sorry to hear it. Truly. You really love her, don't you?"

Solange didn't reply.

Madeleine reappeared. The conversation had been brief, but it had given her a real boost. Her manners all but forgotten, she abruptly brought an end to their meeting with Rachel, much to Solange's relief.

"It's Anamaria. We've got to go, Solange."

"We have to go? Did they find her? Oh thank God!"

"Yes, all hell's broken loose in Rome. I think D'Ambrosio tried to pull a fast one on me. Wait till I get my hands on the little jerk!"

"You want us to go to Rome? Right now?"

Madeleine's sudden change in mood seemed to amuse Rachel.

"Who's this Anamaria?" she asked.

"Michel's ladyfriend. Michel's the child I had when I went back to Quebec," Madeleine replied curtly. "Do you think we'll be able to catch a flight to Italy today?"

"After what's happened tonight, I think that anything's possible. If I wasn't so busy at the hospital, I'd even suggest I go with you. Daddy always took me to France, never anywhere else. Italy remains one of my biggest regrets."

Without further ado, Rachel drove Solange and Madeleine back to their Jaguar at the Port Authority. A little less than four hours and several thousand U.S. dollars later—it was a cry for help from Anamaria, after all—an Alitalia flight catapulted the two women across the Atlantic. Solange and Madeleine had gotten two seats on standby, thanks to two Italians who'd decided they were too drunk to fly home and would rather spend a little more time in New York City. On the ride from the Radisson to JFK, Solange went quiet again. She didn't ask a single question. It wasn't until they were aboard the plane, once the Alitalia stewardesses had taken her coat, that she broke her silence. Simply to tell Madeleine that she didn't want to hear a single word the whole trip and that she had no intention of reading Michel and Gabriel's letters to each other or the Magdalena Berg notebooks that Madeleine had waved under her nose.

"I'm not interested, Madeleine. All I want to do is sleep."

They didn't say much about their encounter with Rachel. Solange simply summed it up with a snide remark:

"Her accent is so annoying."

"Come off it, Solange. She spent some time in France. It's only natural she sounds a bit shrill. And she was more than decent to us. You have to give her that. She kept my cross all those years. Imagine that!"

"That doesn't change a thing about how she talks."

Solange could have stood up to argue the point, but she preferred to sink down into her seat and keep her silence rather than cross swords with Madeleine. She thought about telling her the nun and Old Ma Madeleine had been found dead in the forest in Rivière-du-Loup, but then she thought better of it: Madeleine hadn't been in touch with them since they'd left in 1968. Solange had taken her silence to mean that Madeleine didn't much care what happened to those she'd left behind. She hadn't even been there for the opening of the restaurant in Rivière-du-Loup in 1982; it was Solange who'd taken care of it. Irene Caron had not been invited. Neither had the nuns, a move that Solange had found a little gauche on Madeleine's part, all the same. And so she thought the story about the women's passing could wait. Madeleine was now flying to her little Michel's rescue; no one else—of that Solange was certain—mattered at all.

Solange also didn't ask Madeleine why, when Rachel had asked who Michel was, she hadn't mentioned Gabriel. In other words, it's perfectly reasonable to wonder why poor Solange didn't say a word, not when it would seem the perfectly reasonable thing to do. The explanation is quite straight-forward: while ordinary love is cruel, Puccinian love is merciless. And that's precisely what she'd been suffering from since that day in 1954 when she'd seen Madeleine for the very first time, on the other side of the willow hedge, holding the little cat in Rivière-du-Loup. That day she'd become a Puccinian Suzuki, forever enslaved to Madeleine Lamontagne's teal gaze. It's the same love that allows people to survive misfortune, to recover from the greatest hardships. It is an ordeal in itself, a kind of concentration camp within.

Her seatbelt buckled, she waited in anticipation for that blissful minute when the plane would accelerate down the runway. Nothing thrilled her more than that colossal forward momentum. Closing her eyes, she pictured herself at twenty, on her first motorbike, driving north around the lake toward the immense, welcoming St. Lawrence River. In her mind's eye, Solange was alone, absolutely and marvellously alone on her bike. No helmet on.

As the Boeing growled, she thought back to the green fields of July, the bridge over the river in Rivière-du-Loup, the women off berry picking in the meadows of their northern land. Then she was driving flat out across the Highway 20 overpass, arriving seconds later at that spot on the road above a steep slope that looks down over the blue river in a way that makes you think for a split second that your vehicle has just left the ground, flown over the tops of the fir trees, and taken off like an Inca condor for the mountains of Charlevoix, to the north, the real north, where there's nothing but wind and lichen. As the Boeing left the tarmac, a tear attempted to emerge from the corner of Solange's eyelid, then, realizing it would be all alone in the world, promptly turned back, never to try to escape again. Solange sighed, then fell asleep as she imagined a humpback whale breaching out of the waters of the St. Lawrence. Chances are, it would all end badly, she thought to herself. The good luck they'd enjoyed thus far couldn't possibly hold much longer.

Someone, that much was clear, would have to pay.

Someone would have to die.

Confessions of a Diva

It was the morning of January 2, 2000, and the Red Army was on the march through Gabriel Lamontagne's head. For a good minute, the soldiers stomped their heavy boots as they sang disturbing songs. Then, broad red streamers began to flutter in the sky above a city that was a blend of Montreal, Toronto, Berlin, and Königsberg. In golden letters: "Tosca Must Die." Now roused from his restless sleep, he swallowed a handful of aspirin without bothering to dissolve them first, and tried to fall back to sleep. Gabriel had no idea that the nightmare would prove prophetic and decided to get up and face the new day.

Outside, the sound of fireworks had died down. Nothing is noisier than New Year's Day in Germany. Amused by Gabriel's reaction when the explosions had begun in the sky over Alexanderplatz, Magda had explained to her protégé that the din was designed to ward off evil spirits for the new year.

"And believe me, we've no shortage of evil spirits in Germany!"

The party had ended at some ungodly hour. On the evening of January 1, Gabriel had taken up the invitation of some of the folks from Friedrichshain, but hadn't stayed too late. He'd wrapped up the night in an unspecified place, got home just as the rest of Germany was getting out of bed, and woken up with a brutal hangover and a copy of Margaret Thatcher's biography in his pocket. Convinced that sleep would never come on the back of that discovery, he went down to the basement to pick up the mail that had been lying there undelivered for days. A small envelope like the ones used for sending Christmas cards had been waiting for him since December 31. An Italian stamp. Postmarked Rome. His brother's address. Inside, a Christmas card with a nativity scene.

Mommy Dearest,
I hope you have a very happy Christmas, even if I can't be with you this year. I hope you'll take a little time out to relax over the holidays. Anamaria and I have almost finished filming *Tosca*. Only a few more scenes to go. We'll be back in Outremont in mid-January.

I love you.
Your son,
Michel

Gabriel had to reread the card three times. He laughed heartily, then took the elevator back upstairs, pondering a couple of serious questions. By the look of things, in his haste, his brother had written his address on an envelope meant for Madeleine Lamontagne. "Mommy Dearest," Gabriel snorted to himself as the elevator dropped him off on the ninth floor. More like "Dearest Bitch," he thought. As the water heated for the coffee, his brain slowly fired up. If Michel had put his address on an envelope for Madeleine, that means he'd probably sent Madeleine a letter meant for him. The thought irritated Gabriel. No, there was just no way his brother—a man who got his mathematical mind and colossal memory from his mother—could have done something so stupid. What might he have sent to Montreal? For the first time since arriving in Berlin, Gabriel had an irrepressible urge to hear his brother's voice. Not his tenor's voice. He wanted to speak to him on the phone, to wish him Happy New Year, to do what normal people do. And that was when he realized he'd once jotted down Michel's number at Palazzo del Grillo in Rome, but never called. Gabriel wasn't overly fond of the phone. His mind still enveloped in the mists of the previous night's party, he dialled the number, forgetting the 39 prefix for Italy. Just as he was about to try a second time, he recognized Magda's light but persistent knock on his door. What did she want at this hour? She had to go out for the day, she explained, and was wondering if he'd like to have supper with her when she got back. He said no. He told her about the mysterious card, that his brother's mistake had him worried. He would never have thought Michel capable of such a thing.

"His mind must have been elsewhere," Magda reasoned.

She invited herself in. Dressed in the little felt hat she always wore on holidays and a long green loden coat that had somehow survived the GDR, she looked out of place alongside the unmade bed and Gabriel in nothing but boxer shorts and a white undershirt bearing the imprint of two voluptuous lips, no doubt belonging to the owner of the Margaret Thatcher biography. Magda picked up the telephone and dialled the long number. It rang a couple of times until they heard a loud and virile *pronto!*

The man on the other end was a Brazilian, his job consisting, as he patiently explained to Gabriel, of guarding the Palazzo del Grillo tower to make sure no one escaped. Gabriel told him he was the tenor's brother. No, no one was home, neither Anamaria nor Michel. The Brazilian, who was something of a motor-mouth, told Gabriel that Michel was feeling better and that he'd left early that morning to shoot the final scenes of the film with Signor D'Ambrosio. As for Anamaria, the dangerously talkative Brazilian went on, she'd been found the day before, safe and sound.

"No need for Signor Michel's brother to worry any longer!"

Gabriel hung up, lost in thought. He explained to Magda in awkward German that all was not well in Rome, the awkwardness stemming from the fact that he could think of no equivalent for "All hell's broken loose." No need to worry any longer? So he should have been worried in the first place?

Gabriel heard Terese Bleibtreu again, telling him to look after his brother. He imagined his worst fears being realized. How far had this D'Ambrosio character gone? What did he mean, Anamaria had been missing?

"Are you planning on getting dressed any time soon? Will you come over this evening, Kapriel?"

Magda tried to look elsewhere as Gabriel got dressed and threw a few things into a travel bag.

"What are you doing?"

"I need to go. I don't like what's going on one bit. I need to get there quickly, before Mom gets involved."

"Your mother? Judging from what you told me, she could probably sort everything out just by cutting D'Ambrosio off."

"Yes, but she'll only do that if she thinks there's money to be made. God knows what's going on with Anamaria and Michel in the meantime. No, I've made up my mind: I'm going. Can you call Lufthansa for me, Magda? My credit card's on the table."

Magda looked out the window at the grey, depressing Lichtenberg skyline.

"Take me with you."

"You won't be able to keep up."

"And how are you going to find your way around Rome? You've never been!"

"Neither have you. Need I remind you, you were trapped in a workers' paradise for forty years!"

"Take me with you, Kapriel. Please."

"No way. Besides, I can barely afford my own ticket."

"I'll ask Hilde for money. She'll loan it to me. And I still have some Lufthansa miles from that time I went to Greece."

"Magda, no."

"Don't say no. I want to see Rome before I die! Have pity on me! You know how fascinated I am by antiquity and ruins. You're going to take that away from me?"

"Don't cry. That's not going to work."

"I promise I'll be good."

"You promise you won't be horrible to anyone?"

"I promise."

"Even if we run into any Bavarians?"

"I swear."

"You swear you won't start drinking and lose your temper with complete strangers?"

There was a long silence while Magda stared at the floor, visibly wounded. Then she pulled herself together as only a German can and looked up.

"On Ludwig's head."

Gabriel and Magda caused a sensation at Berlin Tegel Airport. Reduced to silence once she'd sworn not to be unpleasant, Magda smiled beatific-ally at the Lufthansa flight attendants, all from the west. They swooned at the sight of the old woman with the cane accompanied by a beefcake with teal-coloured eyes. Just as the coffee was served, the phone rang back at Gabriel's apartment. Five times. Then the answering machine:

"Hello, Gabriel. I hope you're keeping well. This is Venise Van Veen, the journalist and author. I hope you remember me. I certainly remembe you. Listen, son, I'm calling to talk about what's happened to your brother in Rome. It's an emergency. We need your help. I need you to call me back right away at 514-555-5239. I hope you have a nice New Year's Day in Germany. *Tschüss!*"

Poor Venise. So sure she had a role to play and strings to pull. She'd be waiting a long time for Gabriel to call her back, off as he was to straighten out the mess in Rome. Poor Venise. She'd never know that the fate of Louis "The Horse" Lamontagne and his descendants was governed by forces beyond the ken of a columnist, that there were times when it wasn't about being for or against something, but of moving forward with the wind at your back.

Magda even managed to hold her sarcasm in check when, during the stopover in Munich, the passengers were welcomed with an unmistakably Catholic *Grüß Gott*. She made do with closing her eyes and raising them to heaven, without saying a word. Gabriel and Magda had managed to find two tickets for Rome via Munich. But they had to rush to make it to the next flight, taking one of those little electric buggies from gate to gate, Magda enthroned in silence beside an airport employee with a particularly thick accent and a fondness for small talk. They were the last to board the flight to Rome, taking off from Munich at 10:30. Magda was true to her word. There were no uncalled-for comments, not even when she caught the cabin attendant making eyes at her travelling companion, who said with an embarrassed glance:

"She's got a nerve, doesn't she, Magda?"

"What do you mean?"

"For all she knows, we might be together."

"Husband and wife, you mean? It really is an obsession of yours."

"It would help me get my papers in order with the German government."

"I promise I'll think it over, Kapriel."

Gabriel, having promised himself to never breathe a word of his meeting with Terese Bleibtreu to Magda, nevertheless allowed himself to allude to it, just to ease his conscience a little.

"Would you have married Ludwig Bleibtreu, Magda?"

"Hah, now that's funny."

"What's so funny?"

"Me, marry Ludwig? Why not? We've all seen horses puke outside a pharmacy."

"And what's that supposed to mean?"

"It's an old German expression that means stranger things have happened."

"Why so strange?"

"Because we were so young."

"You didn't see him again after the *Gustloff*?"

"No. I came back just in time to find out his sister Terese had died, that's all."

"What do you mean, his sister died?"

"Terese Bleibtreu died in the final days of the war. They were difficult times for Berliners, women especially. The men were all off fighting, or were half mad. Nerves, you see… Only the women were brave enough to go outside for water as the bombs were falling. All the pipes were shot to pieces, you see. Running water was a thing of the past. Women had to go looking for water with pails, sometimes far from home. Lineups would form at the fountains. Sometimes a bomb would fall on two or three poor women. And the queue would close over the space the explosion had left.

"Didn't the others run away?"

"No, they wanted water for their kids. Anyway, by this point, the living virtually envied the dead. And I know what I'm talking about. The Russians took Berlin that April, as you know. It wasn't the best of times."

"And Terese Bleibtreu died looking for water? Are you sure?"

"Of course I am! I found out from a neighbour on Schillerstraße who was with her. She didn't know what hit her. Such a shame. She played Schubert like an angel."

This last remark plunged Gabriel into an impenetrable silence. His mind was racing.

"You're right, Magda," he said when they landed, before they got off the plane. "We've all seen horses puke outside a pharmacy. And we will again."

"You said it, Kapriel!"

Gabriel and Magda were met at the Hertz counter by an employee who was clearly struggling to keep up with the New Year's Day demand. He didn't have a single car left, he told them.

"You could always take a motorbike. Two crazy women left on a Suzuki barely an hour ago."

But Gabriel couldn't see himself driving an overweight Magda around a city he didn't know.

"We should take the train, Kapriel. Then a taxi."

Magda didn't say a word aboard the Leonardo Express that took them from the airport to Termini station in central Rome, staring out at the ruins and remnants of antiquity from the train.

"Look! Just look at that wall. It dates back to Roman times!"

Lost to a sightseeing frenzy, Magda shared none of Gabriel's preoccupations. He was starting to find the train too slow. What state would Michel be in when he found him? He realized that Magda knew the layout and the street names, even though she'd never been to Rome.

"In the GDR, cities like this were like forbidden worlds to us. We knew them like the back of our hands. I could spend hours looking through books on Rome, poring over maps, ready for the day when I'd be lucky enough to go, at last. And now that day has come, thanks to you, Kapriel."

They had no idea where they would sleep. They had managed to convert a few marks into lira at the airport, before being whisked off to the historic city centre. At Termini, Magda insisted on taking a look around and admiring the clouds of swifts flitting above the station. The two travellers fell under their spell as they formed shifting, complex patterns in the skies of Rome.

"There were the same birds in Königsberg, too. Thousands were strewn across the ground the day after the bombardments. Dead. They're swifts, Kapriel. They fly in tight groups, without ever colliding and without ever really seeing each other. Young birds fly alongside brothers they don't even know. All that matters to them is the ballet they perform in the sky. They don't care about any of the rest."

"Why do that?"

"Nobody knows. But it's beautiful. You know, Kapriel, apparently Puccini, before he composed *Tosca*'s last act, he came to Rome to soak up the sounds of the city. He wanted to hear the bells. One day he got up early and wrote down all the sounds of the bells that rang across the city that morning. The bells we hear at the start of the final act are how Puccini remembered the bells he'd heard. It's a little like being inside his memories. But it's almost noon already! The bells that ring at dawn have been silent for hours. A pity."

The taxi driver recognized the Palazzo del Grillo address right away. He took Via Nazionale, lined with stores and restaurants on either side. The monument to Victor Emmanuel appeared right at the end of the avenue, a giant typewriter that the gods had misplaced in the heart of Rome. The car turned left onto a cobbled street, climbed a slope, then descended the length of Trajan's Market toward the palazzo's square tower, a medieval construction flanked by a crenellated tower. Gabriel asked the driver to wait. At the palace's main door, the Brazilian (who, it turned out, was called Silva) greeted him, surprised to see the brother of the tenor he'd been guarding in the palace's tower for months. He didn't look at all like his brother, he told Gabriel.

"I know. Michel is a little rounder."

Silva smiled by way of reply.

"*Was* a little rounder," you mean. "We made sure he followed Mr. D'Ambrosio's program to the letter. He's changed, you'll see. She has too. Less, but she's changed too. You do know we found her again? She came back! Yesterday morning, like a stray cat. Dressed as a Dominican nun."

The whole film crew, Silva informed Gabriel, was still at Castel Sant'Angelo. He pointed to it, over toward St. Peter's.

"Cross the Tiber. You can't miss it. That's what I told the two ladies who came by a half hour ago."

"Which ladies?"

"Oh, they were probably D'Ambrosio groupies. Or perhaps French journalists. They were on a motorbike. One of them looked like Mireille Mathieu. The other just looked grumpy. They wanted to talk to D'Ambrosio. If you hurry, you might catch them."

Gabriel's heart skipped a beat. Without even thanking Silva, he sat back down in the taxi. Magda had gotten out to admire the ruins of Trajan's Market and its stray cats. He had to shout her name to get her attention. She was gazing down at the Imperial Forum, Piazza Venezia, the maritime pine trees, the domes of St. Mark's, St. Peter's, and Sant'Andrea della Valle, her mouth open, a tear in her eye.

"*Rom, endlich*," she stammered to herself.

Thousands of swifts danced in the sky above Piazza Venezia, beckoning to her.

She came back to the taxi smiling.

"St. Angelo's Castle," Gabriel said to the taxi driver.

The driver didn't move. Gabriel asked again. Silence. Magda, now calm, intervened.

"*Castel Sant'Angelo, per piacere*," she said with a slight German accent.

The taxi began to move. Romans don't believe in foreign languages.

"What would you do without me, Kapriel?"

"I don't know, Magda. I really don't know."

"Can you promise me just one thing?"

"What's that? Finish reading Hannah Arendt?"

"No. That you'll speak."

"Speak? Who to? What about?"

"That you'll speak up when you see injustice, that you'll protest when you hear a lie."

"You sound a little self-righteous, Magda."

"I'm serious. Do you promise?"

"I'm not sure I follow."

"When someone tries to harm those you love, or even—especially—those you do not love, I want you to speak up."

"That's it?"

"No."

"What else?"

"Don't be jealous."

"OK. That's it?"

"That's plenty."

The day before, the same taxi driver had dropped Anamaria di Napoli off at Palazzo del Grillo and was now wondering what was going on inside the palace. Anamaria, still on the run, had hailed the taxi from a side street by the Vatican. He had only stopped because she'd been dressed as a nun. Otherwise, he explained to Magda (who didn't understand a word of his gibberish), he never let illegal immigrants in his taxi. But for a *sorella*, he'd made an exception. Giving a ride to a Dominican nun, African or otherwise, as his first passenger that century could only bring good luck.

The *sorella* in question, poor Anamaria di Napoli, had returned to Castel Sant'Angelo like Joan of Arc to the stake. But the courage and determination of the young woman about to turn thirty was to be applauded. Having readily given in to the increasingly insane demands of D'Ambrosio for months, on December 26 she'd decided to disappear off into Rome after the shoot. Thanks to her talent for observing others, Anamaria had understood right away that she would need her wits about her if she was to escape the director's attention. When he realized she'd gone missing, D'Ambrosio had called on everyone in Rome wearing a uniform, which meant that, as his last assignment of the century, the head of police was ordered to track down a runaway Tosca, an amusing state of affairs that gave the Italians a good laugh.

Right before the Cavaradossi execution scene, Anamaria had managed to slip away from D'Ambrosio and out of Castel Sant'Angelo, which was closed to visitors. It was the day after Christmas. She walked resolutely to a hotel opposite the Vatican, checking in under an assumed name. Two hours later she emerged in the white habit and black veil of a Dominican nun that she'd bought from the costume maker on set a week earlier. A half-million lira for the costume, a million to buy his silence.

For the first three days, Anamaria took refuge in churches, often St. Peter's or in smaller churches where a black Dominican nun wouldn't raise eyebrows. Paradoxically, it wasn't until she donned a nun's white habit that the Romans stopped staring at her dark skin, considered normal for a nun. But even though her costume allowed her to give D'Ambrosio's men the slip, it made her almost too interesting in the eyes of the thousands of nuns who walked the streets of Rome every day in ever greater numbers the closer you got to the Holy See, like ants around their nest. Fearing she might be unmasked, she took care to avoid the other nuns, the Dominicans in

571

particular, and instead melted into the banality of the city's artefacts, a little nun from the third world come to visit the Holy City. Avoiding the nuns of Rome was like a video game where her success depended on her quickness of feet and mind. Aside from that, Anamaria ate during those three days like she hadn't eaten for centuries. She went from one *trattoria* to another, sampling Roman-style tripe in one, sinking her teeth into *mozzarella di bufala* at the next. On December 31, by then repentant and desperate, she went back to St. Peter's one last time. There, at the back of the basilica, right at the very back, on the right, she asked to see a priest who could hear her confession. And so, moments later, sitting in a confessional in the world's biggest church, Anamaria wiped away a tear as she waited for her confessor. Light filtered through the wooden mesh. A man sat down. Aftershave. A priest who smelled good. Vétiver, she thought. The same aftershave as Michel's. She felt her very soul melt.

"Bless me, Father, for I have sinned."

"How have you sinned, my child?"

"In my thoughts and in my deeds."

"Can you tell me your sins?"

"I walked away from an important commitment I made with people I love. May God forgive me. My actions were not out of pride, nor of laziness."

"And what led you to break this commitment?"

"I was asked to do things that are contrary to my understanding of music."

"I'm sorry. I don't understand."

"I'm an opera singer, Father. The clothes I wear are a disguise. I am dressed up as a Dominican sister to hide—please don't turn me in!"

"How can I help you? I still do not understand the nature of your sin."

"It's hard to explain. You must understand, Father. I've been asked to sing Tosca in a production that's being filmed right here in Rome and—"

"You… you aren't by any chance Anamaria di Napoli, are you? All of Rome has been looking for you for three days!"

"Yes, Father. But, for the love of God! I've taken asylum in your church. Please let me stay!"

"What can I do for you? And please try to keep your voice down. This isn't easy for me."

"All my life all I've ever done is sing. It's second nature to me, a God-given talent."

"And your sins?"

"It's funny. We have the same accent, Father. Are you from Quebec too?"

"Yes, but please go on. How have you sinned?"

"My mother is not a rich woman. She could never have afforded the singing lessons I needed to have a professional career. Madame Lamontagne paid for everything. I've been with her son, Michel, for fifteen years now, but lately he's changed. And it's all D'Ambrosio's fault… Madame Lamontagne is funding a good part of his film on *Tosca*. He wanted me in the film at all costs, but Madame Lamontagne would only give him the money if Michel got to sing Cavaradossi. D'Ambrosio lost his temper. He refused, but I convinced him to let Michel sing."

"I still don't see any sins."

"It's simple. Michel and I have been in Rome for months, locked away in a tower in a palace by Piazza Venezia."

"Palazzo del Grillo?"

"That's the one. D'Ambrosio got it into his head that Michel and I are too fat for his production. He wanted us to lose weight."

"Pride!"

"Worse than that, Father. First he had us run on treadmills for two hours a day. Then, when he realized we weren't losing as much weight as he'd hoped, he put us on a diet no one could have kept to. For the past two months, we haven't even been allowed to go outside!"

"But he's the one who should be confessing. What have you done wrong?"

"I ran away. Plain and simple. For weeks now, Michel's been taking pills every morning, some sort of appetite suppressant. I've tried to tell him they're no better than amphetamines, but he won't listen. He'll do anything, D'Ambrosio says. He's losing his mind on those pills. He's stopped sleeping, and he thinks everyone's out to get him."

"How horrible!"

"But that's not even the worst of it."

"Tell me the rest."

"It's Tosca…"

"What do you mean, Tosca?"

"Well, everyone has their own idea of how an opera should be. And usually I try to go along with the director's vision. But D'Ambrosio is asking me to do things that…"

"That…?"

"In the scene we filmed at Palazzo Farnese, for instance, in the Hercules Room, he had me… he had me… I can't even say it…"

"Speak, child."

"We had to pretend Tosca was being raped by Scarpia dressed up as an SS officer. A brutal rape, with slaps and punches. I was thrown against the wall, against the floor. He spat on my face. I…" She began to sob. "Help me! I don't know who else to turn to. Even the police are looking for me! All I want is to sing! Why? Why Lord? Why am I being punished like this?"

"Ssh! Please, keep your voice down. You have nothing to fear from me. We can't talk here… How did you find me?"

"Find you? I just asked for a priest to hear my confession."

"Not so loud. Your voice has a tendency to carry! Listen, I'm one of your earliest admirers, believe me. Here's what you're going to do. You're going to walk out of this confessional and over to the exit, as calm as can be. Once you're outside, turn left and continue up to the entrance of the Vatican Museum, along the wall. Do you know where I mean? Do you have money to pay your way in?"

"Yes. I think so."

"Wait for me in the inner courtyard, beneath the big green pine cone."

"I know it! But who are you?"

"I'm your last hope. Now, calm yourself. I'll meet you up there in an hour at the latest. And dry those tears! Nuns don't cry!"

Unsettled, worried, and shaking, Anamaria walked out of the basilica in silence. Outside, a few hundred pilgrims were milling around the square. On the final day of the century, the museum had only a handful of visitors. Anamaria found the ticket booth in minutes, walked to the inner courtyard, and buried her nose in the copy of the New Testament she'd been carrying around with her in case someone opened her bag. She waited for the priest for an hour and a half, going inside to warm up every now and then before coming back out and reading everything the gospels had to say about the nativity. When she looked up from her page she nearly had a heart attack. The unlikeliest of visions stood before her: a smiling, brown-eyed priest, a little on the heavy side, an almost perfect copy of Michel Lamontagne, but an older Michel, in his sixties, shorter, with greying hair, and a glint in his eye, holding out his hand to her. He was wearing black ECCO cap toe, wedge-heel, four-eyelet bluchers made from the finest quality leather.

"Father Lionel Lecavalier. Pleased to meet you, Miss di Napoli."

Unsure of herself, Anamaria held out her hand to the priest, who was overcome by the urge to take her in his arms.

"How happy I am you found me, Anamaria."

"Do you know me?"

"More than you think. But enough talk. Let's walk and pretend we're looking at the paintings in the Pinacoteca, OK?"

"OK. I've been before with my sweetheart."

"I'm going to tell you a few things that will come as a surprise. I'm counting on your talents as an actress not to start shouting or crying. Act as though I'm talking about the art. No more surprise than need be. They know me here. I'll say you're a nun from... I was going to say Quebec, but given your age, they'll never believe me!"

"From Haiti, perhaps?"

"Why not? Are there Dominican nuns in Haiti?"

"There are bound to be."

Lecavalier and Anamaria began to walk just like the other visitors in the Pinacoteca, looking half indifferent, half fascinated. Since they both knew the museum, it wasn't hard for them to feign surprise in front of the reproduction of the *Pietà*. Lecavalier spoke quietly, occasionally pointing at a painting to stress his words, a subject that was light years from what he was actually talking about.

"Ah, the *Death of the Virgin*. It looks like a painting I once saw in a convent, the Sisters of the Child Jesus Convent in Rivière-du-Loup. I'm sure you don't know it; I can't imagine Madeleine ever mentioned it to you. She seems to have decided that whole world no longer exists. And she's not entirely wrong. Just look at this crucifixion... How beautiful those colours are. If I asked you to leave the confessional, Anamaria, it was on principle. Like you, I am loathe to break my promises. Like you, I'm stubborn and always try to meet the goals I set myself. Or at least 50% of the time... Try not to look at me. I think the nun who watches over this room has spotted us. Let's find another room. Here we go. Now, what do you know about this Da Vinci? It's St. Jerome, the patron saint of translators, removing a thorn from a lion's paw. Let me tell you now who I am. I come from Quebec City, from L'Ange-Gardien to be precise. Since my parents couldn't afford to educate me, off I went to the seminary, at a time when priests were giving up the cloth by the dozen. More than anything I wanted to become a painter and restorer, to help repair paintings for the Vatican museums. I could see myself repainting

Michelangelo's cherubs or touching up the paintings at Palazzo Farnese. Ah? You've seen them? The Carraccis? Wonderful, aren't they? But then I went and met Madeleine Lamontagne. It was in 1968. I was just back from a first stay in Paris. I was certain my time would come soon, that the diocese would be sending me to Rome to continue my fine arts studies. But then the archbishop at the time learned of my artistic aspirations and decided to give me a lesson in humility. The Church is very good at that kind of thing... He sent me to Rivière-du-Loup to answer a very strange request. The parish of Saint-François-Xavier—Oh! Forgive me a moment. What do you think of this *Crucifixion of St. Peter*? Incredible!—well, they wanted me to paint them a way of the cross, no less! I arrived in Rivière-du-Loup in the spring of 1968. I hadn't even set foot in the church when I first met Madeleine Lamontagne, surrounded by all the family you never knew. Her father, Louis Lamontagne, known to the locals as The Horse. Her mother Irene, her brother. I think one of her brothers died in a foolish accident a few years before I got there. It was... how shall I put this? It was love at first sight; it's the only way I can explain it. But diabolical love at first sight, times two. You didn't know the father, or Madeleine's brother Marc. It was absolutely impossible to remain indifferent to either man. In fact, and you must promise me, Anamaria, that this will remain strictly between us, Marc had eyes of such an uncommon colour, like the dark of night. Yes, that's the word. When I say it was love at first sight times two, I mean that from the first time we met Madeleine had already decided that her heart belonged to me; and vice versa. What she didn't see—or what she saw and chose to ignore—was that her brother Marc had the same feelings for me. Yes, Anamaria, Louis Lamontagne's children were very peculiar. They were brought up away from others, and it showed. There was this wonderful young boy, a bit of a simpleton like his father, and his sister, craftier than a monkey, like her mother. And both were handed over to me as models for the stations of the cross, with the blessings of their parents and the parish priest, none of whom saw a thing! There's one thing you should know about Louis Lamontagne: he was a country bumpkin, lacking in education and, by all appearances, something of a simpleton, but he had values. And he had a good heart beneath all that muscle. Do you see that concrete stele? He could have lifted it without batting an eyelid, if you happened to be trapped beneath it. Or *unnerr* it, as he'd have put it.

"Things got out of hand very quickly. First, Madeleine began coming more and more often to the church where I was painting, even on days when

I didn't need her. She told me some disturbing tales about her brother, to the point I ended up believing that Marc was a little too close to her, that there was incest. Solange was already on the scene back then, a bit of a tomboy who couldn't abide me. She'd realized Madeleine was hopelessly in love with me. That Solange was made of the same stuff as Louis Lamontagne: solid rock. But she was a good soul, completely devoted to Madeleine, the poor girl. Her Achilles heel.

"I shared my concerns with one of the Sisters of the Child Jesus. She seemed to know the Lamontagne family very well. A rather homely woman. The Lamontagne children, especially the boys, were a long time growing up, she reassured me. And Marc liked to torment his sister Madeleine, tickling her until she was breathless. But he had no ill intentions, far from it. In fact, had Marc impure intentions, they were much more likely to be directed at the other boys. There were already rumours about him. He talked to me about them once when he was posing for me. What I can tell you is that boy wasn't into girls. And I should know. When Madeleine realized, probably by spying on us, that Marc and I had, well, feelings for each other, she flew into a jealous rage. A real Tosca! You know what I'm talking about! By the end of summer, she was already threatening to tell her father everything—or worse still, her mother. I should point out that Madeleine was as pretty as a picture and, like all the Lamontagnes, as strong as an ox. I'll never forget the day she caught me with Marc in the church while I painted him. My God! Look, Anamaria. Just look at Poussin's *Martyrdom of St. Erasmus*. Now Marc Lamontagne, the boys' uncle, he was the spitting image of the man eviscerating St. Erasmus with his bare hands. Ah, if I'd known how to make better use of the Rivière-du-Loup light in July, I'd have been every bit as good as Poussin! And so in comes Madeleine into the church, only to find her brother half naked, his lips pressed against mine. The poor boy didn't have luck on his side. And to add fuel to the fire, he told his sister he planned on going back to Quebec City with me, which was pure invention on his part, needless to say. But I think Madeleine must have believed him.

"Everything happened very quickly after that. Madeleine got it into her head that, in order to save my soul, she had to take her brother's place, a role she threw herself into the last week of August. I resisted as best I could. But between you and me, I never saw much of a difference between their adolescent bodies. And both Lamontagne children were absolutely stunning at that age. They would just slide in between your arms... Just as good-looking

577

as their father. And what can I say about him? Wait a moment, let's go back this way… Here we are. Reni's *Crucifixion of St. Peter*. Now, just look at that bare-chested man taking St. Peter down from the cross, the one with the huge calves. That's what Louis Lamontagne looked like. Almost exactly like that. That's how I remember him. He didn't have a brilliant mind, he drank, he could be violent, but who wasn't back then? Even the priests would hit each other! When The Horse—that's what we called him—walked into a room, people would go quiet. Everyone wanted to be close to him. How many women said his name at Wednesday confession? How many wives in Rivière-du-Loup had him as a lover? Go there today and just count the teal-coloured eyes. Divide the number in half and there's the answer to your question. Everyone wanted to be Louis Lamontagne. To be able to get close to his daughter or son was—how can I put this?—a privilege for me. I gave in on August 31. With Madeleine. In one of the confessionals in the church of Saint-François-Xavier. After that, I finished their way of the cross and then began mine.

"Around the end of October, Madeleine told me she was pregnant. I was sure she was bluffing. She wanted me to leave the Church, to marry her. When she saw my disbelief, she lost her temper. 'If you don't marry me,' she said, 'I'll tell everyone I saw you with Marc.' I admit, I lost control of myself, Anamaria. I slapped her. Two or three times in front of one of the paintings of the stations of the cross, the one with the women of Jerusalem. I told her she'd have to get along without me. How could I be sure she wasn't making it all up? One week later, her poor brother Marc died from diabetic shock and I left Rivière-du-Loup. I don't know what happened after that. The parish priest told me that Louis Lamontagne died in December 1958, a foolish accident involving a train. He also said that Madeleine and Solange had gone to Montreal to open a restaurant with an Austrian, a food distributor with his own fleet of trucks. Pfeffer? Zucker? That was it. Zucker.

"I managed to put the whole thing behind me. But the Sisters of the Child Jesus hadn't forgotten me. They managed to track me down through the diocese in 1975. It was the ugly one, Sister Mary of the Eucharist, who sent me a newspaper clipping of Madeleine and Solange posing with the twins outside one of their restaurants in Montreal. I was in Paris. I understood right away when I saw Michel. It was me, only younger. It took months until I could get back to Montreal. At the time, I was restoring works of religious art for the diocese in Paris. Touching up a cherub here, redoing a Madonna there, nothing too exciting. But it was a start.

"In December 1975, I asked Madeleine to meet me at a Montreal hotel. She came alone. I asked to see the boys. Do you know what she said? 'I'm managing alone like you told me to, and I'm doing just fine.' She'd changed a lot. She was wearing the clothes of the nouveau riche. She told me if I wanted to see the boys, I'd have to leave the Church and be their father in a real family. It was that or nothing. Madeleine was like her mother: she didn't do things by halves! That was impossible, I told her. I begged, but she replied with nonsense like 'You'll traumatize them' or 'How will you explain it to the bishops?' That wasn't her problem at all. Truth is, she was taking her revenge because I'd abandoned her. Because I hadn't believed her, hadn't loved her. That's what it was. She knew perfectly well that admitting I was the father would have brought an end to my life as a priest. All I wanted was to see them from time to time. She wouldn't even have to tell them I was their father. When I told her that, she got a gleam in her eye, like her mother used to. A week later, she ordered me to go to the Church of the Holy Spirit in Rosemont, on Rue Masson. Father Huot, the priest there, explained that Madeleine had promised to make a generous donation to the church if I agreed to come two or three times a year, at a time of her choosing, to hear her sons' confessions. I was furious. I almost went straight to her restaurant to strangle her with my own hands, and that's what I should have done. Two weeks later, curiosity and the desire to see my sons got the better of me.

"At no time was I allowed to reveal my identity to the boys. That would have meant an end to our encounters. I'd also begun working as a priest at Hôtel-Dieu Hospital, so that I could stay in Montreal. I'd set aside my dreams of Europe. Restoring works of art in Quebec? What works of art? Between Extreme Unctions and confessions, I put in fifteen years at the hospital. Three times a year, I would slip in through the side door of the Church of the Holy Spirit. Always on a Sunday evening. Imagine hearing the confessions of two young boys back in those days! They must have thought their mother was out of her mind.

"I'd sit in the confessional and wait. Michel was always first. He wanted to please his mother. He'd tell me he'd been nasty to Solange. He and his brother used to call her Suzuki. Strange, isn't it? What's that you say? Motorbikes? Ah! That explains it! I thought they meant Suzuki from *Madame Butterfly*! At the start, I didn't know who they were talking about. Then one day I got it. As a child, Michel would describe how he used to torment his poor brother. Michel's every bit as clever as his mom. Perhaps even a little more. You'll be happy to hear that, Anamaria, or perhaps not. When he was a teenager, Michel told me he'd met a girl, a girl who sang like an angel. He admitted many times to having impure thoughts about her. He'd tell me at every confession, until I realized, when he was around seventeen, that the angel had given in to his advances! Ssh! Don't laugh so loud! He was right. I'm very proud of him. You're sublime. But you must really, really love him. Otherwise he'd be unbearable. Let's sit on this bench. Now, look as though you're gazing in awe at all these beautiful paintings and wipe that smile off your face! There we go! Aha! Now I can see the artist in you! You really are wonderful, Anamaria. I cried in the balcony when I heard you sing *Vissi d'arte* at the Montreal Opera. I'd always go hear Michel sing. Not on opening night so as not to run into his mother, but I always went. Every time. You have to explain to him that Puccini isn't his thing. He should be singing Bach! His grandfather loved Bach. And speaking of his grandfather: Gabriel.

"Do you believe in reincarnation, Anamaria? Some say you're the new Leontyne Price, which is a little on the premature side considering she's not even dead yet! No, I mean real reincarnation. The kind the Church still refuses to admit. Well, if I weren't a true believer, I'd say Gabriel was the reincarnation of his grandfather Louis Lamontagne. There's absolutely nothing of his mother in him, nor of me. It's as though The Horse picked himself up after getting run over by the train and chose the little guy to continue his life on this earth. Gabriel was recalcitrant, very recalcitrant at confession. For the first two years, he didn't say a word. He just sat there, stoic and proud. Once I even saw him rearranging his package, like nothing could be more natural. At about age nine, he began to talk. He asked me if it was bad if his brother came into his bed at night to snuggle up against him. I told him no. I couldn't very well say, 'Your uncles did the same thing. Why not you too?' I knew there was no harm. They were very attached to each other, that was all. And, knowing Madeleine, she was bound to have kept them away from other children. They had their own little world. One day, Gabriel told me: 'Father, I think Michel's angry because I won't let him come into my bed anymore.' What should I have said? Then, at age twelve, Gabriel hit adolescence, big time. Without beating about the bush, he told me: 'Father, the English assistant at school sucked me off in the library and I loved it! All I want to do now is read!' Pure provocation.

Pure Louis. The next time, he'd slept with his teacher! By the time he was seventeen, he was up to fifty-nine lovers and, thank God, you weren't one of them, Anamaria. He remembered every one of their names. And do you know what? His only regret, the only thing he feared was that he might be a kleptomaniac since he stole a book from each of the girls after... after... well, you know what I mean. 'I just hope I'm normal,' he said. The poor boy. I had to pinch myself so hard to stop myself laughing. Ah, Gabriel! You know what he's like. I suspect he's not the brightest, I think he probably needs things explained to him two or three times before he understands, but I consider him better than everyone else, with that beautiful body of his and his naivety. He's fragile, a vulnerable Hercules, just like his grandfather. You'd follow Gabriel right up to his dying day, to protect him, because you know he's too dim-witted to protect himself. Not crazy enough to set the place on fire, but in no rush to put it out either. That's what they used to say about his uncles in Rivière-du-Loup. A colourful image, don't you agree?

"When he turned eighteen, he told me: 'Father, I'm an adult now. I don't need to be busting my balls coming here. Mom can say what she likes. Nothing personal. You've been very patient listening to me all these years. But I've one last thing to tell you. About Suzuki, she was the one who wanted it. More than me. But it's over. Mom's mad as hell. She suspects something's going on. Michel too. There you have it.' Even Solange! I almost had to pick myself up off the floor. I was tempted to run out of the confessional and throw it right in Madeleine's face! As it happens, Michel had mentioned it first, but I hadn't believed him. He would often confess his brother's sins, things he'd made up from start to finish. I don't think Madeleine ever really knew, about Gabriel and Solange, I mean. But you suspected something? What's that, Anamaria? The secrets of the confessional? You're so sweet... Pfff! Let's just say revenge is a dish best served cold.

"Gabriel always thought I was Father Huot, who stood in for me. The boys would leave, go back to their mother. She'd be sitting on a pew you couldn't see the confessional from, then Father Huot would come over and say good-bye, as though it had been him who'd heard the boys' confessions. What a rigmarole. I had to put my career on hold for fifteen years, but during that time I learned all about my sons: their fears, their sins (or whatever puerile thing they considered to be a sin), their hopes and dreams. They told me almost everything. But of everything they told me, I can only recall a few things. Michel is hopelessly in love with you. He loves you more than singing, more than music. And Gabriel, the poor devil, I don't even know where he is. In Germany? That's appropriate! So once I was no longer seeing the boys, I no longer had any reason to stay in Montreal. I managed to get sent to Rome when I was in my fifties, to study theology. I stayed. No more paintings, no more touching up Madonnas. I wasn't particularly talented anyway. Once a week, I hear confessions here at St. Peter's where you found me. Apart from that, I'm still involved with a hospital. It's very close to where you're filming, by Castel Sant'Angelo. I saw you both going in there with D'Ambrosio.

"When I read in the newspapers that Michel was in Rome filming *Tosca* with you, I thought it was a miracle. But I said to myself, 'No, I must keep my promise.' Though once God set you down in my confessional a few hours ago, I realized that Providence had decided to stop whispering advice and to start shouting it in my ear instead! I must confess, Anamaria, that one night I sat down outside a restaurant at Piazza del Grillo, right below the tower where you're staying. I knew you were there. A dog collar is like an antenna in this city. You end up knowing everything. Even the cost of luxury apartments and who's staying in them. So one evening I sat there. You both walked out of the side street. You still had all your kilos; you were eating an ice cream. He had his arm around your waist. Before going in, you stopped for a minute to gaze at the Imperial Forum. Then you pointed at a flock of swifts spiralling over the Piazza Venezia at sunset. And you went back up into the tower, without ever suspecting I'd been watching.

"Now you know more or less everything. Let's find the exit. Now, before we leave, take one last look at Da Panicale's *Death of the Virgin*. Did you know the experts all say there used to be another *Entombment of Mary* in the Pinacoteca's collection? Napoleon's troops are said to have taken it back to Paris. No trace of it was ever found. It's also thought to have been a Da Panicale, but a little larger and a little more polished. That's all we know. It's no more than a rumour, if you ask me. If the painting were ever found, the owner would only have one thing to worry about: keeping the taxman's hands off his money. This way, Sister."

The afternoon of December 31 was about to breathe its last on the Viale Vaticano just as Father Lecavalier and Anamaria di Napoli emerged from the Vatican Museum. They crossed the road to walk down the quieter side streets where there were fewer prying eyes. Anamaria's hotel wasn't far. She didn't speak. Then, just as she was about to go her way, she grabbed Father Lecavalier by the arm.

"Father, you never told me how I can work my way out of this. What should I do? I can't go back. It's against every belief I hold as a singer. 'Sing what you believe and believe what you sing, Anamaria.' That's what Madame Lenoir would always say. I can't demean myself to the point of agreeing with D'Ambrosio's definition of singing."

"I know, Anamaria, but I have an answer to your problem. It's quite simple."

"And what is it?"

"Promise me two things and I'll give you the key that, like Angelotti, will help you escape from Castel Sant'Angelo. Believe me, no Scarpia will ever get his hands on you."

"Speak, Father. I'll do whatever you say."

"First, you must promise never to tell anyone we met. Especially not Michel. Promise me that. What? Why the hesitation?"

"I… No. I promise. I swear."

"This time with conviction, Sister."

"I swear on Michel's head."

"That's not enough."

"I swear on my mother's head."

"Please. A little effort."

"I swear on the head of the child I've been carrying for two months," she sobbed.

"There we go. That's what I thought. No woman goes to confession for no particular reason. Which brings me to my second promise. Dry your tears. I'm going to be a grandfather, this is a happy day. Listen! The angelus!"

He took her by the shoulders.

"Yes!"

"There! You're smiling. Now promise me that if it's a boy you'll call him Louis."

"Louis?"

"Yes, Louis. Louis Lamontagne. Come up with whatever reason you like. You're the actress. Then I can die in peace."

"But Madeleine will nev—"

"You must promise me!"

Anamaria nodded, like someone who's just learned of some terrible catastrophe. Then she began to smile at the thought of her child bearing the name of a forgotten demigod.

"I promise! I swear on the head of little Louis Lamontagne! I like that name. It's fit for a king!"

"You're a fast learner. My son's a lucky man. Now, as for your problem, it's quite simple."

"I'm all ears."

"You'll go back up into the tower, apologize to D'Ambrosio and say your nerves got the better of you. Tell him you were dazzled by his intelligence, but now you're starting to make out the new world that the light of his genius has revealed to you."

"That's it?"

"No! No!"

"What else?"

"Keep your good news for later. Don't show your hand... Then you'll ask Michel for his mother's personal phone number. Tell him you want to wish her a Happy New Year. Call her tomorrow night."

"OK."

"Once you have her on the line, tell her this..."

Father Lecavalier's words were swallowed up by the deafening backfiring of a Vespa as a priest drove by, cigarette dangling from his lips, and waved at Father Lecavalier.

"Our cover's been blown! That's Father Tajuelo. He hears the Spanish confessions. He's a real gossip! Apparently he heard the confession of the Queen of Spain last week. Imagine that! Hours of fun! Anyway. If your problem hasn't been settled by Madeleine Lamontagne herself within twenty-four hours, then throw me to the lions right here at the Coliseum!"

"You... You're quite sure?"

"Believe me, Anamaria. This particular piece of advice is as infallible as my boss," he said, pointing heavenwards.

Anamaria went upstairs to her room, got undressed, and fell asleep. On the morning of January 1, roused by the shouts of some reveller or other, she put her nun's outfit back on, just for laughs, settled the bill, and went for a stroll around Rome on the first day of the new century. When she was tired of walking, she hailed a taxi on the Via della Conciliazione. She couldn't believe her luck; cabs in Rome rarely stop to pick up passengers. The driver was charming; he charged her nothing for the ride and wished her a Happy New Year.

At Palazzo del Grillo, Michel fell at her feet as soon as he saw her and cried for a long time. D'Ambrosio was agitated but distant. He accepted her apologies and told her in the same breath that the movie's final scenes would be filmed the following morning on the Castel Sant'Angelo terrace. The director then retired to his room with his little chihuahua, Wotan.

That evening, Anamaria put her plan into action and phoned Madeleine, interrupting her conversation with Rachel Beck. She slept with abandon, feeling she'd risked it all. Father Lecavalier's words resonated in her head. They were so innocuous that she wondered how such banal remarks would ever undo such a critical situation. She had a bad dream that night. Father Lecavalier had fooled her, like Scarpia fooled Tosca, and Michel fell from the terrace of Castel Sant'Angelo, into the void below.

Three minutes after Anamaria's unexpected return, Bruno-Karl d'Ambrosio was on the phone. He knew how things worked: the journalists found out about the happy turn of events even before the stage manager. And as soon as the latter got wind of the news, things moved very quickly. With filming having fallen a month behind schedule, Bruno-Karl d'Ambrosio had only one thought on his mind: to finish the damned thing. They weren't able to shoot the next morning: the orchestra needed more time. And so the RAI orchestra was summoned for the morning of January 3, which would give the crew more time to prepare the set that had been abandoned just after Michel had sung *E lucevan le stelle* at dawn on December 26. But was that really Michel? Having lost thirty-five kilos, he had a mad glint in his eye and a nervous system that had been brought to its knees by all the garbage D'Ambrosio had made him swallow. The tenor was no more than skin and bones, a singing, emaciated nag. In any event, January 2 would be taken up with rehearsals for the last few scenes.

"Rehearsals tomorrow, then we shoot in one take on the third at dawn."

To shoot the final scene, D'Ambrosio was counting on the dawn light to reveal Rome in all its glory. Filming at that hour would also ensure relative silence. At least the production delays had given them one thing, he thought: Rome would be at its calmest. Otherwise the noise of the traffic and the planes flying all across the city skies ruled out any attempts at filming. D'Ambrosio insisted on rehearsing the scene at exactly the same time it would be filmed the following day. And so, at four o'clock in the morning, as Madeleine and Solange were flying over France, the director dragged Anamaria and Michel from their beds for the final day of rehearsals at Castel Sant'Angelo.

They would pick up right after the tenor's big aria, just as Tosca joins Cavaradossi on the terrace, where he is about to be executed. She is clutching the safe conduct she's just prised from the late Scarpia's still-warm hands.

A joyous scene follows. Free at last! We're free! The firing squad will shoot blanks, Tosca reassures Cavaradossi: All he has to do is pretend to fall down dead after the first round of fire, wait for the men to leave, then he can flee with Tosca. They'll make it as far as the nearest port, Civitavecchia, and head to new shores. But Scarpia hasn't said his last word. The bullets are real, and Cavaradossi dies with Tosca looking on, convinced it's all just an act. Tosca walks up to him as he lies on the now-deserted terrace. *Presto, su! Mario!* Hurry! Get up, it's time to go! Her hand touches the bloody body. Dead. Mad with grief, Tosca holds her lover's body in her arms. In the meantime, Scarpia's death has been discovered at Palazzo Farnese. Voices ring out from inside the castle. They're looking for the murderer! Spoletta, Scarpia's henchman, appears on the terrace. Tosca realizes she doesn't stand a chance and, rather than be captured, jumps into the void, crying: *'Ah Scarpia, avanti a dio!'* Scarpia, I'll see you again before God! The opera that began the previous day in the castle D'Angelotti had escaped from ends in the same place, with Cavaradossi executed and Tosca having committed suicide.

According to the initial filming schedule, the final castle scenes should have been shot before the second act, but Kroll's unexpected departure and the commitments of his Polish stand-in had forced D'Ambrosio to reconsider. And so the film crew had taken over Castel Sant'Angelo on that January 2 morning. D'Ambrosio was insisting that Tosca actually jump from the terrace, that no trickery be involved to fool the audience. But to make sure the grandiose ending didn't spell the end for the soprano too, the crew had had to find a way to catch Anamaria. The solution lay in the fact that Castel Sant'Angelo is a fortress built on several levels. Anyone leaping from the terrace wouldn't end up on the cobblestones below, let alone in the Tiber, but on one of the lower terraces, depending on where they'd jumped from. Standing on the terrace, the director explained to Anamaria that she was to jump from the side looking out over St. Peter's.

"I need you to jump with St. Peter's in the background. OK? You see Scarpia's men come up the staircase, you run to the archangel, and you leap into the big net we'll have finished putting up in a few minutes."

"Will it hold?"

"Of course it will!"

D'Ambrosio pointed over at the net the men were busy stringing up in the last courtyard visitors have to cross on their way to the terrace. The nylon netting must have been ten metres by eight, every corner fixed to a ten-metre-high steel pole. A St. Andrew's cross and no small amount of screws held the whole thing together like scaffolding.

"You'll jump a few times now just to get used to it. Otherwise you might balk at the fatal moment. Unfortunately, there's no margin for error."

Five times, then, before the sun came up, Anamaria had to climb up on the parapet and throw herself down onto the net. She ended up enjoying it and insisted on doing it a sixth time to vanquish her fears once and for all. Anamaria loved the feeling as she fell into the void, only to be caught by the net, then float five or six metres above the ground until someone came to help her clamber out. Each of Anamaria's jumps was met with enthusiastic applause on set. Truth be told, all the makeup artists, costume makers, assistants to this and writers of that were applauding the end of a torturous journey that would soon be over. For three days, they'd feared the worst for Anamaria. Most of the technicians had put their money on suicide in the Tiber, some on her running back to Montreal. All had lost their wagers. The singer had explained she was suffering from burnout, and D'Ambrosio had insisted she apologize to the rest of the crew.

"All the same, you made them lose three days of their precious time, Anamaria."

The diva hadn't replied. She'd bitten her tongue, swallowing a barb about wasting other people's time.

Once Anamaria's dive was to D'Ambrosio's satisfaction, he had her go over the scenes Tosca shared with Cavaradossi up until his execution. The extras playing the firing squad still hadn't turned up. They arrived around nine o'clock, at the same time as a delivery of electronic devices that were set up in a room in the castle, the last room visitors walked through before emerging into the fresh air of the terrace. They had to count every step, learn every rictus by heart, every twitch of the finger.

"I want you all in costume in thirty minutes. Do I make myself clear?" D'Ambrosio shouted, accompanied by little Wotan's barking.

Inside the castle, a war room worthy of a sci-fi movie was taking shape. The film's success depended on the singers' live performance, the conductor leading them with the help of a complex system of monitors and cameras, an electronic link to the orchestra in real time. To test the screens that were being set up one by one, the technicians played scenes that had already been shot but not edited, three months' worth of filming, of highs and lows, of problems and solutions, of temper tantrums and tears. One of the screens showed Golub as Scarpia, ordering his henchmen to torture Michel until he could take no more, since D'Ambrosio had insisted—and no one had managed to persuade him otherwise—that Michel suffer for real, that at least part of the blood shed be his own. Another screen showed Scarpia in the church of Sant'Andrea della Valle, while on a third Golub sang at Palazzo Farnese, beneath the wonderful sculpted wood ceiling in the Hercules Room, an enormous portrait of Adolf Hitler on the wall. All of Scarpia's men wore swastikas. A fourth monitor, meanwhile, replayed Michel's moving rendition of *E lucevan le stelle*, recorded on the morning of December 26.

Anamaria and Michel looked on, not knowing whether to laugh or cry at the fate of the gaunt creature that had taken Michel's place. Anamaria compared Michel's features to Father Lecavalier's. There was no doubt about it: one came from the other. No surprise either that Solange had never picked up on the resemblance: Lionel Lecavalier's subtle good looks had never made it through all that adipose tissue and had instead remained hidden for thirty years. The inhuman diet Michel had been subjected to on top of the exercise program had made him a very different person.

"You lost ten kilos too many."

"So did you. You'll need to put some weight back on, Anamaria dear."

"I will. I promise."

But they had little time to dwell on the matter. Hounded by the wardrobe team and manhandled by makeup, the two singers quickly found their focus again. D'Ambrosio and Wotan snapped at everyone's heels, ordering some to hurry up, others to slow down. The ten extras who were to play the firing squad emerged from the cloakroom at 9:45, each dressed in impeccable SS uniform. The whole production crew stood open-mouthed. None of the men looked like they'd been born after 1920.

Weapons slung over their shoulders, the ten hunched old men shuffled forward, one yawning while another rummaged around in his pocket for a pill to calm an imaginary heart condition. D'Ambrosio walked up to them with an interpreter. He was delighted to see them at last. Judging by what Michel and Anamaria were able to make out of the conversation, they were ten authentic SS officers that D'Ambrosio had tracked down and persuaded to play the role of executioner in his *Tosca* film, a twist in the production, a surprise casting decision that D'Ambrosio had kept to himself. The SS men were ordered to await the director's instructions outside on the terrace, where the execution was to take place.

D'Ambrosio had forbidden all communication with the firing squad. The poor men were confused enough as it was, he explained. Best not to distract them from the task at hand: executing Michel while Anamaria looked on. When she had seen the men arrive—men old enough to have walked alongside Moses himself—Anamaria had wondered what they were doing there. Now they were in uniform and she was still wondering the same thing. Unsure whether it was her meeting with Lecavalier that had given her a new sense of authority—authority she could *taste* with each passing second—or whether it was because the shoot was almost at an end, Anamaria nonetheless intended to tell D'Ambrosio exactly what she thought about the age of the men. She took the stone staircase that led out to the terrace, wearing her red dress and her makeup—why on earth did they have to wear makeup when it was just a rehearsal?—and walked up to the SS men, D'Ambrosio, and little Wotan.

"Mr. D'Ambrosio, I'm only trying to understand. These men, you say, they were real SS?"

"Yes, Anamaria! To tell the truth, only three of them were actually in the SS. The others were in the Wehrmacht and the Nazi party. That's what you call a theatrical find! It's how we're going to sell the movie! And how many times? Please, call me Bruno!"

"How can you call that a *find*, Mr. D'Ambrosio?"

D'Ambrosio did not appreciate the shift in Anamaria's tone of voice.

"Miss Di Napoli, need I remind you you've already exhausted my patience with your little Roman escapade? Just who do you think you are? Audrey Hepburn? Running off like that in the middle of the shoot! And then you have the nerve to question decisions that are not only out of your hands, but beyond your intellect? Here's my only piece of advice for you: rest your voice until tomorrow morning if you ever intend on finding work again after this. My memory stretches every bit as far as my influence. Believe me, you don't want to make an enemy of me."

Michel yanked on Anamaria's arm to prevent her from strangling the fool.

"Your *find* is nothing more than a pathetic gimmick! It should be music that sells the movie! Nothing else!" was all she had time to say before Michel clapped his hand over her mouth.

Slowly and deliberately, D'Ambrosio scooped little Wotan up off the ground, tucked him under his arm, and marched solemnly toward Michel and Anamaria.

"If ever you do find work after this, you'll be singing backup for restaurant ads on TV. And I don't mean fancy restaurants."

"You don't scare me. Truth always wins out."

D'Ambrosio walked away, cackling to himself. Michel was in shock, appalled by his lover's outburst. He feared D'Ambrosio's wrath as much as Anamaria's. An irate Anamaria sat on the ledge of the terrace, dangling her feet over the void, looking down over the inner courtyard with the net and the statue of the Archangel Michael. She turned her back on the former SS men, on Michel, on D'Ambrosio who had gone back down with Wotan to what he liked to call his "wolf's lair." She looked out at the sky over St. Peter's, waiting for a sign, wondering if Father Lecavalier might be lurking nearby. A simple shove in the back would have sent her to her death. She knew it, and she didn't care. Suddenly, just as she was about to send a prayer out in the direction of the Vatican, a very familiar voice rose up from the inner courtyard. A slightly nasal voice... no, two voices! A hoot of an owl paired with the quack of a duck.

"Madeleine, look up there! It's Anamaria!"

From down below, Solange and Madeleine had only just got off the Suzuki motorbike they'd rented at the airport and were beating a path between the technicians. Solange seemed overjoyed to see Anamaria.

"That's what you're going to jump into?" she asked, eyeing the nylon net.

Anamaria stood back up, her heartbeat accelerating, her hands trembling slightly. Lecavalier had been right. From that point on, she decided to be happy and went off to find Michel to announce that an end to his torment was now in sight, that real happiness could now begin. She didn't find him on the terrace. Feeling mischievous, she strode over to the old German extras as they sat looking out over Rome, waiting for instructions before they went through their scene. She stood in front of them, looked them square in the eye, and began to laugh. She pointed at each of them in turn, at the missing tooth, the club foot, the stooped back, laughing at how age had transformed their once virile, energetic bodies. Feeling cocksure and giddy, she stroked their bald heads, drummed her fingers on their hearing aids, and tickled their rolls of fat. They were most amused. Then, having decided to give D'Ambrosio his money's worth, she too went down to the video room.

There she fell into Madeleine's arms. Madeleine was speechless when she saw how much weight she'd lost.

"Wait till you see Michel! He's just skin and bones!"

But Michel was nowhere to be found. D'Ambrosio was flitting around, dishing out orders, lighting his cigarette as he went. And it was the smell of tobacco that led Madeleine to him in amid the tangle of machines and the maze the wardrobe and makeup people had made with their folding screens. The director nearly swallowed his watch when he saw the president of Mado Group Inc. heading straight for him. For the first time in her life, Solange had to hold Madeleine back with both hands.

"Where's my son, you little worm?" she demanded, grabbing him by the throat.

Solange forced her to let go. D'Ambrosio gasped for breath. Wotan barked furiously around the women's heels.

"Shut that filthy animal up!"

Madeleine was beside herself.

"Madame Lamontagne! What a surprise. To what do I owe the honour? Shall we go out to the terrace? You really must see the view. It's your first time in Rome, is it not?"

D'Ambrosio was doing his utmost to avoid making a scene in front of the production crew. The old German men, all half deaf, would make a much better audience for the scene that was taking shape. But what on earth was that madwoman doing here with the shoot almost over? Hadn't she given him carte blanche? He found himself alone with Madeleine while Anamaria stayed inside to show Solange the footage of the horrors she'd been subjected to in the second act, never suspecting that D'Ambrosio's fate was already sealed. Solange buried her face in her hands.

"My God, Ana. It's awful!"

"That's not the half of it, Suzuki! Wait till you see the firing squad! And listen to this!"

Anamaria slipped a pair of headphones over Solange's ears and played a scene from the first act. Their love duet.

"Michel's voice has really changed," was all Solange said, oblivious to D'Ambrosio's despicable scheme.

Unhappy with how Michel sounded, he'd secretly dubbed another tenor's voice over the film. The switch was virtually imperceptible to anyone unfamiliar with Michel Lamontagne's voice. A French technician who'd become fond of Anamaria had let her know two weeks earlier. She'd said nothing to Michel, not wanting to obliterate what remained of his self-esteem. Clearly

D'Ambrosio was only waiting for the final scene to complete the dubbing and finish off his diabolical handiwork.

"Exactly! That's not his voice! It's dubbed. D'Ambrosio sends the images off to another studio, where a tenor—I don't know who—adjusts his voice to match Michel's movements. You've been had!"

As soon as she discovered what was going on, Solange decided that, no matter what happened, she wouldn't be the one to tell Madeleine. No. Someone else could do that. Speaking of Madeleine, she found her outside listening to D'Ambrosio go on about just how safe the nylon net was. He was sweating heavily as he pointed at the Vatican to show Madeleine the grandiose closing shot he'd chosen for the movie.

Solange walked around the stone terrace that was decidedly cramped now that it held ten SS men as old as popes, a big-time director, the president of a leading food corporation, her assistant, and a soon-to-be-famous diva. The place had never hosted a more formidable collection of egos.

Solange looked out over the Tiber from the end of the terrace. Too far to jump, she thought to herself. Along the Ponte Sant'Angelo, habitually teeming with tourists photographing the sublime statues on its parapets, two figures were advancing slowly. The first was a man, his silhouette not unfamiliar to her. He was followed by a very old, very fat woman, who moved slowly and stopped occasionally to point over at the terrace or St. Peter's.

"Gabriel!" Solange cried.

Everyone on the terrace, even the Germans, gathered around D'Ambrosio, Anamaria, Madeleine, and Solange to look down toward the bridge. Gabriel and Magda hadn't heard Solange's shout. It wasn't until Gabriel saw the Suzuki motorbike that he realized there was a summit meeting in store.

"Magda, you're about to meet a very strange person."

"Stranger than you?"

"Richer than me, anyway."

It took them fifteen minutes to climb the stairs to the terrace, with Magda stopping to lean on something, read a Latin inscription, and decipher some graffiti along the way. Since she'd arrived in Rome, she'd been as excited as a conservative minister at a strip club. She looked all around for traces of the Rome she'd read about, she gazed out over the Tiber with tears in her eyes, she recited Latin poetry to Gabriel with what she remembered from her time at Sophie-Charlotte-Schule, and she scolded the heavens: why so late? Why Rome today when my legs will no longer carry me? Why did you make me wait so long, Lord? The question those seeing the Eternal City for the first time ask themselves ten times a day.

Magda, who claimed not to be a believer, addressed her question to God directly. With Gabriel holding her arm, they reached the inner courtyard without so much as a glance up at the nylon net. In the video room, Anamaria collapsed into Gabriel's arms.

"I knew you'd come! I knew it."

"Where's Michel?"

"We don't know. You have to crush that scumbag, Gabriel. He's up there with your mother and Suzuki. Please, be nice to Madeleine. Now's not the time to be divided..."

"I know. I saw the motorbike."

"They came from the airport by motorbike?"

Anamaria couldn't believe the effect her phone call had had. Everything seemed to be falling into place at last. Lecavalier was right up there with the Three Wise Men and the angels. Angels really do exist, she thought to herself.

Strange scenes were unfolding on the terrace. Magda had gone up without Gabriel only to come face to face with the ten old fogeys in Nazi uniforms and was now showering them with German vitriol.

"You think you're funny or something? You should be ashamed of yourselves."

The extras told her the truth.

"And you agreed? Ethical considerations never were your forte, were they?"

The old men stared at the ground in shame, suddenly realizing it had perhaps been a mistake to agree to a one-minute movie appearance in return for ten thousand marks apiece.

"He said it was to warn people of the dangers of fascism and authoritarianism."

"Who did?"

"Him, the Canadian."

As if he knew they were talking about him, D'Ambrosio suddenly appeared to join the conversation. Gabriel interpreted for Magda and the director.

"She wants to know why there are swastikas everywhere in your movie, why you're flying the Nazi flag over the castle."

"Tell her it's part of my artistic vision. It's to help simple people understand complex concepts."

"She wants to know if a kick in the ass is complex enough for you."

"Tell her there's no need to be rude."

"She understands everything you're saying, but would like to point out that setting *Tosca* in the middle of a Nazi nightmare is a monumentally stupid idea. She also says that Scarpia doesn't need a swastika to be terrifying. What he sings is enough. If you need to resort to such simplistic methods to express the idea of good versus evil, you're either stupid, performing for an audience that's stupid, or both."

"To hell with your Magda Goebbels! Get her to shut up!"

"She's not done. She says the most important thing—although it's something that seems to be beyond your talent and abilities—would be to show your audience that we're all Scarpia, we're all Tosca, we're all Cavaradossi. That's what she thinks. The oppressor, the innocent victim, and the person who takes a stand. Anyone can be an executioner, anyone can be a victim. I can't make out the rest. She's talking too fast."

"Executioner? She should know all about that, being German and all! I've had enough of all this, Arnold! I don't know who you are or how you managed to get in here, but I know how you're going to leave."

If D'Ambrosio had bothered to ask, he would have found out just how secure the gate to Castel Sant'Angelo was. Times had changed since popes would take refuge there from invading armies. The castle gate was watched over by two security guards, that much is true. But for Madeleine and Solange, a single American $100 bill had been enough to have them look the other way. And for Gabriel, Magda's menacing presence and his own imposing stature had sealed the deal. The guards had assumed they were relatives of one of the extras.

Madeleine had been relegated to the sidelines of the conversation, but had no intention of staying there: she still hadn't told D'Ambrosio what she was doing in Rome.

"Mr. D'Ambrosio, I have some very bad news for you. Mado Group Inc. is withdrawing its funding for your movie. Don't look at me like that. I don't know the first thing about theatre or the opera. All I know is that people like that kind of thing; they find it entertaining. I don't know why everyone is getting so worked up over a few swastikas or the portrait of Adolf Hitler you hung up in the second act. I feel nothing but pity for those old men who don't even understand why we're all shouting at each other. I hope that when I get to their age I won't be reduced to getting up at the crack of dawn to pretend to execute someone. And, by the way, I really would like you to take me to my son. Yes, I saw you, Gabriel. Hello. Sure, it's nice to see you. I'd give you a kiss, but you know how much I hate that sort of thing. Now, about you, Bruno-Karl. Where's Michel? And could you please get that dog to shut up? I can't take it anymore. I'm a little cranky 'cause I didn't sleep very well, you know? So yesterday morning I was in my office reading through a bundle of letters my son Michel sent me—letters he evidently meant to send to his brother Gabriel who lives in Berlin. He'd put the wrong address on the envelope and that got me worried, because my Michel doesn't make that kind of mistake. That's more like something his brother would do. But reading through the notebooks and the letters they'd exchanged over the past few months, I was reassured to see they'd been talking. Sometimes harshly, sometimes tenderly, but they were talking like two brothers. That did me the world of good to see that. And reading through Gabriel's notebooks, I began to understand a ton of things. Just imagine that before coming here Solange and I took a little detour via New York City. Uh-huh. Around the world in one night. I'd something important to sort out. If I'd listened to myself, I'd have stayed in New York for a day longer, then left with Solange when I'd gotten some rest. But then didn't the lovely Anamaria call to wish me a Happy New Year! 'Madame Lamontagne, the place we're staying costs twelve million lira a month.' I beg your pardon? I said. $12,000? And then D'Ambrosio's rent on top of that? For six months? Do you think I'm crazy? Do you know how many waitresses I can hire for that kind of money in Milwaukee alone? Girls with no other prospects? With babies to feed? You know, the kind of morons who've never even heard of your plays. Now you listen to me, sonny. When I go to New York, I don't stay at the Waldorf Astoria, no siree. I stay at the Radisson. I travel economy class, like all my employees, even Solange. But numbers aren't your strong suit, am I right? Too smart to worry about that kind of thing, aren't you? Well, I'm not. Everything I have I got because I know how to run a business. Send me straight to hell if you can find a dollar wasted anywhere in my company. I've the reputation of running my ship like it's a convent, and I'm proud of it. So when news reaches me that a little jerk is in Rome living it up like a prince on my dime, well you'll understand that my patience is being sorely tested, dammit!"

In the next instant Gabriel had to restrain his mother as she tried to punch D'Ambrosio in the gut while Magda held him. She did manage to rough him up a little, though, Magda crushing his Adam's apple with her cane. Gabriel grabbed him by the collar and freed him from their grip, only to mete out his own punishment, holding the man off the ground and shaking him hard.

"So where's Michel? Talk, asshole!"

With emotions running high, Michel suddenly appeared above them. From the mezzanine floor with the huge statue of the archangel that shared his name, he had quietly and sardonically waited for the conversation to turn to him. Minutes earlier, upon hearing the voices of his mother and Solange, Michel had blown a fuse. He would later learn that his behaviour had been caused partly by the amphetamine-based drugs D'Ambrosio had been giving him to speed up his weight loss and partly by shock. He'd wrapped himself in a white sheet that had been covering one of the cameras. Opening it slowly, like a butterfly spreading its wings, he walked forward and found it appropriate, given the circumstances, to deliver his lines stark naked.

Michel's nudity was as embarrassing as it was unexpected, and gave rise to a diverse and varied range of emotions from those party to it. You see, in half a year the man had lost as much weight as the average person weighs. He was unrecognizable. Even Madeleine couldn't believe her eyes.

"Michel, for the love of God, cover up that bass clef!" she told her son.

"Michel, you'll catch cold. Come down from there," his brother told him.

"Michel, my love, you're scaring me. Come down and we'll talk," his lover wept.

But the best line went to Solange. Michel, suddenly bereft of so many kilos, had become the spitting image of his father. His fat—proof of his mother's affection for so many years—had hidden his origins. Now they were in no doubt.

"My God, he looks just like Father Lecavalier, don't you think, Madeleine? He even talks with the same stuck-up accent! It's unbelievable!"

Gabriel helped his brother down while Madeleine stared daggers at Solange. Clearly an enigma had just been resolved in Solange's mind, and she didn't stop chuckling to herself until the plane touched down in Montreal the following day. At the first hint of trouble, the extras had wisely opted for the most German of Irish goodbyes. Everyone gathered around Michel as he sat on one of the ramparts. But D'Ambrosio demanded their attention.

"Pardon me for interrupting this touching reunion, but I've got people waiting down below and an orchestra ready to play the final part of Act III tomorrow. I intend to finish this movie. And I'd like to remind you,

Madame Lamontagne, that if you withdraw your financial support at this stage it will be deemed a breach of contract and I'll take you to court to get my hands on what is rightfully mine. It's important to respect one's commitments in life, *madame*. As for you, you brute, the police will take care of you. Now I'm going downstairs for a cigarette. And if Brynhildr and her gorilla are still here when I get back, I'm calling the cops. Is that clear?"

He disappeared down the stone staircase, his head high and proud. While he'd been speaking, Magda slowly wandered around the terrace, enthralled by the splendid views of Rome. Madeleine went over to her. While the others tried to get Michel to see reason, Madeleine slipped Magda Ludwig's little cross without a word of explanation. Magda held it tight. It was the same little chain. It all flashed before her eyes: Berlin, the little sister who'd been gassed, Ludwig, *Tosca*, the amber barrette, Magda Goebbels' earring, the bombs, the deaths, the freezing waters of the Baltic Sea, the German deaths piling up as if to try to make up for everyone else's dead, an eye for an eye, a tooth for a tooth, a bomb for a bomb, the overture of *The Magic Flute*, and the sound a mad zebra makes galloping off into the night, its mane on fire.

The cross was a little worn, like her memories. She motioned for Madeleine to fasten it around her neck.

"*So schön,*" she said to herself. Then slowly, leaning on her cane, with the speed of a giraffe, she walked over to the edge of the terrace, looked down as though to gauge the distance, cleared her throat, pointed over at the dome of St. Peter's, and sang at the top of her voice:

"*O Scarpiaaa, avanti a Diiiiio!*"

And jumped into the void.

Epilogue

The Santo Spirito Hospital is just a stone's skip along the Tiber from Castel Sant'Angelo. If ever someone feels unwell while visiting the castle, if a tourist is suddenly in urgent need of medical attention after gazing out over Rome from the terrace, they invariably wind up at Santo Spirito. The Italian capital is no stranger to cases of severe emotional trauma, a phenomenon known to some hospital staff as "Puccini syndrome." For every man, three women are affected.

To get to the emergency room at Santo Spirito, you come in through the main door on Lungotevere in Sassia, a busy avenue that runs along the Tiber, walk past the gift shop on your right and continue straight ahead, looking for signs to the *Pronto Soccorso*. Prompt assistance. At the bottom of the stairs, turn right and you'll find yourself in a little waiting room, where you'll stay until someone decides whether you're sick or not. The little room, painted turquoise for reasons patients have never understood, is furnished just as horribly as the waiting room at the Jewish General Hospital in Montreal. The cries of pain are the same. Solange, Gabriel, Michel (clothed, but now silent), Madeleine, Anamaria, and a handful of technicians had followed the ambulance to the hospital, a trip that took just long enough to turn the engine on and off again. Dr. Ruscito came in, plunging the room into almost complete silence. Anamaria was tasked with translating the doctor's sad news. He was very sorry to have to inform the singers that Bruno-Karl d'Ambrosio and Magda Berg were both dead.

"He must have died instantly. He didn't suffer at all. Your German friend was alive when she got here, but I regret to inform you that she succumbed to her injuries. It's quite amazing to think she landed right on Mr. D'Ambrosio's head. She couldn't have aimed better if she'd tried."

"I know. We heard Magda shout out, then nothing. It's just awful," said Anamaria.

"She's at the end of the hallway. We've informed the Canadian embassy about Mr. D'Ambrosio. As for Mrs. Berg, we're waiting for a German diplomat. He should be here soon."

"May I see her?"

No one could refuse Gabriel the chance to pay his respects. He stood there alone, looking at Magda's body. Her head had struck the stone pavement at about ear height. Blood had poured out of her mouth, great gushes of it, drowning the chain and the little gold cross. He managed to undo the clasp, wiped the remaining blood on the sheet, and pocketed it. His mother looked on behind him.

"You'll head home via Bavaria, Gabriel."

"That was the plan. But I'd reserved two seats."

"Will you come back to Montreal after that?"

"I'll have to think it over. I have to get Magda back to Berlin, too. Then I'll have to go to Kaliningrad."

"Where?"

"It's in Russia now. It used to be called Königsberg."

"What will you do there?"

"Look at the beaches."

"Do you need money?"

"I don't need anything."

"Solange says you're to keep an eye out for something important in the mail soon."

"What's that?"

"I don't know. I think she sent you a gift."

There were no tears. That wouldn't have been very German.

Little Wotan, the yappy, high-strung chihuahua, stopped eating and died of hunger following the death of his owner. D'Ambrosio's ashes were, according to his wishes, scattered in the St. Lawrence River just off La Malbaie, federal regulations be damned. The movie was never released and so Floria Tosca was spared the humiliation of having her real age on everyone's lips. She was still out to seduce, after all.

Madeleine decided to bring Michel and Anamaria home with her. Michel eventually emerged from his torpor somewhere over the Atlantic. His voice changed once his son was born. The anxiety that had always been there was gone, as though having a Louis Lamontagne in his Outremont home had brought the singer the peace he'd sought for so long. Madeleine and Solange went on opening restaurants. When Anamaria announced that her son would be called Louis, Madeleine pursed her lips then, drawing on *The New England Cookbook*, went about creating a new brioche with Solange. They called it the Holy Angels Brioche, and it was only available Saint-Jean-

Baptiste weekend. With relish, Anamaria put back on all the weight she'd lost, to everyone's great delight.

Gabriel stayed a day longer than planned in Munich so that he could take a second trip through the pleasant Bavarian countryside. Berta was dressed in black when she opened the villa door to him.

"You? Who told you?"

"Told me what?"

"About Terese. She's being buried this afternoon."

"My God… I wanted to give her her brother's cross. If only you knew, Berta…"

Berta smiled, then, holding the door open, stuck her head outside in the cold air to confide in him.

"Now that she's dead, I can tell you. The undertaker told me this morning. It's the talk of the village."

"What is?"

"Imagine his surprise when he was getting Terese's body ready."

"What do you mean?"

"She had us all fooled all these years. They also found her real papers in a safe she kept hidden away. Before she came to live here in Bavaria, Terese's name was Ludwig! Imagine that! Although with those Berliners, I suppose you can't be too surprised. The Nambergers think she must have been a Nazi and it was her way of disappearing without leaving Germany. But that wasn't it… I always knew something was up. Did you know she was sent to the camps? That's where they… well…"

"Is the casket already closed?"

"No, you can go see her. I'll drive you. We just need to wait for the Nambergers."

In the almost-deserted funeral parlour, Berta thought Gabriel terribly ill-mannered when she opened her eyes after a prayer to find him smiling as he put a little gold cross into the deceased's hands. Berta closed her teal-coloured eyes again.

And far from there, in the land of the cherry blossoms, on that first day of January 2000, people out for a stroll through the cemetery in Nagasaki happened upon something most unusual: an arrow planted in the ground. It lay in front of a white tombstone that belonged to a Canadian nun who'd been killed by the atomic bomb in 1945. No one could explain how the wooden arrow got there. It seemed to have fallen from the sky on New

Year's Eve. The blame was laid on a group of children playing nearby. And the arrow eventually disappeared into the ground, as though drawn in by some inexplicable force.

"red with blood, motionless by the beacon, Captain Nemo stared at the sea that had swallowed one of his companions, and large tears streamed from his eyes." ·

Twenty Thousand Leagues Under the Seas by Jules Verne
Translated by F.P. Walter
Project Gutenberg ebook, 2001

"To be content if neither oak nor elm. Not to mount high, perchance, but mount alone!"

Cyrano de Bergerac by Edmond Rostand
Translated by Gladys Thomas and Mary F. Guillemard
Project Gutenberg ebook, 1998

"A wonderful serenity has taken possession of my entire soul, like these sweet mornings of spring which I enjoy with my whole heart."

The Sorrows of Young Werther by Johann Wolfgang von Goethe
Translated by R.D. Boylan
Project Gutenberg ebook, 2009

"What totalitarian rule needs to guide the behaviour of its subjects is a preparation to fit each of them equally well for the role of executioner and the role of victim."

The Origins of Totalitarianism by Hannah Arendt, 1951

QC Fiction brings you the very best of a new generation of Quebec storytellers, sharing surprising, interesting novels in flawless English translation.

Available from QC Fiction:

Coming soon from QC Fiction:

Visit **qcfiction.com** for details and to subscribe
to a full season of QC Fiction titles.

Printed by Imprimerie Gauvin
Gatineau, Québec